THE EPISODE

About the author

Stan Abbott, who writes his fiction under the name Stan L. Abbott, began his career as a journalist in York and has written for many national and regional newspapers and magazines. For some years he ran a successful publishing business in the Yorkshire Dales and has also worked in the airline industry, and in tourism in the UK and Europe. He has edited several books and magazines and was the author or co-author of three books about the celebrated campaign to save the Settle & Carlisle Railway. The Episode is his first novel. He lives in Durham and the Lake District with his wife and a fluctuating number of cats.

THE EPISODE

STAN L. ABBOTT

First published in paperback in 2019 by Sixth Element Publishing

Sixth Element Publishing
Arthur Robinson House
13-14 The Green
Billingham
Stockton on Tees
TS23 1EU
Tel: 01642 360253
www.6epublishing.net

ISBN 978-1-912218-49-3

British Library Cataloguing in Publication Data. A catalogue record for this book is available from the British Library.

Printed in Great Britain by 4edge Limited (Hockley)

This work is entirely a work of fiction. The names, characters, organisations, places, events and incidents portrayed are either products of the author's imagination or used in a fictitious manner. Any resemblance to actual persons, living or dead, or actual events is purely coincidental.

This book is dedicated to the unsung heroes and heroines who strive uncomplainingly in the Cinderella service that is mental health.

Acknowledgements

I'd like to thank the many people who offered advice, support and encouragement during the very long gestation of this work. In particular I thank my partner, now my wife, Linda, for her love and understanding during the "primary research" for my novel. Especial thanks too to my daughters Hannah and Izzy for their unconditional love and understanding; to my sister, June, my niece Karen, and my brother Mike, now sadly deceased. To all the friends, colleagues and relatives who have supported me, my team at Gravity, who kept the show on the road during my absence, but most especially Dan Kirkby, Gordon Wilson, Angharad Thomas, Rob Mason, Magni Arge, Fran Barry and, by no means least, John Stronach, with whom I developed an unexpected but very special and lasting bond. Thanks too to Marek Gitlin, John Mowbray and Michael Sadgrove for their exceptional wisdom and compassion. Finally, I'd like to thank the team at the Arvon Foundation's retreat at the Hurst, the former home of Angry Young Man and playwright, John Osbourne. It was here, in the company of other writers, that I got close enough to the finishing line to believe I could finally complete my epic.

In memory of my lovely sister, Margaret, who died too young.

Author's note

In 2010, following a prolonged period of stress in my life, I endured, or at times enjoyed, what the psychiatric profession calls a manic episode. For a relatively brief period my brain's chemistry was out of balance and, fuelled by adrenaline, I created a delusional world in which I enjoyed a range of superpowers.

From the perspective of the medical people, my episode was unusual for the fact that my exit from mania was relatively swift: it took a little over a month for me to go mad, but my madness itself lasted no more than three or four weeks.

From my own personal viewpoint, my episode was unusual in that I could explain its onset entirely in terms of the side-effects of an unfortunate injury sustained in an apparently minor and, I thought, inconsequential accident.

My descent into madness, my experience inside a psychiatric hospital, and the delusional world that I created while I was in hospital are the inspiration for The Episode. This is, however, a work of fiction, and while it may draw upon my own delusions, the characters depicted in this book are entirely fictitious and, in time-honoured fashion, I remind readers that any resemblance they may bear to real people, living or dead, is purely coincidental.

CHAPTER 1

Sleepless in Kirkwall

Wednesday, August 18, 2010
The early hours

My name is Pierre Turnbull. Yes, it really is. I always blamed my mum and dad for this. I'm glad I can remember to blame my mum and dad for giving me a French name that would cause me so much hassle at school in the North of England. And for giving me the middle name of Victor, which, in the 1990s, made me sound like a pseudo-French restaurant franchise. These days, people call me Vic. It can make me feel like a strong-smelling therapeutic balm, but at least my name, with all its idiosyncrasies, reminds me who I am and even THAT I am, that I actually exist at all. Because, right now, 340 miles as the crow might fly from my home in Yorkshire, my very being feels like it is falling apart. Right now, in a strange hotel on a strange island in the middle of the night. Right now, in the sleepless wilderness in which I find myself tormented after the worst day of my life. Yes, there have been other terrible days: the one my dad died, the one my mother died, the one I spent in a police cell in Morocco. And of course the day my twin died. But on each of these occasions I knew exactly why it was a terrible day. Last night and now this morning, I have no idea what is wrong with me: only that I feel

~ 1 ~

like I am going mad and that the prospect of sleep is about as real as suddenly finding that I am actually safely tucked up at home in bed in Ripon.

I have got out of bed to write this because, with the light on and something to draw my focus, the terror recedes. Lying in bed, sleepless – utterly incapable of sleep – there's no stopping the games the mind plays. My brain has worked through a medical lexicon of the world's most unpleasant illnesses, hoping to eliminate them one by one as the cause of my malaise. I wrestle with the incubation period of AIDS; when was it that HIV came to the UK? Did I pick up West Nile virus on a recent trip to the States? Could I have caught malaria in India? Once again I am pouring cold sweat into the fetid sheets and pillow. My head feels like an empty box; I look down on it from a position near the ceiling and watch it throb to my racing heartbeat. Outside is an inky moon-free black, free of streetlights and punctuated only by the occasional stars that peer through the gaps in the cloud. My watch says it is ten to three. What can I do that will fill the dark hours till dawn?

I decide to run a bath and take my novel to read. But I can't stop my mind from straying, and reading is a fruitless exercise. I get half way down the page and I have already forgotten how it started. I get out of the bath and pick up the newspaper: I have a little more success tackling the Sudoku. At least I have succeeded in drawing my mind away from the torment of deciding exactly what it is that might be killing me. Away from today... or rather yesterday.

Yes, yesterday had actually begun pleasantly enough. It was my first full day on Orkney. I run a communications business and I like to take time out from the daily grind by doing hands-on research for the consumer travel portal we run, www.travel-knowledge.info. I'd been in two minds about flying north: if I was honest with myself I would admit that things hadn't been quite right for a while. For at least three weeks of the month that had passed since my return from the States. The feeling that my brain is outside my head, for example, is not new. But I am not someone who is used to being ill and I hated to admit to any weakness at a time when sorting out the business was paramount. We'd come through a challenging time that had begun when the banking crisis crossed the Atlantic, but there had been months of long, stressful days and anxiety. Now we were facing increased competition in our core client delivery market and, with the portal, were still struggling to come up with a winning formula for converting web hits in a virtual world into real pounds and real pence. And we had a potential legal battle on our hands with a company that might or might not have stolen another idea of ours. However, I had an investor interested and we were working together on a new business plan with the potential to deliver sustainable growth, albeit at the cost of 51 per cent of the equity in the business I had built up over more than a decade. I had just about reconciled myself to the notion that 49 per cent of a big fruity cake, and the prospect of more cake rising nicely in the oven, was probably better than having my own rather stale fruit slice all to myself. But I really needed to be on top of my game while we assembled all the ingredients for the new cake and made sure the oven settings were right. But I'm rambling again and heating up a metaphor way beyond the point it will burst into flames in the 'oven'. So back to the here and now, or at least to the here and yesterday.

I had got up after what had been a relatively good night; maybe three hours' sleep. An hour or two at best has been the norm for the past three weeks or so. I might have done a bit better, but I'd got over-excited watching the football highlights after a curry at Kirkwall's only Indian restaurant. It's not strictly relevant, but I'd wanted to visit the restaurant as, when I was last there, it had been in the early 90s, before the notorious murder in cold blood of a waiter, only formally identified as a racist crime some 14 years later when the killer was finally convicted. The name had changed, but I was able once again to admire the desire and ability to deliver excellent and original Asian food so far from Manningham, Brick Lane or, indeed, Dakar. Sure, I had sweated, but then it was a curry. The quality was right up there in the top quartile of eating-out experiences, and so too was that of the breakfast in the traditional hotel I'd chosen, in preference to newer pretenders in the boutique, more minimalist style. The kippers were cooked to perfection and elegantly presented, with butter, lemon and an irrelevant sprig of parsley. The porridge, however, was deep and creamy and liberally doused with the local Highland Park whisky. A waste of one of our finest single malts, I hear the purists say, but, hey, a little generous decadence can really make you feel wanted as a guest.

So it was with good humour, having caught up with a few emails, that I chatted with the hotel cleaners and we remarked on the balminess of an August day. But a chill wind was never too far away in this flat landscape, said the women, and so I carefully rolled up my water and wind-proof jacket and pushed it into my day rucksack with my camera, leaving the hotel in shirtsleeves, beneath the gentle warming rays of the late northern summer.

I had a four o'clock appointment back in town with the local tourism people, but plenty of time to devote the rest of the day to the pursuit of stone monuments. I got into the hire car, expecting to find my reporter's notebook on the passenger seat where, I was sure, I must have left it. It was not there. OK, I never have, never do, nor ever will lose a notebook. I learnt to guard them with my life when I trained as a journalist 30 years ago. I rarely throw them out either, because they are my record of conversations, my legal backstop if anyone dare dispute my version of events, and a rich source of information in the form of names, phone numbers, aide-mémoires and bright ideas. These are all jotted in the left-hand margin I create by drawing a rule from the top to the bottom of each page, dividing it into one third for jottings and highlightings, two thirds for my shorthand notes. Now I had lost my notebook and with that realisation the air that had inflated my mood began to seep away. I sat and racked my brain but recollection was not coming easily. Until, finally, after sitting for perhaps ten minutes, my brain achieved some recall. I might, just possibly, have put my notebook down as I collected my jacket on my way out of the restaurant. I would have to wait uneasily until tonight to know if this was indeed the case, and hope that no-one had simply mistaken my notebook for rubbish in the meantime. I called at a newsagent's and bought a new notebook, then headed west towards Skara Brae.

My spirits began to lift again as I drove the five miles or so and I began to get excited about visiting the Neolithic settlement known as perhaps the finest example of such remains anywhere in Europe. I couldn't remember why I hadn't seen the site on my previous visit, so now was the opportunity to make amends.

I soon discovered that the site was indeed impressive. I was looking at the homes of people who lived here 4,000 years ago but some of them were more intact than relics from just 400 years back. Less impressive was the fact that the jacket I so distinctly recalled packing in my rucksack was no longer there. Puzzled and bemused, I tagged along with a small group who were being given a guided tour. It was not cold, though my shirt and no jumper may have looked a little optimistic. The guide was telling the story of the site's 'discovery' by the local laird, William Watt of Skaill, in 1850, after a storm stripped the sand-dune covering from part of the site. I know this not because I can remember what the guide said, nor because I have a good note of it in the new notebook I bought. I am struggling to remember what happened just a few hours ago; I can't read my notes back properly because each sentence appears to fade away into a mess of tangled spidery outlines. What I can remember is that I was worried that my notes wouldn't make sense, so I carefully took photographs in sequence and tried to number paragraphs of my notes so the two would correspond. But I know the story about the laird because the Internet has come to my rescue and it tells me too how Watt excavated four houses before he abandoned his work, with it not to be resumed until the 1920s. And I can remember how the guide spoke about the central hearth in each house, the stone dressers and the little whale bone pots that were found.

As I said, my other prop is the pictures on my camera. But

I'm quite lucky to have these at all. Somehow I contrived to leave my expensive camera on a grassy mound as I wandered back to the café at the visitor centre. It was only as I rose to leave that someone came into the café brandishing a camera that looked very like my own. 'Has anyone left a camera behind?' she asked. I recognised her from the party with the guide and convinced her that I could find her own picture on the camera and thereby prove my ownership. Such deduction felt to me like a triumph of intellectual reasoning deserving of a Nobel prize; I was again struggling with the most basic tasks, like counting out the money to buy my Orkney crab sandwich with lemon mayonnaise.

I wasn't sure how I was going to come across at my scheduled meeting with the tourism people at four, but I reasoned that, if I stopped to revisit the Ring of Brodgar stone circle, I'd get a bit more fresh air and surely feel better. But the Neolithic monument had a nasty surprise in store for me. I had a very distinct memory of this stone circle: a huddled ring of gnarled stones with avenues, giving the appearance, in a bleak windswept landscape, of lots of Macbeth's witches braced against the wind and rain. These witchlike figures stood near a group of houses and there was a grandstand view from a nearby mound. Of all that I was certain, and yet what greeted me when I had driven the short distance to the Ring of Brodgar was a vast circle, perhaps more than 100 metres across and standing in a flat landscape beside the tranquil waters of a loch. Furthermore, the stones were not gnarled, but tall and majestic, forming a complete circle, which it took me about three minutes to walk right round. There were no houses nearby. I felt utterly unsettled: how could my memory have played such tricks. Another circle, the Stones of Stenness, was quite close by, but these too were straight and proud and, again, the circle was twice the size I recalled.

I decided to make a phone call: I needed to talk to someone who might have some understanding of the welling sense of unease that my shifting reality horizon was causing me. I know I'll look back in later months and years and recognise that my actions and decisions were increasingly falling short of the standards I would expect, not just of myself but of any sentient human. I decided to call an ex-girlfriend I hadn't seen for more than ten years. The last I'd heard, she'd run off with her boss, who just happened to be a woman. I wasn't sure how that had made me feel when I heard, but it was hardly relevant now, when I was trying hard to think how best to get hold of someone who might not even remember the last time she spoke to me; maybe not even remember me at all. I should say at this point, however, that there was a logic to talking to Anne Buchanan: she had been with me on my previous visit to the stones. She'd been with me at the curry house, too.

I then enjoyed another triumph of intellectual reasoning: I had a mobile phone signal; if I could get 3G, then surely I could track her down. I could and I did: there was no photo, but there was enough information in her LinkedIn profile to tell me the oil company she now worked for in Aberdeen, and in what capacity. I didn't even pause to reflect on the wisdom or otherwise of making the call; nor did I have time for second thoughts, because the switchboard put me straight through to Ms Buchanan. I don't know if I deluded my muddled self that my call would be welcomed for reviving fond memories (of which, if I'm honest, there weren't too many). The prodigal phone call, indeed.

Anyway, the reception was frosty at best. 'Vic? What do you want?' The emphasis on the word 'You' cast a veneer over layers of meaning. She didn't need to say 'Vic, you'd better have a good reason for calling me at work, given that we parted on indifferent to bad terms and I have since moved on. A long way. A very long way. And when ex-boyfriends ring out of the blue after a decade or more it's usually because they've been dumped by someone and I really don't need this.'

But even in what I was beginning to realise was a deluded state I could hear in that short sentence that she did speak, every one of the words that she didn't need to speak. 'Do you remember when we went to the Ring of Brodgar?' I asked, in a voice that I realised was starting to sound tremulous.

'Vic, I haven't got time, or the desire to play All our Yesterdays with you. Why are you calling me?'

'Anne, I need you to help me because my mind is playing tricks on me. I want you to tell me how you remember the stone circle we saw in the Orkneys…'

'Vic, I don't know what this is about, but I have never visited the Orkney Islands with you,' she corrected me, with the emphasis on the word Orkney. 'So, I have never visited a stone circle with you on Orkney and nor do I understand what any of this has to do with the price of fish.'

'But, what about the curry we had in the restaurant where the guy was shot?'

'My god, now you really are losing it. I have visited a stone circle with you and I have had more than one curry with you, but never on Orkney. Now I'm going to say this once and then you are going to go, because I am at work and you are unsettling me. I went with you to the Isle of Lewis. It's the only Scottish island we ever visited, as it happens. We did go to see the standing stones of Callanish: it was so windy we had to shelter behind them just to stand up, and we had a disastrous curry and a quite memorable argument, in a makeshift café behind an Asian store in Stornoway. I hope the information helps: now enjoy the rest of your life and, as they say, don't call me, I'll call you. Or more likely not.'

It took a moment or two to sink in: wrong woman, wrong curry house; right woman, wrong island, wrong stone circle. But I drew some comfort at least from having made the call: the much smaller circle of gnarled, witch-like stones genuinely did exist — just not on Orkney. I walked the short distance back to the car and looked for my rucksack. No rucksack. I walked back towards the stone circle and began to back-track briskly. I must have looked both worried and purposeful because I had passed no more than three monoliths before a woman asked if I had left a red rucksack. It was hanging on the fence round the other side of the circle, she said. Thank god for honest people: my rucksack was suspended there with its top flap partially open and my expensive camera inside, doubtless thankful for having not been lost for the second time in as many hours.

By the time I got back to the hire car, there was a missed call from my office and I had about 20 minutes to make my 4pm appointment. I realised that I had no idea where the tourism offices were in Kirkwall: I normally bring a carefully printed schedule with me on trips, prepared either by myself or my PA. It might have been in my hotel room, or I might have left it behind, but I had no phone number and couldn't even remember the names of the people I was supposed to be meeting. I rang my office and my right-hand woman was first to the phone. 'Where are you? The Orkney tourism people were looking for you.'

'Yes, can you tell me where my meeting is and who with.'

'WAS, Vic. They were expecting you at 2pm. What is going on with you at the moment? You don't seem totally on the ball all the time…'

'I know, Stella, I thought I was better but I seem to be having the day from hell up here and I've just lost my jacket, my camera and my rucksack in quick succession and for some reason I rang up an ex-girlfriend who seemed less than delighted to hear from me. And I'm not feeling great, but tell me who I was meant to see and give me their number…'

My meeting didn't happen and my phone call was another rather frosty one as three tourism people had cleared their diaries to see me and didn't seem inclined to make further efforts on my behalf. I felt a complete fool and even more alarmed at the apparent shutdown of big chunks of my short-term memory. Maybe if I went back to the hotel and slept for a bit I would feel better. Maybe. But then I probably wouldn't sleep and, if I did, it would stop me sleeping that night. I decided instead to look for my jacket at the lay-by where I'd stopped to take a picture that morning, then head down south to see the Churchill Barriers. These had been built at the command of the eponymous leader in 1940 for the protection of Scapa Flow, following the sinking in these waters by a U-boat of the Royal Oak, with the loss of more than 800 lives. These days, the barriers, built to link five islands, carry the road to South Ronaldsay and I fancied I might gaze across the Pentland Firth and see Duncansby Head on the mainland.

Still jacketless, I stopped en route south to visit the Italian chapel on the island of Lamb Holm. I was stunned by its beauty. The chapel was built by Italian prisoners of war who were brought all the way from North Africa to work on the construction of the Churchill Barriers. At its heart are two simple Nissen huts, joined end to end. But the whole is elaborately decorated so it rivals Michelangelo's ceiling at the Sistine Chapel. I'm serious: it's a place of the utmost beauty and, even if you're not religious, it's worth going to Orkney just to see this curious building. I entered the chapel through the grand portico, built by the Italians, with 'spare' concrete from the barriers. The interior was both simple and functional, thanks to its utilitarian basis – and utterly magnificent. I had wisely left my rucksack and camera in the car, so I used my iPhone to take pictures of the magnificent ceiling decorations, the windows and the wrought iron screen, again built by the prisoners. Here I paused for reflection, lighting a candle each for my twin, my mum, my dad, and another for all the others we had lost. And then I drove off south.

The drive took me over further sections of the Churchill Barriers, across the barren Glimps Holm, the island of Burray and on to South Ronaldsay. This is the island that obtained notoriety in the early 90s when social workers removed children from their families in the mistaken conviction that they were victims of satanic abuse. I drove through St Margaret's Hope, whose name reminded me of the mother in whose memory I'd just lit the candle. St Margaret's HOPE… was this some signal to me to have hope and feel optimistic? I let my spirits rise and took heart from the light of the evening sunshine shimmering on the Pentland Firth, drawing progressively into view as I approached the tiny settlement of Brough, near the southern tip of the island.

It was almost warm as I reached the end of the road and chose to wander the short distance to Brough Ness. It was picture postcard stuff: these oft turbulent waters lay calm and graceful, glinting silver and gold, punctuated only by the odd skerry. I could indeed see Duncansby Head clearly in the near-distance. I would take a picture on my iPhone and send it to my partner, Michaela, so she could share the scene and I might feel less alone than I had as I struggled with memory and context. I put my hand to the trouser pocket where the iPhone had been. No iPhone.

I expected the phone to have slipped out of my pocket in the car. This proved not to be the case and it dawned on me that I must have left it in the Italian Chapel. Twenty minutes later and I was relieved to find the chapel still open – and my iPhone was where I must have left it: beside the candles. I was forming the view that I was increasingly too unsafe to be allowed out on my own. I opened the voice memo facility on the phone and set off for Kirkwall, dictating a running commentary as I drove, slowly and steadily, back towards the north. I thought it would help me maintain some focus in my mind. I tried to give myself the most detailed description of the landscape as I drove. It was a little bit challenging as the landscape changed little and the road was generally flat, rising no more than 100 metres at any point. As I descended from this high point, two motorbikes approached out of nowhere from behind and roared past at something close to 100mph. I nearly jumped out of my skin, a reaction that will be there for me to relive in my extended voice memo. I confidently expected to find one or more bikes wrapped around a sheep or a wall somewhere on the road ahead, but I eventually pulled up at my hotel without further incident and gratefully headed for my room. There I opened my wardrobe, to find my waterproof jacket hanging just where I had seen it that morning before my conversation with the cleaners and the moment at which I had shoved it in my rucksack. Or not.

There was only one possession left for me to retrieve and, after trying without success to get engaged in my novel for an hour, I set off to walk to the Indian. When I got there, the news was good: my reporter's notebook was duly retrieved from beneath the counter. I thankfully put it in my inside pocket and turned for the door, feeling better that I could now once more account for all my possessions. 'Sir!' the voice called after me. 'Your telephone!'

I decided to eat at the hotel that evening and go to bed early. Orkney is not a place whose weather is noted for its stillness, but the air remained calm and quite warm, even as the sun descended beneath the hazy horizon. And that was the signal for the arrival of the midgies: dense clouds of them lurked outside the doors and windows and even the smokers gathered outside the bar weren't able to produce noxious vapour in sufficient quantities to keep the little blighters away. For this reason, the windows of the restaurant remained firmly shut, as did the two glazed fire doors. This might have been fine but for the fact that the kitchen was open-plan, its blazing ovens separated from the restaurant only by a stainless steel counter. It was a touch of modernism belying the otherwise traditional hotel décor. On other days the kitchen's hoods and fans might have made things comfortable enough but tonight they struggled to stop the heat spilling over to the dining area. I began to sweat profusely and embarrassingly. The waitresses couldn't fail to notice and offered to open a door and move me to the table beside it. In the circumstances, being eaten alive by tiny insects seemed like the best bet, but the air outside was so still and humid that the open door did little to mitigate my predicament.

The food was good: a starter of locally reared beef, smoked and marinaded in red wine; a main course of turbot with a red lentil broth. I risked a glass of wine, a very palatable French Riesling, but I can't say I enjoyed my meal: my wet hair clung to my temples and midgies drowned on my sweaty brow; my clothes felt clammy and I had the notion my brain was increasingly distant from my body. My food seemed to take an eternity to arrive, though in reality I'm sure it didn't, and when it did come I ate as quickly as I could and headed straight for bed.

I called Michaela at home without success. Later I got her on her mobile, but I think she was out with friends and I chose not to alarm her by telling her how ill I felt. And then of course I completely undermined that approach by starting to weep with despair at not knowing what was wrong with me. The trouble for Michaela and everyone else is that I don't really seem to have symptoms, apart from my profuse sweating, insomnia and vagueness. Which pretty much brings us to where I began: a sleepless man on a sultry night, in a pool of cold sweat, wondering what disease is burrowing into his brain…

Diary of Stella de Weld,
Head of Operations at Persona Communications
Wednesday August 18, 2010

A very, very worrying day at work today. Charley is right: there's something very wrong with Vic. He needs to see the doctor. He missed his appointment in Kirkwall today and he sounded really awful on the phone, sort of distant but slightly terrified at the same time. After I'd spoken to him I got some of the team together: only those who might have some inkling that Vic's been losing it, as now is not the time to be worrying more people than genuinely need to know what's going on. So there was me, Rog who looks after the travel portal and Vic's PA, Jem, and we Skyped Charley at the London office. Charley's a hypochondriac and she's convinced Vic has a brain tumour. I doubt that, but do want him to go to the doctor's as he seems to have been getting progressively vaguer over the last couple of weeks, ever since he had that bladder infection or whatever it was. Jem's worried about Vic, too, but her concerns are more practical: how's he going to handle the tricky meetings she knows are lined up - she doesn't know Michael Holbeck is potentially going to buy a controlling interest in the company, but she knows he's an investor and she knows as well as any of us that the company's growth, survival even, is constrained by lack of cash. Rog's hopeless: if I'd known how little he'd noticed, I wouldn't have involved him in the meeting. His perception of Vic's

~ 13 ~

behaviour is that it's all been within normal parameters. I just don't get him: of all the geeks I know he's by far the best at finding a productive interface between the online and the real worlds and yet he can still surprise you by turning up suddenly on Planet Zog.

Anyway, between us, we did come up with some sort of plan of action. We'll put it to Vic when he comes back in on Friday. Our view is that we should defer any meeting with Holbeck until Vic's fit to handle it – maybe look to a couple of weeks or more if needs be. In the meantime, we need to sort out the other corporate stuff that's pressing, especially the legal side. It's pointless talking to Holbeck anyway while that's hanging over the company. We did what we could to update ourselves on the issue today: it looks like Vic's given a preliminary briefing to an intellectual property specialist at Immerhutts. However, Rog, bless him, has made a discovery today that might shift the whole issue in our favour. I will discuss this with Vic tomorrow, but I will shadow all the legal stuff with him, both for my own peace of mind and because we need a contingency in place if Vic actually gets worse rather than better.

I feel both anxious and excited. Dead worried about Vic but keen to show I can take things forward, even without him, if needs be.

CHAPTER 2

A face from the past

Sunday, September 19, 2021

Felix took his room key chipcard from the smiling young receptionist. 'Enjoy your stay at the Euphoria Eastertide Island, Mr Merryweather!' The eye contact was firm and her words had more the air of a corporate instruction to guests than a glib throwaway remark.

'I shall do my very best,' said Felix as he returned the smile and turned for the lifts, beyond the potted palms in the lofty hotel atrium.

The bellboy wove the trolley bearing Felix's luggage between the knots of guests who were busily renewing old and not-so-old acquaintances. As a first-timer at a Shared Ambition international workshop, Felix cast his eyes around those present without any real expectation of their falling upon a familiar face. These belonged, by and large, to people in their 30s and 40s, but there seemed few other common denominators. Business suits mixed with casual shirts and shorts; men with women; European faces with Asian and African. The atmosphere was light and airy to match the environment and Felix could hear half a dozen languages above the mono-glottal background hubbub. A few paces ahead, the bellboy pushed the button to summon the lift.

And that was when he first saw her: her profile was caught amid the crowd in the lift like a still from a movie, as the doors faltered before closing for departure, leaving Felix and the bellboy to take the next one. It had been but the briefest of glimpses, but Felix was sure that what, or indeed whoever, he had seen had rekindled a genuine memory. The journey had been long and Felix's body clock was stuck somewhere west of Dubai. Now was not the time to be taxing his powers of recall.

The lift pinged and Felix put the distinctive dark-haired profile and its proud nose out of his mind, for the time being at least. He followed the bellboy to his fifth floor room, where he was warned against leaving the windows open lest the cockatoos come in and wreak havoc. He rewarded the boy's expectant look with a sterling tip. It was the only small change he had. The room was large and spacious, the bathroom and a small kitchenette on the entry level and a king size bed down five steps. A picture window the width of the room provided an inviting alternative to TV in bed. Felix opened the blinds: two cockatoos sat expectantly on the rail of the balcony that overlooked the pool and the broad sweep of Beverage Bay beyond. He eased the sliding door open and the birds flew off. He stood tall at the railings and filled his lungs with the warm early afternoon sub-tropical air. He was exhausted, but it was undoubtedly good to be alive. He knew he'd been privileged to be invited to the workshop: Shared Ambition's reputation went before it and attendance at its events or programmes was regarded as the Holy Grail in personal development by professionals the world over. He'd be challenged but he would enjoy the challenge and it would look great on his CV. But that was for tomorrow: for now, the rest of the afternoon was for free time and acclimatisation and Felix resolved to drag his body clock to Australia by not giving in to fatigue until sometime close to bedtime, local time.

As a freshly showered Felix sat on his balcony in shorts and a loose-sleeved white shirt, leafing through the workshop programme – and, specifically, the orientation activities on offer for the afternoon – one floor directly beneath him, a young woman was also emerging from the shower and pulling a loose-fitting floral dress over her head. Jameela Durrani had been with Aurora, sponsor of Shared Ambition workshops, for eight years. Prior to that she'd worked briefly for an international communications company in Slough before it was taken over by Persona, one of the founder companies in the Aurora empire. But it was the decade's experience she'd gained previously, working, latterly at the highest level, in the UK civil service, that had brought her to the attention of Aurora management. And that experience was now deployed to the benefit of Aurora's Global Policy Unit. Jameela's career was her life: it wasn't just the daily experience of driving forward a corporate ambition with which she identified absolutely; it was the constant repetition of the thrill she felt each time she proved herself or took her performance to a new level. Career success was her opium: she could never get enough of it. For so long as she could continue to climb the ladder and enjoy the respect of colleagues and superiors, she could allow the drug to cast a haze over the arid desert that had been her personal life for a decade.

Tomorrow Jameela would be leading a workshop on how companies could legitimately influence government policies in a variety of different political contexts. It would, naturally, draw directly from her personal experience in the UK and across Europe. In the meantime she could, she thought, allow herself some time to see the island before spending the evening running through her presentation notes.

Felix's next encounter with the mystery woman was almost as fleeting as the first and came as he was being driven round Eastertide Island aboard a golf buggy. As his driver took the track back down towards Beverage Bay, they passed a buggy going in the opposite direction. This time Felix could see the woman's face, or at least the greater part of it not covered by a pair of designer sunglasses.

He saw just enough to strongly suspect he now knew who the woman was, though he could not be absolutely certain. Neither was it possible to tell for sure behind the glasses whether she had seen him, though he suspected her gaze had been towards the opposite direction. He calculated it must have been at least a decade, maybe more, since he had last seen Jameela Durrani and her appearance would surely have changed at least a little in that time; so there was plenty of room for doubt in Felix's mind. And then, Felix wasn't actually the greatest in the world at remembering a face and putting a name to it… Jameela had been working for the Government in communications at the time; Felix had been retained by another section of government on the development of an internal communications network. In Barbara Jones they shared respectively a line manager and a project director and so, although he and Jameela did not work together on the same projects, they did nonetheless meet professionally both inside and outside the London offices where Jameela was based, on days when Felix's project took him to Whitehall.

The last time they had met, however, had been towards the end of Felix's assignment, when they were both on the black tie guest list for an awards event at which Felix's own employers had been shortlisted. It was an evening that had been memorable not just for the fact that Felix's colleagues had won gold in the category for innovation in web-based publications; nor just for the slightly terrifying quantities of champagne that had been consumed as a consequence; nor for the excruciatingly embarrassing revelations about an otherwise forgotten period in Felix's life that Barbara Jones had, quite inexplicably, suddenly chosen to reveal to all assembled. It was memorable too for the rather sad conversation that Felix had had very late in the evening with Jameela.

Felix had realised that Jameela's family must originally have been from Pakistan, but her own accent was an educated South of England; she wore fashionable western clothes and Felix hadn't thought a great deal about her origins. He recognised rather guiltily that she appeared so assimilated into contemporary British culture that he had not given a moment's thought to the process she might have had to go through to become a British person of Pakistani ethnic origin rather than a Pakistani person living in Britain. Because he worked with Jameela he had actually given surprisingly little thought to the person behind the smart grey trouser suits or, on this particular night, the calf-length black cocktail dress, studded with shimmering black sequins.

The dress was quite tight-fitting and revealed a figure that had barely been hinted at through the trouser suits. Jameela usually wore her mid-length raven hair loose over her shoulders, parted at one side and with a hair grip at the other, holding it back off her forehead. Tonight she had gathered the hair together in a twisted bun, pierced and held in place by two gold pins. Her usually discreet make-up was more brash: bright red lip gloss, noticeable mascara above the deep hazel eyes and a blueish eye shadow that Felix noticed toned tastefully with her gold earrings, from each of which was suspended a delicate blue tear drop. The gold chain around her neck was quite heavy and Felix was unsure whether it was designed to partially obscure, or perhaps draw attention to, the hint of cleavage in the deep V neckline. But then, a delicate gold filigree brooch on a pin served modestly to draw the bottom of the V together. She wore a touch of blusher on each olive cheek and Felix fancied she might have dabbed some on her cleavage too. Sheer Nylon could be seen beneath the hemline of the dress, which rose slightly at the front and was slit to just above the knee at the back, as Felix had noticed when she turned to talk to another guest. The shapely calves ended in the most delicate sandals, with stringy gold straps tied just above the ankle. It was the first time Felix recalled seeing Jameela, the woman, and the impression she made was evident.

'Fantastic dress, Jameela,' he said. 'You look great!' He fancied she blushed slightly beneath the dark skin and in the dimmish cocktail lighting.

'Thanks,' she said, with a faint smile. Felix found himself

wondering if he perhaps shouldn't have made the comment; if this was outside the scope of a relationship that had hitherto been essentially defined by the workplace.

Later in the evening, after Barbara Jones's unexpected revelation about Felix's past, he found himself alone at the table with Jameela. Their fellow diners had either wandered off to talk drunkenly with colleagues on other tables or were destruction-testing their cocktail shoes to the strains of the enthusiastic disco. Felix judged that Jameela had drunk quite a bit without being drunk. He himself felt mellow but fully aware. Unaccustomed to her hair being up, he found himself fascinated by the face now revealed. Even in the dim light he could see that her dark hair merged into a soft down on each cheek. The cheekbones were pronounced, the lips nicely sculpted, the chin firm with an alluring dimple. The fullness of her cheeks had the effect of giving a slight appearance that her mouth turned down at the edges, as though deliberately stifling a smile. Jameela's nose, he'd noted when he'd seen her profile earlier, formed a perfect triangle. But now as he looked straight into her face, he observed that it was ever so slightly off-centre to her left; an imperfection he judged added to what he increasingly recognised as her not inconsiderable attraction. There was a similar slight lack of symmetry to her eye line: her left eyebrow was a tad higher than her right and Felix fancied the left eye might be fractionally bigger. The eyebrows themselves were carefully tended, very probably plucked down from their natural size. The forehead was slightly lined, adding to the faintly dolorous look created by her cheeks and mouth.

Now, a decade or more later, as the buggy bounced towards the bay, Felix tried to recall how their conversation that night had strayed onto Jameela's personal life. But he couldn't remember the route by which it got there, only the result when it did. He fancied he might perhaps have asked her what it was that made her so driven by her career and what her other interests were. She was, it turned out, an avid reader of horror novels, both Gothic and contemporary. Fascinated as he was by this revelation, this was not Felix's genre. But Jameela was also, it turned out, a big cricket fan and in this there was more common ground. At some point Jameela revealed to Felix that she had been married to a white man: an accountant from Salford whom she had met when she was in her early 20s and working for the Department of Trade. They had met in a hospitality box at a Lords test match. Sensing that Jameela was lowering the guard that had hitherto kept private and professional firmly separated, Felix leaned towards her across the table and looked into her eyes. She did not reject his gaze; indeed, her eyes widened briefly, but the sparkle Felix had seen was, he realised, the shimmer of tears and he could see in her eyes only the deepest sadness: a melancholy that belied the bright, breezy and efficient woman he knew from work.

Felix wasn't sure whether he had ever seen such sadness and probed her with gentle questions until she had told him how she had fallen deeply in love with the accountant; how she had told him that, to be together, she would have to make very big sacrifices; how the accountant, Phil, had declared his undying love and commitment to her and how, armed with this certainty, she had told her family she intended to marry a white man who was not a Muslim. Quietly and patiently, Jameela told Felix how, faced with the consequent absolute choice between family and the man she loved, she had chosen the latter; she described the intense pain it had caused her and the loneliness that inevitably flowed from effectively turning her back on her community. But it had all been worth it, because they were going to have beautiful children and love would triumph over all. They had been married only a year when it happened: the revelation, by one of his colleagues, that Phil had been seeing another woman; an English woman at his work. Jameela wanted no more detail: she confronted him, he sheepishly confessed, and she put him out on the street, changing the locks the next day. She put his clothes and other possessions in boxes and stood them on the drive. Those he hadn't removed by the end of the day, she threw in a nearby skip. And that had been the end of her dream of happiness, of children, of close companionship. From that day her work was her life and defined the parameters of her happiness. But that was the way it was: she had no complaints, for it was her destiny now to be alone.

Felix had been shocked: shocked at the betrayal but shocked too at the irreversibility of Jameela's reaction to the deception. Was she not prepared to give Phil a second chance? Wasn't she adding to the misery of deception by punishing herself; denying herself the opportunity to bear children? Would she never risk another relationship?

'Felix, I gave up everything for this man and he betrayed me. I gave up seeing my mother, my father, my brothers, my sister, my nephews and nieces, my aunties... I gave up my whole community and I can never go back. There is no forgiveness for me for the choice I made, but I knew that when I chose Phil. And he knew the sacrifices I made to be with him; to hopefully have his children. And then he chose to throw it all away by betraying me.'

'Jameela, he's been a fool and he must know that; but wouldn't you have been happier if you could have found it in your heart to forgive him?'

'Felix, he tore my heart out and trampled it in the dirt. I could never have trusted him ever again. I am soiled goods in the eyes of my community, so I can't go back there. I brought shame on my family so I can not ask them now to understand and offer me sympathy. And I can't ever risk the possibility of feeling such intense pain again. I am happy doing what I do and doing it well. Marriage and children was a joyous ambition but it failed, and I must live with the consequences of the choices I made and my betrayal by someone who chose not to understand the depth of the sacrifices I made for him.'

And then the shutters came down and the glimpse into Jameela's sad soul was closed. 'Come on, you can dance with me, if you want, but no more personal questions.' And so Felix's last minutes with Jameela introduced him, to the strains of the Last Waltz, to her sweet perfume with a hint of rose water, and to the smell of her hair. He felt profoundly sad as he kissed her on the cheek and said goodnight. And then his work for Barbara Jones came to an end without him ever encountering Jameela again. Could this now, all these years later, be the same Jameela, 12,000 miles from home and, miraculously, in the same place as him?

'Welcome back to the Euphoria Eastertide Island,' said the smiling driver as the buggy came to a halt. Felix, jolted from his reflective reverie, thanked and tipped the driver, in euros this time, making a mental note to acquire some Ozzie dollars.

Jameela Durrani decided she would mix a little bit of business with the pleasure of seeing the island. In reality, the boundaries between work and pleasure were pretty informal in Jameela's life. And so, as she left for her sightseeing trip, she took with her in a generous canvas shoulder bag, decorated with a pattern of deep red roses on a beige background, a notebook rather than a tablet or Flexiscreen, the conference guest list, and a few items from her room: an apple, a kiwi fruit, a bottle of water and the striped throw from the wicker sofa on her balcony.

Checking the map in the hotel lobby, she arranged for a buggy driver to take her to Cook's Vantage, towards the north-east tip of the island, from where she could stroll back along the beach to Beverage Bay before the sun sank behind the gentle ridge that traversed the wider southern and western portion of the island.

Jameela laid the throw on the tinder-dry grass at Cook's Vantage, and sighed contentedly as the sun, now sinking towards the horizon, warmed her face as she looked out over the rich blue ocean, dappled with darker areas where reefs approached the surface and becoming a warm turquoise in the shallows, where brightly coloured yachts and cruisers bobbed lazily at anchor. The sub-tropical late afternoon seemed to awaken something deep within her: a sub-conscious recollection of a climate more equable than the one she had become accustomed to in England. This job certainly had its compensations, she smiled to herself, biting into the crisp green apple. She opened her notebook and jotted a series of bullet points, drawing from her own most recent experiences and from national and international events to create illustrations for her session tomorrow. The ideas flowed freely despite her fatigue and she decided to see if there were any names she knew on the attendance list. She quickly spotted half a dozen with which she was familiar, though she couldn't put faces to them all. Then one name jumped out at her. There could be few people called Felix Merryweather. Most probably only one.

In fact, Jameela could think of only one person who might ever have entertained the possibility that there wasn't just one Felix Merryweather in the world. That had been Barbara Jones, her line manager when she worked for the UK Government. She recalled the evening when her own guard had lowered and she had shared with one Felix Merryweather details about her personal life that she had hitherto studiously kept private. She had probably drunk a little too much and for a brief moment had wondered whether Felix was making, or was about to make, a pass at her. Now, she reflected – as she had gone on to do what might have been perhaps ten or more years previously – that Felix was showing not a sexual interest but genuine concern for a colleague to whom he had probably become close. Jameela thought back to their professional relationship: Felix had always demonstrated to her the utmost respect and had never sought to score points or circumvent her authority when, through relative inexperience, she had found herself caught up in the political manoeuvrings so common in government organisations. She also had a soft spot for his name: it was probably more unusual in the UK than even her own. That was why she had been so surprised to hear a drunken Barbara Jones declare: 'Oh, you're THAT Felix Merryweather!'

Felix had revealed to the table in passing something about a failed marriage to a woman who, bizarrely, had at some point become Barbara Jones's next door neighbour, but in a completely different town from the one in which she had lived with her husband. Barbara, who had looked to be about two and a half sheets to the wind, suddenly lit up and gleefully described how Felix's one-time wife's howls of grief could be heard nightly through the thin dividing walls of the terraced properties. Concerned that her neighbour might be tempted to harm herself in some way, Barbara had befriended her. The neighbour, it turned out, was called Merryweather. 'Was it Jill Merryweather?' Jameela wondered. And she had acquired the unusual name by marrying young to a man called Merryweather, whose given name was almost as unusual as his family name: Felix. Barbara's had become a convenient and perennial shoulder upon which Jill Merryweather could cry, and her ear had become an equally convenient receptacle for Jill's lament, the gist of which was that she had been left by her husband who was clearly a cad, a bounder, a misogynist and a man thoroughly undeserving of the fine example of womanhood that Jill represented.

Clearly, Jameela reflected, the picture that Jill had painted of Felix Merryweather had been so at odds with the personable, considerate, amusing and compassionate man that Barbara had encountered in 'the other Felix Merryweather' with whom she now worked, that it had actually never occurred to her that the two men might in fact be one and the same person.

It had been the detail in Felix's reference to his brief marriage to a physiotherapist, when both were too young, that had caused the penny to drop for Barbara and for her to make her gauche 'THAT Felix Merryweather' remark. She'd gone on to make things slightly worse rather than better by saying 'Well, you must have been quite something because she cried every day for a year without showing any indication of getting over you…'.

Jameela remembered how shocked and uncomfortable Felix had looked. He'd only muttered something like 'It was a long time ago, Barbara, and we were both too young'. And now here he was: Felix Merryweather, the bane of Jill Merryweather's life, was surely here on Eastertide Island. Jameela smiled to herself as she thought of how she might greet him when they inevitably met at some point later that evening or perhaps the following day.

In fact, the meeting came sooner than expected. Jameela had finished her work, eaten her fruit and walked back along the beach to the Euphoria. She waited for the lift and, when the doors opened, she found herself face-to-face with the said Mr Merryweather. 'It's Jameela, isn't it? How great to see you. What have you been doing? What are you are doing here?'

Jameela feigned puzzlement: 'Remind me, who are you?'

'It's Felix, Jameela; Felix Merryweather. We worked together…'

'Oh, you're THAT Felix Merryweather!' grinned Jameela, wickedly.

CHAPTER 3

Embarrassed in Nidderdale

Thursday, August 19, 2010

It is, eventually, time to get up for breakfast. I have a morning to kill before my flight but I am terrified of losing track of time and missing it, so I elect to spend the hours in Kirkwall, firstly talking with the hotel owner and then going to sit for a while in the Cathedral. It would be wrong to say I feel better, but at least I don't feel quite as terrible as I did yesterday. I triple-check my room and manage, I think, to leave the hotel with my possessions intact. I even succeed in talking intelligently to the owner and making some notes that appear to make sense. I then feel a sense of peace in St Magnus's and, successfully finding the airport and the car hire desk in good time, begin to hope that perhaps I am finally on the mend. I manage to get myself and my luggage home with no further mishap beyond boarding my second flight, from Aberdeen, with the boarding card from my first flight still in my hand. But the cabin crew check my name on the manifest and find me a seat (the 'missing' card will turn up later in the one pocket I hadn't thought to search when I was on the aeroplane).

Arriving home, I tell Michaela I will go to the doctor's again in the morning and take some time off work.

Another sleepless night begins to unfold and I take myself off to my son Larry's empty bed. In the small hours I go downstairs and make myself a cup of camomile tea. By morning I have maybe drowsed for an hour.

At the surgery I see Dr Gordon for the first time. I am happy enough to make the change: the doctor I've seen on my previous visit didn't respond to my attempts to make eye contact. It hadn't occurred to me that maybe this was neither necessary nor appropriate, but I've been making a conscious effort to make eye contact with people over the last couple of weeks. This has turned out to be quite a revelation (people really respond and open up) and I guess I hadn't expected doctors to be any different from everyone else in that respect. This is my fourth visit all-told to the doctor's, the first two being for an unexplained attack of cystitis now a full month previously. Then I'd gone to see Dr Jones because I was still experiencing pain when I peed and I'd been unimpressed that on my previous visit, the second to Dr Edwards, he seemed to have no recollection of having asked me to come back and see him a week later, simply because cystitis in men was unusual and he would want to check me over again.

I tell Dr Gordon that all the plumbing stuff is still a bit tender and I've had a certain amount of stress and fallen into a habit of not sleeping. He prescribes temazepam. I can't say I'm wildly enthusiastic about this: I have an enduring concern about addictive drugs and would far rather find some way of persuading nature to convince my brain of my need for sleep. Worse, I know that temazepam capsules were the wobbly eggs of street drug culture that had become closely wrapped up with heroin abuse back in the 90s. Dr Gordon persuades me that there is no such thing as a sleeping tablet with absolutely no risk, but that the risk arises with prolonged and excessive use. I resolve it will be my haven of last resort.

I go into the office the following day, Friday, merely to reassure myself that I can confidently leave everything in Stella's capable hands, and am comforted that she quickly grasps the nettle with all the legal business and efficiently renders it into a set of timelines and objectives. I take myself home to rest, but still can't sleep. Michaela arrives home early that afternoon to tell me 'Surprise!', she's booked a night for us at a small country house in the Lake District, with relaxing massages, on Saturday.

Shepherd's Ghyll is a delight: we are greeted like VIPs and dinner is a sumptuous banquet of local paté and melt-in-your-mouth venison. I am wary, however, of drinking more than one glass of wine, having scrupulously stuck to the zero-alcohol fruit cocktail with my appetiser. I manage to log perhaps as many as four hours of sleep until, as the sun rises, I am completely wakeful. I don shorts and T-shirt and set out to walk the extensive wooded hotel grounds that tumble down the hillside towards Windermere. On my return I fill the time till breakfast, in the bath and flicking through the Guardian. I enjoy my massage. (However, I will later come to recognise that this massage also marked the first instance of a new trick that my mind was beginning to play: the notion that often small coincidences were actually much more important than that – rather, events of deep significance preordained as part of our individual destiny. The minor coincidence in question was that my masseuse had quite recently moved to Shepherd's Ghyll to take charge of the health spa with her husband, having previously been in charge of a similar operation in Yorkshire at a hotel that was a new client of ours. It was no big deal really, but I'd clearly made a bit of a meal of it because Michaela commented as we took lunch on the terrace overlooking the lake that she could hear my loud and excitable voice from her own treatment room.)

There is another surprise in store when we get back to Yorkshire on Saturday evening. We'd stayed only one night in the Lakes because Larry was coming home for a couple of weeks ahead of his next term at university. What I was unaware of, however, was that he'd also got tickets for us for the football on Sunday. Now, I may live and have spent much of my life in Yorkshire, but my roots lie somewhat to the north – my mum could trace her ancestry to the Viking lands of the northern Dales of Yorkshire but on my father's side I was of Reiver stock: the wild men who, after the departure of the Romans, continually plundered the so-called Debatable Lands of the fluid frontier dividing England and Scotland. This makes me at least 50 per cent Northumbrian and so I am destined, for better or worse, to support Newcastle United.

Diary of Stella de Weld, Friday August 20, 2010

I didn't need to ask Vic to go to the doctor's. He went of his own accord before he came to the office. He says the doctor showed him his latest test results and they showed he had no infection, even though he says he feels like he's peeing hedgehogs every time he goes to the loo, poor fella. The doctor's given Vic temazepam to help him sleep but I don't know if he'll take it 'cos he's worried about getting hooked, and he never told the doc how forgetful and distant he's become. So we're not much further forward, really. Vic's off to see a homeopath because he says that's always sorted any ailments in the past.

Meanwhile, the doc's signed him off work for a week and I think Vic might actually take the rest, so if it's all just down to stress, maybe that'll sort things. In the meantime, we talked about the legal stuff and he's going to delegate that to me. It's all about the Knowledge America project, which builds on Travel Knowledge with a specific North American website, but also an online and printed magazine and a range of related services, such as links to companies that facilitate migration and visas and such like. Vic got financial support through UK Trade & Investment to do the work to develop the project as an export to the US and Canada and he's done a lot of work finding partners in different parts of the States. But then, just after we've launched Knowledge America online, a company down south comes up with an online magazine called Inside Knowledge that not only covers all the topics ours does but also looks pretty much identical to ours. So Vic writes to them and says that, while imitation may be the best form of flattery, they'd better stop copying us or we'll see them in court. This is all a few months back now and it all seemed to have gone quiet: the other lot changed the look of their website and Vic thought that was that and we went ahead and produced a full print dummy of Knowledge America. What Vic didn't know until I saw him today was the new development: our rivals have actually copied our dummy. We agreed today that we must have a decent case for plagiarism. Even worse, it seems they may have been misrepresenting themselves to our contacts in the US.

http://news.bbc.co.uk/sport1/hi/football/eng_prem

Page last updated at 14:55 GMT, Sunday, 22 August 2010 15:55 UK

Newcastle 6 - 0 Aston Villa
By Mo Durrani

John Carew blazed his early penalty over and from then on it was all Newcastle.

Andy Carroll notched a hat-trick and Kevin Nolan two as Newcastle trounced Aston Villa.

Joey Barton began the rout when he thumped in from 20 yards before Nolan nodded in after 30 minutes and Carroll fired home to make it 3-0.

On the restart, Carroll volleyed a second from near the penalty spot, Nolan added the fifth from point blank, before Carroll completed is hat-trick late on.

If Villa had converted their early penalty then the game might well have taken on a different complexion.

There is a sense of déjà vu as John Carew shapes up for the penalty. We arrive at the match full of hope and expectation and then, within a few minutes, that hope is dashed by the award of a penalty to Villa. Quite inexplicably for a competent striker paid a lot of money, Carew gets his foot under the ball and it sails high into the stands. The miss is greeted with delirium by most of 43,000 people. I reflect as ever that football matches are a metaphor for life at large: so much can turn on a moment, on one bad call...

'That's way up where your Uncle Malcolm used to sit with his mates!' I tell Larry.

'I didn't know he went to the match,' says Larry.

'Just now and then when his mates had a spare seat there... Do you think he's watching?'

'I'm not sure if they get Sky where Uncle Malcolm is now, dad.'

'Maybe they can watch without Sky,' I say. 'The great celestial Pay TV beyond the Pearly Gates...'

With the shocking miss, the Villa players seem to wilt before our eyes. The crowd is baying vengeance for the fact that it was Villa whose goal had consigned Newcastle to relegation two summers and a winter previously. My mood lifts as each Newcastle goal goes in. I don't feel ill, but optimistic for life in general. 'This is one of those special days you won't forget, like beating Barcelona or that David Ginola wonder-goal against Ferencváros,' I tell Larry. It's a prediction whose truth may come to haunt me.

The drive back to Yorkshire is uneventful if more than a little euphoric. But my heart is beating fast and I feel as though my veins are full of adrenaline that is serving no useful purpose: there are no sabre tooth tigers from which to flee; no sharks to swim from. At bedtime my brain is still supercharged with adrenaline and is replaying match highlights in better-than-HD format. I am pouring cold sweat and sleep is no more than a distant and vain hope. For the first time, I take a temazepam. It does not appear to have any effect. I grab a quilt from the spare room and go downstairs to watch 'real' highlights of the match. They appear less vivid than the ones my own head has been playing to me. I try camomile tea. I do sit-ups to burn off some adrenaline but this seems only to produce more adrenaline.

Resigned to not sleeping, I find a film on the movie channels. At some point I think I manage to grab a sliver of fitful sleep, only to find my brain buzzing again at six thirty. A couple of hours disappear in aimless preparation for the day ahead and I decide I'll head for the office, even though I am signed off work. Unsure whether I should be driving, I take my bicycle and stop at the Co-op to buy milk and tea for the office and, after paying, stop to read the back page report in the Northern Echo. It is only later that morning, when I notice the Echo at the office, that I reflect with some concern that I must have walked out of the shop without paying for my newspaper. At the office, Stella tries very hard to brief me fully on what's been going on with our rival and his apparent theft of my contacts in the States. I find I'm getting over-excited by the whole thing and, though I desperately want to see things through, Stella persuades me that I should let her handle the legal business. She's due to see the lawyers on Wednesday. I head for home, stopping at the Co-op to confess my failure to pay for the Echo and straighten things with them.

I spend yet another largely sleepless night. I have taken to roving the house in the dark and have created a series of lairs. These are locations in the house where I can put my small collection of essential night-time possessions and know that if one of these is missing, all I need do is return in sequence to each of my lairs until I find it. In my collection is the book I'm trying to read, Annie Proulx's Accordion Crimes, a handkerchief, a little jar of lavender oil that might help me sleep, my temazepam and my iPhone. On this last I have copied some of that relaxation music they play when you go for a massage, in the hope that it might work with the lavender essence and lure me into the arms of Morpheus. A real plus is that, during these long wakeful nights, I am learning how to get the most out of my iPhone, loading my CDs onto it and downloading material from the Net at dead of night. I have a bigger music collection now than Larry. I also now know the location and dimensions of every piece of furniture in the house, around which I can stalk both silently and safely without the need to switch on a light.

On Tuesday morning I again decide to head for the office on my bicycle, once more stopping to buy provisions at the Co-op. I am almost at the office, when I realise two things: I have, again, failed to pay for my newspaper and I have forgotten to make a sandwich for Michaela to take to work. I'm really concerned about this – I have been working really hard to demonstrate to Michaela that she's in my thoughts, that I'm not locked up in my own mind and to demonstrate behaviour that implies some degree of normality. I've been leaving notes for her during the night: 'Asleep downstairs; better night; wake me before you go to work so I can give you a big hug' or 'Just gone for a walk to the shops as it's such a lovely morning. Don't leave without giving me a kiss, as back soon'. That kind of thing. But when I get home she's getting in her car and anything but pleased to see me. 'You left half an hour ago and now you're back. If you're going, just go...' She snatches the newly-made sandwich and I go to the back of the house where I've left the bike. The path that links our garden to the cycleway has got overgrown as I haven't been using it so much while I've been below par. A trailing bramble wraps itself round my front wheel and clasps it as though in a vice. I'm not moving quickly but my momentum is still sufficient to loft me not so gracefully over the handlebars into a nettle bed. At some point on my descent, the crossbar whacks me hard between the legs. I'm glad it's a secluded spot and no-one can see me. But I'm a bit shaken, so I return indoors and sit down on the sofa. And that's when it hits me and a whole one-armed bandit brimful of pennies finally drops...

The sofa was soft but there was no disguising the pain I felt when I sat down that morning. And there was no getting away from the memories this simple act recalled. Let me wind the clock back to Wednesday July 21, 2010. I was jet-lagged, having returned from California on Saturday, only to head straight to an all-night landmark birthday party. There was a string of other social commitments it was hard for me to back out of and, of course, there were some seriously big challenges to resolve at work. So by that Wednesday, what with late nights and early mornings, I still hadn't shocked my body back onto UK time. It was a pleasant enough summer evening and I suggested to Michaela it might be nice to go for a walk. I fancied some healthy exercise and a few lungfuls of fresh air might do the trick, and get my body clock back on track. We put the roof down and drove out through Pateley Bridge and into Nidderdale. I had a lot on my plate but I didn't feel overwhelmed. Things had gone really well in the States and the Knowledge America opportunity we were building there, alongside the talks I'd been having with Michael Holbeck, a potential and seemingly eager business angel, had given me a real buzz. All I had to do was keep the ship on course and avoid any icebergs. The birds were singing, the sky was blue, it was still pleasantly warm, I was happy with Michaela, and a pint of Black Sheep and wholesome food at the Bridge Inn beckoned. The circular walk we'd planned would take no more than an hour. Out in the open air, I felt young and energetic. I saw a five-bar gate at the edge of the bridleway and told Michaela how good I was at doing the gate vault when I was younger.

'What's a gate vault?' she asked.

'It's a swift and elegant way to get over a gate when you're in a bit of a hurry. I did it all the time when I was on the cross-country team and you didn't have time to stop and open gates. Look, watch…'

Now, the gate vault is a very simple technique that looks harder than it actually is: as you run towards the gate you leap onto its bottom rung, so your momentum carries your body onto the gate, your midriff being roughly level with the top bar of the gate. Simultaneously you grab the top bar with your left hand, while your right remains high and free. As your momentum rotates the top half of your body over the top bar, your right hand grasps the second or third bar down on the far side and you swing your legs over the gate, in a graceful arc, perhaps 45° to the right. Do it correctly and you land on your feet still facing forwards, so you can carry on running without losing your stride.

And so I took a run at the gate and grabbed the top bar with my left hand. But as my body began to arc through the air, the bar snapped towards its left end, depositing me heavily onto the bar below. It was not very graceful. Michaela thought it very funny. I was embarrassed – I only had to look at the gate now to realise most of its components were thoroughly rotten. I had broken the gate and probably the Country Code as well, though I cursed the farmer for having failed to maintain his boundary properly. We completed our walk, ate our meal and headed for home. I had a good night's sleep and woke the next day feeling far fresher.

By that evening, however, I had further cause for embarrassment: my willy looked like a Dalmatian's coat. Distracted by the vivid blotchy brown bruising to my most intimate part, I never gave a moment's thought to the possibility that I might have damaged any other private bits of my body. It would be five whole weeks before I would finally realise that I had indeed done further, and far more significant, damage to myself.

Fast forward to Monday July 26. I am alone in the office at 7pm. Michaela is away so I am taking the opportunity to do some more work on the American business plan. I've had my head in my computer screen for close to two hours and am vaguely aware that I need to go the loo. I must just get this financial section where I want it first, though. It'll only take me ten minutes or so. Perhaps 20 minutes later I stand up to go to the loo and am both astonished and embarrassed that, the moment I am upright, my bladder empties into my trousers. I don't think it's something that has ever happened to me before. At least not since I was a toddler.

It is 10am on Tuesday August 24, 2010 and I am still sitting on the sofa, my pockets overflowing with metaphorical pennies. I am recalling that July Monday evening when my bladder emptied itself, heralding the onset of cystitis. Now, however, I know precisely why I contracted cystitis, so unusual in men, as Dr Edwards remarked at the time. Let's suppose that you take a heavy blow between the legs and all the soft tissues that surround your urethra become inflamed. Let's suppose that your urethra itself swells up, to the point that you can't empty your bladder freely and so you contract an infection – cystitis. Let's suppose that the antibiotics clear up the cystitis but you still have pain when you go to the loo. Yet the tests confirm there's no infection and doctors say 'no infection, no illness' so you think you are just being a bit of a wuss. Let's suppose that it's not just the regular toxins that start to build up in your body, but adrenaline too. Imagine your whole system log-jammed because the simple linear process whereby the liquids you drink eventually exit your body, taking various toxins with them, no longer works. Imagine how your body has to find new routes through which to dispose of the junk it doesn't need – such as sweating profusely, for example… As my homeopath said to me at the time: 'Just because you are sweating, it doesn't necessarily mean you have a temperature.' Christ on a bike: I have spent the last month and a bit living with an injury that's poisoned me with God knows what toxins and with my own adrenaline. And now I have hit myself between the legs again, quite hard, and Things, Can Only Get… Worse!

It is time for drastic action, but it is also my chance to take back control. Control of my own body. I understand. I now know what's wrong. I can sort it out. Yes, with a little help from some ice packs and the entire stock of arnica ointment from Boots, I shall return my urethra to its correct diameter and my insomnia and forgetfulness will gradually recede. All I have to do is ensure that things get no worse after my latest accident. The application of arnica will be frequent and radical – internal as well as external to reach the seat of the bruising – and I'll need to have a supply of ice packs constantly re-freezing. But I will survive. I will be better soon. I will.

Diary of Stella De Veld, Tuesday August 23, 2010

I saw Vic at home today. I'm trying to channel everybody's work projects through me so he doesn't get too stressed by things. I told him the news on the legal front was quite good. I met with Immerhutts yesterday and they think there's a strong case but the difficulty is really in demonstrating what the damage is - how much money this copying might have cost us or how much

It could cost if they carried on imitating us. And then there are issues about the originality of the concept and the extent to which you could say that no-one could have come up with our ideas without actually copying them from us. So, when I got back to the office yesterday, I went through Vic's American contact files and spent the evening phoning people. Almost without exception they'd had calls from the 'other party', and it seemed clear that this lot had been masquerading as us. In fact, I got the distinct impression that Vic's contacts had been stolen. Talking with Vic today he confirmed my fears: many of the contacts that had been approached were people whose details just weren't readily available. Only a moron could think that they had been honestly obtained. Vic was sure we'd been hacked and information stolen.

CHAPTER 4

Chatham House Rules

September 19, 2021
Later that day

Back in his hotel room, Felix resolved to bludgeon his body onto Australian time by not succumbing before at least 10 o'clock to the overwhelming desire to sleep. He looked at his emails and checked some of the threads he'd been following on Blather. He noted that Jameela didn't have a Blather account; nor did she appear on social networking sites; he could find her name only on ConnectPro, the business-based networking tool. Her entry there was functional to the point of minimalist, containing no more than a date list of her job titles, with no photograph or any personal information.

Felix looked at his own profile on ConnectPro and realised he hadn't updated it since he'd been elevated by Back Office to become the company's Head of European Development a full five months previously. It was that elevation that had first registered him on the radar of Shared Ambition, a network dedicated to improving personal performance by encouraging professional links across sectoral business boundaries. He'd attended a week-long course in his home city of York, meeting and learning from a range of people of comparable professional status in the public, private and third sectors. He'd been into a prison and gained a completely new perspective on the drugs scene there, the prison doctor delivering a tragi-humorous address on the relentless traffic that found its way inside, not just secreted on the personage of visitors but inside tennis balls and dead pigeons tossed over the walls into the exercise yard. He'd helped at an early morning soup kitchen for people living on the streets; he'd been behind the scenes at a housing business, a financial services provider and a theatre, and now appreciated the extent to which lessons in one sector could be shared across a wide spectrum of the business world – and the extent to which closed minds could permit bad practice to endure in some companies, and indeed in some whole areas of economic activity.

As a can-do person who liked to roll up his sleeves and rise immediately to the challenges that his work presented to him, Felix was scornful of some people who seemed to dedicate so much of their lives to 'personal improvement' that there was no time left to do their jobs. However, he did feel a particular empathy with Shared Ambition and the simplicity of its model. He read individual 'case studies' and started on a book by one of the network's leading lights, which he found a little too preachy and full of jargon for his own tastes. But he became quite close to some of his new Shared Ambition colleagues and they'd begun to meet for a monthly reunion at which they'd exchange banter and compare notes on how their Shared Ambition experience had modified their approach to day-to-day business and problem-solving. On a couple of occasions he'd got in touch with his Shared Ambition colleagues to pick their brains on ways he could tackle challenges in his new work role. And these dialogues had led him to new contacts both inside and outwith the Shared Ambition network, who had helped him to develop some innovative approaches that had paid real dividends.

At no time did Felix feel that Shared Ambition was anything more than a facilitator; a means of helping people to improve their performance by learning from others in often different walks of life. In his meetings with his Shared Ambition colleagues, however, he learned that there were people in the world who had taken a quite different view of the organisation's activities. Where most might see a desire for learning and improvement, others saw sinister secret networks dedicated to creating a new world order – conspiracy theorists of almost McCarthyist malignancy. One of Felix's new-found friends had described to him how a small band of conspiracy theorists had, in the first decade of the 21st century, dedicated themselves to seeking the destruction of Shared Ambition by trying to discredit its motives and in so doing, cut off its funding by persuading organisations not to enrol on its training courses. The gist of the alleged conspiracy in the UK was that Shared Ambition was committed to replacing the country's democratic government with a new European superstate. In the USA, the conspiracy had gained additional momentum through the simple spin that the goal was to usurp America's 'leadership of the free world' and replace it with a new European hegemony. Felix had seen some of the more extravagant claims that had been made and had laughed in disbelief: the organisation was designed to undermine the police and armed forces, was run by paedophiles and used its network to protect 'members' from disciplinary procedures at work.

Curious, Felix did more research and learned through articles in the business media and marketing publications of the important role played by the Aurora company in turning the tables on Shared Ambition's enemies. Aurora was just one of a number of large organisations that had bought in to the Shared Ambition ethos of personal and business improvement and it had donated its expertise in the design and delivery of campaigns across both social and other electronic platforms, and in the more traditional media. Aurora's approach had been to identify Shared Ambition's greatest vulnerability and tackle it head-on. This was the very simple fact that Shared Ambition's workshops functioned not just in a quite informal way but also, when occasion sometimes demanded, in accordance with the so-called Chatham House Rules. These rules were for the purpose of enabling participants to be frank in the company of other 'students', sharing their own experiences and thoughts without fear that these would then be regurgitated out of context in another forum to their possible discredit.

Most rational people would see this as a simple method of helping to ensure the richest possible debate on professional issues, but the conspiracy theorists discerned something far more sinister: unminuted meetings at which the enemies of Western Democracy were designing their hidden agenda and committing it to memory; the commissars and apparatchiks of the New World Order meeting in darkened rooms to plot the next steps towards realising their fiendish anti-democratic ambitions. The other issue that seemed particularly to bug Shared Ambition's enemies was the organisation's 'use of public facilities', which, they suggested, amounted to tax evasion. This in reality was no more than public sector participants facilitating visits to their establishments. By the same token, Women's Institutes and Scout groups must also be tax evaders.

Felix learned that, with Aurora's help, Shared Ambition had succeeded in marginalising its nay-sayers by campaigning forcefully on the openness of its agenda, presenting countless examples of instances in which sharing experiences across business boundaries had led to improved outcomes for organisations and society at large. Aurora had continued to be a proud and open supporter of Shared Ambition and hosted some of the organisation's highest profile international workshops and forums, including, of course, the one that Felix was now attending in the Eastertide Islands. The 'tutorial' team at the Euphoria Eastertide was made up of people, like Jameela, who were on Aurora's payroll, but also others from a wide range of organisations – governmental, financial, judicial, NGOs... As a global meeting, this one was aimed at senior organisational figures who were already operating on behalf of their own organisations at an international level. Felix knew he was immensely lucky to have been invited to such a significant workshop so soon after his first Shared Ambition experience. That had been at the suggestion of a colleague at Back Office; and now Back Office had been happy to send him to the other side of the world on the basis that he would return a better able, more connected and more ready-to-think-outside-the-box person.

At this precise moment, however, Felix felt neither able nor connected; he would have struggled even to find a box to think outside of. He was tired. Very. But it was still only 7.30. He checked the conference programme again and realised he was missing the informal drinks and canapés reception. He rinsed his face in cold water, changed his shirt and headed down to the reception.

Felix knew people for whom networking was an end in itself. It amused him that something as basic as interacting with other human beings had become so ritualised. These days people used electronic tools like ConnectPro to organise their 'contacts', although in reality they might never find themselves in the same city, let alone the same building or, heaven forbid, in physical contact with these people. They used other tools like Blather, not so much to communicate useful information to other people but rather to demonstrate to the world that they were in there, connected and sentient. And now the ritualised networking of breakfast meetings, after-hours get-togethers, or business 'speed-dating' seemed to be more like an extension of the virtual networking world than real social engagement for its own sake. But then, reflected Felix, it was the same in so many of life's activities: jogging against a stopwatch, or machines in the gym in place of a knockabout with a football or a good long walk; games consoles that did the exercise for you; Internet dating instead of getting out there and playing the field.

'My god, I'm getting old and reactionary before my time,' reflected Felix, who had himself tried each and every one of the social and lifestyle tricks he had just found himself condemning. Truth was he was jaded and wasn't sure, as he entered a room full of people who would be his colleagues for the coming days, whether he was going to be able to deploy his latent wit and charm for another two and half hours.

He glanced round the room and already most other participants seemed to be talking in pairs. Felix hated it when you had to choose which couple to hover beside in the hope that they'd invite you into whatever conversation it was that had been so absorbing them. And then salvation: the only other person at Eastertide whom he already knew entered the room. Jameela did not look like she had just flown half way round the world: rather, she seemed to have gained a second wind and sparkled in a white patterned dress that, it seemed to Felix, was Jameela, rather than high fashion. He caught her eye as she too glanced round the room for familiar faces. She smiled, but quite briefly, as though correcting herself for an informality that she'd decided wasn't appropriate.

Jameela had been a little cross with herself after playing her trick on Felix. She didn't want him for one minute to imagine she was being too familiar or, worse, that she might be flirting with him. He was a former colleague and they had shared the occasional laugh years ago, but perhaps she should have been more professional, especially given that she was, if you like, 'the teacher' at this event, and Felix a relatively inexperienced pupil. She resolved to take the opportunity at some point over the coming days to put things back on a more formal footing.

Back in her room, she lay on her bed but found her eyelids were attached to strings that were in turn fixed to weights slung over the foot of the bed. She must stay awake at all costs... So she served herself a gin and tonic, slipped into the warm sub-tropical night and sipped it slowly on the balcony. By 7.30 she was running on reserve power: she was light-headed from lack of sleep but knew she had just enough in her batteries to make it through the evening, for form's sake if nothing more. She pulled off her floral dress, wiped a wet flannel over her face and neck, then glanced in the mirror: the sun and the sea air had freshened her complexion. She pinched her cheeks and applied the slightest trace of rouge. She chose the crisp white cotton dress with little red polka dots to bring out the colour in her face: no point in looking as though she was way past her bedtime.

Arriving at the reception, she cast her eyes round the room: they fell upon Felix Merryweather and she felt a warm flutter of happy familiarity deep inside that welled up and finally exited her body via her face, where it moulded a smile of recognition. The warmth that seeing Felix again so soon had kindled, alarmed Jameela. So much so that she rapidly extinguished the smile. She would have to be careful. Jameela knew how to flirt and she knew that the discreet application of her sexuality could be a useful tool in business. But she had no need to influence Felix Merryweather to do anything: she might be in danger of sending a signal that could be open to misinterpretation. She could just give him a little wave and head deep into the assembled delegates, but that would perhaps be just too rude. Instead she put on her sternest business face and walked over to Felix. 'Thank God for a familiar face,' he said. 'Do you ever feel like a gatecrasher at these things? Everyone's so deep in interesting conversations that they barely acknowledge you when you hover near them... So tell me about the last, ooh, must be ten? more? years, Jameela.'

At first Jameela had made Felix feel uncomfortable. He had a distinct sense she was looking over his shoulder in the hope of being able to say 'Oh there goes Charlie Smith, I really must catch up with him' or something. She hadn't seemed keen to say much at all about what she'd been doing since they'd last met. He was unsure why the former colleague who had seemed so friendly just a couple of hours earlier now seemed so detached, almost stand-offish. This was almost as painful as trying to get yourself drawn into someone else's small talk. So he decided he would tell Jameela about what he had been doing instead. He told her how he'd left the company where he was working two years after the government contract had ended. He told her how he'd gone freelance, helping companies to build a human interface to very nerdy data systems, but it hadn't quite worked out the way he'd hoped – his aspirations of working short weeks and taking long holidays had never materialised and work seemed always to be a case of feast or famine. Some years on and he had no social life, let alone time to plan holidays with the friends he never had time to even see any more. 'Then I saw this job in York and I thought, well, my folks are getting on and maybe I should take my turn at being the one who's close by. I've two sisters in Yorkshire and they were forever having a dig at me, the busy London lad who couldn't even make a two-hour rail trip home now and then. And when I thought about it I realised I'd never really put down roots in London. I'd gone there partly at least to be a bit invisible and get away from "a situation" and just got caught up in the speed of life…

Suddenly Jameela heard herself say: 'Well Felix Merryweather, you and me too. I went to work for a company in Slough because I wanted to sample the private sector. And then we got taken over by a company up north in pretty weird circumstances. I thought I never wanted to set foot in the North again after my experience with that man from Salford, but I ended up following the work, moving to the North East actually, and that company went on to become part of the great Aurora business empire. And here I am now: your tutor for the next few days, Mr Merryweather.' Jameela blushed. That man was making her lower her guard again. 'Actually, it's nice to see you again,' she said, deliberately and sincerely this time.

Felix fell to sleep like he'd been hit by a mallet. But it was the sleep of a man whose mind and body are in different places: at times fitful and at times filled with disturbing dreams. One such was vivid to the point of being almost tangible. He had gone back in time to the night he'd danced the last waltz with Jameela Durrani, but this time, instead of it ending with a chaste peck on the cheek, Jameela had insisted he come back to her room. There she had read to him from Mary Shelley's Frankenstein, before suddenly plucking the pins from her long thick hair so it fell to her shoulders. Beneath her tresses, she then pulled one shoulder of her dress down an inch or two, tossed her locks behind her and shot Felix a deeply seductive look across her now bare shoulder. Felix woke with a start and was surprised to find that, despite the air conditioning, he was dripping cold sweat. He was also dripping guilt: what in hell's name was his subconscious playing at?

The next three days proved hard work for both Felix and Jameela. The location may have been idyllic, but the exercises were challenging. They began with an examination of a series of business scenarios in which groups of half a dozen delegates were tasked with pooling their knowledge to come up with the best strategy to tackle the problem-solving scenarios presented by the facilitators. These 'scenarios' were real events that had been faced by businesses, some of them having the capability to destroy a company. The groups would come up with tactics and strategies and these would then be compared with those that had actually been implemented by the business in question, and the outcomes that had arisen.

The groups were fluid, with the aim of giving all delegates the opportunity to work with everyone else at least once. And everyone got the chance to work with each of the facilitators. Towards the end of the workshop, the scenarios switched from historic events to real-time issues being faced by a variety of organisations, ranging from private companies, to charities, to quangos, to government departments and global enterprises. All had in common only one thing: they all shared a constructive relationship with the Shared Ambition organisation.

Felix found himself in two separate sessions in which Jameela was the facilitator, the first of them being on the first day of the workshop; the day after 'that dream'. The subject of this particular session, which followed Jameela's earlier group discussion on lobbying, was the protection of intellectual property, and specifically the steps available to smaller entrepreneurs to protect their ideas from bigger players. At first, much of what was being said was drifting right over Felix's head: he was looking at Jameela very carefully, albeit discreetly. Her appearance in his dream had been absolutely unexpected and he needed to know if his subconscious had designs on this woman that his conscious mind was unaware of. Or if, conversely, his dream had been predictive and might actually reflect Jameela's hitherto undisclosed interest in him. However, his surveillance of Jameela revealed nothing whatever to suggest that she had anything other than a purely professional interest in him. On the other hand, however, Felix experienced a dawning realisation that he actually found Jameela more than a little attractive. There was a parallel creeping frustration that he had no idea what, if anything, he either could or should do about it. Felix breathed in deeply, allowing the intake of oxygen to stimulate his brain and focus it on the work question at hand. He had not, after all, flown half way round the world just to ogle his teacher.

Jameela Durrani surveyed the group assembled round the table and invited them in turn to introduce themselves. She instinctively failed to warm to those (usually men) who sought to over-impress at this stage by trying too hard to be witty. Or clever. Like Clive, the Australian guy, who performed to type by cracking a rather limp joke about being in a group with 'a crowd of Sheilas', on discovering that two of his colleagues were indeed called Sheila. Jameela found herself instinctively looking towards Felix to see how he would react to Clive's jest and was surprised to notice that Felix seemed not to have even registered the comment at all and appeared deep in his own thoughts.

She looked at Clive and realised there was an additional reason for her antipathy: he looked disarmingly like Salford

Man. It wasn't so much that he shared her ex-husband's precise features, rather that the combination of his features produced the same effect as those of Salford Man. It was a combination that Jameela now realised she had seen in other faces: it was actually, she was embarrassed to concede to herself, a bit of a film star look – strong jaw line, piercing blue eyes, a mop of hair that was deliberate in its carelessness, designer stubble…

She looked back at Felix, who was by now paying attention to what was going on. He was neither a younger Hugh Grant. Nor a Colin Firth. He was more Steve Coogan than Steve McQueen. That didn't mean he didn't look interesting or just a little attractive. Jameela now found herself looking at him in a new light: the light shone by someone who has made a virtue out of dismissing the opposite sex for a decade or so and is, finally, wondering if life might not, after all, be quite so black and white. Felix had never previously appeared to stand out in a crowd, but now, surrounded by the others at a table, he seemed to glow with an aura that brought to mind Christian iconography of Christ with his disciples at the Last Supper. Now she was just being silly. He was an ordinary man with sort of sandy coloured hair, a fair complexion that was now studded with freckles, probably daubed on as recently as yesterday. He had a wide mouth and quite big lips: a bit too big maybe. His hair had a ruffled look and was maybe a bit too long, but his clothes were tidy: a white shirt with a collar, with a faint blue stripe, the top button undone. He was clean shaven, but his face was really dominated by a nose that was almost too big, but which he could probably just about get away with calling 'Roman', and hence dignified. Despite the mouth and nose, a smile shone through the superficial appearance, enhanced by brown eyes that seemed to exude warmth.

Jameela became aware that Felix was now speaking, describing to colleagues his experience and the fact that he was relatively recently appointed to his position as Head of European Development at a medium-sized company that had developed customer relationship management software customised for individual organisations, whose design features drew upon those of the networking tools that people were familiar with through their everyday business activities… Phew!

'Back Office aims to do what it says on the tin,' said Felix. 'It looks after everything behind the scenes, but it's smart too, because it can spot things like synergies between customers that you may not have realised were there. But the challenge for me is to take it to the next level by ensuring it speaks a language that still means something in lots of different European cultures. And that's why I guess I'm here: to learn from other people who've had experience adapting technological products for people from different backgrounds. Sometimes, though, it's simpler than that: just being in a group like this can get your own mind thinking in different ways, so I'm really looking forward to hearing about everyone's experiences and what they feel they've learned at sessions like this…'

'Hmm, trying hard but just a little pious,' thought Jameela, a little harshly. Introductions over, she passed round the group a typewritten paper, illustrated with screen grabs.

'At the start of the 21st century, people talked a lot about the Knowledge Economy,' began Jameela. 'Knowledge, of course, has historically been the foundation of great civilisations: knowledge gleaned through the work of scientists and philosophers; knowledge handed down by the prophets; knowledge that perhaps sets a certain type of civilisation apart from those built purely upon conquest. In the last 20 years or so we've seen a growing interdependence between the expansion of human knowledge and the evolution of ever more "intelligent" electronic systems. Knowledge itself has become a commercial commodity and yet some of the things that we know are now so dependent on the existence of information technology that we couldn't "know" them at all if, say, we were to find ourselves on a desert island…'

Felix liked the easy way that words came to Jameela and admired her self-confidence and engaging presentation. She'd always been self-confident but the last time he'd seen her, that confidence was designed to protect a fragile interior. If she didn't really know something, she'd wing it, leading those who couldn't see through it to believe she knew more than she really did.

He was happy to let her voice project itself into his head, where it cocooned his brain as he thumbed the sheets she'd passed round the table. The penny quickly dropped: this was the story of the intellectual property case that had famously provided the springboard for the growth of the Aurora business empire, and Jameela, he now understood, had been there at the very beginning and had grown personally as the business had grown. '... find ourselves on a desert island...' said the words, and Felix's imagination found himself right there, on an endless white sandy beach. With Jameela. Sharing a coconut. They didn't send me here just to fantasise about my tutor, reflected Felix again, as he sat up straight and engaged enthusiastically in the discussion about the implications for intellectual property in what was called these days the age of information super-technology.

Felix quickly began to feel that he was gaining something from his participation at Eastertide Island. Even his brain's alarming tendency to lure him into a land of romantic make-believe could be turned into a positive – once he'd acknowledged Jameela's (almost certainly unintended) power to send invisible sexual messages to him across the ether, he was able to harness the energy it gave him so he could make useful, thoughtful contributions to the debate. He was unsure, nonetheless, just how valuable the Aurora intellectual property lesson was to the world at large. The 'victims' in this case had been Persona Communications, one of Aurora's founding predecessor companies. But Persona had been a victim not so much of the greyer end of the scale of intellectual property dispute, such as an alleged case of 'passing off', but of a potentially criminal act that might easily have ended in the criminal rather than the civil courts. Persona's prompt legal action after its intellectual property was stolen by hackers at a rival company meant that it was quickly able to acquire its rival out of liquidation – a liquidation prompted by the seizure by Persona's lawyers of its entire IT system. For every such fortuitous and prompt outcome, Felix knew there were many more cases in which the outlay on legal fees had quickly eclipsed any possible gain.

But there were other members of the group for whom the story both provided inspiration and stimulated thought about new tactics to protect the fruits of their intellectual endeavour. Felix began to learn more about his colleagues; and to recognise that initial appraisals didn't always tell the whole story. Clive had been over-eager to make his mark and had, in the process, seen himself typecast as shallow, maybe even boorish. But Felix increasingly found him insightful and with a sharp mind that was able to think quickly at a tangent. Several times during the workshop sessions, Felix witnessed Clive turn a situation completely on its head by looking at it from a perspective that no-one else had considered. But for whatever reason, Jameela seemed not to have modified her initial assessment of him and more than once Felix sensed she was bristling as she delivered a patronising response to Clive's analysis. Ah, well, she can't be perfect, thought Felix, while Clive, for his part, maintained his dignity, either ignoring the put-downs or feigning not to recognise them as such.

Felix particularly enjoyed one challenge in which the team he was in had to role-play a recovery strategy for a company that had entered a new market with badly translated product names and sales materials. It was a real-life scenario in which a range of harmless children's sweeties had been promoted with slogans that had sexual and other inappropriate overtones. Felix felt vindicated in his own decision to use only native speakers as he developed the marketing materials for his new role at Back Office.

The days at Eastertide were not all work and no play. On Day Four, participants were rewarded for their endeavours with an outing to the Great Barrier Reef, taking a seaplane in the morning to a diving platform, near the eponymous Kidney Atoll. Delegates donned net suits over their swimming costumes to guard against the tentacles of the tiny irukandji jellyfish, the force of whose stings was inversely proportional to their size. Felix was initially delighted to see Jameela in a sky blue bikini, albeit not a skimpy one, that almost exactly reflected the colours of the inviting waters of the lagoon, while contrasting perfectly with her warm skin tones. He was less delighted when she disappeared inside something that reminded him of a giant beekeeper's getup. Felix pretended to be a fish caught in a net, flailing his arms before withering in a mortal heap with his mouth askew, and was pleased to see that Jameela's laughter seemed genuine, rather than polite. The Shared Ambition group, with their snorkels, swam off in a line, like ducklings behind their mother. The crystal clear water teemed with shoals of brightly coloured fish that darted in and out of the multi-coloured corals. It was among the most beautiful and memorable experiences Felix had known. He particularly liked the assorted varieties of clownfish, with their flour make-up and doleful eyes.

The group reached a coral-encrusted wreck, submerged just a few metres below the surface of the lagoon. The waters were dense with all manner of varieties of fish. Colourful shoals shimmered in the light of a sub-tropical sun that pierced the surface of the crystal-clear water. The shoals parted like fly curtains as the swimmers passed and Felix found himself playing a game of hide-and-seek with the fish just so he could watch and see how hundreds of little creatures could behave as one. He reminded himself that, with care and a little practice, he could stay under water for a minute, maybe more, and could swim down the three or four metres to the wreck without undue discomfort. He began to explore different aspects of the wreck, trying to work out the underlying features of the vessel without, of course, harming the corals by touching them. At one end of the vessel he discovered a particularly beautiful sea anemone, its purple-red tendrils like an exotic orchid.

On what must have been his fifth or sixth dive, he rounded what he had deduced was the vessel's wheelhouse and came face to face with another pretty 'anemone'. In fact, they practically banged heads. Felix raised his eyes from the wreck below and so did the woman in front of him. He found himself looking through two masks into a familiar pair of eyes. Mask or no mask, he felt an overwhelming urge to kiss the face beneath the eyes and found himself drifting into Jameela's personal space. Just before his eyes instinctively began to close, he saw those of Jameela widen, perhaps in alarm. He reversed away from her and made a thumbs-up gesture. He beckoned to her and took her hand, leading her towards the stern of the vessel. The anemone had closed but as he pointed it out to Jameela, it slowly opened before them in a quite mysterious, mesmerising display. He turned and smiled. Jameela grinned back. Even through glass she looked relaxed and content in a way he couldn't recall. The pair surfaced and swam to the platform and peeled back their masks. 'It's out of this world,' said Jameela, and Felix noted that, yes, she did indeed look genuinely happy.

On their way back to Eastertide Island, the seaplane put down in Maryport Bay, on the uninhabited island of Whitesands. The aircraft taxi-ed towards the beach where, once in shallow water, the pilot dropped a small anchor and his passengers waded the short distance to shore. The beach shone bright in the early evening sun. 'It looks like chalk,' said Felix.

'And sounds like it too!' added Jameela as the grains of silica squeaked audibly beneath her sandals. Felix didn't want to make Jameela uncomfortable and strode off towards the far end of the bay, where he sat on a washed up tree trunk and watched a group of divers in the water. A few minutes later, a familiar figure approached and Jameela sat down beside him. She smiled and Felix swallowed hard as his heart missed a beat. Felix filled the sound vacuum that followed with some small talk, about the restrictions on visiting Whitesands that he'd read about in his guidebook.

Then he took his courage in both hands and said, 'I've enjoyed seeing you again these last few days.' Jameela smiled faintly and looked thoughtful but said nothing, so Felix continued: 'I know things can be very intense, when you're somewhere new and exciting and a long way from home, but I have enjoyed your company and I think it might be a shame not to see each other again when we get back to the UK.'

Jameela looked down at the white sand and drew a deep breath. 'Nothing has changed for me, Felix. I haven't had another relationship since I told you about my husband from Salford, and I have learned to live without a "significant other" in my life...' The emphasis on 'significant other' was deliberate and carried an ironic overtone as if the whole concept of being close to someone was a ghost that constantly taunted her. 'Besides, my job takes me away a lot...'

'Who said anything about relationships or "significant others",' countered Felix. 'All I said was it would be nice to see you again, as people who can enjoy each other's company, friends even. If in time that became something else, something more, well that's something we could talk about then, but let's not make life difficult by presuming the question is going to arise... We don't live that far apart: we could meet for Sunday lunch, go for a walk; meet on an evening and go to the cinema or the theatre.'

'I do a lot of these things already; on my own or with girlfriends,' began Jameela, but Felix cut in: 'And you get irritated that you have to plan your activities with them around whether or not they are in a relationship, or you smile through gritted teeth at having to play gooseberry. It can be lonely, and I know. We could be a girl and boy who enjoy doing things together, no strings attached.'

Jameela looked up and pushed her sunglasses back so Felix could see into her eyes. The sun's reflection on the beach and the gently ebbing waters of the bay shot teasing shadows up and down one cheek. She placed a hand above her brow and smiled, looking more relaxed than Felix could remember. 'You are very persuasive, Mr Merryweather. I think I might think about giving it a go. But promise me: do NOT pressure me into making this something more than friendship or I will get very cross!'

'I promise,' smiled Felix, daring to kiss Jameela softly on the forehead.

Walking back towards the seaplane, they talked about the approaching long trip home. Jameela, it emerged, was booked on Emirates to Newcastle, but one day later than Felix's own flight to Manchester. Jameela proposed changing his flight, so they could meet up at Brisbane and travel home together from there. 'The Aurora travel team can do that for us,' she said. 'That'll give us an extra day and then you'll get to York from Newcastle just as quickly as from Manchester.' Felix increasingly felt like he was walking on water and had to pinch himself to remind himself that his new 'girlfriend' came with a great many strings attached and absolutely no guarantees that any of those strings would wither. As they reached the group boarding the plane, Jameela tapped him on the arm: 'Felix,' she said. 'Can we keep all this to ourselves?'

'Chatham House Rules,' grinned Felix.

Jameela's suitcase was packed for the flight to Brisbane. She vacated her room, leaving her case with the concierge. As she headed for the poolside café, a helicopter flew low overhead and landed a few hundred metres away on the roof of the small tower whose luxury apartments were rumoured to belong to some of the world's richest and most reclusive film stars. Over a fruit cocktail, she messaged Felix: 'Your flight changed: see you at the airport. J x.' This was without doubt the scariest, riskiest action she had contemplated for years and she felt more than a little trepidation. Would she ever, she wondered, risk it becoming more than a friendship? Could it ever be more than a friendship outside marriage? Every instinct of her upbringing told her there could be no happy medium. No affairs. No 'friends with benefits'. All that was out of the question and so she returned to the simple premise that had been agreed: friendship and nothing more. She found that if she kept on reminding herself of this agreement, the idea of doing something just a bit more risqué in life did have a certain appeal. She began to smile inside. And then a porter approached her with a message, neatly folded into a leather wallet on a tray.

'The pleasure of the company of Ms Jameela Durrani is requested immediately. Floor 15, Eastertide Tower.' Jameela checked her watch: she had no more than two hours before she would have to head for the airport. Who could possibly need to see her so urgently? If Felix had still been there she would have asked him to come with her. She was unsure who else she could ask. She gathered her things and explained to the concierge where she was going. As a precaution, she gave him Felix's details and asked him to contact Felix if she failed to return within two hours. She took a golf buggy up the hill to the tall building where the helicopter had landed. Two burly custodians guarded the lobby. One asked her to look into a camera. 'Ms Durrani, please go straight to floor 15,' he said. Jameela was taken aback: besides the passport authorities, only Aurora would be able to recognise her by her irises alone… She turned and looked at the exit and began to feel anxious. 'Ms Durrani, please, there's no need for alarm, they're expecting you on floor 15.'

She was met at the 15th floor by a young woman who seemed to look vaguely familiar, though from where Jameela could not recall. She was ushered into a large room whose huge one-way windows afforded a magnificent panorama of the island and its beaches. She could see the backs of the heads of two people sitting on a sofa looking out at the view. Hearing her entry announced they both stood up. Jameela caught her breath with surprise: 'Lord Lindisfarne! Lady Lindisfarne!'

'Vic and Michaela is just fine, Jameela,' replied the man.

CHAPTER 5

The slipway to madness

Tuesday, August 24, 2010

Before refining my self-medication, I decide to first revisit all I can remember of each day that has passed since that gate vault on Wednesday July 21, 2010. The knowledge that I have identified the cause of my condition is a strange comfort. On the one hand I now know precisely why I have been so unwell, but on the other, I know I may have only limited time to slow and turn this crazy super-tanker of an illness.

Understanding, however, is key. My diary should open the door to that understanding. It's not a diary in the sense of a record of how I have felt or what has gone on each day, but it is a comprehensive record of what I have done since returning from the States.

My gate vault episode came four days after getting back from America, when my judgement might well have been impaired by both jet-lag and brain overload. On balance, though, I am more inclined to blame bad luck: I've had more than enough practice at dealing with jet-lag and managing work-related stress. A further six days had passed before I realised that I had cystitis in that embarrassing moment when I stood up at the office and my bladder emptied itself into my trousers. Thank God, I reflected, that I was there on my own.

So, it must have been on Tuesday July 27 that I first went to the surgery and saw Dr Edwards. But how was I feeling in the days before that? My diary tells me that I fulfilled a variety of both work and social engagements and I've no recollection of having felt ill at any of them. My diary also says I returned to the surgery on August 6, a little over a week after the infection started. That, of course, was to see Dr Edwards again: the one who'd stressed it would be important for me to return to the surgery, with cystitis being unusual in men. But he hadn't even troubled to read my notes before I went into his consulting room.

In the following days there are two threads to my illness that are clearly ravelled together and yet at no point do I begin to make a connection. Although my urine test has shown that I am clear of infection, for some reason I am still experiencing a burning sensation when I pee. Ejaculation is even worse: like shards of barbed wire. Perhaps it's because I am, increasingly, sweating a lot and, consequently, weeing less, that the importance of painful peeing seems to recede. The other strand of illness is my increasing loss of mental sharpness and focus. This doesn't seem to be a linear progression: on some days I feel OK. I note that on August 9 I drove up to Hartlepool for a meeting and I know that I took a long walk round the docks, where the Tall Ships were visiting, with no apparent ill-effects. On the other hand, I know it was around this time that Charley, our 'London office', began to ask other members of the team if I was OK.

My diary reminds me that the following day was anything but OK. That was the day I had to get Stella to come and rescue me in Leeds. My recollection is of getting up after a sweaty, broken night and hoping that Michaela would tell me I didn't look fit to drive to Leeds. I didn't want to make the decision for myself. But the trouble with a vague, unidentified illness is that you and your symptoms seem to become invisible to those around you. And, of course, not understanding why you feel ill, you want to carry on regardless and not succumb to something so ephemeral. I remember that, driving to Leeds, I was struggling to concentrate, so I gave Charley a call on the hands-free. I must have alarmed her, because I was losing the battle to assemble a sentence. It was probably at that point that I should have turned the car round and gone home. Summoned a taxi, even. But I didn't want to admit defeat. Instead I drove on, ever more slowly as the link between my eyes and my brain, and my ability to react to any messages the former might send to the latter, faded. I did the last few miles on the A61 dual carriageway at no more than 25mph, with the window wound down to give me as much fresh air as possible. I somehow manoeuvred the car into a multi-story and headed for my appointment.

I was supposed to be talking to a major public utility about working on the development of their intranet. They'd just entered into a partnership with a big Danish company and my contact, Bill, now also found himself with additional projects to manage. In fact, he began the meeting by informing me that he was just back from holiday, overwhelmed by all the tasks facing him, and had been on the point of asking his secretary to cancel our meeting… My heart sank: I had just risked my own life and that of other road-users in my determination to prove to myself that I was not ill.

I did my best to keep smiling and Bill told me about another challenge nestling in his in-box on his return from holiday: the installation of 'smart' customer service points, which would need to operate in a number of minority languages in addition to English. The project required the translation of 200 words of instructions into five languages and then these had to be incorporated into a design template. The calculation required was a simple one: five times the normal translation rate of £120 per language per thousand words, plus a mark-up, plus a bit more for the more unusual languages, plus a couple of hours of design time, plus a management fee. My brain, however, was not up to the task. I had to write the calculations down in my notebook and work them out long-hand. I began to sweat profusely and had to mop my face with my handkerchief. I did the calculation three times, taking what felt like ages, and managed to come up with a different answer each time. Struggling to fill the vacuum created by my mental stasis, I plumped for 'somewhere between £x and £y' before wiping another half gallon of sweat from my brow. I was about to say I felt unwell and suggest I leave, but Bill had beaten me to it and had already returned his papers to a document wallet and begun to stand up. 'Another day,' was all he said.

I returned to the reception and sat down. The receptionist asked if I was OK and I told her I wasn't. Could I sit for a minute and recover? But recovery was not in the script... I began to feel even worse and started to sweat even more. The receptionist asked if she should call a doctor but I told her No, I would remove my sweaty presence just as soon as possible. I decided I would try and get a train back to Harrogate and get one of the team to pick me up there. I would recover my car the next day. When I called the office, however, it turned out that Stella was already in Harrogate and volunteered to get the train to Leeds and find me. All I had to do was remember who my car was insured with and get her placed on the policy. I remember thanking my lucky stars that my insurer had a UK-based call centre: I wouldn't have had the mental acuity to deal with any language or cultural misunderstandings. In any event, I eventually found myself sitting outside the multi-storey and, within the hour, safely on my way home with Stella at the wheel.

I took myself immediately to the bedroom where, as I lay with curtains closed, my brain – to the extent that I still had one – slowly packed its bags and floated gently up to the ceiling, leaving behind a throbbing empty shell. It was a quite terrifying experience; that feeling that my brain was no longer inside me. I don't remember feeling pain and yet I felt so ill I thought I was dying. Michaela came home and I hoped she would come and sit with me, but I didn't have the strength to shout for her. Once again, lack of diagnosis seemed to cultivate lack of understanding and lack of sympathy. Eventually, I think I must have drifted off to sleep.

I was upset about the meeting with Bill but wary of not being able to achieve the right tone of voice in a follow-up email, which I wrote when I felt well enough to get up again.

I carefully drafted what I would say and then sent it to Charley to ask her if she felt the tone was right.

This is how it read:

Hi Charley Look at this: tried to call... Bad meet this morn as unwell. Need your opinion. Vic Hello Bill It was good to see you this morning: two years! I can't believe it. That is seriously scary! I'll give you a better idea of translation costs shortly, and let you have an up to date set of creds. Have a good week! All the very best and have a good week. Vic PS: Sorry I wasn't too good this morning. Haven't been ill for for many years, so don't know how to deal with it: thought I was better and looking forward to a great catch up. I know it's hard when back from leave, so

There was no reply from Charley but then you can see that I'm not really explaining either the situation or what I want her to do. And it doesn't look like I have even finished writing or correcting it. I'm not sure it's right at all and I'm glad I don't appear to have sent it.

I think after this low that I must then have rallied as, by two days later, my diary reminds me that I was able to hold a successful client meeting in our offices and, notwithstanding clear evidence to the contrary, was able to convince them that we'd found solutions to all the issues that had threatened to derail another international communications project. My recollection is that this was perhaps the first day on which I even began to feel slightly euphoric: I was on the mend and could talk a good talk and all was going to be good with my world. On the days I had been off work, too, I had been very focused on relating to people. I began going into town more and really engaging with the shop-keepers and stall-holders on the market. I would stand tall and breathe in deeply, to fill my lungs with air and my blood with oxygen. I would seek eye contact with people and felt I could instantly judge whether their core was warm and friendly, or somehow rotten. On one day, the woman in the shop that mends my trousers even gave me a kiss: a man had come in desperate to get his smart pants fixed within two hours and when the woman had said it would be no problem he gave her a kiss, saying 'you've saved my life'. She looked at me and said 'Well, you'd better have one too!' and planted a smacker on my own cheek. You see, I reasoned, all manner of interesting things will happen if you just keep your head high and engage fully with people. Things, for example, that will never happen if you only communicate by text or email or are permanently in a rush. 'Look into a person's eyes and you can see right into their soul' was becoming my maxim, along with Walk Tall, Walk Straight and Look the World Right in the Eye.

And so it was with me in this increasingly buoyant and optimistic frame of mind that, that weekend, Michaela and I headed north for Cynth's 50th birthday bash. In the interim, my diary suggests that another day had passed without major event and so I booked us a room in a Premier Inn a few miles out of Newcastle, not far from Cynth and Ken's. On the morning of the party, I recall, I had persuaded Michaela to come into town shopping with me. I wanted to share with her the relationships I had been building up with my new shopkeeper friends. It was no more than an extension of the philosophy whereby we get our milk delivered to the doorstep: it's not cheaper, and it's probably no fresher than supermarket milk, but it keeps a man running his own business and ensures someone in farming gets the proper reward for milking their cows. But I was a bit disappointed: Michaela said my shops were more expensive than the ones she went to and anyway she liked the people at 'her own' shops…

Michaela drove us up to Newcastle that afternoon and I recall it was a pleasant late summer's evening when we jumped in a cab to run the two miles or so from the hotel to the commuter village where the birthday girl and her partner lived.

Sometimes I'm not great at parties: I'm one of those people who always seems to find himself the third and seemingly unwelcome one at the edge of two people in animated conversation. I never know whether to stand my ground and wait for the moment when I can make some pertinent remark and thereby join in, or for the moment at which I may be invited. Or, on the other hand, whether I should discreetly edge away and find some other exchange in which to engage. But at Cynth's do, I remember being on much better form than this: there were people I knew well and many more with whom I had at least some passing acquaintance. The mood was relaxed and easy and I decided to risk some alcohol: nothing in great quantity and nothing too potent, maybe two or three bottles of beer, tops. Michaela took a picture of me with my arms round the shoulders of some old mates: I have it on my phone here still, and we are all smiling and I can still see in the picture what Michaela saw that night. She could see in my relaxed demeanour clear signals that I was on the mend: it was the smile that spelled relief. I was happy at the relief I felt: I was on the mend, if not completely better, and Michaela told me as much in the taxi on the way back to the Premier Inn.

We went to bed and I went to sleep: such bliss!

In a world in which one's chickens may indeed come home to roost, it may be wise not to count them, if I'm making sense: at about three in the morning I was awake and in pain. My 'recovery' had been no more than a false dawn; or perhaps an unhatched chicken, I don't know; it was all too confusing. For starters, I say I was in pain, but in reality it was neither an ache nor a pain that had woken me. I can only really describe it as an 'extreme discomfort' between my legs and I wasn't able to pee. I had to assume it was something to do with the cystitis: yet I still had made no link with my unfortunate accident at the five-bar gate, now very nearly four weeks previously. Only powerful pain-killers were going to sort this and I knew I didn't have any. I was in too much discomfort to try and do anything about it myself, so, taking my fate in my hands, I woke Michaela. No, she had no painkillers but she would go to reception and ask for me. Hotels have rules these days about not administering medicines to guests, but thank God the young lad on duty was prepared to be persuaded to break them. Michaela returned with distalgesics. The pain eventually subsided and I guess I drifted off to sleep.

I don't recall feeling any ill effects on the Sunday and I prepared myself for my trip north, to Orkney, the following day. And, of course, that pretty much brings me back to the beginning of the story and my day from hell near Kirkwall.

So here I am again: it is August 24, 2010 – more than a month since I knowingly broke a gate and gave myself a Technicolor willy. And, unknowingly bruised all those tender tissues around my urethra, causing them to swell and make it close to impossible to pass water. I know I now need to reverse that damage, but I don't know how far the natural process of healing may have gone, nor to what extent I have turned the clock back again through my recent tumble from my bicycle. Feeling let down by the casual approach of the health service, I consult my homeopath. I have good reason to have faith in homeopathy in general and my own homeopath in particular. Let me tell you about the gunpowder cure… A few years ago, I was out walking in hills on the Norwegian island of Leka, north of Trondheim. Leka is an unusual island, in that much of its topography is created by a reversal of the natural order of things, with rocks from the earth's mantle, normally found beneath the continents, incongruously resting on top of younger volcanic rocks. But, I'm getting pulled off track, I know, so let me quickly tell you how I was walking across rough, coarse mountain grass in an area littered with boulders. The grass was in long dense tufts and it concealed rifts in the surface of the 'magma' below. It was not easy walking. Suddenly I found both my feet tangled in the grass, one foot holding down the grass that consequently kept the other foot immobile. I was falling headlong and put my arms out to save myself, but my arms weren't as long as the sharp pointed rock that was rising fast to meet my mouth. The impact was all broken teeth and split lips. I was shocked but I think my companions more so. No-one likes to see a lot of blood. But I was annoyed that everyone insisted on cutting short the walk and staying with me while a dentist could be found. I didn't want a dentist: the mouth heals quickly, it would be OK, which is pretty much what the Norwegian dentist (when I finally got to see him) said, too. My split lip grew until it looked a bit like those women, somewhere in Ethiopia, I think, who put plates in their mouths to stretch their bottom lip. Mine was not very pretty and the pain kept me awake at night.

When I got back to England, the swelling had only just begun to subside and there was a big open wound inside my mouth that oozed green pus. The doctor, like one I had earlier seen in Norway, said this was just part of the healing process, but, two weeks later, it was still oozing when I went to see my homeopath about something quite unrelated. Almost as an afterthought, I showed her my open wound and told her how long it had been like that and what the doctors had said. She tut-tutted and said she might be able to sort it out for me and sent me home with a remedy made from gunpowder. Now, medical science doesn't like to credit homeopathy because there is no scientific understanding of the practice. I choose my words carefully: it is not that science disproves homeopathy, but the current level of scientific understanding of it struggles to explain how a sub-atomic dose of a substance can have any effect when administered to a 'patient'. The 'formal' scientific explanation will come only when we fully understand the laws of quantum physics: the physics of the small, as opposed to the physics of the big, which does a good job of explaining everything that's bigger than an atom. Sorry, I'm getting sidetracked again, so let me just say quickly that my mouth had healed completely within hours of my taking the gunpowder remedy: that's HOURS, not days, just hours. Even my dentist was impressed the following day when he was at last able to set about making good the damage wreaked by Leka.

'Yes, it won't always work, but when it does it is usually very fast,' my homeopath confirmed. Now, I won't bore you just now with any of my many other first-hand examples of homeopathic triumph but I think maybe you'll understand why, having been failed by the doctors ever since the five-bar gate incident, I should be happy to put my trust in someone else.

So, I speak to the homeopath on the phone and describe everything that's happened but, no, I'm not in a position to drive the 30-odd miles to see her. Yes, more ice packs and more arnica should do the trick. I walk into Ripon, to Boots, and buy up every tube of arnica on the shelf. Back home I spread the arnica liberally between my legs and stick some inside, just for good measure. Then I sit on an ice pack.

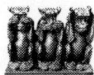

I have launched a full-scale assault on my physical ailment, but now that I understand the damage I have done to myself, I also understand that my blood is full not just of toxins but also of adrenaline. The former explains lapses in my concentration and, I am increasingly aware, in my short-term memory. The latter explains why I can't sleep and why, despite everything, I feel in a strange kind of way that I have a growing insight into things. What things? Well, the sort of life, the universe and everything kind of things…

I have an increasing sense that, somehow, the adrenaline is starting to open up dimly lit and distant parts of my brain and, despite my accumulated lack of sleep, I am feeling very much 'smarter than the average bear'.

I reason that, having identified what's behind the chemical imbalance that's keeping me awake at night, and having instigated a strategy to detoxify my blood and get my waste products out of me the way they are meant to exit, that is via my bladder and urethra, all should now be no more than a simple matter of time and a little patience.

But now I need to explain to you why the idea of adrenaline stimulating the brain isn't really that new to me. When I was a child I thought, as I think a lot of us do, that I was in some way special: out of all the people in the world, I alone was Me. What freakish long odds: I could be anyone else, but the reality was that I was ME. And one of the very special things about Me was that I could create secret worlds. I had my own method and I was as near certain as can be that no-one else could create secret worlds the way I could. The method was quite simple: I would find somewhere secluded where I wouldn't be seen or disturbed and then I would focus my mind on the framework of the 'world' I wanted to create. Now, this 'world' might actually be a world as such: a distant planet with its own lifeforms that I had perhaps begun to sketch out in pictures. But more likely, it would be something more mundane: an imaginary country for which I would need to create cities, transport systems, football teams and stadia and the like. Or perhaps an imaginary airline for which I would work out the fleet and the timetables and so on on paper, but would then have to use my imagination to get the planes actually flying. And to make the planes take off, as it were, I would run up and down or round and round in my secluded place and soon find myself lost in a new world of my imagination as the adrenaline I was generating stimulated my brain.

Now the adrenaline is at work again, just like when I was little, only this time I need to tame it a bit. The homeopath advises me to try and burn off the adrenaline with physical activity, so that it isn't pumping round my brain at night when I should be sleeping. So I try to establish a routine for these days at home while I recover enough to return to work. The weather this week is pleasantly warm and sunny so the day begins with a walk to the Co-op to get the Northern Echo and croissants for breakfast. Today the croissants haven't come out of the oven yet. I buy a notebook with a brightly coloured cover from the stationery shelf and also pay for half a dozen croissants at check-out. I go and sit on the bench by the playing field and begin to write in the book. This will help me to keep track of things that have been eluding my short-term memory these last few days. I read in the Echo that a supporters' trust is trying to raise money to buy Newcastle United from its unpopular owner. I must ring my old friend John, in Newcastle, about this. As a long-standing season ticket holder and local councillor he'll know what's going on. I return to the Co-op for my croissants but they are still not ready, so I hang around another five or ten minutes until they are brought to me by the helpful girl on the till. I try to pay her for them but she won't take my money: I thank her profusely. Hours later I remember that I paid for the croissants when I bought my notebook and newspaper. They were not simply a gift from the Co-op.

Back home, I'm skipping around in the garden when my mobile rings: I see it's John, from Newcastle. 'You'll be calling me about the supporters' trust,' I tell him, on answering the phone, before he has any real chance to tell me why he actually is ringing. 'I guess you'll be leading it, yeah? We need to get the PR wound up a gear, get some real momentum behind it…'

'Vic, slow down, slow down. You sound a bit… hyper.'

'No, I don't think so, it's just I was about to call you about the supporters' trust and then you rang me first…'

'Well, to be honest Vic, I don't know that much about the supporters' trust. I thought it had all gone a bit quiet. I was actually ringing you about something else: we've got a charity dinner coming up in aid of the Better Life Foundation, you know the college for disabled people. I was hoping you and Michaela might be able to join us…'

I run around in warm late summer's morning sun and begin to forget what John has just told me. A mystery local businessman is going to take over the supporters' trust and give it new momentum. I am the victim of industrial espionage; if I can prove it I may be rich. I can see clearly now the rain has gone. It is indeed going to be a bright, bright, sunshining day. Yeah!

Later I walk to the swimming pool. In the changing room is a young man I recognise. He's wearing a Newcastle United shirt. That's unusual down here. Most wear Leeds United, even in these difficult times for the club that 'dreamed the dream', only to see its Enron-style finances unravel in disastrous fashion. As I say, I recognise him, but I can't place the face, however hard I try. We talk about the supporters' trust. I tell him I have an inside track and that I know a mystery businessman is going to come in and front it and save the club for the fans. 'Watch the newspapers,' I say. He tells me to just pop into the shop if I have any more news. 'What shop?' I wonder. I can't for the life of me fit his face into any shop...

As I pound the running machine I see the future so clearly. I am the mystery businessman; I am Chairman of Newcastle United, the people's football club. The world smiles.

My hope is that tonight I will sleep; that my exercise has burnt up my surplus adrenaline. Midnight comes, midnight goes. Michaela is snoring. I head for Larry's bed. I take my new notebook, my phone, my watch, a pen, and place them by the bed. It's dark, it's quiet. I should surely fall asleep. I am a victim of industrial espionage. I have a major football club to run. I have a thousand and one thoughts. I must write them in my pretty-covered new notebook. My brain is gathering speed, not slowing. Suddenly I am in a tunnel of millions of points of light. I am soaring down the tunnel. Faster and faster. The lights begin to turn in a swirling vortex. Faster and faster it all turns. Faster and faster I go. I hurtle through the swirling lights towards a single point of light ahead of me. Faster still and faster. And then calm: I am with my twin brother, Malcolm. I have always known Malcolm is there with me, ever since he was killed. But now he is not just 'there' in that vague ethereal sense. He is here, not there; here, with me!

I need to tell you about Malcolm and how he died. And how, before he died, my mother had a premonition about his impending death. She said it was something he had said to her that set her brain off.

We were not identical twins; nor did we even look that much like each other. Malcolm, with his brown eyes and dark hair, looked a bit like my mum, whereas they say that I take after my maternal granddad, which is to say I'm tall and a bit Nordic-looking. It's almost exactly four years since Malcolm died. It will, in fact, be four years this coming weekend: my mum, Margaret, died exactly one year after Malcolm. Malcolm was very close to my mum; closer than me, really. My mum told me, a few weeks before Malcolm died, that she didn't expect him to be around too much longer. I asked her if he'd been diagnosed with a terminal illness that he hadn't told me or either of my sisters about. She said not, but seemed unwilling or unable to explain why she had said what she'd said. I asked mum to please say nothing to Malcolm: the last thing I wanted was for Malcolm to live his life spooked by some crazy notion that he might die. She agreed, but then urged me to try and persuade Malcolm to stop flying. That was as near as she ever got to saying what the premonition had been until after Malcolm had died. I hate talking about the day that Malcolm died, because I feel so very guilty about it, because the fact is that the last thing that he did was to save my life. And in his dying moments he surely saved the lives of probably a dozen other people. As a consequence of the manner of his death, it's likely that quite a few more lives have been saved.

Malcolm should not have died: he should not have had to give up his life to save me; to save a group of innocent schoolchildren; some senior citizens; or the lives of perhaps countless people unknown. He died because the lessons learned from a fatal bus crash in the Yorkshire Dales exactly 30 years previously, to the very day, had not been applied with the full force of the law. On that day, a bus carrying elderly day trippers ran out of control down a steep hill in Nidderdale, crashing through a wall and landing upside down, trapping and killing more than 30. Its brakes had been defective and the main conclusion from investigations was that coaches should be fitted with an electronic speed retarder to slow a bus in just such an event. Bizarrely, crazily, criminally, however, the fitting of such devices, although good practice and widespread, was never made compulsory. I know all this not just because I did a lot of homework, which I presented at Malcolm's inquest and to MPs and other lobby groups, but also because, by some extraordinary twist of fate, I was actually present in the nearby village of Pateley Bridge when that crash happened in May 1975. I remember them desperately trying to clear the roads of holiday traffic to let the fleet of ambulances through to the scene. Extraordinarily, that accident took place almost exactly 50 years after another fatal bus crash in precisely the same spot.

Anyway, back to May 2005… Despite my mother's premonition, Malcolm's death had nothing whatever to do with flying, unless you count the fact that he and I had been over in Lancashire, to 'test drive' a microlight for a publication Malcolm used to write for. Malcolm was hooked on flying ever since we were young and the comparatively low cost of flying in a microlight had given him the opportunity to fly a lot more than would have been the case if he'd stuck with the Piper Cherokee syndicate he'd belonged to. Plus, combining his flying skill with his writing ability meant he could also spend a lot of time flying other people's aeroplanes and even get paid, a little, for doing so. I was the lucky one, accompanying my brother whenever I could take the time out from work. We had lots of adventures and a few scrapes: Malcolm was always a safety-first pilot, but there are some things you can't legislate for, like the engine failure over the Brecon Beacons, when Malcolm had to bring us down in a field of sheep, surrounded by power lines. I'm still not sure quite how he managed it. But here I am, digressing… again.

Back to that awful day as we drove home by the backroads beneath a high spring sun. I'll tell you what I remember first… Malcolm was driving his yellow VW Beetle and I was in the front seat. We were talking about life and how, here we were, both in our early 50s now and neither of us married. When was I going to get round to making an honest woman of Michaela, Malcolm teased me as he regularly did and I had replied, as usual, that maybe she should think about making an honest man out of me. And he told me he had started seeing someone, had been seeing her, occasionally, for a few weeks. Malcolm wouldn't normally wait so long to tell me something important like that, so I knew then it must be someone special. He might have told me more if he had lived. As it was, I had to find out the hard way after he'd died and I had yet another person's grief to deal with on top of my own, and on top of my own guilt that, really, I was the one who should have died that day.

I remember us crossing the bridge and I remember the schoolkids lined up gazing over the parapet. I remember starting up the hill the other side. I remember seeing the coach hurtling towards us on the wrong side of the road. The next memory I have is of waking up in hospital. I asked where Malcolm was and they told me there was time; I had to be strong and focus on getting myself better. It was my sister Charlotte who had to break the news that Malcolm wouldn't be back. I couldn't understand: my last fleeting memory was of a bus bearing down on me and yet fate had decreed that I should be the one to live, while Malcolm was gone. It only became clear when they pieced together those fateful seconds. Malcolm saw the coach on the wrong side of the road, but as he'd swerved to squeeze through on its left, it had drifted back to the centre of the road, leaving him with nowhere to go; leaving me to take the full impact of the collision, head-on. But even then, it could have ploughed on and hit the kids we'd just passed. They think Malcolm made a deliberate decision to apply full left lock so the coach struck us broadside, leaving him to take the full impact. The coach rode up partially over the Beetle, the pair grinding to a halt before the bridge. They say Malcolm died instantly. When I was well enough I went back to the scene with Michaela and laid flowers. I think his soul left that spot that day and he was at ease. For me, it had been a dreadful burden: the grief of his loss and the guilt that it should have been me. I still feel both now, though neither as keenly nor as often. And through the four years that have passed I still feel close to my beloved twin: he watches over me and in some way that we don't yet understand, he is around, for certain. What helped me get through things was the good that came from Malcolm's death. It should never be thus, but the fact is that it takes people dying for people with power to make changes. The coroner in his finding of accidental death added the rider that the least that should come from this tragedy was that speed retarders should become a legal requirement and now, finally, we seem to be getting somewhere on that. I'm hopeful too that the highways people may at last do something to slow larger vehicles before they reach the hill, maybe a chicane or something. You won't find as much written about our crash as about the earlier ones: after all, only one died. But as the coroner said in not so many words, my brother died that others might live.

So there you have it. The death of my brother, Malcolm. And now, here he is: back again, with me. And he is telling me a whole load of stuff. No, he's not standing there in front of me, reading from a list; nor is he even 'talking' in any real sense you'd understand. It's more like he's all around me and all this information is kind of coming out of him and percolating into my consciousness. There's what I'll call both micro-information and macro-information: the bigger picture, or even the very big picture. At the micro level he's telling me a lot of very sound stuff, not least that it's high time Michaela and I turned the world's longest engagement into marriage. He's setting me a really tough task to bring his son Rory back in from the cold: Rory has pretty much kept his own counsel since Malcolm was killed but it's breaking Malcolm's heart, if that's still possible when you are already dead, that Rory isn't going to show his face at his sister's (my niece, Sheenagh's) wedding. On the bigger picture, Malcolm is revealing to me the truth about so many things: from global warming to the secrets of evolution. He is letting me in on the secrets of Life, the Universe and Everything. There is so much information going into my head that I am having to process it all at super-speed and I know that it will take some time for me to interpret all this data and then share it. And I know I will need to be careful as I share it because some of this information is dynamite: it is the core data from the plan for the universe itself.

I am elated; buzzing; but I feel neither surprised nor shocked by what I have witnessed. Like I say, I have always felt Malcolm at my shoulder, so it is no surprise to me that he should ratchet up his presence in this way. However, this information overload is no real help for sleeplessness. In fact, there's so much information crammed in there now that I'm struggling to take on board any more. If I move around the house, I struggle to remember why I find myself arriving in a particular room. Thank goodness for my new multi-coloured notebook: I can write down things as they occur to me and I can remind myself of the purpose of journeys from one room to another. Just so long as I have my notebook, I have my memory! And here's another trick: I am learning specific routes around the house and, besides the lairs I told you about, I'm setting up little possessions piles in each room. If I can't find something, I now know that all I have to do is visit each possessions pile in turn and I will find it! It's so beautifully simple! I have the whole new memory system in place before dawn. All I have to do now is fill time until I can wake Michaela and tell her about meeting Malcolm.

CHAPTER 6

The Inner Circle

Friday, September 24, 2021

'We'll have your bags brought up,' Jameela, said Lord Lindisfarne. Jameela pinched herself: it hardly seemed like yesterday that plain but charismatic Vic Turnbull had persuaded her to leave Slough for a new life in North East England – a place about which she knew little, where her only friends would be those of her colleagues who might also decide to move north, and which was in the same half of the country as the worst memories of her life.

And now this man was inviting her to take another utterly life-changing decision. Except that it hardly seemed like an invitation. Jameela felt that Vic and Michaela were making her an offer that, despite their protestations to the contrary, she would be unable to refuse. The metaphorical horse's head was already severed and ready to go in her bed. Vic and Michaela were good people who had devoted their lives, and 50 per cent of Aurora Group profits, to doing 'good works' around the world. The Aurora Foundation was legendary and its influence extraordinary, but it could not run itself and Jameela had seen less and less of Vic after moving north. Indeed, she reflected that she probably hadn't seen him at all after her first year – around the time she was herself promoted from Persona to the giddy heights of management in the rapidly expanding parent Aurora Group. Since then, Vic Turnbull's reputation had increasingly gone before him. Except that, more and more often, it would be only the reputation that would arrive, as the man himself became an increasingly enigmatic, indeed reclusive, figure. In the four years since his peerage, Lord Lindisfarne, Jameela knew, had been seen in the House of Lords only occasionally and preferred to use his title and the access it conferred in far less visible ways.

Jameela wasn't happy: the prospect of enjoying some sort of relationship with Felix had actually, if quite unexpectedly, begun to appeal to her. Felix had helped her to recognise the loneliness in her soul and had opened a door to a different way of living her life. One in which she might share new experiences with someone else, wind down with them, exchange views on life and politics. There was even the scarcely admitted possibility that a friendship might one day become something more. Such fantasies, however, would be incompatible with the more radical life change that Lord Lindisfarne had imperiously proposed.

Jameela was also shocked: she had just become aware of why the world saw so little of Lord and Lady Lindisfarne and why rumours persisted around the non-disclosure of the nature of some of the Aurora Foundation's activities. These, of course, were outside the scrutiny of any official body: when it was first created, the Foundation operated only in the UK and to a clearly prescribed set of charitable rules that could be monitored by the country's Charity Commissioners. Latterly, as its activities had become more global and its resources began to derive from parts of the Aurora empire that had previously not existed, so they increasingly fell far beyond the remit of the UK charity. Indeed, the Foundation itself had begun to mirror the Aurora Group, using a variety of different means in its various countries of operation so as to maximise the revenues at its disposal. The other side of this coin was that its activities had indeed become increasingly opaque and there was no one annual statement of accounts that could refute the rumours. Jameela found herself now reflecting, not for the first time, on the irony that the Aurora

Foundation shared some of the less desirable attributes of those it had spent so much of its time campaigning against in the name of Saving the Planet, Promoting Harmony, Teaching Tolerance, or Empowering the Weak. But the activity that Vic had just described to her was beyond the scope of anything she had imagined that the Foundation might be engaged in. And he wanted her to be part of it.

Jameela was also worried: she had made an arrangement to meet Felix at Brisbane Airport and, right now, it was looking increasingly unlikely that she was going to be there. Vic's 'offer' required that she effectively disappear from view with immediate effect. Felix would lose all faith in her and might be very worried as to her safety. Vic had said only that it would be 'taken care of'.

And Jameela was also seduced: one of the world's most famous men wanted her to do an important job. A job with an air of mystery and intrigue. A job that might help change the world: for the better. And a tiny part of her also knew that Lord Lindisfarne's offer would defer, perhaps for ever, the need to make any decision about returning to the land of boy-meets-girl. Jameela had been brought up a Muslim and although she practised little, consumed alcohol and behaved more like an agnostic, aspects of her faith remained deeply ingrained. Not least the notion of fate being in control of her life, of God's Will being done. She was reminded of the guilt she had felt at the break-up of her marriage: the feeling that Allah might indeed be punishing her for choosing Phil, a non-Muslim. Her decision to turn her back on relationships had been not just an act of retaking control over her destiny but also an act of penitence, she reflected. And now she had tasted temptation once again. Was it God who was putting temptation in her way? Was this another test? Or was it actually a signal that she had 'served her time', that she had made amends for her error and was now to be allowed a second chance in the relationship game? She didn't know the answer to these questions. She was not a theologian. But despite the allure of this second chance, Vic's proposition raised another attractive alternative: that of once again turning her back on relationships and being certain to avoid the pain that would, surely, eventually follow...

And so, she reflected, whatever decision she made now, what was meant to be would, ultimately, be... If she was meant to be with Felix, then, one day, she would indeed be with Felix. But for now her fate lay in the hands of Lord Lindisfarne and he had big plans for her.

All these thoughts buzzed inside Jameela's head as she looked down from the heights of Eastertide Tower, across the resort at the foot of the hill. Lord and Lady Lindisfarne had left her to reflect a while on her decision, but time was already pressing: if she was going to Brisbane, she would need to leave within the hour. And then the decision was effectively taken out of her hands: those were her bags that were being offloaded from the golf buggy down below. 'Insha'Allah,' reflected Jameela. Or perhaps Insha'Lindisfarne. She sent a message to Felix, which read: 'Dear Felix, I am very sorry, but something unexpected and very important has come up, to do with work. I am not sure when I will be able to see you. Thank you for your company over the last few days: I enjoyed being with you. Best wishes, Jameela.' The message was returned 'undeliverable'.

Felix Merryweather sat in the departure lounge at Brisbane with only an uneasy premonition for company. Earlier in the day he had received a phone call from the concierge at the Euphoria who told him that he was calling on the instruction of Ms Durrani, whose luggage had just been collected on her behalf. No, he couldn't say where it had been taken. No, he couldn't say where Ms Durrani was. No, he had received no instructions from Ms Durrani herself regarding either her luggage or her whereabouts. Why on earth, then, had he allowed Ms Durrani's luggage to be

taken by strangers? Felix had become angry and frustrated with
the man. He felt impotent. There were no police on Eastertide
Island, but he called the resort manager and expressed his
concerns. He received a call back an hour later to say that Ms
Durrani had been located unharmed and was still on the island.
No doubt she would get in touch with him if she chose. Felix was
far from sure he could take this at face value, but the more he
thought about it, the more prone he was to conclude that Jameela
had simply had cold feet and chosen to run from any threat of a
relationship with him, or indeed anyone else for that matter. His
last message to her had simply gone unanswered.

It was a very disconsolate Felix who finally boarded the long
flight to Dubai.

'I'm genuinely very sorry, Jameela,' said Lord 'Vic' Lindisfarne.
'The difficulty is that once you step into this circle, secrecy is
absolutely essential. We must at all times remain one step ahead
of the people who are out to destroy us, "the enemy", if you
like…'

Vic was drawing breath as he carefully weighed the words with
which he would continue, but Jameela cut in: 'But why did you
cut off my phone and email before I had told you my decision?
What gave you the right to presume my decision. What gave you
the right to collect my luggage and bring it here? What…'

'I know, I know,' interrupted Vic. 'Be assured this is NOT a
kidnapping or a presumption of your choices. If you had declined
the invitation, you could have left and all your communications
would have been restored and your luggage would have been taken
straight to the airport. You have my absolute word on that. But
we simply couldn't run the risk of security being compromised
while you were making your choice…'

'And what about my colleagues at work. Or people I might
have met here over the last few days? What are they supposed to
think when I just…' Jameela paused for effect… 'DISAPPEAR!?'

'Your work colleagues will receive an explanation,' said Vic, 'but we don't think there is anyone else who needs to know…' Jameela contemplated telling him something about her relationship with Felix but, for some reason, she was unsure if she might later come to regret it. So she said nothing.

Instead, she turned and looked Lindisfarne right in the eyes. The peer held her gaze: he didn't need to say 'Look into a person's eyes and you can see right into their soul'. Anyone who knew Lindisfarne well or who had read his book knew this was more than just a maxim of his: it was a fundamental rule that governed his relationships with people; it was intrinsic to his first assessment of strangers and to his evaluation of the veracity of what people said to him.

Jameela felt the clock turn back to the day in late September 2010 when she had first met then plain old Vic Turnbull. It had been a tumultuous time: the company she worked for, Smart Ideas, had been caught committing industrial espionage against Vic's firm, Persona. Well, perhaps industrial espionage was rather too grand a term for it, but Smart Ideas and its boss John Smart had run out of their own ideas and had hacked into Persona's server and 'borrowed' theirs. If the first rule of crime is 'don't get caught' and the second 'have an alibi', then John Smart didn't know the rules. Jameela had arrived at work one September morning to find the doors under guard and men in overalls removing all the IT equipment. As early as the very next day she had received a recorded delivery letter signed by one Victor Turnbull, which stated that his company, Persona Communications, was responsible for seizing the assets of her employer but also that it intended to acquire the company out of receivership and maintain those aspects of its business that were not the subject of a legal dispute between Persona and Smart Ideas. It had invited her to attend with her colleagues a meeting at the Copthorne Hotel, just outside Windsor, the following day. Anxious colleagues from Smart Ideas wore frowns and compared their levels of incredulity while they waited for the meeting to begin.

Jameela hadn't met Vic that day. Instead, it was a blonde of about 5ft 6ins who strode purposefully to the microphone at the front of the meeting room and announced that she was Victor Turnbull's 'first lieutenant'. Stella de Weld explained that she was charged with running Persona's business while her boss and its owner, Victor Turnbull, eased himself back into work after illness. She recognised that this was a distressing time for staff at Smart Ideas and apologised for that distress. However, she and Victor had had no choice but to act in the way they had because of the very serious nature of what had come to light. There was a legal process in progress about which she could make only limited comment but, as a result of that process, she confirmed, Smart Ideas had been placed in receivership.

Jameela remembered how her angry and bewildered colleagues had challenged Ms de Weld at this point, demanding to know precisely what actions alleged against their employer could conceivably justify such a draconian response. She was impressed by the resolute manner in which de Weld faced them down. 'I'm very sorry but I really can't go into more detail while there remains the possibility of criminal charges…'

'Criminal?!' chorused the room.

'Please! …while there remains the possibility of criminal charges against Mr Smart and some of his colleagues. We have no reason to believe that any of you who have been invited here today have knowledge of or were party to the events that are the subject of these allegations, and nor can I say what the legal outcome will be. However, what I can say with certainty is that Mr Smart has acknowledged the seriousness of the situation to the extent that he has placed your company in the hands of receivers because he recognises that Smart Ideas cannot continue to trade in these circumstances…'

'Well, there's not a lot any of us can do with no computers and no records,' complained one of Jameela's colleagues.

Stella de Weld continued as though she had heard nothing. 'Victor has no axe to grind against any of you who have not been involved in the activities that have led your employer to close his business and it is his intention to acquire all the assets of Smart Ideas and to re-employ those of you who wish to work for him on terms that will be at least as generous as those you have been on.'

Jameela remembered the sighs of relief that punctuated what Stella was saying at this point as clearly as she recalled the gasps of disbelief that followed as she went on to explain the unstated 'but' that followed the offer of re-employment. That those who were re-employed would have to demonstrate loyalty to their new employer, seemed reasonable; at least in an abstract sense. Indeed, Stella made it clear that re-employment was otherwise unconditional: there would be no tests of merit or competence, only of loyalty. But on that test, it soon emerged, the bar was set high: the price of re-employment would be relocation to the North of England.

And so it was that, one week later, Jameela had found herself with the majority of her colleagues accommodated at an extremely pleasant hotel in open countryside somewhere near the border of North Yorkshire and County Durham. Stella de Weld had been emphatic that only those who were prepared to contemplate loyalty to Persona should join this trip, but equally she had said that the purpose of the visit was to educate people as to the kind of life they could enjoy in the North and brought with it no obligations regarding the acceptance or otherwise of a position in the transplanted Smart Ideas operation. Indeed, some had joined the trip more because they thought it was the nearest they were likely to get to a Smart Ideas leaving do or a decent wake, and had little, if any, intention of moving north. Jameela had probably considered herself as belonging to this category, but after an intensive three days of sightseeing, culture and meeting people she was feeling herself carried along by the momentum and, she thought, she might just give the move a try. She had, after all, few, no, let's be honest, NO ties in Slough.

What clinched it for Jameela, however, was her first meeting with then plain Victor Turnbull.

Vic had an energetic presence that filled the room when he came to address them at their hotel. Where Stella de Weld had spoken with measured caution and tiptoed around the legal niceties, Vic had no such inhibitions. He told his audience quite bluntly that their employer had been complicit in the hacking of Persona's server, through which product details and the company's contact database, including all its sales leads and partner contacts, had been stolen. While he would fully understand that some staff might hold loyalty for their boss, maintaining such loyalty for a thief would not be compatible with working for Persona. Jameela glanced at Stella, who was sitting behind her boss, and noticed her jaw drop at his bluntness, but Vic shrugged it off, saying: 'My excellent number two, Stella, thinks I may be committing slander or prejudicing any possible legal action, but my view is that Mr Smart wouldn't dare. He has been, so to speak, caught with his hands firmly in the till. Or, to be more precise, in my till. And that's something I take a rather dim view of,' he said, with a smile.

Jameela wondered how Vic could have known that Stella had been uncomfortable, bearing in mind that she was outside his field of vision, and she guessed that he must simply have presumed this to be the case. She was more than a little intrigued by this man who certainly had charisma but who, at the same time, appeared to lack the hard edge she had come to associate with entrepreneurs and, specifically, people like John Smart. No hard edge and no sharp suit either: Vic was wearing jeans, tan coloured boat shoes and a nicely cut herringbone Harris Tweed jacket over an open-necked pale blue shirt. She tried to guess his age but she wasn't that good at gauging people older than she was. Probably 50, she thought. There were no signs of grey in his slightly dishevelled light brown hair and he was clean shaven, which, she reflected, tended to make people look younger. He wasn't thin, but neither did he appear overweight. For someone who, as Stella had said, was just out of hospital, he appeared the very picture of rude good health, with colour in his cheeks and a tanned complexion.

Vic told his audience that he and Stella would meet with each of them in turn to discuss their options and answer any questions they might have. When it was Jameela's turn, she was struck by the way Vic greeted her: he stood up as she entered the room, appeared to breathe in deeply, filling his lungs, and – gripping her hand quite firmly – looked right into her eyes. This was more than just establishing eye contact, she thought: this was something that some might find almost invasive and yet, she recalled, she herself had not felt discomfited by it.

And now, as she remembered that particular moment, another not dissimilar one sprang to mind: the evening she had first told Felix about her personal circumstances. He too had looked into her eyes and she had felt as though he was gazing into her very soul... The inadvertent link she had made between the man who had so easily persuaded her to move north and the man who over the past few days had tempted her back towards the land of relationships did not make her feel especially comfortable. Was she just a sucker for anyone who looked her in the eyes? Was it really so easy to influence her behaviour by looks and aura alone? How could this possibly square with being the tough-skinned woman in charge of her own destiny?

Back at that first meeting, Vic had had to say very little. In fact, it amounted to little more than 'I've read your CV, I like what I've seen and I'd like you on my team'. And Jameela had pretty much said 'Yeah, OK, I'm really looking forward to it'. Now Lord Vic Lindisfarne was at it again. A few years older but essentially unchanged. He'd looked her in the eyes again and told her he wanted her in the Inner Circle with himself, Lady Michaela and a few carefully chosen others. Jameela hadn't said Yes, but neither had she been able to say No.

She smiled at him, albeit a little hesitantly: 'You win my Lord. I guess we'd better get planning.'

CHAPTER 7

The pilgrimage

Wednesday, August 25, 2010

After my meeting with Malcolm I am restless. I want the morning to come quickly so that I can tell Michaela. I write her a message and place it on the floor by the bed in case I am asleep when she gets up. 'I hav somethin very special to tel yo,' I write. 'Lat nigh I met wit Malm.' I notice that I am missing the ends of words, or skipping bits in the middle. My writing hand is incapable of keeping up with my enhanced brain speed. 'I lov yo vey muh, my daring. Don' wake me if I slep.'

Sleep? Pah! Chance would indeed be a fine thing. How could a man, even an exhausted man, sleep after meeting his dead twin brother?

And so morning finds me by Michaela's side of the bed with a cup of tea I have brought her. 'I met Malcolm last night,' I tell her. 'He told me a lot of things.'

'Did you really? What did he say?' Michaela does not doubt me: she knows too that Malcolm has always been with us both since his death.

'He said that we would both live till 103. And that we should stop messing around and get married. Now. In a small ceremony on Holy Island. We can do the big party later. He took me all the way to the Big Bang and showed me how everything was hard-wired for creation. And he explained lots of things to me and then we came back. He told me about what matters and what doesn't. I have to sort out Rory and make sure he's at the wedding this weekend. But that's just the small stuff. He told me all the truth about climate change: how it's all about deforestation and large-scale pollution in the USA and China. He says aviation is just an irrelevant sideshow that's deflecting people from tackling the real issues effectively. And he said he'd given his life for me, those kids on the bridge, the old folks on the bus and anyone else who might still die because of unsafe braking on coaches. And he wants to be recognised for giving his life: he wants to be beatified, you know, made a saint. I have to write to Archbishop Desmond Tutu to get things started...'

'Wow! That's big stuff, Vic.'

'Yes, but there's not too much pressure because I've seen a bit of how time works and anyway, I've got nearly half a century of good life left in me.'

'I think, Vic, you should really take it easy today. I really believe that you met Malcolm last night but all this is hard work for you.'

Michaela sips her tea and sees the note on the floor. I've done my best to replace the missing letters so she can at least read it. 'That's nice! I like how you keep leaving me these lovely notes. But, you know, if you die at 103, then I'll still have a few years on my own... You were thinking we'd go together, weren't you?'

'Oh yes,' I respond, a little sheepishly.

Malcolm has set me a lot of tasks, to which, if I say that the easiest is to arrange a wedding, the adjective 'challenging' might apply. If one was a master of understatement, that is. I have to repair a family rift against a deadline, persuade the Church to make my brother a saint, halt climate change... And all the while the channel of communication that Malcolm has established with me, far from being a one-off revelation, seems more like a gushing tap of information and data. My late brother is telling me more and more about the way things really are, and the rest that Michaela counselled is out of my reach. Each time Malcolm communicates with me anew I feel a prickling sensation at the back of my scalp: do you remember the way eating cold ice cream would sometimes make the flesh on your head creep when you were a kid? I quickly learn how to make this communication with Malcolm a two-way process. I visualise the message I believe that Malcolm is trying to convey. If I am correct, the prickling sensation in my scalp grows palpably and then breaks like a crashing wave across the crown of my head. If I have misinterpreted what Malcolm is trying to tell me then the prickly feeling just gently subsides. Over the course of the next few hours, Malcolm is beginning to disclose to me more important lessons about evolution and about the importance of seemingly trivial events in our lives that are nonetheless significant elements in our destiny.

Have you ever felt that life is full of too many coincidences? I am so convinced that there is an unusually large number of coincidences that visit us that I have developed my own theory about this. I call it the Iceberg Theory of Coincidence because, just like nine tenths of an iceberg lie beneath the surface of the ocean, so for every coincidence that we experience, there are another nine improbably coincidental events that nearly happened but which, for whatever reason, we failed to notice. My most spectacular run of coincidences came about during a train journey through the former Yugoslavia and on to Athens, back in my student days. A week previously I had been at a party up near my parents' place, where I had been staying. I'd been invited there by a girl I knew, but the people at the party were all strangers. I had never seen them before and only once since. That once was in the next carriage of the train as we left Trieste a week later. No kidding!

A few days later I found myself rounding a corner at Omonia, in Athens, to come face-to-face, at the very apex of the corner, with a couple I had met just once at a mutual friends' wedding earlier that summer. Again, I have never seen them since.

And a few days later still, on a beach on the island of Naxos, deserted apart from just two other people, one of those two others had wandered up to me and said: 'You're Vic, aren't you? Aren't you the guy who's moving into our house next term?'

Now, for me, the striking thing about all these so-called 'coincidences' is not merely that they seem to be unlikely events, or even that three such unlikely events should happen within a few days of each other. No, the most intriguing aspect is that these coincidences were recorded at all. Let's start with the train ride: if that party of teenagers had been just one carriage further away from me, I would have remained blissfully unaware of their coincidental presence. If I had arrived at Omonia just 30 seconds later or earlier, we would, all three of us, have passed the apex of the triangle created by two streets radiating from the 'square' and been none the wiser as to the presence of each other in Athens. As for the Naxos incident, well, to paraphrase Bogart, of all the remote unpeopled beaches on all the islands in all the world, I have to choose this beach on this island. At this particular time. AND, be recognised by someone who has hitherto seen me only once, and even then, just fleetingly. The sheer unlikelihood that time and place should have coincided so precisely three times in so few days serves only to highlight the great imponderable: just how many more coincidental events might have taken place in those few days but for the tiniest mismatch in time or place? What if, for example, my first love had been on the boat-train to Dunkerque when I left England, but just happened to have slipped to the loo at the precise moment at which I passed her seat for the only time? What if the step-brother I never knew I had was sitting in the gondola that passed me on the Grand Canal but his sunglasses concealed the telltale family resemblance? What if Michaela, whom I wouldn't actually meet for more than another quarter century, had been among the young children and teenagers with their parents in the taverna in Naxos Town (which is actually not impossible, as she was there at some point that summer)? All these are the ninety per cent of coincidental events that just couldn't quite manage to actually happen. I could go on and, while I am not saying that we are all steered through life by the forces of fate, I am very definitely saying that something is clearly 'going on' here. And I reject as statistically untenable the argument that the sceptics promote, that these coincidences occur in numbers that are entirely consistent with the numbers that represent both the population at large and the size of the social circles in which we move. I say hogwash. But don't ask me to provide an explanation: maybe this is something else that will one day be explained by a new understanding of quantum physics, or what they call the 'Science of the Small'.

Well, I guess you think I am wandering away from the point again, but there is a purpose in my telling you all this. One of the things that Malcolm has told me today is that we as people are the sum of the events that we have witnessed and of the things that we have done, in a far more literal sense than we might have thought. In short, we are all being prepared for a purpose and we will draw upon our life's experience to fulfil our own individual purpose. And so the challenging tasks that Malcolm has presented to me will become that much easier because, in the course of my life to date, I have acquired, in the shape of my experience and knowledge and through seemingly trivial things that have happened to me, precisely the tools I will need to fulfil those tasks. It is all breathtaking in its symmetry and simplicity.

My mind today is untamed and frenetic. And while I'm not going to achieve the rest that Michaela suggested, neither am I going to attempt to go into the office. And so I suggest Stella call round and we work through a few things so I'm up to date.

Not a great deal has happened on the legal front in the three days or so since Stella and I last spoke, since when, of course, I have had both the epiphany of my bicycle moment and my meeting with Malcolm. I get a sense that, unlike Michaela, Stella is not really believing me when I tell her about Malcolm so, over a cup of tea in the garden, I decide to move to less contentious ground, such as the project she's working on at the moment, which is a tourism development initiative in the Caucasus. 'I guess you'll have Georgia on your mind?' I suggest.

'Well,' replies Stella, 'Usettia your heart on something and...'

'It'll Tblisi when you get into it,' I interject.

'Tblisi?' queries Stella.

'It'll be easy,' I explain.

'Let's draw a line now, shall we?' she counters.

'A Caucasian chalk circle?'

'Yep, you knock the ball in the air and I'll hit it!' says Stella as we high-five.

'You'll be as good as Rog, soon!' I say.

Anyway, things, it seems, are under control at the office and it's just a matter of waiting for the lawyers to digest the latest information Stella has passed on regarding the apparent theft of our contacts and data.

I set Stella a couple of additional tasks: to look at taking out some corporate hospitality at Newcastle United and to follow up the news about the National Trust in Scotland having to put the island of St Kilda up for sale because of lack of funds for its conservation, which is something I'm sure I read about in the paper the other day. I want Stella to check out just how close that John Carew penalty might have ended up to where Malcolm used to sit when he went to the match and I'm thinking maybe we can get involved in some kind of fund-raising campaign for St Kilda, an island I have so often pledged to visit, though I have, as of now, still to do so.

It's good to see Stella and it's great to be able to tell her that I have, at last, come to understand the reason for my illness and so, consequently, it will now be only a short time before I am well and back in harness at the office.

The sun shines and, mindful of my homeopath's advice that I should try and burn off excess energy, I take a little jog around the garden and let my mind float to thoughts of the shrines that will commemorate Malcolm's life; the sign that Malcolm sent me through the medium of football; the prospect of success in our plagiarism case. I am an earthly envoy of my late brother. I am his disciple. I will help deliver new truths to the world. I will save St Kilda for future generations. I am the Chairman of Newcastle United.

I need to tell you more about Malcolm's son, Rory. But for you to understand Rory's story, I'll also have to tell you about the woman in Malcolm's life: the woman I think he was about to tell me about on the day that he died. Like I told you earlier, I knew there was someone new in Malcolm's life and I had a good idea she was going to turn out to be someone important. But as we all dealt with our grief over Malcolm's loss and I did my best to come to terms with my mounting sense of guilt, Malcolm's mystery woman was among the last things on our minds. Until the day she turned up on our doorstep.

I remember that day like it was yesterday. I think it was the first Sunday after Malcolm's death that had seemed even vaguely normal. I'd made tea for us and brought the Observer back up to bed and started on Everyman. It must have been about 11.30 that the doorbell rang. Doorbells on Sunday morning are not the norm for us. Opening the door to a slender East African woman accompanied by a teenager in a wheelchair, even less so. She spoke good English, with something of a Leeds accent. 'Mr Victor Turnbull? I am so so sorry to disturb you. I am Ayanna and this is Erasto, my son. You don't know me, but perhaps you do know something OF me. I knew your brother Malcolm. Your lovely brother Malcolm. We were very close. He told me many things about you and said you were a kind man. I know he wanted to perhaps work some things out in his head and, when he was sure of them, I believe he was going to introduce Erasto and me to you and to your partner… Michaela, I think?'

I think I stopped breathing for a moment and then I was

conscious of not breathing because my ribs were still very painful from the crash. 'You'd better come inside. Both of you.'

Ayanna came in and sat herself, quite demurely, on the edge of the sofa. Erasto wheeled himself in and sat, nervously playing with his thumbs. 'I'll make some coffee, OK? Would you prefer juice, Erasto?' The boy nodded. I put the kettle on and slipped upstairs. 'I think you need to come down,' I told Michaela. 'And you need to be prepared for a bit of a shock. It's Malcolm's lady. And she's got a son. In a wheelchair.'

Michaela's face was a picture of suspended animation for a few seconds. 'OK, I'm on my way,' she said finally.

Ayanna seemed kind and gentle, and, considering the pain and strife she had packed into her life to date, relatively unscarred. She was from Somalia and had fled the civil war, claiming asylum on arrival in the UK. In London she'd met a Somali man, who had permanent residency status, and they had moved in together. Then she fell pregnant. And then the abuse started. And so it continued intermittently until, about four years ago, she had fled to Leeds. 'I had fled a war once and, eventually, I decided that I was still living in a war zone and there had to be a better way for Erasto and for me.'

Ayanna had only been in Leeds a few weeks before it happened: Erasto was knocked down by a hit-and-run driver on the edge of the estate they were living on. Although he had not suffered spinal damage as such, the injuries to his legs were so severe that it was unlikely he would be able to walk again. Things were to get worse, however: 'A year ago, they started proceedings to have me deported. I never married Erasto's father so, although Erasto can stay, because he was born here, I can not…'

I looked at Ayanna: even seated you could see the tall elegance in her form. She was ageless in the way that black-skinned people can be, and I could only guess that she must be somewhere in her 40s and Erasto maybe 13 or 14.

'Is that where my brother comes in?' I ventured. I knew Malcolm had been doing some voluntary work with a refugee lobby group in Leeds.

'Yes, Malcolm was helping me to build a case to stay in the UK and he was working with an MP in Leeds and he won for me a temporary stay of execution pending a further appeal. But he also became my friend. He was very gentle, but also very cautious. I think your brother too has known pain in his life and he was not impulsive. He would go away and reflect on questions and then return with a carefully thought-out answer a day or two later. But he was very kind to Erasto too and he would spend so much time with him, helping him to flex his legs so he could try and build up some muscle in them again, and helping him with his studies. Erasto had begun to see him as a father figure and I, well you know it's hard to say, but I was attracted to Malcolm and he was so so kind to me...'

'Were you lovers?' I asked, at the precise moment Michaela, in her dressing gown, came into the room. She shot me the glance that says: 'Don't ask such direct questions, it's rude.'

'Yes, we had become lovers and the truth is that Malcolm had suggested that we should get married. He said we could become a family and that would make my future and Erasto's secure.'

I had no reason to doubt the truth of Ayanna's words, but probed: 'When did he ask you that?'

'Perhaps two weeks before he died.'

It squared with every subtle hint that Malcolm had made to me and in particular with our conversation in the car before the crash. 'How did you hear about the crash?'

'They came to see me from the refugee centre, but of course they didn't know how close Malcolm and I had become. I was beside myself. I try hard not to believe in fate but in my life I feel as if I am being punished so many times for a crime that I do not know I have committed.'

'What's your status now?' I asked.

'I have six weeks and then I must return to Somalia and of course I will have to take Erasto with me to whatever will await us there. I have lost my closest family in the war there and the country is poor and can not feed all its people after the war and the division. I dread it, Victor.' Her deep brown eyes were moist but she was holding back the tears and trying to remain dignified. I knew it must be very hard for her and that coming to us must have felt like the last resort and hardest thing to do.

'Michaela and I need to talk,' I told her simply.

And so it was that I began to repay my debt to Malcolm: with Michaela's support, I threw myself into the media campaign to save Ayanna from deportation and to ensure for young, bright Erasto the best possible future. We garnered cross-party support in both Houses of Parliament and across the media, locally, regionally and nationally and eventually the Home Office relented, granting Ayanna permanent leave to remain. She's a UK citizen now, as, of course, is Erasto, who is blossoming into a fine young man who has come to terms with the limitations that his injuries impose.

Fortunately, Malcolm had made a will and he had made me a trustee with some discretion as to how his estate should be used. After much discussion with Michaela and with Malcolm's lawyer, we had decided that it would have been consistent with Malcolm's wishes for Ayanna and her son to be considered at least as beneficiaries, if not formal heirs, along with his two natural children, Sheenagh and Rory. Although Ayanna did have support in Leeds, we offered her the possibility of moving closer to us. She readily accepted: being close to us would forever remind her of the love and kindness Malcolm had shown to her. We adapted the holiday cottage in Ripon for Erasto and that's where they live now. Ayanna works as a receptionist at a legal firm in Ripon and Erasto is at college in York, where they've been exceptionally accommodating to his needs.

But to every silver lining there is, inevitably, a cloud, and in this case the cloud is Rory…

In the wake of Malcolm's death, we all dealt with our grief as best we could and in our own ways. I had to weigh my grief in a scale against my guilt. The guiltier I felt about being alive, the more I showed my grief. Our mother was tormented by what she saw as the fact that she had misinterpreted a premonition and that, had she done better, she might have saved her son's life. Her guilt was doubled by her perception that the death of a son ran counter to the natural order of things. She was the one who should have died first. We had lost our dad to prostate cancer a couple of years before Malcolm died and now this tragedy was pretty much the last straw. Mum went into a home and never really got over Malcolm. She died a year after her son. Sheenagh had always been the quiet one and although both she and Rory live primarily with their mother, Sheenagh was very much the daddy's girl and her desire to always be close to him meant that she hadn't really extended her horizons far. When Malcolm died it was as though she felt it was now her role to carry forward his adventurous streak. Both children inherited a reasonable sum on Malcolm's death and a larger sum when my mother died, and Sheenagh used hers to learn to fly, though once she had got her licence she seemed to lose interest and then surprised us all by moving to London, where she 'enjoyed' a succession of office roles she found through a temping agency. And then, about a year ago, she had met Paul, a Londoner of Jamaican descent, who worked in an architectural practice. Then three months ago she had made a double announcement: she was pregnant and she and Paul would be getting married. The wedding would be in London, rather than on her 'home patch', she said, as though emphasising that she was now ploughing her own furrow in life.

Somehow, amid all our personal grief, we all seemed to forget about Rory. Poor Rory, Malcolm's elder offspring. In some ways her father's death had proved the making of Sheenagh, but Rory seemed to turn in on himself. His girlfriend dumped him, he lost his job. He moved to Scarborough and stopped turning up at family get-togethers. Then his mother moved back to Dublin and Rory followed, and contact became even more sparse. I always felt that we had collectively let Rory down but now Malcolm is telling me that it's not just our fault, that Rory has responsibility for managing his own emotions and for making something of his life, rather than forever feeling sorry for himself. And Malcolm is so disappointed that Rory has not simply declined the invitation to Sheenagh and Paul's wedding, but has failed even to respond. He wants me in the two days that remain before the wedding this weekend to persuade Rory to travel to London and join the family.

I'm unsure exactly where to start: I know there's a part of Rory that surely feels I don't deserve to be alive; that his father should have been the one to live. I decide to open a dialogue with an email to Rory.

Hi Rory
Such a long time and no see and you've been so important in my thoughts. It would be good to talk, Rory. Perhaps I could give you a call or we could Skype. I've been thinking a lot about your father and what might have pleased him and it might be nice to talk about this.
Fondest wishes
Your Uncle Vic

Another difficult night follows. I am a creature of the night. I navigate my way through the darkness between my little piles of possessions in different rooms in the house. Malcolm is with me and there are many things that I must do to honour his memory. But it all begins at home and home in this instance means Rory. Resolving the Rory issue won't be easy if I go with Michaela to London for the wedding. I decide I should stay at home and let Michaela travel with her mother and my sister, Charlotte. To sugar the bitter pill I decide I will prepare her a wonderful massage to ease away the stress that I know she's been having at work, since the new government dismantled so much of the regional funding her company relied on, albeit indirectly.

I give myself plenty of time and begin by placing scented candles on saucers around the bedroom. I buy some nice scented massage oil at Boots and I put some nice nibbles in dishes so she can have a quick bite to eat when she gets home later. I check the time. Two hours seem to have flown by: I had better start to prepare a meal. The trouble is that the more excited I get about my little massage plan, the more my brain races away: it really has taken me an age to prepare the bedroom because each time I go to find something, I have forgotten what it was I was looking for by the time I get where I was going.

Another hour goes by but I have done no more than locate a few ingredients for a meal when Michaela arrives home. I'm expecting her to be really pleased that I've organised a nice massage, but she isn't... She's had a difficult day, she's late home, she's hungry and the only food I've managed to assemble consists of a few crackers and dips. 'They'll keep you going and I'll do dinner later,' I say brightly, but Michaela's frustration with me is clear. There will be no massage. Michaela cuts her losses and heads to the takeaway.

After eating I tell Michaela that there are a number of critical things going on at work and it would be best if I didn't come with her to London.

'I'm not at all sure if you're fit to be left on your own here,' she says. 'My rational self says I shouldn't go. I should stay here and keep an eye on you. But there's Charlotte... And my mum's so looking forward to going...'

Michaela's mum's on her own and really enjoys doing things with my family.

'I'll be fine on my own. I'll take things easy and I'll keep in touch.'

Michaela gives me a look that hovers been anger, pity and concern.

Come the wee small hours, and I am once again prowling the house. Rory is uppermost in my mind and I face a race against time to deliver his presence at Sheenagh's wedding, as Malcolm has requested. Having failed to evoke any response in my previous attempts to communicate, I fire off a text message in the early morning without pausing to reflect on whether my nephew might have left the sound switched on on his phone, in which case I guess I may be unpopular. But hey, establishing communication when you're competing against the clock is more important than details about etiquette.

Look, here's the message I've just sent him. I have read it very carefully and replaced any missing letters.

Hi R;ory, I am disappointed. U are not listening to me: u are treating me as part of the probelm rather than the solution. I am your godfather, please pause and reflect on that and on the bond I have always had with your brother. I have the answers to all ur questions and can lift u out of this difficult place! Why wait till next week, next month, next year, when I can lift the dark veil now??? Please reflect on this.

With fond and loving care, your uncle Vic x

Michaela goes off to work. I lie that I have had a much better night's sleep. I want her to feel confident that I'll be OK while she is away at the wedding. Later in the morning I receive a reply from Rory. It reads:

Hi uncle vic, just letting u know I got your texts and have sent u an email. Hope u r ok, rory

I reply:

I am fine Rory and very much looking forward to talking with you in your own time! In fact, I don't think I have ever been better! I wd also like to give u help find your way in the world, find the right job for your talents. But most of all in restoring your self-belief and in helping u to understand some of the reasons Y u are the person u are. (My predictive txt just said 'ate' which wasn't at all what I meant!). Anyway, that's enough for now. Do just one thing for me today: go to the beach. Watch the wind suffers [sic] and then gaze out to sea... The next stop is England and coming from there was the 1st big journey your dad made. Close your eyes & say a little prayer to him there! Much love, your Uncle Vic Xx

PS I sent the txt before I read the email! ```I will read it properly later. I will be surprised if there is anything I don't already know. I will help in whatever way I can!! Vic xx

This is progress, but time is very short. Maybe Rory doesn't need to actually go to the wedding if he can just make his peace with the family. It is all I can think about and so the rest of the morning disappears as I traipse around the house, arriving in different rooms and each time not knowing what I intend to do when I get there.

Outside, it's sunny again: I inspect the vines that now cover the front, south-facing wall. They've done well in the two years since we planted them. Last year was their first with any fruit and I juiced the kilo of grapes they produced. This year I am more ambitious. I heard this thing on Radio 4 about people in London who pool their grapes to make London Wine. What's good for London should be good for Yorkshire, I reason. I rattle off a note regarding my ambitions to the local papers, the Echo and the Post.

I walk to the Co-op. I buy more croissants. Six more. I have to wait in the sun at the playground while they are in the oven. I call Stella. Everything is under control before the Bank Holiday weekend. She is a star. She's writing a diary about the legal case and everything. She feels it's a pivotal moment for us. I'll use this weekend to catch up with whatever I can to help.

The sun is shining and I feel a sense of intense optimism starting to flow through my veins. When Michaela gets home, accompanied by her mother, I tell her I can come to the wedding after all. She tells me that would be a bad idea. She doesn't want to leave me on my own, but I'll be even more trouble if I come, or something like that. She asks me to behave myself and not alarm her mother. I'm not sure what she means: I feel fine. In fact, I don't think I have ever felt better. I lift my head high and breathe in deeply, filling my lungs with oxygen, the life gas. I can see clearly now. I can hear clearly now. Everything smells sweet. The world tastes good.

Michaela and her mum disappear to catch the train at Thirsk, where they will meet Charlotte. I am alone.

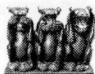

It is Saturday. It is August Bank Holiday but something is not quite right... it is glorious sunshine. The sun's warming rays dance in the garden with my growing optimism. We will win in court and victory will bring with it a new dawn for all the Knowledge team at Persona. I will bring back to the business all the good people who moved on over the past couple of years and make sure everyone's getting the proper reward for being part of this fantastic team effort. I can see the grapes ripening before my eyes. I exchange texts with Michaela. Everything is good. Everything is under control. Nothing has ever been better. Everything is for the best in the best of all possible worlds. Sometimes, if I take things slowly and in methodical order, and breathe deeply to get the gas of life into my bloodstream; sometimes, I can still manage the simple tasks, like cooking, without getting distracted. All I need to make life perfect now is a night's sleep. Malcolm has given me a tip. I must go to the bookie's and place a bet. I feel good but my brain is too active to drive, so I walk to the bookie's. I place a series of bets all based on the presumption of a healthy Newcastle United win and including a goal from new signing, Hatem Ben Arfa. My various permutations come to about £50, but I know I have Malcolm's backing, so the investment will be worthwhile.

Newcastle United one, Wolverhampton Wanderers one.

There must be something wrong! Then I remember that communication with Malcolm has to be a two-way process. In my excitement this morning I have mistaken my own enthusiasm about a chosen outcome, for Malcolm's prediction of that outcome. And it would have been so easy to check. I close my eyes and think of Malcolm and my consciousness forms the question: 'Can you predict football results?' There is no prickly feeling in my scalp. 'Maybe it's not appropriate for me to use your insight to place bets…' My scalp prickles forcefully. I have tried to abuse my brother's powers.

The sky is blue, the grapes are ripening. I am learning how to work with my brother to use his powers for the good. This evening I will make a pilgrimage in his memory to the Cathedral.

I'll tell you about Malcolm and religion, because I am starting to realise just how important this is.

Our mother, Margaret, was always religious in the sense that she'd been brought up C of E and confirmed, and spent most of her life going to church every Sunday. Although as she got older she seemed to lose interest a bit, I think that was more a symptom of her growing ennui with life in general and the fact that she wasn't always that keen on the individual clergy in her parish. To paraphrase, she'd just get used to the new happy-clappy curate chappy when they'd decide to send in a real traditionalist, who'd slosh incense round all over the place. But that's not the point of the story as I am supposed to be telling you about Malcolm. We were both confirmed when we were about 11 but pretty soon we got interested in girls and doing other things at weekends and at the same time I guess we just got sceptical about the whole credibility thing and the relevance of religion to life in the latter half of the 20ᵗʰ century. Our mum tried to make us go and apologise to the vicar, but we politely declined.

Then Malcolm did his VSO stint and at some point, when he was working as a volunteer election monitor somewhere in Africa, he met Archbishop Desmond Tutu. Now, I'm not saying Malcolm underwent a conversion, but I know he was deeply impressed by Tutu and he did start talking a lot about the concept of faith and belief and about the idea of moral compass and that kind of thing. He said it was important for people to have some kind of faith or belief system to guide them: not to make them fanatics, but to give them a framework. I asked him what his own faith was and he would always say that he had faith in the human race and in the innate goodness of people. I would ask him how he squared those ideas with all the evil in the world, with tyrants and mass murderers and so on, and his answer was that these people had never paused to look at their own souls and therefore were outside the faith that the human race represented. Latterly, Malcolm began going to church sometimes and even taking communion. It was not that he believed in God, he said, but he felt the Church was capable of being a power for good and maybe bringing out the best in people's nature. And anyway, he quite liked the pomp and the ritual. My brother. My late brother. My special brother. My saintly brother.

There are some things to do before I make my pilgrimage this evening. If I am very careful I should be able to make myself a meal, though it's important that I keep my mind on the process. Or, I could go to the gym, have some gentle exercise, burn off a little adrenaline and eat there. Then go to the Cathedral.

In the meantime, though, I must catch up with my daughter, Lisa. I don't think I have told you about Lisa. She is my eldest. She lives in Scotland on the Isle of Skye, where she makes jewellery and shares a house with a friend. She's both a dreamer and practical, though not like down-to-earth super-sensible type of practical, like Larry. It's just a regular catch-up call and I tell her I've sussed out what's been making me ill and the practical steps I'm taking to sort it all out, with the arnica cream and everything. And of course I tell her about meeting Malcolm. 'Wow!' she says. 'That's pretty cool.'

I have managed to assemble all the things I need for a trip to the gym: shorts, vest, trainers, swimmers, socks, towel, shampoo, deodorant. Membership card. Locker token. We haven't got a combined pool and gym in Ripon so I belong to one on the Ripon side of Harrogate. Driving is out of the question at the moment so I order a taxi. It'll cost me the thick end of £30 there and back but, hey, I have to look after myself.

I am set to go. I make a cup of tea. The phone rings. It's a journalist. He's following up on the letter I wrote about the grapes. Of course, it's a Bank Holiday. Flat news day. He wants to interview me right now and he wants to fix for a photographer to come round. He's derailing my carefully ordered thoughts and plans. I don't know if I can cope with this. I try patiently to explain that I can't talk right now; that I'll be happy to talk tomorrow and sort something out then. He's having none of it: he wants the story in the bag now and the picture on tomorrow's news list. I feel myself getting more and more frustrated and wound up. This is my life: it's for me to decide when I will do things. 'Let's just do a quick interview now and then we'll get the photographer out tomorrow,' he says again.

'I can't talk now, I have to go, I have a taxi waiting outside,' I lie. I put the phone down. It rings again.

'We got cut off,' he says.

'No, I cut you off,' I respond, and put the phone down again. I am angry. Really angry. I can't remember what happens next. Oh yes, a taxi will come. But I don't want to go in a taxi now. I call and cancel it. I try to make some food, but my mind keeps returning to the effrontery of someone who just won't take a simple No for an answer. Toast, I can manage toast. I find the bread. I find the bread-knife. The effrontery of it. Like I have no mind of my own. No free will. The breadboard. What happens next? I go to the fridge. I open the door. I stare at the contents. The effrontery of it. I have a taxi coming. I close the fridge. I see the bread. I spot the toaster. I cut the bread and put it in the toaster. The phone rings. I ignore it. I get to the fridge. The contents stare out at me: 'What the hell do you want?' they ask me. I don't know. I cross the kitchen and open a drawer. I take out a bottle opener. Why do I need a bottle opener? I must cancel the taxi. 'You have no taxi booking, sir'. I spot the toaster and press the lever. I cross to the fridge. Why am I at the fridge? The contents stare out at me. I find some ham. The smoke alarm goes. The phone rings. I waft the smoke alarm and it stops. I find I am close to the drawer. I find a knife. I have a moment of inspiration:

I cross to the fridge and get spread. Before long I have ham on toast.

I am calmer when I set off to walk to the Cathedral. I take some pictures of the city as I go, and of the Cathedral's central tower above the skyline. I call Michaela and text her a photo. I am going to have a conversation with Malcolm, I tell her. It is Evensong when I get there. I tiptoe in and sit at the back. It is relaxing. I listen to the hymns. I join in with the singing. The world is feeling calmer. More ordered.

After the service, I decide to light candles in memory of all those we have lost, and then my mind focuses on the need to get in touch with Desmond Tutu on behalf of Malcolm. The best plan is clearly to write a letter to the Bishop. I have a pen and there is a box for prayers. I have no paper. I find an empty envelope and rip it open. I begin to write furiously.

In memory of my brother, the late Malcolm Turnbull, to whom I have spoken and now know that he died to save others, namely countless drivers and passengers who would have been killed at Hebden, Yorkshire, and passengers on buses everywhere in the UK. Michaela and me, Vic Turnbull, chosen for each other by Malcolm and now joyously to marry. To Ayanna, the mother of Erasto. To Luc Dubois of Newcastle United, a devout and generous man who played a pivotal role in this extraordinary sequence of events and, I think, miraculous story. Malcolm has asked me to speak to Desmond Tutu, whom he met in Africa. Desmond Tutu and I have a mutual friend, so this is easy to do. Margaret Armstrong (Turnbull), now resting in peace with Malcolm in the woodland cemetery. I believe Malcolm wishes to be and should be beatified. Vic Turnbull, Ripon.

I sign off with my mobile phone number and at the top, I add: *please pass to the Bishop.*

I am about to leave the letter, when it occurs to me that I should keep a record of it. I take it to a quiet part of the Cathedral, a memorial to a family called Aislabie, that's up a short flight of steps. I place it on the floor and get my camera out. The flash attracts attention and a verger arrives. It's preferred for people not to take pictures in this part of the Cathedral, she says. I have to record the letter I have written to the Bishop, I say. It's for my late brother. He has to be beatified, I tell her. She takes the letter and I follow her to some other part of the Cathedral. I can't fail in my mission, I tell myself. I must not fail. I must do this for Malcolm. I am getting emotional. What if I fail him? I start to weep. There is a small round altar in a side chapel, made of black marble. I prostrate myself at the altar and weep, fit to die. The emotional relief is phenomenal. My message will surely go to the Bishop. I weep and weep until they ask me, please, to leave, as it is time to lock up the Cathedral. It is dark as I walk home, but I have done my duty by Malcolm.

CHAPTER 8

Home alone

Saturday, September 25, 2021

Felix began the long flight to Dubai wishing he could somehow rewind time and now find himself on the aircraft with Jameela. Then he wished he could sleep and only wake up on arrival in the UK, but sadness and frustration tore at him and he could manage no more than the odd fitful doze. He half watched another 'new' rom com with Emily Blunt and Ewan McGregor. This one was a pretty unashamed remake of an old Walter Matthau film that Felix had seen on a weekend on the sofa dedicated to 70s and 80s Matthau and Lemmon classics. In the film, Mathau's character, a confirmed bachelor, falls in love with a myopic and accident-prone botanist he had been trying, for complex reasons relating to his inheritance, to murder. Blunt was the scientist and McGregor the Walter Matthau character. A New Leaf, that was what the original was called. This remake was called Plant Collecting in the Amazon and lacked the edge of the original, Felix felt. As rom coms went, it was a bit of a dark one: from murder plot to eternal love in one easy move. Was he now co-starring in his own rom com, with its own dark plot, fashioned around the disappearance, or was it maybe kidnapping, of the woman he was destined to fall in love with? Fall in love... was that something he had ever done before? he wondered. He had not been in love when he got married, he now recognised: the reasons for having tied the knot were complex but, rightly or wrongly, love was not among them. However, he did recall the burning sense of need he'd felt as a teenager over, what was her name, yes, Esme Swallow. He'd never felt such driving need to be with anyone before or since and yet he knew that what he felt for Esme had been just the raw heat of his awakening sexual desire. It was nothing so sophisticated as love and, though he had a pretty good idea how love should feel, he was quite sure he had not as yet felt it. Which was why, he accepted, he tended to drift in and out of relationships without feeling that they were in any way central to his life or his needs or desires.

As they overflew Singapore, Felix realised they were only half way to Dubai, let alone the UK. There was plenty of time for him to reflect on the last few days in Australia; to think about what might have intervened to prevent Jameela travelling with him; to analyse his feelings about the woman who hadn't really stirred especially deep emotions when he had worked with her some years ago.

He watched on the little screen as the aircraft ploughed into the headwinds over northern India, its groundspeed slowing first to 450mph, then 400 and, finally just 350mph. As the aeroplane struggled on as though through treacle, Felix thought this extra time might have been delivered specifically to encourage him to reflect further on things. Which is precisely what he did…

He began with the Jameela question: could it conceivably be logical that he was pining for a woman who had not greatly interested him when he had first met her years ago? He had liked her, yes, but hadn't felt a strong physical attraction. Nor when he had last seen her, perhaps three years after that. On what evidence might he be pining for her now? They still hadn't touched, much less kissed (unless you could count that snatched peck on her forehead) or, God forbid, slept together.

What if he moved heaven and earth to find Jameela, only to find the chemistry was wrong? Clearly he was not being rational in his desires. And yet, if he was a character in a Jane Austen novel, all that would matter little: he would simply feel his destiny to be with Jameela and everything would just work out, which was precisely what he was feeling right now.

Then he had to move on to the next, and related question: did he feel this way only because Jameela was suddenly even more unattainable than she might have appeared a few days ago? That was a harder one to answer: he was very concerned about the sudden unexplained disappearance, which he was increasingly sure was about far more than her just thinking better of risking a modest move towards friendship with him, with no mention of romance, and sex not even on the radar. After weighing his emotions up, he concluded that his disappointment and his anxiety as to what had happened to Jameela were indeed significant in making him feel the way he did. Crucially, however, he concluded that this unexpected turn of events had served mostly to make him confront his true feelings sooner than he might otherwise have done.

In conclusion, therefore, he wasn't prepared to just write off the last few days as some sort of work-based 'holiday romance' that never quite was. Deciding what to do about it, however, was a whole other question. It was, nonetheless, a question to which Felix thought he might well have the answer. And reaching that conclusion had somehow enabled his aircraft to exit the glutinous air over northern India and move at comparatively comfortable speed across Pakistan and southern Iran. At Dubai, he allowed the question to share his bed during his brief hotel stopover. He permitted the question to remain at his heels as he trudged the endless malls to his UK departure gate in the air-conditioned desert dawn. The answer to the question throughout it all remained doggedly the same and, while the answer in many ways surprised him, he recognised it was an answer the implications of which he was going to have to learn to live with. Yes, for the first time in his life, he Felix Merryweather was in love. And so it was now up to him to address the implications of this, the answer to the question, at the very earliest opportunity.

A little over seven hours after taking off from Dubai, Felix found justification for his policy of always choosing a window seat. As the aircraft slipped in from the North Sea, he noted the solitary lighthouse on its little island as it flew over the coast. Sandy beaches stretched away to his left and the animated breakers suggested a fresh and breezy spring day, despite the bright early autumn sunshine. Green fields hove into view, with the city of Newcastle spread out beyond. As they got lower, they crossed a succession of north-south arteries: dual-carriageway, railway, dual carriageway. And then Felix spotted something he recognised. A series of large and dramatic buildings rose from parkland on the edge of the city, but the one that struck him had a very distinctive form. A meld of glazed verticals and a metallic roof, punctuated by more glazing, it was in the form of a particular type of Celtic-style cross – its four arms tapering in and then out again in graceful curves from a circular hub. The outer ends of these 'spokes' therefore presented a gently curved façade of similar breadth to the inner end that butted against the circular core of the structure. The shape was that of the Cross of St Cuthbert and he knew that he was looking at the world headquarters of the Aurora business empire: he remembered the fanfare to which it had opened seven or eight years previously, rather trumping its near neighbour, the not unprepossessing headquarters of the Sage software group. Felix now knew how he would begin to answer what he suspected might just become the biggest question of his life to date.

Rather more than 30 minutes and long Immigration queues after the sighting from the aircraft window, Felix found himself in the airport taxi queue. 'The Aurora HQ, please,' he instructed.

'You work there?' asked the driver. 'Take all sorts there, mate. Arrive from everywhere. Wish I understood what goes on there...'

'You and me too, mate,' Felix found himself answering. 'I thought you said you worked there,' the driver said with a laugh. 'Did I?' said Felix. Anything might be possible after flying half way round the world. Felix had defied a powerful urge to jump on the Metro, then catch the first train to York and, after a brisk ten-minute walk, let himself into his flat and collapse on his bed. He suspected he might be due at work the next morning and risked being in no fit state. Better check that! But he had reasoned that his assignment at Aurora might take no longer than 30 minutes or so and he could probably get home no more than 90 minutes later than would otherwise have been the case. In fact, by getting home around tea time, he would be able to get a few provisions in, have a bath, maybe even pop to see his parents and then take a wondrous 12-hour sleep, if his body clock would let him.

'There you go mate, that'll be just £20...' Felix came to with a start and realised he was unprepared for what to do next. He settled the fare and wandered away from the grand entrance to Aurora House, to sit with his carry-on luggage on a bench overlooking an ornate fountain that fed a large lily pond. Sheltered from the wind, it felt sunny and pleasantly warm and Felix was conscious of the risk he might fall asleep. 'Focus, Felix!' he scolded. He took his VSP from his pocket and switched it on. The Very Smart Phone ('all the attributes of a tablet in the palm of your hand') fired up quickly and found the 5G link. He clicked on Eureka and found Aurora's Global Policy Unit. Jameela's name was not listed and, confused and fuzzy with the shock of being transported 12,000 miles, Felix even began to wonder if she had ever been more than a figment of his imagination. But the warmth of her smile on the beach that day had been too real for his imagination to have concocted it. 'Acting Head of Unit, Rebecca Flowers,' he read.

'Would you like me to give her a call?' asked the VSP. It scarcely waited for an answer from Felix who just had the presence of mind to ask the device to switch on its secrecy function.

'Rebecca Flowers speaking,' he heard before cutting the call. He was surprised Ms Flowers had answered her own phone but that was all he needed to know.

Felix strode purposefully through the sliding doors and past a not particularly attentive security guard, presenting himself confidently to the receptionist. 'I've an appointment to see Rebecca Flowers in the Global Policy Unit,' he said.

'Sign in and I'll give you your badge, love. Who shall I say is here for her...? Merryweather?! What a lovely name: I'm pleased you've brought it with you, mind. Good job you're not called Mr Stormcloud, eh! Felix! That means happy, doesn't it? Or does it just mean your mum and dad thought you were a cat? Anyway, take a seat and I'll let Rebecca know you're here...'

'I'll just use the loo if I may,' said Felix, thinking on his feet and resisting the urge to tell the chuckling receptionist that he was actually Thor, the God of Thunder, and he'd only been called Felix Merryweather as a joke by parents who had a deep sense of irony.

'Just down the corridor, on your left, love!'

Felix found the toilets but, instead of going in, he glanced over his shoulder, saw he wasn't being watched and moved quickly on down the corridor towards the central hub of the cross, making sure he was already out of sight by the time Ms Flowers or her PA had answered her phone. He was a bit self-conscious, pushing his little wheeled suitcase along, but he knew that to do anything else with it would only spark a security alert. The hub, when he reached it, was impressive, with more water features and something resembling a sub-tropical forest at the heart of the central glazed atrium. Unlike a hospital, this was not a building designed to facilitate navigation by outsiders: Felix had no idea in which of the four spokes the Global Policy Unit was situated, nor on which of the four levels. He turned left, as much to be out of sight of anyone who might be in pursuit as anything else. A lift bell pinged in a familiar way and, as the door opened, his heart almost missed a beat with the expectancy of catching a glimpse of Jameela inside. It was, in fact, empty, so Felix got in and pressed for the fourth floor.

'Can I help you?' asked a casually dressed man of about 30.

'I'm looking for the Global Policy Unit but I think I may have gone wrong at the jungle,' Felix improvised.

'GPU! You must be a big cheese! And yes, you must have gone left at The Med instead of right. You're in the Americas and GPU's in Australasia, across the bridge over the Med.' The young man gestured vaguely towards the central atrium, where Felix now saw there was slender walkway stretching through space towards a corridor that was a mirror image of the one he was standing in.

'Australasia?' queried Felix.

'Yes, you'll have come in through Africa then, when you reach The Med, you've got the Americas here, on the left, Eurasia straight ahead and Australasia on the right. Anyway, GPU has its own section at the far end of the Australasia. You can't miss it.' It was said with a smile and, Felix reflected, very little thought for the security implications of a guy wandering around, lost, with a suitcase and looking for one of the principal nerve centres of the entire operation.

He strode over the bridge: on the floor below, a similar structure ran at right angles, linking the third floors of Eurasia and Africa. The spokes of the lower floors were linked by galleries that encircled the hub, The Med. It was not a building for the vertiginous. Felix reached a door that blocked off the rest of floor four at the end of the corridor. Unusually for the building, it was labelled. Global Policy Unit. Just as the man had promised. There was an iris recognition unit beside the door and an intercom. He'd got this far. Now was not the time to become faint-hearted. 'Felix Merryweather for Rebecca Flowers,' he said with confidence as the intercom responded. To his surprise, the door opened a few moments later and a tall blonde woman of about 45 ushered him in.

'I'm Rebecca,' she said. 'You'll have to excuse me, my PA was at lunch when you arrived and I'm not quite to grips with my diary...' Felix followed her into the office, where she sat him at a table. A dark-haired woman of about 35 came through the door and hung a coarse-knitted cardigan with a kind of Fair Isle pattern on a peg behind the door. Felix guessed it might be the late-lunching PA and, sure enough, Rebecca invited her to bring tea or coffee. 'I'll be with you shortly,' she said over her shoulder as she retreated into an office partitioned from the open-plan layout. Felix noticed a patch of brighter paint where perhaps a name plate might have been removed.

'Hi Felix, I'm Tracy,' said the dark-haired woman as she arrived with coffee. She also had a large old-fashioned desk diary that reminded Felix of the 20th century. 'I'm very fond of pen and ink,' said Tracy, perceiving Felix's surprise and by way of a defence-cum-apology. 'It's actually quite hard to put an appointment in the wrong day in one of these,' she continued. 'And it really wouldn't be like me to forget to put an appointment in at all...' Felix began to get the first sniff of an accusation. He'd been lucky, but now his cover was beginning to fall apart. 'Why the suitcase?' asked Tracy.

'I've come straight from the airport,' said Felix. 'From Australia,' he continued, anticipating the next question. He fancied he could see cogs whirring and two and two being added together.

But then Rebecca returned, pulled out a chair, placed her computer tablet on the table and began: 'So Mr Merryweather, you were seeing me about...?'

The question hadn't hung in the air long before Tracy answered for him: 'Felix has just got off the plane from AUSTRALIA, Rebecca.'

The women seemed almost to be speaking in code, so Felix took a chance: 'My original appointment was with Jameela Durrani but I understand she's moved on. My office called and I'm pleased you were able to see me instead.'

Rebecca looked Felix straight in the eyes and said: 'We don't have a Jameela Durrani.' She paused after Jameela and pronounced Durrani slowly and deliberately as though she were saying the name for the first time. Out of the corner of his eye, Felix fancied he saw Tracy's eyebrow rise, but Rebecca continued. 'Remind me why you wanted to see me.'

Felix's brain was racing as fast as it could, given his fatigue, but to say he was becoming confused was an understatement. Had he completely imagined Jameela's existence? Had she indeed been kidnapped? Was something even stranger going on, to which his present company was in some way party? Felix allowed his instincts to take over and took his wallet from his pocket. From it he produced two business cards and passed one to each of the women. 'Felix Merryweather, I'm responsible for European Business Development at Back Office, in York.'

'Do you need me now?' asked Tracy and, on being released from her duties, she retreated to a desk close to the office with the phantom nameplate, still within earshot.

Felix entered into his standard presentation of what Back Office's strengths were and the areas in which it might add value to a big operation like Aurora. Rebecca let him talk and then said, 'Very interesting, but you probably should be talking with our comms team rather than me.'

Felix paused and took a gamble. 'Look, my contact here was Jameela Durrani. I spent the last few days with her in Australia. We were supposed to travel home together but she appears to have, effectively, disappeared and now I find you, Acting Head of Unit,' he paused for effect. 'ACTING as if you don't have the faintest idea who you are ACTING in place of. I'll level with you, Rebecca, my interest in Ms Durrani, which is actually quite easy to pronounce, is personal and, specifically, I am getting very concerned for the safety of someone who is an old friend…'

'I'll see you out now, Mr Merryweather. This is a professional environment and I can only talk to you about professional matters. I suggest you speak to our comms team if you feel there's an opportunity there for your company. Now follow me, please.'

Felix had no desire to find himself at the centre of an embarrassing scene. He stood up, turning towards Tracy and calling, 'Goodbye Tracy, lovely to meet you!' Tracy half turned towards him and gave only the slightest acknowledgement.

Rebecca walked all the way to the front reception with Felix, where she paused and said to the jovial woman who had joked about storm clouds, 'Mr Merryweather didn't have an appointment and shouldn't have been allowed in.'

'Excuse me, Ms Flowers, but Mr Merryweather went to the gents' and when he didn't come back I checked with your PA and…'

'OK, fine, but Mr Merryweather won't be having a follow-up meeting with me, if you understand me.'

Felix felt humiliated as he walked out of the building towards the fountain where he had hatched his plot to get inside the Aurora headquarters. His immediate thought was that he should call the police and report a missing person. But he still had nagging doubts and wondered if it might be better to wait a while or perhaps make some more enquiries of his own. And the behaviour of Rebecca and Tracy had been strange, to say the least. His train of thought was then interrupted by his VSP: 'Hi Felix, you have a text from an unknown person.'

'Felix. Meet me at 6pm at the Brandling Villa in South Gosforth. Be there. Delete this message. Tracy.'

Felix felt his heart pause before choosing to resume its duties. He took a deep breath and looked at his watch: it was not yet 3pm and he had been back in the UK for only a little more than two hours. He could still be home for five. Or he could amuse himself for three hours and then get some clue as to what might be going on at Aurora and what might have happened to Jameela. He was extremely tired, but it was no contest. He took advantage of a taxi that was dropping off at Aurora and rode with it into Newcastle and headed for the Central Library. There he found a quiet corner, plugged in his tablet and began researching Aurora. It wasn't so much the public face of the company that was likely to be interesting; rather, what people might be saying about this global empire. It turned out that quite a lot was indeed being said and it was the entries that dealt with the Aurora Foundation that Felix found particularly intriguing.

One such read: 'Aurora channels a large proportion of its

global profits into what are described as its charitable activities, which fall under the loose umbrella of the Aurora Foundation. Some of the activities of the Foundation are well known and widely publicised, such as its support for reforestation in the Amazon basin and for a raft of environmentally-focused research projects. However, while the costs of a number of individual projects and strands of activity are in the public domain, the Foundation does not publish a global set of accounts to give a full picture of its activities. Some of these activities have for some time been the subject of speculation and one popular view is that the Foundation is engaged in a war against the Freemasons and the mafia. The Foundation's policy of making no comment on such speculation has allowed such ideas to flourish, along with rather less flattering interpretations. One such, favoured by some on the political Right, is that the Foundation is engaged in a campaign to subvert democratic government and free market economics.'

Another presented a profile of Aurora's founder, Vic Turnbull, now Lord Lindisfarne, the speed of whose rise to the stellar heights of international business had been more emphatic than Branson's, and rivalled that of Bill Gates or the late Steve Jobs. But the most telling 'detail' of the Turnbull story was the near total lack of detail for the last four years. This paucity of information was reflected in the websites; although, in the way that – just as nature abhors a vacuum, so vacuous comment will flood an information black hole – some sites did venture explanations for the seemingly reclusive behaviour of Lindisfarne in recent years. One hazarded simply that the peer had tired of being in the limelight just as quickly as he had been seduced by its attractions and had 'done a Howard Hughes', living a life hidden from public glare like the 1960s American business icon. Another suggested that Lindisfarne's invisibility was born much more of necessity and was indeed connected with his Aurora Foundation's determination to expose and defuse the influence of freemasonry on business and political life. It speculated that elements of the American mafia had placed a multi-million dollar price tag on his life. What was very clear was that Lindisfarne maintained no more than a loose grip on the workings of the Aurora business itself and was far more concerned with whatever it was the Foundation was engaged in.

Felix reflected on his reasons for not having called the police or taken any other steps to locate Jameela. In truth, his initial conclusion that she had simply got cold feet about meeting up with him again had become clouded by the thought that things somehow didn't quite seem to 'add up'. And so he then took a bit of a punt and entered 'Aurora missing persons' into Eureka. He was both surprised and intrigued by the outcome. The search turned up several pages of results, in which three names were recurrent. One, an Emily Frances Black, had apparently disappeared about 20 months previously, prompting a police search in her native Devon, where she had last been seen while on leave from Aurora headquarters. Chillingly, her disappearance had coincided with a 'virtual' vanishing, her phone number, email and all her personal online accounts seemingly closing down simultaneously. Then a news site announced that she had been 'found', having returned to Devon after what she called 'a sabbatical'.

'I just needed some time on my own and never thought taking three months out to go travelling would have caused such a fuss.'

Others who had apparently gone missing had not reappeared: there was Nils Boateng, last heard of at an Aurora office in Cape Town more than a year previously. And there was Monique de la Rochelle, who had last been seen en route from Québec City to the French overseas territory of St Pierre et Miquelon, off Newfoundland. She had, it seemed, simply failed to arrive.

What struck Felix as particularly odd was the fact that there did not seem to be any indication that anyone anywhere had recognised the unlikely coincidence of these disappearances and set out to turn any stones. He could find only one such piece of investigative journalism, in a UK Sunday newspaper, and yet the manner of its presentation rather had the effect of making the idea that there might be links between these three and two other possible disappearances seem fanciful and no more than the stuff of conspiracy theorists. And now, thought Felix, there's Jameela.

At a little after 5pm, Felix walked to Grey's Monument and took a ten-minute Metro ride to South Gosforth, from where he was directed the quarter mile or so to the pub, a stone building, whose location on a busy intersection detracted from what might otherwise have been a handsome demeanour. He installed himself in a seat that combined an element of privacy with the ability to see and be seen from both entrances to the substantial bar area. The latter boasted an impressive array of beers from both UK micro-breweries and from Continental establishments Felix had not heard of. A banner over a food servery invited the clientèle to Enjoy Belgian Week at the Brandling Villa and a chalk board listed such delicacies as rabbit in sour beer, or Flemish beef stew and chicory in cheese sauce, alongside waffles with Belgian chocolate sauce. Felix decided to risk a foamy lager from Antwerp on the basis that he had successfully stayed awake all afternoon and wasn't about to succumb to the soporific qualities of alcohol now.

Time seemed to crawl towards 6pm and Felix had to check the speed at which his drink was disappearing. The alcohol might not be sending him to sleep but it was going to his head; the head that was trying to exercise control over his various jet-lagged systems. Six o'clock passed, then 6.05. Felix fidgeted uneasily and wondered if he should leave. Perhaps if he went to the loo his absence would cause Tracy to arrive. But then if she didn't find him waiting for her, then she in turn might just head for home. He remained where he was but it was nearly ten past when Felix eventually saw his rendezvous come in. She went straight to the bar where she turned and swept her gaze round the room. She appeared not to register Felix at all as she did so, turning her back to him and talking to the barman. Felix was about to cross the room to her when, remembering how she had instructed him to delete her message, he thought better of the idea. Soon she left the bar with a glass in her hand but still she did not walk towards Felix. Instead she headed for a notice board on the wall, which she made a point of reading before, finally, approaching Felix and asking: 'Do you mind if I sit here?'

'Sure, I'm leaving soon anyway,' replied Felix, feigning absorption in his VSP. Another five minutes passed before Tracy, who had been casually thumbing a magazine, said softly: 'You'll have to excuse the cloak and dagger stuff, Felix, but it's important that I'm not seen by anyone from work. That's why I chose a pub that's not too close to you know where. Now, you'd better explain to me your interest in Jameela.' The tone was friendly, spoken in 'posh Geordie'.

Felix suddenly felt apprehensive: what if Tracy was foe rather than friend. 'How do I know I can trust you?' he ventured cautiously.

'You don't. But you'll have to accept that I am taking a risk seeing you here and I'm only doing this because I don't entirely approve of what's going on at Aurora; and because I was a bit impressed that you were concerned enough about Jameela to pull the wool over the eyes of our receptionist and our "Acting Head of Unit".'

Felix could all but see the inverted commas that Tracy inserted round the title and so he ventured: 'So she's not really the head of your unit?'

'Not in my book, she's not. She's a perfectly nice person but my head of unit remains Jameela Durrani until Jameela herself tells me that she's not...'

Felix felt his heart pause and skin prickle at the mention of Jameela's name. He could feel his face flushing too and, gathering his wits, he said, with a tone of voice reminiscent of a parent who has just caught a child telling fibs, 'I thought Jameela Durrani didn't exist.'

'On one level, she doesn't exist any more. She's been called "upstairs", to the Inner Circle. Although of course I don't "know" that because I no longer know Jameela. In fact I never did know her; the name Jameela is a figment of my imagination...'

'So she's been kidnapped?' said Felix.

'No, kidnap implies force: Jameela will have gone of her own free will.'

'Gone where?'

'To the Inner Circle.'

'We're going ROUND in circles, what do you mean, "the Inner Circle"?'

'She'll be one of Lord Lindisfarne's selected trusted disciples. We're not supposed to know what they do, or even that they exist, and, really, I don't actually know what it is that they do do. But I have known about enough of these "moves" to have some understanding of what's going on and why it is all so secret.'

'And that is?'

'There's a level of danger, or at least there is thought to be a level of danger in what this Inner Circle gets up to. In the early days of Aurora, the charitable foundation did fairly uncontroversial good works: funding academic research into Lindisfarne's pet topics; helping projects to reinstate rainforest; fighting repressive practices, you know, all the usual "good" things that wealthy people who still have a conscience do get up to. But there were some things that the foundation did that were less than popular with some powerful people and organisations. I don't know how much of it is paranoia and how much is genuine concern for the safety of the people in the Inner Circle, but when they join it, their previous lives are pretty much erased.

'In that respect, Jameela would have been the ideal candidate and maybe I should have seen it coming, because she was also very highly thought of – IS very highly thought of – but she's estranged from her family so when she vanishes, as she has, there's no-one to ask too many questions.'

'What about her friends? What about you?'

'I'm not supposed to ask questions; there's an acknowledgement that I know what's going on but it's also understood that I won't speak out of turn.'

'And Rebecca?'

Tracy snorted a half laugh. 'She's lucky: she doesn't know

Jameela and has no reason to believe that she ever actually existed...'

'Do you like her?'

'I hadn't even met her till a few days ago. I was expecting Jameela to be back soon and then they came in and removed her name one night and I thought "Aye aye, here we go," you know...'

'No, I don't think I do know.' Felix looked straight into Tracy's eyes. They were brown, quite warm and sat beneath quite dark eyebrows. The face was framed by shoulder-length dark hair; the lips neatly symmetrical, above a dimpled chin. Her complexion was at the tan-easily side of Anglo-Saxon. 'An Armada girl,' thought Felix: those dark-haired, Mediterranean Geordies with a genetic link that, if anyone were to bother, might be traceable back to marauding Spanish sailors who passed the Tyne hundreds of years ago. Or perhaps more likely, to Spanish-crewed merchant ships that may have docked. Or, indeed, further back to the troops that Hadrian brought in to build and garrison his great Wall. Tracy held his gaze, which was a good sign. If all this was some charade, she might have only tolerated a second or two of his looking directly into her eyes. Who was it who said, he wondered: 'Look into a person's eyes and you can see right into their soul?'

Tracy gave a weak smile, as of resignation. 'Felix, this has happened before and I'm not sure that it's right. But then I'm not sure what can be done about it and I wanted to meet you today to save you from what I think might turn out to be a lot of heartache.'

'I know it's happened before: I've been researching,' said Felix.

'Then maybe you'll understand that there are two reasons why it might be a bad idea for you to pin your hopes on getting something going with the woman I suppose I now have to call my ex-boss.'

'Two reasons?'

'Yes, two. I know Jameela as well as anyone, probably better and I'm guessing she may have flirted with you a little. She may even have thought for a minute it might be nice to get to know you better. She may even have wondered for a few minutes about breaking her vow of "no relationships". And then she may have woken up the next day and thought better of the idea: she's been alone too long and she's still too hurt. She knows she can survive without putting her soul on the line again. So, on that level, I think you might be wasting your time.'

Tracy paused, before continuing: 'The second reason is that I don't really see how you can find her. No-one else who's vanished, or been vanished, this way has been found, except when they've returned of their own free will.'

Tracy wore a look of genuine sympathy, but it was a little too close to pity for Felix's liking. He thought carefully before responding at length. 'You're pretty bold, presenting me with your conclusions, which are based essentially on guesswork. You don't know what might have gone on between me and Jameela and you can't second-guess what either of us may have thought or felt or, for that matter, what I might feel now. But I understand your concern and what it is that brings you here now and I even appreciate your warning me off. But you have also pretty much confirmed my suspicions about what has happened to her and maybe that makes me just that bit more determined to try and follow her and find her. And I'm not saying it's love and nor am I saying that I'm being either sensible or realistic, but I think maybe something not very healthy is going on and I'm in a position to perhaps do something about it. Maybe you are too…'

'Maybe I am, but I won't. I'm neither a crusader for justice nor a risk-taker, Felix. But I could save you a lot of trouble and, I think, near certain heartache. Jameela is not the only single woman in the world who's been hurt and who might just possibly take a risk with another man, but only if she could be sure of his constancy and commitment. There's another woman in this room who's bright, attractive, intelligent, interesting. And who might just be prepared to take a chance on a guy who's gallant enough to even think about chasing after the uncatchable in the name of love. But this woman isn't uncatchable and might just go for dinner with you if you wanted to ask her.'

Felix was taken by surprise and gave a slight start. He saw Tracy blush and turn her gaze away from his. The intensity of the blush increased, and then she said, 'I'm sorry, that was much too forward of me, but shy bairns get nowt in this world, as my mother would say and, as the world might say, "You know where to find me if you change your mind".'

'I haven't said No yet,' said Felix.

'No, I know that, but I thought I'd save you the trouble. Shall I run you to a Metro station?'

'That would be very kind,' said Felix, who had had quite enough shocks for one day.

CHAPTER 9

The lion's den

Monday, August 30, 2010

Flintstones: meet the Flintstones. They are, as everyone knows, 'the modern Stone Age family', from the town of Bedrock.

Yes, I am meeting the Flintstones. It is close to 30 hours since I got back from my pilgrimage to the Cathedral and delivered the letter to the Bishop, regarding Malcolm's being made a saint. I have created a nest for myself on the sofa, which I have filled with familiar objects: my handkerchief, a book to read, my glasses, my iPhone, some lavender from the garden to calm me down and perhaps help me sleep, my arnica cream, my brightly coloured notebook, a ballpoint and marker pens. It is 2.30 in the morning and I can't sleep. Although I arrived home from the Cathedral feeling calmer and more serene, there is nothing I seem to be able to do that will make me sleep. And so, I am meeting The Flintstones, whom I have found on a distant channel somewhere at the furthest reaches of the TV remote.

I don't remember having been all that impressed the first time I watched the first Flintstones movie – now, in the hours heralding yet another unwelcome dawn, it is somehow capable of capturing my wandering mind. Because it is (unusually) holding my attention, I spot things in it that passed me by in its first watching back in the 90s. I decide it's a very clever movie indeed: one to be watched on two levels, adult and juvenile, like the Simpsons. I remember wondering in the 90s what had been gained by turning an animated cartoon series into a film with real people. Back then, of course, I wouldn't have known that Halle Berry would become a Bond girl eight years later, or that the headline in the Daily Granite, Middle East Peace Talks Break Down Again, would remain as apt now as it was a decade and a half ago. I am tickled at the thought that Israel had been an awkward question even back in the Stone Age and begin to elevate the Flintstones movie to special status. A cult movie that all who know me should make a point of watching, and as full of special meaning as the coincidences that have been occurring in my life with increasing regularity.

I will add the Flintstones to my growing list of essential watching and reading for all the disciples who will spread the word. The word of Malcolm. The Truth.

It has been a strange day. Michaela has reassured me she will be coming home tomorrow. Larry is already home but, most odd, his mother is also here, staying in my house. She phoned this morning to say she didn't think it was a good idea for Larry to be alone in the house, responsible for me, given the 'condition' I was in. She had formed this view after Lisa called her and said I'd claimed to have met Malcolm. 'Well I did meet Malcolm,' I retort. 'Larry would be happier if I stayed,' she said. 'Whatever,' I responded.

Then I had an email from that bloody journalist, pressing me again to be interviewed and photographed. 'It's a really good story,' he wrote.

'Being a reporter isn't just about being pushy,' I responded. 'You need manners to earn respect. I will speak to your editor!' In fact, I know that reporters are so hard-pressed these days because local papers just aren't the cash cows they once were. It's really hard. I will set up a school for journalists, I decide. I will bring in the best trainers I know to create a centre for excellence in regional journalism.

But right now, I need to tell you about how Michaela and I met and what all that has to do with the Newcastle United player, Luc Dubois. I am increasingly understanding that a great many things in my life have happened for a very specific purpose, to prepare me for the important work that I now have to do. So many seemingly trivial events that, in reality, have a deep and special meaning and importance. Meeting Michaela is one of those events, although by that I certainly don't mean to say that meeting her was a trivial occurrence. Michaela had been working at the time for a company that was developing a major visitor attraction in the North of England. The principal backers of the project were French and, indeed, the technology behind the venture was also French. My own company, Persona, had been appointed to deliver supporting promotional communications on behalf of the French side as the development progressed. The French partners had wanted a French face to the project in the UK and an obvious choice was Dubois, whose mesmerising ball skills had earned him admiration across the wider footballing world during eight or ten years with Newcastle United. The French were very clear, however, Dubois was their man and was not to be made available on an open-ended basis to the UK partners. It had been my job both to recruit and then manage Dubois, and now to set out his terms of reference to the UK side, for whom Michaela was the key point of contact.

There had been a certain amount of e-mail sparring and one or two terse phone calls before we actually came face to face. To be truthful, I had built her up into a bit of an ogre as she had seemed quite determined to get from me something that I had been instructed quite clearly not to deliver. We met, finally, on neutral ground, away from both my office in Ripon and hers in Manchester, in an hotel off the M62, near Huddersfield. I know it's corny to talk about love at first sight, but for both of us, it really was. I'd seen her picture on the company website, but the real Michaela bore only a passing resemblance: she was just so much more real. She seemed to fill the room with her personality when she walked in. I'd expected her to greet me with something approaching a scowl, but it was the warmest of smiles. She looked great: she wore a dark suit, with a skirt, something like you might expect a lawyer to wear, with a discreet pin stripe and a jacket that wasn't cut to fasten, but shaped to reveal a light blue blouse, a chemise maybe, with a delicate lace edging and centre trim. Her tights, I recall (they were more likely to have been stockings, I now know), shimmered slightly blue, while her shoes were modest, with mid-height heels and quite round toes. They were navy. Her hair was thick, brown and shoulder-length with what I guessed was a natural wave; her eyes blue, where hazel or brown might have been more expected. Her lips were glossed, not coloured, and her light blue eye shadow brought the colour out in her eyes, as though she had dripped belladonna into them.

All this I remember today as though it were yesterday. It took no more than 30 minutes to agree terms over the use of Monsieur Dubois, and so we moved on to subjects that had little to do with work and much to do with what we each enjoyed in our spare time, me overstating my interest in sailing and she overstating hers in 1980s French cinema.

The rest, as they say, is history: a change of job a year later enabled Michaela to move east of the Pennines. I moved out of the cottage (where Ayanna now lives) and we bought a nice place, with a big garden, on the edge of the city. We got engaged and all seemed set fair. And then there was Malcolm's death, then my mother's, then her father's and a string of misfortunes afflicting friends and, somehow, it was never the right time to get married. Malcolm does not want us to be in the kind of situation that Ayanna found herself in and that's of course why he has told me we should marry quickly, conveniently and without fuss, leaving the pomp and celebrations for a later date.

I, we, also became quite close to Luc. He trusted me more than he trusted his agent and so would use me as a sounding board for things. We also enjoyed a friendship outside the close circle of football, so we'd sometimes go away for the weekend as a foursome with his English wife, Chloë, in the close season, or meet up after a match. We became godparents to their first child, which made us feel both proud and honoured.

So there you have them: Michaela, Luc Dubois and Chloë. And here you have me, again: a man awake, drooling over the Flintstones and with two hours yet to run before dawn. I am beneath the duvet that is the cover for my den on the sofa. It keeps out any moonlight that might jeopardise my chances of sleep. These, however, remain infinitesimally slim. My brain is still on fast-track. But it is an unordered frenzy, without any glue to hold the thoughts together. And there are many thoughts: there are new thoughts coming to me every few minutes. As I appear to have lost the ability to remember even the simplest of things for more than ten seconds, I know I have to record all these thoughts or risk losing the very scaffolding that supports my consciousness, what makes me me. But I don't want to introduce light: I must maintain dark in the hope that I may sleep. I do my best to keep this record of my thoughts sequential, turning pages of the coloured notebook in the dark only when I think they may have filled.

In the murk beneath my duvet I also search for soothing music, downloading tunes onto my iPhone in the hope that they may calm me. I use the camera on my phone to take a picture of my den: it is part of what I now call my 'evidence collection'.

Eventually, another journey through the wakeful hours of the night is drawing to a close: it's seven thirty, and I send this message to Michaela:

Hi darling!

I am going to take the rest of the week off except my meetings (michael holbeck on thursday), which are very important...

I need total rest for a while as I am in DEEP deep shock and it will take a long time to adjust to having to wear my undies on the outside and for people to get used to seeing me like that (ho ho ho)...

I'm not even sure wearing a Big S on the font [sic] of a blue tunic will even go with my other clothes now I have lost wight... [sic] Nor is there kryptonite at Sainsbury's. Please do as I say and ask me nothing more until I tell you I am ready and be assured that I will love you always...

I will need you to send me back all the messages I have sent you and remember as much as you can of what I have said and what terrified you the most and what made sense!

I think this will prove to be the greatest breakthrough in SCIENCE for a long time... A lot of the time I have been scared I would forget but now I don't think I will!!!

I may have to go in the bin and recover all my scribbles!!!!!! I have just watched the Flintstones movie and had an absolute belly laugh... I didn't even like it first time in 2000 BC, sorry in the 1970s....

The truly astonishing thing is that I feel so much cleverer...

The solutions to problems I have discovered in this hideous journey are little short of miraculous if they (I think they will) work!

I have a whole new purpose in life and can't want [sic] to get going when I am stronger!!! You will make the journey with me but as I will be at home you will call me when you are heading home and say exactly what you want when you arrive and it will be ready for you. I want to be your househusband while I do this work!

Love to all my adorable one!!!!!!!!!
XXXXXXXXXXXXXXX

PS together we can change the world and have everything we dreamed of without making anyone else sad!!!!

The sun shines again and I walk to the Co-op. Once more, I find myself returning to the shelves after I have paid for my shopping, to pick up a newspaper. I note that it is dated Wednesday September 1 and the headline is about a big fire on an industrial estate in County Durham. Then I panic: tomorrow is Erasto's birthday and I haven't got him anything.

Realising I haven't paid for the paper, I take it back into the store and pay. Something strange is happening: at home, the TV information says it's August 31. So does my iPhone and my watch. Time, I begin to understand, can be different in different places. It is tomorrow at the Co-op: it is today here at home. I have a day's grace to get a present for Erasto.

I have another conversation with my homeopath, who says she's sending me some 5HTP. This is a natural product to boost serotonin levels and the idea is that it may help me to sleep and counter any depressive tendencies. She also advises me to buy Aconite 10m from the online homeopathic pharmacy. The '10m' suffix indicates that this is an extreme dilution of the product, which comes from the poisonous plant, aconite. In homeopathy, the greater the dilution, the 'more powerful' the remedy. This is to counter the anxiety I describe as arising from my increasing confusion.

Michaela arrives home at about lunchtime, having put her mother on a train to Manchester, at York. Charlotte has headed for home too. Michaela tells me two things:

– Rory sent a good luck tele-message to the wedding.
– She has booked a doctor's appointment for me that evening.

So, I have accomplished my mission; in part anyway. Rory is back in the family fold, a little bit at least. The doctor's appointment, I am unsure about. I tell Michaela I will see the doctor, but only on condition that the doctor 'has faith'. She has booked me to see the doctor who didn't make eye contact with me, earlier on in my illness, but if she indeed has faith, she can redeem herself.

Before we go to the doctor's I tell Michaela more about what happened in the Cathedral and about my journeys into the very engine of life itself. I tell her about the Flintstones. She promises we can watch it again. I tell her that time really can move at different speeds: that I have already seen tomorrow's front pages. I remind her that she has always been able to make time travel faster, using her Michaelo-minutes, as I call them. This is when she gets her head down and gets really deeply into something and, after an hour has passed, thinks that only ten minutes have actually gone by. And of course, she's always saying she'll just be two minutes, but it's invariably 12. I tell her it's been hard for me to cook but maybe she'll play chef/sous-chef with me, where I'll be the chef and she'll provide all the ingredients as I need them. Tomorrow, she says. Larry will sort something out for us today.

We arrive at the doctor's. Michaela tells me to wait and slips in to ensure the doctor, who looks as if she's of east Asian origin (maybe she's a Buddhist), does indeed have faith, as I have stipulated. A couple of minutes later, Michaela emerges, confirms that the doctor is a woman of faith, though Michaela can't confirm precisely which faith. I go into the surgery with her. This time the doctor does look at me and I explain how I have had a meeting with my dead brother who has tasked me with lots of big challenges and how it's a big responsibility and I've not been getting any sleep. She listens quite intently, wearing a serious frown. Eventually, she writes a few notes and looks me in the eye. 'This is all a bit outside my knowledge and experience,' she says. 'The best thing is probably if I have a chat with a colleague who knows more about these things.'

After my visit to the doctor's I realise that I must get some sleep: I have very important things to do; places to go; people to eat, as they say. Who said that? I don't know. It was someone funny. They do say that, don't they? Maybe it's me: maybe I'm the one who says that. Maybe I'm the funny guy. Anyway, I need sleep. I take a temazepam at bedtime, but by the small hours I'm wide awake again and heading for my sofa den. I download more soothing music: I'm becoming a whizz at this iPhone stuff. I look for more Flintstones or something else with meaning. I watch a nature documentary instead, but note that there's a nice rom-com this evening, called Leap Year.

Again the sun shines. I sense the sun is shining on our legal issues too and that this could mark a new beginning for us. Stella rings with some news about St Kilda: there's no big campaign but the Scottish National Trust needs funds and clearly if a buyer came along who could guarantee the future and safe guardianship of the islands and thereby relieve the Trust of that burden, then it would be a good idea. When the money starts to roll in we'll rescue St Kilda, with just one condition: that we can visit and stay once a year with all our friends in one of the traditional houses that will be reserved for our use.

The helicopter sweeps low over Village Bay. The mountains behind the island rise steeply from a rare calm blue sea, disturbed only by the rise and fall of a modest swell. It is a wonderful October day in the westernmost outpost of the UK, bar Rockall (and no-one's sure if that even belongs to the UK and there's 'rock-all' there anyway). There are no service personnel on the islands these days and we've made the military building and the Puff Inn bar look much better: more like what you'd expect to find at a double World Heritage Site.

The helicopter lands and we walk to the main street that was home to that hardy race of islanders until 1930. All our friends are amazed: we are so lucky and so privileged. I take the chance to slip away and clamber to the hilltop above the village. I turn and look back over the village from near the summit of Connachair. Behind me, the initially gentle slope will progressively plummet seaward on the opposite side of the island. Before me, I fancy I can just make out the tops of the Cuillins, on the far horizon. It is a perfect autumn day in a perfect place in this, the best of all possible worlds. How fortunate I am to have acquired the right to stay with my friends on St Kilda. I smile; I feel warm inside; I slowly wander back down the hill, passing the feral Soay sheep and keeping a wary eye on a bonxie. It's not the nesting season: he should leave me alone.

Michaela has gone to work; I get a visit from some people called the Crisis Team. Something to do with my visit to the doctor's. They must be the people who know about these things. They take some blood and give me some drugs.

Larry is up and about. Stella calls, en route to the lawyers. 'I can't be long,' she says. 'I just wanted to see how you were.'

'We can all belong somewhere,' I rejoin.

'But I'm quite short…'

'Then you should have shortbread with your tea.'

'Well, there's not much wrong with your brain,' she says. 'At least nothing that wasn't already causing problems in your bad jokes lobe.'

'I think I'm on the mend,' I say. 'I just need to find a way of burning off this excess adrenaline so I can start to sleep again. But then I've got so much I have to do…'

'You should rest and let the rest of us worry about things,' says Stella. She brings me up to speed on all the projects and workstreams and how everyone is taking my absence and, yes, she says the word, my illness. I've managed to make two cups of tea: that's good. I even remembered the shortbread: that's good too. I close my eyes and tilt my head back to feel the sun on my face. Things are going to be OK: soon. Stella is still talking. I am not interrupting: the passage of our individual time is in synch. Stella stops talking and only then does my mind fill with something else…

There goes Stella,
Walking down the street.
She's looking for a fella,
Who'd be nice enough to eat.
But I think I'd better tell 'er,
That his name will not be Pete.

The doggerel rolls off my tongue and I think, 'she's right', my brain is still on the case.

'Have you just made that crap up?' she asks. 'How did you know about Pete, anyway?'

'Pete who?'

'The Pete I've had my eye on…'

'Pete who? Pitot? Henri Pitot, the 18th century fluid scientist?'

'Now you've lost me…'

~ 134 ~

'I know: too smart for my own good. Are you really seeing someone called Pete?'

'That probably depends if I'm brave enough to make a move. Speaking of which, it's time I made a move now. I'll let you know how it goes.' She heads off to Leeds, to the offices of Immerhutts. As she leaves, she adds: 'And, I'm putting Holbeck on hold until you're better, OK?'

I'd completely forgotten about Holbeck, but if this legal stuff comes good, we might not even need him... 'OK, I trust your judgement,' I say.

Stella gone, I tell Larry I am off to the shops and that, as it's a nice day, I may stop off in the park, so not to worry if I'm more than half an hour.

I don't set out with the intention of doing a big shop, but life is good and getting better and I feel like I can taste everything even as I look at it. The woman who comes to vacuum and clean once a week has been telling me about which brands have the healthiest and most ethical ingredients and, as I pass the freezer, I spot the Scottish ice cream she's been telling me about. My basket's already pretty full, what with the ten croissants I have to buy and all that fresh fruit. I put three tubs of ice cream in the basket and it tips. I ask someone if they wouldn't mind watching my shopping while I run and get a trolley. I have no £1 coin to release the trolley from the rack. An old woman is sitting on a chair by the door. I ask her for £1. 'I'll bring it straight back,' I say.

She gives me the coin, muttering, 'I want it straight back, mind you.' I transfer my shopping into the trolley and return to the door of the store.

'Where's my £1?' demands the woman. I shunt my full trolley to another and slot the release clip in and return the £1 to the woman. But now my trolley and the shopping in it are marooned on the wrong side of the till.

'Can I borrow a pound?' I ask. She grudgingly gives me a pound; I release the trolley and resume my shopping. We're all square.

I gather some more goods, now I have a trolley with room to put them in. I get to the till again and pay. I head for the door, pause and return to the newspaper stand. The front page of the Echo is about a pensioner who travelled to a Swiss clinic to end his life. It is dated Thursday September 2. I head for my shopping at the door. I haven't paid for the paper. I go to the till and pay. I exit the store and a voice whines, 'Where's my pound?'

'I gave it back to you,' I say.

'And I gave it back to you,' she replies, with a slightly aggrieved, almost threatening tone. I make to leave and a man appears from behind and invites me to come back into the store.

'We've been watching you, sir. I'd like to check your shopping.'

I'm floored: I realise I have been behaving erratically in this store for days now, but so far as I am aware, I have paid for everything I have taken, even if once or twice I have had to make a return visit to do so. I take the receipt from my pocket, but I am panicking as he begins to check the goods in my bag against the receipt. I honestly don't know what he's going to find. It's entirely possible I have got stuff I haven't paid for. I feel a wave of nausea and terror. I call Larry: 'You've got to come to the Co-op. They think I've been shoplifting.'

'Dad: don't say anything; don't do anything. Stay calm and quiet until I get there.'

'You can bring the car to be quick,' I say. I watch the process of comparing the contents of my shopping bag with the little slip of paper.

'He owes me a pound n'all,' the old crone chirps. It feels like the final straw. Kick a man while he's down, why don't you. I ask the girl at the till to change a fiver for coins.

'Here's the bloody pound I don't owe you!' I shriek, almost throwing it at the woman, who can only grunt at me.

After what feels like an eternity, Larry arrives. 'Go home, wait for me there and DO NOT stop at the park or anywhere else,' he says.

'Why not?' I ask, tears welling.

'Dad, I can handle shoplifting, but just think about what people might think about you hanging round the park… It's more than I can take right now, OK?'

The penny drops. Or maybe it's a pound. I head home. Larry arrives 15 minutes later with my shopping. 'So?' I ask.

'You'd paid for everything,' says Larry. 'But this has got to stop. You stay here, you don't go to the park and you'd better steer clear of the Co-op for the next few weeks.'

'I'm so sorry, son. Thanks, you're a star. But that old bag nicked a pound off me, you know.'

'Really?' His look is withering.

If I can't go out, I'd better be productive at home. With Rory to some extent 'sorted', at least for now, I turn my attention to Erasto. I go on-line and buy him the Flintstones films boxed DVD set on Amazon for his birthday. 'He'll enjoy that,' I think. Michaela has told me that things haven't been going quite so well for Erasto at York and he's come home for a few days to be with his mum. Then I remember something: Ayanna was supposed to be coming in to feed the cats for us while we were both away, but Michaela must have forgotten to cancel the arrangement after she left me at home. Now I have a recollection of having seen Ayanna in the house when I was a bit muddled, sometime during the day-night that I've been living through since meeting Malcolm. I'm not sure what she must have thought as I think I was probably half naked and not expecting anyone else to be there…

I focus very hard on getting all the spelling and everything right and email her:

First of all, I'm sorry if I scared you: I think you called the other day and didn't expect to find me home. And I'm really sorry I haven' t been in touch for a little while, but as you may have heard, I've not been too well and then, last week, I met Malcolm. I think I probably told you this or maybe Michaela did. I know this will be a shock to you, but it is true. Then, at the weekend, while Michaela was away, I had a bit of a crisis in the Cathedral. I was trying to get a message to the Bishop because Malcolm needs to be beatified for giving his life for others. You know, to be made a saint by the Church.

I haven't been sleeping and I'm on some medication. I have had 9 temazepam but the doctor told me last night that's OK and I can take more... I have also got something longer term to help me sleep better and to calm my mind down... You now join the small group of people who 'know everything about my conversations with my late brother'. He is my 'guardian angel' but I'm so confused I don't know what I have and haven't told you... Essentially I was working against the clock at the weekend to 'mend Malcolm's family', and I'm pleased to say that his son, Rory, is now speaking with the family again. I guess you'll know about Rory even if you haven't met him. I now need a long rest, possibly years!

You see the work of a guardian angel is very busy and you'll know that I've been your guardian angel since you and Erasto came to us after Malcolm died... But it's time now for me to find a new guardian angel for you as I have other work to do after I have rested.

A dear friend and colleague of mine, Charley, will be in touch with you soon to help you sort out the problems I hear Erasto's been having at York. I think she may be your new guardian angel.

They have taken bloods today and want me to have a brain scan. Frankly I am exhausted and need a good night's sleep but people are trying to micro-manage me... I have to forcefully tell them to back off. But you'll understand I gave too much info to my own family and they were terrified when I started telling various people I had 'met Malcolm'. I think they were close to sectioning me so I had to use all my powers of persuasion with the doctor last night and it was important that she had faith, ANY faith will do, including science. This very big Ayanna and I will coach you through it in small bits.

I'm sorry if this email is a bit all over the place. It kind of 'fell apart' and had to be put back together again!

Vic x

PS I got stopped today because they thought I was shoplifting.

I read the mail: I am pleased. With a few corrections it looks OK to send. I get a response quite quickly.

Victor
You are not my guardian angel: that is profane. You are a friend who has been very good to me and to Erasto. But now you are upsetting me. My Malcolm did die a hero, but it is of little comfort to me that I lost my Malcolm. Michaela still has you. I have, as you know, some difficulties at present as things are not working out very well at York for Erasto with his disability and he is unhappy. It is my lot in life to deal with this however and I have dealt with far worse. If there is an angel in my life it is my Malcolm, not you and not your friend Charley.

As for you, Victor, you are unwell and I worry for you. You must listen to what the doctors say and you must listen to Michaela and Larry too. They will know what is for the best for you and you are fortunate that they are there to care for you.

For now, though, it may be better if you don't send me emails.
Ayanna

'I didn't have a very good day today,' I tell Michaela when she gets home from work. 'They thought I was shoplifting at the Co-op. And I think I've upset Ayanna.'

I see Michaela sigh the sigh of a woman close to the end of her tether. And I thought she understood. 'Did the crisis team come?'

'Yes, they gave me some medicine and talked about a brain scan.'

Michaela goes off to talk to Larry. When she comes back, she says: 'So you tried to steal £1 from an old lady...'

I protest and say I will draw a diagram to demonstrate how the pound coins moved around and how I ended up having to give her an extra pound.

A little later, she says to me, 'I'll do that chef/sous-chef thing with you now.'

This is going to be real fun! I gather up the ingredients for a couscous and take up position by a large frying pan. The radio is on Radio 4. Michaela takes her station on my left. 'Chop me the onions,' I say. I notice as I say it that the volume of the radio goes down. When I stop talking, the volume rises again. It is just as though I was turning the volume knob. Yet another amazing new power: I can adjust the radio by telepathy. I wonder if I will soon be able to change channels too.

'How do you want them?' asks Michaela.

Again the volume goes down when she talks, rising to where it was, until I say, 'Chunky, please'.

'Tomato purée and spices,' I instruct. Then I hear Michaela's response of 'which spices?' and tell her 'coriander, paprika and cumin'. I am saying the words even as she asks the question. Her next question will be 'what next?' but, again, I hear this a full half-second before she has voiced it. 'Prepare the meat,' I say. Again I am responding to her question as to how it is to be prepared before the question has even reached her vocal cords. I could be reading her mind but I don't think that's what it is: I think it's that our times are out of synch. For me, time is simply moving faster than for her, so I hear what she says before she has said it. To her, however, it simply seems as if I am talking on top of her all the time.

'I've had enough of this,' she huffs, slaps down the knife and leaves me to it. It's not easy, but I manage to complete the meal by preparing all the vegetables and the meat and then carefully cooking all the ingredients. I try singing to myself and, again, the volume on the radio subsides as I do so. This is much better than the fiasco of the massage that never was: I have successfully cooked a meal, which the three of us sit down to eat together.

'Tell us again how you tried to diddle that old lady, Dad,' says Larry.

'I'm telling you, she did fleece me for a pound, the old grump,' I insist.

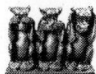

Diary of Stella de Weld, Wednesday September 1

Met with Immerhutts today. The case is indeed much stronger and, clearly, there may have been criminal activity going on, over and above the intellectual property stuff. They want to get affidavits from everyone in the US and Canada and they want to secure a court order to confiscate the other party's computers so they can search for evidence. On the face of it, this could put them out of business. Vic wants us to look at bringing their best people up here and maybe taking over all their other activities. What an arrogant dummy their owner must be. He's called Smart. What a laugh!

I had been hopeful of a better night but, when I found myself still awake at about one in the morning, I decided to take a temazepam. I could find them nowhere: I had systematically moved between my storage dens in each room and the little bottle was in none of them. And now I know it is going to be a long night.

Michaela has been reading a book about feline behaviour. I'm not sure I go along with some of its claims about why cats do what they do. Specifically, I'm not at all happy with the suggestion that cats bring dead animals into the house as a kind of love token to their master or mistress, the 'dominant cat'. I'm also not all that sure that the experts have quite got cats right when they try to explain the relationship between two cats living in the same household. We have two cats, Bafta and Nada. Bafta was originally going to be called Oscar, but Michaela got worried that a guy she worked with, who seemed to have taken a bit of a shine for her, might get the wrong idea if he heard she'd apparently named her cat after him. Nada is so called because of what he sometimes seems to have between his ears. So you'll not be surprised to hear that Bafta appears to be the dominant cat: he was slightly older when we got them both and Nada was unwell, so Bafta quickly established a relationship with us, while Nada acquired a mistrust of human handling nourished over several trips to the vet. By the book's theory, Bafta should bring in dead animals to please us, while Nada, if he brings them in at all, should do so only to please Bafta. Furthermore, logic suggests that Bafta should bring home little presents at regular intervals, lest he fall out of our favour. Observation has told me that none of the foregoing is true. In fact, the dead animals seem to appear, as a rule, when the cats either have no food in their dishes, or when they have gone on one of their battle-of-wills hunger strikes, during which they turn their noses up at the food given to them and it gradually goes rancid as we resist replenishing their bowls until they have eaten what's already there. Furthermore, both of them bring corpses, and their principal objective seems to be to avoid sharing their trophy at all costs, not to donate it generously to Michaela and me.

As I lie in my den, Bafta pokes his little black nose in to see what's going on. I begin to wonder how cats first came to be domesticated and what their role was, compared with the more obvious hunting and guard-dog role of the first domesticated wolves. Earlier today, Bafta nearly made me jump out of my skin, when he leaped about two metres up onto a high shelf after something scared him. I'd never seen him jump so high and I think he was a little embarrassed that I had spotted him doing it, and being seen to be a bit of a wimp.

I decide to observe the cats in their natural, nocturnal environment. I set off into the garden jungle, armed only with my iPhone to give light. I crawl through the bushes down towards the old netty at the bottom of the garden, where, a few months previously, I'd uncovered what was clearly a local drug dealers' lair, with tin foil, scales and other essentials. I hear a noise and shine the light of my iPhone screen. It's a hedgehog. 'Hedgehog at two o'clock, Captain Biggles!' I chuckle. And it is, indeed, two o'clock, I notice on the screen. Then the light from the iPhone catches an old tin can, which glints and, in turn, illuminates a wider vista. Among the branches and the old dead roots, I spot Bafta approaching. I hold out a hand, one finger extended. He pokes his nose forward and sniffs it, before giving a contented mew of recognition. Together we crawl through the undergrowth, Bafta in front. He seems to move quite systematically from one location to the next, each time stopping to sniff and sometimes scratching the earth or scent-marking a branch or stone. A penny drops: Bafta is doing precisely what I have had to learn over the past few nights. He is moving from one safe place to another in a set sequence that he has learned.

I return to my den to record my findings and draw a picture to show how the domestic cat has evolved to complement the dog. It shows a cave, with a fire deep inside. At the mouth of the cave are the wolves, or proto-dogs. The humans sleep around the fire. The cats, too, seek out the warmth of the flames. But they sleep with one eye just 20 per cent open, ever watchful and never in deep slumber. In short, they cat-nap. In the roof of the cave the rocks conceal tiny pieces of quartz that reflect the light of the fire. The cat's part-open eye watches these glinting rocks and it will spot any movement outside the cave. And if that's cause for alarm, the cat will bolt, waking everyone and setting the dogs baying. The perfect burglar alarm; or sabre tooth alarm, or whatever. I'm proud of my deductions and reason further that cats bring dead animals home because the furthest corners of the house where they place these prey are the safe spots on their routine patrols. I will pursue my line of enquiry tomorrow.

The police set up a security camera to monitor comings and goings at the 'drugs den'. With a little bit of adaptation, it also served as night-vision camera to observe the cats going about their nocturnal business. We

produced what may appear, on the face of it, to be THE most prosaic nature film ever: the life of the humble domestic pussy cat. However, The Man Who Stalked His Cats is far more than this: it is the story of how an ordinary man re-wrote the books on feline behaviour and how his observations were extended to cast new light on the hunting practices of aboriginal peoples. Of course, the footage of me hunting with aboriginal people in the harshest deserts of Australia does make more exciting TV than the opening footage of Bafta and Nada strutting their stuff in a back garden in Ripon. It's great that we've been able to embark on this kind of activity as an offshoot to the core business, and fantastic that we've been able in the process to create work for Gerry and Tom (yes, yes, I know, if you were called Gerry, the last person you'd choose as a business partner would be someone called Tom, but there you go!) who have been a bit down on their uppers since the regional TV market imploded. The scene I like the best is when we are all preparing for going out hunting by dancing and chanting to enter a kind of trance. We are connecting with the Dreamtime and sharpening our senses for the long days and tough thorny conditions underfoot beneath the scorching sun. When I was fighting my illness, it took me weeks to enter this similar heightened state of awareness in which I was able to connect with souls of the departed. Here in the Outback, these people are so practised that they can connect with the Dreamtime in tens of minutes, not tens of days.

And here am I, so privileged to be there with them, connecting with the Dreamtime, so close to the Earth, so close to their ancestors, so close to the souls of those who lived and those who are yet to live.

In the morning Michaela shows me the little bottle of temazepam on the mantelpiece, where she put it. The unsaid words are: 'Why don't you use your eyes?'

'You can't take things from my den,' I say. 'I can't see things in the dark if they are not in the places I know. They need to stay on the routes that I follow.'

On the other hand, my homeopathic remedy has arrived but I

am unsure about taking it as, over the last few days, I have had my temazepam and the drugs that the Crisis Team gave me. Normally, you need an element of stability and 'being clean' before you take a homeopathic remedy. Furthermore, the homeopath has warned me that the 5HTP should not be taken alongside 'conventional' anti-depressants. I must talk to the homeopath about this. However, my challenge today is to build on my initial cat work last night. I need to conduct an experiment to establish if it is possible to alter the dynamics of a group of two humans and two cats so that each cat can enjoy a primary relationship with one human.

At present it is Bafta who enjoys that relationship, with both of us and pretty much to the exclusion of Nada. My task today will be firstly to unteach that relationship. I am sitting in the sun in the garden and Bafta approaches. As ever, his first approach is tentative, even though he is pretty sure of his ground. He extends his nose and sniffs my outstretched finger. Content that it is indeed me, he lies down, rolls on his side and stretches. I tickle his tummy. This, I realise, is cat yoga: the stretch fills his lungs with oxygen and my tickling stimulates his circulation, taking that oxygen around his body. Such a simple technique: I must try this later with Michaela.

Now, however, it's time to unteach Bafta: I call him a second time but on this occasion, when he sniffs my finger, I surprise him with a dollop of strawberry yoghourt on the end of his nose. He sneezes and rushes off in disgust. Mission accomplished: now, all I have to do is find Nada...

When Michaela gets home, I tell her about the cat massage and sit her on the sofa: I perch on the back of the sofa behind her.

'You see, the first touch by the cat is so soft, it's almost imperceptible. It's the gentlest of signals, by which he establishes he's in his comfort zone with you.'

I run the softest of tickles across Michaela's neck and ears.

'When he's really comfortable and relaxed, it's yoga time and he wants your help to oxygenate his body. It begins with a tickle, then it's a gentle massage and then a more robust one.'

I gradually increase the pressure of the massage until it's quite robust. Larry comes into the room. 'What the hell's going on?' he exclaims.

'I'm just showing Michaela how Bafta does a massage,' I explain.

'I think that will do for now!' says Michaela. 'You're hurting.' I think maybe she's embarrassed too...

That evening the three of us watch the rom com, Leap Year. I love it! This American woman lures her boyfriend to Ireland so she can propose to him on February 29 because she believes Irish tradition demands that he will accept her proposal. At first it seems to present a parody of Ireland, but gradually you realise that the joke is on the Americans and, of course, in the end, the rough-edged Irish guy gets his gal who is, natch, our American heroine. I decide it's a very symbolic film that has important lessons in understanding cultural difference. I must put it on the reading and watching list for the disciples.

If I am honest, I have to accept that, while I may have sorted out my physical injury with all that ice and arnica, things are not right in my head. I am as far from sleep as ever and I know that not everything is working quite right in my brain. On the one hand, I have acquired superpowers and rare insight into life, the universe and everything. But on the other, this is certainly causing me difficulties in everyday life. This elasticity of time, for example: it's hard to conduct a conversation when you have heard the answers to a question before the person you are talking to has uttered them. And this inability to retain focus and concentration... And then, while sometimes I just feel a bit weary, at others I am feeling quite unwell: strange, distant, out of control... Maybe if I can just get a decent night's sleep tonight. I take a temazepam but an hour later, it's had no effect. Furthermore, my mind is full of feline behaviour. I decide to conduct a further experiment, the objective of which will be to work with the cats to establish a series of outdoor feeding points in different parts of the garden, as well as a series of 'safe stations' that they can use. The idea is that they will stop bringing dead birds and mice indoors because they have these safe stations in the garden at which they can always expect to find food, whether it's a dish of food that we have put down for them, or something they have caught, a 'takeaway' as we like to call it.

I set about scent-marking various entry points to the house: the cat flap, the conservatory door. I use a combination of cat food, urine and lavender. The cats will get to know that this combination means safety. I introduce the cats to these new smell signals. I'm not sure if they have understood yet. I return to my own den, but sleep is elusive. I think dawn comes without it.

I feel really quite fragile and I just can't get my time synched with other people's. Michaela has gone to work, leaving me at home with Larry. I have a brainwave: I find a full length mirror that used to be attached to the door of a built-in wardrobe. I lug it downstairs and take it into the garden, where I prop it against the Torbay palm. I take a chair out and sit in the sun, a couple of metres from the mirror, so I can see my full face and, specifically, my mouth. I call Larry and ask him to stand behind my right shoulder. I can now see his mouth too. The idea is an immense success: I can coordinate my own words as I speak them with the movement of my lips in the mirror. More importantly, I can see Larry's words as they exit his mouth. Now, we can have a conversation again, without my talking over him.

I am sitting quietly in the garden: I am carefully minding my own business. I am trying hard to be uncontroversial. Larry asks why the patio door smells. I explain. He gives me a rather strange look.

I try to read a book, but it's just not really possible. Suddenly, I feel really quite unwell and start to panic a little. I can't recall having panicked since that awful night in Kirkwall. How long ago was that? I reason it can't be much more than two weeks. It could be two minutes; it could be two lifetimes. Time, after all, is elastic. In any event, it's two weeks with next to no sleep and that wasn't even the beginning: there was a good week of wakefulness before that and probably a week before that when sleep was not the most abundant commodity in my night-time warehouse. That's not a lot of sleep for a man who has superpowers to manage and a campaign for beatitude to run.

Yes, I'm feeling really quite unwell: I call Michaela at work. 'Can you come home? I really don't feel well…'

'OK, I'll come just as soon as I can. Has the Crisis Team been?'

'No, I don't think so… No, yes. No, that was yesterday. Is it Friday today?'

I think Michaela is a little alarmed to find I have transported that big heavy mirror downstairs. I am now sitting on a rug on the grass: she strokes my hair then disappears. I feel too tired to get up off the blanket. I think Michaela is inside with Larry and I wonder what they are talking about. I call the house phone on my mobile. 'I'm hungry: is there any chance of some food?'

'Larry's making you something.'

Some time passes: maybe 45 of my minutes, but I'm unsure how much time has passed for Larry or Michaela. I ring the mobile again. 'Is it coming?' I ask, exasperated.

'Yes, for God's sake, it's coming.'

Finally, a small sandwich arrives on a big white plate: I am unimpressed. I need a man-sized sandwich and they've given me a blini. The more I look at the food, the smaller it gets, and the bigger the white plate it is sitting on appears. I ring the phone again. 'That'll never keep me going! I'm a hunter, I need REAL food, not something from a cocktail party!'

Michaela and Larry appear together and suggest maybe I should go to bed and rest. I think maybe that would be a good idea. But I struggle to get to my feet and the stairs become a mountain. I am a hungry lion; I have been wandering the Serengeti for days; I have chased but failed to catch ten wildebeest and I am at the end of my energy reserves. But I can at least still roar. I can ROAR! I CAN ROAR VERY LOUD!! I am now crawling up the staircase. I am spent. Michaela and Larry have to help drag me upstairs. But at least I can still roar. The man who stalked his cats has become a lion; a very hungry lion. I have for a fleeting moment the strange sensation that I must sound like Ian Paisley in full flow...

I am in bed. Larry has confiscated my phone. Something about not wanting me to call people I work with. I need my phone. I have to keep on top of these work things. And I need some way of communicating with Larry and Michaela downstairs. I am getting hungrier and hungrier. Eventually Larry brings me my food. The blini has shrunk further and the plate has expanded. Not only is time elastic, but so too is space and this is no food for a hungry lion. 'I need carbs! Bring me carbs! A lion needs a proper plate of food!' I roar. 'CARBS!!!'

An eternity passes. Larry finally arrives with a big bowl of pasta. This looks more like the food for a hungry lion. I wolf down a big bowl of pasta. No, I LION down a big bowl of pasta. I don't finish it but I feel full. I am the sated lion in the Serengeti. My belly aches. I push the tray to the foot of the bed. I close my eyes. The hot afternoon sun bakes the dry grass of the plain beyond the shade of the acacia.

The Crisis Team arrives again. 'I'm Charlie and this is Simon. You saw our colleagues yesterday. How are you feeling today, Vic?'

'I don't know; I don't feel so good.'

'Did you feel better after you had the tablet last time?'

'I don't know. Maybe. Did I have drugs?'

'We're going to give you a slightly higher dose and then we'll come back and see you later this evening, OK?'

They've been rummaging through my meds with Michaela. They are looking for the homeopathic remedy. Now there's a funny thing. Sceptical medical people say homeopathy doesn't work, yet here they are trying to confiscate my homeopathic remedy. They think I have hidden it, but I have nothing to hide. The remedy is still in its jar, precisely where they were looking for it. If only people would use their eyes now and again.

'They're in this bottle,' I say, 'but I never actually took any.' I think Michaela thinks the remedy has contributed to my worsening condition, but that would be hard if I hadn't actually taken even one. Unless, of course, it really is just a placebo effect.

More time bounces past. It no longer moves at any speed that I can identify. I guess mostly it goes forward, but that's all I can say. Michaela comes into the room and tells me the doctors are coming back with the Crisis Team and she'll need to talk to them before they see me. She seems agitated.

I think it's quite late in the evening when they come. I decide this would be a good time to have a shower and put on a brighter face for everyone.

The sub-tropical rain drives down in sheets of warm water. The acacia tree offers little shelter and the lion's coat is thin, from the dry season. But at least the big cat's belly is full...

'Are you going to be much longer?' asks Michaela, at the door.

'Just a few minutes,' I say.

I am in my dressing gown: Michaela is in heated discussion with all these people in another room. I think they are going to try and take me away. I really can't allow this to happen: I can manage this on my own at home. I can make myself well again.

Larry says, 'Dad, can I talk to you?'

'Of course,' I say. 'I'll get my mirror.' The full-length mirror is still in the garden. I lug it indoors and prop it against the sitting-room wall, and position Larry behind me. But I don't watch his lips. I am angry. They simply must not take me away. I can manage this on my own at home. I am dealing with it. I am OK. Everything will be OK. I begin a tirade at Larry, insisting I can manage here at home and why it would be wrong to take me away because I'm OK, I really am OK. 'I'm OK, I'm OK, I'm OK! OK?'

'Dad, dad, DAD. Stop. Please listen to me for just one moment...'

'I am not going to be taken away!!!'

'Dad, just one minute, please. PLEASE!'

I quieten down and Larry comes close and whispers in my ear, 'They're going to Section you if you don't go voluntarily.'

Section Two of the Mental Health Act, 1983. Taking someone into hospital for psychiatric assessment, for their own or others' safety. They can be detained without their consent for up to 28 days. I know about that.

'Oh,' I say. It is not an exclamation. It is more a sigh. I am defeated. I feel like the air has escaped from the balloon. The big cat is past his prime. The lionesses have had their eye turned by the handsome young male. The old cat trudges off through the still damp savanna grass. He will be a long time alone... 'You'd better tell them to come in,' I say.

Enter Michaela, the two guys from the Crisis Team and Dr Gordon. I hadn't expected Dr Gordon. I haven't seen him for a while. The last doctor I saw was the Oriental lady, Dr Macduff.

'What's happened to you in the last two weeks?' he asks me. 'You were fine when I last saw you, just missing a little sleep.' He looks at me and his face says 'man in dressing gown; will only talk to me through a mirror; looks terrible...'

'I don't know, doctor. I'm not sleeping and I can't concentrate.'

'Why are you talking to me through a mirror?'

'It's the only way I can have a conversation, doctor. It helps me deliver my answers to people's questions at the right time: when they have finished speaking.'

'When else would you answer someone's question?'

'I hear what people are saying before they have said it.'

'Victor, we think you need a little time in hospital to help you get better and we'd like to have your consent to be admitted....'

'I understand, Dr Gordon. I know that if I don't consent you will Section me and I understand that there are all sorts of additional implications if that happens.'

Dr Gordon nonetheless explains some of those implications as if to underscore the seriousness of the pretty pickle into which I have got myself.

'I would have preferred to stay at home and manage this myself, but I am prepared to agree to go to hospital.'

Jean-Paul Sartre: Les Chemins de la Liberté. The existentialists argued that even in the direst circumstances we still retain choice. The man at the gibbet waiting for the hangman to pull the trapdoor can choose whether to shriek vengeance before he hangs. Or he can choose to drop quietly. I can choose not to make a fuss and go to hospital. Or I can choose to argue and make it very much harder for myself ever to come out again. Yes, ever. I know why the doctor is here. I know why it is late at night. They all have the tools of Sectioning at the ready but I can thwart them in their endeavour by agreeing to go quietly.

'I'll put some clothes on,' I say.

'I'll help you pack, Dad,' says Larry.

Together we pack a small holdall. The ambulance doesn't come. I hear them agreeing that it will be safe to take me in a car.

Autumn night is falling, we drive through the edge of town, towards Harrogate. We enter an NHS site in open countryside on the fringes of the Dales. I had noticed it before but hadn't appreciated it was a psychiatric unit.

I arrive at reception. They show me to my room. It is clean and bright, with an en suite toilet and shower. The bed is single. It boasts a rubber-covered mattress. Michaela makes it up with the sheets she has brought, to help me feel more at home. At my bedside she places my coloured book, a novel, glasses, my handkerchief and a little brass ornament consisting of the three wise monkeys, who respectively Hear no Evil, See no Evil, Speak no Evil. I can't recall why they are here. She places my laptop on the little desk in the room. There is a sheaf of papers that explain the rules of the unit. That can be for tomorrow.

'Will you come and see me in the morning?' I ask.

'Soon,' she says. 'But now you must sleep.'

I am drugged. I go to bed. I feel a strange sensation; one I had almost forgotten. It is the taste, the smell, the sight of sleep drifting over me. I close my eyes and submit to its advance.

CHAPTER 10

Home truths

Monday, September 27, 2021

When Felix eventually got back to his home in York he did little more than tumble into bed with a cup of herbal tea that would remain undrunk. His body sank into a deep slumber, but his mind slept the fitful sleep of one shorn of its compass, adrift between time zones and battered by seas of doubt, disappointment and despair. He dreamed of airports where the security zone was a maze without exits and flights for home left without regard for passengers still trapped in its web; of glimpses caught, and then agonisingly lost, of long forgotten faces; of finding himself at a conference podium, naked before his audience.

Somehow the hours dragged themselves past his tossing, fretful form till the sun rose, its first rays casting rods of light through the blinds and across the dishevelled bedclothes, waking their equally dishevelled occupant with a start. Felix was surprised and confused to find himself at home and more so that the first face to come into his mind was not that of Jameela Durrani, but Tracy's. Tracy who? He didn't know the family name of the woman with whom he had had the disarming conversation in the pub the night before. Was it the night before? Had yesterday taken place? Had the past week happened? Felix got out of bed and confronted the mirror with his face: the mirror didn't look so good. It bore the image of a tired, haggard man who might be suffering from stress, or jet-lag. Maybe both. Felix filled the basin with cold water and scooped it over his face, achieving little. He ran a basin of hot water, had a shave, cutting his upper lip. He slopped more cold water over himself and thought that, if you could ignore the stream of blood, the mirror was looking a little perkier now.

He switched on the 24-hour news: it was approaching 6am. The Americans were still in Kalamistan: as they had been at five; as they had been last week; as they had been two years ago. Stock markets were down again in Japan and there was more friction in the Eurozone over China's expanding asset base around the Mediterranean. Plus ça change, thought Felix, now realising that it was Monday, the first day of a working week. Had he said he would be back at work today? He couldn't remember. Could he face work with his mind so distracted?

Felix checked the calendar on his VSP: he had fortuitously allowed himself two days' recuperation, which was helpful, given that he was back at home a day later than originally anticipated. He slipped on a T-shirt, shorts and trainers and stepped out into the bright early sunshine, pausing to apply a piece of toilet roll to the wound on his top lip. He headed for the river, where he sat on a bench and watched a mother swan and her sooty-coloured adolescent offspring as they swam towards him in the hope of breadcrumbs. His life had become an ugly duckling: what would he have to do to find the beautiful bird within?

The city still slept and, tempted by an absence of people other than Felix and a lone jogger, the river yielded its secrets: an otter surfaced in mid-stream and swam for the shore, sending the swan and her cygnets scurrying for the water's edge. Felix was even more surprised to see the dazzling plumage of a kingfisher as it dived from its perch on a piece of driftwood at the other river bank. The countryside was marching into town; the sun still shone and Felix reflected that, yes, there was indeed much in life to feel good about. He would make a plan.

Felix's plan would begin with Tracy Whatsername. Should he take her up on her offer of a date and see if he could glean more about the secretive world of the Aurora Foundation. Trouble was, Tracy was not unattractive and, without the cloud of Jameela's disappearance hanging over them both, he suspected she could be witty and intelligent company. If they were to meet, it would be either in York or Newcastle and then there'd be a real risk that geography would dictate that somebody would spend the night at someone's. The next morning Tracy would reflect bitterly that she had played her ace too soon and that Felix would be just the latest in what he suspected might be a succession of false handsome princes, if he might be so bold as to describe himself thus. And Felix would be riddled with regret at his betrayal of Jameela. No, he should get in touch and tell Tracy he was flattered by her offer to date him but that were Jameela suddenly and unexpectedly to return, she might not be best pleased that her PA had been carrying on with the man she was toying with starting some kind of a relationship with. Then he realised he had erased Tracy's number when he deleted her text and the alternative of contacting her through her work might not be a great idea.

No, now was not the time to add further complications to life. In fact now was the time for Felix to begin some spring cleaning. Because, as Felix reflected, his life over recent months, years even, would earn him no prizes for the way he conducted his relationships. He would start by going to Doncaster to collect Mr Merryweather.

Mr Merryweather was lodging with Wendy while Felix was in Australia. Wendy was an old friend of Felix's. To be more accurate, Wendy was a former girlfriend of Felix who, some might observe, had acquired a status over the last couple of years that not everyone would categorise as 'ex'-girlfriend. There were certainly some people on Planet Earth who would regard Felix and Wendy as 'an item'. Felix, however, was not among them, though whether this was delusional on his part is another question.

Felix had met Wendy through a dating site when he was in

London, at a time when his chaotic working life made it close to impossible for happenstance alone to lead him to a girlfriend. Wendy was the third woman Felix had struck up any kind of rapport with on the website, but on actually meeting, neither of the others had greatly interested him. Wendy, on the other hand, was intelligent and they appeared to share aspects of their outlook on life. Plus, they found each other attractive. Wendy worked for a large charity engaged in a variety of projects in the Third World. Like Felix, she was frustrated by living in London: so many people, but so few opportunities to meet the right ones in the right places. They began to go for days out, to the coast, to art galleries; for evenings at the theatre and cinema. In time they became lovers, though they had been in no great hurry as both had enjoyed the suspense of what was almost an old-fashioned courtship. After they became lovers, Felix waited, confidently expecting to fall in love with Wendy. He waited to feel what he anticipated would be a sense of urgency, of needing to see her as often as possible; of finding himself bereft without her; of experiencing an all-consuming desire for every inch of her body. He was unsure why he didn't feel this way: he liked her; he liked being with her. But although he was happy to sleep with her, he found this mechanical, rather than driven by passion. Although he never told Wendy he loved her (nor she him), neither did he share with her what was now becoming for him a conviction that theirs could never be a partnership for life.

So life went on for Wendy and Felix for about a year. They would see each other once, maybe twice a week and would take the occasional weekend in the Cotswolds, or Dorset, when both could wring the time from their busy working schedules. Then Wendy announced that she had had her fill of living in London and wanted to enjoy a more civilised lifestyle, having negotiated with her employer to work from home three days a week and visit the office in London on no more than two. Wendy was going to become a Doncy, but some 30 years after that tongue-in-cheek term had first been coined. Back in the 1980s when acronyms like 'dinky' complemented marketing people's social descriptors, such as yuppie, someone came up with the term Yorkie to describe the small band of financially blessed people who commuted from York to London on what was then the UK's fastest rail line. With larger numbers commuting more regularly from as far afield as Peterborough, a property boom was predicted for Doncaster, which lay between the two, and the term Doncy (pronounced with a hard C, like a member of the horse family) fleetingly entered the language. Fleetingly, because there was scant evidence of either the predicted house price boom or of the new breed of commuters who might have driven it. Wendy, however, reasoned that for a fraction of what it would cost her to buy a studio flat within five miles of central London, she could acquire an entire Georgian town house in Doncaster and become part of a community, instead of a worker ant in the London termite mound.

Soon after Wendy's move north it became apparent to Felix that, although she had never said as much, she was hoping that Felix would follow her. He made token visits to Doncaster and though he admired the home she had created, he did not feel part of it. On the days she had to work in London, she would stay with him. But this did not necessarily suit him: it was hard to predict his work patterns and he would often have to toil, leaving Wendy to let herself into his flat and amuse herself. In the time that she was there alone, she would busy herself tidying and reorganising things. One day he came home to find all his books and vinyl rearranged by alphabetical order of author or artist. He had not asked for this. He began increasingly to reflect on what he enjoyed about Wendy and what annoyed him. Since she had moved out of London there were more things in the latter category and he began to struggle to remember things in the former. Besides her penchant for doing things unbidden, there were two other things that, increasingly, grated. One was the way she responded to his jokes: instead of laughing or indeed groaning at how bad they were, she would always return the same withering look and say 'Ha, ha'. With others, even a bad joke was a form of engagement and they would rejoin with an even worse pun, or trump his joke with a funnier one. He began to think Wendy took life too seriously. And then there was football. For Wendy to dislike football was, Felix thought, OK. That was her choice. But she went further: she hated Felix enjoying football and would sulk if he wanted to watch a match on TV or, worse, go and see one live.

Eventually he said, 'Wendy, this just isn't working for me, I'm sorry. I like you and I like doing things with you, but our souls live in different universes and I think we should accept that and move on...'

Wendy's response was resigned and she didn't force Felix to say the uncomfortable things he hadn't really wanted to say. Equally, he never heard from Wendy the frustrations that she felt about him but had chosen not to express for fear of rejection.

For six months they went their separate ways. Felix had other girlfriends, but all were casual and at best occasional relationships. No-one lit his fire. He did not know what Wendy did, or if she was seeing anyone. Then, out of the blue, she emailed him and asked if he would partner her at a friend's wedding. She dreaded the idea of turning up alone. She didn't want to be Fiona in Four Weddings and a Funeral. Perhaps Felix would have done well to reflect on some of the finer detail of Fiona's character in that 90s classic, and specifically her unrequited love for Charles, as played by Hugh Grant. In any event he saw no harm in doing the favour asked and long enough had passed for him to be curious about what Wendy had been up to. He left the arrangements to Wendy and turned up at the appointed time and place, a country house in East Anglia. Wendy had reserved a double room for them. Felix had not even thought about sleeping arrangements. She looked well, fantastic even, with colour in her cheeks, a smile replacing the slight scowl he had remembered; her now blonde-highlighted hair hung in waves in a bob that suited her slightly slimmer face. She wore a summer-blue dress that brought out a shimmer in her eyes and her bronzed skin was revealed by the low back and neckline, sculpted to showcase an inch or so of each breast. Felix realised why her face appeared narrower: she must have lost five or six kilos; not an excessive loss, but just enough to complete the picture of health and reveal a figure as near perfect as Felix could imagine. He must have been crazy to dump her, was his immediate thought. Not for one moment did he suppose that he, Felix, might have anything to do with this new, improved Wendy.

'You look really great,' he told her. 'The bride doesn't stand a chance!' To which Wendy gave a giggle and flushed slightly.

Much to Felix's surprise, she had made a real go of getting involved in her new community, joining not just a gym, but a ramblers' group and a theatre restoration project, for which she had become an enthusiastic and tireless advocate. She had also become a Samaritans volunteer. Felix was pleased to see her looking so good, so attractive, so healthy. He was pleased she had taken her life by the scruff and moved on from him. He felt absolved from guilt.

After the wedding, Felix pondered whether he should get in touch with Wendy again but reminded himself that the fundamental dynamics of love and attraction would not have changed: it would be the wrong thing to do. Eventually, it was Wendy who contacted him, posting pictures from the wedding on her Nimbus page, and reminding him what an enjoyable weekend they had shared. Felix admired the pictures and agreed with her about how nice the weekend had been, saying once again how pleased he was that she had looked so well and so happy. 'It was for you, you blind fool,' she replied, leaving poor naïve Felix unsure how to respond.

And then, not many weeks later, Felix made his own move north, to York, just 20 minutes up the line from Wendy. He decided after some thought to invite her to see his new city centre warehouse apartment. And they succumbed to the temptation so common among former lovers: better the devil you know. Indeed Felix was pleased that they became close friends; friends who slept together but who were not a couple; who were not bound by presumptions of exclusivity or fidelity. Felix thought it was an arrangement that worked well for both of them and it was one that had, by now, endured for the best part of three years.

As Felix watched the strangely graceful ugliness of the now redundant cooling towers of Ferrybridge describing the horizon beyond the train window, he reflected he would be pleased to see Wendy and naïvely expected to enjoy her support in resolving what he was now calling the Jameela Crisis. Half an hour later he was at her door. Even in jeans and an old T-shirt, her hair hastily pinned back, she looked good, he reflected. Equally, though, she was not and never could be Jameela. 'Welcome home, globetrotter!' she smiled, putting her arms round his neck and kissing him, just once, on the lips.

'You look good,' he said.

'And you look terrible. Come in and sit down.'

It was only lunchtime, but Felix was happy to accept the glass of wine offered. Mr Merryweather, curled tightly on the sofa, raised his head in response to Felix's tickle behind the ears and purred softly. Felix had never really thought about owning an animal: he had never imagined he would be responsible enough, but Wendy had demanded once too often what a man named after a cat would call his pet cat. Tiddles was a black and white kitten advertised in a shop window, who was looking for a home. Felix, on impulse, had acquired him and, naturally, renamed him Mr Merryweather. For once Wendy had achieved a faint smile in response to one of his jokes. She now provided a second home for Mr Merryweather during Felix's frequent absences on business. Felix failed to appreciate that for Wendy, Mr Merryweather provided the best guarantee that she would see him again sooner rather than later.

And so, like an innocent marched unwarily into the Valley of Death, Felix unfolded the story of Jameela Durrani; his unanticipated attraction to her; the elusive promise of a relationship of some kind; the bizarre circumstances of the cruel disappearance of that promise; his meeting with Tracy, though, out of modesty, he did not mention that she too had appeared to hold a candle for him. If Felix had paid more attention, he would have noticed the colour fading from Wendy's face and seen how the corners of her mouth began to descend so her lips assumed a straight line across the visage now crowned by doleful eyes. Had he observed these changes, he might not have gone on to describe how he now planned to negotiate time off work to track down Jameela. Remarkable as it may seem, he was taken by surprise when Wendy erupted.

'And I'm supposed to share your joy? I'm supposed to be happy standing on the touchline rooting for you in your search for the Holy Grail of love? I've given up years for you. Years when I might have been happy with someone else, having babies with them, having some purpose to my life instead of being trapped by my own idiotic love for a blind, stupid idiot like you. A fool with a cat's name. Felix the happy man, Felix the selfish uncaring oaf…'

'But I thought we were just friends…' a shocked Felix attempted to counter.

'Pah! Don't you think I'd rather have at least something of you than nothing at all? Don't you think I live in hope that one day, one day, you might just look me in the eyes and say "Wendy, I love you"? Don't you know the pain I feel when I know you're with someone else; why you always wait a day before you come to see me after one of your "business trips". You think I don't know about Helga in Helsinki, Françoise in, in… France! and and and, and Maria in in, in Moscow! You visit your women and then you spend 24 hours shaking off your guilt and then you come to see me and take your stupid cat home.'

Felix felt like saying 'Don't bring Mr Merryweather into this,' but thought better of it. As for the other things, well the detail was wrong but he was in awe of Wendy's perceptiveness regarding the generality of his behaviour. He began to feel more than slightly ashamed.

'You are a complete dreamer, Felix Merryweather. Life isn't about dreams, it's about pragmatism and compromise. Do you think for one minute it was love at first sight for me? Do you think there aren't things about you that drive me mad? Quite apart from the fact, now proven, that you are not just a complete dick but a completely uncaring dick. But I was prepared to make a life with you and because I gave it time, I found I grew to love you and even when you dumped me I didn't rush out to find someone else, either to replace you or just to sleep with. I looked at myself in the mirror and thought about things that I realised were getting in the way of you loving me and I did something about them. And if you would just stop for a moment and imagine yourself living in the real world like the rest of us, you'd realise that there are far worse things in life than spending time with me and having a proper, adult relationship…'

Felix was utterly lost for words and Wendy was like an empty balloon that had landed on the floor, shrivelled after rushing noisily round the ceiling. And then, with something between a sneer, a snarl and a scowl, she added: 'I presume she's a Muslim. How will you feel about adopting a pure and clean sex life? She won't want to do some of the "unclean" things you like to get up to with me.'

'That's cheap and unnecessary,' said Felix, finally sensing a sliver of moral high ground.

'I'm sorry,' conceded Wendy. 'But you'd better go. You can call me when you haven't found your crazy love and you can make the most of a proper life with me instead. If I haven't found myself a proper man living in the real world in the meantime that is. And by the way, calling your cat Mr Merryweather wasn't funny either.'

'Come on then Tiddles, time to go home,' said Felix, ushering the feline into his travelling basket. 'I guess I'll see you when I do, then…'

'Maybe; maybe not. But for now, just go,' said Wendy.

Back home in York, Felix reflected on the lesson in life that had been delivered to him so precisely. He had seen what he wanted to see, believed what he wanted to believe and he had hurt someone who, despite everything, was very dear to him. But what was love if it didn't merit real sacrifice? What was hope if a dream wasn't worth pursuing? And what, for that matter, was humanity if people could simply vanish – be vanished – without anybody trying to find them? He would follow his dream and live in hope and aspiration. And if he found Jameela and his love turned out to be unrequited, only then would he be pragmatic and return to Wendy. If she still wanted him, that is. Until that moment, he would carry on searching. For Jameela and Shangri-La.

The following day, Felix returned to work, where he was surprised to find on arrival a rare package that had been delivered by 'snail mail'. It was marked 'Strictly for the attention of Mr F Merryweather'. Inside was a letter: from Tracy Davenport.

Dear Felix

I'm sorry if I was a bit gauche yesterday. Please pretend I didn't come on to you and accept that I will do what I can to help you find Jameela, without compromising my own position. I enclose some essential reading for you, but take good care of it as copies are very hard to come by, either online or hard copies like this. You should also read Lord Lindisfarne's autobiography, Luck and Judgement. You shouldn't have any trouble finding a copy of that one.

The note concluded with a list of names entitled 'Others who have vanished', followed by 'And one who returned'. There were contact details for Emily Black, the woman Felix had discovered who had disappeared and then returned, and family contacts and 'last seen' notes alongside some of the other names. It was all written in the same neat hand he had seen Tracy use to compile her boss's desk diary.

Tracy signed off 'with all best wishes, Tracy Davenport'. A PS provided her personal contact details.

The 'essential reading' to which Tracy had referred comprised a paperback of about 350 pages, entitled The Secret World of the Aurora Foundation. The sub-title read: What one of the world's most powerful companies would prefer you not to know. The cover design comprised a cartoon of Lord Lindisfarne, with a finger held to his lips.

Felix resolved to read both works over the coming days, while arranging his affairs as best he could to enable him to take an extended sabbatical. He was unsure how his bosses would respond to this request, but he could see no other way.

At home that night he reflected on what he was coming to recognise was the fairly despicable way in which had been conducting his love life. It was time to wipe the slate clean and begin a more mature phase of his life. A far more respectful phase. He would begin by calling Katrina in Copenhagen. He'd seen her occasionally when in the Danish capital, having first met her three years previously at a conference. He told her he'd met someone and thought it would be best if they stopped seeing each other. Katrina said she was sorry to hear that as she had felt that, with a bit of effort, they might have been able to create something together. 'That's life, I suppose,' she sighed, with all her Scandinavian pragmatism.

Encouraged, Felix called Ute, in Berlin, who responded by saying, 'Why are you telling me this? It's your life and you do what you want with it. If I see you, I see you, if I don't, I don't. Tschüss!'

Well, at least Felix hadn't misread one situation. Finally, he called Genziana, in Florence, and repeated the story of his resolve to find the woman of his dreams. 'You are beeg bastard, Meester Felix Merryweather. What kind of woman you think I am? You take for granted my virtue and you are full only of bad intentions. May you rot in hell, you bad man!'

Felix reflected that he had thus far in his life no more than scratched the surface of cultural difference and of the female psyche. He hoped he was properly equipped for the voyage he was about to undertake.

CHAPTER 11

Into the cuckoo's nest

Saturday, September 4, 2010

I awake in the morning. I'm going to say that again: I awake in the morning. From that you'll quickly recognise that I must have gone to sleep. It may just be the first proper night's sleep I've had in weeks. It is 8.45. Someone knocks on my door and tells me it's nearly time for breakfast. My room is a neat little affair with an en suite loo and shower. I take a shower and feel the warm water breathe fresh life into my body. I look down at my belly: it is a distended ball, like the stomach of a gorged lion or the pot bellies you might see on aboriginal people. I always thought it was a sign of undernourishment, but perhaps it's a sign of different eating patterns: after all, the aboriginal people of Australia are renowned for their ability to survive for days with little water and only grubs and insects to eat. So if a big meal comes along, I guess they'll gorge and run round with big bellies until it's all converted to energy or fat or whatever. As a privileged First Worlder on a regular diet, I usually start my day with a good healthy poo, but there seems to be nothing doing on that score today. Maybe a bit of breakfast will bring it along. I pull on some clothes and, popping the three wise monkeys into my pocket, set off to locate breakfast.

The place seems strangely quiet. Those people I do see are either staff who seem busy with morning routines, or one or two patients shambling along the corridors, heads bowed. My room is not far from the reception area. I notice that the staff behind the desk have to kind of crouch forward to see their computer screens, which are located beneath the 'counter', at which I guess the patients – maybe I should call us guests – come to ask questions. This arrangement is going to give these guys terrible posture problems, I think, but before I can pass comment a man in a nurse's uniform comes round the corner. 'You look a bit lost,' he says. 'Can I help?'

'I'm Vic. I'm new. Arrived last night. Where do I get breakfast?'

'Ah, you're Victor... Vic,' says the nurse, emphasising the 'you're' as though to suggest he's been expecting or looking for me. 'The night team said you'd arrived. It was me who knocked on your door earlier. I'll take you to the dining room and then I'll get one of the guys to show you the ropes. I'm John, by the way.'

I follow John, wondering about his accent: he has Yorkshirisms, but there's something else in there. 'How long have you lived in Yorkshire?' I ask.

'Moved up ten years ago when I married a Yorkshire lass, but you'll probably guess I'm not from here.'

'No, I didn't think so,' I say. And then I have an inspiration. 'You're from London, aren't you? North London, I'd say, probably brought up in Crouch End. But I reckon you spent a year or two somewhere else before you came here. Maybe in the Midlands somewhere. Not Birmingham though.'

'Bloody 'ell Victor, me ol' shiner, you psychic or you just been goin' through the HR files, mate?' laughs John, exaggerating a cockney East End accent.

'No, I don't think I'm psychic. I just have heightened senses. It's the adrenaline. I've friends in London and you know, up here, we like to pretend that everyone down there speaks the same, you know, "You orll right, guv?" and all that cockney stuff, but you can detect differences between different southern accents, different London accents even. You just have to tune in and listen. And anyway you've started laying it on now. So, am I right, then?'

'Pretty much: I was raised in Hornsey, just by Ally Pally, between Crouch End and Muswell Hill. I did my nurse training in Derby, which is where I met the missus. She's from Skipton and I followed her to Yorkshire: never looked back, really. Love it, mate. Love it.'

John isn't laying it on any more but I notice he still pronounces Crouch End like Craach Ind and the O in his love is more like an A.

'I was probably making a bit of a lucky guess,' I venture, though I am quite seriously impressed with myself: I am detecting nuances of sound and language I don't ever remember being able to before.

'So here's the dining room, Victor. Breakfast at nine, then lunch at 12, or dinner as you'd probably say. Tea's at six and then there's sandwiches on the trolley about nine, before medication, and you can make yourself a drink in the little kitchen next door.'

While he is explaining all this to me, a guy in his 40s ambles up. Unlike the others I've seen so far, he's looking ahead, not at his feet. He has bright blue eyes: I immediately see into his soul. He is a good man. Beneath those eyes, the nose is flattened and a little crooked. The way a nose only gets through contact sport: football, rugby, boxing maybe.

'Dave, this is Vic, our new guest. Can I leave him in your capable hands?'

Dave extends a hand: it's powerful but his grip as he shakes my own is comfortable and warm. 'Welcome to the madhoose,' he smiles. 'What're ye in for?'

'Too much adrenaline.'

'Me too,' he says with a cross between a smile and a chuckle.

'Yeah? How come? How long have you been here?'

'Lost the plot a bit, mate. I was a pro boxer and they play with your mind; promoters and people, ye knaa. Bad scene. Got to drinking and lost me way. It's me second time in this kind of place. Voluntary this time: been here a couple o' months but not deein' so bad. Maybe another week or two'll see me oot again if I can sort oot me livin' arrangements.'

I feel my linguistic gift nudging my tongue again and before long my mouth is asking: 'How long have you been living in Yorkshire? You're from County Durham originally, Blackhall way, aren't you?'

'Hey, ye're good, mate! Where d'ye learn that trick?'

We've drifted into the dining room. Dave pulls me a chair at a table where a lad in his early 20s is already sitting.

'Jeff: Vic. Vic: Jeff,' says Dave.

'What you in for, Vic?'

'Too much adrenaline.'

'Yeah? Me too!'

Jeff is on the chubby side: a pile of buttered toast is submitting to his steady assault. Breakfast doesn't amount to much: cornflakes, toast and a choice of marmalade or jam, with orange juice and tea, served from a hatch in the corner. I collect mine and return to the table and start to yabber. I know I'm yabbering but my brain is winding up again and it just kind of happens. Dave looks straight at me and places a finger to his lips. I stop. We eat in silence.

'Tidy yer plate and stuff up, Jeff,' says Dave softly as the last piece of toast succumbs and Jeff makes to leave and abandon the untidy jam smears and piles of crumbs he's created at the table.

'Sorry, Dave. See you for a ciggy in five?'

'Naa lad, I'm tryin' te keep 'em te afternoon 'n evenin'.'

Dave turns to me again and gestures that we too should clear and tidy our places before leaving the dining room. We place our dishes on a serving trolley by the hatch and then I follow him across the corridor. 'Games room, Vic. D'ye play pool?'

My heart soars: the thrill of doing something as normal and brilliantly enjoyable as a game of pool is fantastic. 'Later,' says Dave. 'I've somethin' te show ye forst.' He beckons me through the games room: beyond is a generously-sized garden, accessed via double patio doors and enclosed on three sides by the hospital buildings; on the fourth by a quite high wooden fence. We have the Indian summer for company as Dave starts his guided tour, beginning with some plastic buckets, in which he has planted seed potatoes in fresh compost. These stand on the paved terrace, to the right of the doors as we go into the garden. Beyond them, and filling most of that end of the garden, is a raised wooden compost-filled bed. Dave tuts as he removes cigarette butts from the buckets. 'The other garden, off the dinin' room, is for smokin', not this 'un. I'm tryin' me best ter keep it tidy in 'ere and I've been larnin' aboot the different plants, but I divn't knaa aall the names.'

He takes me into the part of the garden that lies to the left of the patio doors. This comprises a wedge-shaped lawn, surrounded on its three longer sides by quite densely planted borders, which I now realise are filled not just with flowering shrubs, but herbs too. 'D'ye knaa the name of this 'un?' asks Dave, rubbing a needled sprig between his finger and thumb.

'That's rosemary, Dave,' I say. 'My favourite herb.'

'And this 'un?'

'That's thyme.'

'And this?'

'Curry plant: what you smell is what you get!'

'What aboot this?' Dave points to a low shrub with small, bright yellow-green leaves.

'It looks like another variety of thyme,' I suggest. But when I crumple it between my fingers, there's no smell to speak of. I put some on my tongue: pretty tasteless. 'Some sort of false thyme: I don't think you'd use it in cooking.'

But Dave's attention is now elsewhere. The morning air is still a little cool: the sun hasn't really done its business yet. A small bumble bee hasn't enough warmth in its body to get busy and it's shambling (just like the guys in here) along a stretch of patio, in the shade of a bush of blazing yellow broom. Dave is gently nudging it onto the end of his finger. He carries it a few metres and softly places it on a flower on a buddleia bush that is enjoying the full force of the sun's gathering rays at the end of the garden that is furthest from the raised compost bed.

'We 'ave te help the bees,' says Dave. 'They're under attack frae the wasps: the wasps are stealin' their food.' He frowns. 'The wasps are evil: they are the only living creatures it's right to kill – they carry the souls of people who are stuck between heaven and hell. The tormented souls. If we kill the wasps, we can release these souls from torment. Have you noticed how there's more and more wasps and fewer and fewer bees?'

I have read a lot about the decline of bees in recent years and seen much conjecture as to why this should be. Some blame lice, some an accumulation of systemic pest-killers in the environment. I like Dave's neat explanation that the wasps are getting the upper hand in a battle for food resources that's been going on for thousands, millions of years. My charity wing will finance research into this theory at one of the region's top universities. It will bring ground-breaking advances in the worldwide battle to save the honey bee.

The idea that wasps carry tormented souls that are trapped in purgatory rings a bit of a bell: isn't there something like this in Danté's Inferno? I'll have to check this out...

I do my best to help Dave with the names for some of the other shrubs, but they're not all my strong point. In time, we find ourselves back where we began: at the rosemary bed. Dave puts his hand in his pocket and pulls out a delicate string of beads. 'This is my rosemary,' he says. 'I always carry it and I hold it tight when I need strength.'

I look into his eyes: again I see the warm soul and an almost childlike glow of enthusiasm that belies the weight of fundamentalist, or is it just Catholic, theology.

'Rosary, Dave,' I correct him, not for a second imagining that he may be making a joke. I fish in turn in my own pocket. I surprise myself a little as my hand falls on the three little brass wise monkeys. 'This is my talisman, Dave. The three monkeys See no Evil, Hear no Evil and Speak no Evil: see how one covers his eyes, while this one has his hands on his ears and this one, his mouth?' My mouth continues, for I realise that it must be Malcolm who has made sure I have arrived in hospital with some kind of talisman of my own. 'It symbolises my own faith: the faith I hold in humanity and scientific truth,' I continue. 'But you know, I don't believe that religion and science are so far apart. In fact, one day, religious faith and our collective faith, as humanity, will come together in one ultimate Truth.' I recall how important it was for me that my doctor had Faith that day when I was feeling I was starting to lose the battle, and I know that all religions are just different routes to, different attempts to unravel, the mysteries that science has yet to explain. Dave nods gently and smiles as I conclude: 'The important thing is that we all have a belief system; that we have Faith.'

'Aye, yeah, I think that's true but ye knaa, there's not so much time. We 'ave te act now te save the world; te save 'umanity.'

His look now is earnest and concerned.

'Yeah, that's right Dave…' I pause before deciding quite easily that I can trust him with my frightening truth. 'My brother was killed in an accident – an accident in which I was the one who should have died,' I begin. 'He's spoken with me and told me the Truth: huge Truths, in fact, about humanity – about Life, the Universe… Everything!'

Dave listens carefully as we stand outside the patio doors while I take him, first, through the car crash and then through the swirling coloured vortices of my meeting with Malcolm and my subsequent understanding of how to verify whether I have correctly grasped the meaning of the hugely important life-changing, world-changing things he is telling me. Dave looks elated. 'So d'ye understand already that me 'n ye, we've been sent heor for a porpose? That we are meant to meet, because the destiny of the world is in wor hands?'

'I think I do, Dave. And I think we have just seven days to save the world. But it's not literally seven days: that's the trouble they got into when they wrote the Old Testament. The seven days in Genesis aren't seven days as we would understand it,' I tell him. 'You see, my brother has shown me the future and he's demonstrated to me that time isn't constant, it's elastic, so one person's minute is another person's day and God's seven days when he made the world, if you take all that literally, is millions of years in geological and evolutionary time. So, like, we've no time to lose if we're going to save the world but at the same time, we've got all the time in the world!'

'Aye, aall the time in the world,' Dave, echoes, with a smile. 'Time enough for a game of pool any road!'

He gestures me back inside, through the patio doors, and begins to assemble the balls on the pool table.

'Let's start,' says Dave. 'But remember the idea isn't te win: it's te improve yorsel'. And ah think ye'll find that we're very evenly matched, as it happens. But forst we'll play a little game just te sharpen up a bit. We just play the balls in numerical order until we've cleared the table, aall reet!'

Dave hands me the cue. 'Ye break!'

Before I square up to the balls, I step into the fresh outdoors and raise my eyes to the sky. I breathe in deeply, ensuring the oxygen is drawn deep into my lungs. I repeat the exercise four or five times to be sure my brain is fully oxygenated. My focus is acute as I slam the cue ball into the pack, with a little side. Two balls go down.

'Now tyek 'em in order,' reminds Dave.

I rewind my mind: I can see the two balls zipping into the pockets. I slow down the rewind action. I can see on the rewind slo-mo they are the Two ball and the Four. The One ball presents me with a difficult challenge: I draw in another breath of the oxygen nectar. My shot becomes clear: I triangulate it, seeing the invisible lines that demonstrate where I must strike the cushion with the cue ball so as to come back to gently side the One into the centre pocket. My shot is sure: the cue ball hits the invisible mark on the cushion and nudges the yellow ball into the pocket.

'Nice shot,' says Dave.

I realise I haven't been thinking ahead: I am snookered on the Three. I attempt an audacious chip and the cue ball indeed hits the three but fails to direct it towards the pocket.

'Nice try!' Dave takes the cue and sinks the Three, Five and Six in quick succession. We move on through the pack, sinking balls in roughly equal numbers.

'OK, let's have a game,' says Dave. 'Ye break again.'

The game unfolds in much the same way as our practice: I pot two; Dave pots two; I pot one; Dave pots one. Predictably we end up both going for the black, having downed all our own balls. Then Dave sees the black kind of squirt back out of the corner pocket instead of dropping into it, leaving me with an easy winning shot. The rematch follows a not dissimilar course, only this time it's me who holes the black, but the cue ball rebounds into the centre pocket.

'I should look beyond where the object ball is destined to go,' I say.

'Aye: ye can practise and improve yor game. Table tennis?'

'Table tennis!?' I chirp. Can life get any better? I've never been better than average at most games, but I've always felt I can more than hold my own at table tennis. 'Where's the table?'

The table in fact comes in two halves that sit on top of the pool table. We begin with a practice knock-up. We seem pretty evenly matched.

Before we begin a 'real match', I again slip outside and inhale fresh air deeply.

I serve my totemic backspin backhand low over the net and the ball bounces low and awkwardly, giving Dave no chance. 'Nice one,' he says. I take the next two points before Dave manages to get the measure of my serve, taking the next two points. He then evens the game at ten-ten. And so we go on, until I eventually win 23-21. Dave wins the return 21-19.

'Funny how the games are so even, isn't it?!' says Dave. 'But, ye knaa, it's not the winnin' that coonts, it's the takin' part and improvin' yersel'.'

Dave suggests we go to our rooms and meet again in the dining room for lunch in 15 minutes. In my room, I try my iPhone and find I can just about get a signal if I stand on the window sill and put the phone outside. Not very practical. I walk back along the corridor to Reception and my signal gains an extra bar. 'I see reception is best at Reception,' I pronounce to no-one in particular. I text Michaela and ask her to bring my table tennis bat and maybe some cash, when she comes to see me.

There are more people around now, but most are in silent reverie, deep within their own worlds. I need to lift them from this torpor.

Lunch proves something of a revelation. Dave signals me to join him at a table near the serving hatch. Jeff blusters in and asks if he can sit with us too: Dave silently motions him to a table further back. Jeff looks a little crestfallen. A much older guy, with sunken cheeks indicating an unscheduled absence of false teeth, is permitted to join us. 'Aall reet Jimmy?' asks Dave. The reply is incomprehensible.

A young lad is also permitted to join us, though he seems to have trouble holding up his head and flops across his table place, his chair screeching back on the wooden floor. 'Siddup Jake!' says Dave. 'Siddup!' Jake pulls himself up. I can't work out whether he's looking at Dave or just staring into space.

Gradually the half dozen tables pretty much fill up: Dave explains that a lot of the guys find it hard to get going in the morning. I'm not quite sure what he means: I haven't felt better in days.

Dave puts his finger to his lips: he's looking at me, like he's saying I'm talking too much. Can't say I'd noticed I was talking at all. He whispers to me something about a rule that we should keep the noise down over lunch. It's anathema to me for whom meals are social occasions, but hey ho, when in Rome...

'Let's say Grace,' says Dave. 'Jake, siddup, lad!'

'Bless us, O Lord, and these, Thy gifts, which we are about to receive from Thy bounty. Through Christ, our Lord. Amen.'

He speaks the words clearly, if quietly, his rosary in his left hand, his eyes closed, head slightly bowed. I place the three monkeys on the table, respectfully.

John the nurse is supervising and he's joined by another nurse, who I gather is called Sophie. At 12 sharp the serving hatch rises and Sophie selects a table to come forward.

'Nay Sophie, why them? Why them not us, it's alles them first, ne'er us!' The voice is young Jeff's.

'Quieten down, Jeff, yor torn'll come in good time!' says John.

'Ah hey, why do I alles have to wait?'

Jeff's waiting will continue a while yet, as it's our table that's called second. I'm pleasantly surprised by the food on offer, though – because I wasn't around yesterday to book my choice – I have to wait until the end to see what's left. I needn't have worried too much: apparently there are nearly always one or two guests who, for whatever reason, choose not to pitch up at meal times. So I eat well: healthy food, nicely prepared – something between brunch and lunch. Even the fried bits are sparing of fat. If this is hospital food, give me hospital food!

Old Jimmy struggles a bit with his food and the nurses have to chop it up for him and mash it. He keeps kind of jabbering and they can't quite understand what he's trying to say, though I'm impressed by their patience with him. Then I make a bit of a remarkable discovery: if I close my eyes I can hear and understand him pretty much perfectly. It seems like an extension of my ability to turn the volume of the radio up and down without touching the knob. I guess it's like shutting off all other stimuli to my brain except the one that's especially important at any given moment, in this case Jimmy's words, contorted as they are by his shortcomings in the dental department.

'He's telling you he doesn't like peas,' I tell the nurses. 'And that you're trying to shovel in too much at once anyway!'

I open my eyes: the nurses are looking at me nonplussed: 'Yes, thank you Victor, that's MOST helpful,' says John with a distinctly sarcastic tone.

After lunch an attractive nurse of 40-ish, called Julia, summons me and sits me down in one of the quiet rooms, near Reception.

There are a few books and magazines and games, including a chess board and draughts.

Julia takes a comfy seat opposite me: she has an auburn bob and bright, intelligent green-blue eyes. 'You joined us in a bit of a rush, Victor, so I've a few things to catch up on with you.' She has a distinctive kind of Yorkshire accent.

'How long is it since you lived in Wensleydale?' I ask.

'Ooh, a good ten years, I should say... Who told you I lived in Wensleydale?' The accent has both a deadpan edge and a lilt to it.

'No-one, I recognised your accent. I'd guess you're from round Bainbridge, or at least somewhere in the upper dale.'

'Eh, Vic lad, tha's a clever 'un,' she teases. ''Appen aa'm from Askrigg ter tell't truth, but tha's near enuff! But back to the matter in hand, yer clever bugger: we'll be needing to settle your medication, which'll mean a bit of trial and error with your dose. How did you sleep last night?'

'Like a bairn,' I tell her.

'OK, so you can see how you go and just take the temazepam if you feel you need it to get to sleep. Dr Honeydew won't see you till he does his rounds on Monday...'

'Who's Dr Honeydew? I was hoping I'd be back home by Monday...'

'Well, you know Victor, going home isn't just your decision. We need to know that your wife and family are ready for that...'

'Oh they'll want me back home just as soon as!' I tell her confidently.

'So tell me a bit about your family, Victor,' says Julia, uncrossing and recrossing her elegant legs below the prim blue uniform. I can see her warm, caring soul behind, or rather through the windows of her eyes. I can see her genes: she's of the Viking stock of the northern hill country...

I join some of the other guys in the games room. Jeff is sitting like a sack of spuds, his chin collapsed onto his chest.

'Will ye be gannin' te chorch tomorra'?' asks Dave.

'Aye,' says Jeff and, seeing me standing by the pool table, adds, 'Ist tha' comin', Vic lad?'

'Where's the church?'

Dave replies, 'There's a chapel just doon the corrido', other side of the ward doors and alang te the left. Should be a good show tomorrow. Important time: world te save.'

'No time to lose, eh Dave.'

'But we've all the time in the world!' we chorus, me touching the monkeys for reassurance as I do so and Dave, rosary in hand.

'Are ye allowed off the ward?' Dave asks me.

'Dunno… no-one's told me…'

'Ye'd best ask John or Julia.'

So. It's going to be an important event at the chapel on Sunday morning. I'd best check I'm allowed to go and then I'll make sure Michaela can come in for the service. I guess it must be about having to save the world and news is getting around that the team is being assembled to do just that.

'Ah'll mek sure as many as possible know aboot the service and come along,' says Jeff, and makes to leave the games room.

I notice he's still slouched, even if his chin is no longer glued to his chest.

'Jeff lad, stop there!' I call.

'W'supp?'

'Look at the shape of you!' I stand behind him, raise my knee to high on his back and pull his shoulders backward. He feels very tense.

'Relax, mate! You're depriving your body of oxygen here. Let's get those shoulders back.'

He relaxes a little and I manage to grow him a couple of inches by getting his spine to describe something close to a vertical, but more work needs to be done.

'Come outside and sit on the bench!' I order. Now I can lever his spine more effectively and I can massage some of the tension out of his shoulders. Then I place a hand either side of his neck and cup his chin in both hands before pulling his head up, stretching his vertebrae in the process.

'Now breathe in deep, Jeff, and hold the oxygen in your lungs… How does that feel?'

'It's good!'

'OK, now try and hold your spine straight and keep your chin up: I don't want to see you shuffling round with your chops on the floor. Where were you born? Leeds?'

'Aye.'

'Support Leeds United?'

'Aye.'

'OK, say after me: "Proud to be a Tyke, proud to support Leeds United, proud to be Jeff, proud to be alive!".'

'Are you mad?!'

'Of course I am; we all are; that's why we're here, you moron! Now, this is good for you and it will help you get better and it will help you do the important work you've got to do…'

Jeff raises his chin and breathes in: I see him stretch and grow in front of me and with it I see his confidence grow too.

'Proud ter be a Tyke; proud ter support Leeds United; proud ter be Jeff; proud ter be alive!' he says.

'That's great, Jeff. Now remember that as you walk round all day: keep your mind focused on being proud of who you are and of your roots, and remember you're an important part of what needs to be done!'

'Ah'll be getting folk lined up for the service then,' he says, heading back through the games room and onto the ward. 'Proud ter be a Tyke; proud ter support Leeds United; proud ter be Jeff…'

The mantra fades as Jeff, now on a mission, disappears.

'That was good, mate,' says Dave. 'Impressive! What de ye de for an encore, like?'

'We've got to get these people working properly, Dave; turn them from zombies back into human beings!'

I have a brainwave: we need to get everyone doing yoga and we need to pull them all out of their own little worlds. Too many of them are zombing round with iPods and headphones.

'We can turn these guys into true disciples, Dave. It'll just take a little time…'

'There's nee time te lose, though but.'

Chorus: 'There's all the time in the world!'

That afternoon Dave tells me a little more about his life and the places he has fought bouts. He mentions a place in Holland. 'I think it was near the border. Began with M…'

'Maastricht?'

'Aye, that's 'im!'

Suddenly I hear Malcolm. He's right inside my head, telling me that Maastricht is significant. I remember Stella's missing sister, from whom none of the family has heard for years, and realise that this is where she is: Maastricht.

I take my iPhone and find a sliver of reception at the far corner of the garden from where I can tell her the good news about her sis.

'I don't think so, Vic. Why would she have gone there? And, you know, I prefer not to dwell on it really…'

'Have faith, Stella: you'll see it's true – I've received word.'

'OK, Vic, OK. Where are you anyway?'

'Hospital.'

'Hospital!! Are you OK?'

'Yeah, never been better: I'm here for a purpose.'

'That's good Vic,' she says, though I sense a little hesitantly. Then a few moments later, she adds, 'I'll get Michaela to bring me up to speed and see you soon, OK? Gotta go now!' And with that she is quickly gone.

Ooh heck, I'd better call Michaela… She takes a while to answer the phone and when she does, she sounds only half awake…

'Listen, there's a very important service in the morning, you've got to be here for 11, OK! And get me a yoga mat and will you tell Stella I'll be back at work soon but I've got to get this important work finished first…'

'Listen Vic, I need a bit of a rest and maybe I won't come to see you today, but Lisa's driven down and Nat's arriving at the airport later today so we'll come and see you tomorrow…'

'Nat?' That's fantastic news: Nat's our daughter, well Michaela's really, younger than Larry and Lisa, and we don't see so much of her since she moved to Amsterdam. Amsterdam! It must be another sign about Holland and Maastricht!

'Be sure you're all here in time for the service at 10.30, OK!?'

I guess I'd better make sure I'm allowed to go there, so I head at speed for Reception, where there's now a crowd of guys all queuing to ask questions.

'Stop crowding, boys!' It's a new voice: Yorkshire with heavy German undertones. I wait my turn.

'What's your name? Whereabouts in Germany are you from?'

'My name is Ute. I am from Harrogate; I haven't lived in Germany for years.' The English is precise, if adorned with a thick veneer of Yorkshire.

'Willst du mit mir Deutsch sprechen?' I ask, pleasantly surprised at how easily the sentence forms.

'No, I do not want you to speak German with me. I must always be improving my English and it will not help if you speak German with me.'

'But speaking German will also help your English.'

'No, it will not and now I am busy, OK?'

'Oh! OK… Am I allowed to go to church tomorrow.'

'How do I know that? You must ask Julia, or perhaps John, as Dr Honeydew will not be here until Monday, yes?'

As luck has it, Julia is passing.

'Can I go to church in the morning?'

'You're in here voluntarily, Victor, but I'd prefer you to check with me first. Let's talk about it at medication but if Dave goes with you it should be OK.'

'And Michaela, my fiancée: she's coming in with her daughter, Nat.'

'Oh really! Is that so!? I shall look forward to meeting them, then.'

CHAPTER 12

The learning curve

Wednesday, September 29, 2021

When Felix arrived at work the following day, he was unsure exactly how he should proceed. The reality was that he would have a considerable amount of research to do before he could sensibly set off to find Jameela. He had little idea how long such a quest was likely to take, but he guessed it might run into months; which shone a light on the very difficult negotiation he was going to have to have with his (he hoped) benevolent employer. The same employer who had just sent him all the way to Australia and back that he might bring the benefits of a Shared Ambition residential workshop event to his work across Europe. He decided he should take his research further before broaching that contentious topic. And then there was the question of what he would survive on, with travel costs to bear and no income coming in. He checked his savings on-line and reckoned he could probably muster about £25,000 without incurring any significant financial penalties. Twenty-five grand: was this, then, the price of true love? The gnawing loss he felt for Jameela right now told him that, yes, it was.

Felix delved into his briefcase and looked again at Tracy's list of the disappeared: besides the returnee, Emily Black, in Devon, there were a couple of others in the South of England. Felix would endeavour to set up some meetings around a forthcoming trip south. Emily Black should be relatively easy to trace. And Tracy's information ought to provide a good start towards locating the other families. Felix had meetings scheduled in Southampton and, two days later, in London. Emily Black's address was in a village not far from Exeter, on the edge of Dartmoor National Park. Two of the families that Tracy had listed were in Tunbridge Wells and Windsor.

Felix left the office on the pretext of buying a sandwich for lunch and called Emily Black's parents' landline number on his VSP. He had been unsure what to expect and the possibility that Emily herself might answer the phone had been one that he had not really considered.

'I'm sorry to bother you,' he said. 'I'm trying to contact an Emily Black.'

'And you are?'

'My name is Felix Merryweather…'

'Is this a wind-up?'

'No, I just have a slightly unusual name… Is Ms Black at home, I wonder?'

'I'm not sure Emily knows a Felix Heatherberry…'

'Merryweather!'

'As I say, I don't think she knows you…'

'No, she doesn't know me, but we do have mutual acquaintances and I'm very much hoping she might be able to help me to get in touch with one of those acquaintances.'

'Mr Merryweather, I'm Emily Black but I'm not at all sure I want to get involved in any kind of missing persons thing, because I'm guessing that's what you're calling about…'

Felix decided to try a different tack, avoiding confrontation over the issue of 'missing persons'. Instead he told Emily the story of how he had met someone he hoped might be the woman of his dreams, and of his desolation and frustration at his inability to begin even to guess where she might now be.

'What makes you think I might be able to help? What makes you think I've even heard of her?'

'I just think you might, but all I'm asking is that you meet me: I promise I will meet you just once and that I'll leave you alone after that. Look, I'm going to be in the South of England...'

'Where do you work?'

'Where do I work? Why?'

'Just tell me where you work, OK.'

'I work at a company called Back Office, in York and...'

'Goodbye Felix, it's been lovely talking to you!'

And with that, the line went dead. I've blown it, thought Felix, resolving to adopt a different approach towards the other families. He returned to the office, did a bit of work, clarified his diary commitments in the South and then did something that he wondered if he should have already done some time ago. He did a Eureka search on the name Jameela Durrani, in Slough. The difficulty, he knew, was that, while he knew Jameela had worked in Slough and he could tell from her accent that she had been brought up in the South, he had little idea as to precisely where.

Felix's heart missed a beat: on the 20th page of search results was something quite unexpected. 'Roger Smart and Jameela Durrani pictured at last night's meeting of Slough Small Business Forum,' he read. The website was the online version of a local 'society' magazine, Berkshire Business and Social Life. Felix searched Roger Smart and soon realised that this was the man whose business had been taken to the wall by the Aurora empire in its very early days. This was the very man who had featured in the case study in Jameela's workshop at Eastertide Island. Felix then did a further search on Roger Smart and found it appeared he was still in Slough, having to some extent rebuilt his life after the Aurora incident. Felix had the makings of a plan.

Before leaving for home, Felix arranged with his boss to take a day's holiday 'to catch up with old friends in London' during his trip south. He then walked the short distance into the city centre and called at Waterstones, where he looked in the Business section. There were three copies of Lindisfarne's Luck and

Judgement on the shelf and he bought one, before walking the ten minutes across the river to his flat.

He was surprised when he got home to notice that he had missed a call from Wendy. He pressed the call-back key.

'Hello shit-for-brains,' said the woman he'd thought of as a friend.

'It's nice to talk to you again too, my sweet.'

'Well, don't think I am even close to even BEGINNING to think about forgiving you, but I thought you might be interested to know something.'

'Really? What?'

'You don't have to sound so eager.'

'OK, I'm not eager, just curious…'

'Well, you know this Lord Lindisfarne character? Well, not that long ago he used to be just plain Victor Turnbull…'

'Yes, I know. And?'

'Well, when he was just plain Victor Turnbull, my sister went out with him for a while.'

'Your sister went out with Lord Lindisfarne? You mean Jean?'

'No Anne. With Victor Turnbull, like I said.'

'How bizarre…'

'More bizarre than you think. Let's say it was 15 years ago that she went out with him…'

'Hang on, I thought Anne was supposed to be gay…'

'She's tried both, but that's not the point.'

'And the point is?'

'Maybe if you shut up for a moment…'

'Sorry.'

'Anyway, as I'm trying to tell you, Anne has heard nothing whatever from this Victor Turnbull guy for years, when suddenly, right out of the blue, she gets a call from him, at her office in Aberdeen, and he sounds really weird. He's asking her about some time they'd visited some stone circle somewhere in Scotland and he wants to know how she remembers it, because he is there again and, he says, it all looks completely different. He told her he thought he was losing his mind.'

'So what did she say to him?'

'She told him to get off her case and not bother her again.'

'So... is that it?'

'Well, yeah, pretty much. Except that, obviously, Victor Turnbull subsequently became rich and famous and is now Lord Lindisfarne. The reclusive Lord Lindisfarne, I think you'll find. The formerly mad Lord Lindisfarne, who may still be mad for all we know. And he's the one who's kidnapped your imaginary woman, Felix.'

'Real woman, Wendy. She may have disappeared and vanished in a virtual sense, but she does very definitely exist.'

'Whatever you say, but I thought that might at least give you a line of enquiry, you know, mental records of Peer of the Realm, that kind of thing.'

'Thank you, Wendy. It's very thoughtful of you to let me know.'

'That's OK, you pig. I'll think about what you owe me. Maybe payment by reward, only back to front. No payment if you find her and, if you don't, then you have to come back and have a proper relationship with me. And in the meantime you can take me out for dinner.'

'I'm not sure that's...'

'Oh Felix, don't be such a wimp. I'm not going to slip Rohypnol in your drink and drag you off back to my place.'

'So you want to make peace and be friends?'

'Yes, I think I'd rather have at least some of you, so if I can't have your body and your seed, I'll settle for your mind, such as it is. And I promise I'll behave and also, just so you know, I'll be looking for a new man and you mustn't be heartbroken when I find one, OK?'

'OK, Wendy, that would very nice. I'll take you out before I go away.'

Felix still hadn't done a 'proper shop' since returning from Australia. This was unlike him: he normally made a point of cooking well for himself and he realised that he'd been no more than a whirlpool of jet-lag, anxiety and emotional mess since he got back. He should sort himself out, he thought: tomorrow. For now, he ordered an Indian for delivery. He looked in the fridge: there wasn't much, but what was in there included two bottles of Cobra and one of Old Peculier.

He took his reading matter and sat on the sofa with the bottle of Old Peculier to hand.

He looked first at the cover notes on Luck and Judgement, which read:

The road to business success is strewn with the corpses of those who had great ideas for new businesses but who failed to realise their dream. The missing ingredient may have been adequate finance; the right advice; perseverance. But above all, the successful entrepreneur needs luck: without a decent helping of luck, all the sound judgement and inspiration that lie behind a business idea will come to nought. This is the central thesis behind this fascinating account by one of the UK's, indeed the world's, most inspirational and successful business figures of the 21st century. Lindisfarne argues that once a natural entrepreneur has enjoyed luck as the catalyst to business success, he or she will acquire the self-belief that is, along with the consequent belief of others in his or her circle, the foundation of serial success. That the good fortune required may arrive in bizarre or paradoxical circumstances merely serves to illustrate the cunning disguises worn by Lady Luck. This story traces Lindisfarne's extraordinary success to three weeks in psychiatric hospital that were to change his own and the lives of many others for the better.

So that confirmed what he had suspected, even before his conversation with Wendy. Yes, he had had that nagging suspicion that what Wendy was telling him was not entirely new, and so sister Anne's relationship with the said Peer now assumed the rank of curiosity rather than useful fact.

Felix ran his eye down the contents, which comprised chapter titles and a short summary of the contents of each. Chapter One was called In the Beginning and comprised the story of 'How a small company called Persona Communications became one of the world's most important communications businesses'. Chapter Two was called Method in my Madness and the summary read: 'Some of humanity's greatest minds have drawn their most significant inspiration from the use of artificial stimulants. Lord Lindisfarne's stimulation occurred naturally but was no less influential.'

He turned to the chapter and read…

In 2010 I went mad for two months. The medical people would say that my manic episode was just one of those things that happens when a brain gets over-stressed and its chemical balance is compromised. For my part, I knew that my illness was caused by an injury to my urethra when I made a hash of vaulting over a gate. This led to a build-up of poisons in my body, leading to sleeplessness and, in turn, to a build-up of adrenaline in my brain.

It was this adrenaline build-up that, for a short time (perhaps just two or three weeks), gave me an intellectual and creative force that I had never hitherto known. From this period of intellectual super-power was born the Aurora world business empire and, indeed, its associated charitable foundation. If this may sound a haphazard and somewhat happenstance origin for a hugely successful enterprise, let me say the following. Firstly, the dividing line between what we regard as 'normal' and what is often described as madness is a fine one: I suggest that it is a line that is trodden regularly by the greatest figures in the arts and in business and, indeed, across all walks of life. Secondly, let me say that the type of mania during which I enjoyed my greatest business inspiration is a very close cousin of the state of heightened awareness that great minds have habitually induced through the use of drugs and other stimulants. I cite you the historic examples of Wordsworth and his laudanum, and Wilde and his absinthe, and submit that many successful business people have been (and indeed are) no strangers to illegal stimulants.

The chapter went on, without dwelling greatly, to describe in more detail some of the build-up to the then Vic Turnbull's stay in psychiatric hospital, and Felix was amused to read the following:

After my accident, it was some time before the penny dropped that I was slowly poisoning myself with my body's own waste, and I endured some alarming moments before my adrenaline surfeit gradually took over from blood poisoning as the dominant feature of my illness. On one occasion I 'revisited' a stone circle on one of the islands of Orkney. I had a very distinct memory of this stone circle: a huddled ring of gnarled stones with avenues, giving the appearance of a bleak landscape filled with lots of Macbeth's witches braced against the wind and rain. They stood near a group of houses and there was a grandstand view from a nearby mound. Of all that I was certain and yet what greeted me when I arrived at the Ring of Brodgar was a vast circle, perhaps more than 100 metres across and standing in a flat landscape beside the glassy waters of a loch. Furthermore, the stones were not gnarled, but tall and majestic, forming a complete ring, which it took me about three minutes to walk right round. There were no houses nearby – it was, all told, quite unlike the circle I recalled. I felt utterly unsettled: how could my memory have played such a trick? Another circle, the Stones of Stenness, was quite close by, but these too were straight and proud and, again, the circle was twice the size I recalled. It was only when I telephoned a former girlfriend that I learned that I had confused that circle with another, far smaller one on the Isle of Lewis...

Elsewhere in the chapter, Lindisfarne detailed the legal process by which his company, Persona Communications, had acquired Smart Communications from the Receiver after the latter had been forced to cease trading by seizure of its assets, most importantly its IT systems, following a court order obtained by Persona's lawyers. He talked too about the key personnel who had chosen to move north and take up new but similar roles with Persona, and about how that legal success had inspired other successful legal actions.

All this was going on while I was either in hospital, or in recovery from illness, at home. It was my trusted 'lieutenant', Stella de Weld, who conducted most of the negotiations with our lawyers and it was the same Stella who went on to head up the new Persona business on a day-to-day basis while I, in my new role of Executive Chairman of the emergent Aurora Group, worked on the company's strategy for expansion. So what has all this to do with my illness? some may ask. And the answer is a very simple one: without my massive adrenaline injection there is simply no way that I would have had either the ability or the imagination to create that strategy and oversee its subsequent execution. In the first instance, I had the inspiration of seeking legal solutions to other areas of Persona's business. Specifically, I conducted an audit of all our business relationships over the previous 24 months, with particular reference to whether contracts that we had won through tender had been correctly executed by the other party, that is, the party letting the contract. My audit revealed a number of instances in which it might be argued that Persona had been a victim of the failure by the client to permit our business to fulfil its contract properly. In all such cases this had led, to a greater or lesser extent, to financial loss on our part. This encouraged me then to extend my audit to contracts that we had failed to win, when well placed. It became clear to me that, almost without exception, we had, in these instances, been victims of a flawed tender process in which the outcome had been either pre-decided or the evaluation process had been 'fixed' so as to ensure another contender would be selected.

Persona's lawyers had, in respect of each of these cases, been instructed to go in bristling with weapons from their legal armoury, Felix read. But the account in no way suggested that they had simply bullied their way to legal victory by force of greater resource. Indeed, Lindisfarne himself appeared to have effectively invited his adversaries to a Day of Judgement, at which they might see the error of their ways and repent. The repenters might make good their misdemeanours through paying compensation or by re-engaging Persona on the correct terms, or, if Lindisfarne judged it more appropriate, make a donation to a charity relevant to their own field. In a few instances in which repentance was not forthcoming, Persona's lawyers would pursue their quarry remorselessly; on a very few occasions, culpable individuals were actually bankrupted. It was in this way that Persona created for itself a cash mountain from which it was able to fund a process of expansion through acquisition, with each such acquisition bringing to the company new skills and expertise.

Of the process by which the Aurora Group grew from being a mere holding company for a small basket of businesses of quite modest size, to being a major player on the world stage, Lindisfarne wrote:

The skills that I acquired during my illness included an astute tactical imagination and the ability to create a coherent strategic vision, as well as the ability to quickly make a valid judgement as to the commercial possibilities presented by an opportunity. One of the most significant such decisions concerns the acquisition of Framboise, which of course provided us with the people, the skills and the infrastructure from which to launch Blather, the product for which Aurora is perhaps best known and the one that made it a very rich and powerful company. Framboise was scarcely known outside the French-speaking world and the company's failure went effectively unnoticed in the UK and US. This is, in part, a cultural thing: I would go so far as to say that there is in instinctive blindness in the English-speaking world to ideas that originate from non-English cultures. This is not necessarily wilful: rather, I suspect that business people in the English-speaking world actually have to work at a disadvantage. It is the disadvantage of belonging to the lazy majority; the indolence of the lingua franca. And I use that term intentionally, rather than talking of English as 'the language of business' or the default language of people doing business across cultures. Why? Because if we, the English and the Americans (and the Australians and others), were as open to French (and other) ideas as we have been to the importation of their vocabulary, where it will add a certain je ne sais quoi to our own expression, we, collectively, would do so much better.

Quite literally because of my manic episode, the default settings of my brain were more open to the opportunities in the Framboise failure than were those of my English-speaking rivals. It was entirely because of this that we were able to move in and obtain, for a song, the intellectual property of Framboise and indeed the services of the best brains at the company. It was surely the best single decision that I have ever taken, because we all know what Blather has achieved for Aurora and indeed the extent to which this simple electronic communications medium has changed the world. Blather succeeded because the development work had already been done by the fabulous people at Framboise, at Sophia Antipolis, near Cannes. However, it almost certainly needed to move into the English language medium to achieve its full potential. Aurora enabled that process and was able to use Framboise's bespoke and highly original system for the monetisation of the facility to ensure not only that Blather was widely used, but also that it made an awful lot of money for Aurora.

Felix flicked on further:

While I was in psychiatric hospital, I was part of a group of patients that also included the ex-boxer David Nixon. David was a born-again Christian with a strong belief in charity. Whenever we went to the hospital shop, David would always take his change and divide it 50:50 with the charity box on the counter. 'One for me and one for Good Works,' he would always say. I adopted this motto with enthusiasm, sometimes varying the split up to 90 per cent in favour of the Good Works. However, it was the simple one-for-one formula that formed the basis upon which the Aurora Foundation still operates. Quite simply, 50 per cent of the Group profits are reinvested and the other 50 per cent are used in pursuit of the Foundation's 'Good Works'...

Felix's train of thought was interrupted by the doorbell. Curry! Felix served about half the takeaway onto the plate he had warmed (or overheated) in the oven, helped himself to a Cobra from the fridge and returned to his reading.

One of the most significant events that took place during my period of adrenaline surfeit was my meeting with my late twin brother, Malcolm. While some people might view such a meeting beyond the grave as merely symptomatic of the illness that would soon see me become a voluntary psychiatric patient, this meeting was very very real to me. Indeed, even now that I am deemed completely sane again, I am still of the conviction not only that I met my dead brother (or some assemblage of the sub-

atomic forces that make up his soul) but also that he gave me a variety of missions to fulfil.

On a very personal level, I have been able to ensure that a process is now in place to formally assess, in a religious sense, Malcolm's sacrifice of his life to save others. But my late brother's discourse with me was very much more about delivering further Good Works than being recognised for what he had done when alive, albeit in death. Thus, in its early days, the Aurora Foundation focused primarily on a variety of issues that Malcolm had identified to me. These included, on a global scale, reducing deforestation, most particularly in the world's tropical rain forests, and, more prosaically, funding a variety of research projects, such as that which helped provide solutions to the decline in the bee population. Rather less in the public eye has been the Foundation's work in ensuring more openness in the allocation of business contracts, and in the reinterpretation of religious texts with the aim of reducing causes for conflict.

It was the final 36 words of the extract, so blandly delivered, that caught Felix's attention. He thumbed through the book, in particular the later chapter addressed specifically to the subject of the Foundation, for further references to the 'reinterpretation of religious texts' and anything about business contracts. He suspected, because of other things he had heard or read, that this was actually a quite specific reference to challenging the influence of the Masonic movement.

Felix turned his attention to The Secret World of the Aurora Foundation. He was already beginning to get an idea of 'what one of the world's most powerful companies would prefer you not to know'. The book had been published in the USA and was less than a year old. The authors were listed as Arbuthnot, Baker and Clarke. The foreword confirmed his immediate suspicion that the ABC initials did not indicate the real name or names of the author or authors. 'The Aurora Foundation is not, as it would have people believe, a benign agent for good. The authors of this work have, therefore, elected to remain anonymous so as to safeguard their future well-being.'

That sounds ominous, if a little hyperbolic, thought Felix, as he turned to the first chapter.

The Aurora Foundation was created by Lord Lindisfarne, the Englishman behind the international communications company of similar name. It was his intent to use a proportion of the Aurora profits for so-called charitable works and, in its early days, this was at least partly the case. More recently, however, this organization has gone way beyond any such legitimate activity and has gotten to be a threat to the very fabric of the democratic world.

A slip of paper fell from the book. It was in the unmistakable neat hand of Tracy Davenport and read: 'I hope you enjoy your essential reading, Victor. I suggest you skip all the rantings about socialist and European conspiracies and focus rather on the bits about "intervention" and the section on people who have disappeared. You may also find the bits on the foundation's early history and the profile of Lindisfarne useful background. Good luck and happy hunting! T x'

Felix acted on the advice and went straight to the profile of Lord Lindisfarne, where he read:

Lord Lindisfarne used to be plain Victor (Pierre) Turnbull. Until the summer of 2010 he was just a regular kind of guy who ran a regular kind of Internet communications business, mostly in the United Kingdom, although he had been to the USA to carry out the groundwork for a product called Knowledge America, which was to be an extension of his UK enterprise, www.travel-knowledge.info. The www.travel-knowledge-us.com site is today just a small part of Persona Communications, which in turn is but a tiny part of the Aurora empire.

Victor Turnbull was made a Lord by the Labor Party, probably as a reward for 'political services'. He assisted a female candidate for the party's leadership (a self-confessed Marxist). This gave Turnbull access to the Upper House of the UK Legislature, with immense power and scope to influence.

Running the business of the Aurora Group has been increasingly left to its President, Ms Stella de Weld, who was a close servant of Turnbull for some time before the change in his fortunes. Now Turnbull/Lindisfarne is a non-executive chair and devotes his energies to the supposed charitable functions that his organization bankrolls.

Turnbull married Michaela Larkhill in 2010 and she became Lady Lindisfarne when he was made Lord. They are a deeply secretive couple, whose permanent address is understood to be a private island, Jacqhou, off the coast of France, and part of the UK tax haven of Jersey.

Today Lindisfarne rarely gives interviews and his precise whereabouts at any particular time are difficult to predict. In addition to their home on Jacqhou, the Turnbull-Lindisfarnes are known to have a number of other homes in different parts of the world, only some of which can be identified with any certainty, on account of the secretive nature of the couple. Many of these domiciles are on islands, further emphasizing the reclusive nature of these people. Those that are known about include the French territory of St Pierre et Miquelon, off the coast of Canada, the Scottish island of St Kilda, Amorgos, in Greece, a remote Norwegian island called Sør-Gjæslingan, and the island of La Digue, in the Seychelles. However, these people lead the life of gypsies, perpetually on the move, and there are other locations at which they have been known to have resided but which appear no longer to be visited by them.

Lindisfarne claims to have been inspired by some kind of Road to Damascus moment in 2010, when he claims to have met with the soul of his brother, Malcolm, who died in an auto accident in which Lindisfarne was a passenger but survived. He spent some time in a psychiatric unit at a hospital in Yorkshire, England, and it was during that time that he claims to have received his business inspiration.

After his release from hospital, his business seems to have grown like crazy and the Lindisfarnes seem to have started moving around not many weeks later. We know that in the first instance this was to locations in or close to the United Kingdom and that latterly they've gotten further and further away from home. Regular guys may ask themselves why people who claim to lead honest lives should appear to live their lives permanently on the run, or so it would seem. Well, there's an answer to that: Lord and Lady Lindisfarne head an organization that campaigns with all the vigour of an evangelical cult. It is committed to ridding the *world of what it sees as evils and its targets include such worthy ideals as those who cut down the rain forests and religious extremists. However, the Lindisfarnes' definition of extremism ain't necessarily your or our definition of extremism. In particular they appear to take some delight in disrupting the law-abiding activities of some American citizens whose views they choose not to agree with.*

All this would be no more than an irritation if these people hadn't gotten so damn rich and powerful. Because they have both wealth and power they can get away with these attacks. Should we be afraid? Yes, we damn well should be afraid!

Felix began to tire of the ranting, partisan style of the book and flicked to the section on the early history of the Aurora Foundation.

The Aurora Foundation was established late in 2010 and was at that time registered as a legitimate charity in the United Kingdom. Its declared aims were listed with the UK Charity Commission as: 'To deploy a proportion of the profits generated by the Aurora Group in pursuit of charitable works, with a focus on securing harmony between faiths, and supporting initiatives to reverse deforestation in the Tropics and reduce dependence on fossil fuels. Secondary aims may include, although not exclusively, the promotion of the language and culture of the part of England formerly known as Northumbria, and the support of scientific and other academic research projects based at universities within the same area.'

Charities in the UK have legal obligations: they have to satisfy the Charity Commissioners that they meet the legal requirements to be a charity and thereby to enjoy the tax and legal privileges that this special status brings. It seems the Lindisfarnes found this straitjacket too restrictive and, in 2013, it seems that the management of the charity moved offshore, outside UK jurisdiction, although the extremely complex nature of the Aurora accounting conventions leaves it unclear whether the UK charity remains in place as a tax-avoidance device. But the reasons for moving the Aurora Foundation offshore are about far more than avoiding paying a bit of tax. The move was clearly designed to ensure

that the Foundation could escape the scrutiny of the UK's law-makers
and the guys who police the laws, such as the Charity Commissioners.

One of the areas that gives rise to most concern is the Aurora
Foundation's unwarranted attacks on the legitimate work of Christian
religious organizations in the USA, as part of Lindisfarne's crusade
against 'religious extremism'.

Felix chuckled at the paradox of a 'crusade against religious extremism', but then George W Bush had proved long ago that Americans could be ignorant of the derivation of the word crusade. Or at least he had if you were charitable about it. He continued to read about the Foundation's alleged assault on a variety of 'legitimate businesses in the USA and elsewhere' and, fascinating as it surely was, he decided to devote more attention to his lamb passanda. Nothing he had read thus far really provided any clue as to how he should set about tracking down Jameela, the love of his life, should she eventually turn out to be that.

He began to wonder if he was deluding himself: was it the idea of her unattainability that made Jameela seem so attractive? Did he really know her well enough to spend a smallish fortune? Was it realistic to think he could trace her when others in an apparently similar position had seemingly vanished off the face of the Earth? Would he be a sadder but wiser man in 12 months' time? What if Jameela didn't even fancy him? Might York City get promoted again?

Felix moved from unanswerable, imponderable questions to a more abstract world of unanswered ones: Was there a Loch Ness Monster? What about the Yeti? And giant cats on Dartmoor? How do some people manage always to keep their shirt tails safely tucked into their waistbands? Why do Americans travel with such insanely big suitcases? Is there anything after death? What is the answer to the ultimate question of Life, The Universe and Everything? In a moment of inspiration, Felix found an old DVD of Douglas Adams's Hitchhiker's Guide to the Galaxy and re-watched it to the last bottle of beer, idly wondering what had inspired the late Douglas Adams to choose the number 42 as the anti-climactic answer to that 'ultimate question'.

Later, as he lay in bed, he thought he might fantasise about an intimate encounter with Jameela but, try as he might, he simply couldn't create such a scene in his mind: it somehow seemed disrespectful. Yet, if he tried to fantasise about anyone else, that seemed equally inappropriate. Oh great, he thought, not only am I now celibate till no-one can predict when, but nor can I even commit a solo act of infidelity. What have I embarked upon?

On arrival at work the following morning, Felix was surprised once again to find himself the recipient of a hand-written piece of snail mail. It was post-marked Exeter and the letter inside read: 'Dear Mr Merryheather, Meet me at Carluccio's, Exeter, next Sunday morning for breakfast, nine-thirty. I'll wear a Barbour jacket and have a pink hair grip. Don't ring me. I'll be there. Yours, Emily Black.'

CHAPTER 13

Of Life, the Universe and Everything

Saturday September 4, 2010
Later that day

In the tea-room that evening, people shuffle in and out. They slop their tea bags on the bench and over-stir their mugs, spilling tea, coffee and hot chocolate everywhere. I must ask Michaela to bring me in my I Love my Dad mug Lisa gave me years ago when she was little. And some fruit and herbal teas.

'Come on lads,' I say. 'Show a bit of respect and keep the place tidy.' Mostly they ignore me, though one guy, whose pock-marked face scowls beneath short-cropped ginger hair, spits in my face: 'What the fuck ist tha goin' ter do abaat it, like? Na shuttit, raat?!'

There's a tray of sarnies on a trolley: I haven't been early enough – they look like they've been trampled by stampeding gerbils. I make a mental note to show up sharper tomorrow.

Soon there's a queue forming outside the medication room, though it's only 9.15 and we don't get our meds till half past. I'm not sure I see there's much point in queueing when I can be otherwise occupied: so much to do and so little time to do it in. Or should that not be: there's no time to lose; but there's all the time in the world? Of course, because of the elasticity of time itself these two seemingly contradictory statements are not, in fact, mutually exclusive. So I may as well join the queue in that case.

My neighbours in line are a motley crew: some are lost in themselves; some sitting against the wall with their heads in their hands; some more engaged with the world; some even in conversation. 'Fuck off, cunt!' says ginger acne man as he passes me to take his place in the line.

'Such eloquence,' I mutter.

'Cunting well fuck off, cunt!'

I shall keep my own counsel, I reflect.

There's a flurry of what might pass for excitement when Julia and another nurse I don't recognise walk past the queue and unlock the door to the pharmacy.

When my turn comes, they weigh me, take my blood pressure and then sit me down and give me a tiny little waxed paper cup. Julia drops my medication into the cup but it leaps straight out and goes flying across the room, as though propelled on the legs of a flea. I try hard but can't really understand how or why this has happened. I can only guess that my super-charged body is vibrating, but at a speed that's too fast for me to detect.

Julia gives me a look that I can't quite fathom.

'I didn't mean to do that, honest,' I say.

Julia begins again and then adds a second tablet to my medication pot: temazepam, I believe.

'You should be OK to go in the morning,' she says.

'What, home?'

'No, to church…'

It is the morning of the church service. This is important because Dave and I will receive instructions about what we must do next in the seven days that we have in which to save the world, remembering of course that, thanks to the elasticity of time, these are not 'days' in the terrestrial sense, so it's not that we have to have everything done by next Saturday. That would be silly. But even so, the task of getting the whole world to live in harmony while simultaneously removing any man-made threat to the planet is not one to be underestimated, I know. I'm excited now that I understand that I am here in the hospital for a purpose; that this is less a place of convalescence, more a retreat in which those of us who have been chosen can gather strength for the task ahead.

It is already working: I have had another good night's sleep and have finally remedied my lack of bowel movements so I can get back to the traditional daily routine. When I got up this morning, I looked down at my belly and it was like a distended ball and once again it brought to mind the gorged lion in the Serengeti, lying in the shade beneath the baobab, his belly swollen by fresh wildebeest; and the aboriginal hunter in the Australian outback, sated by the luxury of fresh kangaroo meat. Last night, at medication, I'd told them about my little problem and the other nurse, who's called Janet, suggested running water might do the trick. My 'en suite' is actually a toilet pedestal and a hand basin in a little sort of wet room, so after a few minutes straining to no avail I'd stepped off the pedestal and turned the shower on and, sure enough, first a wee and then, my god, time to get back on the throne! The result had been the biggest poo I think I'd ever done in my life: days' worth of erratic gorging in one big dump. It was a big steaming bowlful, like an elephant's. And already my belly lump was receding.

So it had been in a good frame of mind that I had gone to breakfast and Dave and Jeff had spoken of spreading the word to make sure as many as possible turned up for church. Michaela hadn't seemed to really welcome my call at 9.30, reminding her of how important it would be for her to come, but she said maybe she'd try and bring one of the girls along. I don't think Larry will come as he's very sceptical about the whole religion thing. But then so am I; it's just that now is the time for religion and science to work together in the name of Faith and to realise the ultimate Truth that will save the world. And there really is no time to lose.

The sense of expectancy grows as the morning passes: Dave and Jeff are busy recruiting for the church service at 11. This will be the beginning of the Great Plan to save the world. But it will also be an important day for missing people everywhere: I must remind Stella what I have learned about her sister, Violet. I find a signal by walking to Reception. 'Reception is best at Reception,' I muse. I text her: 'Your Violet in Maastricht. I've had a message from Malcolm.'

I am surprised to receive no reply but it does not diminish my own excitement and anticipation.

At 10.50 Michaela arrives with Nat, who gives me a big hug. Apparently Larry will come in later with Lisa to see me once more before he goes off to his mother's.

'It's great that you could come because it's so important,' I say.

'Well, some of us might have quite liked a rest,' says Michaela, taking me aback slightly. Let's get things in proportion – which matters most, saving the world or having 30 minutes extra in the sack!?

'It's for Malcolm, not just for me,' I rejoin. 'And for the future of us all. Everyone.'

Dave and Jeff turn up at Reception and make all the introductions.

'Let's go,' says Dave, and leads the way. We go out through the exit door: it's the first time I have been out since my arrival on Friday. We go down a corridor to the small chapel, where Michaela seems to make a point of having a word in private with the vicar. Inside, I take a seat at the front as I know it will be up to me to lead parts of the service this morning. It's nearly 11 and there are a lot of people arriving. Dave was right when he said this was going to be a big one. The vicar asks Jeff to go and find some more chairs somewhere. There seem to be people arriving from all over Ripon and Harrogate, so the word must have really gone right round town. There are one or two guys I have seen in the hospital and some women I haven't seen before and then lots more besides.

The vicar remarks on the good turn-out as he introduces the service and notes that we have some additional guests, nodding towards Michaela and Nat, who tucks her hand into the crook of my elbow and gives my arm a gentle squeeze. She's a good girl and very much like my own daughter really. The vicar tells his congregation that the service will be not about the urgency necessary to save the world but, rather, about lost people. 'Like Stella's sister, Violet,' I say to myself, as it dawns on me that so many people have come this morning precisely because they are looking for hope to find lost loved ones. This is actually the beginning of a great movement that will return all missing people to the bosom of their forgiving families and from today, hope shall eternal spring.

The service continues with a couple of hymns and then, after a prayer, the vicar talks of the perils of our collective voyage through the ocean of life and how we need protection from being washed onto the reefs of despair, loneliness or loss and then he says we'll sing the hymn, For Those in Peril on the Sea. I know this one and remember it as a rousing anthem. The vicar catches my eye and it is, I realise, for me to help him out and lead the congregation in their song. I take a step forward and turn to those gathered, inviting them to really put their lungs into the hymn as the vicar starts some music on a CD player.

Eternal Father, strong to save,
Whose arm hath bound the restless wave,
Who bidd'st the mighty ocean deep
Its own appointed limits keep;

I gesture everyone to really give it some oomph as, with a subtle change of key, the words implore:

Oh, hear us when we cry to Thee,
For those in peril on the sea!

My flock follows me through the next two verses, until the hymn concludes:

Thus evermore shall rise to Thee
Glad hymns of praise from land and sea.

Amen, I say, and retake my seat, pleased at a job of leadership well done. The vicar then invites us to end the service with the Lord's Prayer and, as the praying begins, I am suddenly overwhelmed, almost like that evening in the Cathedral, and I prostrate myself at the front of the congregation, saying the words of the prayer as loudly as possible, for Malcolm, for my soul, for the souls of all the Lost.

At the end of the service the vicar asks all those with missing relatives or other loved ones to write the details on sheets of paper and he commandeers our Nat specifically to collect Japanese and other Asian details, as he must know that she once learnt a little Japanese.

'Are you OK, Vic?' asks Jeff. 'You seemed a bit emotional in there.'

'I'm fine, Jeff, just fine. But there's work to be done. Much work.'

The church service has left me a little drained, but I feel exhilarated for all that. It's still the weekend, so at lunch I have to just eat what others haven't already ordered. But I've already ordered my choices for lunch and tea tomorrow. Michaela has gone, leaving me a few clean clothes and a promise to see me 'in a day or two'.

But today is a day to learn a few more of the ropes here. Some of the guys, like Jeff, have already seen the light and understand that there is work of the most critical importance to be done. Others continue to shuffle around, their chins on their chests and lost in their Walkmans or iPods. Somehow I need to fashion this ragamuffin bunch into an army fit to save the world. And the place to start is with the few troops we already have and hone their skills as best we can.

'Look at this lot, Dave. They've all got their eyes glued to the floor and their rib cages have collapsed into their diaphragms. They're getting no oxygen, Dave. And people are lost in their music machines, Dave, they're going to damage their hearing and totally internalise themselves.'

'Ah knaa, Vic, lad, but people are heor for a reason. They're unwell, Vic mate. Unwell.'

'Aye, well, mebbes we can make them better, quicker, ' I suggest, just as another young lad shambles up to us.

'See, look at this one! He carries himself like a sack of coal. His body's so crumpled he can't even breathe.'

'Eh, ist tha talkin' abaat me?' asks the lad, who turns out to be called Bryan.

'I am indeed! Now, come with me!'

I march him out into the garden to the little bench at the far end, by the buddleias. I sit him down and walk round behind him.

'Relax, Bryan, and hold your chin up!' The head tilts back a little but everything is still in a heap. 'That's useless, Bryan lad. Here, let's get you sorted!' Once again I put my right knee in the middle of his back and pull his shoulders backwards until they are broadly above his hips. Then I cup my hands beneath either side of his chin, and – with my knee still holding his spine straight – I pull his head upwards, gradually extending his spine until it is somewhere near its correct anatomical length. I work his head to left and right, progressively untensing the muscles. Then I massage his shoulders and I can feel his body begin to relax. I raise his chin and stretch his neck again.

'Now breathe in deeply and fill your lungs with oxygen. Do it three times and feel the life begin to flow back into your veins. Where are you from Bryan?'

'Harrogate.'

'Who do you support, Bryan?'

'Leeds United.'

'Are you proud to be a Tyke?'

'Aye!'

'And to be from Harrogate?'

'Aye, mebbe.'

'OK, Bryan lad, now stand up and let's get you sorted!' I swear he's grown six inches already, but there's still room for improvement: I work on his neck and spinal extension again. 'Now repeat after me: "Proud to be a Tyke; proud to be from Harrogate; proud to support Leeds United; proud to be Bryan!"'

He repeats the mantra dutifully.

'Now, you do that every morning, first thing when you get up: come out here and get the fresh air into your lungs; get the oxygen into your heart and let the world know you are proud and it better watch out!'

The Indian summer is still with us: although the early mornings have a bit of a September edge, once the sun finds its way into our garden it becomes a little slice of Shangri-La. Michaela took my shorts away for washing and only left long trousers, including a pair of sort of thin tweedy ones that I never liked all that much. I hacked the legs off with my nail scissors, leaving one an inch or so shorter than the other in places. It wasn't the best of jobs but hey, if people don't supply the right kit, what can I do?

In the garden, I love the feel of the grass between my toes: shorts, T-shirt and barefoot is my uniform now. I have a solution to the Walkman/iPod problem: I have discovered that, if I put my iPhone in my shorts pocket, playing iTunes, I can 'adjust' the volume mentally, just like I found I was able to do at home before they came and took me away. With my heightened sense of hearing, it's easy to listen to whatever music is playing in my shorts pocket. Typically now, this will be my native Australian album, The Aborigines, so when I begin my barefoot garden patrol, I am very quickly in the outback, poised on the tips of my toes, boomerang or spear in hand as I spot an unwary roo drinking by a coolabah. Ancient skills are coming back to me, not just the skill of walking on tiptoe and hunting, but my own ability, the one I had as a child, to create new worlds in my head simply by walking or running in circles.

I now have a clearly beaten path round the perimeter of the lawn: it brings to mind a memory from my 20s of a Scottish wild cat in an enclosure at Edinburgh Zoo. It was pacing round the edge of its own lawned enclosure and I had thought it was the walk of a caged, frustrated animal. But for me, pacing my perimeter track is a creative process: a simple device to pump my excess adrenaline into my brain, where it can be used constructively to create the best intellectual outcomes. Already I have audited our entire US operation and been able to brief Stella on how to take our case forward with Immerhutts. I have also gone on to conduct a complete mental audit of all our contracts (including failed tenders) over the last three years to identify examples of immoral or illegal behaviour in public office on the part of those who were responsible for awarding or subsequently managing Persona contracts.

I have been able to look into all these arrangements with a new objectivity and new incisiveness. The trouble is that, although the tender process is intended to enable a fair, evidence-based choice between a range of potential suppliers, the reality is often somewhat different. Those buying the services often have a view as to who they want to perform a task and will manipulate the tender process, including the scoring matrix, in order to achieve the outcome they feel most comfortable with. And such an outcome is always very difficult to challenge because the 'evidence' will be there to support their decision: all the scores stipulated by the tender will be correctly entered as empirical evidence, whereas they are really just numbers derived from a subjective assessment of each offer. Tenders were supposed to bring fairness into a world that had been dominated by Old Boy networks, political graft, corruption, tit-for-tat and, of course, Masonic loyalties. The trouble is that, now we have tendering in place for the contract to wipe the council leader's nose, everyone blithely and innocently thinks well, everything's all right Jack. Here we are in the Best of all Possible Worlds, so how could there possibly be any system better than tendering as a way of awarding contracts. The private sector, at the sort of level of contract I'm talking about here, has a different way of going about things: it's about not just who you know, but also about making sure that the right people do know what you can do. That's not to say that you'll get work on a nod and a wink, but that, if you're in the frame for some work, it's because someone somewhere has recommended you and your ability to fulfil the requirements and, if you can demonstrate your ability to deliver through a series of discussions, then you may well get the work, or at least the opportunity to be compared with just one other similarly capable outfit. Is that any more perfect than an open tender process? No, of course it isn't, but it's a sight more honest and, I suspect, functions in a system that is less endemically corrupt and perverted by Freemasonry.

So, I've done my little audit, focusing on the contracts that we either lost or which, having won them, failed to live up to our expectations. There's the tourism contract that was abruptly terminated for no apparent reason. With my heightened awareness I was able to identify a probability that a near-identical piece of work had been commissioned elsewhere. Once I've briefed Stella to ask some probing questions of the right people it turns out that this is precisely the case. Verdict: client incompetence, coupled with illegal termination. Then there's the charity that terminated our contract because they didn't want to hear the professional advice we were giving them, as it was out of kilter with the chairman's ego. Verdict: client incompetence, coupled with unsound internal structures and unfair termination. The one that continues to bug me though is the largest single contract in the portfolio of 'contracts gone wrong'. This was actually a public-private IT systems venture, but the management was by the public sector team, which replaced the project leader part way through our third term of successful delivery. She terminated our contract on the 'grounds' of 'budget changes' and then let a new tender with another supplier. Another supplier that, to me, has always smelled strongly of fish: old school, class and society connections. Talks gold-dust, delivers shit. This debacle now bears all the hallmarks of masonic back-scratching and yet Freemasons are men, so that can't be the case, can it?

Anyway, I could go on and on about this contract thing because there are many more examples and I really don't want you to think that Persona has been a failing organisation. Far from it: our portfolio is still ram-jammed with blue chip operations and that's without even considering travelknowledge. info or the American project. But I've briefed Stella and, once the Smart Ideas case is settled, we'll use the cash to pursue these other cases. Not viciously, but in the knowledge that we will have the financial muscle to force a swift out-of-court settlement in each case. I have graded each case provisionally into Innocent Mistake, Incompetence and Malice, although there may in each be also both mitigating and aggravating circumstances. Innocent Mistakes will generally require only reinstatement on a comparable programme of work. For Incompetence, the 'punishment' will vary in-line with the humility of response and willingness to learn and eliminate unhelpful traits, like arrogance. Typically it may include a substantial gift to charity in lieu of compensation. In cases of Malice, however, our pursuit shall be resolute and, yes, it will get personal. If an individual has acted in a way inconsistent with their public duties, we'll have no hesitation in going for their personal wealth. We are not unfair, however. Repentance at any stage will lead us to 'call off the dogs'. For mercy is a great attribute in a civilised society, n'est-ce pas? I suspect the big IT systems debacle will end up going down this route eventually. For two reasons: firstly, my incisive powers of memory have uncovered a previous meeting 'in another life' that will demonstrate that she has 'previous'. Secondly, having briefed Stella on my findings, she has now uncovered what looks like a campaign of disinformation about Persona, about me specifically and my professional competence. Some of the written evidence, based as it is on untruths, is clearly libellous and certainly calculated to damage my personal reputation with my peers. Damages could be substantial.

I find myself leaving the garden behind, for a place far distant…

The aboriginal hunter ties the legs of the felled roo together and hangs the carcass over his neck and shoulder and begins the long trek back through the bush to the camp, where, nights previously, he and his fellow huntsmen had danced and chanted in the firelight until they had entered the state of euphoric trance that would best equip them for the dangers of the bush and the challenges of the hunt. Now he is returning from the Dreamtime. With food. His family group will eat and there will be much joy.

Of course, I am far more than just the guy from that movie, The Man Who Stalked His Cats. I am also the man learning to live in this little oasis, Priestley House Hospital: this place of recuperation and preparation for the immense challenges ahead. I am the man on the threshold of Greatness; the man with the power not just to save the world but to change it for the good into the bargain. And I am the man who, through the medium of his dead brother, is acquiring almost more knowledge and wisdom than he can feasibly cope with.

Life at Priestley House is settling into a routine as I learn the ropes. I have discovered that this is not just a very short temporary respite: I will have to play a number of games to meet the criteria for my escape from incarceration. On Monday I met Dr Honeydew for the first time: an odd cookie that one… he doesn't really make eye contact so all my efforts to look into his soul have come to nought. I have a distinct feeling that his approach is empirical rather than empathetic. I think he is deriving his agenda from conversations with Michaela that I am not party to. Julia, on the other hand, is a whole different prospect altogether. I can see a good person inside, far beyond the sea-green eyes, and that goodness permeates through every pore.

'Do you have to stare at me quite so hard?' she asks.

'I believe in making eye contact, Julia. Look into a person's eyes and you can see right into their soul…'

'Oh really. And what do you see today, Mr Turnbull?'

'Only goodness, Julia.'

'Well, thank the Lord for that, then!'

She talks to me about my medication. It's a drug called olanzapine and she asks me if I have noticed any side-effects. I think long and carefully about this. I really think there's just the one and this will surely be important for the medical people as they build a more complete picture of the drug's action.

'Reduced seminal emission at ejaculation,' I suggest.

Julia reddens. 'Yes, well, I think we'll move swiftly on.'

I change the subject for her. 'So, when can I go home?'

'Well, Vic, that's not just up to me, or even to Dr Honeydew. You're a voluntary patient, but this isn't just about you: it's about those who have to live with you and be responsible if things start to go wrong. They have to be comfortable that you are well enough to be at home.'

'So, maybe this weekend, then?'

'Victor, my sweet, it is just far too soon to say, OK?'

'But there's a chance?'

'No, Victor. You will have to be patient.'

'I am a patient.'

'Indeed, ho ho ho.'

'Yes, and patients are a virtue, are they not?'

'Well I guess you all keep the wolf from the door. And if it wasn't for the occasional interference from upstairs, this wouldn't be such a bad job. In fact, it's a job I love, to tell you the truth.'

Julia has a best pal, Roberta, 'Bertie' to her mates. 'We're like this,' says Julia, interlocking her fingers. 'We've both been here ten years and we live each other's lives. We're a proper double act.'

Bertie is big and buxom, with a no-nonsense demeanour, which I guess complements Julia's more demure stature and less self-assured personality. With John, these three are the A-team, one of whom must be on duty at any given time.

In fact, pretty much all the staff (and there are many) seem to have hearts of gold, though I did have a run-in with one right at the outset. Part of my routine comprises going through the newspapers each morning, which demands only that I get to the newspapers before any staff whip them off for their coffee break. But Michaela, when she has time, also drops by with the Northern Echo from home, and the day before's Guardian or Inde if she's bought one.

I sit at 'my desk' in the games room and go through these papers carefully, looking for 'signs'. These might be articles that echo childhood memories or that can be read as portents. I mark the headlines and copy them into my coloured notebook. If it's a shared newspaper, I sometimes cut out the story or the page at the end of the day.

I had only been inside a day or two when it happened. I was lying on my bed, watching a DVD on my laptop, which was on my stool at the foot of the bed. I was idly abusing myself. Just a little. My Northern Echo was on my bedside shelf, to my left, the side away from the door. Suddenly the door bursts open and an elderly member of staff leaps across my naked body, her hand outstretched to snatch my newspaper.

'Have you got the newspapers?' she's shrieking.

'How dare you burst in? Get out, get out, get out!!' The nurse retreats and shuts the door firmly behind her.

I pull my dressing gown on and storm off to Reception. 'I want to make a complaint about invasion of my privacy!' I am well upset.

The next morning, Jeff says to me: 'What have you said to Mavis. She's really upset and she's my favourite of all the staff here.' I'm puzzled as I am still seething with outrage.

Later, John takes me aside. 'I hear you had a bit of an incident with Mavis, Vic.'

'Yeah, she burst into my room without knocking when I was naked on the bed and accused me of stealing the newspapers.'

'Are you sure that's what happened? Mavis doesn't put it quite like that.'

'Quite sure, John.'

Only later does the reality of what's occurred dawn on me. There has been a mis-synch of time. My hyper-sensitive brain has actually seen Mavis flying across my bed towards my Northern Echo before the event has actually happened. It's just like at home when I could hear people's responses to things I said before they had actually said them. Mavis had never made that leap, or at least not within the time frame to which she herself related. I'm still unhappy about the whole principle of assuming that I steal newspapers and of people not knocking and waiting before entering, but I am persuaded, mostly for Jeff's sake, to make peace with Mavis. It is best to get on with the staff.

And I've had another minor run-in with acne-face, or Willy, as he's really called. This time it was over smoking, or more precisely where he stubs his ciggies out. I suggested this shouldn't be in the buckets in which Dave's seed potatoes are growing and, furthermore, this garden isn't the smokers' garden: that's the other one, on the other side of the games room and the dining room.

'What's it to you, cunt? Now cunting well get off my cunting case, OK?'

Dave tells me he knows this guy: reckons he's killed a guy down Pontefract way. Some 'unsolved murder', but everyone in Pontefract knows who did it.

I have my place at a dinner table, near the front, though I know when the time is right I'll be able to move towards the back. Right now though, it's the table at which Dave and I can offer support, help and reward to those who may need it. Like Jimmy: I'm the only person who can understand what his toothless, gummy mouth is saying, though my secret is simple, if counter-intuitive. Most people focus their eyes on his lips and try to decipher his words that way. But we don't hear with our eyes, do we? I just close my eyes so the only sense I am dealing with is my hearing and I'm cutting out all that static created by sight, smell, touch. I can understand him perfectly now and act as his interpreter.

The other inmates have varying degrees of 'illness'. Some have tried to top themselves in the face of life's overwhelmingly complex challenges, and they're basically depressed. Many of the younger ones have become psychotic through drug abuse. Some, like Dave, have just run into a bad scene and are trying to piece their lives back together. Most are decent guys, though the jury is definitely out on Willy, as it also is on a slightly creepy guy, called Thomas, whose response when I told him I would die at 103 was that he knew he was destined for a violent end at 61.

I have my routines: scanning the papers, writing notes on my MacAir, pacing the lawn. I have my table tennis bat; I've got Michaela to buy a yoga mat so I can give everyone yoga lessons, and a football made by sweated labour in the Far East as a World Cup fake. I spend long periods playing 'spot' against the raised seedbeds in the garden. One of the challenges is to kick the ball hard off the seedbed so it will travel the full length of the garden and score a goal under the bench at the other end of the lawn, where I gave Jeff and Bryan their massages. One day I stub my toe on the football and turn my nail back. I discover that the 'false thyme' in the garden is a good disinfectant and painkiller.

The Viking warrior scrapes his foot against a barnacle on the hull of the longboat as he jumps ashore, but he knows the herb that will ease the pain.

I gently push the nail back into place and continue playing.

Dave and I continue to build our plans: time is of the essence and each time the troops ask for instruction they are reminded: 'Ask once only and never again; you will only waste time.' Gradually we find that Jeff and the younger lads are listening better now, as we no longer have to repeat instructions.

We add arm-wrestling and chess to our games repertoire. Remarkably, I can hold my own against this former boxing pro in arm-wrestling, but he totally wipes me out in chess. From arm-wrestling we develop our comrades' 'good handshake'. It's an honest handshake to challenge secret masonic gestures and is simply an extension of the arm-wrestling grip into a hand greeting.

I am thankful for the greater peace that has become my environment, for Malcolm is now adding a range of scientific

Truths to the social Truths he has already shared with me. Chief among these is an equation to define the elasticity of time:

$$2^\infty = \infty^2$$

Or two to the power of infinity equals infinity squared. Or, put another way, in a closed-loop universe in which time begins and ends at the Big Bang, the time taken to travel from the Big Bang to the End of the Universe is equal to the time that it takes to travel from the End of the Universe to the Big Bang. That is the only inelastic part of the equation: within those parameters time is elastic and free to pass at different rates in different circumstances. Like Michaelo-minutes or God's Seven Days, for example.

I am struck by how similar the symbol can be made to look to the number 42: Douglas Adams's digits that are the huge computer's disappointing answer to philosophers' 'ultimate question of Life, the Universe and Everything'. I think Adams may have known things he didn't get a chance to share before his untimely death.

Michaela has also brought me in some pocket money and I have started to go beyond our ward to the little café in the hospital foyer where, as I mentioned earlier, Dave and I will always split our change equally between the charity box and our own pockets or 'One for the Lord, one for me,' as Dave puts it.

I suddenly realise the significance of the clock in my bedroom. It reads 11 minutes past 11. My mother was born at that time on November 11, 1911: 11/11/11/11. The clock becomes my anchor: my unshakeable reference point that is forever correct and unchanging, unlike the clock in Reception which is always wrong.

Diary of Stella de Weld, Monday September 6

Two days of very hard work trawling our North American contacts again at the end of last week. Almost without exception they've received correspondence from 'the other party'. Absolutely without exception they are confused and have thought they were communicating with us or at least another branch of our company. I got as much of the material forwarded to me as possible and printed it all out for today's meeting with the lawyers. There is material in these emails that is known only to Vic and me. So either there's a mole in our own company or we've been hacked. I can safely rule out the former.

It's refreshing to see lawyers acting with a genuine sense of urgency. I think they may even be starting to get slightly excited, heaven forbid. But, at the end of the day, they are lawyers and not given to acting on impulse or impetuously. They want more prima facie evidence of intellectual property theft and cyber crime to be sure that a judge will grant the necessary orders. Needless to say, all this is going to cost an eye-watering wadge.

Rog has been working with the IT people to try and find evidence to back up the idea that we've been hacked. The thinking is that if we can identify the method used it may be possible then to tie that up with evidence from the computer used by the hackers.

Wednesday September 8

Today has been one of both good and bad news. The good news is that Rog and the guys identified a Trojan that the hackers used to give access to what is effectively a remote desk top of one of our computers. So someone had access to everything on our server, including the file with everyone's individual passwords, so they were also able to log on as different people in turn and copy whatever they chose from people's emails. The bad news is that this really makes us look like a bunch of total muppets. More good news is that Immerhutts have agreed to act on a no-win no-fee basis, once the not inconsiderable external costs have been covered. And the other bad news is that if we were to lose we'd be saddled with costs that we'd struggle to pay and we might have to bite the bullet and shelve the whole North American project.

CHAPTER 14

Deep South

Thursday, September 30, 2021

Although Felix had lived in London, he had never before been to Tunbridge Wells and his only 'knowledge' of the place was that it must be some sort of southern version of Harrogate, but rather more poncy on account of its 'Royal' moniker, in addition to its being, like Harrogate, a spa town. He was therefore rather pleasantly surprised, following his drive across the similarly unexpectedly green and pleasant slice of England to the north and east of Southampton, to find it was actually a not unattractive place. One that was without Harrogate's at times rather dour Georgian grandeur and with a twee and jaunty collection of shops and cafés, in one of which he was now busy finessing the speech he would deliver on the doorstep of the parental home of one Kenny Marchant, apparently unheard of in more than two years.

Felix had chosen to fly down to Southampton, where he had hired a modest car – one of those new VWs, the obscurely-named Cavolé – and successfully fulfilled his day's business commitments by lunchtime on Wednesday. It was now about 4pm, it having taken him a near three hours to drive the hundred miles or so, thanks to some incident on the M25. Even without that hold-up, Felix was bemused at the distance he had to cover, having, as ever, been caught out by the fact that there remained a pretty hefty wedge of England beneath London and before reaching the South Coast. His plan was to arrive at the Marchant residence at about 6pm, when he figured the odds on finding someone at home would be good, and so the delay had saved him having to kill time hanging around Tunbridge Wells.

On rechecking the information from Tracy, Felix realised that the Marchant home was actually a few miles out of town, in a village that Felix judged, from what he had seen on the Internet, to be impervious to the misfortunes that life regularly visited on communities in other less blessed parts of the country.

As the little Cavolé hove into the village, its driver was still far from sure exactly what he should do next. Yes, he'd drafted his little speech, but he was aware that there remained every chance the Marchant door might be politely closed on him if he wasn't able, quickly, to negotiate his way inside. The Marchant address was close to a village green, on one side of which stood a pub. Felix parked and decided that a little bit more research might assist in the task ahead and that the bar of the Duke of Kent might be as good a place as any to conduct said research.

A couple of men sat on bar stools, in conversation with a youngish blonde woman behind the bar, who was separated from them by an impressive array of beer pumps, each charged with, Felix quickly noted, a different locally-brewed ale. He hoped this wouldn't turn out to be a house of the notorious 'local pub for local people' template.

'I spy stranger!' declared one of the men. Felix's heart sank, then rose as the man then engaged with him quite warmly, enquiring as to the reasons for his arrival in the village at this, the end of a mid-week working day. Felix decided to go with the flow and said he was in the area and had decided to look up an old friend, Kenneth Marchant. The man's eyebrows rose.

'Hey 'chelle, I think we've got another one of those reporters here,' he said, in the general direction of the barmaid. Felix feigned puzzlement. What made them think he was a reporter, he quizzed?

'You mean you didn't know that the young Marchant boy had gone missing? Off the face of the Earth if you were to believe his old man. We had a succession of reporters down here a few months back but they ran out of things to write after a few days and left us to get on with our quiet uneventful lives.'

'I'd no idea,' lied Felix. 'It must be five years since I last saw Kenny. We were working on an IT project together, in London,' he risked. 'The last I knew he was working for Aurora, the Blather people…'

'Well, they reckon he had something to do with Aurora when he went missing, but it's been a fair old while since he lived here with his old man and his ma, so I'm not sure why you'd have expected to find him here today. I should have said I'm Derrick, by the way, spelt like a crane…'

'And I'm Felix, like the cat. Kenny was commuting from his folks' place when I worked with him so this was the only address I had and his mobile's dead so I guess he's changed provider at some point…'

'Changed it to the Great Provider in the Sky for all we know,' the second man chipped in. 'I'm Tony, by the way: what'll yours be?'

'Driving,' said Felix.

'Pull a Jolly Vicar for our friend here, 'chelle. It's only 3.5 per cent so he'll be OK to drive.'

'Let the Jolly Vicar pull himself, the dirty old bugger,' sniggered Derrick.

'That's only the fifth time this week you've cracked that one,' groaned the woman whose full name, Felix deduced, must be Michelle. Protesting against being bought a drink didn't feel like the most worthwhile of exercises. Besides, he sensed this trio might prove a source of information that might just cast a little more light on the 'Marchant boy'.

'So when was Kenny Marchant last seen?' he asked.

'You'd best ask young Michelle that one,' replied Derrick with what Felix detected as a definite smirk.

The barmaid's eyes rose in their sockets as, with a look of

resigned acceptance, she sighed, 'I had a couple of dates with the guy, it wasn't heading anywhere in particular, he moved to London, we lost touch, and these two jokers like to tell everyone either a) that I kidnapped him and now keep him in my wardrobe as my sex slave or b) that I terrified him so much that he's in permanent hiding somewhere...'

'Atta girl, we like the sex slave idea best!' chortled Derrick, his rather ample sides beginning to heave.

'For what it's worth, if you'll all be serious for a moment, Kenny wasn't a very happy bunny when he was living here with his folks,' said Michelle. 'His dad was forever on his case and he felt he had to find his own place again. If you want my opinion, he decided he wanted nothing more to do with his parents and then his mother says to his dad, "Now you've done it, he'll never come back!" and so his dad invents this story about him disappearing in supposedly mysterious circumstances to cover his own backside. That's what I think.'

Felix wasn't overjoyed to hear what Michelle had to say. No disappearance; no Aurora involvement; no light cast on Jameela and her all-too-real vanishing.

'But why would his dad invent a story like that?' he asked Michelle.

'Well, I don't think it was something he planned to do, but then he read about some woman down in Devon or somewhere who'd apparently gone missing while she was working for Aurora and I think, you know, one of those little lights just came on. And I really think he'd had all hell from his wife about Kenny leaving home and then not really going out of his way to visit or even keep in touch. It was just a way of maybe getting himself off the hook with his missus, I think.'

'You said there'd been a lot of reporters down here, following up the story,' said Felix. 'But I don't think I ever saw anything in the newspapers or on-line at the time.'

It was Derrick who replied, 'No, that's very true, young man. That's the funny thing. I guess they all just decided there wasn't much of a story after all...'

Felix turned to Michelle. 'Do you think that's true? How did you get on with his dad?'

'Well, apart from the fact that Gordon, that's his dad, didn't really think his precious son should be wasting his time on a barmaid, I actually got on OK with him and we still talk if I bump into him in the village. He's a bit of a harmless old buffer really, military man.'

'Disgusted, Tunbridge Wells?' said Felix, recalling the traditional address for the old Tory man of the Shires that you might find at the foot of a Private Eye cod-reactionary spoof letter.

'Disgustin'? No, not at all,' said Michelle, the remark having clearly zoomed right over her head. Then she lowered her voice and leaned towards Felix. 'In fact, if you don't mind waiting till Lucy comes in and I can leave the bar for 30 minutes, I'll take you round there so you can see for yourself.'

Bingo! thought Felix and whispered his reply: 'Yeah, sure, if it's not too much trouble…'

Felix now faced a dilemma. His plan had been to spend Thursday in Slough and Windsor on the trail of Roger Smart and the family of one Katie Brown who had, apparently, left Aurora to go travelling in Australia and New Zealand. Her parents feared the worst: that she had endured a fatal encounter with a madman somewhere in the Australian bush or had got lost in the rainforest and died a lingering death from starvation. After all, she wouldn't be the first to suffer either fate. At the same time, though, what little Felix had found out had also revealed that their greatest solace now lay in the notion that she was still alive and, indeed, still somehow in the employ of the Aurora giant. Their adherence to this ray of hope enjoyed an element of justification, in a paradoxical way: it was Katie's concurrent virtual disappearance that allowed her parents to think that she might belong to that small and as yet unproven group of people who had vanished while working for Aurora. So it was almost as though the less they knew about her whereabouts, the more hope they might have that she was still alive somewhere. And the especially exciting thing for Felix was that it seemed highly likely that, like Jameela, Katie had been an employee of one Roger Smart, who had moved north and had been with Aurora during its rapid rise to its current giddy heights.

If Felix left Kent in, say, an hour and half, he could still get to the Premier Inn at Slough and arm himself ahead of tomorrow's challenges with a good night's sleep. He had, after all, prepaid his room at Slough and with a looming sabbatical and possibly months of one-way cash flow, he wasn't too keen to start by wasting a £80 pre-booked hotel room. On the other hand, however, there was every chance he might not get away from the village much before nine and, were he to spend even longer there, he might yet discover something really valuable. Perhaps even more appealing, he could sink a few pints and escape from the strictures of the task he had set himself, if only for a few hours.

'Is there a B & B near here?' he asked Michelle.

'About two metres, I'd guess,' came the reply. 'Just above your head. Jeff and Sandra, the landlord and landlady, have a couple of rooms here in the pub. Nothing special.'

'Trouble is I've already paid for a room in Slough...'

'In Slough!' interrupted Derrick. 'Have you any idea how far away that is? Bleedin' miles, sunshine. Bleedin' miles.'

'Yeah, bleedin' miles,' echoed Tony, helpfully, if a little half-heartedly.

'Look, I'm in charge for Jeff and Sandra while they're in Tenerife,' said Michelle. 'We've no-one staying tonight so there's no breakfast chef tomorrow, but if you don't mind just letting yourself out in the morning, you can have the bed for twenty quid.'

'Well, I guess that's an offer I can't really refuse,' said Felix, who then called the Premier Inn and told them they could release his room.

'What d'yer do that for, Felix?' said Derrick again. 'They could get paid twice now and all you've got out of it is losing the cost of a phone call!'

'I suppose I'm just that kind of guy,' sighed Felix.

'There's something you need to know,' said Michelle as they walked the few metres to Gordon and Miriam's elegant detached house.

'Oh no,' thought Felix. 'Not another woman about to hit on me...'

His anxiety increased as Michelle stopped and turned to him. He began to feel defensive.

'You need to know two things really,' Michelle continued. 'First, I don't believe for one minute that Kenny was just on the run from his dad.'

'And second?' enquired Felix anxiously.

'That's the main reason why I'm hanging around this place working behind a bar. Gordon and I are trying to trace Kenny but those two jokers back in the pub know nothing about that. And nor does anyone else in the village and that's important, OK? We had more than a couple of dates, too, me and Kenny... I used to get the train up and stay with him in London and I thought we might, you know, have something. But he got kind of unhappy and a bit restless and maybe I tried too hard and crowded him when what he really needed was more space...'

Felix felt both relieved and a little excited.

'Why are you smirking?' asked Michelle. 'This is a really serious business.'

'I'm sorry,' said Felix, who found himself having to think quickly. 'It's just it's almost a relief to find that you're not the only person in the world chasing shadows.' He then shared with Michelle the truth that his especial interest was in the whereabouts of one Jameela, rather than Kenny, whom, he confessed, he had in reality never met.

Michelle decided to return to the subject of the smirk, and said, 'You thought I was going to say something else, didn't you?'

'Like what?'

'Like I fancied you or something.'

'Don't be ridiculous!' said Felix a little overenthusiastically.

'Well thanks for that, Mr Chivalry!' Michelle feigned offence and turned to complete at a brisk pace the last few steps to the gate in the brick wall that surrounded the generous garden. 'Just let me do the talking, Mr Tactful, OK?'

Felix had expected Kenny's father, Gordon, to wear a somewhat stern countenance and was surprised when the man who came to the door after Michelle had tugged the old-fashioned bell-pull turned out to have a round, ruddy face that broke into a smile on seeing who was on his doorstep. The smile quickly faded, however, on seeing that she was not alone.

'I've brought another seeker after The Disappeared,' said Michelle. 'Don't worry, he's kosher. Not Press.'

'You'd better bring him in then...'

Gordon ushered them into an ample sitting room, in which two Chesterfields were surrounded by period furnishings. Felix was unsure exactly which period. It was all a little formal and something of a mishmash. One wall was adorned with a large print that might have been a Rembrandt; on another was what Felix guessed might have been a regimental line-up.

'I'll not fetch Miriam,' said Gordon. 'She doesn't like to have to dwell on it all.'

'I know,' said Michelle, touching Gordon on his arm, reassuringly.

Michelle introduced Felix and Gordon gestured Felix to sit on one of the Chesterfields while he occupied the other with Michelle. Felix felt a little like he'd just arrived for an interview.

At Michelle's invitation, he began his story at the beginning: his reunion with Jameela on Eastertide Island. She and Gordon were especially interested in his account of his visit to the Aurora headquarters in Newcastle. And, as he told of the purpose of his 'business trip' to the South of England, it emerged that they too had had a meeting with Emily Black, whom Felix was due to meet in Exeter in a few days' time.

'Emily was very reticent when we met her,' said Michelle. 'Either she had had second thoughts about meeting us or someone had got at her somehow. I hope you have more luck than we did.'

'And what about you,' asked Felix. 'What have you actually managed to find out?'

'Dispiritingly little,' said Gordon. 'Only enough to persuade us that Kenneth is more likely to be alive somewhere than to have disappeared and died.'

'What gives you that confidence?'

Before Gordon or Michelle could answer, the door to the sitting room swung open and a shortish woman in her late 50s, with neatly permed grey hair, entered.

'Is this a private party?' asked Miriam. 'Not much of a party when the guests don't even have a cup of tea,' she added, turning on her heels and drawing the door shut behind her.

'Oh dear,' said Gordon, who then picked up where he'd been before the interruption. 'We had a message from Kenneth,' he continued. 'Well, not directly from Kenneth, but from a woman called Katie Brown.'

'From Windsor?' asked Felix.

'Yes, that's right. Katie got in touch to say she was a colleague of Kenneth's at Aurora and was aware he had apparently gone missing. She said that we really shouldn't worry for him and that, in time, everything would become clear…'

'And then she disappeared off the face of the Earth, just like Kenneth,' interjected Miriam, bursting back into the room with a tray, laden with a floral china teapot, bone china cups and a plate of ginger snaps. 'Gordon tries to protect me from all this, Mr…'

'Merryweather, Felix Merryweather.'

'What an elegant name, if you don't mind me saying so,' continued Miriam, extending her hand and introducing herself, rather superfluously, as Gordon's wife. 'As I was saying, Mr Marchant doesn't like that I get visibly upset when people talk about Kenneth. He belongs to the stiff upper lip school. But just because I get upset doesn't mean that I don't have my own views and one of those views is that, while I will never give up hope,

I'm less able to cling to the thread of hope that my husband and Michelle seem to derive from the message from Katie Brown. Because, as I say, she has vanished just as completely as Kenneth.'

Miriam pulled the stool out from beneath the upright piano on the internal wall and perched on the edge of it, as though she'd be out of the room at the first polite opportunity.

Felix asked what other leads Michelle and the Marchants had followed.

'Well,' replied Michelle, 'we've followed a lot of leads on line…'

'But every time we feel we're getting somewhere, the leads seem to dry up,' Gordon interrupted.

'As though they'd never even existed in the first place,' continued Michelle. 'You know how impossible it's supposed to be to permanently erase something from the Internet? Well, it's as though things about the Disappeared don't follow the normal rules. You can find something one day and then start following up from it and then you come back the next day and it's as though you'd just imagined it all. So now we hard-copy all the links as soon as we find something and keep all the material in a master file. And we've started timing things to see how long it takes for anything to vanish, or be removed…'

'So someone very clearly doesn't want you to follow these trails,' observed Felix.

'Well yes, I mean it could hardly all be coincidence, could it?' Michelle's look wasn't quite withering, but Felix was embarrassed that he had, perhaps, rather stated the obvious.

'They're like people with a dodgy TimTom, or whatever you call them, Mr Merryweather,' sighed Miriam. 'They keep finding themselves up country lanes that lead nowhere but they haven't the courage to just turn round and follow their own common sense.' And with that, she was gone.

'It hasn't all been such a waste of time,' said Gordon. 'Let me show you something.' Gordon took down a thick ring binder from the built-in bookcase and came and sat beside Felix. Michelle joined him at his other side. Gordon opened the file: it was filled mostly with print-outs from websites, but divided by coloured tabs, some of which bore labels that Felix quickly recognised – Emily Black, Katie Brown, Monique de la Rochelle, Nils Boateng and a few others from Tracy's list – and some that he didn't.

Gordon flicked through the file until he reached the section devoted to information about Katie Brown. 'I told you that we had a message from Miss Brown,' he said. 'But what I didn't tell you was what kind of message.' Katie's section in the file was thicker than most and from it Gordon removed a plastic wallet, from which he then removed a postcard. 'I find it rather comforting in this age to come across something as old-fashioned as a real postcard with a real postage stamp on it. We started to print out the Internet searches when we realised things were beginning to change and then this came along as if to say "trust me, I belong to a different time, when information was more certain and things were more what they seemed to be".'

Gordon handed the card to Felix. The stamp featured a bird Felix recognised as a dodo and looked pretty much like any innocent holiday postcard. Felix reflected on the endurance of the postcard: it had outlived the hand-written letter and was perhaps living proof of the contention that, when we go on holiday, we are forever subconsciously seeking to return to the security of our youth. We may be in Casablanca, Cape Town or Cairns, but the Holy Grail we seek in these places we never visited with our parents is nonetheless the happy memories of the warm childhood environment. A time when others took responsibility for us and looked after our wellbeing and happiness.

The writing on the card was a throwback to that same age of untroubled tranquillity – the briefest of messages in hand-writing that reflected lack of practice in an age when the medium of the keyboard or hand-held prevailed. 'Having a great time here in paradise with Vic and Michaela. So much to do and see – off to the crocodile farm tomorrow.'

Felix noticed that the word tomorrow had an extra M, crossed out. The kind of mistake you make when having to hand-write. It was signed 'In haste and with much love, Kenny and Katie', followed by two crossed kisses. Felix turned the card over: the reverse was a picture of a looming grey mountain that might have been in Scotland had it not been for the foreground, which featured a tropical lagoon, surrounded by open-sided thatched buildings and golfers in Bermudas.

He turned the card again and read the caption: Le Morne, Mauritius.

'So, do you think Kenneth and this Katie had become an item?' he asked no-one in particular.

It was Michelle who responded, and quickly. 'No, absolutely not! This may look like a very mundane object. It's just a postcard after all. But it's the only postcard we've turned up in all the leads we've followed.'

'So, what do you read into it?'

It was Gordon's turn to respond: 'We don't think any of these people are free to communicate and we see this postcard as a solitary successful attempt to breach what we've come to call "the wall of silence".'

'OK, so what have you done to try to get the bottom of it all?'

The older man and the young woman looked at each other. Gordon turned his head to the side as though to avoid both Michelle and Felix's gaze.

Michelle, however, turned her face to look Felix in the eye, so far as that was possible in the sombre light. 'In truth, not a lot,' she said. 'But you shouldn't judge us too harshly. It's not that we haven't wanted to do something constructive, it's just that it's very hard to know where to start. And, having started, how to keep going.'

Miriam chose that moment to come back into the room. She looked at the three occupants in turn before remarking rhetorically, with what seemed like a kind of perverse glee: 'Stuck in a cul-de-sac, are we?'

Felix walked the short distance back to the Duke of Kent deep in thought.

'A penny for them,' probed Michelle.

'My thoughts?'

'No, your trousers, stupid,' said Michelle, hastily correcting herself. 'I mean your shoes, yes, your shoes.'

Felix guessed Michelle was blushing, so chose to spare her, replying: 'I dunno, I s'pose I just hoped you might have found a little more to go on. If you've been trying to follow a trail for ages and all you've got is lots of sheets of paper of web references that no longer exist and a single postcard from Mauritius, perhaps I should just give up now.'

'There's more than that,' said Michelle.

'Like?'

They'd arrived back at the pub and Michelle said quickly, 'Don't rush off in the morning, OK?'

Michelle was quickly back in her place behind the bar, where the second barmaid, Lucy, was now being ribbed by Tweedles Dum and Dee, as Felix now thought of Derrick and Tony. Michelle's return brought instant relief. 'Been out for a quicky with young Felix, have we 'chelle?'

'Well, Derrick, it's nice to have a real man in the village again,' she returned.

'Ooh er, please excuse ME!' Derrick stroked what was left of his hair and attempted to suck in some of the fleshy rolls that overhung his thighs.

Felix wasn't sure he could cope with the banter for what remained of the evening, but he realised he was hungry and there was still time to grab a bar snack. He used this as a pretext to leave the boys at the bar and take a seat in the dining area, where he took out his tablet.

It was Michelle herself who brought Felix's lasagne to his table 15 minutes later, by which time Felix had drawn a blank in his efforts to retrace Nils Boateng and Monique de la Rochelle. The bookmarks he'd created and copied to his VSP when he'd done that first search in the library in Newcastle now returned an ominous 'The page you are looking for does not exist; it may have been moved, or removed altogether', or 'The URL you entered does not exist. Please check and retry'.

'I see what you mean about the mysterious disappearing web searches,' he told Michelle, discreetly. 'If I'd any idea that could happen, I'd have pasted everything into Word documents or something.'

'Or printed everything out, like we did,' replied Michelle. 'Dressing for your salad?'

'Yes and a knife and fork might be nice…'

That one earned him a withering look and when Michelle returned, she said, 'Give me a shout when you want to turn in and and I'll show you your room. Or you can eat up quick and come and save me from Bubble and Squeak over there.'

'Bubble and Squeak? I'd called them Tweedle Dum and Tweedle Dee.'

'Tweedle Dum and Tweedle Dee; Bubble and Squeak; Bodger and Badger; Rosencrantz and Guildenstern…'

'Blimey, are you into Shakespeare?' asked Felix.

'Not that I'm aware of,' came the rather baffling reply.

The lasagne was pretty standard pub fare, but welcome for all that. Another Jolly Vicar might just wash it down nicely. Felix returned to the bar, where Derrick and Tony were in heated discussion about something that Felix couldn't get a handle on to start with.

'Yeah, I used to love sucking them off the bone and letting them just slip down nicely,' said Tony.

'I used to like 'em with a glass of Guinness: take the salty edge off and get the bones away.'

'Jellied eels, young Felix!' said Tony. 'Bet you love 'em like we do.'

'Can't say I've ever tried them…'

There was a clunk as both men replaced their glasses firmly on the bar and chorused: 'You've never 'ad jellied eels?! Where you been all your life?'

'In civilisation prob'ly,' said Michelle. 'Eating sensible food.'

At which the two men broke into a song that Felix had never heard but was clearly something to do with jellied eels. He had to laugh: they were such a cliché.

'How about I buy you each a pint and, in return, you shut up and give us all a break.

'It's a deal!' said the pair.

They downed their pints in comparative silence, drew breath and Derrick said: 'What do we not have to sing about for you to buy us another one?'

'Sing as much as you want: I'm off to bed,' said Felix, departing upstairs with Michelle to a predictable chorus of catcalls.

Michelle showed him to a room towards the back of the pub, equipped with a double bed, a small sofa and an en suite bathroom, with shower. The floral wallpaper was doing its best to outshout the rather larger flowers on the carpet. Neither design said to Felix: 'I am a brave statement of interior design in the UK as we find ourselves in the third decade of the 21st century.' The duvet cover had been cowed into submission and wore a restrained pattern in light blues, while the counterpane's role in life seemed to be to clash with just about everything else in the room.

'Cool décor,' said Felix.

'Hmmm, isn't it just,' replied Michelle. 'Look, my sanity tells me I'd better not hang round here too long if I don't want to overstimulate the imagination of our two friends at the bar. But remember what I said: don't go in the morning before I've seen you, OK?!'

'Where's your place?'

'Room in a house at the other end of the village: my parents left the village and moved to Tunbridge Wells. It's not the greatest; not when you feel you should be getting some substance to your life, you know, proper job and everything. But I'm caught in an eddy in the stream and it's the same one that's probably going to catch you soon.'

'Nice turn of phrase,' said Felix, chastising himself for having earlier jumped to the conclusion that Michelle worked behind a bar because she wasn't all that bright.

'You will find that I'm not just a pretty face,' said Michelle, emphasising the 'will'.

'WILL I?'

'Yes, I think you very possibly will, but, like I say, I'll see you in the morning.' And, with that, she turned and went.

Felix got ready for bed and slipped beneath the blue duvet. He took out his VSP and thought he would try something. He wasn't a great Bleater, having always felt that life was really too short. But now he wanted to know if the rule about the incredible disappearing search terms applied across all media, or just the 'Internet-proper'. He began by setting up a new Smartmail account, happiness@smartmail.com, then created a pi-blah tag, πlesdisparus¿. He looked for and found both Michelle and Tracy, but drew a blank when he looked for Emily Black. He used the encryption function in Blather and invited them both to follow him, wondering if he had, in the tag alone, offered enough clues.

He put the VSP away and fell asleep reading another chapter of the Secret World of the Aurora Foundation.

CHAPTER 15

The Man of Many Tongues

Wednesday, September 7, 2010

The sun is shining again, as it does every day in this special place, to which I have been called. It is September and its first task of the day is to remove that autumnal nip that descends each night, and which now lingers in shaded corners of the hospital garden, where I find myself, ahead of my toast and cereal.

I look at the path that the Scottish wild cat has beaten in the grass: it accurately describes the extreme perimeter of the irregular lawn, following the lawn's sculpted edge, rather than taking a straight line from A to B. I pace the path I have worn over the past days of my assignment here at Priestley House Hospital.

In my pocket, my iPhone, as ever, emits the soothing tones of the didgeridoo as it plays the Aborigines collection. It seems a long time and some distance from those early sleepless mornings before they sent me here, during which I created all my playlists.

I feel the cool, fresh September dew between my toes: I stand tall and draw the morning oxygen deep into my lungs and feel the life infusing my body. I shake my hands and loosen the muscles; I shake each leg in turn: the oxygen has reached the tips of my toes and now, the nerve endings freshly fuelled, they probe the spaces between the blades of grass – I feel a little curly worm cast; the petals of a late daisy; the forked tail of an earwig as it runs across my big toe. I rise to the tips of my toes and stride out into the hospital outback. We huntsmen are high on adrenaline; we've prepared ourselves with dances invoking the Dreamtime and are at one with our environment.

The celebration of the marriage of Victor Turnbull and Michaela Larkhill was a notable affair for two main reasons: the 500-odd guest list encompassed the world of sport, politics and entertainment across the North of England; yet notwithstanding this, it went entirely unreported in the media, the region's leading news agency having been retained by the couple to do precisely what wouldn't normally come naturally. The blanket media silence delivered by the agency ensured the guests could enjoy the party, while comfortable that the world at large would not then derive its own enjoyment from viewing unguarded moments caught candidly on camera.

The bride and groom had, of course, already completed the formal marriage ceremony: an even more private affair, with just their closest family and friends, in Lindisfarne Castle, Holy Island. Then — as the helicopter arrowed across the rolling foothills of the Cheviots; over the fastness of Hadrian's Wall, austere atop the Great Whin Sill; and on into Cumbria — the guests assembled expectantly in the former stately home, carefully crafted into that most special of landscapes, the land of lakes and mountains, where England's green and pleasant sits cheek by jowl with England's most dark, dangerous and dramatic.

They had come from far and wide: people from the couple's present but, significantly, some who had last featured in Vic Turnbull's life years, decades even, previously. Those who were now arriving from afar would not, in most cases, have registered the significance of a first meeting with Vic at the time. Since his meetings with Malcolm, however, and the revelation by his late brother of the imperative of his 'seven-day' mission to save the world, the importance of many of these half-forgotten acquaintances had become not merely apparent but glaringly obvious. And so they had travelled from six continents, the helicopter having been kept busy over the previous 24 hours transferring these international guests to the grand pile in the Lake District.

There they had been joined by other partners in the great mission – politicians and well-intentioned celebs who had elected to deploy some of their wealth to good purpose, on environmental works or projects to mitigate poverty through sustainable development. Some of the couple's 'more prosaic' friends – who were not completely up to speed with the scale of the mission that Vic and Michaela were embarked upon – found themselves unexpectedly sharing tables with people they had only ever previously encountered through the pages of Hello!. Vic and Michaela had laughed aloud at some of the unlikely encounters they'd created in this way.

The matrimonial couple surfed into the hall on a tremendous wave of expectation, riding the applause as it rolled across the assembly to the top table, the éclat eclipsing the gentle melody of the Northumbrian pipes, whose rich, warm, evocative tones had woven an emotional tapestry of sound that had filled the room just seconds earlier.

The speeches were warm and witty; the menu, created by the northern lads who'd become the nation's favourite TV chefs, reflected the very best of the region; the drink flowed, and surprise revelation followed surprise revelation, as laughter turned to joy, and joy met the advancing evening with music and dance, the happy couple taking the floor to lead their smiling guests through jolly jigs and riotous reels.

It was, all concurred, the best wedding ever: the best wedding ever that The World kept as its little secret, in the knowledge that it signalled not just the start of a great marriage, but also the beginning of a mission that would lead to its own salvation.

Hunting in the outback is gruelling and very demanding on the human frame. Returning from the bush I can especially feel the strain on my calf muscles from having stridden on tiptoe for so many miles. Also, no amount of surplus adrenaline can disguise the reality that, although I am now super-fit, and my reactions are keenly tuned, I am nonetheless in my 50s and it takes time for the body to readjust to behaviours it thought it had left behind 20-odd years ago. I quickly run through the inventory of body parts: mostly in order, but – besides the calves – I've an ache in my left hip bone and tenderness in the groin on the same side. I address these with a little stretching, gentle movement and self-massage. As I'm doing this, Jeff lurches into the garden from the games room, carrying his surplus fat in a way that reminds me of a Dr Who monster, the ones that look like a big bag of sticky phlegm that can morph into a human form. Jeff badly needs to morph, but today he knows it.

'Eh Vic, canst tha gi' us a massage, mate?'

Just over Jeff's right shoulder I see Bertie, the nurse who's best mates with the lovely Julia.

'What do you mean, Jeff?' I feign puzzlement, as I'm unsure whether administering my own therapy to other inmates is strictly allowed.

'Tha knaas, like where tha puts tha knee in us back and pulls us head up in t'air...'

'I hope you're insured!' says Bertie, shaking her head with a puzzled expression.

After his massage, Jeff looks a bit less like an extra from Dr Who and so we run through the 'Proud to be...' routine and get his neck and head held up: he looks inches taller.

'Now follow me, Jeff,' I say, as we stride off down the corridor, filling it with our presence and the world with our happiness to be alive.

Dave joins us and we're a trio singing the Johnny Cash song as we arrive at Reception, where – as usual – two staff are scrunched up below the level of the counter, their eyes glued to their computer screens. A third, John, comes by: 'Jesus Christ, lads, where do you think you are? The madhouse?'

I have established a number of routines during my stay at Priestley House, besides my morning exercise in the hospital garden. After breakfast I usually take a walk to the main reception area at the hospital – that's not just the place I've been calling Reception, which refers only to our own ward. I have made a very important discovery: the hospital comprises other wings that radiate from a core, such as the women's psychiatric wing, which is just over the fence from our own garden. Apparently that's where a lot of those at the church service the other day had come from.

Anyway, in the main reception area there are, wait for it, receptionists! One is a really nice Italian woman, called Valentina, and I've been doing the eyes-shut comprehension thing with her too. I did Italian at evening classes once but, you know, normally you have to live immersed in the language for your ear to tune in and for your brain to learn to think in a new language. It's a long process and one that I can only really do properly in one language other than English, that is, French. However, if I close my eyes and Valentina talks slowly in Italian to me I find I can understand every word – it seems like it's just French with frilly bits. So easy! Valentina wants to learn French and so we spend a few minutes each day on French and Italian vocabulary.

Bonjour. Je m'appelle Victor. Comment allez-vous?
Ciao Victor. Il mio nome è Valentina. Come stai?
Je vais bien, merci!
E io sto bene, grazie!
Quel est le nom de votre mère?
Il nome di mia madre è Margherita. Qual è il nome di tua madre?
Ma mère s'appelle Margaret aussi! Est-ce que vous avez de la famille ici en Angleterre?
Sì, ho una figlia. Ha sedici anni.
Et moi, j'ai deux filles et un fils. Vous êtes très belle, Valentina.
Io sono bella? No! Ah, stai scherzando!

After these conversations, I'll pick up the Northern Echo and get a coffee and a biscuit from the cafeteria. Today I've run out of the loose change Michaela gave me and so I put the few coins I have in the charity box and ask the server if she can just put the coffee and biscuit on my tab, like previously.

'You can't have a tab here: it will have to stop. We just can't do that. I'm sorry…'

I can't understand what has suddenly changed and now I'm in debt and on the wrong side of hospital law…

Quite a lot of people gather here and I've come to recognise them. I guess some are doctors, some nurses, some trainees, some admin staff. A young woman, possibly Indian, always smiles at me. I like it here, even if they don't want to give me credit any more. In the Northern Echo there's a piece about the Labour Party leadership. I've been backing Gloria Turnbull, partly because it amuses me that someone who looks so unlike me should share my Border Reiver name. Gloria doesn't just look unlike me: her background is as dissimilar to my own as it possibly could be. She doesn't know who her birth parents were, as she's a product of that long and murky period of Australian history when it seemed like a great idea to remove Aboriginal children from their parents and place them with white families. Her adoptive parents were Ten Pound Poms, who then returned to the UK with their adopted daughter back in the 70s. Although she probably only spent about the first ten years of life Down Under, Gloria still has a bit of an Ozzy lilt and, combined with her naturally blunt nature, this can make her come across as sharp and not as cuddly as received wisdom would have it the British people prefer their political leaders.

The other, and more substantive, reason why I support Gloria's leadership bid is because she is a woman of substance, character and colour in a race that's being run by grey men cloned from a party mould.

So, when she first declared her candidacy, I offered not just my own practical support, but also persuaded Charley to help her with some screen coaching, as she just isn't as good on camera as she'd like to think she is. Of course, there's no way she's going to win this time, but if she can build some momentum, then the future's a whole new ball game…

The piece in the Echo confirms Gloria's campaign isn't really getting off the blocks and a grey man will surely prevail. I will call Charley and get her to bring my old lobbyist pal Jack on board.

After chatting with Valentina, reading the papers and supping my coffee, I then will head back to the men's wing, my route taking me past the central lawned courtyard. Here they've installed a kind of adults' playground: there's a series of broad wooden stakes driven into the ground, arranged so they create a gently ascending and descending obstacle course. You have to jump across from one stake to the next and I've got pretty good at doing this at speed, thanks to my heightened sense of balance and poise.

As I head back through the garden courtyard via the stake challenge today, I notice something new: mushrooms! They must have used horse manure when they laid the turf, because there's a healthy crop ripe for the picking, an invitation I can hardly refuse. I quickly collect a couple of pounds and, saving half for Michaela when she comes later, I return to Valentina's desk and make a gift of the other pound.

'Oh, Victor grazie. Tu sei così gentile.'

'De rien, ma chère dame!'

Do you remember how, when you were a kid, if you got lippy with someone, they might ask if you liked hospital food? I just wanted to say a bit about hospital food because, like I said earlier, the food here isn't at all bad. So, this lunchtime, I paid *mes compliments au chef* and it turns out all the 'chefs' here have to do is turn a knob on a special oven; an oven whose purpose in life is to correctly reheat the meals, which have been cook-chilled. Well, I guess I shouldn't be surprised; was I really naïve enough to imagine all our meals were individually cooked to order here at Priestley House? Perhaps I was for a little while, as the food's so nice. But what I discovered this lunchtime was that the food isn't prepared in some central kitchen in Harrogate or somewhere, but in Wrexham, of all places. And that's the kind of anomaly that's created by the wonderful world of tendering: a world in which monetary considerations trump common sense; or a world in which corrupt practice can create its own inefficiencies. Who knows?

I found out something else at lunchtime: that Thomas guy is making me feel not just uneasy, but a little queasy. He's the one who said he knew he was going to die suddenly at 61. Well, over lunch, he dropped the strongest possible hint that he was going to get lynched in a couple of years' time and mentioned he was on the sex offenders list.

That afternoon I find myself with Dave in the games room. 'Aye lad, you have to see this place like any other "community" where they lock people up, yer knaa. So there's yer killers, like Willy, reet, and then there's yer sex offenders, like Thomas, and then there's aall them that's oot te make a bob or two anyways they can, so there's the black-market in ciggies and the black-market in porn...'

'Porn?'

'Aye, they try and get young lads like Jeff hooked in: I keep tellin' him it's wrang but, ye knaa, he's young and impress-impression-impressionable – phew!' Dave smiles contentedly at having eventually managed to get his mouth round the challenging word.

We draw a couple of games of pool; draw a table tennis match; draw an arm wrestle and agree to meet later for draughts and chess, as I have just been summoned by nurse Julia.

'Can you spare a few minutes to have a chat with a couple of the student doctors, Vic?' she asks.

Sensing the opportunity to share with a wider audience the news about the great project we've got going on in here to save the world, I naturally agree. The first of my interviews turns out to be with the young Indian girl I keep seeing in the main hospital reception. I tell her how pleased I am to have the chance to share with her the important developments that are going on here at

Priestley House and suggest she'll get more good evidence if she talks to Dave. Stressing the original nature of the data she'll end up gathering through talking to the pair of us, I tell her she'll be a nailed-on cert for a first class degree. I do my best to help her by nudging her towards the most important aspects of the work that Dave and I are doing: saving the world in seven days; eliminating corruption; saving the bees; reversing global warming... But she seems to have her own agenda to pursue, which seems to me like a missed opportunity.

After half an hour or so, tops, she says: 'Well thank you for your time, Mr Turnbull...'

'Wait... Hita...' I say, a little experimentally as I recall her name from earlier in our conversation. 'Where are you from?'

'Manchester.'

'And your parents?'

'Chenai.'

'Are you Hindu?'

'Yes.'

'Can you speak Hindi?'

'Only a little: I spoke a lot as a child but much less recently.'

I close my eyes and ask her to tell me the Hindi for mother. What I hear is remarkable: the word is almost identical to 'mummy' in English.

'ममी – mam'mī'

'That's incredible,' I say. 'Can you write it down?'

'I can't write Hindi...'

'Can you say some more.'

'No, I can't do this, I'm sorry...'

She collects her books and papers and goes. I'm disappointed. I had wanted to test the theory that my Italian comprehension method could work equally well in Hindi...

Another student is waiting to see me in another of the little consultation rooms.

'You're a very bright young man and your involvement in the amazing things we're doing here at Priestley House will ensure you get a first,' I tell him.

I leave a message on Michaela's voicemail asking her to bring all my language books into hospital with her at visiting time this evening.

'But where's my Icelandic grammar?' I ask Michaela.

'I really don't know, Vic. I've brought you about 20 other language books and all you can do is tell me that there's one I've forgotten…'

'Icelandic is the nearest modern equivalent of the language we would all have spoken a few hundred years ago, with all the original syntax; all the original grammar. It's like Latin, only more relevant because it's still spoken by people today. If a Viking invader at Lindisfarne somehow got whisked off to present-day Reykjavík he'd have no trouble making himself understood. The Viking legacy here may have been submerged by more recent invasions, but in Icelandic that part of our history lives on. I think that's why people like William Morris were so interested in Iceland…'

'Victor, how's about you drop this and just thank me for taking the trouble to go home to collect all this lot' – she executes a broad sweeping gesture to enclose the several small piles of books – 'before coming here to see you, which hasn't for me, up to this point, actually been a very rewarding experience…'

'Oh, yeah, sorry. I should be more thoughtful, I guess.'

'Yes, you should. There's a whole world going on OUTSIDE your mind.'

She continues: 'I spoke to Dr Honeydew this morning.'

'And?'

'I reminded him that he said you should be referred for a brain scan.'

'And?'

'It's going to take some time for you to get better, Vic.'

'But I'm already much better: that's why I'm able to get on with all this important work with Dave, saving the world…'

'I know Vic, it is very important.'

Something strange is happening this evening: while I am talking German with Ute again and trying my very hardest to convince her that keeping her German alive will prove the best way to hone her English, I am having a strange experience when I speak English. I never really had a strong regional accent, but – having spent most of my life in Yorkshire – it's easy for me to slip into Yorkshire dialect when I am with Yorkshire folk. Equally, my parents lived in the North East and I have spent time there too, so when I speak to Dave, for example, I can find myself slipping into something like Geordie, or at least maybe something a bit generic North Eastern. But tonight a strange thing is happening: I can begin a sentence in one dialect and by the time I reach the end I have completely switched to the other. It's as though my tongue is struggling to keep up with my agile brain and it has echoes of when my timeframes were de-synched and I was able to answer other people's questions before they had asked them.

'Naa then, Ute, tha should keep thissen up to date wi' thi' German, ye knaa.'

Or: 'How Dave, are wuz playin' chess marra, dost tha know?'

I'm aware, while all this is going on, that Thomas is watching me and listening.

There are a couple of rooms in hospital where you go just to be a bit quiet, away from the telly, but a bit more connected than staying in your own room. One of these has some books and games and is where Dave and I play chess and draughts. As I sit in there, alone, this evening I am feeling a very strong connection with Malcolm: he is telling me something of great significance. I have the Post-its and magic markers Michaela brought in for me to help with my daily monitoring of the newspapers. I take a green, an orange and a bright pink Post-it pad. Green notes are 'good to read'; orange mean the reader should exercise caution; and the bright pink require a very definite pause.

What Malcolm is telling me flows, pardon the pun, from this thing about running water and bowel and bladder movements. He's telling me about the very building blocks of the evolutionary process. I scribble 'poo' and 'wee' on two green Post-its, and 'lion' and 'wildebeest'. I scribble 'the chase' on an orange one and plant it on top of the others. So, the lion is in control: he watches his prey and only he can decide the right moment at which to give chase and the right target for that chase – a younger or weaker animal at the edge of the herd. The lion will have emptied his bowels after he last gorged and he won't be needing a wee either. The wildebeest, on the other hand, never knows the moment at which danger will rear its head, so he can wee small and often and, most importantly, he does little round poos – he can even do these 'on the run' if he has to, though it may slow him down. I then scribble the magic word 'adrenaline' on a pink Post-it. This is the key. The lion's adrenaline build-up ahead of the chase flicks a switch in his prostate so he couldn't wee even if he wanted. He will never be slowed down by a call of nature while he's on the chase.

I write 'water ahead' on another Post-it… So the lions are chasing the wildebeest and they're in full flight and suddenly they're confronted by running water: the whole herd stops and relieves itself and then the ones that have best learnt to pee on-the-hoof are the first to wade into the river and swim, where the lion won't follow. He, on the other hand, can choose his prey, but he's not immune to the effects of the running water: he'd like to pee but adrenaline has ensured the tap is firmly switched in the other direction, so the only liquid that's going to escape is seminal fluid. He's killed his prey and the fastest of the lionesses has arrived. There's only one answer. Eureka: natural selection in a nutshell and, now here's the new bit, the prostate is a two-way, not just a one-way, tap and its over-function is not to be confused with disease, just with over-enthusiasm. 'Prostate is two-way tap!!' I write on a green Post-it.

The following morning, as I sit at my 'desk' in the games room, that Thomas drifts into the room again.

'Naa then, Victor, what's tha writin'?

'It's just a bit of a diary,' I reply.

'I'm a bit of a writer missen...'

He leaves the statement hanging in the air so I've no alternative but to ask him, 'So, what do you write then, Thomas?'

'I'm a crime and mystery writer.'

'Yeah? Published?'

'Aye, one or two...'

He sits himself down at the old PC in the corner of the games room and bashes away feverishly with two fingers.

A little later he disappears to return with a sheaf of papers including some that he says are from his latest novel. They are printed in 10-point, single-spaced on A4 paper. There are, despite the lack of space for them, a few manual author's corrections, though the sheets are clearly photocopies, not originals.

'Take a geek at some of these,' he says. 'Keep 'em, see what you think. And you give me something of yours.'

'I haven't really got anything...'

'Well, lend us one of thi' books.'

I have a pile of little books on French philosophy among the several that Michaela brought in for me. I can probably spare one of these for a few days.

'You can borrow this one, if you like, though I'll need it back...'

I'm not normally one to deface books, but I have written a lot of notes on the title page of Renan's L'Avenir de la Science (The Future of Science). This is regarded as the pivotal work of the French thinker, who wrote in the latter half of the 19th century. Renan's thoughts remain highly relevant today, as one of his central tenets was the idea of religion as a kind of 'human science' and of the biblical stories being a human rather than godly creation. It is, of course, especially relevant for Dave and myself at this current time of a coming-together of science and religion to one common purpose. Renan was seen as a very enlightened figure during his lifetime and his ideas on democracy were very advanced for the mid-19th century, but – as with so many 'great thinkers' – he had his paradoxes and his ideas on nationhood, nationalism and hierarchy can appear regressive in the context of his more liberal ideas on democracy and anti-clericalism. Indeed, even Mussolini drew inspiration from the work he did after France's defeat in the Franco-Prussian war.

'Cheers mate. What's it about?'

'Science, religion. Life, the universe and everything…'

'So, like he's a sort of French Douglas Adams?

'Well, not exactly…'

'Joke, mate. Joke!'

I guess my first impression of what Thomas gave me was that it couldn't possibly have been written by a 'proper writer', but I could hardly accuse him of not being a proper writer. Here's an extract from something called Eurochallenge. It seems a bit all over the place to me.

Hector had not minced his words or watered the whisky as he joined the debate.

'You lose job, money, home, freedom or your life if you challenge orders,' Hector warned those who thought a cop or a spy led a life of glamour. Models had claws and teeth for more than just smiling with. Every business was a fight.

Every boss like Dan Pistol is the same – a reject from a bad B movie. Some guys retire and do weeding or pruning but Lance's hobby is risking people's lives and then discrediting any who may survive. My Dad the Hero is something kids can be proud of; My Dad the Nutcase and Liar is the way Dan paints his disposable people!

There's lots lots more, of course, but it all seems full of names and rushing round like an express train. Maybe he did write it, but that doesn't make him a writer.

'Don't read it now. Look at it later and let me know what you think.' And then Thomas leans across and grabs my evolutionary theory Post-its from last night.

'What's all this then?'

I'm cornered, so I tell him: 'I've got this theory about evolution and adrenaline and the reproductive urge and the idea that the reproductive urge flows directly from the fight-or-flight response.' And I tell him about the idea of the hunters and hunted suddenly finding their path blocked by a river and the first female on the scene gets laid.

'Aye, and what if the second lion is a tom cat, eh Vic? What 'appens then, lad?'

'You tell me, Thomas.'

'Well, he gets shagged, if he's lucky enough, or if he doesn't like it that way, he'll fight. And if he doesn't mind which way he gets it then he's got twice the chance of finding a mate, 'asn't 'e, eh?'

'So you mean evolution might positively discriminate for homosexuality?'

'Well, bisexuality, at least. That's why I lean that way missen. Double me luck, eh?'

I'm tempted to say 'You'd need it', what with his nicotine-stained teeth and greasy hair, but I'm uneasy about where this conversation is leading so I choose the blandest response I can: 'Well, it's an interesting proposition, I guess.'

Perhaps prompted by my discussion with Thomas, I receive this evening a further visitation from Malcolm, helping to develop ideas, truths, about evolution. The first and most important of these concerns the evolution of the human race itself. The need for fight or flight is increasingly marginal to the needs of humanity. Indeed, fighting ability is at best an irrelevance in the evolutionary picture and, at worst, counter-productive, as it can override the primary goal, which is intellectual advancement, enabling humanity to overcome environmental challenges and continue to build a society that thrives and prospers for all. Malcolm is predicting a series of potentially huge events that will tend to remove the most aggressive people from the gene pool altogether.

At the same time, there's a pressing need to replenish the intellectual gene pool in areas where human intellectual advancement is most concentrated, most especially in Europe, the seat of modern civilisation, but also in North America and in the world's great cities. Modern migrants self-select through a determination to better their station in life – their ambition is an intellectual rather than an aggressive genetic trait and their movement will refresh stale gene pools here in the UK and elsewhere, with go-getting African and other genes from the 'developing world'.

Finally, with advances in science and medicine meaning that populations can remain stable with only minimal reproductive activity, quality of intellect trumps brute strength in the evolution game. That's why gays are already, statistically speaking and according to much psychological commentary, over-represented in most creative fields. So we may expect to see increased selection of the 'gay gene' in the future.

'So you're suggesting that sexual orientation is genetically determined and that some people are pre-destined to be gay,' says Michaela when she comes to see me later.

'Yeah, pretty much I guess. But there's not so much new in that, just like you can't be socialised into being male when you are actually female, and vice versa.'

'Hmmm, it still sounds a bit dangerous to me, like eugenics or something.'

'I'm only telling you what I was told by Malcolm, Michaela, but for all that, it's not something I feel a great urge to argue with…'

'OK, OK. Did you see Dr Honeydew today?'

'No.'

'You really need to find out about that brain scan…'

'I'll ask John or Julia.'

'OK. Look I'm going to go now, OK? Sleep tight and I'll try and call tomorrow.'

I am on my own again.

My sister Charlotte is coming to see me today and I have plans. Charlotte's a linguist and works very hard, translating novels from Portuguese, Romanian and Spanish into English. Curiously, her services have been significantly more in demand since the advent of the Nordic Noir crime genre, because publishers are now falling over themselves to find the next undiscovered detective hero in a backstreet in Bucharest or Bilbao. Sadly, it's not something that will make her rich, because the translator is never more than unsung hero, even though a good translation can make a book, every bit as much as a bad one can kill it stone dead (I'm still haunted by memories of the first English translation of Françoise Sagan's Bonjour Tristesse, which so failed to capture the essence of the original at a time before people fully understood how to translate a work of fiction).

I'm a lesser linguist than Charlotte: languages are not my main line, but they're important nonetheless and, besides my French and smattering of German (and my Italian, of course), I also have some knowledge of the Nordic tongues and my aim is to impress Charlotte today with my Norwegian. I have a Norwegian friend who is front of house at a restaurant over towards York and this is our destination, now that I have firmly established that, as a voluntary patient, I am completely free to come and go as I please (I could even discharge myself if I so chose).

I call my favourite Viking, in Trondheim, and get him to take me through my pre-prepared routine.

Charlotte arrives and is pleased to see me: she was actually a bit scared when she came last week, because she was really struggling with the whole thing about my meetings with Malcolm.

It's great to really get out of Priestley House again as, although it feels safe and secure inside, I am increasingly aware of the oppression of confinement.

Our lunch venue is a gastro-pub in the 'golden triangle' – the affluent commuter belt, centred on Wetherby, and lying between east Leeds, Harrogate and York. As we arrive, my friend Gunhilde is waiting to greet us. 'God dag, Gunhilde,' I say. And, introducing Charlotte: 'Detter er min søster. Hun herter Charlotte.' Gunhilde in turn wishes us 'god dag' and then says something else in Norwegian that I can't understand and Charlotte doesn't actually seem all that impressed. Perhaps she just assumes I speak Norwegian anyway...

After lunch our next mission is one that I haven't yet explained to Charlotte. Like the lunch date, I have already set this all up on the phone. A few years ago I set out to learn to play the Northumbrian small pipes, which is a bit of a musical challenge, as well as a physical one that demands an ability to perform simultaneous but quite different repetitive actions with each arm. The one has to pump a set of bellows, while the other must ensure a constant stream of air from the bag of the bagpipes, through the drones and the chanter, which, in turn, requires dextrous agility from the fingers. I got on OK last time, but the bagpipe-maker ran out of patience with me and said I had to either return my loan pipes or place an order with her for my own set. Now that I am gifted with new acuity, I believe I can easily pick up where I left off and, indeed, quickly advance to the point where I can order my own set of pipes.

When I was in my teens I recall being introduced to the 'last Northumbrian pipe-maker' at a party near my parents' home. He looked so frail he might pass to the other side at the first gust of wind. I supposed that that was signalling the end of the road for Northumbria's traditional instrument. But a lot has happened in the years since then, not least the arrival on the scene of one Kathryn Tickell, who is to Northumbrian folk music what Scarlett Johansson is to cinema. Not only did Kathryn make playing the pipes look like an activity for young sexy people, rather than old gadgies, but she also became their disciple, teaching a new generation, and going on to be a leading light in the promotion and teaching of the pipes and other folk music at the Sage Gateshead.

As for me, well ever since I can remember, the sound of the Northumbrian pipes has had the ability to make me feel really emotional – their rich, melancholy tones seem to penetrate into my very bones and sometimes I can feel the tears well up, even with the happy tunes. I've always wanted to be able to play them and today is another chance to achieve that ambition.

The huge resurgence of interest in the traditional instrument has in turn driven the establishment of a new generation of craftsmen and women to make the pipes for these musicians to play. You can find them all the way from Newcastle, Tyne and Wear, to Newcastle County Down, and Catriona Fenwick is just one of those in the wider North of England, crafting not just the small pipes, but Irish and Scottish pipes too, in her little workshop near Knaresborough.

'So, Mr Turnbull, is this round two of the Turnbulls versus the Fenwicks?' she teases, referencing the family rivalries of the days of the Border Reivers, as we get out of Charlotte's car outside the former railway cottage, where she has her home and workshop.

'I hope it's the signal for a victory by one Turnbull over the best set of pipes a Fenwick can make,' I reply.

'So, are we talking a set of pipes for the man from the Turnbull clan, or are we talking about another of your indefinite loans?'

'We're talking about a short loan, followed by a commission,' I assure her.

Catriona goes off to her workshop and returns with a set of pipes, which she tests and then carefully puts into a large case. 'So, you remember how it goes: practise rubbing your tummy with one hand and patting your head with the other whenever you've a spare minute, and give me a call in a month to let me know how it's going. And that'll be £60, please.'

'Charlotte, would you mind lending me £60?'

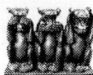

Our final call on our little run-around today is to Waterstones, in Harrogate: I need a book on linguistics and phonetics to help me get to grips with my Faroese grammar book and I want to get my teeth into the Girl with the Dragon Tattoo trilogy, too. I ask Charlotte for a further sub for my purchases and suggest she treat herself to something too, as we get chatting to the young woman at the till. She's disillusioned: the role of the high street bookseller is being constantly eroded by Amazon on the one hand, and the likes of Tesco on the other. Investment is needed to inject a new level of excitement into the process of visiting a bookshop and browsing. I suggest that we might invest in creating a new vibrant concept in book-selling, starting a bookshop that's also a kind of cultural hub, with books in languages that reflect the wide diversity of people living in Harrogate in 2010, a coffee shop, a small cinema...

Anna, who turns out to be the assistant manager, is excited and we leave with her phone number. She will be our manager just as soon as we set the business up. It will, of course, be just a little sideline as Persona Communications has much bigger works to accomplish, but it will be part of our new corporate social agenda.

It is the evening of the day: a very good day. I thanked Charlotte profusely when she dropped me off at Priestley House after our little adventure. Now I place the pipes safely out of sight in my little room and then make myself comfortable on my little bunk and scan the first volume of my Swedish crime trilogy. I quickly conclude that it's either not very well translated or badly written in the first place. I reflect on my conversation yesterday with Hita and how extraordinary it is that the word for mother should be the same across thousands of miles and thousands of years of linguistic evolution. It gets me thinking about how language must have evolved from the most primitive grunts to the simplest sounds a tiny baby can make.

I reflect that our written language, with its imposed structure of grammar and spelling, can never be any more than an interpretation of what went before, that is to say the spoken language that evolved from those post-Neanderthal grunts and squeals. Take, for example, the words 'pose', 'paws', 'pause', and 'pos', as in the plural of the word for a chamber pot. Grammatically, these words are unrelated and yet they are first cousins, or closer, by sound. We like to play with words like this, as in 'Tiddles emerged from behind the pos, paused, struck a thoughtful pose, and licked his paws to cool himself, as he had no pores.' Wordplay, I conclude, must be a driver in the evolution of language: that's why those of us who work with words enjoy so much indulging in such play. I begin to set down the opening to the forthcoming blockbuster, Two Flew Over the Cuckoo's Nest: The Unsequel.

At supper I clean up the kitchen: again. I then wander into the games room. The screen of the old PC is aglow and I glance at what is on display: it's a page of text, headed The Man of Many Tongues. I start to read: 'Charles was one of Eurochallenge's greatest assets as he could slip effortlessly from one language to another; he could even speak sentences that began in one tongue and ended in a quite different one…'

There's no doubt about it: that Thomas has been building a character based on his observations of Me! I feel slightly invaded; violated even. Just then, the very man himself comes in: 'Hey, eyes off! That's private!'

'Yeah? So why is it left up there on the screen for the world to see? And why are you writing about me?'

'About you?' Thomas sniggers unpleasantly, ejects a disc from the PC, turns and disappears.

I return to my room and take out the sheaf of papers that Thomas gave me yesterday. I hadn't noticed the newspaper cuttings: they are all about the date June 6, 2006. There's an advert for special cinema showings of a remake of The Omen on this day. It reads: 'On the sixth day of the sixth month of the year 2006, the Antichrist will be reborn.'

'In cinemas today

6+6+06

'You have been warned.'

Then there's a cutting from the Daily Star: '20 evil facts on the cult film release.'

Then there's a collection of photographs of collages and graffiti, comprising words made out of cut-out letters, a bit like a ransom note. There's a lot of 666, but also words like 'hearse', 'death', 'rage', 'war' and, curiously, 'Santa Clause' (sic), and very curiously, 'paws' and a picture of a dog. Strange that only an hour or so ago I was playing with that very word, 'paws'.

Then I notice the defining link between all the pictures: they are all dripping deep red blood from a source at the top of the image.

'I'm in the madhouse,' I reflect. 'I must work on my release.'

Diary of Stella de Weld, Thursday September 9

Wow, what a day! Certainly the most momentous ever in the short history of Persona and absolutely the most memorable in the life of a company in Swindon called Smart Ideas. Immerhutts got the orders from a judge sitting in chambers yesterday afternoon and at nine o'clock this morning the bailiffs arrived at the Smart Ideas offices and removed their server and all the individual work stations. They then took everyone's home address and confiscated a number of laptops from people's homes. These are now all being forensically examined. The Fraud Squad has been informed but it's not clear yet whether this will become a criminal case. Of course, all the Smart Ideas staff were sent home but they'll get a lawyer's letter tomorrow explaining why the company's equipment has been seized.

Diary of Stella de Weld, CEO Elect, Persona Communications
Friday September 10

Things have moved incredibly fast. The computer guys found the 'smoking gun' quite quickly and it appears that all the hacking was done after hours from one particular work station at Smart Ideas. It's not clear how much Mr Smart himself knew or how much he chose not to know, but faced with the overwhelming evidence from the computer people and the affidavits from the States he quickly concluded he was on a losing wicket and was poised to put the company into receivership. We in turn moved quickly and acquired Smart Ideas as a going concern, or as much of a going concern as it could be without computers for people to work on. The deal is that any value left in the company would be offset against damages due to Persona but that will be for the lawyers to work out. In the meantime, Smart Ideas staff will be getting another letter inviting those who want to, to come and spend three days in the North of England so they can decide if they'd like to relocate with the business. Vic and I decided to acquire a struggling publishing company in County Durham as the vehicle to take forward all of Smart Ideas' projects - it's got decent sized premises, which we haven't got in Ripon, and there's a good chance we'll get grant support for moving the jobs up there. The ambition is to have everything up and running within four to six weeks so that there's as little disruption as possible to the Smart Ideas income. Once all that's sorted, we'll bring in Michael Holbeck, who'll be buying into a business with a real prospect for growth. Even Vic's getting a smile back on his face: he wants to call the new set-up Aurora, because it's like a new dawn for the company and for all of us. And he wants me to be Aurora's first Chief Executive, while he's Executive Chairman, at least while things get started.

CHAPTER 16

A journey of discovery

Friday, October 1, 2021

When Felix awoke, he did not feel in the least refreshed. Sure, he'd probably logged seven and a half hours, but they hadn't been quality hours of rest, especially not the ones spent dreaming that he was being tempted by a half-dressed woman waving a feather boa – who was, and at the same time wasn't, Jameela – while scantily-clad dancing babes sought to distract him. Half the blue duvet clung desperately to his sweaty body, while the other was trying to make a dash for the door.

'What the hell am I doing with my life?' he asked himself rhetorically. Yesterday had done nothing whatsoever to reassure him that pursuing Jameela was either a wise, realistic or even possible idea. His suspicion that virtual pursuit simply wasn't going to work had pretty much been confirmed by the Marchant experience and yet, if he were indeed to set off in a real-world pursuit, where on earth would it end? Where, for that matter, would it even start?

For want of anything better to do, he went back into his new Blather account. There was an encrypted connection request for πlesdisparus¿ from the address carty@smartmail.com and an invitation from the same address to join πlespoir¿. Felix needn't have worried: clearly Tracy had understood straight away both who was getting in touch and what the objective was likely to be. He elected not to connect the two *ficelles* and sent slightly different messages to each. 'Join my experiment in the introduction of volatile words,' was added to the first *ficelle* and 'Can words self-destruct?' to the second.

He was just finishing off as a confident double knock sounded at the door. 'Come in!' he replied without thinking, allowing Michelle to enter. Her gaze surveyed the wreckage of Felix's bed and the disarray of its dishevelled occupant.

'Perhaps you should have asked for a moment to tidy your hair and put some lippy on, love.'

'I wasn't thinking...'

'She must have been hot, whoever she was. And I thought you were playing the dutiful faithful one.'

Felix delivered a withering look and said, 'I've not been sleeping so well.'

'Join the club, Felix, though I can't say my bed looks like a one-woman orgy in the morning.'

'Perhaps you just need to try harder.'

'Perhaps, but listen, we need a bit of a pow-wow. Let me knock us up some breakfast and we'll have a chat downstairs in ten minutes, OK?'

Felix took a quick shower, gathered his possessions, rearranged the tangled bedlinen and headed down. Michelle had made eggs Benedict with crispy bacon: Felix was well impressed.

'So, what's your next move, Felix?'

Felix reminded Michelle of his plans to visit the Brown family and track down Roger Smart, before heading down to Devon. He then confessed to the wave of doubt that had washed over him on awakening that morning.

'So that was doubt, was it? And here's me thinking it was just sweat.'

'You seem cheerful today: in fact you seem decidedly more upbeat today than you did when I met you yesterday.'

'Well, last night, I felt you'd brought me some hope: that

Gordon and I weren't the only people in the entire universe bent on hunting phantoms.'

'And now?'

'Well, I still feel that hope and I think maybe we can work together. First, though, I have some more things for you.'

Michelle handed Felix a memory lozenge.

'What's on here?' he asked.

'All sorts, but mostly things I've pulled together to try and give a bit more of a picture of Lord Lindisfarne and Lady Michaela.'

'That should be interesting,' said Felix, trying genuinely to sound interested, and adding, 'And I've set up an experiment in Blather to see how long it takes for references to disappeared people to disappear from there. I've sent you an encrypted message: you and a woman called Tracy who still works at Aurora and knows Jameela. You'll need to create a new Smartmail ID first and then you can sign up to the pi-blah *ficelles*.'

'I don't really do Blather…'

'That's not really the point,' replied Felix. 'This is in the name of science and research.'

'OK, I understand. But first things first. You've seen how difficult this task is if you try and do it all on-line. It's like tracing shadows. So it's a while since I decided the only solution would be to actually get out there and go looking. You know, turn a few stones; follow a few leads. My gut feeling is that the answer lies in tracking down Lord and Lady L and only by finding them can we find Kenny and Jameela and anyone else. So, I'm going to suggest we form a team: that I come with you to find our lost lovers, or not as the case may be…'

Michelle found herself interrupted by Felix's spluttering.

'Oh dear, is the idea of my company really so repulsive?'

'No, no,' protested Felix. 'It's just I kind of imagined it was something I would do all on my own and, anyway, it'll cost a lot of time and money…'

'In reverse order: Gordon will give me money; and two brains should be better than one, even if one of them is the one that I know you thought yesterday was a bit feeble and always missed a joke.'

'And supposing we find Jameela and she sees me with a beautiful blonde with whom I've been sharing the past several weeks of my life?'

'Well, if she doesn't trust you, she's not the woman for you, is what I say. Oh, and thanks for the compliment. You're not so bad yourself.' She continued, 'We work together as a team but go our separate ways when that's more efficient. That way we don't just double our costs for the sake of it. But, also, we make sure we meet regularly to share our findings and brainstorm next steps.'

Felix was yet to be 100 per cent convinced, so he decided to buy some time. 'Yeah that might work, but before we do anything I need to have a difficult conversation with my boss about some extended leave. So how about I finish off this little research trip and come up with my own draft plan. Then I'll resolve things at work and maybe we can take it from there. And I think we'll need some safe way of communicating: we should never mention Aurora or the names of Kenny, Jameela or any other *disparus* in any formal communication channel.'

'OK,' said Michelle. 'So Kenny Marchant, March hare, rabbit, snuggle-bunny… that kind of thing?'

'Snuggle bunny?! Well, if you must. Jameela, jam, eels, jelly, jellied eels…'

'Snuggle-bunny and Jellied Eels it is, then!'

'OK, so what about Aurora?'

'How about Our Friend Dawn for the company and Dawn's Friends for the Foundation?'

'Sounds good,' said Felix. 'And maybe we change these once a week. Let's weave a private *ficelle* on Blather and create two new Smartmail IDs to support it. You can be Shell2021@ and I'll be TopCat2021@.'

'I think we'd better write all that lot down,' suggested Michelle.

The Cavolé left the Duke of Kent behind as Felix's VSP intoned directions to the M25 and onward to Slough. After he'd first found the reference to Roger Smart, Felix had gone on to locate a website for Roger Smart Associates and had both phoned and emailed, requesting a meeting on behalf of Back Office. Although he had no more than a Post Office box address, Felix was reasonably confident this part of his mission need not be such a wild goose chase. But he was puzzled: it seemed inconsistent that he had been able to find any reference on-line to Jameela, even if it had been on far from the first page that came up in his search.

Of far greater concern right now, however, was the question as to whether he should permit Michelle to join him in his pursuit. Part of him was attracted to the idea of simply living off his own wits and being answerable only to himself. But at the same time he knew himself well enough to acknowledge that his greatest concern lay in the fact that Michelle, not least as she progressively demonstrated that she was a great deal smarter than she sometimes teasingly allowed others to believe, was also very attractive. The fact that this truth worried Felix led him in turn to ask more searching questions of himself and his motives: the sea he currently found himself swimming in was indeed a bounteous one, with many highly attractive fishes swimming in it. Not just swimming, but displaying their rich colours to him at every opportunity. With such pretty fish abounding, what was it that continued to attract him to the one fish that was permanently not on display and, even when on display, was known to be a shy creature, at best uncertain in the game of finding a mate? Frustratingly for Felix, he wasn't sure what the answer to that question was and, worse, there was an annoying little monkey sitting on his shoulder who kept whispering in his ear: 'Go on Felix, me old son, you've got their sympathy, they all want you, you can have 'em all; and you can still have that Jameela if you ever find her.'

If Jameela really was so special, why had he not done something about it when he'd first met her years ago? The answer to that question was rather easier: he could not at that time have trusted himself to live up to the standards Jameela would have set and to have tried and failed would have been to further cement Jameela's rather sad conviction that she was destined for a single life.

So what had changed that Felix now felt able to trust himself with that precious responsibility of creating a joint life enterprise with another person; an enterprise founded on trust, sharing and fidelity? There were several answers: Jameela was someone very special, who made his heart miss a beat if he only looked at her; he really did want to have a proper enduring relationship based on equality; Wendy had finally taught him that it was possible to delusionally interpret a relationship so as to salve one's own conscience without consideration of the other person's needs.

And then there was the annoying fact that, just as Jameela had begun to inch open the doors of Heaven before him, she'd changed her mind, slammed them shut and thrown away the key. Or there was the more scary possibility, however remote, that she had been taken somewhere against her will... Both of these possibilities fuelled Felix's sense of adventure and romance and, he recognised, created a heady cocktail that gave the idea of an adventurous pursuit its own attractions.

That Roger Smart had come down in the world was evident in the unprepossessing frontage of the terraced home on the north side of town, the front downstairs room of which now served as Smart Associates' office. Felix had picked up Smart's email response on arrival in Slough that lunchtime, and he now understood the latter's reluctance, on the phone, to meet with him 'at the office'. A reluctance overcome only by Felix's insistence that the address was right between two other appointments.

Smart himself had opened the door. He was wearing beige chinos above light brown brogues, and a white shirt, open at the collar. He had a slight paunch and sported a tan to his face, which in turn boasted a neatly trimmed brown moustache, to make up for the lack of hair on top of his roundish head. Felix delivered one of his standard Back Office presentations and talked to Smart about opportunities for working together, particularly bearing in mind Smart's involvement in various overseas markets. He admired Smart's 'lean and clean' virtual operation: 'Why weigh yourself down with unnecessary overheads, like an office and a payroll?'

Smart responded in kind, though Felix suspected that, since his ruination by Lindisfarne, he was a man more of straw than substance, but one who was, nonetheless, easily able to allow his mind to slip back to a time when he really was master of his own little universe.

Eventually, Felix leaned back and said, 'So, Roger, what do you think you might be able to bring to the party? I work to the simple rule that every new business I bring into our network must, in turn, bring forward another ten good international businesses with a strong on-line presence...'

Smart began to wing it and Felix's suspicion that he simply enjoyed pretending he retained the influence he once had was confirmed.

'It must have been hard for you: adjusting. I bet you'd like to wind the clock back. It's something I'd quite like to do myself, though in my case, only by a couple of weeks, tops.'

Smart sighed and slung one leg over the other knee, revealing a white branded sports sock. 'So you know about the Aurora business, then? I guess I'll be forever the guy whose company built Aurora...'

'Or the man whose business could have destroyed Persona Communications before Aurora was even a glint in Lord Lindisfarne's eye?'

Smart bristled visibly. 'You shouldn't believe everything you read. The rich and famous have a habit of bludgeoning the truth till it supports their version of events. Lindisfarne, or plain old Mr Turnbull as I believe he then was, was pissing on my patch: he'd got some government grant and he was going to build a business in precisely the same e-space as my team had spent years working on. But he paid some fancy lawyers and I didn't stand a chance: they walked in and seized all my gear "for evidence-gathering purposes," they said. And then they stole my best people. I was ruined. It was just as the big slump started: I had to sell my house in a falling market; barely covered the mortgage; wife left me, mistress left me. And then I started again, trading on my reputation. Except that my "reputation" wasn't quite what it had been. I get by doing consultancy and I use my notoriety as my selling point. Like Gerald Ratner, the jeweller who lost his fortune after describing his own products as "crap", I provoke curiosity.'

Felix thought Roger was perhaps still a little above his station in comparing himself with someone as well known, or notorious, as Gerald Ratner. 'Didn't your guys hack into Persona's files?'

'Yes, one of my team got a little over-enthusiastic, but which is the greater crime: doing what my guy did or doing what Turnbull went on to do when he trawled through all the stuff seized by his lawyers and used it to build his own business?'

'Well, I guess one act was illegal and no-one has ever questioned the legality of the other, but at least you've got your place in history.'

'Well thank you, Mr Sundowner or whatever your name is, maybe we'd best just call it all a day…'

'I'd like you to tell me everything you know about Jameela Durrani first.'

'Jameela? Why?'

'Because she has vanished while in the employ of said Lord Lindisfarne.'

'What do you mean, vanished?'

'Precisely that. Jameela and at least half a dozen Aurora employees I could name.'

'Jameela was my best; my right hand. Do you think she's in danger?'

'I've been working with other people whose loved ones or relatives have "disappeared" like this. I don't think any of them have truly vanished. In fact, on Sunday, I'm meeting up with one-who-disappeared-and-then-reappeared.'

'So is this Lindisfarne and his fancy Foundation? No-one really knows what it's up to, do they?'

'The very one, but what can you tell me about Jameela?'

'Why should I tell YOU anything? And what's she to you anyway?'

'She's an old and dear friend from since before she ever worked for you and you should tell me because she was loyal to you while you worked within the law, and because maybe you can get one over on Lindisfarne.'

Smart's eyes brightened at the final suggestion. 'OK, what do you need to know?'

'Everything you can tell me about Jameela: family connections; how she came to you and how she left for Lindisfarne.' Then Felix had another thought. 'And we might need someone who can build an encrypted e-comms system that can't be compromised through the Internet.'

'I may know just the man for that, but he'd need to be paid.'

'Find out how much and see if he'll do it on the basis of a small amount now and something 'down the line' if we get to the bottom of all this. Now tell me about Jameela.'

Roger Smart lay back in his chair, sucked his bottom lip, and drew breath.

'Jameela Durrani was always a dark horse,' he began. 'She came to me from the Government because I think the bureaucracy was driving her mad: that and the incompetence of some of her seniors and their lack of accountability for that incompetence. As for her personal life, she never discussed it. She really was a closed book and I asked no questions because that was how she preferred it and, in return, she gave me absolute loyalty till that bloody end. All I do know is that her family still run a business in Luton but that, for some reason, she never sees them.'

'In Luton?'

'Yes, I know it sounds corny but she did once mention her dad owning a restaurant, Pride of Kashmir, or something…'

'In Luton?'

'Yes, I think that's where the family settled when they first came here but, as I say, Jameela's a loner.'

'Are you bitter that she left?'

'She had no choice, really. I was finished. Lindisfarne said he would take anyone who would move up north, providing that they signed a document of loyalty and confidentiality.'

'How did that all come about?'

'Lindisfarne, that's Turnbull, sent down some woman with a funny name, Stella someone, who held a meeting at the Novotel and invited anyone who wanted to work for Persona to go up north for a two-day visit to see how they liked it. I think Jameela would have gone even without the two-day holiday and certainly one or two people just went on that for a bit of a laugh, last hurrah for Smart, bit of a wake, have a bit of a laugh at the northerners...' Smart paused a moment. 'Of course I wasn't allowed and nor were one or two others, including Luke, the guy who'd do the encrypted comms for you. Luke was the hacker, you see, though I hadn't realised at the time that he was putting the whole business at risk, 'cos I hadn't actually appreciated exactly what he was up to, though I can't blame him for it. I think Jameela, as management, was on their original blacklist but she talked to this Stella woman and persuaded her to let her meet the Big Man himself... 'Course, he was a fruitcake, you know. Just out of the loony bin when they all went up there. But somehow he had the gift of the gab and half my guys, that's about ten, moved up to Yorkshire or County Durham and I guess they must have liked it because I never heard of any of them coming back; and then I guess some moved even further north, to Newcastle, when Aurora got really big.'

Felix interrupted: 'What can you tell me about Katie Brown?'

'Katie? How did you know her? Nice kid, she was. Such a tragedy. She hadn't been with us long and she had no real ties here. She fell out with her dad big time, so I think she was happy to move up north but then she went off travelling and the rest, as they say, is history...'

'Why, what do you think happened to her?'

'She went missing in Australia.'

'Or perhaps she didn't: I'm seeing her folks later today. She's one of the Disappeared, Les Disparus.'

'Oh really, is that so?'

Smart may not have been quite up to speed on the possible status of Katie Brown, but the meeting with him had been invaluable: not only did Felix now have a potential new lead on Jameela, but he also had additional background on the internal strife at the Brown family and a possible means to make communication with his 'search team' more secure. Furthermore, Roger Smart had looked with him at the picture of himself with Jameela on the Internet and pointed out something that Felix kicked himself for not noticing. There was not just one, but two errors in the caption on the picture, which Felix now saw actually read: 'Roger Smart and Jameelah Durani pictured at last night's meeting of Slough Small Business Forum.' An erroneous H in Jameela and an R missing in Durrani. Felix had asked Smart what he thought about the idea of retrospectively removing material from the Internet so as to make it invisible to searches, and Smart had responded: 'Eminently feasible, I would say. I'm sure government agencies do it all the time. You'd just need to set off a worm that would be programmed to rewrite web addresses as it found them. The material would still exist, but the Internet reference would be gone. My guess is that everything the worm found could still exist on a secret server somewhere…'

So, his immediate plan was now to visit the Brown household that evening and then pay a call on the Durrani family on Saturday morning, before driving down to the West Country.

Smart had actually called Mrs Brown on his behalf: the couple were estranged and Katie's disappearance lay at the heart of that. Smart had commended Felix to Mrs Brown and had commented to Felix as he left: 'She really does believe that Katie's alive, doesn't she?'

The Brown house was a substantial semi-detached in the Royal Borough of Windsor (My second royal town in two days, thought Felix). Mrs Brown was a nervous woman of close to 60 and Felix surmised she had had her family late.

'Katie was, Katie IS a much treasured person for me and for Ralph, my husband,' confirmed Mrs Brown, without Felix having to ask, as she led him into another anachronistic sitting room. This one appeared to be stuck in a more recent period, the Fifties or Sixties. The furniture might have looked modern then, but now it looked both dated and insubstantial: a far cry from yesterday's Chesterfields. The room was filled with foolish knick-knacks: coloured glass ornaments and a Home Sweet Home embroidered sampler above the wooden fire surround. Mrs Brown's attire seemed to be from a yet earlier period, possibly even the wartime, raising the perverse possibility that she might in reality have been not quite the age she looked. She had a round, worried face, and nervous, unsettled countenance. Losing a treasured child heaped tragedy and despair upon a natural anxiety.

'I had to ask him to leave in the end, Mr Merrybody. It was his fault, you see. He couldn't abide that she wanted to be her own woman. In fact, he couldn't abide that she was a woman at all. To him, she was still just the little girl he used to scold. So he kept trying to control her: always wanted to vet boyfriends, sniffed at the jobs she chose. Of course he tried to stop her moving up north after Roger Smart went bust, but she thought it was an exciting opportunity and she settled in well up there. We went to see her a couple of times but Ralph made it hard: he would turn his nose up at everything and say it was uncivilised. She rented a lovely house in Durham and then not long before she disappeared, she moved to Newcastle as she was, by then, working in the big new Aurora headquarters there. That was a nice place, too: expensive, but lots of lovely shops nearby and little bistros and cafés. Jezborough, was it?'

'Jesmond?' corrected Felix.

'Yes, Jezmond,' that's right, said Mrs Brown, with a curious emphasis on the Z she had invented.

'Did you ever get to meet Jameela Durrani? The two of them worked together for Smart and moved up north together.'

'Yes, but only briefly on one of those trips north, with Ralph. She was visiting Katie, but Ralph took an instant dislike, so she left. Katie was furious with him and so was I but there was no telling him. He has funny ideas. I think that was probably the day Katie decided she would have nothing to lose by cutting her ties, because she said to me that she was not coming home for so long as her father was going to be there. I only wish to God that I'd thrown him out then and there and perhaps she wouldn't have taken that next step.'

'Which was?'

'She went on some big training conference with Aurora; Majorca or somewhere.' Mrs Brown pronounced it with an ugly J in the middle. 'Then she phoned me and said she was going to take a few months out to go travelling and the last we heard was a postcard that came from Mauritius, or somewhere. I gave that to Kenneth Marchant's father: they seemed to have a better idea how to look for these missing people.'

'So what made you decide she was missing?'

'Well, there was a horrible story about a young British woman being kidnapped by a madman somewhere in the Australian bush: they knew it had happened but they didn't know who the victim was, but then two people came forward and said they were sure it was Katie. That's when I told Ralph to leave, I felt it was all his fault. Then a month or so later they found a body and it wasn't Katie after all. And then two young people went missing in the forest in the Blue Mountains in Australia and again someone came forward and said they were sure it was Katie and it was all over the newspapers again. And then this young man turned up, all dehydrated and very ill and he insisted he'd been alone: he'd spent a day with a woman but she'd gone her own way before he began his forest adventure.'

Mrs Brown galloped through the whole account, scarcely pausing for breath. There were tiny beads of sweat on her forehead beneath the tight curls of grey hair and Felix detected a tear trickling slowly down one cheek. He felt very sorry for her and wanted to give her a hug. But she was off again before he had the chance to decide whether or not that would be a good idea.

'And then, Mr Weathervane...'

'Felix, please!'

'Cynthia, Felix. And then, as I was saying, another postcard came last week, so Katie is alive, because it's her writing, that's for sure. I haven't told Ralph. He doesn't deserve to know.'

'Another postcard!' exclaimed Felix. 'Where from?'

'Oh, somewhere hot and dusty; let me fetch it.'

Cynthia returned with a rather battered card that looked like it had had its work cut out getting through the mail. It was an old-fashioned design, the colours rather wishy-washy. It was divided into four illustrations: one showed a wide river with a bridge and people bathing or washing clothes in its waters. Another was a wide aerial view of a city that might be anywhere; a third was a picture of a green tuk-tuk, auto-rickshaw. The final illustration was in sepia and showed Mahatma Ghandi, sitting on the floor in his khadi, beside a spinning wheel. Across the middle of the card, between the two pairs of illustrations, text in red italic read, rather incongruously: 'Ahmedabad – the Manchester of India.'

Felix turned the card over and read the ample caption: 'Ahmedabad, largest city in the state of Gujarat, is a major centre for the production of cotton textiles and is the largest producer of denim in the world, earning it the sobriquet, the Manchester of India. It is also today an important centre for pharmaceuticals and other high technology industries as well as the site of Mahatma Ghandi's Ashram National Monument, beside the River Sabarmati, where he lived with his wife Kasturba for 12 years. It was from here that Gandhi began his famous 1930 march against the British salt laws.'

So lengthy was the caption that there wasn't a great deal of room left for the message, which was written in a neat hand in distinctive green ink. It read: 'Mum – Enjoying a fascinating time here in Gujarat, seeing the temples and the mosques and, of course, Gandhi's shrine. Very busy city. Jameela great company (remember her?). Give dad a hug and tell him it's OK. All my love, Katie.'

Felix had to re-read the message several times to take it in. If Katie had genuinely been with Jameela, then both of them must have been in Ahmedabad as recently as... Felix looked at the postmark: it was smudged, but it looked like 25/9/21. Just days after he'd last seen her in Australia: could that be possible? How bizarre that an old-fashioned postcard should emerge with evidence of her whereabouts, just as all e-evidence was disappearing as fast as it could be found.

Felix scoured the postcard for any other possible clues: there were none, so he took a photo of the card on his VSP and handed the card back to Mrs Brown. 'You know, Mrs Brown, the best thing that you could do would be to make the peace with Ralph, for Katie's sake. People need to stick together in difficult times and it's clear that Katie can forgive him so perhaps you should too. Talk things through with him and be strong for each other, eh?' He reached out and gave her the hug he felt she needed. She sobbed a little into his shoulder and thanked him. Yes, she said, she would think about initiating a reconciliation. And Felix, for his part, promised to let her know of any developments in his search.

After leaving Mrs Brown's home, Felix made a brave decision: he would spend the night in Luton. The Cavolé ploughed a furrow through the evening rush on the M25: Felix reflected that, by the time he had reached Luton, he would have navigated more than half of Thatcher's most fitting legacy – a featureless road with no beginning and no end. He found a cheap room at an Ibis, not far from the airport. The following morning, he took the train into Euston and, on completing his business in the capital, returned to Luton and headed for the address, on Hitchin Road, of the Pride of Kashmir. The restaurant extended across three adjacent terraced properties on the busy artery. It was far from the only

'Indian' restaurant in the neighbourhood, but was differentiated by boasting a neat forecourt, bounded by black metal railings, that extended a couple of metres out from the restaurant frontage. This compound was just wide enough to accommodate a small number of tables for al fresco dining, should the weather permit, which, tonight, it did not. The three buildings appeared to house flats or maisonettes above the restaurant: just as Felix had hoped.

He took a seat near the window and perused the menu, whose special feature was the opportunity to 'bring your favourite guests and share our special Kashmiri Wazwan banquet of many courses'. Perhaps another day, he thought as he chose a lamb pasanda and a couple of side dishes and elected to accompany them with a savoury lassi yoghourt drink, rather than a Cobra. It was very good: in the upper quartile of curries he had ever enjoyed. When the young waiter brought the bill, Felix plucked up the courage to ask, 'Does the Durrani family live here?'

'Why would you want to know that?' The waiter seemed to have to fight to even say the words.

'I'm a friend…' ventured Felix.

'If you're a "friend", why don't I know you?'

'You're a Durrani?'

The man turned his back and walked away. A few moments later, he returned with an older man: a man old enough, thought Felix, to be Jameela's father.

'Now, what is all this about?' asked the older man. His accent was that of a first generation arrivé in the UK.

Felix quickly began to realise two things: firstly, he did not have a plan for this meeting and, secondly, he was toying with walking into the politics of a family, a Muslim family, about which he knew precious little and in which he had the capacity to cause significant upset. He realised he had two broad options: feign that he had made a mistake and withdraw, politely and quietly; or choose the nuclear option and come clean about Jameela. Deciding it was already too late to deploy the first option, he said: 'I'm a colleague of your daughter, Jameela, and I believe she's in danger…'

'There is no Jameela in our family,' said the younger man, threateningly.

'Hamza,' said Mr Durrani, reproachfully. He addressed his son sternly in a language Felix did not understand: Kashmiri, he presumed. Hamza scowled and walked away. The older man continued: 'I am not knowing who you are, or what your business may be. My daughter has been bringing shame on our family but, although my son is not agreeing with me, she is for me still being my daughter. You tell me your name and you are coming back in morning. You coming upstairs to our home and you are telling me what it is you must tell me, Mister...'

'Merryweather,' said Felix.

Mr Durrani looked puzzled: 'Merr'wazir?' He made it sound exotic and Oriental. 'You are coming at ten o'clock, yes.'

The following morning, Saturday, as the Cavolé found itself once again on the M25, this time heading in an anti-clockwise direction, its driver reflected on a bad plan badly executed and the desirability, nay the necessity, of always having a good plan before embarking on any course of action. This was particularly the case, reflected Felix, when dealing with the uncertainties of cultural difference (a subject about which his work, he reminded himself ironically, required that he know more than a little).

As the Cavolé slowed to walking pace somewhere north of Heathrow, Felix replayed the events of that morning and tried to determine if there had been anything in the least bit useful that he had gained from his meeting with the Durrani family. Almost the entire Durrani family...

He had returned to the Pride of Kashmir, as bidden, a little before ten and sounded the bell on the door that he judged would give access to the flat above the restaurant. Mr Durrani himself had invited him to follow him upstairs, where members of the family were grouped as though in a scene from the Inquisition. At the centre, behind a large table, sat a woman of about 60, whom Felix judged must be Jameela's mother. She was flanked by Hamza and another young man of similar age, who might even have been Hamza's twin. A little behind sat an older woman, still elegant, though surely in her 80s. Mr Durrani had to sit on the end of the row beside Hamza's brother and, despite the fact that he clearly was not a leading player in this inquisition, it was he who had instructed Felix to sit down opposite the line-up and had then introduced all the family. Besides the two brothers, there had been another, younger, man – not much more than a teenager, sitting completely apart from the others, his feet raised disdainfully on a chair in the corner of the room. Of all of them, it was he who had exhibited the least acknowledgement of the presence of Felix.

As the traffic ground to a complete and inexplicable halt, Felix tried to recall at exactly which point the discussion had nosedived. He reflected it had not really nosedived at all, as it had never really had the chance to get airborne in the first place. Hamza and his brother Abdul had been hostile from Felix's first breath, let alone his first word. The boy Rahman had said very little, just staring coldly into Felix's eyes whenever the latter had tried to escape the drilling, chilling gaze of his primary inquisitors.

'What on earth did I think I was going to find out,' he asked himself, as the Cavolé took up a bit of slack that appeared in the chain of vehicles. Hamza and Abdul had had only one agenda and were strongly supported in this stance by their mother and by the matriarch in the chair behind. The latter spoke no English and Jameela's mother very little, but Felix had been able to infer the general meaning of what was said, alongside the unambiguous core message delivered by the two young men. This message was simple and ran something like this: Yes, we once had a sister, but she brought shame on the family by marrying a non-Muslim, indeed a non-Kashmiri not approved of by the family. Ergo, she was no longer a member of the family and must deserve whatever fate might have befallen her as a consequence of her actions and Allah's judgement upon them. That another non-Muslim was now coming into their house to talk to them about this non-person could bring only more shame upon the name of Durrani. The Durrani family could have no interest in what had become of Jameela, for only the most miserable life imaginable would be suitable punishment for the pain and shame brought upon her family.

As emphatically as it had ground to a halt, the traffic started moving again and the Cavolé found itself carried along by the tide, crossing the Thames at a healthy 50mph as Felix reflected on his own contribution to the 'debate', such as it had been.

He'd used words like 'compassion', 'forgiveness', 'family bond', 'love' and 'humanity'. None had cut any ice and, finally, Hamza had stood and told him: 'We think it is best that you leave right now, that you never think to darken our door again.'

Shaken, he had been escorted downstairs by Mr Durrani, who – on reaching the door – had gripped Felix's hand in both his own and said, 'I am sorry Mr Merr'wazir: my sons are very, what is the word, "inflexible". My daughter was very dear to me and I am missing her always. Like a limb that is missing, do you understand? My wife and her mother are very traditional and it is from them that my boys take this attitude. Not from me. I am wanting to know that Jameela is well and if you are finding news, you will tell me.'

'How can I do that?' asked Felix, both puzzled and suspicious. He was unsettled by the sons' hostility and wary of sharing with anyone in her family Jameela's whereabouts – should he eventually find her.

'You will send email to my brother,' said Mr Durrani, thrusting a business card into Felix's hand at precisely the moment the young Rahman appeared down the stairs.

'I loved my sister,' said Rahman, turning his fearsome gaze onto Felix. 'You must take me to her.'

Now Felix was genuinely confused and at a loss as to what to do or whom to believe.

'You say she has been recently to Ahmedabad? You must take me there.' Felix now regretted having earlier shared the information on the postcard from Gujarat.

'I'm sorry, Rahman, I can't do that as I won't be going to Ahmedabad,' he replied, slipping out of the door and walking briskly away from the Pride of Kashmir.

Felix had elected to take the M25 and then the direct route to Exeter, via the A303, rather than stick to the motorways, via Bristol, and, as the Cavolé finally left the M25 for the M3, he made a decision: he would find out as much as he could from Emily Black, sort out things with his boss, make a plan with Michelle, and then head for Ahmedabad.

CHAPTER 17

The Masons

Tuesday, September 13, 2010

It is another Indian summer's day in the garden. I have had breakfast but the sun is still September low and the dew lies on the grass as I follow Dave's example and look for bumble bees to help. The aboriginal hunter is at one with nature and knows it is his role to work in harmony with the Earth and the creatures that walk upon and fly above it. The sun is arcing up into the sky and it won't be long before it once again bakes the earth hard and red. The hunter will soon turn for home with his quarry…

The hunter returns from his mission and he can feel the strain that walking on tiptoe has placed on his calf muscles. He greets his extended family, presents them with the prey he has taken and sits quietly to permit the adrenaline to subside.

I return from my morning garden exercise to the games room and conduct a quick audit of body parts: the calves again feel a little strained through striding round on tiptoe and there are the familiar aches in my left groin and left hip. The Aborigines are playing in my pocket and, using the techniques of mind control that I have developed, I reduce the volume by simply thinking that the music on my iPhone is less loud, and then head for breakfast.

Michaela has given me a bit more cash, so after breakfast I make for the main reception and settle my debts. Disappointingly, there is no Valentina today. 'She's on this afternoon,' her colleague tells me. I return to the men's ward as I have a 10.30 appointment with Dr Honeydew.

'So tell me Victor why you think you are ready to go home?' Dr Honeydew is asking me this very important question but his face is turned not towards me, the person with whom he is (supposed to be) engaging. I've heard he's like that: it seems strange that someone whose job it is to see inside your mind doesn't seem to want to use the portal of your eyes to look there.

'Well I never really expected to be in here very long: I had a bit of a crisis, but now I'm sleeping well and I feel a lot calmer.'

'I've seen a lot of you, here and there around the ward...'

'Really? I don't recall our paths crossing...'

Dr Honeydew now turns his gaze toward the ceiling and draws his breath. 'Victor...' The pause is so long that I start to speculate on just what he might eventually say. Then he lowers his eyes until they are pointing vaguely in my direction and the words finally start to exit his mouth. '...It isn't just about how YOU feel. I, we, need to feel comfortable that people are ready to have you back at home.' Dr Honeydew removes his glasses as if to emphasise his point. They are quite heavy-rimmed, so he looks rather different without them – he's maybe about 45, short dark hair, flecked with grey. He wears an earnest expression and speaks with a bit of Lancashire accent, almost certainly Rochdale.

'People? You mean Michaela?'

'Yes, Michaela. You have to understand the stress it can place people under when someone is going through the kind of difficult experience that you've been going through.'

'So how do you think I'm doing?'

'Well, there are significant signs of improvement and I note that you no longer take the temazepam, but equally that we've had to increase your dosage of olanzapine...'

Oh yes, I realise I'd forgotten about this: John and Bertie marched me off to the dispensary a couple of days ago because I was getting too excited in the ward reception area and winding people up.

'Yes,' I say. 'But it's been much better since my dosage was right: I haven't caused any trouble.'

'How are the massage classes going?'

He catches me slightly off-guard with that one, so I measure my response. 'I'm trying to discourage that, but I do try to encourage people not to shuffle round with their chins glued to their chests.'

'Some of the people here need their own space: they don't want to be told to be proud of anything...'

'I know: I leave those people alone.'

'Good, I'm pleased to hear that: now, do you have any side-effects I should know about?'

I guess, on the basis of Julia's reaction, he's not wanting to hear about the seminal fluid issue, so I decide not to mention this... 'I don't think so, Dr Honeydew. I know it causes some people to pile on the pounds, but I've been getting good exercise and haven't been eating excessively.'

'That's good. Now at what point do YOU think that it might be reasonable for you to go home?'

'When I'm calm enough not to be any trouble?'

'I think so, Victor: maybe if we see how things are in a few days after I've spoken with Michaela again?'

'OK. There's another thing I need to ask... I understand you think I should have a brain scan.'

'Yes, it would be a sensible precaution and I have referred you, though I've not heard anything back as yet and it might be best to wait until you're as stable as possible.'

'You're from Rochdale way, aren't you?'

Dr Honeydew looks slightly surprised: his furrowed brows indicate that his eyebrows have risen behind his glasses. 'Yes, why?'

'Just my ear for accents,' I say. 'Though I'd guess you've been this side of the Pennines for, let's say, ten years?'

'Pretty much correct, Victor. Quite impressive.'

After lunch I propose a table tennis match to Dave and we meet in the games room. I step out into the garden to oxygenate my body before we get going.

There's enough room around the table to permit a decent game of table tennis, though occasionally the space at either end can be a little bit restricted. Today I have the garden end, so I'm playing close to the double garden doors. Where these join the walls, there's a 45° angle and so the top of the skirting board presents a bit of a sharp point at the precise location at which the wall turns towards the door.

As usual, our game is finely balanced, with each of our scores pretty much tracking the other's. We're both enjoying taking the opportunity to try a smash whenever it arises. I step back in anticipation of Dave's smash. He doesn't get quite the top-spin that he was looking for and the ball rises temptingly. I leap and smash an unreachable return to the far backhand corner of the table. However, returning to earth, my left heel strikes the sharp corner of the skirting board at full velocity. My God, it hurts: thank the Lord for my adrenaline surfeit... I let the adrenaline wash the pain away though I strongly suspect a hairline fracture, such was the force with which I hit the skirting. I rise on my tiptoes again. 'Play on!' I say. I recall that earlier incident in which I tore back the nail on my big toe while playing football barefoot, as I do each day. Then it was a combination of adrenaline and the unidentified non-aromatic herb that Dave and I discovered that helped the pain subside when I rubbed the crushed leaves into the injury. The Vikings would surely have planted this natural poultice and made use of it at the same time as they planted angelica everywhere.

After our game, I take a closer look at the skirting. It does look to me like a hazard that's the product of shoddy workmanship. John told me the other day that Priestley House was built to a Norwegian blueprint, but at eye-watering cost – it's one of those Private Finance Initiatives, which means that the NHS will pay a large sum each year to the developer, Fantabulon, without ever coming to own the buildings. There's a worse sub-text to this: Fantabulon is paid a fee for maintenance and this means that every time there's a small repair job, the NHS Trust has to pay Fantabulon a £75 call-out fee – and that's even before a hammer or a spanner has been raised in anger. For example, you can have a bath in Priestley House as there's a private bathroom on each ward and all you have to do is tell the staff you're in there. The bathroom door has a spring-loaded return on the inside, but the spring has a habit of springing out of its runner. I have to date saved the Trust no less than £225 in call-out fees alone by fixing this myself.

The nursing team love the hospital but are frustrated at the maintenance costs and numerous examples of shoddy workmanship. I chat about this with Dave: we sniff something rotten in the state of Vale and Dales NHS Trust. I sense a Masonic stitch-up.

That stitch-up will be just one strand in the drama that will be the work of fiction that I am writing, based on my time at Priestley House and, more importantly, the mission with which Dave and I have been charged. I have played with this a little on previous days on my laptop but this afternoon, perhaps because my heel injury has got the adrenaline pumping, I really feel the creative juices flowing. This will be both my own story, the story of the project to save the world in 'seven days', and the inside story of life in a psychiatric hospital.

As I write the words, they begin to exhibit a certain symmetrical quality on the screen: I play with the text until each of five paragraphs is exactly the same length. Here's how it looks!

Prologue

I was born at home. In a city. I was raised there. I went to junior school there. And to secondary school. I always pined for my city; the wild open lands and beautiful beaches that surrounded it. It was, and still is, part of an ancient kingdom whose name has oft survived the cruelty of conquest. I tingle each time I cross its mighty river; each time I fly over the lonely lighthouse that saved so many lives on what my mother called the German Ocean. I am nearly home. I am home.

I was born with a gift. I didn't use it. I hadn't discovered it. I was Just Seventeen (YOU know what I mean). And before too long I sailed the German Ocean. As had my elders; to the land where the sun never rises and never sets; where time is elastic. To the Far North where day meets night, colliding gently to create one wondrous summer's day. There it was that I was chosen to mine the rich but latent seams of linguistic skill deep within my brain. I chose to change me. I still change now.

I took my gift for languages back to school. A year passed. I took it to university in another city. I stroked and nurtured it. It came to life. I took it to another land. It took me to new continents; across oceans; to islands of the imagination; and of reality. I made mistakes; I was despatched by my studies to France, to the hinterland of the Mediterranean shoreline. Opportunity knocked, and although my tormented heart turned a screw in my ribs with each day away from my love back home, I moved on. I was reborn.

I had a fear of heights that grew fiercer. I didn't understand why. A cookie hypnotherapist began to prospect among the long forgotten slack of the deepest catacombs of my mind. I thought she was not just scary, but weird. And yet, she got closer to the terrifying cause of my escalating vertigo than anyone. Until, that is, that terrifying night, when 2010 gripped my shoulders and threw me to the Cathedral floor. I was again reborn. So was my dead brother.

I am of the most robust constitution. Yet nature said I should have died of whooping cough at six weeks. Since I was 25, my sick days could be counted on the fingers of one hand. In 2010 all that changed. A butterfly flapped its wings in Amazonia. A man fell off a broken gate in Yorkshire and then from his bicycle. He embarked on a terrifying journey. No-one heard his cries. He left his body and stared down the tunnel to the Big Bang and the end of time. That man was me. He is me. He is Pierre Maçon.

Or perhaps I'll choose some other pseudonym. Then I play with the title, which everyone loves, to produce this idea for the title page:

Two Flew Over the Cuckoo's Nest

The Unsequel

Ron Curt-Butvill
&
Victor Turnbull

A work of fraction, faction, friction and fiction

Α β γ δ ε ζ η θ ι κ λ μ ν ξ ο π ρ σ ς τ υ φ χ ψ ω ϑ Υ φ ϖ

Α Β Γ Δ Ε Ζ Η Θ Ι Κ Λ Μ Ν Ξ Ο Π Ρ Σ Τ Υ φ Χ Ψ Ω

(It's all Greek to me)

It is the evening and Dave and I have played draughts, or checkers as Dave insists on calling it. Once again, our parity in table tennis, and even arm-wrestling, is a concept that has deserted us and I am soundly beaten here in the quiet room.

'Aye lad, ye need to focus a bit mair! But I'm off to me bed after medication, mate. A'am knackered!'

After medication, Dave indeed heads for bed, but I have a sense that Malcolm wants to talk to me again, so I return to the quiet room with my Post-its and marker pens. I can feel Malcolm's presence: his message concerns the bigger picture about our descendancy – the bit that comes long before the traceable family tree; the bit that concerns the key genetic markers that define who we are, or more significantly, who we were.

I make sure I have the room to myself: I can feel the fuzzy ice cream sensation creeping across my scalp. I sit with my notebook and the Post-its on the low coffee table in front of me. I can feel Malcolm inside my head, telling me great Truths. This is not about Life, the Universe and Everything: this is about Life, Me and All My Yesterdays – my own particular place in the universe. We live in a mobile world; we are on the move; people move and mix; movement strengthens the gene pool. But, Malcolm tells me, we are also homing pigeons and, though our homing instinct is no longer near the surface of our consciousness, it is latent and can be awakened. It manifests itself most frequently in the yen we may feel to visit particular places: my own yen has always been for the distant North, to satisfy my fascination with people who live good lives close to and far beyond the Arctic Circle. I have travelled through Iceland; to the far North of Norway; to Europe's North Cape; to Hudson Bay; Greenland; northern Alaska; by terrifying sea journey to the Norwegian island of Jan Meyen, astride the North Atlantic Ridge, its simmering volcano so at odds with its bleak icy presence in the Arctic Ocean, north of Iceland; to Spitsbergen, where a few thousand souls practise science and coal mining just a nod and wink from the North Pole itself. Now I understand why I have done all this: it is the Viking genes that are calling me: reminding me that it is written in my code to survive at high latitudes.

Malcolm tells me I am descended from Thor himself, Viking God of Thunder, whose seed spread out across the Viking world in ancient times, even unto the furthest northern reaches of Norway and the other Arctic lands. The tendrils of that genetic web have never entirely let me go and hence I am called to return from time to time to recharge the subliminal DNA matrix. People these days talk all the time about things being 'in my DNA' but this, Malcolm informs me, is the true meaning of the expression and should not be taken lightly.

So much for the Viking side of my paternal descent, now feverishly recorded on a succession of green Post-its. I place an amber Post-it atop the greens: 'Caution – pause before proceeding!' it reads. Malcolm then drives me on; it is a whistle-stop journey back through the generations. We are with the marauding gangs demanding their protection money from those eking a meagre agricultural living in the unclaimed Borderlands between England and Scotland. We are cattle-rustlers. We have arrived here from the Celtic fringe, to where we travel back, to lands peopled from the Atlantic edges of Europe: my maternal roots are in the Isle of Man, where the Celtic tongue has withered from first-language use within the last century. Small wonder I have felt such fascination, not only with the Isle of Man, but also with Scotland's Western Isles, the Arran Islands, the Isles of Scilly.

It is time for another amber Post-it: Malcolm is telling me of the drivers that lie beneath today's great migrations: our northern European gene pool – fashioned from the ancient Britons, overlaid by such dynamic and diverse conquestorial interests as the Romans and those from the widest reaches of their empire, the Angles, the Vikings, the Normans – is in need of further refreshment. We have been becoming genetically complacent: lacking in ambition, drive and innovation. We have become lazy couch-potatoes. Evolution's response to this challenge is manifested in new migrations – from Central and Eastern

Europe, from Africa, from South America – of ambitious and dynamic people; strong, healthy, young people.

So, immigration isn't a question of whether you're liberal or just plain xenophobic: it's about survival of the species, so, you xenophobes, oppose it at your peril. At the peril of all of us; at the peril of the human species.

Time now for a red Post-it… Time for my readers to pause, take stock of the revelations they have read. Time for me to draw breath, sit up and permit the torrent of information flowing into my head from beyond the grave of my brother to subside.

As the cerebral electricity dies down, I collect the pile of Post-its, slip them into my notebook and head for my bed.

It is morning and the sensation that Malcolm has more to share with me is as strong as ever. The drugs mean that people here rise late: that's why we enjoy only the sparsest breakfast of cereal and toast, but our midday meal is more of a brunch as, everyone who is going to get going, has just about got going by noon. So, the 'private' rooms are still free right after breakfast and I can secure a bit more solitude, in which to receive Malcolm's messages. Today he is taking me into the areas in which ancestry and evolution pass into matters of language and Faith. You'll have understood already that we like to play word games in the office, but you probably need to have a better understanding of this. Typically, one of the team, usually Stella, will seize on some remark one of the others has made and this will then become the subject for a wordplay challenge. So, for example, Rog was talking about a project in Arizona and was telling the others how, around Phoenix, it ought, by rights, to be a desert but in reality so much of it is a manicured green, interrupted only by the turquoise of innumerable swimming pools – that's thanks to the bounteous waters of the Colorado River, syphoned from miles and miles away to lubricate the golf courses of Phoenix suburbia. But I digress, again. What I'm trying to get to is that Stella interrupts him and says, 'Ok guys, puns on deserts starting now!' It'll go something like this...

Stella: 'OK, I'll get you started – such a lovely day today... dunes bursting out all over, baboom!'
Jem: 'Atacama time of my life I might have found that funny...'
Rog (getting into the swing of it): 'Gobi an angel, Jem, and put the kettle on!'
Stella: 'Yes, I'd "erg" you to do that Jem...'
Me: 'What's "urg" supposed to mean?'
Stella: 'It's a type of sand dune...'
Jem: 'Wadi y'expect from a smarty pants like her?!'
Me: 'Sinai I should have seen coming, really;'
Stella: 'Is that a dirty cravat you're wearing, Rog?'
Rog: 'No, I don't think so...'
Stella: 'Oh, my mistake: I can see it's just some cacti...'
Groans all round: 'Cacti – cack tie...'

You get the picture?

But all this is important and I now realise just how important: Malcolm is telling me that word play lies at the very heart of the evolution of language. We can make a pun out of cacti and cack tie, which look quite different when written down, but the spoken word lived for many thousands of years before the written form decreed that the words 'pose, pause and paws', for example, should all be written differently, despite sounding so similar. When language first came to be recorded, it was down to some very clever people to find a way of rationalising the verbal spaghetti that had evolved over thousands of years of people playing with sounds and, later, words. These clever people discerned patterns and logic and called this grammar. Curiously, the older and 'more pure' a language was, the more complex this grammar. At the same time they had to find ways of expressing the subtle nuances of sound, devising symbols to define the consonants or, in some languages, pictograms to set down instead concepts deriving directly from the intended meaning, rather than from the sound used to express that meaning. Other systems created symbols to represent the vowel sounds too, and accentuations to convey subtle differences between these sounds.

What Malcolm is saying is that the formalisation of spoken language into the written form is a bit like rolling Tarmac on a gravel track: it obscures the subtle differences between the myriad stones that lie beneath the Tarmac: sharp pebbles, white pebbles, grey pebbles, small irregular stones, misplaced shards of glass. So, while paws, pose and pause may seem unconnected to us now, that does not necessarily mean that they don't share a connection that predates the written language form. Maybe we need to go back to our earlier evolutionary model: you know, the one in which the cat is the lookout, deep within the cave, and first to respond to the slightest sound or to the play of light on a lump of quartz in the cave roof. Perhaps our ancestors gazed at the mighty cat and constructed a whole lexicon around his movements, sounds and habits?

It's easy to see, in character-based languages, like Chinese, how the written form evolved from the idea that people wanted to express: the symbol for a horse, for example, evolved over centuries from something that was not unlike a picture of a horse.

Languages like Chinese represent an extraordinary feat of the imagination, in their traditional form at least. In languages written using the Latin or Cyrillic alphabets, once you know the individual rules of pronunciation you can work out roughly what a word will sound like simply by knowing the letters on the page. In Chinese, characters generally represent a whole word and you need to be able to recognise thousands of them to understand what's written. Interestingly, recognising what's written is no guarantee of being understood when you speak: words in widely differing dialects still have the same written character. Although the Communist state brought in a simplified version of many characters, Chinese remains a language in which there is no guaranteed correlation between what you read on the page and the corresponding sound made by a Chinese speaker.

I'm telling you all this because, in languages like English, the correlation between the written and spoken form has given rise to a degree of complacency. We have been lulled into thinking of written language as an absolute representation of what people are saying and, by inference, what they think. We've made the mistake of understanding language as absolute and unambiguous – in much the same way as economists tend to delude themselves that they are scientists, whose models accurately reflect the behaviour of both macro- and micro-economic worlds. Here're two words to illustrate how delusional this thinking is: Lehman Brothers.

Malcolm has been reminding me of why such absolutism in the field of languages can be not just erroneous, but actually dangerous: abstract thoughts can be bashed into shape to 'fit' the demands of the 'science' that is the written language. And that can be the start of the slippery slope… subsequent generations increasingly see the written word as absolute and ignore the sentiment, the wringing of hands, the agonising that made up the abstract process behind the creation of the 'summary' that is the written language. This erosion of meaning, he suggests, lies behind that great social disease of our times: the over-literal interpretation of religious texts. I understand that, as part of the process of saving the world through the unity of Science and Faith, it will be necessary to reinterpret the Scriptures; to understand the role of prophets; and to steer people away from literal interpretations of complex works of the imagination.

Given the complexity of this task, it is little wonder that I felt the need, earlier in my hospitalisation, to ask Michaela to bring to me all my language books: not just French and German, but other Romance languages, like Spanish, Portuguese and Italian; Nordic languages, like Faroese and Norwegian; languages like Welsh and Turkish, in which words change their form in different grammatical contexts; artificial languages like Esperanto. My only frustration has been that she didn't locate my Icelandic grammar: the one modern language that can reveal so much about the origins of our own tongue.

I realise that our modern communications technology now provides the opportunity not only to reinterpret the Scriptures in their original tongues, but also to disseminate their 'new meanings' to the widest number of people in the shortest possible time.

All this is a lot to take in so I must take some time in the garden.

Charlotte Turnbull had always enjoyed translating novels and bringing new discoveries about less familiar cultures to an English-speaking audience. Her especial love lay in translating Romanian novels from the Ceausescu period, which created such an unusual backdrop, against which mysteries could unfold. As not all that many linguists, with English as their first language, specialised in Romanian, she had the market pretty much to herself and, in her own limited sphere, had made something of a name. Why Romanian? Well, Charlotte's forté was the Romance languages, which share Latin as their common root. By some schools of thought, Romanian is among the closest living languages to the tongue spoken by the Roman conquerors in the time of the Empire, and it had therefore seemed logical to her that she should complement her Spanish and Portuguese with this language. So she took a job with a company facilitating the acquisition of holiday properties on the Romanian Black Sea coast, got a voluntary position working at a World Heritage Site, and spent two years learning the language and culture.

The death of her brother, Malcolm, had hit her hard and was the catalyst for a move back to the UK, which happened to coincide with the rise in interest in Eastern European crime and Gothic fiction that came to be dubbed Slavic Noir (although, of course, Romanian was not itself a Slavonic language). So she tended to think her move into translating fiction was pretty much 'meant to be'.

That said, she had been pondering a new challenge, and preferably one that paid a bit better, even before her brother, Victor, had made her an offer she was unlikely to refuse. Now she headed up the Aurora Foundation's Languages Division from her office secreted in a picturesque village on the Northumbrian coast, having built the operation from small beginnings just a few months after spending a day with Victor, in Yorkshire.

The scope of the Languages Division was quite wide, but at its core was the fundamental truth that no language in the world can wholly reflect something as abstract as belief and sentiment. The Foundation attached a lot of significance to this fact, on the twofold basis that language may not represent an abstract concept accurately in the first place, and also that language itself changes over time. So the Foundation saw language and all its vagaries as a significant contributor to what it called 'the problem with religion'. Religions, the Foundation contended, would generally share benign origins but would subsequently become corrupted by zealots who chose to misinterpret language and, worse, add new pieces of text to bring 'religious authority' to their oppressive and violent interpretations of Faith.

The Foundation promoted the view that Faith and Science could, should and would work as One to save the World.

Charlotte's job was to develop and manage the teams that were responsible for systematically working through the principal texts from all the major religions with the aim of reinstating the original words and meanings. This was one of the most sensitive areas of the Foundation's work, as well as one of its most important strands of activity, with the potential to ignite clerical fury, and it was for this reason that the Division was located in anonymous buildings far from the beaten track, with only the sea and sand dunes for immediate company.

A particular area of work that Charlotte enjoyed had only a tangential religious element – the development of a modern Northumbrian lexicon, combining previously published grammars of the historic language, closely related to Scots, with modern vocabulary and usage. The objective was to halt the decline of the regional tongue and to seek to give it the status of a written language with its own syntax and grammar, deriving from its original position as one of four languages spoken by the descendants of the Angle settlers.

It is a new day: one that, Michaela has told me, will include a visit from my other sister, Leanne. She is a few years older than me: a war baby, who grew up with Chris Barber, Elvis and the Everlys. She's had to work hard to get where she did, which was a pretty senior position in a leading architectural practice. There weren't that many women in the profession when she finished her training and there were even fewer who stuck at it and climbed the career ladder. Leanne had demonstrated in her life a degree of application and determination that surpassed that shown by her siblings. There had been a price, however. She had entered her first marriage in the expectation of an equal partnership and had not envisaged a situation in which her own career success would be a source of resentment for her husband. The reckoning had come when Leanne had said she would be happy to start a family, but only if she could get back into the career driving seat as soon as possible. Her husband could not share her vision. They went their separate ways and, so far as I know, Leanne never got seriously involved with anyone else until she was in her 40s, when she met her true soulmate, Dennis. It was getting too late for her to have her own children, but she inherited two lovely step-kids, a teenage boy and girl. They live in Shropshire, where they now share blissful retirement.

Because of the dual separations of age and geography, I'm probably not quite so close to Leanne as I am to Charlotte. I am not so close to either of them as I was to Malcolm. But bonds of fraternity (is this the right word when it involves both a brother and sister – maybe it should be fraternity AND sorority) are strong and I am very much looking forward to seeing Leanne, getting her take on Freemasonry in the building industry, and maybe even escaping from Priestley House for a little while.

It'll be the afternoon before Leanne makes it, but after breakfast I have a surprise visit from Stella. As it's outside visiting hours I agree to meet her over coffee in the main reception area.

Stella is excited: if visual confirmation were needed, she's doing that thing she does, twiddling the ends of her long back hair while she talks. Her hazel eyes are animated.

'Things have moved on, Vic. I have to go down to Slough for a meeting of Smart Ideas staff – I've spoken with the regional development agencies both here and in the North East because I want their help to showcase the kind of life that Smart Ideas people could have if they moved up…'

'Move up? Is that what we want? Can we trust them? Have they got good people?'

'That's what I intend to find out, Vic. They are, after all, part of the assets of what remains of Smart Ideas and we are uniquely placed to enable them to add value to the new business.'

'Can we afford them, Stella?'

'It's almost a case of can we afford not to have them, Vic. If we don't get at least some of the key staff on board, we'll struggle to maintain the flow of business and cash that we've already acquired.'

'What does Holbeck think of all this?'

'Ah, Holbeck,' says Stella. 'I don't think we need him any more Vic. I think we should ditch the Holbeck investment idea…'

'…and go on our own?' I reflected on the hours I'd spent negotiating with the man, manoeuvring him towards the point at which he might elect not just to put his good money into Persona Communications, but do so on terms that would allow me to salvage both self-esteem and a decent stake in the business I'd toiled so long to build up.

'Yes, I've worked through the cash flow figures with the Smart business integrated and once we've got through the squeeze around the cost of integration, we're laughing.'

It is the laughter-free period just round the first corner that worries me more, but Stella has anticipated my questions on this subject and produces from her bag a letter she's drafted to our suppliers. This amounts to a request to bear with us while get through the next three to four months – a period that will presage one of exciting growth and prosperity. In return for being part of this brave new future, Stella is asking suppliers to extend credit terms to 90 days for three months and 60 days for another two.

'I've talked to the main players and they'll run with it, providing we incur some pain too,' said Stella.

'What sort of pain?'

'A month's salary holiday…'

'Wow, will the guys do that?'

'Well, I've set up personal loans of £3,000 for everyone if they move their bank accounts to our corporate bankers, and then the company repays the money to them across six months, starting in three months' time.'

I am impressed, not least because I can't be sure that I could have persuaded the team to go for the salary holiday.

'OK, so who tells Holbeck?'

'Well, Vic, I think in the circumstances…'

'That has to be you, OK! I'm very grateful.'

I feel both proud of the team and truly vindicated for having placed so much trust in my Number Two. But now I have something I want to show her. I tell her about my plans for Two Flew Over the Cuckoo's Nest: The Unsequel and produce my laptop with the Prologue on it. She reads it in studied silence.

'Now take a look at the next bit,' I say, opening the file I have been working on since the Prologue. This is it:

1. (alpha)

Genesis

And in the beginning. And at the end. And at all the bits in between. As it was then and is now... Look, can we just suspend belief and disbelief for five minutes? OK? For the sake of argument, let's just take it as read that time is elastic, OK?

So here I am, sitting waiting for you at the Bistro at the Beginning of Time. Just over the road from the Restaurant at the End of the Universe. You know the one, Douglas Adams wrote all about it. But, then again, you probably doubt its existence. Well, it does exist, as sure as I am drinking a Pangalactic Gargleblaster with a brown ale chaser... Not...

And here am I (or there was I) at the mid-point of my life on Earth. It's a precise mirror of the time I was, am and shall also be at the beginning and end of the Universe. Follow me?? You at the back! Yes, you the 'scientist'!! The one with the closed mind... Let's make it easy for you reborn flat-Earthers... Here is the story of me and of my late brother and of the strange, so strange night when we supped together at the end of time.

Celestial time

I am the spirit of Thor, the God of Thunder and Lars Le Boeuf is my spiritual ward. As is Victor Turnbull, the author of these biographical words on the late and much mourned Bro. Much mourned, that is, in the Dreamtime. He writes of Malcolm, son of Tommy Turnbull. Me? I am a Viking; my legacy had, has and shall acquire strength and zest from other races and it has passed, passes and shall pass through many kingdoms and many generations; always the guiding cosmic hand that gives succour to those who inherit of my patrihood. Lars Le Boeuf is a Viking; he is of the ancient Kingdom of Northumbria; he is, on the maternal side, a Manx and Faroese Celt and, on his father's line, a Border Reiver. He is a Geordie.

[Author's note – Use this bit for context and sense of place]

Dream time

I am Lars Le Boeuf. I am in Room 13. In my room in the asylum it is ten past ten and 10 seconds on the tenth of October, 2010. It is always ten past ten here. My mother, God rest her soul, was born at 11 minutes past eleven on November 11, 1911. All is as it always is and always shall be. It is my lighthouse; my safe anchorage. I am in the cuckoo's nest now for almost two weeks. My brother is gone. At rest once more, the weight of the message he brought to me lifted from upon his celestial shoulders. I am 55. I shall live to be 103. My brother (the 'dead' one) says his baby's good to me, you know he's happy as can be you know, he said so! That baby is me. I have 48 years left to run.

How did I get here? I was conceived is the easy answer. But how did I get HERE?? That's a toughie...

Perhaps it's best if I begin at the 'front end' and go through things in terrestrial chronological order. The only difficulty here is that Dream Time is elastic, whereas as you, dear reader, will be perpetually preoccupied with the passage of hours, days and weeks. To try and make some kind of sense, therefore, I shall tell my story through the eyes of those who have witnessed the events to which I refer.

[Use this bit for ideas factory, including evolution]

Ancestral time

My name is Malcolm, son of Tommy Turnbull. I am, with my brother Victor, equal third of four. My sister was born in a primitive village in the south of England. It was just after the war, the second big one. The war ended when she was yet to become a twinkle in my parents' eyes. My brother and I were born back in the city of my mother's birth. My mother was and is, in universal time, Daisy Irvingsdottir (Le Boeuf). My mother left the city to escape the threat of war. She traded northern comfort and security (the city where I would spend my childhood escaped the war relatively unscathed) for a no-mod-cons existence at the edge of Salisbury Plain. There, my father, a conscientious objector, was made to walk predominantly in circles for the duration of that terrible war. My mother was unwell when my brother and I were born, her teeth taken from her by the blight of a fruitless and vegetable-free life, coshed by stress, fear, loneliness and thieving postmen who knew a box of contraceptives when they arrived by mail (or femail) to coincide with rare periods of military leave.

My mother's Christian faith engaged me and I began to lay my sickly infanthood to rest. And yet I can't say mine was an untroubled early life…

[use this bit for historic narrative]

'That's as far as I've got,' I tell Stella. 'But do you feel how the words have kind of flowed from my mind and out through my finger tips?'

'Yes, well. Yes. Wow! Yes. Amazing.'

I can't quite tell if Stella is being sincere. But why wouldn't she? After all, the quality of the prose and the importance of its content are self-evident.

'Buongiorno, Valentina!' I smile, upon seeing my Italian friend is back on reception duty, as I wave goodbye to Stella at the hospital doors. Valentina returns my smile. She's wearing a white cotton dress with a blue printed floral pattern. It buttons up the front and I notice it reveals just the tiniest hint of body shape. Her head sits high on the slender neck; her makeup is sparing, as ever – just a hint of eye shadow visible behind the rather unfashionable black-framed glasses. Her hair is pulled back and tied in a pony tail. A tiny blue coral stone dangling from each ear complements the eye makeup. Notwithstanding earlier conversations, I realise for the first time that she is not plain, as I had initially thought, but very attractive. An old Walter Matthau film suddenly springs to mind, in which Matthau's character is plotting to kill off the female lead, played by Elaine May (probably better known for her later direction than as an actress) because he wants to get his hands on her inheritance. Against his instincts, he saves her from a river in Amazonia. Then, if my memory serves me right, he lifts her spectacles and says something like: 'Why, Henrietta, but you're beautiful!' I'm sure that filmic moment must be the inspiration for countless subsequent takes in TV adverts for products as diverse and unconnected as gravy browning and bras.

'Come stai oggi?'

'Oh, you speak to me in Italian today! How nice!' Her smile melts me – disarmingly – and I'm struggling to find my next words, or indeed the best language to say them in, when there is an interruption from behind me.

'Don't listen to a word he says to you, love.' Valentina looks puzzled, but I know that voice and turn round, just as she's adding: 'He's a terrible smooth-talker, my brother!'

'Leanne! It's great to see you! You're looking well.'

My sister looks me up and down and I can read her thoughts – she's thinking: 'My brother's in hospital but he doesn't look ill…'

'You're looking pretty good, yourself,' she now ventures.

'Valentina, questa è mia sorella, Leanne.'

'I am very pleased to meet you,' smiles Valentina, whose attention is then taken by someone needing to ask directions to a hospital department.

I turn to Leanne. 'Would you like to go out somewhere? We'll have to go back to the ward so I can tell them I'm going out.'

'Will that be OK?'

'Yes, I'm a voluntary patient…' I lead Leanne back through the hospital gardens, taking in as usual the 'commando course' of sawn-off wooden stumps, leaping from each to the next, barefoot. I take her to the locked doors to the ward: from here there's a straight corridor leading directly to the ward reception, maybe 50 metres away. I have recently learned that it's possible to gain access to the ward by pressing a buzzer by the door and the Reception, on confirming who you are, can let you in. Originally I thought you had to attract attention by dancing up and down and waving your arms around. The staff seemed to find this amusing.

So, I take Leanne to Reception and introduce her to Ute, the German nurse, who – as usual – chastises me for speaking to her in German. 'Victor, I try to learn English, OK!?'

'Hast du Dave gesehen?' I ask.

'I am not answering you if you are not speaking English!'

But there is no need for her to answer: I can feel Dave's presence right behind me. I turn round and sure enough, there he is.

'Wow, that was like I had eyes in the back of my head: I could FEEL you were there somehow, before I KNEW you were there. It's like the kind of sixth sense that animals have...'

'Aye, ah feel that sometimes, n'aall,' says Dave, introducing himself to Leanne. 'We're good marras, me and yor kid: gonna save the world together!'

As he's talking, I seem to recall another snippet from my most recent communication with Malcolm. Didn't he say something to me about the expression of having eyes in the back of one's head? Something about latent skills that we, as humans, have lost because they are no longer crucial to our survival as a species. Suddenly the penny drops: I have often wondered why I have two small but easily discernible bumps on the back of my head, on either side, towards the base of my skull. I now realise that these are all that remains of the organs for perceiving what goes on behind us. I feel my skull-bumps and, sure enough, there they are. And they feel as though they've been busy: kind of warm.

'Dave, let me feel the back of your head...' Sure enough, he has the bumps too. And Leanne. I feel a few of the heads of the other guys milling around the reception area like they always do. At least half have the bumps. 'It's a gift,' I say. 'It's all we have left of our sixth sense that enables us to detect when there's something behind us that we need to know about, like danger. Our vestigial backward-facing radar system!'

'You are talking nonsense!' says Ute, as Leanne prods me and suggests it would be better not to get sidetracked if we want to go out.

'You better must then behave yourself,' says Ute, when I tell her that Leanne is going to take me out for a while.

'I will, I will.'

Leanne hasn't spent that much time in Yorkshire: when she's come up, she's tended to head straight for the family home in the North East and visits have been less frequent since our parents both died. So, I suggest that we head up Ripon way and take a wander round Fountains Abbey.

It's a long time since I've been to Ripon's World Heritage Site myself, and so I'm pleased with my idea as it will give Leanne and me the opportunity to explore the place together. We wander through the ruins of the abbey and on into the Georgian grounds of Studley Royal, pausing among ornate statues and watching the deer grazing. We climb up the little rise to Anne Boleyn's Seat, from where there's a view across an ornamental lake, down to the ruins of the Cistercian abbey. Leanne and I drink in the gentle view: we don't exchange many words.

It's over lunch in the café that I decide to tap Leanne's lifetime's bank of knowledge and experience. There are four things I'd like to know: did she ever come across instances of the corrupt award of public contracts? what does she think about PFI contracts? has she ever come across female Freemasons? has she ever come across the Norwegian hospital design that is the blueprint for Priestley House.

'It's a tough call, Vic. "Open" tendering is there precisely to avoid the old "jobs for the boys" system, but I'd be the first to acknowledge that any system can remain open to abuse. I can think of many occasions when tender awards seemed open to question, perverse even. Was it down to Masonic influence? Well I can't know the answer to that question because I'm not a Mason...'

'Could you be?' I ask.

'You mean can a woman be a Mason?'

'Yes.'

'Well, the popular belief is that they can't, but I've been invited once, so I guess popular belief is wrong!'

'You were invited!?'

'Yes, it was a few years ago, but a guy who owned a building business we'd worked with took me out for a drink and suggested it might be good for both of us if I were to join his Lodge.'

'No kidding! What did you say?'

'Well, part of me wanted to duck the issue and just say I'd think about it, but then my principles kicked in and I told him I really didn't believe it was morally correct and what was the point of a tender process if some participants effectively had a head start.'

'So what happened?'

'We never worked together again and I made two decisions. Firstly, the forces that he and his cronies represented were far too big for me to take on and, secondly, I no longer had any interest in public sector tenders.'

'So you think it's worse in the public sector?'

'On balance, yes, and – ironically – it's because the tender process is mandatory. The thing is that those running the tender often have a favoured outcome. This may be because one of those bidding is in their Lodge but, equally, it might simply be because they already have a view as to which bidder will do the best job, or offer best value for money. So they pervert the tender system by bending the subjective part, which is just about every bit of the process except price. That's the bit in which the bidders are given points for the quality of different aspects of their submission, so it's really quite easy to get the outcome you want, unless your preferred bidder has really screwed up. So, the top and bottom of it all is that there's often not much point in entering a tender process unless someone has tipped you the wink that you're the preferred bidder, or the people running it are in your Lodge.'

'So doesn't that happen in the private sector?'

'Yes, of course it can do, but private companies – unless their rules state otherwise – do have the option of awarding work without a tender process, which may seem less fair, but at least everyone knows what's going on. And I genuinely think that the Masonic movement doesn't have so much of a foothold in the private sector in general, because it is just so very anti-competitive and anti-efficiency. Of course, there are exceptions and I suspect it's rife in banking, some sections of the law and maybe some areas of finance.'

'So how did your company get work after your Masonic incident?'

'Well, I told the other senior partners what had happened and that process in itself flushed out one Mason in our ranks: he was told leave the Masons or leave the company, which may have been an illegal ultimatum, but it had the desired effect. And we built our business instead on building our contacts by legitimate means, mostly in the public sector, and by trying to be the very best and then evidencing it through awards and so on.'

'What about PFI?'

'Well, it's a neat way for governments to use smoke and mirrors to reduce their capital spend, but it's lousy value for money and will saddle future generations with debt and ensure the country has a diminishing stock of assets. I can't say if it's corrupt but I can say that there's only a tiny number of companies that seem to pick up these construction and maintenance contracts.

'As for Norwegian hospital designers, well I've spent a lot of time over there but not really in that field. Why do you want to know?'

'Well, I want to make a film about life in a psychiatric hospital and I thought the set could be a real replica of Priestley House, only without the shoddy building and the PFI maintenance contract hanging over it. Then, after we've finished the film, it could become the best psychiatric hospital in the country, maybe run by a charitable trust…'

'Wow, yes, what a great idea…' said Leanne.

After lunch I suggest we go back to our house in Ripon. It's the first time I've crossed the threshold since I was admitted, and it's nice just to relax and have a cup of tea. Then something unexpected happens: Michaela comes home early. She's clearly taken aback to find me at large in the community and, indeed, sitting in a chair in my own home.

'What on earth are you doing here?' she demands. Then, turning to Leanne: 'What the hell's he doing here?'

'Whoa, whoa, hold on,' I say. 'Leanne took me out to Fountains Abbey and I just thought it might be nice to set foot in my own home before they put me back behind bars…'

'Oh, stop being so melodramatic, you're not supposed to be here!'

'Now, hold on,' I say. 'I am a voluntary patient in a psychiatric hospital: I can walk out of there for good any time I choose, so who's the one who's being melodramatic?'

'Yes, and then they'd come round and section you.'

'Well, we don't know that. I'm past my crisis, but I'm happy enough to play the game while my recovery continues. But, for now, we have a guest, so sit down for five minutes until Leanne takes me back to Priestley House.'

Michaela sits down, if a little uncomfortably. 'Like I said, we've been at Fountains Abbey,' I say. Michaela rolls her eyes but I choose not to draw attention to this and switch the subject. 'Leanne and I had a nice lunch there and we had a nice catch-up.'

'Yes, Vic was asking me about the Masons,' says Leanne – a little unwisely, I suspect, given that Michaela's eyes are rolling again. But, taking my sister's cue, I say, 'Leanne has confirmed my suspicion that there are female Masons. And you know who might be one of them…'

I'm referring to the boss of one of our projects that began to go particularly pear-shaped when this particular woman took over, until the point at which we eventually lost the contract to another well-connected but, in my view, not particularly good supplier. What I know about our ex-boss includes information that she doesn't know that I know: I have chapter and verse on a previous business fiasco that cast serious doubt on her integrity. In the Persona reckoning of clients who have sinned, you may recall that this particular one falls into the category of wilful transgression and injury, the latter because she has repeatedly questioned my professional integrity and competence both verbally (slander) and in writing (libel).

'I've been looking at our client list and assessing whether

we might have a legal case against some of them over the way they've broken their contracts with us,' I tell Leanne. 'Now that my suspicion that the boss of one particular contract may be a female Mason may actually be correct, I think we can build a really strong case for libel and slander.'

Now it's Leanne's turn to roll her eyes... 'I'd be very careful where you go with legal action, Vic: in my experience the only people who consistently win are the lawyers.'

I could tell them both about the success of Persona's action against Smart Ideas, but that's something I really want to keep under my hat for the time being, so I defuse things by saying: 'Yeah, I guess you may be right.' Michaela looks suspicious: she's used to me arguing persistently these days.

After Leanne drops me at Priestley House and sets off on the long drive back to Shropshire, I'm keen to share some of my news with people who'll welcome it. John, the nurse, is coming towards me in the corridor, so I stop him and tell him all about Two Flew Over the Cuckoo's Nest: The Unsequel and about my plans for the film version of the book.

'So, we'll build an exact replica of Priestley House, only we'll build it well: properly. There'll be no doors that don't close right, no dangerous skirting boards, no clocks that don't tell the time,' I say. 'Then, when the film's finished and we don't need the set any more, we'll set up a charitable trust and open the best ever psychiatric hospital and there'll be jobs on the best terms for all you guys.'

'Wow Vic, lad, that's fantastic. I can't wait!' says John.

Then I see Dave and we exchange the comrades' good handshake, developed from arm-wrestling. 'I've made an important discovery in the battle against corruption,' I tell him. 'Women can be Masons!'

We agree that this is an important piece of intelligence in the war to save the world from diverse evils.

But there's another recent discovery that I badly need to share: the news of my ancestral family tree and confirmation of my paternal Viking line and maternal Gaelic one. Who better to share this with than Persona's business partners in Iceland and how better to do so than by text message?!

I rattle off the following message:

Hi Skúli, my dear Viking godfather. I am todl that u have been told that I am in hospital... Bad news is I may not get out till Mon, though enjoying says of home leave... V unlikely I will make conference in Reykjavík... But I do have a lot of ideas for shared cost promotional activity for the world's favourite Atlantic island.... Plus, I may have told u before aobut the strength of the force that pulls me northward. I feel I am Thor's Viking from the ancient Kingdom of Northumbria, with Faroese and Manx blood in my female lineage. This much I know... I am a Border REiver (robbers and killers after the Romans left Northumbria); and I shall c u soon in your wonderful land! All best wishes, Vic ... Cc to Knut and Hildur... Feel free to pass on to Birgit etc as do not have mobile numbers here...'

I hit Send without giving it a second read: after all, my mind is in tip-top form and there won't be any mistakes.

It is another day and once again I take a walk to the main reception to chat to Valentina while I wait for another special visitor. This one is my old pal Danny Mason, who's coming up from London. He's early, and arrives even before I've had my French and Italian practice.

'Danny, great to see you! Meet Valentina.'

'Buongiorno Signor Danny,' she smiles.

I already have plans for Danny: we're going to take lunch at one of my favourite restaurants in Harrogate. It's a place I often take clients and I've booked my favourite corner table. The team have been careful what they tell clients about my whereabouts during my hospitalisation and I figure it might do no harm if one or more were to just happen to see me, alive and well, at lunch in Harrogate.

In the event, there's no significant encounter at Bistro HG1: I only exchange a brief hello with one occasional acquaintance as we go in and with the restaurant staff, of course.

Sitting talking with Danny Mason, it occurs to me for the first time that someone, somewhere in his ancestry must have been a mason: a skilled artisan who crafted stone. Subconsciously perhaps, I have also chosen Maçon (French for Mason) as a possible pseudonym for myself in Two Flew over the Cuckoo's Nest: The Unsequel. Then there are my own maternal ancestors in Cumbria, the Stanleys (probably some generations after leaving the Isle of Man). The name Stanley means a stony place, or a rocky clearing.

'So Danny, my ancestors, the Stanleys, went up the quarry to hew the stones and your ancestors, the Masons, carved them to build great buildings! What a team, eh?!'

'Yeah, what a team!'

Diary of Stella de Weld, Wednesday September 15, 2010

Went into the hospital to brief Vic today. On the one hand he seems right on the ball: he fully understands all the issues around Smart Ideas and he's OK for me to go down to Slough and talk to the Smart Ideas staff and to present to them the opportunity for some of them to move north. I've also briefed him on our cash position and on my recommendation that we no longer need to bring an investor on board. Specifically that we no longer need Michael Holbeck.

On the other hand, however, Vic showed me the manuscript for his proposed book: the title is very funny – Two Flew over the Cuckoo's Nest: The Unsequel – but that's where the joke ends. Vic is very proud of what he's written but it reads like he's on speed or something. I didn't like to tell him, but it seriously freaked me out. But it's what I learned later today that is more worrying: Vic sent a crazy text message to all the guys in Iceland. Skúli copied it to me and it's just so embarrassing as Vic seems to have copied it to other people up there.

My sincere hope is that we can all hold this ship on course until Vic shows signs of returning to sanity.

CHAPTER 18

The Mystery of the Stones

Saturday October 2, 2021

'My castaway this week is a man whose name was scarcely known to the British public just a few short years ago: now it is synonymous with one of the UK's biggest and most influential companies, and a world leader in Internet technology and social media. He was born 63 years ago in the North East of England and is a passionate advocate of the North in general and of his beloved "Kingdom of Northumbria" in particular. Elevated to the House of Lords following his support of the Labour Party's leadership aspirant, Gloria Turnbull, he is of course the completely unrelated Victor Turnbull, now Lord Lindisfarne. Yet, just as the profile of his name has risen, this man and his family have increasingly withdrawn from the media spotlight; so it is a very real privilege, Lord Lindisfarne, to have you with us today…'

'Thank you, Kirsty,' replied Lindisfarne as the Cavolé played back the lozenge that Michelle had given Felix two days previously. Felix had slipped the lozenge into the sound system as the little car had left the M25. It was now pointed resolutely towards Devon and was already gobbling up the miles.

'So, Victor Turnbull, Lord Lindisfarne. How did you acquire the Midas Touch?'

'Well, to be honest Kirsty, I don't believe I have the Midas Touch. Indeed, I'm not convinced anyone in business possesses such a touch. I guess you're suggesting I have some sort of innate entrepreneurial ability, but I've always maintained that – above all else – the successful entrepreneur needs a really big slice of luck. The skill of the good entrepreneur lies in harnessing the natural resource that is luck to his or her own sound judgement.'

'And to what extent would you say you've made your own luck?'

'Well the paradox is that my "lucky break" came when someone tried to steal my business idea – you probably know the story. So I wouldn't say I made my luck at all, but I then used my own skills to turn that situation to my advantage, and exploited my own personal knowledge and contacts to turn it all into a great opportunity.'

'And the rest, as they say, is history, as your Aurora Group is now mentioned in the same sentence as the likes of Apple and Microsoft. Your first record?'

'I grew up just as the Beatles were rising to fame and Britain began its evolution from post-War austerity to the vibrant society we know today, so it has to be the Beatles, and this one is the first single I bought with my own money, and it also reminds me of family holidays in the Channel Islands…'

As the racy beat of Lady Madonna oozed into the Cavolé, Felix turned up the sound so it filled the vehicle. 'I like this but I'm not sure I've even heard it before,' he said to himself, reflecting that Lindisfarne was of a generation quite distinct from his own.

Lindisfarne then began recalling his teenage years and wild uninhibited parties, as he introduced a song by a band that was also named Lindisfarne, called Lady Eleanor. It was all about some goddess of the party circuit, Eleanor…

'So that's two ladies for the Lord already and we've barely started!' quipped Kirsty.

After that track, Kirsty broached what Felix judged was the difficult question: 'Your story, Lord Lindisfarne, is remarkable enough without considering the fact that the "moment of luck" you described earlier occurred when you were, shall we say, otherwise detained...'

'Indeed Kirsty, though I've never sought to brush over the fact that I was a voluntary patient in a psychiatric hospital when we found evidence of the industrial espionage and hacking that created the big opportunity that I spoke of earlier.'

'How was that experience?'

'It was many things, Kirsty: challenging, humbling and yet – at the same time – inspirational. You see, I believe some of civilisation's greatest artistic and intellectual accomplishments are the product of minds in a state of unusual stimulus. If we think of the Lakes poets for example – Wordsmith and Coleridge and so on – they took drugs to fuel their creative juices. Could we have enjoyed Sergeant Pepper without the Beatles' experimentation with mind-altering drugs? But at the same time it's my belief that people from history who were inspired by what they described as "visions" were undergoing a similar kind of experience – one stimulated not by drugs, but by the adrenaline surfeit associated with a manic episode, like my own. People like Joan of Arc, St Paul on the road to Damascus...'

'Are you condoning illegal drugs?'

'No, not at all: I'm just drawing a parallel between an artificially induced state of euphoria and the kind of naturally occurring euphoric state that I and many others have experienced; and I'm thinking of the high incidence of mental illness, including bipolar disorders in particular, among creative people.'

'Your next record.'

'My God, she's cut him off at the most interesting bit,' thought Felix as Lindisfarne chose a Van Morrison number that reminded him of his university days and teenage love. It was The Way that Young Lovers Do, from an album called Astral Weeks.

As the Cavolé maintained course, the miles continued to flash past in the opposite direction, and Lindisfarne's selections came and went: a Senegalese one called Lale Kouma, by Lamine Konté, which Lindisfarne said recalled carefree times when he lived in the south of France; the Dire Straits ballad, Romeo and Juliet, from his early career, and a song by The Travelling Wilburys, featuring, Felix acknowledged, a towering vocal performance by the late Roy Orbison, You're Not Alone Any More.

'But of course, Lord Lindisfarne, "alone" is precisely what you will be on your desert island. How do you think you'll cope?'

'Well, Kirsty, when I was ill, my partner, Michaela, now of course Lady Lindisfarne, was a tremendous support and it was incredibly difficult for her, because she had her own challenges and here was I, behaving like a crazed madman, and she had to both temper my excesses and somehow also acknowledge that I was dealing with some very real events that would prove life-changing for both of us. So she was, is and always shall be my soulmate and it will be very hard to be without her, but – at the same time – I am also a very self-sufficient person at ease with my own company, so I guess I'll get on OK.'

'You have over the last couple of years rather shrunk from the limelight and the media reports say that you and Lady Lindisfarne are spending more and more of your time engaged in delivering the ambitions of the Aurora Foundation, your company's charitable arm.'

'Indeed, that's so: we've been building a lot of partnerships with other charities in sustainable development, research…'

'It's suggested that some of your work in the religious sphere hasn't won you many friends.'

'That's true, Kirsty. We do promote an interpretation of religion that seeks to take faiths back to a moment before they became autocratic and dogmatic. Most religious doctrines began life in just such a way, but they have pretty much all at some point been subverted by those who would seek to impose them by violence and indeed defend them by violence. We don't believe religion is "wrong" per se, but want to remind religious people of the fundamental values of tolerance, understanding and human kindness.'

'That sounds all very reasonable: who are your enemies?'

'They are many and varied, Kirsty, and that's why you don't see so much of us. Michaela and I live our lives on the move and away from the public glare.'

'Next record.'

'This one's an old ballad to remind me that love and separation can be painful and to recall to me a place that's very dear to my heart. It's The Waters of Tyne, sung here by Kathleen Ferrier. Although Sting and Jimmy Nail have done it very nicely more recently, Ferrier had a truly magical voice.'

Felix certainly hadn't heard this one before and he vowed to find out more about Kathleen Ferrier when he reached his destination.

'You're a great lover of the North of England, Lord Lindisfarne. I suppose your desert island will be rather different...'

'I'm sure it will! And so I think for my final choice I must select one of my favourite Kathryn Tickell tunes. Kathryn is a great Northumbrian and was pretty much single-handedly responsible for ensuring that we can all enjoy the wonderful tones of her favourite instrument, the Northumbrian small pipes, today. This one's called the Wild Hills o' Wannie and it will take me back to the rolling heather uplands of the Cheviot Hills.'

For his book, Lindisfarne chose Proust's À la Recherche du Temps Perdu – in Search of Lost Time. 'For two reasons: one, it will keep me busy, trying to understand it and, secondly, I'm fascinated by questions of time and its passage or otherwise. Does time flow, or is it simply something that's all around us?'

'I don't know, Lord Lindisfarne. Perhaps you can tell us? And for your luxury?'

'Well, I know you won't allow me a computer and Internet access, so maybe I'll have a nice hot whirlpool bath...'

'On a desert island, with hot sun and warm water all around?'

'Oh, OK then, I'll have an expensive food processor instead, with solar power.'

'It shall be yours: thank you, Lord Lindisfarne, for sharing your desert island discs with us today.'

'Thank you, Kirsty.'

For the first time, Felix felt he had enjoyed a glimpse into what it was that made the man behind the organisation that had stolen his love, tick. And, although Lindisfarne was his elder, Felix found himself feeling a certain empathy, not least because he too was of the view that luck was an indispensable catalyst in the formula for business success. His mind slipped to the telephone conversation he had had with Wendy before their recent reconciliation: the one about the stone circle and phone call to Wendy's bisexual sister in Aberdeen.

Felix then had to grasp the steering wheel and pull the Cavolé back on track as his heart skipped a beat, for – bang on cue – a huge circle of giant stones had appeared in his view, just slightly to the right of straight ahead. As the Cavolé veered left and the monument swung behind him to the right, Felix made an impulsive decision, just in time to take the next exit, for the Stonehenge World Heritage Site.

The Cavolé pulled up close to the smart and still quite new visitor centre, but Felix had research to do first: he reasoned that if he could put himself into the mind of Lord Lindisfarne, it would significantly help in his quest to locate Jameela.

He had hoped for a more definitive answer, but his VSP told him that there were more than 1,300 known stone circles in the British Isles and more than a hundred in North East Scotland alone. Three in other parts of Scotland, however, did seem to stand out: two in Orkney and one on Lewis, where it was among a large number of other smaller such circles. There was only one thing for it, and Felix found himself engaged in an exercise identical to one that the then plain Victor Turnbull had carried out, in Orkney, a little over 11 years previously.

Anne Buchanan was, of course, Wendy's older sister – by more than ten years – and Felix reckoned that Lindisfarne must be another decade older than that, maybe more. Despite the passage of time, Anne Buchanan was as visible on the Internet to Felix as she had been to the then Victor Turnbull in the moment of madness and delusion that, it was now clear, had been a curtain-raiser to his time in psychiatric hospital.

Here goes, thought Felix as he pressed the phone link on his VSP.

'Anne Buchanan!'

Bingo! thought Felix, as he heard the bright, efficient voice, which, he sensed, had more of a Scottish overlay than he'd last remembered.

'Hello, Anne,' he said. 'Bit of a voice from the past here; Felix Merryweather, Wendy's friend...'

'You mean the guy who's been fucking with my sister's head for the last several years?'

'Yeah, I guess, though we have made our peace...'

'Yeah, sure, of course you have, because she'd never do what I keep telling her to do and cut you adrift completely.'

Oh dear, here we go again, thought Felix. Perhaps this wasn't such a good idea after all...

'So, what do you want, Mr Merryfucker?'

Felix got the idea that Anne Buchanan must not only have her own office, but one with pretty soundproof walls, as he had to hold the VSP away from his ear.

'Very little, Anne, and I'm sorry to trouble you with this, but I understand from Wendy that you once visited a stone circle with Victor Turnbull...'

'What the fuck is all this about? What is it with these bloody stone circles and Victor Fucking Lord Bloody Lindisfarne who, incidentally, is every bit as much of a jerk as you are?'

'I'm trying to understand him?'

'Well good bloody luck on yer, laddy. For the record, it was Callanish, if that's your question. Now goodbye, and don't call again.'

Felix began to wonder what hope he ever had of getting inside Lord Lindisfarne's head if he could so badly misjudge the minds of people he actually knew. He got a picture of the Stones of Callanish on his VSP and took the little shuttle to Stonehenge: the two monuments really were very different and, Felix recognised, different again from the two big circles on Orkney. He sat and contemplated the conundrum of the Neolithic circles and indeed the wooden Mesolithic ones they may have superseded. How could those who built them have had the wherewithal to move such huge stones? How could they possibly have acquired the knowledge of the cosmos implied in their structure? He reflected on Lord Lindisfarne's closing Desert Island remarks about time and thought of some of the documentaries he'd seen about quantum physics and other elements of scientific rationale that were yet to be fully formed; the concept of Time as something that's all around us, rather than something linear. It was all as wondrous and mystical to him as the stars and their alignment must have seemed to the builders of Stonehenge. Was this what Victor Turnbull had been thinking in his confused state, at the Ring of Brodgar?

Over lunch in the visitor centre, Felix thought about finding out more about Kathleen Ferrier and was alarmed to discover he must have left his VSP by the monument, during his moment of contemplation. He was particularly perplexed as it was so very unlike him to do something like that. He got up from his table and moved to tell the serving staff to hold his Portland crab sandwich and soup while he headed back to retrieve the VSP.

'Excuse me!' Felix spun round. 'I think you left this at Stonehenge,' said a middle-aged woman, holding his VSP in her hand. Had he turned just moments sooner, he might have noticed that the woman had shown more than a passing interest in the content of the VSP and noticing that might, in turn, have helped explain some of the events that would follow over the coming days and weeks.

However, he said: 'Ah, thanks so much! I was just on my way back to find it – not really like me at all to do that. I can prove it's mine, if you like: just run through the camera roll...'

'No need for that: I recognise you, but I didn't quite manage to jump on the same shuttle back as you. Anyway, I'm getting used to this now.'

'Really?'

'Yes, I've been visiting stone circles for years and I can almost guarantee that every time I do, someone will leave an expensive phone, or a camera or something behind. It must be something about the incompatibility of modern gadgets with a mystical past, or something. I even reunited that Lord Lindisfarne with his camera on Orkney once, though he wasn't Lord Lindisfarne back then: I only realised it was him years later, after he got famous…'

Reunited with his VSP, Felix looked up Kathleen Ferrier: hers was a sad story – her marriage to a bank manager in the Cumbrian town of Silloth ended unconsummated, and she died of cancer at just 41. Felix reflected that life can be cruel and it demands that we act quickly and never do tomorrow what we can reasonably do today. With which he got into the Cavolé, selected the next item on Michelle's lozenge, and headed for the A303 and Exeter.

'And now it's time for Woman's Hour, with Jenni Murray.'

'Good morning and welcome to Woman's Hour, where today I'll be talking to Michaela Lady Lindisfarne, wife of the celebrated peer and Internet entrepreneur, about the challenges of being the woman on the outside when your husband or partner is in psychiatric hospital.'

Could be interesting, thought Felix.

'So Michaela, can you take us through the events that led to your husband being hospitalised? It must have a been a very difficult time,'

'It was Jenni, and perhaps the worst thing is that, at first, you don't quite realise it's happening. Vic would have some days when he was acting really quite normally and then on others it appeared he was losing touch with reality, and the problem is that you cling to those good days and persuade yourself that things are getting better when, in fact, they're actually getting worse.'

'Your husband suffered what's called a manic episode, which

of course could be a precursor to more long-term mental illness, such as bipolar disorder.'

'Yes, indeed. In Vic's case it seems the chemistry of his brain was upset by many many nights with very little sleep, combined with a restriction to his ability to process his own waste, if you like, after he suffered a minor injury.'

'How did that injury occur?'

'It was very silly, Jenni, we were out walking near our home in Yorkshire and he decided to demonstrate a gate vault to me, only the gate collapsed beneath him and he took a rather painful blow to somewhere quite delicate.'

'Goodness me, Michaela, my eyes are watering just thinking about it.'

'Indeed, though we did laugh about it at the time… The thing is that, during those sleepless nights, Victor was actually very nice and considerate: he seemed always to be thinking about me, leaving little billets-doux for me to find in the morning and so on, and I guess that fuelled what I later came to recognise as my complacency about his condition.'

'So how did he eventually come to be admitted to hospital?'

'Well, his behaviour began to get more and more erratic: he would only talk to people if he could watch the movement of both his own and their lips in a big mirror, for example, and he began to think he was a lion.'

'A lion!? Did he threaten to eat you?'

'No, but he did roar a lot and that's when I called the NHS Crisis Team for the first time. That was also when he was first given drugs for his mania: olanzapine, to calm him down, but with hindsight, he was already too far gone and the dosage just wasn't sufficient.'

'So what happened next?'

'Well, the Crisis Team came back with Vic's GP and the idea was that he was going to be sectioned. Vic thought I was in a conspiracy with all of them to have him taken away, but in reality I was negotiating desperately for a more benign solution, for him to go to hospital voluntarily.'

'You say a more "benign" solution... what exactly do you mean by that?'

'Well, if you're sectioned under the Mental Health Act, it's a bit of a one-way ticket because you then have to be "unsectioned", so to speak, before you can leave hospital again. This means that a psychiatrist is putting his head on the block and he's not going to discharge a patient if there's so much as a thread of doubt about their condition. And, of course, there's real stigma attached to being sectioned.'

'Indeed! So how was it once Vic was in hospital?'

'Well, for him, it was a godsend: he thought he was at Butlin's and spent his days playing table tennis and kicking a ball around. But, again, he was convinced I was in some sort of conspiracy with the doctors and nurses to keep him "inside" as he called it, when he thought he was perfectly fit to come home. The thing is that I'd asked the Crisis Team right at the beginning how long it was all likely to go on for, and they kind of shook their heads and frowned and said they remembered one case where someone got better in as little as six months, so – to me – it just seemed like a life sentence: my world was falling apart and, all the while, I was trying desperately to present a normal façade at work and everywhere.'

'Did people know Vic was in a psychiatric unit?'

'Well, close friends knew, yes, but not his work colleagues other than his immediate team and, you know, I practically begged the staff to take his mobile phone from him as I was just terrified who he might call at some dreadful hour. You see, for people like Vic, professionals, hospitalisation is as much about protecting them and their reputations from themselves as it is about protecting the rest of us from them.'

'I suppose some of it must seem a little amusing in retrospect?'

'Well, you know, Vic was very plausible and charming and he persuaded an old friend, Danny, that they should take lunch at one of his favourite restaurants: I was furious with Danny about that afterwards as so many of his business contacts could have seen him. And then there was the day he led his sister a right merry dance and he ended up with a set of bagpipes that I thought he'd paid £2,000 for.'

'Bagpipes?! Well it sounds like that one takes the proverbial biscuit!'

'Yes, the Northumbrian small pipes – they're a more tuneful cousin of the Scottish ones. He was convinced he had superpowers and would be able to play like a maestro as soon as he got them out of the box.'

'And could he?'

'In a word, no. No more than he was the best table tennis player in the world or had solved all the major challenges in quantum mechanics, or was going to save the world in seven days…'

'All of which he believed?'

'Give or take… They call it grandstanding, I believe.'

'The psychiatric people? But of course in your husband's case, it wasn't just about "delusions" of grandeur, was it?'

'No, it wasn't: there really was something very, very big going on, in respect of which I guess I have to be thankful now that they didn't oblige me by confiscating his phone.'

'Which, of course, was the fact that he found out his business had been hacked into and it was his legal recourse in response to that illegal act that enabled his company to make its first big leap forward.'

'Yes, his Persona Communications company was the victim of hacking by a rival company in Reading and, despite being in hospital, Vic, with his number two, Stella de Veld, was able to instruct lawyers and thereby seize the assets of his rival.'

'And all this happened when he was suffering from mania, from delusions.'

'Yes, that's the paradox and that was another huge difficulty for me, because it was actually very hard to distinguish between his manic behaviour and the quite rational behaviour around instructing lawyers and so on.'

'Indeed. Extraordinary. Was there a risk that you might have jeopardised all this because you thought Victor was just "grandstanding".'

'A very real risk, yes.'

'And so, when your husband was doing all this wheeler-dealing, did you take that as a sign he was getting better?'

'To be truthful, a lot of it I didn't know about and nor did the team at the hospital. He had a quiet spot he went to in the hospital grounds to make all his phone calls, and Stella would come in to update him every couple of days and, in the end, the whole thing happened very quickly and, quite soon after he came home, that's when he and Stella held the first show-round for the new people who came in from the other company.'

'The decision as to when Victor came home, because he hadn't been sectioned, was very much down to you in the end.'

'It was, yes, and here I have the utmost admiration for the staff at Priestley House…'

'That's the psychiatric hospital Victor was in?'

'Indeed, yes, the staff at Priestley House never put me under any pressure to free up a bed for them or whatever. It was always "Are YOU ready for him to come home?". "Will YOU manage OK if he comes home?".'

'So how long after he was admitted did this happen, and were things OK?'

'He came home for a "day visit" after two weeks and when I rang and told the hospital he was OK, they said he could stay the night.'

'Ooh, lucky you!'

'Indeed, it was a bit like treats for teacher! Then a few days later, he came home on extended leave that ran right through to the following Sunday, and then he only went back to the hospital to discharge himself on the Monday.'

'Tell us just a little about what happened next.'

'Well, one of the big problems upon discharge for people who have suffered a manic episode is the "coming-down". It can be very depressing, finding out – as Vic put it – that you don't actually have superpowers after all. But, of course, in his own case, he didn't need superpowers, because his whole world had just taken off big time.'

'And could he manage that?'

'He was quite delicate for a time, so he delegated all the real graft to Stella.'

'Is he at risk of another episode?'

'Statistically speaking, yes, he is certainly at risk, but there's been no threat of a relapse in the years since, and his experience was very unusual in that it was really a very brief, if quite severe, episode, caused by a physical injury. So, once the brain chemistry was righted by the drugs and once he re-established a sleeping pattern, he was OK.'

'Well, and long may that be so. Thank you so much, Michaela Lady Lindisfarne. And Lady Lindisfarne will be back on the programme later this week to talk about some of the work that her own and Victor's charity, The Aurora Foundation, is doing to ease religious discrimination against women. And now let's talk about sex…'

The remainder of the drive to Exeter was uneventful and Felix decided to save the second episode of Michaela on Woman's Hour for another time. Felix had found a decent room-only rate at the Rougemont, in the city centre, which offered free WiFi and was only a couple of minutes from his morning rendezvous at Carluccio's.

He set up his new TopCat2021 Smartmail account and logged onto Blather. There were by now lengthy piblah *ficelles* on πlesdisparus¿ and πlespoir¿ involving the smartmail addresses, Shell2021@ and Carty@. No-one had as yet inserted any trigger words, such as Aurora, or names of those who had disappeared and Felix judged it would be worth letting these *ficelles* run their course a bit longer rather than compromise the identity of participants on the open Internet.

Shell2021@: Snuggle-bunny disappeared at dawn

Carty@: Hear Catman likes jellied eels

Shell2021@: Yes, gone south west to meet the one who came back

Carty@: I knew that one. Good kid. Interested to hear her views on daybreak

And so it went on… Felix added: 'In city of David, Italian breakfast in prospect. A funny thing happened at big stones today.' He then reworded it to: 'Funny thing happened at big stones today; now in city of David; Italian breakfast in prospect.' This he attached to the second *ficelle*, without being especially sure what implications, if any, this might have.

Opting for an early night and Match of the Day in bed, Felix was surprised when his VSP rang.

'What the hell are you doing, taking the piss out out of my sister?'

'I'm sorry, is that Wendy?'

'Yes, of course it's Wendy, how many other women's sisters have you been harassing today?'

'None at all, and that includes your sister, who was actually pretty unpleasant to me.'

'Why would she be anything else, you moron?'

'Well, with hindsight, that's a question I maybe should have asked myself before I rang her.'

'So what were you playing at?'

'I was at Stonehenge and I remembered what you said about Lord Lindisfarne and the stone circles and I was trying to get inside his head…'

'My god, Felix, if you only spent some time sorting out the inside of your own head or understanding the inside of mine… What did you say to her?'

'I asked her which stone circle Lindisfarne was at.'

'She thought you were having a laugh at her expense.'

'Well, I wasn't, but I accept it wasn't such a great idea.'

'And did you form any conclusions?'

'No, but something a bit strange happened: I left my VSP by Stonehenge and this woman found it and brought it back to me in the visitor centre and then she told me that kind of thing was always happening to her at stone circles.'

'As you do!'

'As I say, she said she was always finding phones and cameras and things that people had lost at stone circles, and one of those people was Lord Lindisfarne, and the stone circle was in Orkney, so it must have been the day he rang your sister, Anne.'

'Hmm. I agree, that IS strange. Strange, but probably of no consequence whatsoever, so I wouldn't lose much sleep if I were you.'

'I don't suppose I shall. So are we OK?'

'OK, yes, but no more than that. Good night!'

And with that she was gone.

Sunday dawned sunny and slightly autumnal and Exeter, Felix thought, looked pretty good as he left the Rougemont at 9.15 to ensure he was at Carluccio's in good time. A handful of diners were already seated when he entered, but no single females, with or without pink hair grip and Barbour jacket. He ordered a cappuccino and picked up a Sunday newspaper (reflecting that the final demise of print media, so long predicted, seemed no more likely now than it had ten years previously). He chose a table as far as possible from the other diners, while still reasonably easy to spot for someone coming in from the street. Which is precisely what somebody did, just moments after Felix had taken his seat.

The first thought that struck Felix when the woman in the Barbour jacket came in was that he couldn't have seen any pictures of her in those reports on the Internet that he knew he had seen, but which had so infuriatingly since disappeared. Had he seen her picture, he would naturally have remembered that Emily Black was, well, black. The woman's thick black hair was gathered up at the back and held together by a large pink hair grip: it had to be her. Felix half stood and gestured to her to join him. Emily smiled, unwound the voluminous woolly scarf she was wearing and sat down.

'Coffee? Breakfast?' asked Felix.

'Both please.' Then she paused and said: 'I'd better just check:

you are Felix Wotsisname, aren't you? Just before I tell you my life story.'

There's something deeply pleasurable about taking breakfast out on a Sunday: this is the day it's permitted to take your time and indulge yourself with fine Italian coffee and lovely pastries; flick through the news; do the crossword; chat casually as though at home.

Felix and Emily blended easily into the milieu and could have been just another youngish couple indulging in breakfast out, although the eagle-eyed might have spotted a greater intensity to their interaction.

They hadn't wasted long before Felix cut to the chase: 'So, you worked for Aurora, disappeared, vanished from the Internet and all social media – seemingly ceased to exist – then reappeared and asked everyone what all the fuss was about, because you'd just been away travelling.'

'Correct.'

'So do you want to paint a bit more of a picture for me.'

'I don't know, Felix. How do I know I can trust you? How do I know you are who you say you are and your motives are what you say they are? Maybe you're just another journalist.'

'Maybe I am, though I can tell you categorically that I'm not.' He looked straight into her eyes; he saw a sadness and vulnerability but he also saw sincerity. What he didn't know was that the last person who had looked at Emily in this way – seeming to gaze directly into her soul – was none other than Lord Lindisfarne himself. Instead of looking away, she returned the stare and, in turn, saw an idealistic man in his 30s; a man who would speak it as he felt it.

After what might have seemed to an onlooker like an extended exchange of mutual love and admiration, Felix and Emily averted their gaze simultaneously. 'It's OK, I know enough. I can trust you,' said Emily. She took a big sip from her large cappuccino, wiped the froth from her top lip with the back of her hand, drew breath and said: 'I'm going to have to start at the beginning.'

Emily shuffled her chair towards the corner of the table so

she could lean towards Felix, who then mirrored her movement so Emily could talk in a soft voice that wouldn't play that trick that voices sometimes can in a crowded place, like when you're sitting there minding your own business and suddenly a sentence flies through the ether and reverberates in your ear. It's invariably something you weren't intended to hear and which perhaps you didn't want to hear: 'Yes, our Cynthia's thrush just never seems to get better.' 'Jack's had a back, crack and sack: smooth as a baby's arse.' Emily's conversation with Felix, however, was not going to travel any further.

'You might not have noticed, Felix, but I'm not really from round here; I don't necessarily fit in. I was adopted and my adoptive parents are very lovely and they gave me a wonderful upbringing. I love them dearly, but you can't escape reality. I know who my birth mother is and I have met her and I understand why she felt she had to give me up. She had poor health, poverty, mental illness and an abusive man in her life and, although giving me up was the hardest thing she could do, she did it for me.

'So I recognise that I'm what some black people call a choc ice or a coconut: I'm a white person wrapped up in a black skin, though it's not a term I like, because it just stereotypes people and I don't see anything actually wrong with being like me, providing you're comfortable with it. But I wasn't all that comfortable: I felt both loved and rejected at the same time and that's something I carried through into my 20s, after I left university. As you know, I ended up working for Aurora and I was one of the company's rising stars and that brought me to the attention of the main man, Lord Lindisfarne himself.

'Lord and Lady Lindisfarne – Vic and Michaela – asked me to start working for the Foundation. It was tremendously exciting: I was helping to run a reforestation programme in Amazonia, working in partnership with a big charity started by a rock star. Then one day I got summoned to a workshop I was told was for Aurora Foundation team leaders. It was in a Foundation property in Barbuda, in the Caribbean, and was all a bit hush-hush. You probably already know that the Lindisfarnes spend their lives between islands, though you may not know exactly why. Anyway, it was long, long journey. Firstly, I had to go by river boat to where I could get an air taxi to Manaus, then from there it was a 14-hour trip to Antigua, with a six-hour layover in Miami. Then I had to overnight in Antigua and catch a tiny plane to Barbuda the following morning. I was pretty shattered when I arrived and I was surprised to find it wasn't a workshop at all: there was just me, three other Aurora Foundation workers at my sort of level, and Lord and Lady Lindisfarne themselves.'

'Who were the other three?'

'I can't tell you that Felix: they're still with what's called the Inner Circle, though nobody knows about the Inner Circle.'

'You mean, like nobody expects the Spanish Inquisition?' chipped in Felix, recalling a celebrated episode he'd seen from the old Monty Python TV series.

Emily looked puzzled: 'You've lost me.'

'Sorry, carry on!'

'OK, so I found myself at this former luxury resort on Barbuda, which is, incidentally, notwithstanding the efforts of Hurricane Irma, still officially the least spoilt island in the Caribbean, not to mention one of the hardest to get to. That's important, because, as I said, the Lindisfarnes really don't like being easy to find. So, there was no workshop, as such, just a series of discussion groups on various topics and Vic and Michaela, the Lindisfarnes that is, kind of came and went on the periphery of it all. Then after a couple of days I was summoned: I had to go, alone, to the Lindisfarnes' suite, and Vic said we'd all been brought to Barbuda to assess our potential to join the Inner Circle. The Inner Circle comprises the most trusted members of the Aurora Foundation team and absolute discretion and loyalty are essential. The Inner Circle is responsible for the delivery of aspects of the Foundation's work that are wholly outside the public's gaze and, indeed, outside any form of scrutiny, so you absolutely have to believe in the rightness of these projects if you're going to be in the Inner Circle. Our activities during those few days on Barbuda had been designed precisely to establish whether we would identify 100 per cent with the goals and objectives of the Inner Circle projects and would do whatever was necessary to defend them.'

'It must have all seemed a bit scary: what do these projects do?'

'It was scary: I can still feel my palms sweating now, but I'm sorry, I can't tell you about the projects. I am compromising myself and breaking promises even just by meeting you today and certainly by disclosing geographical locations and that kind of thing.'

'OK, I understand and I really appreciate all that. So what was the deal.'

'Well, the deal was simple: on the face of it there was a choice – I could join the Inner Circle and enjoy a really challenging, stimulating and useful life or I could decline and return to my old role in Amazonia.'

'I'm guessing it wasn't that simple.'

'No, it wasn't: it was subtle, but Vic had manipulated things so that saying No would be really very difficult. It's partly just about this way he has of looking at you, like your eyes are just a window and he's looking right into your very being. I think you understand what I'm saying, don't you? And the other thing was that saying Yes came with a big down-side, because in saying Yes, you immediately "disappeared", both in a real sense and, almost more importantly, in the virtual world. But despite all that I was very attracted to the offer, because it brought with it a very real sense of family and belonging and that really appealed to a vulnerable side of my character. So I said Yes and within hours, no minutes even, it was as if someone had plugged a big vacuum cleaner into the Internet and sucked out every single reference to Emily Black. To all intents and purposes I no longer existed.'

'And then at some point you changed your mind about it all.'

'Precisely so, Felix.' (Felix reflected that this was a slightly unusual turn of phrase and wondered how Emily had acquired it.) 'I was becoming disillusioned with some of the projects and no longer felt able to identify 100 per cent with them. In fact, I thought some were at best misguided and at worst dangerous and possibly immoral. I really felt the Foundation was involved in things that were much more complex than its own interpretations and that it might be riding for a fall. And I really missed my mum and dad!'

'So you reappeared. Was that easy?'

'No: there are terms and conditions and one of them is to deny in your own mind that what you know happened actually did happen. And you must never talk of what you know or do anything that might compromise the Foundation's projects.'

'So why are you here today?'

'Two reasons: firstly, my concern about some of the Inner Circle projects has actually grown since I left, and the more I think about things the more I think I have a moral duty to open the door a tiny bit in the hope that maybe someone like you can put a foot in it and perhaps allow the light eventually to shine...'

'Eloquently and flatteringly put, Ms Black, if I may say so.'

Emily continued as though she hadn't heard Felix's comment: 'And the second reason is that I know Jameela and I think she needs to put the fulfilment of her soul before the fulfilment of her mind.'

'Meaning what?'

'She's more a prisoner of her background than even I am of mine: her upbringing makes her feel guilty for just wanting to be happy, so if ever there's a threat that she might be happy she'll do something perverse and then blame it on fate or God's Will, yeah.'

'I think I know what you're saying... Do you know where she might be?'

'I can only guess and I can't tell you what those guesses might be.'

'I believe she was in India very recently. In Ahmedabad.'

Emily visibly started and moved her face away from Felix's, her eyes wide. 'How on earth do you know that?'

Felix told her about the postcard and about Katie Brown.

'A postcard? That's a shocking breach and yet so simple. It may mean that Katie has doubts too. Ahmedabad is where the Faith Team have their initial training, yeah.'

'The Faith Team? What's that exactly?'

'I'll tell you only that it's about replacing religious dogma with tolerance, which sounds all very well, but in practice it can have nasty side-effects and that was one of my concerns.'

'What do you know about Nils Boateng and Monique de la Rochelle?'

'Only their names.'

'What do you know about Kenny Marchant?'

Felix had an immediate sense that if Emily could have turned red, she would have. This might be tough news to share with Michelle.

'Kenny's a nice guy but he didn't share my concerns or rather he felt that, on balance, the benefits outweighed the risks.'

'Were you close to him?'

'That's not relevant.'

'Well, it might be actually, because a woman who very much holds a candle for him wants to zip off round the world with me in an effort to find both Kenny and Jameela.'

'That must be Michelle… I'm not sure it's requited…'

'OK, let's get right to the point: what should I do? What should WE do?'

'Well, first, "we" does not include me, yeah? Second, I can't tell you where to go because I just can't, it just wouldn't be right and I don't know where exactly Jameela will be now, as she will almost certainly have left India.'

'So, for example, is it still worth going to India?'

'Oh yes, they say the Taj Mahal can look beautiful this time of year, yeah.'

'Very funny.'

'That means, Felix, that it MAY be worth going to India but I can't say for sure. You might begin at Gandhi's Ashram. And it might be worth finding the main man himself because where he is, his closest protégés will also be from time to time.'

'Where do I begin?'

'Well he and Michaela began in the Lake District and it's impossible for anyone to cover their tracks completely. Think in terms of the most isolated hotel there is.'

'You are infuriatingly cryptic, why can't you just tell me?'

'Because I just can't, Felix. Please understand. I've told you all I can and all I will. Now, what have you seen of Exeter? I propose a little bit of sightseeing and maybe some shopping, if you'd like to join me.'

CHAPTER 19

Crimebusters

Wednesday, September 15, 2010

The hunter is in the outback again: his mind is wired, his senses keenly attuned…

'OK, so let's summarise the key points,' said Frank, pausing to reassure himself that he had the undivided attention of everyone in the private room at Shepherd's Ghyll. Frank had run his news and picture agency, North Words and Images, for a quarter of a century and knew pretty much all there was to know about news management and maximising both the impact and the earning power of a story. In this kind of scenario he was the perfect complement to a PR professional, thanks to the breadth and depth of his contacts across so many news media and his instinctive feel for the news value of a story.

'I remember when I was a junior reporter, there was an old hack on our paper who was responsible for selling on to the nationals or the Press Association any stories in our newspaper that were of wider interest. He was probably my inspiration, really. Anyway, this guy, Sid Hughes, always reckoned there were certain key ingredients to the best human interest stories – good or bad luck, conspiracy, money, love (preferably unrequited),

revenge and, of course, sex. So your real classic news story intro goes something like one I still remember writing myself and which made old Sid proper squeal with delight. It was something like: "It's going to be a heartbreak Christmas for rags-to-riches pizzeria owner Luigi Spinosa after an arson vendetta attack at the restaurant he set up with his lover." But I'm drifting off the point, because I think we need to add a couple more to these key ingredients – religion and the spirit world. And these, of course, are the extra ingredients we have in this story...'

'I don't see much sex, revenge or conspiracy,' interjected Cynth, Frank's wife and long-standing business partner. While Frank looked after the words side, Cynth was the pictures expert. 'Like, stick to the point, Frank!'

'OK, so we've got a potentially huge story about a guy who meets his dead brother, who sends him on a mission to ensure he gets better recognition for his "good works", or specifically his good work in dying so that others might live, so to speak, and whose formerly struggling business suddenly starts to soar to hitherto unknown heights. There you are, see, it's a rags-to-riches story after all!'

It was a very select group: Frank and Cynth, me, Michaela, Stella, Charley. We'd all recognised the need to carefully manage the news about Malcolm's revelations. There was clearly scope for ridicule and we needed to avoid this at all costs. Frank believed the best approach would be to issue one simple factual version of events while selling exclusive insights to individual news media, the proceeds going to the new charitable foundation whose establishment would follow the creation of the Aurora Group.

That strategic mini-conference – hidden from the eyes of the world – would, of course, come to prove a masterstroke in media management. If we hadn't got that one right, maybe so many other things wouldn't have turned out quite the same.

Michaela arrives at the hospital with Danny. I have had a busy day today, after Danny and I went to lunch in Harrogate yesterday. Malcolm has been to see me again while I was in the quiet room resting this afternoon. I just sat down ready for a bit of peace and me-time and then it all kicked off: Malcolm wanted to reinforce to me the notion that Faith, or the desire to have a Faith, is genetically implanted in us. It is an essential component of evolution as it helps in the process of natural selection. Violence, however, is a deviant genetic trait whose usefulness has long since been outlived. It is being bred out, but it's a slow process. On the one hand, we see the movement of so many modern cultures away from violence as a means of problem-resolution. But then, on the other, violence continues to prevail in some societies, often in the name of Faith. And then, of course, there is war… And it may be that some kind of seismic event will be required to eliminate violence from the human genetic blueprint. What Malcolm is impressing upon me is that the required blueprint changes from time to time and new 'instructions' are handed down through Faiths, by means of messages to the prophets. I had to scribble all this down in the margins of my Sudoku puzzle book.

I try to explain all this to Michaela but for some reason she doesn't seem to grasp its significance, or she has other things on her mind. This is frustrating, given that so much of our future together is being mapped out at the moment. Then Michaela disappears to try and have a conversation with John or Julia or one of the other senior staff.

'I got an absolute bollocking from your missus last night,' Danny tells me. 'She asked me if I was completely mad, taking you to HG1. I said I didn't take you, you took me and, anyway, it was no big deal. But she started going on about how you need protecting from yourself and how easy it might have been for us to bump into one of your business contacts and what a disaster that could have been.'

'Oh!' I respond, unsure, in fact, how to respond. 'She needs to remember that, when we boil it all down, I am here of my own free will and I don't need a special pass to go to HG1 with you…'

'Try telling Michaela that,' says Danny. 'Or maybe don't bother.'

It's a shame Michaela is winding herself up about this as something else has happened today that I need to share with her… Ayanna came in with Erasto this morning: yes, the same

Ayanna who seemed to have quite deliberately expunged me from her address book, if not her consciousness. Anyway, this morning she turned up unannounced in the games room, with Erasto in his wheelchair. Erasto appeared deflated, slumped in his chair with his chin on his chest. He looked like a discarded set of bagpipes. Ayanna had anxiety etched across her face, her brown eyes sad, tearful almost. I locked my own gaze onto those brown eyes and sought to peer into her soul: I could see only sadness and the heaviest heart.

'What brings you here?' I tried to sound cheerful. 'You look well,' I lied.

'You Victor. It is you who bring me here. I heard you were here; that you were unwell.'

I tried to catch Erasto's eye and, perhaps a little reluctantly, he did respond, lifting his head and allowing a weak smile to travel on a one-way ticket across his face.

'I'm fine, Ayanna, never been better. My mind is so amazingly fertile. And I have a new friend, Dave. We are going to save the world.'

'Pah!'

'What do you mean, "Pah"? This is all very serious; very important. We have just seven days to save the world, but the good news is that these "days" are not Earth days; they are days from a universe in which time is elastic so I'll be getting on with saving the world just as soon as Dave and I are out of here.'

I couldn't quite figure out what was going on in Ayanna's head: although she looked a little less sad than she had just moments previously, her mouth now hung open slightly and she looked as if she was waiting to say something, or to cut across me.

'What is it?' I asked.

Ayanna sighed the sigh of a winter wind. 'It's nothing Victor, I brought Erasto in to see you and maybe to say sorry for saying some of the things in the last email I sent to you. I was angry with you because I did not understand that you were ill...'

'I'm better now,' I said. 'But they won't let me go home until Michaela says I can come home. Can you talk to Michaela for me?'

'No Victor, that is for you and for Michaela and for your doctors.'

'Well, we'll see,' I said. 'But what of my friend Erasto?'

'He is not good, Victor. York is not good. He is unhappy and I am thinking that this is not working out and that we should both leave and go back to Leeds and be among our own people.'

'But you are among "your people": you have friends in Ripon – a job...'

'Pah!' she said again. 'You do not understand what it is to be so alone.' And she looked at Erasto and Erasto looked at her and yet I could see that there was no electricity: she wasn't looking into his soul, even though he was her own son. She was more preoccupied with her own sadness than with her son's problems, even though she appeared superficially to be focusing on the latter.

'You are not engaging with him, Ayanna. You talk about him but not to him and certainly not with him. Look into his soul, let him grow!'

I turned to Erasto and beckoned him to wheel his chair towards me. Then I turned him round so I was behind the chair and placed my hands beneath his chin and gently lifted his head and extended his spine. 'Now breathe in! Fill your lungs with oxygen and feel your heart pump the life force around your body... And again! And now tell me: "Proud to be a Tyke, proud to be black, proud to support Leeds United, proud to be Erasto!"'

He mumbled the mantra at first. 'Come on Erasto, you can do better.' He could and he did. 'Come on, you can do it even better: lift your head high, breathe deeply!'

I spun the chair round and he was smiling at me: there was air in the bagpipes and they were making music. Then something quite remarkable happened: young Jeff came into the room and, seeing me oxygenating Erasto and hearing him chanting the mantra, puffed up his own chest. That was unremarkable, but then he said: 'Hey, Erasto, me ol' mate, how's tha doin'?'

I couldn't see Erasto's face but I could see his ears move as he smiled and spun his wheels so he met Jeff near the door. 'Hey, Jeff, man, it's like real good ter see yer!'

'So you two know each other?' I looked at Ayanna and she returned my surprised expression.

'Yeah man, we was at school in Leeds together.'

'Proud ter be a Tyke, proud ter support Leeds, proud ter be ME!' they chanted in unison and then Jeff took Erasto's handles and spun him off down the corridor, singing, 'Walk tall, walk straight and look the world right in the eye'.

'No man, it should be "Wheel tall, wheel straight and look the world right in the eye"!' I heard Erasto rejoin, and then the pair of them dissolved into giggles.

'You see,' I said to Ayanna. 'You've got to engage with him, connect!'

'Give me a break, Victor Turnbull. Life is hard and my heart is still broken. If only you could be Malcolm; if only you could be single; if only you were not mad.'

'I'm sorry, Ayanna, I can't be Malcolm, but I am your link to Malcolm and I talk with him often, even just this afternoon. I'm sorry I'm not single and I'm not mad either.'

'You are mad, Victor, like the man with the hat in the children's story, but maybe one day you will be not so mad but by then maybe I shall be gone.'

'No, you should stay: Erasto has friends here.'

'He has refound an old school friend in a madhouse, Victor. That does not help and it changes nothing.'

I was sorry when they left and puzzled as to what Ayanna meant. Did she really mean that she'd settle for me now Malcolm was gone if only Michaela wasn't around? I thought about it very hard and recognised that I probably shouldn't speculate on this when Michaela came, as the last thing that Ayanna might need would be friction with Michaela who was, after all, one of her friends in Ripon. I didn't think Ayanna and Erasto should go back to Leeds and I didn't want to add another reason for them to do so.

So, now I'm sitting with Danny and Michaela returns from wherever she's been.

'I meant to tell you, I think we could make six figures from the auction of the film rights to Two Flew Over the Cuckoo's Nest: The Unsequel,' I say.

Michaela looks at me strangely and tells me to 'drop it!'. She looks tired.

'You should take a step back and not get so hung up on things,' I suggest.

'Oh really, thanks for the advice.'

'I'm serious about selling the film rights.'

Michaela seems to pretend she hasn't even heard me, so I in turn change the subject and tell her about Ayanna's visit. 'She's talking about leaving Ripon and going back to Leeds. You've got to stop her.'

'I have to stop her?!' Michaela placed emphasis on the 'I'. 'She's a grown woman, Vic, she can do as she pleases.'

'Erasto met an old friend: young Jeff. They know each other from Leeds. He had a great time here this afternoon.'

Michaela still looks distracted. 'I've been talking with Julia and I've told her I don't think I'm ready for you to come home just yet.'

'What do you mean, YOU'RE not ready? How do you know how I feel inside? I am ready and I need to come home, even if it's only for the weekend.'

'That's not the way it works, Victor, my love…'

'Look,' I say, 'I've got something to show both of you that may change your mind.' I go to my room and collect the Sudoku book, with the notes on natural selection and human race, and all the Post-its from yesterday that tell the story of my own genetic inheritance. I place them all on the table in front of Michaela and Danny. 'You need to read this: it's a whole new set of revelations, but you have to go carefully. Be wary when you see an orange Post-it and don't go past a red one until you are sure you're ready. This is truly ground-breaking, mind-blowing stuff so maybe you'll understand its commercial importance too and why I need to be getting back to the world outside so I can make us financially very comfortable.'

I leave them at it and go to look for Julia.

I find her with Bertie: they are thick as thieves, standing near Reception.

'I think it's time for me to go home, Julia.'

'It's not just about what you think, Victor. There are other people to consider...'

'Yes, and those "other people" have been telling you they don't want me underneath their feet, or whatever?'

'Victor, it's not like that: all of this is a partnership aimed at finding the best solution for everybody.'

'So how much longer?'

'Victor, we need time to be sure we are happy for you go home, but that can only happen when Michaela and everybody else is comfortable with you going home.'

'Like never?!'

'Victor, don't be silly. Just learn to be more patient.'

'More patient? How can I be? I am 100 per cent a patient – in the loony bin and although I'm "free to go" I'm not really free to go, because if I do go I'll just get sent back here by Michaela and if I object I expect you'll come along and Section me even though I'm no longer mad. I'm not, you know. I'm not mad, I'm just someone whose senses are hyper-alert and who's having to learn to deal with that...'

Then Bertie interjects: 'Of course, Victor, you're not mad and none of us has eyes in the back of our heads, you know!' She seems to be smiling, slightly mockingly. I return to her a signal that's designed to say 'Of course no-one has eyes in the back of their head'. I now absolutely realise that I will just have to play their game if I want to get out of here. Then I can get a research project set up to find out the truth about sixth sense and eyes in the back of the head.

'OK guys,' I say. 'Let's be realistic about this: how's about we aim for some kind of day-release this weekend?'

Julia this time: 'If Michaela agrees and Dr Honeydew is happy, then that might be possible.'

'OK, fine,' I say, turning back towards the games room, where I left Michaela and Danny.

I find the pair of them studying the Post-its carefully. 'It's serious stuff, isn't it?'

'Yes, Vic, it's really amazing,' says Michaela.

'Yeah, amazing, mate,' adds Danny in a voice that doesn't sound quite as amazed as it might.

'Did you take care with the amber and red Post-its?'

'Yes, yes, that was really helpful,' chirps Michaela, but the smile she is wearing looks like she popped into the Oxfam shop for it on the way here.

'You do understand the implications, don't you?' I ask. 'Forget about the family tree and Who Do You Think You Are? This is our inheritance on the big stage; this is about the defining moments in our individual evolution and how that evolution then fits into the big picture about what's happening to the human race.'

Then Danny says, 'Look, mate, I agree, it is amazing and it's been helpful that you've warned us with the amber and red wotsits, but you know, it's a helluva lot for us to take in, so just give us a bit of time.'

'Yeah,' says Michaela. 'Give us a bit of time: we aren't as supercharged as you and for us time is still moving at the same old speed, so cut us a bit of slack, OK?'

I think they're both being sincere.

'Bertie and Julia say I might be able to come home at the weekend now…'

'They say what?' screeches Michaela. I think the Oxfam smile will be going back to the shop.

If I want to go home this weekend, I am going to have to play their game more effectively. I will have intelligent conversations with the nurses and steer clear of subjects that seem to upset them, like my discovery that we have vestigial eyes in the back of our heads.

So I have an intelligent conversation with John about the mobile reception and WiFi signal in the hospital (there isn't one). 'So,' I suggest, 'people like me who can be trusted could have WiFi that would plug in under the bed, which is just a solid base at the moment of course. And if you've got "guests" whom you won't be able to trust, then the equipment can just be locked away under the bed and they'll be none the wiser.'

'Yes, that sounds like a great idea, Victor. We could maybe run with that one.'

Bearing in mind Michaela's reaction yesterday to the idea of my coming home at the weekend, I'm hoping I might get the chance to talk to Dr Honeydew, as he's the one who seems to really have Michaela's ear at the moment. It's hard to get to speak to Dr Honeydew: I suspect that's the way he likes it. So I'm both pleased and surprised when he finds me at Reception talking to Ute and once again trying to help her to understand that exercising her German holds the key to improving her English.

'Victor, for zer last time, pleeease,' she says. 'I do not want to speak German, so please do not be making me!'

Then suddenly the vestigial 'eyes' in the back of my head sense a presence: I turn round and it's Dr Honeydew himself. 'Mr Turnbull, are you annoying the staff?'

I feel like a scolded schoolboy. 'Not at all, sir, I mean Dr Honeydew. I'm just trying to persuade Ute that her German language is an asset, even when she is learning English.'

'Hmm, that may be for Ute to decide, rather than for you, Victor, but for now I think we perhaps need a little chat.'

Dr Honeydew leads me from Reception to the little room where he usually holds his meetings with the team. Once again, he has failed completely to make eye contact and he sits with his head in what I presume to be my 'notes'.

'Your partner tells me you want to visit your home at the weekend. Do you feel you are ready for that?' Still no eye contact.

'Yes, I believe I am. I am very much improved.'

'Michaela is a little less sure, Victor. She says you are still getting very agitated about some things – about these "communications" you say you have with your late brother.' He labours the word 'communications' in a manner that seems to cast doubt on his belief in the veracity of my ability to communicate with Malcolm.

'Well, it's pretty agitating stuff that I'm being told, Dr Honeydew. I think you might be agitated if you were having so many of the secrets of the universe presented to you in just a short space of time. It's quite hard to keep up.'

'Indeed, quite.' STILL no eye contact.

Dr Honeydew continues: 'You know Victor, this is a team game, making you well again, but all of the team have to be able to be ready to kick the same way and at the moment Michaela's not very sure, if I can extend the analogy, Michaela's not very sure if the ball's even on the pitch or indeed if SHE'S even on the pitch.'

'That's a shame, she should really be on my side.'

'Oh she is, Victor, very much, but you know she has a big advantage over us: she knows what you SHOULD be like when you are completely well, so she is a very good judge of how well, or indeed unwell, you are.' This time he measures the word unwell, as though he is reluctant to pin a label on me. Then he continues: 'On the other hand, I'm minded to give you a chance, so I'm asking John and Julia, and Bertie, to keep an eye on you and then, if they're happy and Michaela agrees, perhaps you can go home on Saturday afternoon and then come back for your medication.' No eye contact, but the words are music to my ears.

'Thank you very much,' I say. 'I shan't let you down.'

I have seen little of Dave in the couple of days during which this debate over whether I should or should not go home at the weekend has been evolving. My only recollection is of him heading swiftly from one of the consultation rooms to his own room, head down, signalling that he did not wish to engage with anyone else – even me. I know that he is working hard to resolve issues in Priestley House that some of those in authority would prefer to turn a blind eye to. I believe some of his work in this regard is coming close to its climax.

I decide it might be best if I were not to hang around Reception as this seems to be taken as a measure of one's state of mind by some of the hospital team. So I wait instead for one of them to pass. Soon enough, John is coming towards me, with a purposeful look on his face.

'You seen Dave?' I ask.

'I think he's resting, can't stop, Vic mate.' He hurries by. I need Dave to help me: I need my rocks, my anchors, to demonstrate my sanity. So I head instead for the main hospital reception desk in the hope of seeing Valentina. I am in luck and her smile warms my soul. I close my eyes and, once again, we exchange words, she in Italian and me in French. I learn a little more about her. She came to England, met a man and had her daughter, now a teenager. Things haven't worked out with the father of her daughter. And now her mother is growing old in Sicily and she is torn two ways. Her daughter has friends and an education here but her brothers are telling her robustly and repeatedly that her place is back at the family home that she escaped 20 or so years ago. 'Droits et obligations familiaux,' I say.

'Diritto di famiglia; obblighi familiari,' says Valentina. I open my eyes again to find a sadness in hers, which are not only open but locked on some point in the mid-distance. 'Cosa devo fare?'

'Que dois-je faire?' I respond. 'You must first do what is right for you and for your daughter.' Valentina's faltering smile tells me it can not be so simple. And then work beckons her: people to greet; people to direct.

I go outside into the main grounds of Priestley House: it is an extensive site. Much of it is taken up by uniform rectangular blocks, with a 60s look about them, but Priestley House itself is set apart, its wards forming the spokes of a wheel. When I first arrived here I hadn't appreciated that there was more than just our own, men's ward in Priestley House. In fact, as I say, other wards and an administrative block radiate off the central area where my adventure playground is. I think back to that first

Sunday and the service in the chapel, when I thought all the people had come from all over town. In fact they had come from the adjacent wings, in particular the women's wing, which is just over the fence from our garden.

Dave and some of the other guys have been going for a run starting here in the grounds lately and taking in a few nearby fields. I thought my superpowers would mean I could do this too, but when I tried to join them one time I actually didn't get very far: they are younger than me, and fitter. I guess my superpowers improve my eye and my speed of decision-making; they can make me strike a football more truly; hit the winning shot at table tennis or pot from an impossible angle. They can't make me run further and faster.

Notwithstanding, I set off on a gentle jog round the buildings. There are even more mushrooms than the last time when I was picking them from the central courtyard, so I swap jogging for mushroom-picking and present Valentina with an even more impressive collection.

'Ah Victor, who will pick funghi for me if I have to go back to Italy?' I don't know the answer to that. I think about saying she should never go back to Italy, but then I guess it's not really my business. But I look into her soul and see only sadness.

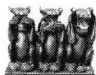

I think maybe it would be nice to play a melancholy ballad for Valentina on the Northumbrian pipes, whose subtle harmonies make me feel so emotional. I haven't actually got the pipes out of their box since that day with Charlotte, so I guess it's not before time. I lift them out and attach the reed and the chanter and strap the bellows round my midriff. I pump the bellows and equalise the pressure in the bag, beneath my arm. I focus on the mantra: 'Pat your head and rub your tummy.' This is not to say that you have to literally pat your head and rub your tummy, it's just good practice for playing the pipes, as you have to allow your body to keep the bellows and the bag going at the same time without consciously thinking about it. It's not as easy as it sounds: just try the belly and head exercise. But Catriona has always said I have the knack for it.

So the bellows are blowing and the bag is full and my fingers are on the holes of the chanter. I expect my superpowers will mean that they will spring straight into melodic perfection, but there's a horrible screech and then the bag deflates and the sound dies. I am shocked. My superpowers don't extend to music as I had not unreasonably expected them to.

It is the morning and Dave is still keeping his head down. The staff say he is sleeping. I see him just once, walking purposefully along the corridor, his mind clearly elsewhere. Just before lunch he comes and finds me in the garden. 'Remember ah telt ye how it's just like prison here? Ye knaa, rackets goin' on with the ciggies an' that? An' how that Willy, the guy who killed someone, is sheltering on the inside here? Aye, well, ah've been busy, so keep yer head doon and watch carefully what happens…' And with that he is gone.

At lunch he makes only the briefest appearance, leaves me to say grace, and is gone again. To where, I'm not sure. I look for him in the smokers' garden and sit with the guys for a while. Jeff is out of ciggies and is trying to 'borrow' one. Thomas 'the writer' gives him two, saying, 'And another 'un for later. You know the deal.' I wonder what 'the deal' is, but don't ask.

I head for Reception in the hope of finding Dave around there. He isn't there but there's a new guy just arriving. He's called Nigel. Julia asks me to 'show him the ropes'. This is a sure sign they think I am getting better if I can be trusted with this responsibility. Nigel seems a nice guy, but exceptionally nervous and on edge. He keeps repeating to me that he shouldn't be in here, that he's not mentally ill, that he's suffering from extreme anxiety and lack of sleep. Whatever his problem, it appears to be exacerbated by the fact that his eyesight is clearly quite poor. He wears bottle-bottom glasses and, as I show him the basic hospital instruction sheet, he holds it just a couple of inches from his face.

'I shouldn't be in here,' he says again as we find a quiet corner in the games room. 'Do you know when I last slept for a whole night?' The question is purely rhetorical as he quickly snuffs out any opportunity for me to respond. 'Six months; six bloody months; I'm wrecked; I'm persecuted…'

'Persecuted?' I take the floor for a very short cameo.

'Yeah, I reported a couple of my superiors for misconduct. I should have known better. They conjured up a spurious set of charges against me instead…'

'Are you in the police?'

'Yeah. Well maybe: I can't be sure any more. I'm suspended on full pay for alleged gross misdemeanour.'

'But you filed the first complaint?'

'Yeah, a couple of quite senior officers on the take; confiscating drugs then selling them on; taking bribes to keep local crime bosses out of gaol…'

'And you blew the whistle?'

'Yep. It seemed the right thing to do; it WAS the right thing to do. But I feel like now it's me who's the criminal.'

'So,' I ask him. 'What charges did they come up with against you?'

'Well it began with tripping me on a couple of minor procedural things, like not writing up my case notes quite quickly enough…'

'Was that true?'

'Yes, it was: I got hit on the head while on duty and I was too ill to write up my notes on time…'

'Bloody hell, that's not very fair…'

Nigel presses on: 'That was just the beginning. They falsified records so they could pin the collapse of a trial on me. In fact it had collapsed because the very guys that I had reported made sure it collapsed! Eventually they came up with a charge of gross misconduct against me for "making allegations against colleagues while knowing them to false".'

'Is there no-one who'll back you up?'

'No. That's where I made my biggest mistake. I didn't recognise how deep all the corruption goes and that means I didn't recognise how scared anyone who might have wanted to support me would feel. We good cops might be in the majority. In fact we are in the majority, but we don't hold the majority of the power. Everyone was scared to speak out because they knew what the consequences might be. Now, with me, they have actually seen the consequences.'

'What about the police ombudsman, or the police committee? What about a lawyer?'

'The system's rigged against me. The biggest problem is that there are people involved in this who are, frankly, above suspicion. That was another big miscalculation on my part. I thought the really senior officers would back ME...'

Nigel pauses, sighs. I think he might be about to cry, but he takes a deep breath, tries very hard to focus his challenged eyes on mine and says, 'I've hit a brick wall. My best hope is to withdraw all the charges and try to leave the force with my reputation intact, if they'll let me. I joined the police because I thought I could help it to be a force for good. But now I realise the police is like a supertanker and it will take a hell of a lot to turn it onto a better path. There's something very rotten and it runs very deep...'

'Funny handshakes and things?' I ask.

'Yeah, well, I reckon the Masons do have a lot to answer for.'

'You'll have to meet Dave: he and I are going to save the world from the Masons and all forms of corruption and evil. And this place isn't immune: there's a killer lying low in here and there's rackets, just like in prison...'

'Really, is that so?' asks Nigel. I sense he doesn't completely believe me, so I decide to share more detail with him. 'Well, there's Willy: Dave says he knows for sure he's killed a man. And there's Thomas, who seems to be running a porn racket, like he gives out cigarettes in return for "favours", you know... He says he writes crime novels, but it feels to me like he's just saying that to try and ingratiate himself with me. He gets very touchy if you try to read what he's been writing on the PC. I think he's got something much more sinister he keeps on there.'

I nod towards the old PC in the opposite corner, and Nigel says, 'I could have a look at that; I used to be in cyber-crime.'

Later in the day I see Dave in the corridor, head down. 'Can't stop,' he says. Then I see Jeff: he's walking away from me with the shady Thomas. I'm relieved to find Dave making an appearance for dinner. He still seems preoccupied, but I nudge him and say: 'Thomas has been up to something with Jeff. But the new lad, Nigel, has been looking at the PC to see if Thomas has left any porn stuff.'

'Nigel?' queries Dave.

'Yeah, he's a cop: whistle-blower. Been suspended. Reckons they've fitted him up.'

'More 'n likely,' shrugs Dave, as he turns to young Jeff. 'What've ye been deein' wi' Thomas, Jeff lad?'

'Watching porn,' says Jeff without shame.

'And?'

'Well, the things you do when you watch porn.'

'Ah've telt ye, Jeff lad: ye can nae watch porn – it's evil!' responds Dave, with animation.

'Why?'

So I chip in: 'Well, Jeff, because it exploits people.'

Jeff reddens and a penny drops: he's not just been watching porn, but making it. Suddenly Nigel's investigation of the PC acquires a new significance. I glance around the dining room: Nigel is nowhere to be seen.

It is morning and still no sign of Nigel, though Dave has rushed past me once again. 'It's aall coming to the boil, Vic lad,' he says and rushes off. In the games room, the PC stands forlorn in the corner, but it's at a slight angle and the disc that was in the drive seems to have vanished.

Yesterday Nigel gave me his phone number. I decide to head for the front reception, where there's a decent signal. As I pause to do my traditional commando exercises in the garden en route, I hear sirens. When I arrive at Reception, a single squad car is outside. It is unoccupied. 'They'll be here for Willy,' I think. 'Maybe Thomas too.'

I call Nigel: 'Where are you?'

'Who's this?'

'It's me, Vic!'

'Vic?'

'Yeah, Vic. We talked yesterday. Where are you?'

'Ah Vic! In the hospital? Sorry, Vic. I discharged myself. I'm not ill. I'm just stressed and fatigued, you know.'

I'm disappointed: I had foreseen Nigel helping me and Dave bust the gangs in Priestley House. I try to mask my disappointment. 'Well, mate, I hope you beat the bastards: hang on in there, because we have to win all the battles to win the war! What did you find on Thomas's disc on the PC?'

'Well I had a look, but there was nothing I could pin down...'

'But the cops are here now? Is that for Willy then?'

'Willy?'

'Yeah, Willy: the killer!'

'Oh I dunno, Vic, my friend. I'm just thinking about how I can get some sleep and stay sane, you know...'

I slip back indoors. 'Big day,' I tell Valentina. 'The police are here to bust the gangs...'

'The gangs, Victor?' She gives me a puzzled look. I guess she isn't up to speed on what's going on and decide that maybe it's best I don't alarm her about all the crime in Priestley House.

Later, Dave is flying around the place, head-down again. 'I saw the cop car and heard the sirens– I guess it's the end-game!'

'Aye lad,' is all Dave says, but I am relieved to know that at least Willy must now be safely inside.

After dinner I decide to slip into the garden. I'm astonished to find Willy there.

'Naa then, Vic,' he nods. He is, for the first time, almost smiling.

CHAPTER 20

The sabbatical

Sunday October 3, 2021

Felix settled the bill, while Emily waited outside, nervous that they might be seen leaving Carluccio's together. Felix wondered how Emily proposed that they should go sight-seeing without creating the appearance that they were, in fact, together. He chose not to ask the question.

He exited into the gentle massaging warmth of the mid-morning autumn sunshine. Emily was shading her eyes from it: she projected a gesture that lay somewhere between a wink and a shrug in the general direction of Felix as he came through the door, and turned to walk in what Felix judged was a roughly northeasterly direction until they intersected the city walls. Here, Emily sat on a bench and waited for Felix. 'I think we should be OK now,' she said.

'You're very cautious,' said Felix.

'It comes with the territory these days,' she replied with a resigned shrug. 'So, here begins your tour of historic Exeter: you can walk close to me now.'

'That will make conversation easier!' said Felix, as they began their tour by heading from the old city walls.

'Exeter's pretty unusual as about three quarters of the old city walls are still standing,' said Emily, with a look resembling local pride. It occurred to Felix that for all her feelings of not quite belonging, this was still her home. 'We'll do a circuit and end up at the Cathedral, OK?'

'You were going to tell me about your misgivings,' continued Felix as they began to follow the neatly tended masonry remains.

'How much do you know about the origins of the Aurora Foundation?' Emily asked him.

'Well, there's what I've read, and there's what I've been told.'

'And how do those two match up?'

'A little inconsistently, if I'm honest.'

Emily hadn't responded to Felix's observation when she halted in a pleasant area of parkland beside the castle, called Northernhay Gardens, and began to describe how the walls had originally been built by the Romans and then rebuilt in the Middle Ages. The gardens themselves provided something of an oasis in the city centre and family groups and individuals were making the most of the autumn sunshine, strolling among the lawns and a curious combination of statues that ranged from the historic to what looked to Felix like representations of mythical beasts.

'Let's sit down,' said Emily, choosing an area of lawn that sloped gently towards the sun. Felix spread the jacket he'd been carrying on one shoulder and the pair of them squeezed onto it: a little more intimate than Felix, or indeed Emily, might have expected.

'So, OK,' said Emily. 'The Aurora Foundation, as I think you will have guessed, is nothing if not cagey about what it does. And the absence of hard information, naturally, invites speculation. So some of the things you will have read or heard about are just that: pure speculation. So it's maybe worth beginning by establishing what the Foundation is not...'

'I'm all ears,' said Felix.

'OK, well, it's not a communist conspiracy or hell-bent on world domination as some of the more fantasist American commentators might have you believe. But, at the same time, you have to take some of these commentaries with an even bigger pinch of salt...'

'Meaning?'

'Well,' continued Emily, 'the Foundation is not above creating its own spoof attacks that look a bit right-wing loony, just so people will tend to label all criticism as loony right.'

'That wouldn't by any chance include The Secret World of the Aurora Foundation, would it?' queried Felix.

'I'm not sure about that one, but quite possibly,' Emily replied.

'OK, well putting all that to one side, what IS the Aurora Foundation?' said Felix, seeking to steer the conversation to more fruitful pastures.

'Well,' said Emily, 'you'll remember how I told you about what I liked about the Foundation and what persuaded me initially to join Lord Lindisfarne's Inner Circle, yeah? What I was interested in was building partnerships with other charities and NGOs and so on and I think the Foundation was doing some really good work in cooperating with others, for example, to help provide alternative livelihoods for people in South America at the heart of the deforestation issue. And I think the problem was that, as the money came flowing in ever faster as Aurora profits grew, the ambition began to outstrip what the reality was calling for...'

'And?'

'Well, that began to lead the Foundation into areas in which, in my opinion, the potential gains just weren't worth the risks involved, yeah.'

'Like?'

'Well, I think all the anti-corruption work was very worthy – but once it moved from tactical actions to counter organisations like the Masons and started on the Russian and Nigerian mafias, you know, well, work it out for yourself!'

'What happened?'

'We lost a couple of people and Lindisfarne ordered a rethink and we shared what we knew with more "official channels", for what little they were worth.'

'Lost?'

'Yes, a couple of the disappeared will never reappear.'

'Who?'

'I can't tell you, Felix, yeah.'

'That's serious stuff, Emily.'

'Like yeah, very! But it's the religious thing that was the decider for me.'

'Tell me!'

'Well, like, the whole basis of Lindisfarne's and the Foundation's ethos, if you like, yeah, is that both science and what we call Faith should lead to the same ultimate truth: the truth about Life, the Universe and Everything. The Truth that will save the world and save humanity from itself. So Lindisfarne believes there should be not only no conflict between faiths, but no conflict between Faith and lack of faith.'

'Which sounds like a bloody good idea to me!'

'Of course it does: it's like at Miss World when they used to say "my hobbies are dancing, make-up and creating eternal peace and happiness", but these are just words and the real world is very different, yeah?'

'OK, tell me how the Foundation sets about promoting peace and love and concord between faiths.'

'OK, yeah. The starting point is what Lindisfarne sees as the mismatch between the scriptures as written down and the intended meaning when all these prophets and saints and people were visited by the Lord or whatever. And for all of this, understand it means all supposedly holy tomes in all faiths, OK, yeah?'

Felix wondered if there was any way he could turn off the 'yeah' function in Emily's vocal cords or if he should point out to her that it was getting a bit annoying. He decided that the appropriate moment was long since past and he'd just have to live with it.

'So the Foundation's language teams have worked on all the big holy books – the Bible, the Qur'an, the Torah, the Bhagavad-Gita, the Tipitaka…'

'Whoa, whoa – what's the "bagavadikka"? What's the "Titicaca"?'

'The Bhagavad-Gita' (Emily pronounced it slowly and deliberately) 'is a sacred Hindu book and the Tipitaka' (again, the word was carefully enunciated) 'is the core Buddhist holy book.'

'So how many people have been doing all this work? It sounds like it could take for ever,' said Felix.

'Well, maybe not for ever, but I don't think even Lindisfarne quite realised what he'd bitten off. Take the Tipitaka, for example. It runs to about 40 volumes in English but the original is in an Indian language that's reckoned to be something like the language that the Buddha himself spoke, yeah. So it's not just a question of finding linguists who are Arabic or Hebrew specialists, or whatever, but finding linguists who are also talented historians with familiarity with theology... The difficulty right from the start has been knowing where the main focus should be and defining the task – that is, taking something that's too vast even to begin and turning it into something that can at least be contemplated over a given timescale, yeah.'

'So was that achieved?' asked Felix. 'I mean, was the task made achievable?'

'Well, yes and no, really; and that's one of my issues, because I think some of those doing the work maybe find it hard to take the full number of steps back that Lindisfarne was looking for, so as to get back to the roots of these sacred texts and distil out, if you like, yeah, their original meaning. OK?'

'OK, yeah,' Felix found himself saying.

Emily gave him a slightly quizzical look... 'Let's push on!'

A little further on, the magnificent building that was Exeter Cathedral came into view. 'Nice little chapel!' observed Felix.

'Cheeky monkey! That's our rather fine cathedral!'

Felix and Emily sat down to admire just how fine on a seat across the grass from the Cathedral itself. It didn't have the grandeur of York Minster or the sheer majesty of Durham, thought Felix, but it successfully disguised its bulk with a series of adornments that gave it a squatter, though handsomely more decorative demeanour than its older aforementioned cousins.

'So, you'd say it all got too big, then?' ventured Felix.

'What, the Cathedral?'

'No the Aurora stuff!'

'Yes, that's part of the problem,' said Emily. 'But it's not just about the religion, it's also about simply trying to fight on too many fronts at once. I mean, yeah, if your "core business" could be something as big as just "doing good" then maybe it wouldn't matter so much. But "doing good" seems to encompass everything from saving the bee, to countering corruption, to rewriting the scriptures to saving the bloody planet!'

'Yeah, that's quite a lot!' said Felix. 'But you said it wasn't just about scale or lack of focus or whatever…'

'No. As far as the religious thing goes it's about whether it actually works and I think that there's good evidence that far from "working" the Foundation has actually made things worse. In short, it's a bit of a disaster, yeah.'

'Explain!'

'OK, then. Let's say that the method behind the religious thing is a presumption that all faiths began as the generally benign and even helpful instructions of the prophets: people who had a big religious experience, you know a Road to Damascus revelation, Moses coming down off the mountain, Jesus and his miracles or all these female saints who had these enormous self-induced orgasms…'

'Beg pardon?!'

'You know what I mean, like Joan of Arc, she'd say she's had the vision but in reality she probably rode her horse too hard and came big time, yeah, I mean…'

'Are you serious?!' interjected Felix.

'Pretty much. If you read the accounts of these women who have been canonised after witnessing so-called "miracles" they sound pretty much like the sort of orgasm you might have if you were really frustrated, yeah, like you'd never really had a proper one before…'

'You almost sound like you're speaking from experience,' said Felix. He thought Emily might have blushed at that point, but it would have had to be quite some blush, he thought, to penetrate the rich warm chestnut of her remarkably smooth (he observed) skin.

'Imagination and not so much of the experience,' she countered, with almost a mutter.

'Sorry, I didn't mean to embarrass you, but what about all the blokes? I mean are you telling me that Moses had an involuntary ejaculation on top of the mountain; and what about Mohammed?'

'Mohammed? Best not to go there really, which brings me right back to my point.'

'Go on…'

'Well, Lindisfarne's basic premise is that, as I say, faiths begin as benign but once things get "organised" they're corrupted by people who use what we might call the "blind faith" of the, let's say, "common people" as a means to exert power over them and exploit them. So you get these self-appointed "priests" who invent a whole load of rules that the prophets would never have dreamt of imposing in their worst nightmares and then they "adjust" the so-called "holy books" to justify the rules they've made up. So, like yeah, you get in Christianity, for example, the idea that only men can be priests and then over time women become not just unable to be priests but actually second-class citizens. Or in Islam, people like the Taliban come along and say that the Qur'an says that women can't be educated and can't for that matter even be seen… And then faiths can get quite mature and enter another phase in which religious people can become almost as tolerant as the rest of us… you know, women priests, gay marriage, the lot – nothing's taboo any more.'

Felix wasn't very sure where all this was heading, but just as he was about to ask, Emily continued: 'So Lindisfarne's idea is to bring every Faith to its tolerant phase, be it an early tolerance or a mature tolerance, with the idea that all Faiths can always live in harmony and there'll be certain, if you like, "golden rules"…'

'And they are?'

'Well, the over-arching one is that no-one shall do physical harm to anyone on account of their religious beliefs, which is a pretty good catch-all, as it were, yeah, like 'cos it covers punishment for adultery, apostasy, blasphemy…'

'But it puts you pretty firmly in the sights of the fundamentalists, I guess…'

'And the not quite so fundamental, for that matter. I mean, as a principle, none of this squares too well with Sharia law and other laws that various faiths have managed to extrapolate from their core beliefs. And then there's the whole question, not just of female genital mutilation, but male circumcision…'

'Because you are doing harm but dressing it up as health benefit? I guess you'll be taking on not just Islam and Judaism, but the entire American medical profession with that one.'

'Pretty much, yeah.'

'So what are the other core principles?'

'Well, freedom of religious belief and the right not to believe, while at no time imposing your faith on others. Sex equality in work, education and everyday life, including the rights of gays not to be persecuted…'

'Pretty much what we might take for granted in the West, then, but I guess it all comes across as the West imposing its own morality on the rest of the world and who's to say who's right and what's wrong…'

'Exactly, which is why there was, or is, more than one strategy to try and get people "converted". Where there are more benign interpretations of faith, this is seen as a potential intermediate phase, for example. So Sufism is seen as a potential counter to the kind of extreme interpretations of Islam that US and UK foreign policy have managed to provoke. But there's also the Foundation's "new prophets", whose liberal teachings are disseminated through the Internet and social media. Though, of course, no-one knows they have anything to do with the Foundation…

'My God, I'd no idea. How come I've never heard about this? I mean it's dynamite and I can't imagine encouraging one sect at the expense of others, or introducing a whole new interpretation of a faith, is a recipe for peace and light. I mean it's not as if the

Catholics and Prods or Shi'ites and Sunnis have been models of peaceful coexistence…'

'Precisely! I think tackling religious extremism is just an impossible dream. I'd like to think that increased prosperity might bring increased tolerance, yeah, but if Saudi Arabia or Northern Ireland are your base line, then that doesn't begin to be true. So I came to believe that the whole religious angle was a waste of time and resources and was actually more likely to make things worse in the world than better and that there were better things for our highly paid linguists to do than to try and rewrite religion, as it were…'

'Yeah, I can imagine, but back to my other question: how come I know nothing about all this?'

'Well, it's not something that the powers that be would ever want to advertise, is it? There are lots of vested interests that have worked together to keep it all invisible.'

'So did you talk about your misgivings?'

'I did and Lord Lindisfarne is not stupid, but despite not being stupid he still believes that, over time, Faith and Science will "be as one", as he puts it, and we just have to accept that the road to this goal may sometimes be a bit rocky, yeah.'

'Yeah!' Felix involuntarily repeated. 'So, is that why you left and how easy was it?'

'Well, I had to make it really clear that I would not compromise the security of the Foundation in any way and I s'pose that was a bit of a dilemma for me because I did have other misgivings: about the use of tax havens, for example, when we are supposed to be actually challenging corruption, which, incidentally, is what I believe should have been and should be now the fundamental role of the Foundation. But, I badly wanted out, so I agreed to keep my thoughts to myself and say nothing. In fact, Felix Merryman, you are the first person with whom I have had this conversation. Not even my parents know about all this.'

'Should I be flattered?'

'Yeah, I think you should.'

Emily smiled a mysterious smile… He wasn't sure what to

make of what he'd been told. Nor how it might all fit in with the disappearance of Jameela.

He caught Emily's enigmatic gaze and smiled: she reciprocated. 'Jameela's not stupid,' he said. 'I can't imagine she would sign up to all this…'

'Lindisfarne is very charismatic. That's all I'd say. Sometimes he even seems like a prophet himself…'

Felix thought he saw a wistful look in Emily's eyes, like she was transported back to a time and place that she missed but to which she could never return. 'You miss all that, then?'

'You mean, do I have regrets, yeah? Of course I do…' She left the statement hanging in the air. 'C'mon,' she said. 'Let's go in.'

They entered the Cathedral and presently each took his or her own course beneath its fine vaulted ceiling. Felix admired the astronomical clock, which he fancied reminded him of the one in Prague, with its Kafkaesque connections. He felt that here was a poignant reminder of just what he and Emily had been discussing: once upon a time, Faith and science were coincident and shared a common purpose in unravelling the mysteries of the universe, albeit a universe that might have been created by a God. Was it conceivable that the two might one day be as one again?

Twenty or 30 minutes later, Felix was browsing in the Cathedral bookshop, admiring a tea towel with all the Shipping Forecast names on a map of the British Isles, unsure what its connection with organised religion might be, when Emily found him. 'I wondered where you'd got to,' she said. 'It's time we were moving on.'

'Sorry, I was in North Utsire,' said Felix.

'You what?'

'Oh nothing, just day-dreaming…' Emily threw him a quizzical glance that withered slightly on its way to him.

As Felix and Emily came out of the Cathedral, a movement in the mid-distance caught Felix's eye. Now it was his turn to act paranoid. 'Don't stop now, but I think someone might be watching us,' he said. 'Keep walking, and when we get to the gate, stop suddenly and turn round, OK?!'

The pair reached the gate simultaneously, where they spun on their heels, as agreed. Emily somehow missed what Felix saw: it was a sight that was as unwelcome as it was unexpected and it momentarily froze the blood in his veins. The glimpse of the young man had been fleeting in the extreme, as he had slipped into a huddle of tourists, but there was, Felix was quite sure, no mistaking his identity. The last time Felix had seen that sullen face it had been over the shoulder of his father, on a doorstep in Luton. Although Rahman had spoken of 'love' in the context of his hitherto absent and now missing sister, Felix's abiding memory of the encounter was of the seething resentment harboured by other family members, and by his brother Hamza in particular. Felix had no more than Rahman's word that he did not share the family's sense of shame.

'What's going on?' asked Emily.

'I think I just saw Jameela's younger brother,' said Felix. 'In fact, I'm certain I just saw Jameela's younger brother.

'How on earth would you know what Jameela's younger brother looks like?'

'Because I went to her family's house. In Luton.'

'You did what? Are you crazy?'

'No, I don't think so, but I am wondering if I was a bit naïve.'

'Skip the wondering, starry-eyed boy: you WERE naïve, yeah, OK?'

'You think he's hoping I'll lead him to Jameela, then?'

'Er, yes!' Emily drew out the Y-E-S as though she was saying 'doh', Homer Simpson style. 'I think it's pretty important that you shake this guy off, yeah!'

'I can't even think how he's got here, Emily. I can't be sure he's even old enough to drive.'

'Maybe he's not alone...'

Oh my God, thought Felix, what if he's got the hideous brothers with him?

'OK,' said Emily. 'You have the advantage here: they may have got lucky and been able somehow to follow you to Exeter, but, assuming they're in a car, there must be a hundred and one ways to make off without them spotting you.'

'Do you think they could have put a tracker on the car?'

'Who knows? But it's a hire car anyway, so you'll be returning that soon, I guess. So how about we take your car to the airport tonight, then you get a taxi back into town…?'

'I'm flying tonight anyway…'

'Maybe you should change that…'

'Or maybe we shouldn't be quite so paranoid…'

'Or maybe you should take the car to the airport, get a taxi back to town and catch a train.'

'Emily, I know I freaked out when I saw Rahman, and I know there's no easy explanation as to how or why he should suddenly appear on my tail here in Exeter, but I think I should stick with my plans: I can't see him suddenly appearing on the plane…'

'Well, it's your choice Mr Merrydown. And in the meantime I think we should find somewhere quiet where we can discuss your masterplan, OK?'

It was a confused and rather nervous Felix who found himself at the airport that evening, perpetually looking over his shoulder for a stalker who never appeared. Maybe he had imagined Rahman after all. Or then maybe not. But that wasn't the only reason for his confusion. He had half hoped that Emily might present him with a simple route map to Jameela… a map of Treasure Island, on which there was a label that said, 'Here be dinars and much gold' or something like that. He suspected that he might be able to go to Ahmedabad, locate the Aurora HQ there and simply find Jameela, perhaps sitting behind a desk, or in some sort of classroom. But Emily, despite what Felix had earlier taken for her encouragement in this regard, had been quite insistent: no, he shouldn't go to Ahmedabad, Jameela would be long gone now; yes, he needed rather to follow the original trail left by Lord Lindisfarne, then Victor Turnbull.

'Or why can't I just go to that Channel Island where m'lord and lady are supposed to hang out?' he'd asked.

'Far too risky, and anyway, no-one knows for sure if they are ever there...'

Felix ended up with a distinct feeling that he wasn't actually being told everything; that he was almost a pawn in a larger game of life.

Just as his flight was called, he sent an encrypted message to Michelle, suggesting she come to York and that they spend the following weekend in the Lake District.

'Ooh, I thought you'd never ask,' came the encrypted reply.

Felix's arrival back in the North was without further unwelcome eventuality and, once in the sanctuary of his flat in York, he decided to peruse some more of the contents of the lozenge that Michelle had given him.

He looked first at a collection of PDFs of newspaper and magazine articles. One was from the Free Radical and he immediately found himself kicking himself: why had he never realised that this politico-scientific liberal journal that he had thumbed through from time to time in WHSmith was the creature of none other than Victor Lord Lindisfarne himself?

The headline on the first article, an early-page opinion piece, screamed: 'Why I'm backing Gloria – by Victor Turnbull, Publisher.'

The article read:

Since establishing The Free Radical as an independent voice that encourages innovative thinking in UK politics, often outside the constraints of traditional party lines, my philosophy has been at all times to remain out of the limelight myself.

In stepping out of the shadows to write this leader piece today, therefore, I do so not with the intention of abusing the position conferred on me by ownership, but because it is surely essential that someone stir up the turgid pond of platitudes that has become the so-called 'race' for the Labour Party leadership.

I say 'so-called' race because, by my definition, a race involves an element of competition, of excitement – in short, of inspiration. The current Labour leadership battle offers none of the above: it is the soporific shuffle of the half-dead towards a wake to which they haven't been invited.

Like their counterparts in the other mainstream parties, our putative Labour leaders scratch their heads and perplexedly ask themselves why UK society, and its younger members in particular, are currently so indifferent to the political process.

Well, people, it's because you are so very boring and uninspirational! Let's recall for a moment the days when politicians had charisma; when the Labour Party stood for radicalism, social justice and new ideas; when a politician might dare, once in a while, simply to speak his or her own mind. Now, name me just half a dozen Labour politicians who might dare to break free of the party straitjacket; who might even have the breadth of life experience that would enable them to think and speak out with such disregard for the party line.

Let me save you the trouble: I will name you just one Labour politician who fits that bill. I concede that Gloria Turnbull may lack the temperance that has come to characterise our political leaders; she may at times be frank to the point of brutality; she calls it how she sees it and how she sees it is as often as not how it is; she oozes humour and what she may lack in free-flowing natural charisma, she more than makes up for with her forcefulness of argument and passion for truth and justice.

With such attributes we might expect that Gloria would be a front-runner for the post of leader. That she is not reflects no scandal, no lack of empathy among her modest but dedicated band of supporters. Rather, it is a reflection of all that is wrong with our party politics: the 'race' is between shades of grey – grey men who enjoy varying degrees of support within the various power blocks; grey men whose common trait is safety, caution and aversion to risk.

The reality, I know, is that one or other of the Bumbelowski brothers shall prevail in the leadership contest, but I believe that, if nothing else, my intervention can help stimulate at least a semblance of real debate, real politics before the final outcome.

Already some of the best members of my team are working with Gloria, not to temper her natural charisma and enthusiasm, but to help her drive home her key messages and to help her improve her tactical game. Above all, to help build her relationship with real people as opposed to party people.

At the very least I hope it will inject some life into the race of the undead.

Felix had not paid a great deal of attention to the Labour leadership election at the time and had not been aware of Gloria Turnbull as anything but a rank outsider in the contest. The notion that Victor Turnbull had helped her was intriguing: more so than anything else about the election, which had indeed – as Turnbull had predicted –been won by one of the Bumbelowski brothers, though not the one everyone had expected.

The next PDF was a news cutting from The Phoenix, from New Year 2012, and was a report of the New Year Honours list.

The e-commerce entrepreneur, Victor Turnbull, is among new life peers named in the New Year Honours list.

Turnbull, who will take his seat on the Labour benches, is among 15 new political appointees to the House of Lords and arguably the most interesting of these, given his near complete obscurity until the remarkable rise of his Aurora Group, which began little more than a year ago and which continues to wrong-foot more established names in the technology world.

Turnbull will assume the title of Lord Lindisfarne, after the Holy Island off the Northumberland coast, reflecting his allegiance to what he calls 'the ancient Kingdom of Northumbria'.

Although he did not back the winning horse in the Labour election race, preferring instead to throw his weight behind the outsider, Gloria Turnbull, who shares a surname though no other familial connection, Turnbull has nonetheless earned significant respect within party ranks, where he is seen as an important element in leader Jon Bumbelowksi's efforts to reconnect the party not just with its traditional support but also with young people and new audiences in the business community.

Only in The Phoenix, thought Felix, would it be possible to find a sentence of more than 100 words and with two subordinate clauses, in a news story. Once again, Felix reflected that what he had read contained no new information, but was something he should really have been more aware of.

Then there was another article by Lord Lindisfarne himself, published in Psychology Now.

Lord Lindisfarne, one of the newest peers in the House of Lords, gives a fascinating insight into what it is like to experience a manic episode...

They told my partner, Michaela, she could expect me to be like this for a year; maybe six months if she was lucky.

But hey, life is short and time is of the essence. Why waste time being mad for a year if you can pack it into a month or two? And so it was that, three weeks and two days after being admitted to psychiatric hospital, I was formally discharged. I had been ill for two months — mad for one.

My friends and family will forever remember my manic episode for two great highlights: my creation of a vast global business, 50 per cent of whose profits are devoted to doing good works in all corners of the world, and my conviction that I had had a beyond-the-grave rendezvous with my brother, who had died in a car crash a few years previously, from which I had escaped largely unharmed.

For most people, of course, the creation of a vast global business during a manic episode will prove ultimately to be delusional. I am deeply fortunate in that the inspirational qualities of my mania did, in reality, spark just such a development and for that element of my mania I can only be deeply grateful. Equally, I do recognise that this creation might, in different circumstances, have proved to be nothing more than the product of a fevered imagination.

Most important for me is my conviction that the cause of my mental illness lay in a physical injury sustained when I was vaulting a gate. This knowledge is a tremendous crutch for me when I am reminded by the psychiatric experts that I am statistically much more likely now to experience another manic episode than is the population at large.

So a butterfly flaps its wings in Amazonia and causes hundreds to die in a cyclone in the Philippines…

My own brush with chaos theory began with a minor accident and led me on an at times exhilarating and at times terrifying journey that included three weeks in psychiatric hospital. In something close to other people's descriptions of near-death experiences I believed I had been shown the very codes of evolution itself; I rediscovered long-lost talents and acquired an extraordinary sense of infallibility. But I encountered the darker side of humanity and terrified those closest to me.

My 'butterfly moment' began when I vaulted over a gate, which then collapsed beneath me. Although my tenderest parts took a hefty whack from cross-members of the gate, I was convinced it was my pride that was most at risk and was happy to note that no-one other than Michaela had witnessed my inelegant acrobatics.

Over the coming days and then weeks, strange things began to happen. I became forgetful and distant, and prone to cold sweats. Then I broke down, sweating, in a business meeting and had to get a colleague to come and take me home. I had the distinct feeling that my brain was somewhere outside my body and that I was going to die. I couldn't remember the last time I had had a proper night's sleep.

It was quite a long feature and it began to put a lot more flesh on the bare bones of Felix's understanding of Lord Lindisfarne. It went on to describe in some detail the visit to the stone circles on Orkney, of which Felix was already aware, then there was an account of football match, which Newcastle United had won 6-0. This appeared to have been something of a watershed in the then Victor Turnbull's descent into a manic episode.

It described Turnbull's self-diagnosis of his condition and his attempts at self-medication. It was when Lindisfarne described his apparent meeting beyond the grave with his dead brother, that Felix really began to pay attention…

I wasn't really challenged by anyone about having met with my brother. In fact some, including Michaela, believed that in a quite real sense I had indeed met with him. Do I believe now that I met him? Well, a quite senior man of the Church very kindly made time to discuss my experience with me at some length about five months after the episode.

He suggested to me that, in my heightened emotional state, I might actually have been communicating with my own sub-conscious. My brother's words, then, were perhaps no more than expressions of my own concerns: a family schism at a time that should be joyful and uniting; not focusing on the most important things in my own and Michaela's life; wanting to believe that my brother might have died for some greater purpose.

It's easy now to look back on my manic episode and to find more rational explanations for some of the things I experienced. At the same time, however, it can be quite challenging and sobering to reconcile this more conventional reality with what seemed at the time to be a very real, if alternative, universe.

Just how alternative was the universe I was living in? Well, alternative enough for my GP and the NHS Crisis Team to form the view that I needed to be in hospital, at least for my own and possibly for other people's safety. That's because the problem in my brain went from being, perhaps, a surfeit of adrenaline compounded by sleep deprivation to what was by now in all likelihood a much more complex chemical imbalance. I found myself locked in a cycle in which I now suspect that my own increasingly bizarre behaviour served to stoke up that imbalance. My little old engine was now not just running on methanol but had a turbocharger fitted too. My short-term memory was such that if I crossed the room to find something, I would have forgotten what I was looking for by the time I got there. In my dimly lit night-time world I began to accumulate possessions in little piles in different places. If I lost something all I had to do was work from pile to pile; even if I forgot what I was actually looking for I would find it simply by following the trail from pile to pile. Was this how animals remembered where things were? I wondered.

Then Lindisfarne described bizarre behaviour, when he had stalked his own cats at the dead of night and then created what he called a new feline evolutionary theory.

I figured that for early cave-dwellers the newly domesticated cat must have become a great look-out; curled up half-asleep by the fire at the back of the cave, its half-open eye would detect any external movement from a glint in a seam of quartz in the cave roof, picked out in the glow of the firelight. My feline evolutionary theory saw cats as incredibly quick learners, moving on from and never repeating behaviours that produced bad outcomes. In return for warmth and scraps of food, the cat would keep watch and deter vermin. The cat would also use humans to help him unwind after the hunt, only stretching and aerating his body when he was completely comfortable and feeling unthreatened by human presence.

The feature told how Lindisfarne had stalked his own cats and how this in turn had prompted his further mental decline.

I found myself feeling disproportionately proud of what seemed like an immense leap forward in cat psychology, but it proved the catalyst for the next catastrophic deterioration in my behaviour. Locked in stalking mode, my brain was surging to new levels of hyperactivity: I could no longer follow a conversation. It seemed to me that I was hearing people's responses to anything I said long before they had even opened their mouths. Indeed, I was already responding to their response before they had actually had time to think about responding. I was seeing tomorrow's newspapers on sale each day and was always convinced it was a day later than it actually was. I found I could turn the volume of my hearing up and down to cope with different levels of background noise. I mitigated the communication problem by insisting on talking to people with the aid of a mirror. That way, I could watch both my own lips and those of other people and synchronise my conversation accordingly. Worse than that, my nocturnal life as a cat had turned me into a lion. I became fearful about where the next food would come from and yet I needed food to be sure I had the energy to hunt. My son would bring me a plate of big sandwiches but I would see only tiny blinis with the odd prawn on top.

That Vic Turnbull then found himself close to be Sectioned under mental health regulations came as little surprise to Felix, though he found the actual account compelling. Once in hospital, he'd met up with an ex-boxer, called Dave Nixon, and gone on to form an allegiance that had clearly been central to his ultimate recovery.

Dave kept a rosary in his pocket, or rosemary, as he called it. I discovered Michaela had slipped into my bag a small brass casting of the three wise monkeys who neither saw, heard nor spoke evil. It became my own rosary and never left my pocket during my hospitalisation.

Dave had made it his job to look after the hospital's sensory garden: we tended all the herbs and I helped Dave with the names of some of those he didn't know. It was an Indian summer and my hospital uniform became shorts and T-shirt. I soon cast off my shoes, determined to feel the grass and the texture of the floors beneath my feet. I rose to my tiptoes and would pace round the edge of the lawn in rapid circles. I was reminded of the Scottish wildcat I'd seen years before in Edinburgh zoo, wearing a track round the perimeter of its enclosure. But I wasn't a cat or even a lion any more: I was an aboriginal hunter in the Australian outback. Other patients were often lost behind their iPods or Walkmans, but the hunter needed to feel and experience his surroundings, so I developed safe iPodding, my iPhone sitting in my pocket and churning out incessant aboriginal dreamtime music.

When I was a child I indulged in creating make-believe worlds. I'd map some of these on paper, but to 'turn them into reality' I had to fire up the most powerful motors of my imagination. I found I could do this quite easily by running in circles or, more usually, back and forth along a circuit of 20 metres or so in length. I guess some of the adrenaline I created from physical exercise was channelled into the creative part of my brain and my fantasy worlds acquired a near tangible reality.

Looking back, it seems to me that the surfeit of adrenaline in my system during my illness had found its way back into the part of my brain that had once been trained to create fantasy worlds. This time, however, there were two problems that simply hadn't existed when I was a child: I wasn't too good at distinguishing between the real world that my brain observed and the imaginary one that another part of it was creating; and I had lost the ability to switch the fantasy on and off, even if and when I could recognise it. Again, with hindsight, it's clear that the fantasies had begun a week or more before my hospitalisation. The underlying premise was that my business, far from being forced to adjust to the reality of an economic downturn and changed government policies, was actually very successful and enabled me to achieve many things.

Although the article was unusually long, Felix was gripped as he tried to put himself in Lord Lindisfarne's shoes. In his delusions, the then plain Victor Turnbull had, with Nixon, come up with a plan to save the world in seven days and a whole new theory about the 'elasticity' of time, that he expressed in the formula $2^\infty = \infty^2$. Felix found himself shaking his head in disbelief and wonderment. 'I could use a bit of this insanity myself,' he thought.

The article continued:

I could probably write a book about all the curious things that happened while I was 'inside'; about all the curious thoughts I thought; about the many eureka moments I experienced as suddenly a whole new universe was beginning to make sense.

Gradually, as the days passed, I was aware that I was beginning to slow down and my primary focus moved to getting myself out of captivity and back home.

All the while, of course, my able business deputy, Stella de Weld, was coming in to hospital to meet with me and then working hard on my behalf to lay the foundations of what would become the Aurora Group.

By the time I first came home, the Aurora train had left the station and was steaming strongly ahead — it was an immense relief to me to discover that Aurora was NOT in fact a figment of my imagination, as I concede some things during my hospitalisation, in hindsight, were.

In these more fantastic episodes, the hospital staff exercised the utmost patience and helped nudge me gradually back towards normality. I have only the utmost respect for them, if rather less for the buffoons who paid through the nose for the hospital they work in. But that, of course, is another story…

Then there was a piece from Wired that aimed to unravel the story of Aurora. It talked about the Framboise take-over, and about Aurora's subsequent move into different areas of e-business: the search engine, Eureka; the messaging tool, Blather; the encryption tools; and the hardware, including the VSP. Taking a transatlantic position, it questioned how the major American players had managed to fall asleep on the job and permit this European unknown to steal such an unexpected lead in so many areas.

'No-one could say even that Aurora's products have that must-have quality that we see in, say, an iPhone – Aurora is actually a triumph of functionality over brand to the point that the brand has acquired its strength through the reliability and efficacy of its products rather than by being, above all, seductive,' ran the commentary.

Felix reflected that he himself had chosen the VSP simply because it was the best. But it wasn't unsexy and he fancied the Gallic influence permeated many aspects of the device. Then again, would he ever have bought it if it hadn't had that cute little raspberry logo on it?

Within a few days of his return north, Felix had moved things forward: he had broached the subject of his proposed sabbatical and dodged the grenades that flew as a consequence. Ultimately his boss had said to him, despairingly: 'You're a good operator, Felix, and I had high hopes that you were ready to move on to the next level, but – however much I'm angry from a business perspective – I know that questions of work and loyalty to colleagues are no match for affairs of the heart. I'd like to say you go with my blessing, but you don't, because I think what you are doing is, frankly, madness. It's so mad that I'm not even sure I should keep your job open until it all turns sour on you. But, like I say, you're a good operator and I hope you will come back to us, even with your tail between your legs...'

Felix struggled to find the words to reply and ended up saying, simply: 'OK, thanks!' It seemed hopelessly inadequate.

And now here he was, on the platform at York station awaiting the train from London. He spotted Michelle quickly, as did she him. The pair marched purposefully across the pedestrian bridge towards the exit. And then Felix glimpsed something, or someone, he really hadn't expected to see.

'Oh my God, Michelle,' he said. 'We're in trouble!'

CHAPTER 21

Home leave

Thursday, September 16, 2010

I am disappointed that my safe iPodding hasn't been adopted with more enthusiasm here at Priestley House. I still see guys walking the corridors with big earphones on their heads and their eyes glued to the floor. Perhaps it is more than one man can achieve on his own. And yet my Walk Tall campaign achieved so much. The Aborigines are giving it wellie on the didgeridoo as I step out once again into the warming rays of the morning autumn sun. Soon the sun is burning my back and hot sands sear the soles of my feet...

Rog Reid felt an enormous weight of responsibility sitting on his shoulders. It hadn't been so long since he'd been just a young man who liked computers who happened to work for a small company that had become the victim of a hacking scandal. He was proud that Victor had shown faith in his ability as little Persona had morphed into the Aurora giant and its charitable foundation had blossomed in the fertile ground created by its share of the Aurora Group's spiralling profits. Of all the activities funded by the Foundation – from research into bumble bees

on the one hand to its proactive anti-corruption campaigning on the other – Rog's line of work was by far the most controversial, not to say potentially dangerous.

Aurora's Anti-Fundamentalism Unit was highly secret, its mere existence known only to those who worked in it and to Lord Lindisfarne himself. No-one in the unit knew for sure whether even Lady Lindisfarne was fully aware of what went on inside the walls of its 'bunker'. Nor for that matter was the location of the unit in the public domain. If Rog or one of his team bumped into anyone else from Aurora the story was that they were working on a project to extend literacy in the developing world. Indeed the World Literacy Project actually had a plaque on an office door in the Group headquarters, in Newcastle, and Rog would be seen from time to time going in and out of the office, whose permanent residents were half a dozen people in charge of allocating funding to third party work in the field of literacy.

Most days, however, Rog's place of work was about 500 miles north west, as the crow flies – deep inside a rugged mountain on a windswept archipelago in the North Atlantic. There had been various ideas mooted as potential uses for the former Nato listening post in the Faroe Islands, but all would have demanded significant capital to make the entrance to this giant bunker more accessible, as a tourist attraction for example. Accessibility, however, was the least of Aurora's concerns when it bought the giant complex and its associated 'barracks': a turf-roofed building with a commanding fellside view down a dramatic fjord. Security, on the other hand, was paramount and this was delivered by virtue of the old base's containment within a mountain of basalt and through its only access being by means of a twisting single-track road that climbed to close to 2,000ft to reach the securely guarded entrance to its labyrinths.

The departing Nato forces had filled some of the spaces with concrete to entomb forever equipment that was too bulky to remove and yet too secret to leave behind. Aurora had excavated some of these tunnels again and had dug new ones. And had reopened the 'jewel in the crown' – a tunnel leading to an opening in the side of the mountain, high in the cliffs above the boiling ocean.

One might have thought that, in an archipelago of 50,000 souls, the presence of strange people inside a mountain might have sparked at least some curiosity, but Aurora had, once again, created a smokescreen.

As far as the Faroese people were concerned, the mountain housed just a small team of researchers in the Centre for the Study of Cetacean Populations. Small team it may have been but its work was prolific, not least in the field of the controversial Faroese grindadráp – the practice of harvesting often quite large numbers of pilot whales from a population accepted to be more than capable of withstanding it.

Given this output, there was no appetite in Faroese society to ask questions about what else might go on in the mountain. Rog's local friends would jokingly call him a troll or one of the 'hidden people' and he would play up to it by describing how he had slunk out of the huge tomb at night and moved sheep from one side of the mountain to the other.

It's hard to say how these same friends might have responded had they known that Rog's true purpose was the movement not of sheep but of human beliefs – and on a near industrial scale.

The objective was to nudge followers of the world's various faiths away from dogmatic interpretations of supposedly holy scriptures and towards more benign, tolerant creeds. These new faiths would be represented to communities by the arrival of a new prophet who would extol universal values like individual liberty, the decriminalisation of apostasy, sexual equality and the separation of faith and state.

These days, however, there was little call for prophets to toil up mountains and descend with books of rules, or indeed to have themselves martyred in the cause of reinforcing their prophetic status.

Health workers and aid workers had recognised for some time that large populations in the less developed world could most easily be reached and engaged with via the mobile phone network. Simple health messages could be shared with large numbers of people who did not necessarily even need to be literate.

It was the same with the new faith messages, which were based on the simple principle that the 'new prophet' advocated a return to the original roots of the faith. These original roots, of course, represented an interpretation of the scriptures which, while very different from the version of the religion that most would know and maybe even love, was really every bit as valid. Indeed Rog's team of researchers had quickly reached the conclusion that pretty much every faith had begun on the right track but its rules had soon been manipulated for the purpose of meeting the aspirations of a self-serving elite and denying the 'common people' control over their own religion, and indeed their own destiny.

Rog's team had begun experimentally, verifying that the 'sacred messages' could under no circumstances be traced back to either Aurora or the Faroe Islands. Indeed, they were disseminated via the channels of what was, in effect, a private Internet, with banks of servers not just here in the mountain headquarters, but in secret locations across the globe. The first campaigns were quite gentle, nudging adherents towards liberal religious interpretations and giving theological validity to such liberalism. There had been measurable success within the Anglican church, in which the so-called Re-Scripturing movement had helped to marginalise less tolerant views.

But now Rog was increasingly uneasy about rolling the strategy out into other faiths and other parts of the world. Specifically, he wanted to sit down with Lord Lindisfarne and talk about Islam, as he feared strategies for change could be, at best, ineffective and, at worst, incendiary...

'Victor, don't you want any breakfast today?' It's the voice of Julia. The aboriginal hunter must leave the dusty red heat of mid-day sun; leave the Dreamtime.

I stroll in to breakfast, where there are even fewer of the guys than normal. I have a sense of something in the air though I can't quite put my finger on it. I have seen very little of Dave these last days and I have missed him: he's the only one on my wavelength really. I wander to Reception but no-one there is sure of Dave's whereabouts. I ask Julia if I can have a chat and we go into a small consultation room. An unfinished game of chess is on the table, suggesting Dave's presence here at some point not too long ago.

'So, Vic,' says Julia. 'What can I do you for?'

'I'd like to go home this weekend – see how things go...' The words have been only half planned but I feel it's time for me to press for progress. I see the familiar rolling of the eyes and I know what's coming, so I save her the trouble: 'You see Victor, it's not just about what you want, it's about everybody else as well…' I say, with oozing sarcasm.

'Well, that's just exactly it, Victor, so you can mock as much as you want, but not only do you have to feel ready, but Michaela has to feel ready and Dr Honeydew…'

'And Uncle Tom Cobley and all…'

'Look, Vic, how about we have a plan? It's Thursday today. Get Michaela to speak with me when she comes in to see you and then you try and speak to Dr Honeydew in the morning. But I'll promise you one thing: it won't be a whole weekend and it probably won't even be overnight.'

I am unsure whether to feel pleased or deflated: I make the mistake of calling Michaela at work and telling her about the conversation with Julia. I immediately think I would have done better not to give her advance warning, and that view is borne out when she arrives later, on her way home from work. I don't think she has forgiven me for my previous 'commando' visit home with Leanne; or for my 'escapades' around the county with Charlotte; or for my lunch out with Danny.

'So what makes you think you're ready for a home visit?' she asks me.

'Because I am a lot better; a lot calmer; and I know I won't be any trouble.'

'And how are the plans for world domination?'

'Oh, of course I still have ambitions and you're very much part of them, but, you know, I just want to see my home, see you at home, see Bafta and Nada… start getting back to normal.'

'You know, Vic, you're not the only one in all this: I'm having a stressful time at work – and your calls there really don't help, because I'm trying to make sure no-one at work knows where you are – and I really can't cope with you coming home and going crazy. And anyway, Phil and Jean are going to come down from Durham and come and see you so it's not like there isn't something to look forward to…'

This is news to me; good news... Phil is an old friend from student days and, of all my university friends, they have been perhaps the least changed by work, wealth and ambition. It would be good to see them, but for just a couple of hours?

'So, all the more reason for me to come home, surely?!'

'Vic,' says Michaela. 'This isn't just about you...'

I feel hurt and annoyed. 'No, but it's not just about you either and, given that it's my life, it has to be at least a little bit about me.'

Later in the evening, before she goes off shift, Julia calls me to one side. It's clear she has been my advocate in her meeting with Michaela. She tells me she'll leave a note for Dr Honeydew and to be sure I catch him in the morning.

At tea, there's still no sign of Dave but, last thing, after meds, we pass in the corridor.

'Great news, Vic, mate, I'm being discharged tomorrow. I'm off doon te Brighton to stay with me sister.'

I say my goodbyes to Dave on Friday morning. I guess one man's joy and all that: the thought of time stretching ahead here at Priestley House fills me only with dread. There's a crowd milling round Reception and I know the best place for me is somewhere else. As I leave, Dr Honeydew arrives and disappears into his office. I head back towards my room to check that it is still 11 minutes past 11 and to see if I can get a phone signal today by standing on the window sill. I need to catch up with Stella – life would be that much easier if there was an Internet signal.

I'm aware of someone on my shoulder and the thought flashes through my mind that perhaps Dave isn't leaving after all. However, it is nurse John.

'How's it going, Vic lad?'

'Oh, not so bad, though I've lost my soulmate today...'

'Dave? Yeah, you two've been as thick as thieves these last two weeks…'

'Yeah, there's no-one else I really get on with; at least not on an equal basis. It mightn't be so bad if there was Internet, but at the end of the day there's only so much TV you can watch; only so many games of pool and table tennis you can play. And anyway, I only like playing with Dave.'

'Aye, well the Internet is a problem here, but of course there are some people we could never allow near the Internet…'

'Like Tricky Thomas?'

'I'm saying nothing!'

I remind John of my idea of putting an Internet connection under every bed. 'You could keep the connections locked and only open them when you had responsible residents who could be trusted.'

'Residents like you, I suppose?'

'Yes, of course,' I say. I can't quite read his expression.

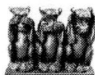

I succeed in getting a message to Stella by holding the phone out of the window and at 11.11 (plus 15 minutes) I judge it should be the right time to approach Dr Honeydew.

It is Ute behind the desk. I think very carefully before speaking in English: 'Is Dr Honeydew available, please Ute?'

She looks surprised to hear me address her in English. 'Because you are being so polite, Victor, I shall ask.'

Dr Honeydew invites me to walk down the corridor to a private meeting room.

'I haven't seen you hanging around Reception so much, Victor,' he begins, his gaze, as ever, directed towards a point half a metre below and to the left of my face. 'I expect you're wanting to know if you can go home for a little while tomorrow, so I won't waste time talking about the weather. I've watched your behaviour and talked to all my colleagues and it's clear you are responding to the drug treatment well, now that we have the dose right for you. So I have talked with Julia, who feels you should be allowed home, and I talked with Michaela this morning and was able to reassure her that she can send you back here the minute you start misbehaving. So, shall we call it a Day Pass for Saturday?'

'It would be very nice if we could,' I smile.

That afternoon I take a trip to see Valentina but she is not on duty. I am disappointed as I feel we have a connection, but nonetheless haven't connected for a while. I return via the obstacle course and leap from wooden stake to wooden stake: I can feel the energy within and hurry back to the garden, where I lash the football against the flower bed a few times. The thwack of leather on wood feels good against my tough leather feet: wood-on-wood; flesh-on-flesh; leather-on-leather. The Aborigines are playing in my pocket as I begin to beat the path around the lawn. The day is drawing to a close but the sun still incinerates the parched earth; as the sun reddens, so too does the scorched landscape. The heat rising from the baked desert plays tricks on the horizon and conceals a group of red kangaroos pounding towards the aborigine. He raises his spear above his shoulder and confidently takes aim...

The Embraer jet takes off from Leeds Bradford Airport and climbs out over Otley and Wharfedale, before gently turning slightly to head to the north-east of the Lake District, then crossing the border north of Carlisle. The invited guests are a cross-section of everyone who has supported the Aurora project through its early months plus one slightly unexpected passenger: the man they call the Hermit in his home town of Ripon. The Hermit lives in an uncharacteristically, for neatly presented Ripon, shabby little single-storey house, its roof of cracked red pantiles untidily adorned with rambling rose and bindweed, with its deceptively attractive white parachute flowers. The windows are cracked and dirty, the paint peeling, the front door rotten, the garden overgrown with cow parsley in

Spring, and willow herb and nettles in Summer; so the Hermit's house attracts the unwelcome attention of under-occupied groups of youths from time to time.

Yet the few privileged to have been invited to witness the interior of the little house are surprised to find it scrupulously clean and tidy; uncluttered, its walls lined with erudite rows of books, an enviable collection of vinyl, and ornaments and artefacts bearing testimony to a life lived and a road well travelled. No-one is particularly sure how the Hermit came to be so shy and reclusive and, while they have nothing at all against him, this being a well-heeled town, they do have concerns that the appearance of his property is knocking a few per cent off the value of nearby homes.

This is not the primary concern of Victor and Michaela, whose property is among the closest to the Hermit's. Rather, Victor has identified the small piece of undeveloped land that is separated from their own garden by the Hermit's as the ideal spot in which to create a small 'garden of rest' for the family to visit and reflect on the life of his brother Malcolm, and indeed all others 'lost', albeit in less dramatic circumstances.

Vic's aspiration is for the Hermit to leave to enable this to happen and then the house could be tidied up and perhaps adapted to provide a suitable home for Ayanna and her disabled son. As the Embraer continues its flight north, Victor is walking up and down the cabin, talking with guests while, internally, congratulating himself on having engineered a possible future for the Hermit that will enable his plans for the house and land to be realised. Yes, the Hermit has agreed to look at some even lonelier places to live, consistent with his core desire for comfort and a more romantic location, perhaps, than Ripon.

Only a few people on board are privy to the Hermit's identity (he has been given a smart suit and a haircut for the occasion), much less to the fact that it is the Hermit's future that has shaped the itinerary for the next two days.

'The Hermit's a sucker for lonely dramatic islands,' Vic assured Michaela as the plans for the trip were laid.

'I trust you're right,' she replied, sceptically. 'It's a lot of money...'

'A lot of money we no longer need to worry about,' he reminded her.

From the little airport at Islay, the bus made its way across the surprisingly benign landscape, bathed by the warm waters of the Gulf Stream Drift. Some of Scotland's most celebrated distilleries adorn Islay's sandy shores, but today's destination was another island altogether.

For twins, Islay and Jura have little in common – in relative terms, Islay positively bustles, with more than 3,000 residents; Jura can't muster 200, though it has a great many deer. Islay's highest point is only about 1,500ft above sea level; Jura's dramatic Paps push towards twice that. There's but one distillery to Islay's eight, at the last count, but this is today's first destination, the idea being that the Hermit can compare the relative merits of two contrasting islands.

Freshly caught and cooked local lobster at the hotel next to the distillery is washed down by Jura Origin – very much its own whisky despite the proximity of its famous neighbour to the south-west. Vic is hoping the associations with George Orwell, who holed up far along the single track leading north from the village to write 1984, will appeal to the Hermit's literary pretensions.

Blessed by the long still rays of a North Atlantic evening sun, departure from Islay is magical as successive island vistas unfold as the Embraer resumes its seemingly serendipitous journey north. The next stop, however, will have a greater purpose, and one seemingly more connected with Victor himself, and indeed the Aurora Foundation. A few years previously, back in the days when Aurora was just plain old Persona Communications, Vic and the Icelanders had set up a meeting with potential new partners in the Faroe Islands. Towards the end of a successful series of meetings to explore the scope for joint working and, indeed, for establishing a North Atlantic IT hub, the Faroese delegation had unveiled a surprise for everyone: a trip to the far west island of Mykines – an island that holds a particularly fond place in the hearts of the Faroese people, to the extent that, while you could count the population comfortably on the fingers of one hand in winter, those numbers could swell easily to a few score in summer.

The idea had been to take the helicopter out in the morning and *return by boat later in the day. But the fickle Atlantic Ocean had had other ideas and the little ferry had had no choice but to escape the rapidly rising swell before it had been able to take on board a full complement of passengers. For most of those left behind, the inconvenience was neither severe nor especially unexpected and they simply returned to summer homes that had been in their families for generations.*

Vic and his colleagues were less fortunate and the only option was to bunk down in what passed for an occasional guesthouse. Its owner was not on the island to sort out bedlinen, or – for that matter – food and drink. Vic had always thought Mykines would benefit from somewhere more suitable for the weary traveller to lay his or her head and had set up a local fund to raise the resources to ship over the materials to erect just such a facility. By the time Persona had become Aurora and the latter in turn had begun to generate profits beyond the younger Vic's imagination, he had all but forgotten about this early charitable venture. So it was with surprise and some delight that he had recently discovered that the fund set up those years previously had not just gathered dust but had actually grown to a point at which a decent injection of cash from the newly established Aurora Foundation would enable its realisation.

This evening, therefore, would see a reunion with the Icelanders and the Faroese at the new building – bearing a plaque in memory of the lives of local sailors and seabird-hunters lost, and a short dedication also to Malcolm Turnbull – to be followed by a banquet of Faroese fish soup and slow-cooked Faroese lamb. The party on the Embraer would then be the first to overnight at the new premises, built in the local tradition with a fine new grass roof and brightly coloured doors and windows.

It was a remarkable, some might say foolhardy, leap of faith by Vic, given the real risks that this new party might just as easily be stranded as was the very one whose failure to get off the island ahead of the approaching storm had driven the creation of the new lodgings. And yet, with high pressure settled across the islands, the Embraer had flown up the narrow fjord to the precariously situated Faroe Islands Airport, at Vágar, to kiss the ground immaculately, before disgorging its payload to the waiting helicopter.

Vic was delighted to see the Hermit enthralled by his dramatic new surroundings and had high hopes as the chopper collected the party again in the morning for the return journey to Leeds, via another improbable island.

The Embraer landed at Sumburgh near the southern tip of Shetland, where this time the band of passengers was transferred onto three small waiting aeroplanes for the short hop to Fair Isle, one of the two most remote permanently inhabited islands in the United Kingdom, but one with a relatively thriving local economy, thanks to its home-knitting tradition and its reputation as an extraordinary place at which to see rare birds, blown astray during long migrations across the ocean.

To facilitate that interest in the birdlife, the island's bird observatory, doubling up as the only 'hotel' and 'bar', had recently been substantially rebuilt and extended, though it remained a not particularly attractive edifice to look at. However, another early bequest by the Aurora foundation had been to work with the National Trust for Scotland to create another communal building in a more vernacular style and more inclined towards supporting 'wool tourism', rather than bird-watching. The intention today was for Vic to unveil a modest plaque and, of course, for the Hermit to inspect the small number of empty homes on the island, whose rugged horizon belied its tiny size.

Taking off from Sumburgh that evening and turning to the south, Vic reflected that, not only had his own and Michaela's – and indeed Aurora's – guests enjoyed a thoroughly unusual and enjoyable trip as thanks for their help in the Foundation's formative years, but surely the Hermit had also seen enough that he might be tempted to vacate the little tumble-down cottage in Ripon…

'Victor, aren't you having any tea tonight? Vic slipped from the skies over Scotland and found himself back at Priestley House.

'Yeah, I hadn't noticed the time,' I say. With Dave gone, and as I enjoy little real empathy with many others in the dining room, I move to a table at the back of the room, realising as I do so that there is, actually, a kind of hierarchy of sanity: the further back you are, the saner you are, and indeed, on the whole, the more quietly you conduct yourself at meal times, the further away from the serving hatch you'll be, and the closer to sanity you'll be.

When the meds are given out that evening, I remain thoughtful: I look at the setup in the little communal drinks kitchen: there's sugar and coffee granules all over the worktop. I clean it all carefully. Fifteen minutes later it is back to the same condition. I am despairing of my fellow inmates, especially now that Dave is gone. I can't wait for home leave tomorrow.

I awake at eight, full of hope and anticipation, though I must restrain myself from calling home as the morning is unaccustomed to seeing much of Michaela on a weekend. I wonder what time Phil and Jean are due. They are much more early risers. I believe they are bringing their bicycles down on the train, so I guess they'll be wanting to get going in decent time. At 8.30, showered and feeling fresh to face the world outside, I stick the phone out of the window and risk a text to Phil: they plan to get a train around 11, to Thirsk, from where they'll make the hour or so's ride to Ripon.

After breakfast, I chance a text to Michaela, suggesting she pick me up about 11.30 or 12. I walk round the ward, round the games room, round the garden. Strangely, Priestley House seems to have lost some of its mystique since Dave left. I wonder how I would have coped here at all without Dave; for the first time in two weeks I actually feel a little flat, subdued.

'You know I'd have come for you in plenty of time without you hassling me,' says Michaela.

'Since when did one text constitute hassling,' I ask.

She doesn't answer.

'If it's really so very much trouble, I'll stay here,' I say. 'I'm sure you'll have a wonderful time without me with Phil and Jean and you'll be able to do the cooking…' I really feel this whole visit thing is taking place under severe sufferance.

'Or, if you are going to take me home, at least do it with good grace…'

'Vic, I'm tired; I'm stressed. I don't really want company, so maybe you can look after Phil and Jean…'

'Fine; whatever…' We ride in silence towards Ripon.

On arriving home, I decide to keep my own counsel and retreat to the 'den' where I do the odd bit of painting, creative writing or, more often, paying bills and such like. There is a rather large pile of post on the desk. As I flick through it, I discover to my horror that most of the letters are pretty much the same. They are from insurance companies, organisations I belong to, credit card companies and the like, and say: 'We note that you have cancelled your direct debit with effect from [date] and we shall therefore be closing your account should we not hear from you by [date].' I find a bank statement: I have been over my overdraft limit for more than two weeks, from shortly before I was admitted to hospital. Letters from the bank refer to there having been insufficient funds to meet my various direct debit obligations.

I look for Michaela and ask: 'Why didn't you tell me about all these letters – they're after cancelling my life assurance and everything!'

'I thought you'd been cancelling them all yourself,' she replies. 'That's what the letters say.'

'That's because there's no money in my bank…'

'And you expect me to do what exactly? I've already put £8,000 in your business account because Stella said there wasn't enough to pay the salaries or to pay Charley…

'Or to pay me by the looks of things – my salary seems strangely absent from these statements,' I add, unsure what to say next.

I retreat to my den, organise the letters into groups and then slip downstairs and quietly park myself in front of the TV.

Phil and Jean arrive about 1.30 in not exactly the best of humour: it's still hot and some of the ride has been on quite busy roads. Michaela sticks her head round the door to say Hi and leaves me to find cool drinks and knock up a snack. I suggest we keep things simple and go for a walk to the edge of town. There's a lane with a lot of fruit bushes and trees and I fancy collecting some for jam. In the event, we find a bumper crop of just about every hedgerow fruit: brambles, crab apples, quinces, sloes, rosehips, damsons… Jean is quickly into the spirit of things and collects bagfuls of fruit, which I presume she will take home with her. Over the picking we chat about why I have been, why I am, in hospital and when I might be able to come home. I say I hope it won't be too many days and that I'm hoping Michaela will deem me fit to stay at home tonight.

We arrive back home and wash the fruit and I wonder what Michaela's plans are for an evening meal. Finding minced beef in the freezer and rounding up sufficient other ingredients, I reckon spag Bol is going to be the safest bet and begin the prep work, aided by Jean and Phil.

'Did you know,' I ask, 'that spaghetti Bolognese no more comes from Bologna than Newcastle Brown comes from Newcastle these days? In fact I believe the people of Bologna actively seek to disown it…'

'So where does it come from?' asks Phil.

'Well, I think they make a meaty ragù in Bologna, but they wouldn't dream of putting it with spaghetti…'

'Well, I guess the rest of the world can't be wrong,' says Jean, just as Michaela reappears.

She seems in better humour, but asks why on earth we are cooking when she intended to order a take-away. I suggest none of us is telepathic and, in any event, the spag Bol is half done and will taste twice as good as any take-away.

As we sit down to eat, two bottles of wine appear on the table:

one white, one red. I can think of few things I would like to do less than drink wine. I serve the spag Bol and Michaela serves the wine.

'I don't think you should have any of this,' she says.

'I feel like I would die if I did,' I reply.

She looks relieved.

As we eat, Phil and Jean are intrigued to hear the story of how I came to be admitted to Priestley House and so I explain all about the accident with the gate and the subsequent mishap on my bicycle. I want to tell them in as credible and measured a fashion as possible about how I met my brother, or his 'angel', and how I have been able to communicate with him and seek his affirmation in answer to important questions. It occurs to me that this is something that has been happening rather less often in recent days. I tell them how I feel my senses have been heightened – about my ability to look into people's eyes and see their soul; about the vestigial organs that derive from our lost ability to perceive what's going on behind us. I explain to them how I have seen the genetic map of my own family history; how they have come to call me the Man of Many Tongues and how so many hitherto seemingly unconnected little events in my life have come, collectively, to make sense. I do this all in as deadpan a way as possible lest I alarm them or they make a judgement as to my sanity.

I mention that things Malcolm has told me hint at some cataclysmic confrontation to come, between the USA and Islam, though the detail of this event – while it has come up more than once in my 'conversations with Malcolm' – remains hazy.

Phil and Jean tell me the story is 'extraordinary', 'fascinating', and then the conversation moves on to more mundane things, like the evolving football season, or Phil's passion, Rugby League (he's an exiled Lancastrian, originally from St Helen's). We talk about the quality and abundance of this year's hedgerow crop and Jean says she'll donate everything we've picked this afternoon to me. I promise sloe gin and hedgerow jam, while caring not to dwell too much on the idea of actually drinking the gin. Then the conversation switches to the Hermit, as we had earlier passed his house and Jean is curious.

I explain my ambition to create a family garden of remembrance beyond the Hermit's garden and mention that it might be nice to instal Ayanna and Arasto there. Out of the corner of my eye, I see Michaela's eyebrows rise at this. So I go on to explain how transformational developments in my business mean I, we, will have the resources to achieve many things, including a great many good things for other people and, ultimately, for society and the world at large. I have to go back to basics and explain how Persona Communications is acquiring the company that hacked us and how we are pursuing a number of can't-lose lawsuits against other companies that have 'wronged' us. I tell them about the aeroplane trip to visit the islands and to show the Hermit that there are many places he might like to live that will be better suited to his lifestyle than the tumbledown house at the bottom of our garden...

Phil and Jean remain 'fascinated', but again the conversation moves on and, as more wine is drunk, becomes, not raucous, but louder... Too loud for me: I am used to eating in near silence and I can't process all the conflicting noises I am hearing. I need to go and sit on my own, I tell them, as I'm struggling and need a quieter environment.

After 30 minutes or so Michaela comes looking for me. 'You're not being very sociable with your friends,' she says.

'I'm sorry but all that noise and chatter is making my head throb. I'm not used to people trying to out-talk each other round the dinner table. We eat in near silence at Priestley House...'

'Priestley House!' interjects Michaela. 'You're supposed to be going back there...'

'Well you're not driving me given the quantity of wine you've put away and I'm certainly not walking. You'd better ring them and tell them I'll be back tomorrow. Good job they sent me off with my meds for tonight...'

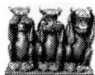

The following morning I wake up in my own bed, next to Michaela. It's very comforting, but I sense Michaela won't wake for some time yet and so I get up and help myself to cereal and toast. I have an urge for croissants and toy with walking to the Co-op, before remembering that I am persona non grata there. Jean appears, blurry-eyed, and asks me how I'm feeling.

'Probably rather better than you are,' I suggest. 'I feel OK, and it's been good being at home, but I think maybe I need to get back to Priestley House.'

Eventually Phil and Michaela also appear and we spend what remains of the morning drinking coffee and reading the papers. At Priestley House I have religiously scoured the Northern Echo each day making sure no significant linkages and connections escape my attention. Now, at home, one of the broadsheets has a big piece about climate change, which mentions that deforestation in Amazonia is a kind of a double whammy because not only are there no longer trees to absorb carbon dioxide, but they are often replaced by cattle ranches, and cows are among the biggest producers of unwanted methane and hence a big part of the global warming problem. Another story mentions that the National Trust for Scotland remains in a precarious financial position and speculates that it may struggle to maintain its costlier assets, like St Kilda. I feel warm inside with the knowledge that I will soon be able to come to the rescue. I mark both stories with ballpoint, date them and ask Michaela to be sure not to throw them out.

Phil and Jean head off on their bicycles after lunch and Michaela suggests it's time for me to return to Priestley House. I don't disagree.

'That didn't go too badly,' I venture, as we drive back.

'No, it didn't,' replies Michaela. 'Better than I expected.'

'And I wasn't mad,' I add.

'No, though I think Phil and Jean did find some of the things you told them a bit hard to take in.'

'Like meeting Malcolm?

'No, not that so much as the stuff about the Hermit and how you're... we're going to be wealthy and generous...'

'Well, they'll get used to it when it's just the way it is, I guess...'

Michaela changes tack: 'You know, Dr Honeydew mentioned to me that he sees you far less often around Reception. It's one of his measures of people's progress, including yours. He says when people's minds are agitated they buzz around Reception like bees round a hive or flies round a cow-pat...'

'I think I prefer the former,' I say.

After breakfast on Monday I return to my room and take out the various bank and credit card statements and letters from insurance companies I have brought from home. The mobile signal is being unusually cooperative today and – after transferring £2,000 from the Persona account to my own – I systematically ring each company to explain I have received a letter suggesting I have cancelled my payments. Painstakingly I reinstate each one. It takes more than an hour, during which time the mobile signal continues to behave.

I decide to take a walk to the main reception and see Valentina. As I leave the ward I pass Dr Honeydew, who stops me. 'How was your day at home, Victor?'

'It went well, I think, Dr Honeydew. In fact, it turned into nearly two days...'

'You mean Michaela decided you could stay?'

'Well, I'm not sure she had much choice, given the amount of wine...'

'Really?'

Oh dear, I think; I have probably put my foot in it, and add hastily, 'Don't worry, there's nothing that would appeal to me less – I took myself off and spent a quiet evening.'

'I'm pleased and relieved to hear that, Victor!'

I continue: 'I'd like to think I might be able to go home for longer, or even permanently…'

'All in good time, Victor, all in good time. Let's see how this week goes. Oh, and by the way, a little bit of positive news on that front. There'll be a chap called Marius will come to see you sometime this week. He's part of our team in the community. He's there to soften the blow when you are ready to return home.'

And with that, he is turned on his heels and is gone, without once having looked me in the eye.

As I complete the obstacle course in the garden near the main Reception, I reflect that the reason why I am headed here is because Dave is gone and I have no kindred spirit on the ward.

I'm thrilled, however, to find that Valentina is at work, though when I look into her eyes I see her soul is hurting.

'What's wrong,' I ask.

'It is my mother in Sicily. She is more ill and my brothers say I must return to help them look after her.'

'And you don't want to go?'

'My daughter especially does not want to go: she is English, she is not Italian and she is scared. And, for her, I too do not want to go and, you know, although I do not have, you know, romantic interest here, I think I am happy and, no, I do not want to go either to Sicily.'

'And perhaps if you stayed, there might be romantic interest? But then there might be romantic interest for you in Sicily, no?'

Valentina looks at me in a way that makes my heart miss a beat. For a fleeting second I think she might even have romantic designs upon me. Then she says, 'I do not want a Sicilian man unless perhaps he is Inspector Montalbano…'

'Don't leave without saying goodbye to me,' is all I can find to say. It feels decidedly limp.

'I fear it may be addio rather than arrivederci…' says Valentina.

I feel I am choking and my eyes feel wet. I am being ridiculous, I reflect, as I leave Valentina to her work.

I return to my room to reflect on things: Dave is gone; I have been home and stayed a night; I am to meet a man called Marius to help me prepare for a return to the outside world. I look at my pile of language books: I recognise that I haven't actually opened most of them since Michaela brought them in and I made all that fuss about the Icelandic grammar being missing. I look at my Sudoku book: it has many scribbles on most pages but I haven't tackled a single puzzle. I look at the artist's sketch pad a visitor gave me one day: there is what I had once thought was a neat drawing of my plan for the Garden of Remembrance, but all the other pages are blank and the tips of the pastel crayons that came with it are still, for the most part, sharp. I open the file on my laptop marked Reading List, expecting it to be a full and comprehensive list of books to be read by all those joining the team that will change the world. There are just three titles: Elias Canetti's Auto da Fé, which I remember adding to the list because I recalled that, when I was attracted to it in the 1970s, the cover notes read something like 'Diary of a mind on the slipway to madness'. Another says simply 'Magnus Magnusson' and the third says 'Manx Gaelic'. My list of films is a bit more comprehensive, though I am unsure what was the thread I identified to link them: Lost in Translation; Leap Year; Airplane; What's up Doc?; two Flintstones movies and a Danish film, set in the Faroe Islands, called Barbara. Language and cross-cultural understanding might be there; alongside love, both requited and unrequited. My thoughts stray again towards Valentina. I tell myself to stop being ridiculous.

As I try to make some sense of all these observations, I reflect that I do feel much less agitated than when I arrived here; I also recognise that I may need to be calmer still before everybody agrees that I can return home. I think hard about all this and, settling back on my bed, I try to contact Malcolm. There doesn't seem to be anyone at home.

At lunch I make a conscious decision to adjust my place in the dining hierarchy by moving to the very back of the room, reinforcing my observation about there being an informal division that places those of us who are least ill furthest away from the serving hatch. We have more patience than the newer patients and so are capable of waiting longer to be served.

After lunch I head for the games room, where I'm alarmed to find that there appears to have been some sort of invasion. A new arrival has pinned newspaper cuttings about the war in Afghanistan on practically every available piece of wall. My own 'workspace' – the table at which I sit myself each morning to run through the papers and identify significant stories – has also been taken over, with sheafs of paper headed Happy Homes for Heroes: Business Plan. Worst of all, the table tennis surface is on the pool table, but not so that people can play table tennis... the net has been removed and the table is covered with pictures of soldiers and architectural plans for some kind of residential complex. They are very neatly arranged, the whole framed by snooker cues, while the set-up triangle has been placed upside down at the head of the table in a king of giant letter A, so that the whole has a sort of quasi-ritualistic appearance.

'What's going on here?' I ask.

A middle-aged man with an anxious look on his face is buzzing frenetically between all the different cuttings and piles of papers. In the corner of the room a woman, perhaps a few years younger, sits at a table and is patiently carrying out instructions issued by the man.

'What's going on here?' I repeat. The woman looks at me and pulls a kind of face that's seems to try to say: 'I'd like to tell you but, in present circumstances, I'm afraid I can't.'

Then the man notices my presence: 'Ah, I know you; I've been waiting for you…'

'Really? Why's that?'

'You're going to be part of the plan.'

'Which plan is that? And who are you?'

'Ted Hughes,' he says. 'Property developer turned charity chief.'

'Not THE Ted Hughes,' I tease, but he just ploughs on…

'We're building homes fit for heroes. You'll have heard of Corporal Dave James, OK?'

I tell him I haven't, so he produces another picture, in a frame this time. 'Dave James, from Wetherby. Killed by an IED in Helmand. His widow made a small bequest and it's my job to turn it into a big bequest and build homes fit for heroes to return to…'

And then he looked right into my eyes and said, 'I do know you and I see your soul and you're a good man; a man with skills; the skills we need to turn Homes for Heroes into reality.'

Now, my feelings about everything to do with injured servicemen and women and the difficulties they often face returning from conflict and trying to live in 'civvy street' are troubled. Fundamentally, I believe that many young people sign up for the forces on the false implicit pretence by government that they will never go to war; never find themselves thrown, ill-equipped, into an extremely dangerous and frightening conflict zone. Ultimately, it is the Government's disingenuity that has duped them. And so my belief is that it is very much the Government's responsibility to take care of these young people should they return home badly injured, traumatised, or both. Shamefully, the Government seems all too eager these days to wash its hands of such responsibilities wherever and whenever it can. Deeply traumatised individuals go on to harm themselves or others and may end in places like Priestley House, or indeed far less pleasant institutions for the mentally ill. Many end up on the street, homeless and out of work. And some with terrible injuries seem to miss out on the kind of support a caring government would afford them.

This is a long way of saying that I think the rash of charities that has broken out since the start of the ill-advised Afghan campaign, and indeed the Iraqi conflict before it, while generally well meaning, has the ultimate effect of letting the Government off the hook. Today is the first time I have heard of Happy Homes for Heroes, but instinctively I feel it must fall into this category.

'I don't think this is something I'd be the right person to help with,' I tell Ted. 'It's not really my area of expertise.'

'But we've been brought together for a reason,' he complains. 'We are destined to cooperate...'

'Honestly, Ted, I think you've got the wrong guy. And I think I need to say that this is the hospital's games room and people come here to play games and that's going to be very difficult this afternoon, don't you think?'

With this, I leave the games room. Moments later I sense someone hurrying up behind me. It's the woman from the corner of the room, with the exasperated expression. 'Susan Jeeves,' she says. 'I'm Ted's secretary; I'm sorry about all that.' Then she asks quite straightforwardly, 'Are you a patient or one of the staff?

'I'm a patient but I'll probably be going home before long as I'm much better...'

'Why were you admitted?'

'I had a surfeit of adrenaline in my blood and I was suffering from lack of sleep, which made me quite unwell but they've given me medication and I'm much calmer now. And sleeping well too. Come to think of it, I was probably a little bit like Ted just a couple of weeks ago...'

'So you can see how hyperactive and wound-up he is. How delusional?'

'Yes, I can be objective about that. I probably wouldn't have seen it two weeks ago. It's very supportive of you to be here with him.'

'Well, someone has to be. His wife walked out on him because she said he was becoming obsessed, but really, back then, life was a picnic compared with the way things are now. Someone had to stick by him, so I got someone in to look after the business and eased him out of things, but Celia leaving seems to have tipped him over the edge and that's why he's here now. They'd have Sectioned him if I hadn't been able to persuade him to come voluntarily. You see this Happy Heroes thing has completely taken over his life and I was worried it would ruin him financially too. Please be understanding with him, won't you?'

Her words of explanation cause me to reflect: I don't have the Aborigines playing in my pocket today; I couldn't reach Malcolm this morning; I am losing patience with some of my fellow inmates to the point that I have moved to the back of the dining room in part, I now realise, to avoid having to tell people to sit down, wait their turn, not demand seconds when others haven't even had their firsts, to hush people during grace... I had been heading for Reception to demand the return of the games room to Games Room status, but when I reach Reception, I turn instead down another Priestley House spoke with the idea of taking a walk in the hospital grounds. I'm pleased, on reaching the main reception, to see – not just that Valentina is at work – but that she is also smiling.

'I have chosen to defy my brothers and stay here with my daughter,' she says. 'I will make only a short visit on my own to Sicily.'

We chat a few minutes, but there are people arriving and she has work. 'I hope it all works out,' I say. 'If you go soon, I may be gone when you get back.'

'Oh, I don't think it will be quite so soon, Victor. I will see you before you leave. I am pleased you are leaving but sad that I shall miss our conversations...'

Priestley House not only has showers in each bedroom: there is also the private bathroom I mentioned earlier. I love my baths and so I decide to take a bath this evening.

The bathroom is plain, very plain but the hot water, once I have cleared up the wet towels, mopped the floor, and rinsed the hair from the plughole, is copious. As I may have mentioned, the door is equipped so that it can be opened from the outside by staff in an emergency. It has a self-closing spring, but this keeps popping out of its groove and obstructing the closing mechanism. I take the single plastic chair in the bathroom and climb up to the mechanism. It is quite easy to return the spring to its groove and once again I reflect that my action will have saved the hospital a couple of hundred quid at least in call-out charges.

The TV room is another facility I've discovered: arriving here on a Sunday night when I was first admitted deprived me of the full staff guided tour.

Refreshed by my bath, it is to the TV room that I head: there's a match on and, another thing I've discovered, I have the attention span now to watch a match.

There are about three of us watching, when we are joined by Thomas, who sits down, not facing the TV, but in the same plane as the TV screen, as though to watch the watchers, rather than the programme. He tries once or twice to catch my attention but I remain resolutely absorbed by the match.

When the match ends, the others drift off to join the medication queue or to make tea or coffee in the communal kitchen. Thomas stays behind.

'So how about it?' he asks.

'How about what?'

'You and me. You and me an item,' he says.

'Nothing could revolt me more,' I tell him candidly. Even if I did fancy men – I don't – it would be hard to imagine a man any nearer the back of my queue.

'You don't know what you're missing!' he says and stomps off.

Two things happen the following morning. First of all, Dr Honeydew spots me and calls me to one side. 'Michaela called me and reminded me about your brain scan yesterday,' he says. 'I just wanted to reassure you that I've made the referral and

I'm sure you'll hear something very soon after you've been discharged.'

I thank him, though I think we are both increasingly confident that neither a tumour nor other brain injury is what's behind my arrival at Priestley House.

I feel a great comfort that people are now increasingly talking in a way that suggests I may return to the community in days rather than weeks. That feeling of optimism is reinforced when, later that morning, Ute tells me that Marius wants to see me.

'Marius is a nice man,' says Ute. 'It is good that you will be seeing him.'

The said Marius is in a private room with another patient, but arrives shortly. 'Victor Turnbull, I presume,' he says, with a smile. He's a man of, say, 35, maybe 40, with long blond hair in a pigtail and gold-rimmed glasses. He's wearing jeans, soft brown leather shoes and a blue Aertex T-shirt with a nautical motif on the breast.

'And you must be Clare in the Community,' I say.

'You mean like the Radio 4 comedy,' he says, immediately on my wavelength. 'Nice one! But I think you'll find she's female and I'm male. And she's a local authority social worker and I'm a freelance adviser in mental health. But that apart, good joke, Victor.'

'Vic'll do,' I say. 'And I guess you'd prefer Marius to Clare.'

'Probably, yes,' he says, beckoning me to follow him into a private room, where he explains that he'll be my main support during my transition back to life on the outside.

'I'll call and see you a couple of times a week in the first instance,' he says, 'but I'll give you all my contact details so, if you have any sort of crisis, you just call, OK?'

'So when will all this happen?'

'Well, I think they're thinking in terms of you going home for a night this weekend and then, if that works out OK, you might go home on Monday, so I would then call and see you probably on Wednesday.'

Buoyed by my meeting with Marius 'Clare in the Community', I take another bath in the evening, save the Trust another two or maybe five hundred quid by fixing the door spring again, and head for the TV lounge.

I've not long settled down to watching nothing in particular when young Jeff runs in. 'Hurry, Vic! Dinin' room now!'

We run down the corridor and into the dining room. A young man is standing on a dining chair, quivering.

'Help me get 'im down,' says Jeff. And turning to the young man, who's probably about 21, says, 'It's all right, son, tek it easy. Tha'll be all right, son, we'll get you down.'

We take an arm each and are able to persuade the lad, Tony, he'll be safe. Eventually he steps down and, as his feet touch the floor, I can feel the thumping of his heart slow.

'Thanks guys,' he says. 'That was real scary stuff. I was going to jump but you got me down.'

When he has gone, Jeff turns to me. 'They picked him up off the viaduct at Knaresborough,' he says. 'Apparently it's not the first time.'

Later that evening I decide to take a walk to the games room, just to see the extent of the Happy Homes for Heroes paraphernalia. I open the door and am astonished to be confronted by a hairy arse suspended over the pool table at my eye level. A single large turd emerges even as I arrive. I turn tail and dash to Reception, where I nearly collide at full speed with John, the nurse.

'Games room, quick!' I shout and, as we run down the corridor, more quietly: 'That new guy's just done a shit on the pool table!'

When we reach the games room, Tony is gone, but the evidence of his recent presence is still there steaming on the table.

'Hmm,' says John. 'Brown in the top corner, I'd say.'

CHAPTER 22

Tall stories

Friday, October 8, 2021

'I'm struggling to imagine how he could have known we would be here,' said Felix, as he and Michelle sat in the little café at York station. On spotting Jameela's brother – for he was sure it was he – he'd spun Michelle though 180 degrees and marched her back across the long bridge and on to the station's final island platform.

'You're going to need to bring me up to speed here, Felix,' said Michelle.

Felix realised he hadn't fully shared his most recent adventures with Michelle and now he found himself once again running through what had happened at the Durranis' restaurant in Luton.

'You did what? Are you crazy?'

Felix felt a distinct sense of déjà vu, or perhaps déjà entendu. His brain processed the same reply to the rhetorical question as he had not long previously delivered to Emily, in Exeter.

'No, I don't think so, but I am wondering if I was a bit naïve. And now you're going to say to me something like "Skip the wondering, starry-eyed boy: you WERE naïve, yeah, OK?!".'

'Yes, I think I might just do that, though I'm not sure it needs the "yeah, OK" on the end…' She continued: 'So let's get this straight, we don't KNOW if this young Rahman is dangerous, but then, even if he isn't, he might have his brothers with him but out of sight. Is that right?' She didn't wait for an answer, and pressed on: 'And from your perspective, quite apart from any danger, you really don't want anyone from Jameela's family jumping to the conclusion that you're chasing after Jameela while also running around with an attractive blonde.'

'You being the attractive blonde?'

'Of course!'

Working on the basis that it would be harder for any pursuer to track both of them at once, Felix had helped slip Michelle through a disembarking crowd and onto a Transpennine train, with instructions to await him at Betty's, in Northallerton. For his part, he hurried back to his flat, and hastily assembled enough clothes for a few days, along with his walking boots and waterproofs. He then headed south out of the city. At the superstore on the edge of town, he drove several times round the car park before finally parking and walking ostentatiously towards the store entrance, wearing a bright red waterproof, and carrying a more subdued jacket in a carrier bag. In the store he slipped into the toilets, swapped the jackets and then, for good measure, swapped the carrier bag for a differently branded one that he had brought in the first carrier. He pulled on an old cloth cap he liked to wear when out walking and then waited until two other men were exiting the toilets and followed them closely, head bowed. He employed similar tactics to reach the exit, before making his way across the car park, doing his best to keep his face out of sight. He felt it unlikely he could have been followed and took the ring road back north and on up the A19.

The railway between York and Northallerton is fast and straight in a way that the A19 is not and, by the time Felix was clear of the city's northern suburbs, Michelle had had time to find her way from Northallerton station to the town centre, locate Betty's and enjoy toasted teacake and a pot of tea; and then cakes and tea; and then coffee and ice cream. So, when Felix eventually showed up, she was in danger of merging into the very furniture of the place and was less than delighted at Felix's suggestion that they might enjoy a pot of tea before hitting the road.

'OK, OK, keep your hair on!' said Felix, slightly taken aback at Michelle's sharp response, as he took her bag. 'Christ, what've you got in here? How the hell did you lug this all the way from the station?'

'With difficulty,' replied Michelle, electing not to share with Felix the fact that she had actually taken a taxi.

There's nothing like the feeling of ticking off the miles for lifting the spirits, reflected Felix, once they had made their way across country to the new motorway and then onto the A66, now finding themselves climbing steadily towards the roof of England.

'You get your kicks on the A66!' they sang in unison. It might not be the iconic old American highway heading from the industrial heartland to the wide open spaces of the west, but, reflected Felix, there were parallels. They powered onward across the rolling grazing plateauland of the Durham prairies towards Stainmore Gap and the nick in the highest ridge line that had made this a good point to cross the Pennines, even back in Roman times. Down to their left, Felix pointed out to Michelle the metal sign alongside the old railway, affirming that this summit was – despite the 'gap' moniker – still more than 1,300 ft above sea level. They had indeed been climbing steadily for 20 miles since leaving Scotch Corner.

The dual carriageway descended more steeply on the western escarpment of the backbone of England, affording a magnificent view north and west across the Eden Valley towards the rugged profile of the Lake District fells, backlit by the autumn sun as it began its afternoon descent.

'Wow, that's pretty,' said Michelle. 'Really dramatic!'

'So, I guess we've left the Great Plains and now we're looking at the Rockies,' mused Felix.

'If you say so – but I think I like this Route 66 better; more civilised. I just love that view; I don't think I ever imagined the North could be like this.'

'Oh you sheltered southern lass,' said Felix, as he wondered whether things would work out with her as his travelling companion. What was particularly nagging him was that, thanks to the change of plan prompted by the unwelcome sighting at York Station, they had taken Route 66 with no real 'plan' in mind. Even the Oakies escaping the dust bowl on the great American migration must have had a clearer sense of purpose. 'We're leaving Route 66 in a minute, so we won't be getting our kicks any more,' Felix told his companion.

'So what's the plan, northern man?'

'I don't really know exactly, to be honest. Emily said to start the journey where Lord and Lady Lindisfarne began their journey, in the Lake District. She said I should think of the most isolated hotel there is. I've looked at all the stuff written about Lindisfarne and Aurora and I think they must have started out at Wasdale Head, which is right round the far side of the Lake District. I've booked two rooms there…'

What Felix didn't tell Michelle was that the booking was for the following night: it had been his original intention that they should stay in York on this, their first night on the trail of loves lost.

'Isn't two rooms a bit extravagant?' ventured Michelle. 'Don't you think we can be trusted?'

Notwithstanding his resolution of fidelity, Felix nonetheless preferred not to have to run the gauntlet of potential temptation. Equally, he had been loathe to presume that Michelle would agree to sharing a room: she might have thought it highly inappropriate. Or perhaps she just wouldn't have trusted herself to keep her hands off him. He smiled to himself at the thought that he might be so irresistible.

'What are you grinning at, Mr Cheshire Cat?'

'Nothing at all! I was just thinking about garden birds?'

'Garden birds?! Why?'

'Well, it's just one of those daft things that comes into your head sometimes. You know the tongue-twister about the woodchuck?'

'How much wood would a woodchuck chuck if a woodchuck could chuck wood. That one?'

'The very one.'

'What the hell's that got to do with the price of fish. Or birds. Or Route 66 for that matter?'

'Like I said, we're not on Route 66 any more,' said Felix, who had just exited said highway to the southwest to take them towards Kendal.

'Don't change the subject, tongue-twister man. You said you were thinking about garden birds and it made you laugh. Or smile at least...'

'Oh yes, I was thinking How many nuts would a nuthatch hatch if a nuthatch could hatch nuts?'

He glanced across at Michelle. She was looking at him like he'd just stepped off a spaceship from Mars. 'That's really crap! You're either barking, Felix Winterweather, or you just said all that nonsense to avoid saying something else. Something about whether or not we should share a room.'

'Absolutely not,' said Felix, reflecting that he would be unlikely to pull the wool over this one's eyes. He was, however, slightly anxious that he might have to confront the question of sleeping arrangements sooner rather than later. They must be still at least two hours from Wasdale Head – maybe more – and it was already time to think about eating. Or at least it was time for Felix to think about eating: he hadn't spent an enforced afternoon in the custody of Betty's tea-room. Pending a conversation about biting something of more nutritional value, Felix decided to bite the bullet on that evening's accommodation arrangements. 'We're not booked in at Wasdale till tomorrow and, in any event, we wouldn't get there till pretty late. It might be best to stop off somewhere...'

'So... singles or a double?'

'What would you prefer?'

'Don't pass the buck, Mr Avoid-the-Subject.'

'Well, OK, a double would save money.'

'Oh dear Felix, I'm not sure that's the right answer: I don't think I'll be able to keep my hands off you!'

He took his eyes off the road and looked anxiously in Michelle's direction… 'Joke, Felix. Joke, Mr Vanity!'

Felix felt his anxiety turn to something closer to relief, although he was no closer to an answer to questions regarding what they should do next. He continued to harbour concerns that, against all apparent logic, they might still have been followed and, given that, he was unsure whether they would be better off staying in a town, like Kendal, where they might be inconspicuous among the crowd, or somewhere right off the beaten path. That said, he really was at even more of a loss to understand how young Rahman might have followed him to York, or even followed Michelle from London, than how he might have earlier tailed him to Exeter.

Such speculation, however, was not going to find a bite to eat or a bed for the night. He tapped his VSP to wake it and instructed it to link up with the nav screen in the car. 'Show me routes to Wasdale Head!' he instructed. The screen responded with three choices, none of which could be described as even remotely direct – one would have him make a U-turn and rejoin the A66 and head, via Penrith, through the northern Lake District and down the coast, before heading inland to Wastwater and Wasdale Head; another described a similar hooked arc, but to the south of the Lake District; the third was the most direct, taking them through the centre of the Lake District, then almost reaching the coast, before turning back north-eastward. While the shortest route by distance, at less than 80 miles, this latter would nonetheless take the longest, at somewhat more than two hours. The other routes came in at about the same distance and both at a little under two hours and so, finding the idea of backtracking abhorrent, Felix asked Michelle to tap the southernmost route and then asked the VSP: 'Find me somewhere to stay half way to destination.'

'You asked for somewhere to stay half way to the station?' queried the VSP.

'Still room to improve this technology,' mused Felix, instead suggesting to Michelle that she select a point roughly half way along the route.

'Broughton-in-Furness,' said Michelle slowly, pronouncing it so the first syllable rhymed with 'cow' rather than 'caw'.

'Find me a hotel in Broughton-in-Furness,' Felix instructed the VSP, gently correcting Michelle's pronunciation.

His companion flicked through some options on screen: 'This one looks nice… The Black Cock Inn. Sounds interesting too…'

Felix shot her a quizzical glance but was unsure whether she was being smutty or risquée, or quite innocent.

'Would you like me to call?' demanded the VSP.

Michelle took charge and booked the only remaining room at the 16th century coaching inn. The chunky wood faux rustique furnishings had appealed to her, as would have the picture of the puff pastry-topped steak and ale pie, had she not still been replete from Betty's.

'This will for sure test my resolve,' reflected Felix, prompting him again to ask himself just what it was about Jameela that had inspired him to embark on a quest that was, he had to admit, quite out of kilter with the way he had lived his life previously. He drew a deep breath and sighed as he swung left to join the motorway just as the carriageways separated and the road entered the valley of the Lune.

'Life?' asked Michelle in response to the sigh.

'Yes, and the Universe and Everything else, I guess.'

'Did you ever see that old film, the Hiker's Guide to the Universe or something?'

'The HITCH-hiker's Guide to the Galaxy, wasn't it?' said Felix, choosing not to let on that he'd re-watched it so recently.

'Yes, that's the one: do you remember how they built this big computer to come up with the answer to the "ultimate question"?'

'The question of Life, the Universe and Everything: and the answer was 23…'

'I think you'll find it was 42,' corrected Michelle. 'Douglas Adams. He was the guy who wrote the books. Died young, in California or somewhere.'

'Have you read them?'

'No, but I did see the film and Kenny was really into it. It started on radio and he had all the series on CDs and the TV series too, as well as the film. It was good, clever, about this guy who hitch-hikes through space in a dressing gown.'

'So, do you think we're overdressed then?' asked Felix.

The pair left the motorway and turned west, passing to the south of Kendal and on past the southern tip of Windermere. To their left, occasional views of the vast expanse of Morecambe Bay shone gold in the evening light. They cut across the neck of the Furness peninsula, glimpsing the sea again at another estuary, the Duddon, before turning briefly inland up the hill into Broughton, where it was close to seven when they arrived at the Black Cock Inn. Felix stooped through the low front door and they found themselves in a cosy bar with a fireplace laden with logs, seemingly eager to be to be introduced to some flames. Escorted up the tight stairway to their room, its décor proved broadly reflective of what Michelle had found online. Felix noted that, for all its exaggerated presence, the heavy-timbered double bed was actually quite small: not even Royal Pretender size, let alone Queen or King, he thought, glancing towards Michelle as he supposed she too was contemplating their forthcoming nocturnal confinement.

Dumping his own and Michelle's more substantial bag and getting away from having to face the question seemed the best bet and they headed back downstairs. Although Felix could quite happily have eaten then and there, Michelle persuaded him to wait till later, and so they left the pub and headed uphill to where they found an attractive Georgian square that hinted at times of greater glory. They continued their circuit of the old market town and came across a small group queueing outside an attractive public hall, with pale blue render. A poster on the wall of the grandly named Victory Hall was promoting Broughton Film Club. 'Look,' said Felix. 'Isn't that the Lindisfarne film?'

'October's film is Two Flew Over the Cuckoo's Nest: the Unsequel,' he read from the poster. 'Arthouse 2012 English film that has become a cult classic.'

'And it's on now!' exclaimed Michelle. They joined the short queue and bought tickets, a little bottle of wine each and a bag of Jelly Babies, picking up a copy of the film club programme as they took their fold-away seats with maybe three dozen others.

'Look,' said Michelle, pointing Felix to the programme notes on the film they were about to see. '...explores the shifting boundaries between madness and sanity, challenging conventional notions of where the real world ends and fantasy begins...'

Felix picked up the thread: 'Paul McGann shines as Victor, a role broadly based on the time Vic Turnbull (now the celebrated entrepreneur, Lord Lindisfarne) spent in psychiatric hospital. Cameo appearances by Hugh Grant and Brenda Blethyn contribute to the film's lasting appeal.'

'What did you make of that, then?' Michelle asked Felix.

'You know, what puzzles me is that I never caught it when it first came out and now it's a "cult movie". How did that pass me by?'

'Well, I did see it,' Michelle continued. 'But I'd pretty much forgotten it. I think it might have been one of those films you have on in the background when you're also reading the papers, talking to your sister and trying to knit a pair of gloves.'

'I know the feeling well. Except for the knitting. And the sister. But to get back to the film, I'm not sure it's greatly illuminating as far as we're concerned...'

'Well, like it says in the blurb, it's a bit hard to work out what's meant to have actually taken place, and what's just Victor away with the fairies. But all that stuff about time being flexible, that was a bit spooky after we were just talking about Douglas Adams and Life the Universe and Everything.'

'Yeah,' said Felix. 'You mean all that two to the power of infinity equals infinity squared stuff? Do you think there's anything in the idea about time passing at different speeds? I mean, I often get the feeling both ways, you know, sometimes that time's just standing still and sometimes that time's already gone before you can reach out and grab it.'

'Definitely, but that's just in people's minds, surely? It's a big leap from that to suggest that the physics of time is sort of bendy.'

'Yes, you don't really hear of anyone trying to test the formula out for real, do you?'

'Whereas,' said Michelle, 'that thing about the bees did come to something.'

'Meaning?'

'Well,' replied Michelle, pausing for effect. 'I never realised it at the time, but the research I did for my PhD was funded by Lindisfarne.'

Felix stopped in his tracks, unsure which was the most surprising: that Michelle had a PhD, or that she might have been funded by Lord Lindisfarne himself. Then he mentally chastised himself for doubting the possibility that Michelle might be not just a little bit more accomplished than the average barmaid, but considerably more so. 'You're going to have to walk me through this one, Michelle.'

'Well, when I had graduated at Newcastle…'

'Whoa, Newcastle? You said you'd never been to the North before!' exclaimed Felix.

'I didn't: you just presumed that I hadn't because I happened to comment that the view was nice earlier today. Anyway: bees… I was researching environmental reasons for the possible decline in bumble bee populations.'

'And?'

'Well, not that much. I mean nothing earth-shattering. The biggest problem for bumble-bees is loss of habitat, which is pretty much the case for any species that's in decline, so I didn't win any prizes.'

'You're just being modest…'

'Well, OK, my work did help provide the evidence that was required for significant changes in agricultural policy that have helped populations to recover. Though I say so myself!'

'And until just now you didn't know where your money came from?' asked an incredulous Felix.

'No, I really didn't: I thought it was just university departmental money until the idea came up in the film and that's when the penny dropped.'

'But in fact it was part of that one-for-me, one-for-charity thing that goes right back to when Victor, or Lord Lindisfarne, I guess, was in psychiatric hospital. What did you make of the rest of the film?'

Michelle paused for a few moments. 'I thought the plot was a bit improbable, to be honest. That a bunch of guys in a nuthouse, 'xcuse my French, rumble a corrupt clique at the council and save the bumble bee…'

'And challenge the Masons,' added Felix. 'And defuse racial and religious tensions… But then isn't that the whole point of the film? Isn't it really just a flight of fancy in which everything turns out all right in the end and anything can seem possible?'

'Yes, I guess it's just a feel-good movie and it doesn't pay to dig too deep and analyse too much,' said Michelle as the pair found themselves going back into the Black Cock.

'I've remembered something,' said Felix as he pulled out two chairs at a table near the door. 'They built a set for the film and then turned it into a real hospital. It's supposed to be state of the art. It's in Yorkshire, just off the Harrogate road, from York. I hadn't really given it that much thought, but it's a private psychiatric place funded by the Aurora Foundation.'

'Do you think we should pay it a visit, Felix?'

'I don't know: there are lots of things that are funded by the foundation and we couldn't possibly visit them all,' replied Felix, by now somewhat more interested in the bar menu.

'I'll take the snake-and-ale pie with chips,' he told the young woman behind the bar. 'And my friend will have the salmon steak.'

The woman glanced at her watch. 'Just in time – kitchen closes at nine, last orders at quarter to. Do you want to order a pud now?'

Felix declined and turned back towards their table in the low-ceilinged little timber-beamed bar-room, carrying a glass of cider for Michelle and the pub's own bottle-conditioned ale for himself. He was only half way back to his seat when he saw out of the corner of his eye a face he fancied he recognised. This time it wasn't that of a young Asian boy, but a middle-aged woman of perhaps 55. He felt confident he had seen her somewhere before, but was still struggling to think when or where as he sat down again next to Michelle.

'You look puzzled,' she said.

'I am,' Felix half-whispered. 'Don't make it obvious, but I'm sure I know that woman over there. The one on her own with the wavy hair and glasses.'

Despite the scant description, it was clear to Michelle to which other diner Felix was referring. There were only half a dozen tables in the main bar area and only one of them was occupied by a woman sitting alone. She was wearing a chunky-knit cabled pinkish jumper with a pale blue and fawn pattern. Her spectacles were rimmed in a similar blue, giving her a studious look, amplified by the fact that she was intently reading what looked like a sheaf of printed papers.

'At least it's not our special friend,' said Michelle. 'She looks pretty harmless.'

'Yes, but it's all getting a bit spooky they way things seem to happen as though they were all pre-planned: Rahman, the Lindisfarne film, our conversation about Douglas Adams. And I'm sure this woman's presence is going to turn out to be something else that just "happens" to happen. I mean, Michelle, until this morning we weren't even going to be in the Lake District today and it's only by chance that we're here in Broughton. If that last room had gone or if we'd thought better of sharing a room we'd be somewhere completely different now. Or if we'd taken a different route to Wasdale we'd be in Ambleside, or Keswick or somewhere else miles from here. And then, what about her? What if she's only here because she missed her flight to Ibiza and decided to take a break in England instead?'

'What if? What if?' interjected Michelle. 'What if someone's deliberately set out to test our sanity by lining up loads of improbable coincidences? I mean, which is more unlikely? That these events are just coincidences or that someone could conceivably go to all that trouble and orchestrate them?'

'I guess…'

The philosophical conversation was curtailed by the arrival of food, which Felix assaulted with ravenous glee.

'So, what are we going to do when we get to Waspdale?' said Michelle as she addressed her own food with more restraint.

'WASdale,' corrected Felix, between chips.

'I was TRYING to be amusing,' said Michelle.

'Sorry, Michelle: you are very amusing, but I'm just not sharp enough to see it coming every time – I'm not quite on your wavelength yet and anyway I thought bees were your thing, not wasps. But to answer your question, I think we try and place ourselves in their position: ask ourselves what they went there for and what they were trying to achieve while they were there, and turn as many stones as we can to find evidence of what they were up to.'

Felix paused, poured the last of his ale into his glass and continued: 'Nice pie, how's yours?'

'My god, Felix you don't hang about! I've only just started mine!'

Felix was about to rehearse excuses for eating too quickly when he was interrupted by a voice that he immediately recognised and which enabled him straight away to place where he had seen the bespectacled lady before.

'Excuse me, don't I know you?' enquired the woman.

'Yes and no,' said Felix. 'No, you don't really know me but, yes, we have met, and quite recently. At Stonehenge.'

'Of course,' exclaimed the woman, who was now standing at their table between Felix and Michelle. 'This is a coincidence! May I join you?'

Felix motioned for her to pull up a seat from the unoccupied table next to their own.

'You'd left your phoney-ma-jigammy by the stones! And now here we are again: are you going to Swinside? My name's Flora, by the way…'

'Felix; Michelle,' said Felix. 'What's Swinside and should we know?'

'Oh forgive me, I thought after seeing you at Stonehenge you must be a circle-bagger like me! I'm making my way round all the stone circles in Cumbria. There are more of these Neolithic monuments round here than even on Salisbury Plain. And Swinside's one of the best – it's one of the biggest and most important. It's just a few miles from here and they only properly opened it to the public in the last year or so.'

'We're not "circle-baggers" I'm afraid,' said Felix. 'But it does sound interesting.'

'Where are all the circles?' asked Michelle.

'Well, in Cumbria, there's Long Meg and her Daughters, over in the Eden Valley, and Castlerigg, near Keswick. They're the biggest, and Swinside's probably next, unless you count Mayburgh Henge, near Penrith, of course, which is massive.'

'Why wouldn't you?' quizzed Michelle, confused.

'Because it's not standing stones. Or at least there's only one standing stone and it's in the middle of the circle. But the circle itself is more like a rampart built out of lots of small stones… Look why don't you come with me to Swinside in the morning and I'll tell you what I know.'

'Have we got time to do this?' queried Michelle as they made their way upstairs. They had agreed to meet Flora after breakfast at nine and drive together to Swinside before completing the journey to Wasdale.

'Well, isn't time flexible? We can borrow time in the morning from later in the day, can't we?! But, you know, I still can't help thinking she's turned up here for a reason. Otherwise, it's just too much of a coincidence.'

'And, as I said before, a coincidence is less improbable than the idea that she's here because of some greater force,' said Michelle. 'And now let's deal with the improbability of squeezing two of us into this bed...'

Felix did not sleep well. He was used to sleeping naked and having to wear a T-shirt and undies already meant he was hot and uncomfortable, even before allowing for the hot female form beneath the cotton jim-jams that was doing a good job of raising the temperature still further – in both a literal and metaphorical sense.

'I really don't know what the fuss is about,' Michelle had told him as she rummaged in her ample travelling bag for her pyjamas. 'I often sleep with my girl friends.'

'Yes, and boys don't sleep with their male friends unless they're gay. I'm just not used to sharing a bed like this...'

'You mean narrow and built from big bits of wood?'

'Yes, Michelle, very funny.'

Felix had been relieved that Michelle, who'd set off early from the other side of London, was ready for sleep and was already pretty much out for the count by the time he'd cleaned his teeth. He'd slipped quietly under the duvet and turned the TV on low while he wound down a little, his mind still struggling to embrace the improbable reality of so many coincidences.

Vaguely watching a reality TV show about two teams of minor celebrities sent to an Arctic island to see which could dig coal quickest, he'd suddenly started as his head clunked onto his chest. Recognising that he hadn't taken in what had been going on on-screen in Celebrity Ice Mine for a few minutes at least, he turned the TV off and wriggled down beneath the covers.

But the sleep was fitful and in no time at all Felix found himself gasping for breath as he was woken from a particularly unpleasant dream, in which he found himself stumbling across a fractured glacier, hotly pursued by Rahman's brothers.

Michelle moaned softly as her deep slumber was punctuated by Felix's nightmare. She shifted her head and Felix inhaled her hot breath and caught a draft of her perfume, spiced with slightly sweaty armpit as she turned over.

Felix lifted the duvet to allow things to cool a little and his hand brushed against the small of Michelle's back, the skin bare where her top had ridden up. He felt his pulse quicken and his loins stirred as her pheromones threw the switch on his equipment. The situation was completely insane, he reflected. He left the bed and slipped into the loo, where he sponged himself down with a cold, wet flannel.

When he went back to bed, he placed his left arm above the duvet so as to create a barrier between himself and Michelle and in this way he was able, eventually, to salvage such slumber as he could from the remainder of the night.

'You smell nice,' said Michelle, prodding Felix awake as her VSP alarm sounded. 'I could almost fancy you…'

'Don't,' said Felix. 'It's not been exactly easy trying to sleep with you lying there being all, all WOMANLY in the same bed.'

'Wasn't it such a good idea then?'

'No. I mean I don't know; maybe I could get used to it.'

'Ooh I hoped my potency might be a little longer lived…'

Why was Michelle flirting with such application? Felix found himself questioning the wisdom, not just of teaming up with her in this way, but even of his very pursuit of Jameela. That pursuit, he reminded himself, was based on the premise of chastity until such time as he might track her down.

As if reading his mind, Michelle said, 'We'll get by Felix, don't worry. We're just finding our way at the moment. And this whole process should help us both get our feelings for our missing friends fully into context.'

Felix wondered if Michelle's true agenda was to weigh her feelings for Kenny against the thrill of the new that perhaps he, Felix, might represent. He chose for the moment not to dwell further on the question. They spoke little as they dressed and headed down for breakfast.

'All these circles have their own legends,' said Flora as she turned to face her new companions, Swinside's ring of 50 or so stones framing the view immediately behind her. 'The legend here is that they were trying to build a church by day, but every night the devil would pull down the stones and use them to make his circle. That's where its alternative name of Sunkenkirk comes from.'

They had arrived at Swinside, or Sunkenkirk, by way of a minor road that climbed up the flank of a lowish fell and was not a great deal more than a track. In the field opposite the one in which the circle was located, a small parking area had been constructed and a little plaque proclaimed that enhanced public access to the site was thanks to an agreement made in 2019 between the national park and the landowner. 'Something to do with death duties,' Flora had said.

'It's not exactly Stonehenge, is it?' asked Felix rhetorically, observing that the diameter of the circle – notwithstanding its third place ranking among Cumbrian stone circles – wasn't much more, or indeed any more, than the length of a cricket pitch.

'No, but there are people who genuinely believe this is the most wonderful circle anywhere in Europe,' responded Flora. 'And I have to say that my first impressions are very favourable.'

'Small but perfectly formed, then?' suggested Michelle.

'Yes, I'd say so!' said Flora, turning to lead the small group the short distance to the circle itself. 'There would have been more stones at one time, and of course they would all have been upright.' She was referring to the fact that perhaps a third of the stones appeared to be fallen or partially buried. Of those that still stood proud, the tallest was about Felix's height, or a little more.

'What now, then?' he asked, wondering why they had agreed to this diversion.

'Just be reflective,' said Flora, impervious to Felix's impatience. 'Sit quietly and absorb the atmosphere and just follow where your mind takes you.'

Sitting still and being meditative had never been Felix's strongest suit, but this time it was Michelle's expression that seemed to be telling him to do as he was told and go with the flow. Without prior agreement, the three people found themselves heading for different spots on the circle's perimeter, where they each sat down on a fallen monolith. Felix found himself looking south-east, in the general direction of Broughton and the double standing stones that had been placed, Flora had suggested, to coincide with sunrise at the winter solstice. Flora was at his ten o'clock and Michelle at his three. The October sun was slowly taking the morning chill off the air and a gentle breeze blew off the sea and up the valley onto Felix's face. A large bumblebee buzzed past his head and zoomed so close to Michelle that she had to duck. 'We have an understanding,' she called across to Felix, grinning.

That grin was Felix's last recollection before he slipped imperceptibly into the arms of Morpheus. Morpheus then took him to a world in which he could see Lord and Lady Lindisfarne, or at least plain Victor and Michaela. They were visiting a stone circle that seemed not dissimilar to Swinside. They seemed uneasy, taking turns to glance over their shoulders towards where the road approached over the fells, while at the same time quite clearly looking for something. Victor at one point got down on his hands and knees and appeared to rummage around the base of one of the taller stones, which – even in the changed reality of dreamland – he recognised as close to the one on which Michelle had been sitting. Suddenly a gang of armed men appeared to storm through the gate from the road and Victor hastily got to his feet. Gunfire cracked out and Felix woke from his dream with a start…

So realistic had the episode appeared that Felix felt he was able to step directly into the action he had just 'witnessed'. He strode across the circle to where Michelle too appeared to have nodded off. 'We need to look under that stone, 'chelle!' he said.

'I know!' replied his companion, as they made for the tall stone with the slightly stooping profile. 'I just had a dream.'

'You too? How very bizarre!'

'What on earth are you two up to,' demanded Flora a few moments later. 'This is a scheduled ancient monument: you can't dig things up!'

Felix had cut away a square of turf at the base of the monolith with his pocket knife, under Michelle's loose direction. Now he was digging further beneath the stone itself.

'Don't worry, we'll put everything back,' said Felix as Flora stood watching, jaw dropped.

It wasn't long before Felix was able to push his arm into a deep hole beneath the stone. He withdrew it, triumphantly clutching a metal tin, about ten centimetres long. The damp environment had taken its toll but the words 'Farrah's Original Harrogate Toffee' and the boast 'Estd 1840' could still be made out. He opened the tin: it contained an old-fashioned mobile phone, clearly predating the Aurora revolution. There was nothing else inside.

'How on earth did you know you'd find that?!' asked Flora.

'We didn't,' chorused Felix and Michelle.

'How are we going to power it up,' asked Michelle as they drove on over the fells towards Eskdale.

'I really don't know,' replied Felix. 'Those things went out with the ark.'

'But it'd be useful to know what was on there before we get to Wasdale, wouldn't it?' said Michelle. 'I'll ask the VSP.'

On the VSP's advice, they made a detour towards the coast, arriving at Seascale, in the shadow of the huge old Sellafield nuclear complex, where the obliging electrician in the little shop on what passed for a high street not only found an old-fashioned charger to power up the phone but even showed them how they could bypass the password. 'Haven't seen one of these in years,' he commented. 'Where the hell did you find it?'

Felix resisted the temptation to say 'Under a monolith, of course' and muttered something about it belonging to his dad, who no longer had a use for it.

Although eager to reach Wasdale Head and explore the phone at their leisure, there was something about the pub at Santon Bridge that caused Felix to pull over and suggest they grab lunch. On a roll from the phone discovery, Felix felt a curious conviction that the Bridge Inn would have secrets of its own to reveal.

The wood-floored bar struck them as being unusually quiet, even for a mid-week lunchtime. A family was eating at one table, while a lone figure was sitting at a bar stool, in conversation with the man behind the counter. Felix again had a distinct sense of déjà vu, recalling the day he had walked into the pub in Kent and first encountered Michelle behind the bar. Now he and Michelle stood at the bar and thumbed through the menu. Michelle watched the barman closely as he pulled a modest half-pint for Felix and poured a glass of wine for her.

'Can't help it, I'm afraid. Once a barmaid always a barmaid!' she smiled. 'Any visit to a pub's a busman's holiday for me...'

'Buswoman's,' corrected Felix.

The man at the bar was listening to their exchange intently. He was tall and rangy, ruddy-faced, with white whiskers, of which those above his top lip bore traces of yellow nicotine. A cloth cap in faded tweed lay crumpled on the bar beside a half-drunk pint of Jennings, which was responsible for the frothy residue partially masking those yellow stains. He wore a thigh-length waxed jacket that had clearly seen better days and his muddy boots bore conclusive testimony, if any more were needed, to a life outdoors.

'Ye'll be them mystery shoppers, I s'pose,' he ventured.

'Us? no way!' chuckled Felix. 'Whatever made you think that?'

'It'll be my probing gaze,' interjected Michelle. 'Sometimes I can't help myself in pubs – I work behind a bar myself.'

'Oh aye. That'll not be hereabouts, then?'

'No, down south, in Kent.'

'Oh my Lord, th'art a lang way fra' hame, lass.'

Michelle wondered what the man might have said had she revealed she was from the south of France, or even the south of India and was pondering whether to pose some witty reply, when the man continued.

'Tackler's the name,' he said. 'Ned Tackler from the famous fell-running family.'

'You're a fell-runner?' inquired Felix, perhaps a little too incredulously.

'Well, I was, my man. But these days aa'll leave that te younger fowks. The nearest I get to competition these days is sheepdogs and tellin' fibs.'

Michelle and Felix searched each other's faces for a sign that one or the other of them might have understood what Ned was driving at, before the barman came to their rescue.

'Ned's a regular name in the World's Biggest Liar competition,' he explained. 'It's held here every Autumn. The Tacklers have always been keen entrants and they've won more than once. Ned's the current champion, though some say his lie last year may just have been true...'

'And that, young man, is the secret of a good lie – it should always come wi' a ring o' truth te it.'

'So what was your lie?' asked Felix.

'I'll show yees,' said Ned, taking his audience by surprise as he pulled the latest VSP model from deep within his jacket pocket and beckoned Felix and Michelle to gather round. He began to play a clip that had clearly been recorded in the pub in which they now stood. In it, Ned held a microphone close to his lips and began to recount a story about a mysterious couple living in a submarine deep beneath the surface of Wastwater, which was – he reminded his rapt audience – the deepest lake in England.

'Na' some say these two were on the run: fugitives from international crime; hiding from the law; on a mafia hit list. Others say they weren't on the run at all, but were Russian spies, keeping an eye on Sellafield or terrorists hatchin' a plan for world domination. But I can tell yees that the truth was none of these: they were carrying out genetic engineerin' beneath the surface of our beautiful lake.'

Ned went on to describe how he had, quite literally, he said, 'got to the bottom' of the mystery, bringing in his own mini-submarine from Aberdeen and launching it alone into the depths of Wastwater.

'It took us a while to master the controls of th' submarine and at first it were leading me a reet merry dance, loopin' th' loop an' dippin' n' divin'. For a while I thowt I were aboot te meet me maker when the sub went into a dive. Everythin' aroond were pitch black and I could ownly sense I were headed strite doon. Ye'll o' heard o' the monster that splits his time between Wastwater and Loch Ness? Well, he was so terrified when I shot past 'im, he scuttled strite off back up te Scotland.'

Eventually, recounted Ned, the little sub stabilised deep below the surface of the lake's eastern shore, where the daunting screes that tumble close to 2,000ft continue their plunge beneath the waters, only stopping close to 300ft further down and 50ft lower than the shores of the Irish Sea, nearby.

'Imagine my surprise to find I was not alone: the strangest beast I've ever seen. It were somethin' between submarine and cinema; I kid you not.'

Ned described how he edged his bucking bronco of a submarine alongside the generously proportioned craft, which was anchored to the lake-bed by three steel cables. From the top of the curious craft, an air line rose to a buoy on the lake's surface, disguised as clump of driftwood. Beneath the vessel could be seen an airlock of some kind. Ned described how he watched as a smaller craft descended from somewhere near the shoreline and docked with the airlock, enabling a man and a woman to move from the smaller to the larger vessel.

'Well, by now I'm gettin' th' hang of steerin' me underwatter ship and so I edges it towards the airlock after the l'il submarine's moved awaa.'

Ned's tale described how he'd slipped silently into the big submarine, where he'd spied upon a man and woman in white lab coats tending a menagerie of the strangest looking creatures, all captive in cages.

There was an oversized red squirrel with an elephant's trunk, a two-headed monkey, and other bizarre beasts. Quick-thinking Ned returned to his mini-sub, but not before painting the end of the air line with a sugar solution he had conveniently brought with him. Then he headed for shore and collected a hive of bees from his farm.

'Aa sails up to th' end of the air pipe, pops a funnel in and lets the bees find their own way down to the submarine.'

At this point, Ned's narration became increasingly complex. Suffice to say, the Cumbrian fellsman emerges the hero of the hour, persuading the 'mad scientists' of the folly of their ways and, with one notable exception, discharging the hybrid animals into the custody of the Biological Sciences department at Lancaster University. The 'notable exception' was a small winged horse, which now roams the high fells above Wasdale and can occasionally be seen circling high above the little church at the head of the dale.

'So what became of the mad scientists, then?' asked Felix, with a grin.

'Well, once they'd seen the error o' their ways they chose to devote their lives to doin' good works, savin' unfortunates from poverty and the like. They calls 'em Lord and Lady Summat or Other – Michael and Victoria.' Ned said the names slowly and looked straight into Felix's eyes, to the point at which he felt compelled to avert his gaze. Then Ned swiftly moved on…

'Taek a leuk at some o' th' previous winners,' he said, flicking through a gallery on his VSP. Many of the frames showed a chap in his 50s who looked not dissimilar to Ned. 'An' this is the year the unthinkable 'appened…'

'The unthinkable?' said Felix, obligingly filling the pause.

'Aye, a lad frae Essex won wi' a tale aboot the fells n' lakes 'avin' been pinched frae Essex.' Ned showed them a picture of a bespectacled man of 40-something, with a scarcely buttoned white shirt and lurid trousers, but that wasn't what immediately caught Felix and Michelle's eye.

'Do you see who I see?' said Michelle.

'I do indeed,' said Felix. 'Do you know who this is?' he asked Ned, pointing to a man sitting at a table quite close to where the man from Essex was performing.

'Aye, aa've sin 'im aboot but I'm not sure aa ken his name.' Ned looked at Felix as if inviting him to challenge him on the veracity of this assertion. 'Aa might have more pictures wi' 'im in.'

Ned found another gallery, filled this time with images of men and women pulling faces while wearing a horse's halter around their necks.

'Crab Fair up the road at Egremont,' said Ned, as if those seven words explained everything, then expanding. 'It's the gurning contest at the annual crab apple fair and yes'll perhaps recognise this chap.'

The face was contorted, though by no means as hideously as some of the others in the collection, some of whom had clearly turned a lack of sound teeth into an artform. Despite the contortion, there was no doubting the owner of the visage.

'Lord Lindisfarne!' exclaimed Felix and Michelle in unison.

CHAPTER 23

The homecoming

Wednesday, September 22, 2010

Waking the following morning, I feel like I've been running a marathon and the stadium, with the winning post, is in view but I've somehow got to haul myself the last half mile and then, once inside, I'll have to run another 400 metres. It is Wednesday and it's already been agreed in principle that I will spend Friday night at home and, if all goes well, Saturday too. On Monday they'll reassess me and see whether I may be ready to be discharged.

I catch Jeff at breakfast and ask what more he knows about Tony. 'He did a shit on the pool table last night.'

'You're kiddin' me,' says Jeff. 'I think he were trippin' on summat. I'm not so sure he's really ill.'

'Maybe not, but he must be a danger to himself if he goes up on viaducts and acts like he did on the chair in the dining room?'

'Mebbe, but he never jumped when we were with 'im, did he? He just wanted to get down safe.'

'I guess so…'

Jeff persuades me to give him a massage in the garden and, a while later, Tony appears.

'Thanks again guys for looking after me yesterday,' he says. 'And Vic, I'm really sorry about last night. I can't believe I did a shit on the pool table. Anyway, I'm leaving now, so thanks again and sorry again.'

At lunchtime John indeed confirms to me that Tony has been discharged, though he's not at liberty, he says, to tell me why he was admitted to Priestley House. Then I hear news of another departure: that of Thomas. I smile the smile of a turnip lantern.

It feels altogether a time of great change here at Priestley House, which shall, before long, witness my own departure. I wonder how I'll fill the next two days and begin by concluding that it's now high time I took possession of my 'office' in the games room once again. I tell John that Ted Hughes has effectively rendered the games room out of bounds to the rest of us and suggest this is not very fair. Within an hour, it's sorted and I'm able to resume my daily perusal and marking of the papers.

Then I have an idea: maybe I can short-circuit my exit a little. I open my sketch pad and look at the only picture: the plan for my Garden of Remembrance. I text a friend who does garden design and tell her I've been resident at Priestley House for two and half weeks but am better now. I suggest she pick me up at Friday lunchtime and take me home, where I'll brief her on my ideas for the Garden of Remembrance. At the same time, I put in a call to the builders who did our kitchen extension and arrange for the boss to meet me at home after his 'builder's week' ends on Friday afternoon. All this means that Thursday may well be my last complete day at Priestley House, while today, Wednesday, is now nearly half gone.

I step out into the garden and kick my football against the wooden raised beds. I run round the perimeter of the lawn and am able to build a more complete picture in my imagination of the Garden of Remembrance. However, the Aborigines are again switched off in my pocket and there is no trip to the desert today.

'I'm very bored,' I tell Julia. 'I want to go home.' She's interviewing me and watching me closely. 'It might not be quite so easy as you think when you go home,' she says. 'You know a lot of people end up back here surprisingly quickly. The old revolving door. We really don't want you to be one of them, so we have to be cautious and not count all our chickens too soon. So another quiet day here will do you absolutely no harm at all.'

In the event, Thursday turns out to be not such a bad day as there's a trip to play football organised by a volunteer with a minibus. I play in goal and am delighted to find that my reflexes are as sharp as ever, as I pull off a series of superb saves, though one of them wrenches my knuckle and causes me to reflect that there is now less adrenaline in my bloodstream to mask any pain.

Buoyed by my performance, I follow some of the other guys when we get back to Priestley House. They're going for a run, which was something Dave got them going with when he was here. Once again, disappointingly, I fall behind after a mere 200 metres. I am brought right back down to earth. I am at the edge of the hospital grounds and look left and right to the horizon, noticing for the first time that the hospital sits on a hilltop in a direct line between two other hilltops, one of which has some kind of folly on the top. 'We must be on an important ley line,' I reflect.

At last it is Friday: I meet with Dr Honeydew who repeats the little pep talk I had from Julia on Wednesday. He stresses to me the importance of taking my meds and ensures I have enough to see me through until Monday. 'I've told Michaela to ring in tonight and tomorrow and then have you back here at teatime on Sunday.'

In celebration, I turn up the volume on my iPhone and select the Aborigines, and head for the garden. I run round the lawn a few times, then pause, sit on the seat at the far end and watch the bumblebees. One is stumbling in the damp, dew-laden grass. I rescue him and place him on a buddleia flower.

At noon I collect my bag, check I have my meds and wander through the hospital to the main reception, where I'm delighted to see that Valentina is on duty.

'Just in case I don't see you again, I'll say *arrivederci*.'

'I hope we will see each other again, Victor,' she says, and, coming out from behind her counter, she takes my hands and kisses me once on each cheek.

'Who's that?' asks Alice, my garden designer friend who has slipped in through the door without my noticing.

'That's Valentina; she's helping me with my Italian and I'm helping her with her French.'

'Really! Is that so…?' says Alice, with a knowing look.

'Entirely innocent, I assure you,' I say, as we walk out to Alice's car.

Once at the house, I produce my little plan for the garden and walk Alice through it. I show her where the plaques should be placed for Malcolm and for each of my parents, and for Michaela's relatives. We discuss some modest landscaping and the choice of flowers for each bed, with the aim of ensuring that there should be colour for as much of every season of the year as reasonably possible. A wooden bench beneath a rose arbour will be a place for quiet contemplation. I show her where I plan to erect a simple shelter so the little garden is not out of bounds in the worst weather. Bang on cue, the builder arrives, but I'm surprised that he is not alone, but accompanied by an electrician, a plumber and a roofer. I'm struggling to work out what I might have said to him to lead him to presume that this would be such a big project. I am slightly embarrassed and scared to admit that I neither own the land where the garden is planned, nor have I negotiated a right of access across his land with the Hermit. Although, of course, it remains my hope that the Hermit will move on. For that matter, I haven't even got so far as to have an architect's drawing prepared for the builder. I mutter an apology about 'crossed wires' and ask him instead for some ball park figures for building a shelter, giving him the rough dimensions and a pretty high grade spec, with walls of Yorkshire stone and Welsh slate roof. To save a bit of face, I suggest we duct in an electric cable and water pipe to make it easier to tend the plants. By the same token, the plan suddenly acquires a tool shed, discretely hidden in one corner of the plot. The builder says he'll come back to me with a price, but I suspect he won't.

'I'm sorry about all that,' I tell Alice as we cut across back to the house. I spot the Hermit at his window and remember that there has not, as yet, been any flight of fancy or otherwise to the remoter Scottish isles or the Faroe Islands and the Hermit can not possibly know anything of my intentions for him or his property. I hurry Alice along as he pops his head round his door and begins to raise a hand. In anticipation I offer a friendly wave. I suspect it was a fist that the Hermit intended to raise.

Once indoors I carefully tear my garden plan from the sketch book and give it to Alice, asking her to scan it and email the scan back to me once she's done her sums. I do my best to reassure her that this is indeed a real plan, notwithstanding the fiasco with the builder. Somehow, however, I suspect this will not find itself at the very top of her in-tray. Rather too late, I think to text Michaela to say that she does not need to collect me on her way home as I am already here.

'It's good to be back home,' I tell Michaela as she marches into the sitting room, where I am idly flicking between TV channels, sipping a cup of tea.

'Well, I hope it's good to have you back, Vic, but you erode my confidence when you go making your own arrangements... What have you been up to? How did you get home?'

'I got a lift from Alice, the garden designer.'

'Alice? Who the hell's Alice?'

'I told you, she's a garden designer I met at a networking event ages ago. She came with me to look at my plans for a Memorial

Garden in the spare land beyond the Hermit's house – for Malcolm and everyone else who's died. Just a quiet place to relax and be contemplative…'

'You know, you really do take the biscuit, Victor Turnbull. You seem to have completely forgotten that I was supposed to collect you from the hospital and the team would go through all your meds and everything with me. And remember, this is a two-night visit: you'll be going back to Priestley House on Sunday afternoon.'

'Don't start sending me back when I've hardly arrived,' I counter, going on to tell Michaela that I've also seen the builder and how he arrived with a whole army of tradesmen. She gives me an exasperated look, prompting me to reassure her about my meds and suggest that, perhaps, we might just start again and not set out to make the weekend go wrong before it's even begun.

'OK,' she says. 'I got another ready meal. And some popcorn and ice cream. There're some decent movies on: I quite fancy watching Atonement – we missed it when it first came out. It's the Ian McEwan novel adaptation. The book was very good: quite sad.'

I feel immense relief at the prospect of doing something so normal as sitting watching a film with my loved one, indulging in the guilty pleasure of popcorn. We eat the ready meal at the table: it's some Marks and Spencer deal that comes with a 'free bottle of wine'. I look at the bottle and try to imagine how it smells; how it tastes. I shudder at the prospect of the bottle opening and the smell of the wine wafting into my nostrils. It's as if my brain is saying: 'Enough! No more poisons in this body, please!' My mind goes back to last weekend when Phil and Jean were here and I had to retreat from the table because it was all getting too rowdy. But it wasn't just the noise, I reflect: it was the presence of alcohol too. I begin to understand that life on the outside is going to require a certain amount of adjustment. I resolve, however, to keep my own counsel. I am on probation: my imaginary electronic tag will ensure I don't run off and do my own thing this weekend. But the probation officer will be observing my behaviour very closely. As I watch the arrival of the food I draw imaginary timelines in my mind: I am running through everything I can recall from the last few weeks, and from the last three weeks in particular, during which my thoughts have been more ordered. I am able to rationalise that only events that happened in hospital can genuinely have happened. By that rationale, it is unlikely that I have travelled to St Kilda; it is even less likely that I have travelled to Australia. But then, I rationalise again, I don't think I have ever believed that I have already made these journeys: my brain has simply experienced very real manifestations of events set some time in the future. I have, however, made some journeys: the journey to Knaresborough and Harrogate, with Charlotte, when we got the bagpipes for me to resume learning the instrument, and made plans for a new style of bookshop. These were realistic ideas, not flights of fancy – even the bookshop idea: any ambitious entrepreneur might identify this as an opportunity and run with it. So, by extension, why shouldn't saving St Kilda be a realistic ambition? And this leads me in turn to the very foundation of the events that I am beginning to be able to separate in my mind into things that have or haven't happened yet. That foundation is the suite of legal actions that have changed the fortunes of my company, Persona Communications. With a degree of horror my consciousness is struck by the possibility that, not only has no legal process even begun, but that such a legal process might not even be possible...

'Vic, Vic! Wake up! Your tea's in front of you!

I start: 'Sorry sweetheart, I was just thinking some difficult thoughts...'

'Really?'

'Yeah, some of my recent dreams and aspirations may not be realisable,' I say, rather pompously.

'What do you mean?'

'Well, my mind has been living some of the last weeks in some kind of Candidesque Best Of All Possible Worlds and some of the things that I thought were happening and would happen either didn't happen or won't now happen. I'm no longer sure I wear my underpants on the outside any more; I'm not sure I have or ever had superpowers…'

'What the hell kind of a word is Candidesque?!' asks Michaela.

Atonement turns out to be a very good film, with James McAvoy, Saoirse Ronan and Keira Knightley and, later, Vanessa Redgrave. Michaela says it's very true to the original novel, though I can't judge that, having read only a few of McEwan's books, and this is not among them. If you don't already know, the theme of the book is a young girl's error in giving false testimony that leads to McAvoy's character being convicted of a rape that he did not commit and Saoirse Rohan spends her adult life seeking ways to atone for what she's done. It's one of those stories, like The French Lieutenant's Woman, that has both a happy and a sad ending. And, as is always the case in such stories, the happy ending is full of hope and joy, but the sad ending is devastatingly sad. Worse, in this story – unlike the French Lieutenant's Woman, in which we can choose to cling to either ending (or even both) according to our mood or disposition – the only 'real' ending is the sad one. One that condemns Ronan's character to having to face the reality of her childish misdeed not just throughout the adult life she has lived but for what remains of her old age to her very grave. The story feels as real as one of my constructions of a new reality running around the hospital garden. Perhaps I should add it to the essential reading list of my 'disciples'. But then perhaps there will be no disciples and no reading list. I shed a few tears, not just because it's a sad film but at the way my false reality is gradually dissolving – I am saddened and deflated by my own loss.

'You're a bit of a softy really, aren't you darling?' says Michaela. 'Let's go to bed, shall we?'

We spend Saturday morning reading the papers in bed and life feels remarkably normal. I am unsure if this is a good or a bad thing. The sadness I began to feel last night is beginning to feel a little like a heavy cloud forming and drifting across the sky above me. I decide to get up and survey the boundaries between where I think reality lies and where it really is.

I begin by looking at the texts and emails I have sent recently, and especially in the days leading up to and immediately following my admission to hospital. There's a lot of traffic to and from Ayanna containing much talk of 'guardian angels'; some to-ing and fro-ing with Rory in the run-up to Shenagh's wedding; a text to Iceland about my Viking heritage. Even quite recently, a lot of messages to and from Phil and Jean about traffic conditions between Thirsk and Harrogate. The overwhelming impression I get is of the sheer volume of words exchanged, or perhaps, rather, words that I have sent to people. Or perhaps it might be better to refer to simply 'collections of letters', as I have sent messages comprising no more than approximations to real words.

I open the pictures folder on my phone and find one that makes me smile: it's from soon after I went into Priestley House and shows a strange looking fella sprawled on the chair in my bedroom. His head is the football Michaela bought me in my first week. It's wearing a 'hat' comprising an upturned leather and canvas overnight toilet bag I got on an Emirates flight once. The torso must be my clothes stuffed into a jacket, and there's a mug balanced close to where the football's mouth should be. The legs are a pair of shorts, with Crocs stuffed in the bottoms and rested on a stool, close to the chair. The whole bears a rather demonic expression, thanks to the reflection of the rest of my room in the lenses of the skiing sunglasses I have plonked on the football. I think of my three monkeys: my football-headed mannequin has neither ears nor mouth, notwithstanding his mug, and nothing from his surroundings can pierce the opaque mirrors of his spectacles. I'd forgotten all about my little creation in the world of his own; but now I remember how I excitedly went to fetch the nurse, John, to show him. 'Ah, I get it: Wilson out of Castaway!' I remember him saying.

Another picture shows the 'den' I created on the sofa when I was spending the nights prowling the house prior to my admission. I remember that I thought this den was hugely important and that I got upset after my admission when Michaela and Larry told me they had dismantled it and that it smelled.

Also in the picture folder are shots of the letter I wrote that night in the Cathedral. I have to be honest and say that I'm not really surprised that the Bishop didn't get in touch – they look like the work of a madman. All of which causes me to reflect that I have crossed a line: I am reaching a point at which I am probably no longer mad. I am feeling uncomfortable with this discovery and head outdoors: the grapes are doing well and should be ready to pick early in October.

I look in the fridge and notice that the large quantities of fruit we picked a week ago are getting past their best. I put them in the freezer ready for conversion to jam, sloe gin and chutney. With the wrinkly-skinned fruit gone, there is now very little in the fridge, so I decide to go shopping, though not, I resolve, at the Co-op. The only problem is that I can't find my wallet. I slip upstairs and ask Michaela...

'I hid it to stop you going mad with credit cards...'

'Where did you hide it?'

'I can't remember...'

'Can you offer me a clue?'

'I'm not sure. Probably in a drawer or a cupboard underneath something else. But then it wouldn't be hidden if I knew where it was, would it?'

I wrestle with the logic of this last statement and suggest that maybe Michaela might give me some cash to shop with.

'I'm right out of cash,' she says.

I shrug my shoulders, bite my tongue and trot back downstairs, where I systematically open all the drawers and cupboards one by one. On each occasion I look behind and beneath whatever I find in the drawer. I am just beginning to think this is all too much like looking for the proverbial needle in a haystack when I have a moment of inspiration: Michaela used to always hide things behind the books on shelves when I first met her, and so I look for books that may appear to be sitting a little proud on the shelves in the room we euphemistically call the Library. I notice that the central volumes of the Harry Potter series are jutting out and, sure enough, my wallet is there behind them. So too are my car keys! Feeling an extraordinary sense of autonomy that I haven't known for weeks, I head for the centre of Ripon.

I wake on Sunday morning. In my own bed. Next to the woman I love. As Wordsworth might have put it, Bliss is it in this dawn to be alive! And yet it is a strange and curious thing… I have been ill: that I know – that is why I permitted myself to be admitted to Priestley House. I am much, much better. This I also know. I was not tempted last night to prowl the house in wakefulness, nor to build little dens anywhere. I recognise that this behaviour was unusual. Meeting Malcolm was also unusual, but that does not mean that it didn't happen or, indeed, that it may not continue to happen, even if he no longer seems to be sitting on the other end of the metaphorical phone all the time. It is possible, I concede to myself, that there may be things other than my liaisons with Malcolm that I have imagined will happen or to have happened already. Michaela is still fast asleep: I slip out of bed and downstairs, closely followed by Bafta.

The shopping I bought yesterday is where I stowed it in the kitchen: I made a real trip to real shops yesterday and spent real money, or at least enjoyed real credit on a reinstated card. Nada comes in through the cat-flap and paws at my dressing gown as though I hadn't been away, but I am sure at least that I have indeed – with the exception of last weekend's brief interlude – not been around for a while. I feed the cats, pop a croissant from yesterday's shopping haul in the oven, and put the kettle on for coffee. I take the papers and sit on the sofa with my snack and

Sky Sports for company. At ten, I'll take tea for Michaela and we can watch Saturday Kitchen Best Bites. It'll be just like normal: proper normal.

It is Monday morning and I have spent three nights at home. The weekend has proved remarkable only for its lack of remarkability. It was ram-packed with the normality of doing normal things at a normal pace. The stand-out moments were a trip to the Curzon cinema on Saturday evening while, on Sunday, we drove across to Whitby and walked along the beach at Sandsend. I think I could get used to this not being in Priestley House idea.

Before Michaela left for work this morning she phoned the hospital and told them she felt I was now ready to be discharged and return home. I have a meeting scheduled with Dr Honeydew at ten, when my revived status of Free Man will, I trust, be confirmed. I am allowed to be very grown-up and actually drive myself to the hospital to collect all my things and, I guess, say a few farewells.

'So, Victor, you've made contact with Marius and I believe he's already introduced himself to you,' says Dr Honeydew. 'And I've written to Dr Scholl in the community psychiatric unit, so you should be getting a letter for an appointment in a month or so's time. You've enough olanzapine to see you through the next ten days, but you should make an appointment with your own GP to get a new prescription before that runs out. That just leaves your brain scan and I should imagine you'll get a letter from Harrogate about that quite soon.'

'I'm pretty confident that'll be OK, Dr Honeydew,' I say. 'I'm increasingly sure my episode was caused by my tubes getting clogged up after I broke a gate and then came off my bike...'

'That's as may be, Victor, but what I must remind you is that people who endure a manic episode as you have are statistically very likely indeed to suffer a recurrence and we must be extremely mindful of that. That is why your medication is important and why we must be sure that all the "team" are on board, which is to say that it's terribly important that those you live with are mindful of your risk of relapse.'

'You make it all sound a bit like leaving prison and the possibility I might reoffend and find myself in the old revolving door…'

'Well, sadly, as you'll be aware, we do have our own revolving doors in the mental health sector, Victor, and it's my fervent desire that I never see you here ever again.'

Just for once I succeed, albeit fleetingly, in catching Dr Honeydew's eye: I think he may even be forcing a smile…

'I just would like to say, Dr Honeydew, that I am very grateful to you and all the team here and for all the professionalism and understanding. You read a lot about services letting people down, but the only complaint I would have is down to the PFI company that built this place and the idiots who must have drawn up the contract.'

'Not my field, Victor, not my field…'

And with that I head for my room to gather my remaining belongings and reflect on how little use I have made of some of the things I was so adamant Michaela had to bring in for me. The yoga mat is a particular embarrassment in that regard, but I have to concede that most of the language books in the big pile on the desk in my room remain unopened. At the very bottom of the pile I find a three-page guide for newly admitted patients at Priestley House, complete with a questionnaire, which I have never filled in. I take my bag to Reception, leaving it to conclude a brief farewell tour.

Most of the guys are in the smoking garden and, with the exception of young Jeff, my imminent departure is greeted with not much more than a casual acknowledgement, causing me to remind myself that this is, after all, a psychiatric unit, in which people are living strongly medicated lives. Jeff, on the other hand, gives me a hug, wishes me the best and says he hopes I won't come back through the revolving door, or at least not too soon. I tell him I'll be watching out for him and won't forget.

'One more time!' I tell him, and he responds: 'Proud to be a Tyke, proud to support Leeds United, proud to be Jeff, proud to be alive!' We high-five and I cross the corridor to the games room.

Ted Hughes's presence in the games room is a little more restrained than it was: he has Happy Homes for Heroes posters on the walls but they are no longer spread across the tables. The pool table is no longer a shrine to fallen soldiers, or whatever it was intended to be that day, and Ted himself is a little less frenetic, though he is keen to tell me once again of his disappointment that I have failed to join the project he believed I was destined to support.

In the garden I find Willy sitting on his own. He wishes me an unexpectedly warm farewell. I feel guilty for having taken Dave's assertions about his murky past at face value.

'What about you?' I ask. 'Do you think you'll be able to get home soon?'

'Pah! What's so good about getting home? Aa's better off in 'ere lad. 'n safer...'

'What do you mean?'

'Let's just say, Vic lad, that I'm not the most popular guy in town...'

At Reception I wind Ute up by saying Auf Wiedersehen, for which she rewards me with a withering look; nurse John shakes my hand; Julia gives me the briefest hug (probably slightly more than the rule book actually allows) and I ask her to say my goodbyes to Bertie when she's next on duty. And with that I am gone. There is no Valentina at the main reception as I leave for the last time, and I wonder if perhaps she is making the trip to Sicily that she spoke of.

CHAPTER 24

First base

Evening of Saturday
October 9, 2021

'What did you make of "Michael and Victoria"?' Felix asked Michelle as they sat on a bench in a little room just off the main walkers' bar at the Wasdale Head Inn. Such conversation as they had had on the short final drive up the dramatic dale from Santon Bridge, when not constrained by Felix weaving past oncoming traffic on the narrow road, had been focused on the very specific subject of precisely why Lord Lindisfarne would have not merely stuck his head through a horse's collar, but then pulled a ridiculous face and – perhaps most unbelievably – permitted himself to be photographed while doing so. It was a question the answer to which was still in orbit somewhere beyond the asteroid belt when they pulled up at the tiny settlement, in which the inn seemed by far the largest single element, a mile or more beyond the head of the lake. Heading to their separate rooms, they'd agreed to reconvene for a late lunch in the bar.

Michelle was wearing a frown as she considered the best answer to Felix's question, in which she could practically SEE the quotation marks around Michael and Victoria. Eventually she said, quite slowly: 'It has to be just too much of a coincidence, surely? Victor and Michaela: Victoria and Michael.'

'Well, it wouldn't be the first of those we've encountered on this trip, would it?' was Felix's rapid response. 'Let's weigh up what we've got… we've got a surreal visit to Egremont Crab Fair and the gurning picture, which – let's face it – might or might not have been faked up in some way; we've got a clearly fanciful story about a couple who may be modelled on Victor and Michaela Lindisfarne that is, by definition, a lie, because it was entered in the World's Biggest Liar competition; and then we've got an old-fashioned phone found in highly mysterious coincidental circumstances, the contents of which we may know once it's finished charging in my bedroom.'

'Let's work through that lot backwards, shall we?' suggested Michelle. 'I've been thinking about the phone and, you know, even if the Lindisfarnes had deposited it nine or ten years ago when they were here in the Lake District, it would already have been a bit of an antique. People were already using smartphones then, so it's almost as if that phone was deliberately chosen and deliberately hidden…'

'And if that's true, then who was meant to find it? Us?' interrupted Felix.

'Well, possibly, though I'm struggling to work out the dynamics of that. And then, how do you explain the fact that we just happened to find ourselves in the pub at precisely the right time to meet a man who just happens to have strange pictures of our dearest Lord on his phone…'

'Well, to be fair, I suspect Ned Tackler can probably be found at the bar in Santon Bridge most lunchtimes,' suggested Felix.

'Possibly… but to continue working backwards: we're here at Wasdale Head now, so let's find out everything we can about what the Lindisfarnes were up to when they were here and see if that then throws light on the other questions.'

'OK,' said Felix. 'How about we begin with the visitors' book, then chat with the staff, examine that phone, and then follow up on any local leads…'

'Sounds like a plan,' said Michelle. 'Except I think we should do the first three in the opposite order!'

The phone could not by any stretch of the imagination be called smart, but it did have email functionality and could take pictures. And once past the password, its contents were not encrypted in any way. The last entry in the picture library was what appeared to be a selfie, dated Monday December 3, 2012, and had clearly been taken at Swinside stone circle, although in somewhat different conditions, as the pair were both dressed against hostile elements and a moderate fall of snow covered the area within the stones and submerged those monoliths that had fallen. The white fells in the background merged into a white-grey sky. Other pictures showed the pair at other stone circles, which Felix could not immediately identify, but guessed might be Long Meg and Castlerigg. There were shots of the inn at Wasdale Head and, perhaps significantly, there was one taken inside the bar there, in which none other than Ned Tackler was standing between the Turnbull-Lindisfarnes with an arm around each. All three were smiling broadly. Even more significantly, there were separate pictures of all three with their heads through a horse's halter, gurning into the camera. The one of Lord Lindisfarne was distinctly familiar.

Felix and Michelle chose to presume that the phone had been hidden on December 3, 2012, but that then raised new questions as there was more recent content on it. The logical conclusion was that it must have remained synchronised with an email and diary account after its burial. There were a lot of emails in what was clearly Victor's Persona account. They ran from early 2010, but did not end until February 2013. The diary appeared to have remained synchronised to a similar date.

'Look, one thing we know for sure is that Victor Turnbull was extremely mindful of the notion, true or otherwise, that people were out to get him,' said Michelle. 'Hence Michaela and him effectively going on the run. So leaving a mobile phone with all this data on it would appear at best extremely careless...'

'Or,' chipped in Felix, 'it's all an elaborate smokescreen. Perhaps the intention was that the phone would be found by their pursuers back in 2012.'

And yet, for all that, the emails bore all the hallmarks of being genuine. There was an extended thread that began in March 2010 with a man called Michael Holbeck, who had clearly been contacted by Victor with a view to investing in Persona to develop its Travel Knowledge portal. There were a lot of internal mails, particularly to and from a Stella de Weld, culminating in a series of summaries of a legal process against a company called Smart Ideas, which had begun while Victor was in hospital. For a period from around the middle of August, Victor's mails became increasingly erratic, with spelling errors and many repetitions. However, Victor appeared to recognise he wasn't functioning well, as a long thread with someone called Charley was devoted to ensuring that a coherent message was sent to someone Victor had gone to meet but in whose office he had broken down.

Most outgoing mails then seemed to cease for a period of about three weeks, starting around August 20, 2010. Then, around September 14, they resumed, with a flurry of exchanges with Stella regarding the takeover of the Smart Ideas company. One mail specifically confirmed to Stella her role as acting CEO. Around ten days later, Victor sent emails to a small number of contacts who must have known about his hospitalisation, confirming that he was now home again, feeling well and very excited about developments in his business that he was sure they would hear about shortly.

After that, business emails on the account appeared to come to a stop, but there were personal mails to Michaela. When it got to 2012, these appeared bland in the extreme, referring to 'packing for two weeks' or arranging 'for Bafta and Nada to go on holiday to my sister's'.

The diary on the phone was more explicit, although the information was still quite sparse. The entry for December 4,

2012, stated simply, 'BHR Rye'. But on closer examination, the photograph with Ned had, on the face of it, been taken on the fifth. Then there were gibberish entries alongside other dates that followed: Shellty cheese; Bah! Ade mad; Mile so fan; Van Luco; Haj quoc; Aer and fossil.

'These are just bad anagrams,' said Michelle. 'In fact, the more we look at it, this phone seems less like a golden bullet and more like a piece of junk.'

Felix couldn't help but agree: there just seemed no rational explanation as to why the phone should have been hidden and, more particularly, why the head of a high-tech company would choose to hide an obsolete phone with information on it that was at best thinly disguised and, at worst, not disguised at all.

'He hasn't even tried to encrypt such information as there is,' he said. 'So I think we have to ask ourselves just who, if anyone, was actually meant to find this phone...'

'And how it came to be that we had a sixth sense it was indeed hidden there, given that it appears to be of very little consequence,' chipped in Michelle.

'Let's "take it from the top", then,' said Felix. 'So a man and a woman who may or may not be "on the run" go to a remote stone circle, where they hide a previous generation mobile phone containing a few scraps of information. And that "information" includes a photograph that appears to have been taken a day after a diary note referring to, what was it?'

'BHR Rye,' said Michelle.

'So,' resumed Felix. 'The first question: was someone meant to find the phone or was it hidden to avoid someone finding it? What if the idea was to lay a false trail but whoever they expected to find the phone simply didn't?'

'Or what if it wasn't even put there by them in the first place?' suggested Michelle. 'Perhaps it was put there recently and it's we who are the target, so to speak.'

'Oh, you've got to be kidding, 'chelle! That would really start to complicate things, wouldn't it? Maybe we should just park the phone thing for the moment and look at the visitors' book.'

They found the visitors' book in the little entrance lobby where walkers removed their muddy boots or donned their waterproofs before going out. Next to it was the day's weather forecast and a log book in which guests were encouraged to write their walking plans for the day and estimated time of return, lest they get into trouble on the fells. Frustratingly, the guest book went back only as far as 2014 and the log book to 2016.

'I think my boss might have them in her archive at home,' said the woman at reception, who had just the faintest trace of an accent, possibly German. 'We haven't room to be stashing things like that here,' she added, glancing up towards the low ceiling where the staircase went up, directly above the head of whoever was running the reception desk. 'I could ask her to bring them in tomorrow if you can tell me what it's for...'

'Well,' began Felix, thinking on his feet, 'we're doing some research for a biography of Lord Lindisfarne, if that name means anything to you, and we're trying to fill in some blanks from the early days of the Aurora Group...'

'Well, I might be able to help you there,' said the woman, 'because I actually began working here round the time that Victor and Michaela stayed here. It would be hard to forget because it wasn't just them, but every time a room fell vacant, they took it over and then more of their, I guess, support staff would arrive.'

'Gosh, that must have been good for business,' said Michelle.

'Well, yes and no... we're a walkers' and climbers' hotel and it got to the point at which walkers and climbers stopped making enquiries because they would know the hotel was full. In the end we said that, much as we loved having everyone here, it might be better if they moved on. And Victor said they were about to move on anyway...'

'Do you know to where?' asked Felix.

'Well, they were very coy about that, said they didn't want "certain people" knowing where they'd gone, but I can tell you that we did overhear conversations and there was a lot of talk about islands.'

'Can you remember which ones?'

'Well I do recall they talked to each other about somewhere with a strange name, like Silly, and the Isle of Men and somewhere else with a sort of French-sounding name, like Jacques, or something.'

'So, the Isles of Scilly, the Isle of Man and maybe one of the Channel Islands,' suggested Felix.

'Yes, yes, that could be correct! I'm Greta by the way. Greta from Austria. I came here when I married a farmer.'

'So, Greta the greeter!' said Felix, feeling pleased with his wittiness.

'Beg pardon?' said Greta. 'I do not understand.'

'Never mind, just my English sense of humour,' said Felix, who then had a flash of inspiration and showed her the pictures of the gurning Lindisfarnes and Ned Tackler.

'Oh yes, that's Ned. He's a second or third cousin of my husband and he created these pictures for a joke. They are amusing, no?'

The following morning, Greta's boss arrived with a number of leather-bound books, which she presented to Felix and Michelle in the breakfast room. Felix and Michelle were feeling buoyed, not just by the rather fine breakfast, including succulent Waberthwaite Cumberland sausages, but also by the continuing 'research' they had done the previous evening.

This had been prompted by a message on the secret Blather account that had come from Carty@, asking TopCat2021 if he'd finished his homework. Two things had occurred to Felix as a consequence: firstly, they hadn't concluded their experiment to see if the secret *ficelle* would disappear if they used sensitive terms like Aurora; and, secondly, there remained a couple of items on the lozenge given to him by Michelle that were still to be read or listened to.

'Carty being Tracy,' Michelle had reminded herself, adding: 'And we should try and solve those anagrams from the phone, if that's what they actually are.'

Felix bleated to Carty@ and Shell2021@ using the tag, πlesdisparus¿: 'Concerned at the disappearance of a number of young people working for the Aurora Foundation... any news of Kenny Marchant?' The encryption function was turned off.

Michelle watched the message arrive on her VSP, while Felix noted its presence in the ficelle on his. They then both watched as the bleats simply faded away before them. Michelle then tried to bleat to Felix, using the same πlesdisparus¿ tag, only to be greeted by the message: 'This is not a valid Blather tag, please choose again.'

'Well,' said Felix. 'That seems to answer that question... The shifting sands of the Aurora virtual world.'

Then he clicked the WiFi link on Michelle's lozenge and opened a file called Michaela's Blog.

'Haven't you read that yet?' asked Michelle slightly accusingly.

'I just wanted to check something in it,' lied Felix to Michelle's doubting expression. 'Well, I think it's worth reminding ourselves of our quarry, don't you?' he continued.

The blog had turned out to be a disarmingly candid account of 'living with a loony' as it had been catchingly, if not terribly politically correctly, titled.

September 6, 2010 Ripon

I'm writing this blog because I feel I need people to understand things from my perspective and because I want to be able to look back one day and know that I have a record of how everything felt at the time that I felt it. Of course nobody will actually know that it's me who's writing this because, for very obvious reasons, I am writing it under an assumed name. But it will make me feel better if I can at least get things off my chest.

I'm calling it Living with a Loony because it has a nice ring to it. In the old days, they called people lunatics because it was believed that bipolar episodes were linked to the cycle of the moon. I think there is actually something to this but of course my partner, Chuck (not his real name either!) is not bipolar: he's just having a manic episode.

It took me some time to recognise that he was entering a manic episode because, firstly, I've never seen someone become manic before, and secondly, because I have to admit that I keep kidding myself it wasn't going to come to this. I buried my head in the sand because I couldn't really contemplate how awful it would be if they took Chuck into hospital.

I don't mean that it would be awful being separated from him, although, of course, there is that. It's more that, whatever anyone might say, there really is a terrible stigma attached to mental illness. So my own trauma began with trying to find ways to manage living with someone who was, I realise now, increasingly losing touch with reality by the day, and then doing everything possible to make sure that no-one discovers the secret about where he is now.

Every day when I go to work I'm in dread of the secret getting out. When I'm at home in the evening I dread the phone ringing because I may have to tell more lies about where Chuck is. I feel like a kind of pressure cooker simmering on the hob, but the slightest knock, or too much, heat, could make me just blow. Pfsssst!! There I go!

Today I called to see Chuck at the hospital – I'd best not call it the loony bin! – and he's convinced that he's going to be able to sue all these companies and get ridiculous amounts of money from them. He's got one of his team already running round seeing lawyers. I don't honestly know if his business can even afford lawyers' fees.

And then he told me he was expecting a six-figure advance for the story of how he met his dead brother somewhere beyond the grave and even more for the film rights. He said we would never have to worry about money ever again, which would be nice, if only it were true!

Davina Peregrine

Subsequent blogs described the strain of never knowing whether something might cause that pressure cooker to blow and, in particular, 'Davina's' fury when friends and family of 'Chuck' allowed him to persuade them to take him to restaurants or, more surreally, to buy a set of bagpipes. And then there was a change of tone, and, on the 18th, 'Davina' wrote:

It looks like I am going to have to eat humble pie as it turns out that some of what I took to be figments of Chuck's vivid imagination may actually come to be true. His company's lawyers have shut down one of his rivals and it looks like he has acquired the company as a result. Perhaps what worries me even more is that Chuck is still not well and the last thing he really needs is more stress if he is going to make a full recovery quickly.

'You know what struck me when I first read these,' Michelle said. 'It was just how quickly Victor must have gone from being a complete fruitcake to being a millionaire-in-the-making.'

Felix could only agree, but he was more curious as to how Michelle had come by the blogs and who had worked out who had written them.

'They were sent to me anonymously,' Michelle continued.

'And that didn't strike you as just a little odd?' queried Felix.

'Well, yes, of course it did, but the contents seemed more important than the origin.'

Felix said, 'It's just that that whole thing with the phone and what happened at the stone circle and everything is all seeming, well, odd... Don't you begin to get the idea that someone is just playing with us?'

So Felix and Michelle then turned their attention back to the phone and the curious diary entries and appeared to make a breakthrough.

Working on the basis that the entries were indeed anagrams, Felix wrote out each entry on its own sheet of paper: BHR Rye; Shellty cheese; Bah! Ade mad; Mile so fan; Van Luco; Haj quoc; Aer and fossil.

It wasn't long before Michelle ventured, 'Could "Mile so fan" be "Isle of Man"?' And added: 'You can solve anagrams online, you know.'

Soon, with a little WiFi help, they were able to add the Seychelles, and Faroe Islands. BHR Rye and Haj quoc proved more problematic, but with the aid of Eureka they identified the tiny Scilly isle of Bryher and the even tinier channel island of Jacqhou.

'I'm not sure that necessarily takes us much further forwards,' said Felix. 'Greta heard them talk about the Isle of Man and the Scilly Isles, but all this happened years ago and I can't help thinking that the trail must have gone cold.'

'So why are we doing this instead of trying to work out where the action's going on now?' asked Michelle.

'Because Emily Black was adamant we should begin at the beginning,' replied Felix.

'And what if she has a different agenda to us? What if she's still loyal to Aurora?'

Felix pondered for a moment, before saying, 'I just felt I could trust her.'

'You know, Felix, your easygoing way with women might just make it a little easy sometimes for them to squeeze one past you...'

'I'm not sure I know what to make of that,' said Felix. 'But look, as I see it, we're here now, we've got a visitors' book and a log to check through and then we can look again at our strategy.'

And so Felix and Michaela looked through the pile of books that Greta's boss had brought. The visitors' book was of marginal use only, because, of course, it recorded just the dates on which people had left the hotel.

Checking with Greta, however, they were able to establish that the extended stay began in late August 2012, while Vic and Michaela recorded their thanks to all the staff in a message on December 12th. Another familiar name was that of Stella de Weld, who left two days after Vic and Michaela. It was possible to deduce that others in the party included a couple called Frank and Cynth, and a woman called Charley. All of these had left the hotel by Christmas, while January was also marked by a continuing roll of departures.

Of potentially more interest was the walkers' log, which revealed that Vic Turnbull and Michaela Larkhill appeared to have been especially fond of walking the screes route, along the south shore of the lake. It was a route that they appeared to have taken almost daily, starting about a week after they had first moved into the hotel.

Felix had some experience of fell walking but had never

previously witnessed at first hand the immense grandeur of remote Wasdale. Today England's highest peaks loomed menacingly on all sides of the hotel as the fine autumn weather began at last to break. Had he looked at a weather chart, Felix might have observed that a deep area of low pressure was powering in from the Atlantic. And had he then looked at the forecast, he might have seen that those who knew about these things were expecting the fast-moving cyclone to slow right down as it began to butt up against the high pressure that had been in charge. As a consequence, there was now a risk that a cold front would become stationary across the Lake District, bringing deeply unsettled weather and very heavy rain.

It was now late morning and the sky was becoming increasingly leaden. Felix had had it in mind to take a wander round the lake in the footsteps of Victor and Michaela but had been firmly put in his place when he casually mentioned the idea to Greta.

'The screes are not an afternoon stroll,' she said firmly. 'It is a day's expedition to walk around the lake. You must be correctly footed and coated and you must be taking food and water. And you should not be setting off without you have a good and fair weather forecast.'

Recognising that the day would not now extend beyond the walls of the hotel, Felix engaged Greta in longer conversation and was able to get a better picture of the early days of the Aurora Foundation as it had taken shape in Wasdale. Crucially, he learned that, not long after the last members of the Aurora party had left in January 2013, a group of four American men had arrived and had been very interested indeed in what Vic and friends had been up to prior to their arrival. And very disappointed to have missed them.

'So did you tell them where Victor and everyone had gone?' Felix asked Greta.

'No, I did not. I really did not like these men and I felt that they did not have Victor's best interests at heart. And anyway, if you will recall, I did not know for sure where he and Michaela had gone.'

'Do you think I could possibly have a look in their room,' Felix risked.

'You mean Herr Victor's room or the room of the Americans? I remember exactly which rooms they all stayed in. The room that was occupied by Victor is empty today, but you know that this was a long time ago and you will find nothing in there now.'

'I think I'd like to look,' insisted Felix. And so he and Michelle headed up the stairs, armed with a bedroom door key but no more than modest expectations of finding anything of either value or interest.

As might have been expected, the room was one of the larger ones in the hotel and had a large bed, with a patchwork spread, and an en suite bathroom. The room was at the front of the hotel and might have offered a view of Scafell Pike, had the cold front not now arrived and cloaked the mountains in low cloud, the contents of which were starting to fall in near monsoon quantities.

All of these observations, however, faded into insignificance as Felix and Michelle cast their eyes to the bedroom walls, where, above the centre of the bed-head, hung a photograph of a stone circle, whose identity was unmistakable.

'Swinside!' exclaimed Felix, while Michelle, simultaneously, declared, 'Sunkenkirk!'

Without hesitation, Felix removed the picture from the wall, and then the backing paper attached to the back of the frame, to reveal a hand-written note on a folded piece of A4 paper.

The writing was that of someone clearly more accustomed to hitting a keyboard, wandering up and down and written with the frustration and impatience that tends to be felt by anyone used to creating words quickly on a keyboard. It read:

To whomsoever may find this short document...

We are writing this on paper because paper leves [sic] no trail on the Internet. So we can be sure that the person who first finds this letter will also be the first person to read it. The Wasdale Head Inn has been a valuable base from which Michaela and I and our initial team have been able to lay the first building blocks of the Aurora Foundation.

This foundation, thanks to the continuing and rising profitability of the Aurora Group, shall become an immense force for good in the world – in countering issues around climate change; religious discord; corruption; and scientific research. Its overriding mission shall be to facilitate the coming together of the two great universal truths, represented by science on the one hand and religious faiths on the other.

We might have wished to retain the Foundation's headquarters here at Wasdale, but already we are not without enemies and we have reason to believe that these enemies will soon find us here and so we must now be gone. I stress that we shall not be going underground, but we shall go down before we go wide and far. Our personal and corporate safety will be guaranteed not merely by secrecy but also by our best possible insurance policy: we have already taken steps to establish safe centres of operation on islands both close to home, in and around the UK, but also very much further afield.

We are leaving this message because even our extensive precautions can not guarantee our safety and we therefore feel it is important that we leave this old-fashioned physical trail as a backup to more modern records.

Victor Turnbull and Michaela Larkhill
December 2012

'So when was he knighted?' asked Michaela.

'You mean made a Lord? Dunno… 2013 maybe. But what do you make of it? Do you think it's real. And why didn't the mysterious Americans find it?'

'Because they hadn't been to Sunkenkirk,' said Michelle confidently. 'And maybe because Greta wouldn't have let them into this room anyway.'

'What do you make of going down before going wide and far?' asked Felix.

'I haven't the faintest idea,' said Michelle.

To say that the following day dawned would be to presume that the sun not only rose but was also seen to rise. In the event, the former truth could be inferred only because at some time in the morning the sky became marginally lighter than it had been during the night. Of the sun itself, however, there was no sign. It was presumably obscured by the mountains, which were in turn obscured by cloud, which in turn was indivisible from the unremitting deluge. The beck behind the hotel boiled and spat and had created a new torrent that tore through the yard between the building and the legitimate watercourse.

Michelle and Felix had spent the previous evening sifting through the remaining contents of the lozenge, re-reading Michaela's blogs and listening again to Vic's appearance on Desert Island Discs, and establishing via Eureka that he had in fact entered the Lords as recently as 2015, which appeared to question the presumed link between this event and his unsuccessful espousal of the leadership cause of Gloria Turnbull in 2010.

Another 2010 blog by Michaela appeared to leave the question open.

I can't believe that it took me so long to finally understand that Chuck had actually lost the plot, or at least so I thought. Now I'm really unsure what to believe. When he first told me he was helping Gloria Turnbull's election campaign I had no reason to disbelieve him. Then, after he'd been in hospital a few days, he started to talk about how there would be forces of evil out to get us, that's me and him, and how we would have to go on the run, hiding on islands, so as to always stay one step ahead of them. Well, I didn't want to believe that and so at that point I started to question lots of things he'd told me, including the Gloria Turnbull idea, especially as he has subsequently told me it would be his fast-track to the House of Lords and hence a place near the seat of power. I realised all of this – and his constant talk of legal action against half the world – was consistent with what the hospital team told me was called grandstanding.

And then of course, as I said in my last blog, it turns out the whole legal action thing is in fact true and so, I guess all of these 'fantasies' could, in fact, also be true. Perhaps I shall become Lady Muck, or whatever title he decides to take. Perhaps we shall have to lead a life on the run. It's not a prospect I'm sure I relish.

Both Felix and Michelle felt increasingly frustrated by the weather: they had toyed with bailing out, armed with such new information as they had been able to garner, but Greta advised them that the dale was effectively cut off from the world by floods, and suggested they pass the time at chess or Scrabble. They chose the latter and the game would have been unworthy of record but for the fact that Felix opened by placing the word 'auroras', scoring 50 bonus points and prompting Michelle, somewhat freaked-out at the coincidence, to complain firstly that he must have fixed it and, secondly, that the plural of aurora should surely be aurorae.

It had still been lashing down when Felix and Michelle, and several other guests who now found themselves marooned at the hotel, satisfied themselves that the roaring torrent behind the hotel, for all its ferocity, had risen no further in the course of the evening and, thus reassured, headed for their beds.

Now a new day had dawned and, were it not for a small river still making its way down the road at the front of the hotel, and what looked like a new lake in the fields at the head of Wastwater, Felix might have been forgiven for thinking he had imagined the deluge. As it was, the sun seemed to have found renewed confidence as it cast its rays the length of the dale and in through his window.

Over breakfast he and Michelle resolved to set off for the screes and to circumnavigate the lake.

'You must be taking sticks and a towel,' cautioned Greta. 'You must cross the beck to reach the path along the shore and you know it has been in spate and there will be much water everywhere. If I am you I am not attempting this walk today.'

But Felix and Michelle, frustrated by their confinement and inactivity, decided that valour was in this instance the better part of discretion. As a precaution they made a detour via the campsite at the lake head so as to cross the beck by the bridge rather than stepping stones, splodging on towards the point at which the fells began to rise sheer above the lake's southern shore. Their progress quickly slowed as the path narrowed and climbed ever more vertiginously above the now glassy waters. From time to time the walkers had to negotiate new watercourses that had sprung from the fellside above them and continued to cascade down the loose scree. In places the path had been replaced by deep gashes in the scree, which the pair had to pick their way across cautiously.

As the stones got larger, the scree appeared more stable, but soon larger stones gave way to boulders, with no clear indication as to the correct route by which to move forward. The greasy boulders became increasingly slippery and progress slowed to a crawl.

'This is hell,' said Michelle, picking herself up after having lost her footing for the umpteenth time. 'I really can't see what we hope to achieve by this torture.'

Felix felt disinclined to argue and would happily have turned back had it not been for his reluctance to recross the boulder field.

Eventually the path became recognisable again and appeared to lead round the head of a gully, filled today by what looked like another impromptu river. As they looked more closely it became clear that there'd been a landslide, as clods of earth and the remains of scrubby bushes poked out at odd angles either side of the waters. The path was completely submerged beneath the debris: there was nothing for it but to take their boots off and pick their way through the torrent. Felix ventured across first – it was a struggle to keep his footing without completely immersing his arm into the bed of the new watercourse above him. He was thankful for Greta's reminder about taking walking poles, using his own to avoid overbalancing and sliding down the rapids. Once he had made it to the small shelf where the path resumed, Michelle threw across their boots and day bags for Felix to catch and then began to trace his steps. As she got close, she held out her pole for Felix to grab, but then got impatient. Stumbling onto the little platform, she tugged on the pole and wrong-footed Felix, who tumbled in the opposite direction, landing on his back in the water.

'Michelle, look!' shouted Felix as he dragged his dripping body upright. 'Look, up there!'

Michelle followed the line to where Felix's pole was pointing. She could see where the flood had dislodged a substantial chunk of scree, but it was what had consequently been uncovered that caused her to catch her breath: protruding from the watercourse was what looked like a large pipe of perhaps three feet in diameter. It was clear that it had until recently been concealed beneath the scree, as too had what looked like some kind of doorway, which was now perched on top of the pipe for all to see.

Felix was by now almost oblivious to the fact that he was soaking wet, as he and Michelle followed the line of the pipe down to where it disappeared again beneath the scree. It seemed probable that it continued in the same direction beneath the surface of the lake.

'I think we need to find our friend Mr Tackler, don't you?' said Felix.

'You think it leads to something in the lake?'

'I certainly do,' replied Felix, slinging his day-bag on to his wet shoulder.

The going remained difficult for another couple of hundred yards and then eased as the loose scree gave way to a more thickly vegetated slope and then to a near level track towards the foot of the lake. The sheer force of the storm had, however, caused the lake to overtop its banks and the pair found themselves trudging through a foot of water.

Eventually reaching the road, they decided to take a chance on finding Ned and – instead of returning to Wasdale Head along the road up the western shore – chose instead to walk down the dale to Santon Bridge.

'What the hell have yous two bin up te?' asked an incredulous

Ned Tackler, who looked as though he hadn't left his post at the bar since Felix and Michelle had first come across him there two days previously.

'We've been round the screes searching for submarines,' said Felix, haughtily.

'You've walked the screes today!?' exclaimed Ned, with what looked like genuine shock. 'Are yes completely mad? Do yes knaa how many fowk 'as died on them screes – and that's in good weather. There was that French lass and then that woman who wes murdered…'

'Aye, but it was her husband who chucked her in the lake,' interjected the barman.

'Aye, well, that's as mebbes but it's still no place to be goin' after the rains we've bin seein' these last twa days…' Then he continued: 'So what's aal this nonsense about submarines, then?'

Somewhat to their surprise, Felix and Michelle soon found themselves in Ned's Land Rover, heading back towards the foot of the lake. 'The polis'll be after better things to be doin' today than seekin' out fowk as had a couple of drinks afore gettin' ahind the wheel,' shrugged Ned, when Felix raised an eyebrow at the idea of him driving.

Ned let the Land Rover plough its way through the waters as far as the pumping station, from where they retraced the route taken by Felix and Michelle earlier in the day.

'Aye, well, yes, mebbes I do knaa summat aboot this,' said Ned, when finally confronted by the pipe within the wreckage of the landslide. 'I alus thowt it might be an idea to make a up a tale aboot his and her lord an' ladyship but I nivver thowt anybugger else'd ivver be findin' it.'

Michelle looked bemused, as though Ned were talking a completely different language. 'I think he's hinting he worked "on the inside" with Vic and Michaela and never thought he'd be rumbled,' explained Felix.

'Aa'd best be showin' yes what's doon the pipe,' said Ned, climbing onto the step of the door that now appeared to float incongruously in mid-air.

Descending the narrow pipe at a steep angle was neither especially easy nor comfortable, and induced a distinct sense of claustrophobia. Felix reckoned they must be about 20 feet below the lake's surface when, finally, they arrived at a larger chamber, fitted with what appeared to be an airlock.

Ned invited them to follow him into the airlock, prompting Michelle to reflect that they must surely now be in far greater danger than had been the case on their 'walk' along the screes. They exited the airlock into a kind of mini-submarine, with a proud-looking Ned explaining: 'It's my job ter keep 'er shipshape, so ter speak; keep the batteries charged 'n suchlike. Nah, 'old on ter yer 'ats 'n awaa we go!'

The little craft set off in a gentle descent away from the shore; everything beyond its little windows was pitch black and the strobe light on its nose struggled to illuminate the inky waters. After no more than a couple of minutes, they arrived at another airlock.

'Welcome to 't mother ship!' exclaimed Ned proudly. 'This beast is anchored to the lake bed, which is another hundred feet or so down from 'ere, 'n we're aboot 80 or so feet below the surface. There's an air line runs up ter 't surface, where it's attached to an 'ollow buoy, so's not ter attract attention.'

'Why are you showing us this?' asked Felix. 'If they went to all this trouble to make this place secret, I don't understand...'

'Mebbes aa'm just not so good at keepin' a secret... aa've been bustin' ter tell someone ever since the pair o' them left an' I reck'on'd mebbes now's 't time, what wi' 't access gettin' exposed by 't flood an' aall. Yer see aash'll a' ter move 't mini-sub any road lest someone try ter get inside 'er.'

Ned ushered Felix and Michelle through the airlock, as though he were an estate agent presenting a highly desirable property. The mother ship was not especially large, comprising a chamber of no more than 15ft long and perhaps eight or so wide. But it was quite comfortably fitted out, with a couple of sofas, a large TV screen and a small kitchen. At one end, Ned showed them, you could access a compact bathroom with shower, adjacent to what could at best be described as a sleeping 'compartment'.

But it was what was at the other end of the vessel that made Felix and Michelle once again catch their breath: they could feel the heat coming through the slatted door even before Ned inserted his key and pulled it open to reveal an array of what Felix quickly concluded were computer servers.

'Where the hell's the power come from to run that little lot?' exclaimed Felix.

'T'owd cable on't lake bed,' said Ned. 'We took it ower when they lost 't supply up top end o't lake, like. So it runs these li'l babies 'n it recharges me li'l submarine 'n aall. Naa, aam goin' ter tell yers everythin' aa knaas but here's 't deal. First off, yes are goin' ter tell me 't truth aboot what yer really after deein' here. Yer see aa don't buy this cock 'n bull tale yers telt our Greta aboot writin' some kind o' biography or summat…' Ned stretched word biography for emphasis, as though it were a piece of clay; dirty clay you wouldn't want to soil your hands with.

'Yer see, she's a nice ship but she's not exactly somewhere as anyone would CHOOSE to live or sleep for want o' sharin' a li'l bit o', like, specialist, knowledge.'

The words felt to Felix uncomfortably like a threat; less so to Michelle who continued to grasp no more than half of anything that Ned said.

'I think we need to tell Ned about Jameela and Kenny,' said Felix. 'Otherwise we might not see much daylight for a while.'

Michelle's eyes opened wide as she glanced involuntarily towards the sleeping quarters. 'Are you going to take us hostage?' she asked bluntly.

'Nay lass, not if yes are good boys 'n girls!'

'So, it's aal aboot unrequited love and nowt ter de wi' espionage or owt, then?' said Ned.

'Since you put it that way,' replied Michelle, sullenly.

'So what do you suggest we do?' added Felix, more positively.

Ned scratched the whiskers on his skin and furrowed his brow. 'Well, from what you tell me, ye'd be best followin' the route that Michaela and Victor thissens took. Yes'll only find out where any of their Aurora people are if yes can ask 'em yersels. And 't ownly way yes'll track 'em down is by sniffin' the ground behind 'em.'

'And you think that trail won't have gone stone cold since they left here?' asked Felix. 'I mean, it's years, after all.'

Ned shrugged in a couldn't-care-less fashion. 'You got a better idea?'

'Well, how about I go to Ahmedabad and look for Jameela there?'

'Pah – be like lookin' fer a needle in a haystack. C'mon!'

And with that Ned led both of them back into the mini-sub and pointed its nose up the lake: 'I can't be leavin' 'er back there with that access exposed. I'll moor 'er at 't jetty near 't campsite.'

Somehow Felix found the strength to drag his sodden self the mile or so along the road back to the hotel, where Greta was relieved to see them both again, though alarmed at both their condition and the fact that Ned Tackler was with them: that could only spell trouble, she thought.

After a hot bath, Felix made his way back to the bar to meet Michelle. They found Ned – marooned at the head of the dale with his Land Rover at the other end of the lake – propping up the counter in the walkers' bar.

Thankful not to have been kidnapped and held hostage in a submarine, they decided to ply him with more drink in the hope that he might yield better clues than he had earlier.

By the end of the long day Ned Tackler remained as adamant as ever that they had no choice but to follow in the footsteps of Michaela and Vic. His only concession was regarding where those footsteps had actually led the day they left Wasdale. Michaela, he said, had travelled to the Isle of Man to make financial arrangements for the Foundation and had then intended to travel on to Bryher, in the Scilly Isles, to establish a new safe operations base. Vic, he said, had travelled to the island of Vulcano, off Sicily, though he was unsure precisely what his mission there was. Ned had repeatedly stonewalled any attempt to pin him down on the couple's current whereabouts.

'T'ownly communication I 'ave is through their private Internet, so aa's no way of knowin' where they might be.'

Felix and Michelle struggled to find much to smile about over breakfast the following morning. Even the Waberthwaite sausage – which had been casually arranged beneath her egg and tomatoes – to form a hideously grinning face – did no more than cause her lip to twitch slightly.

'They're all just playing with us, Felix,' she said.

Felix struggled to muster any argument to the contrary.

'I know I can only understand half of what he says, but that half is enough to tell me that he's slippery and hiding something for sure. And don't forget that he was perfectly happy to kidnap us.'

Felix wanted to find something – anything – optimistic to say in response.

Michelle continued: 'I'm seriously wondering if we should abandon the whole idea…'

Felix had been wondering the same thing, but felt now was not the time to rush to judgement. Nonetheless, he could find not a single word of encouragement to utter. It was the arrival of Greta that saved him…

'So I am hearing that you spend your evening with Ned,' she

said. 'It feels to me like an unnecessary punishment after all you have been through on the screes yesterday. He may be in my husband's family, for sure, but he is a man who can sometimes be too full of his own importance. I do not know what he must have arranged with Mr Victor and Miss Michaela but am very sure that they would not have intended that he should use his knowledge to taunt people…'

'You think he's taunting us?' asked Felix. 'It certainly feels like that to us.'

'So, if you perhaps tell me what is your real purpose to find Victor and Michaela, then perhaps I will try harder to help you than cousin Ned.'

Once again, Felix and Michelle found themselves laying their souls bare, to which Greta responded: 'So, it is being all about, how you say, "unrequired love" and it is not about writing biographies or spying, yes?'

'Unrequited!' said Felix.

'Yes, yes, unrequired love,' reiterated Greta, continuing: 'I was not completely truthful when I am first telling you about their time here and where they went afterwards. I do know exactly where they both went when they left here, because they gave me postal addresses. They tell me to not tell anybody about these, but I feel that time has passed and I can see no reason not to be telling you any more. Because that is all history now, no?'

Greta disappeared and returned a few minutes later with a carefully folded piece of paper on which she had written four addresses. 'You must tell nobody where you got these, you understand.'

Michelle took the paper and noticed that, on the other side, there was what looked like a four-line verse that had been scribbled out. She did not give it a second thought.

By lunchtime, Felix and Michelle had a clear plan of action: Michelle would head for the offices of an accountant in Douglas and then on to the Scilly Isles. Felix would skip Vulcano and instead travel to Ahmedabad. They also had a promise from Greta that she would get in touch if any new information were to come her way.

And so it was a much more buoyant pair who were so absorbed in gazing across the lake in wonderment at the black screes while driving out of Wasdale that they somehow failed to notice the occupants of either of two cars travelling up the dale. These they passed on one of the few sections of road that was wide enough for two vehicles. In one car were two British-born Pakistanis; in the other, two Americans. The occupants of the first car cursed, but by the time they had travelled on to a place wide enough for them to turn their car, Felix and Michelle were already beyond the fork in the road near the end of the lake. Their pursuers chose the northern fork; Michelle and Felix had taken the southern. The Americans, who had no idea as to their shared interest with the occupants of the car that had made such a hash of a three-point turn on the narrow road, were equally unaware of their potential interest in the identity of Felix and Michelle.

CHAPTER 25

The road to recovery

Monday, January 3, 2011

And so a New Year has begun: it is time to reflect on the direction my life should take henceforward, and to come to terms with the curious lanes along which it led me during 2010.

When I returned home in late September it was with a gloomy expectation born out of experience on the part of all the experts that I would, in due course, be returning to Priestley House. More than three months have drifted by and this has not happened. What's more, I can't really imagine it happening. Do I feel OK? Yes. Do I feel positive about the future? No, not really. Do I feel happy with my life? No, not especially… How could anyone feel happy with their life after having tasted a parallel one in which they were blessed with superpowers and everything they touched seemed to turn to gold?

At Priestley House, there were no real challenges: my time there was just one big solution to all the problems that had weighed upon my shoulders before I went in. As I now reflect on my time back home, I realise that there was no great eureka moment at which I recognised that I had created an elaborate fantasy world during my 'confinement'. Equally, however, I was aware even before my discharge from hospital that I had indeed constructed just such a fantasy world. So, I now conclude, rather than any eureka moment, it was more as if my world existed on two planes: the reality plane and the fantasy one. For a short time I lived life almost entirely in the latter, but by the time I left hospital I was almost entirely back in the former. In between, I do believe there were times when I existed on both these planes simultaneously.

The curious thing is that it now feels a little like being bilingual: you usually speak automatically in the tongue appropriate to the company in which you find yourself, but if you try and think too hard about things, you can come unstuck. I guess I am saying that, with the passage of time, I have lost the ability to slip from my real world to the fantasy world I created. Bluntly, as I have said to Michaela more often than I can remember over the last few weeks: 'I don't wear my underpants on the outside any more and it's very hard to get used to that!'

When I left hospital, it was with a packet of olanzapine and an instruction to continue taking these each night, and to make an appointment with my GP, ahead of my anticipated summons to see Dr Scholl sometime towards the end of October.

When I went to see my GP, Dr Gordon, he smiled widely and said I looked unrecognisable from the previous time we had met: that, of course, was the fateful night on which I escaped being sectioned by the skin of my teeth, and largely thanks to the intervention of my son, Larry, and – I now understand – Michaela. I reflected that in a short space of time Dr Gordon had seen three distinct versions of me.

We discussed how I was feeling and I told him that I did not feel in danger of relapsing and that I would like to wean myself off the olanzapine. He suggested I begin taking the drug only if I felt I really needed to, until such point as my supply was exhausted. I recall Michaela's surprise when I told her of Dr Gordon's verdict: she clearly felt that this was a premature step, but I was firm in my own resolve that I should follow my GP's advice. From that point on, I took olanzapine only if I felt my head was buzzing so I couldn't sleep.

The loss of my superpowers and the slipping away of the tectonic plate that bore my alternative reality had induced a feeling that I was now living my life beneath a fug. I was reluctant to attach the particular label, but I guess I was mildly depressed. Few aspects of my life retained the sharp edge and meaning that I had been accustomed to before what I had begun to call, for ease of reference only, my 'breakdown'.

I found I had an acute aversion to alcohol when I got home – as though my brain was saying: enough poisons! I have still scarcely touched a drop; even at Christmas and New Year.

Physically speaking, I was mostly without symptoms, though the aches induced in various muscles by my time prancing about on tiptoe 'in the Outback' continued to punish me at times. And, if things were quiet, I could always hear a gentle singing in my ears. I called this 'low-level tinnitus'. I suspect this is something I will have to learn to live with, as it has shown no sign of diminishing.

Shortly after returning home, the promised appointment for my brain scan came through and I went through the motions of attending, while being completely confident that there was nothing wrong, physically, with my brain: it had just suffered an overflow of adrenaline and toxins and had needed some more chemical prompting before it could return to normal.

I eased myself back into going into the office. It didn't take me long to take on board the true state of affairs at Persona. My own extended absence was probably irrelevant to the general decline in the company's fortunes and it looked like the 2008 downturn had finally caught up with us. Mr Holbeck's interest had waned, unsurprisingly, as there is no compelling case for investing in a business that is demonstrating neither growth nor the potential for it. I took a step back and reassessed the whole Knowledge America project and concluded we did not have the resources to launch this without an investor. Nor, given the competition from Smart Ideas, is there any guarantee it would generate a return anyway. And speaking of Smart Ideas, I have been unable to substantiate the theory that they stole our IP.

Given all this, a piece of news that I might have considered disastrous actually came as something of a relief: in early October, Stella told me she had been offered a job in Australia and wanted to leave Persona as soon as possible to get her life in order before emigrating. I told the rest of the team that we would probably have to shed more overhead and needed to be leaner and fitter to survive and prosper. I wouldn't be standing in anyone's way should they choose to follow Stella's example. It all seemed a far cry from Stella being acting CEO of what would become a hugely successful world business. Or from Rog, dear head-in-the-clouds Rog, running a secret propaganda network from inside a mountain in the Faroe Islands.

If I was grudgingly finding myself having to admit to my depression, my return to work was proving far from being a tonic to revive my spirits.

For the first month or so I limited myself to a couple of days a week in the office, though I was simultaneously building up the hours I could manage from home. Marius – or Clare in the Community, as I still liked to call him – came to see me two or three times a week initially, and we would talk a bit about life, the universe and everything. The subject to which we continually would return was the concept of the revolving door: the simple fact that so many mental health patients – however 'cured' they might be upon discharge – would end up back at Priestley House, or wherever, a few weeks or months later. That was why, Marius said, the follow-up work was so very important. But we were – we are – living in an age of austerity. And, notwithstanding fine government pronouncements on the importance of mental health services, the Trust that ran Priestley House was feeling the pinch.

Marius was retained by the Trust on a consultancy basis and, just as I had become used to his support, he told me he would have to move on and look for new work elsewhere. I would be visited instead by a young community mental health nurse called Jenny. In the meantime, Marius said he would press to get me an early appointment with Dr Scholl: I was looking like a potential success story and he didn't want that good outcome compromised by lack of adequate follow-up.

In our final little consultation we chatted about mental health from a class perspective: it hadn't really occurred to me but, on reflection, I had to agree that most of my fellow patients at Priestley House had been 'working class', for want of a better description. Indeed, Marius said that me, Dave and Ted Hughes all being there around the same time had been unusual – middle-aged, middle-class blokes, he observed, without implying any kind of judgement. Though I'm not sure whether Dave would have embraced the middle-aged bit.

Speaking of Dave, it was around the middle of October when he got in touch with me again. He had been living down in Brighton with his sister and together they had now come up with a plan for him to live down there somewhere where his sister and a brother would be on hand to support him if he went into a difficult phase. Now, though, he was going to come back up to Yorkshire to collect his remaining belongings and wondered if I might fancy calling in to Priestley House to see how everyone was doing.

Both Dave and I felt grateful for the treatment we had received at Priestley House and we decided to demonstrate this by buying a big tin of Roses for the staff. We drove up there together and I quietly hoped that Valentina might be on reception. 'No, Valentina's not here any more: she was just agency staff,' said a colleague of hers I remembered from my time there.

'Do you have any contact details for her?'

'No. I think she may have gone back to Italy, but to tell you the truth I don't even know which agency she was with.'

I felt deflated: Valentina had been real but now it felt like she too was no more than a symptom of my madness.

As I look back on that day now I'm not sure exactly what reaction I expected from the staff when Dave and I walked in. I think I honestly anticipated some kind of fanfare: a killing of the metaphorical fatted calf as the two prodigal sons returned. In reality, though everyone was very nice and Julia at least seemed quite pleased to see us both, no-one seemed especially inclined to break off from the work at hand to say they were glad to see us both looking well. More depressingly, familiar faces stalked the corridors: Willy, Bryan and Jeff were all still here. Worse, they were all slumped down into themselves. I wanted to say 'Come on lads, tell me you're proud to be Tykes', but I couldn't summon up the enthusiasm.

Dave came back to ours for tea and we shared with Michaela and with Dave's sister (she had driven him up all the way from Brighton) our sadness that Priestley House was less of an improvement centre and more of a revolving door. Dave and I were the lucky ones, but a lot of this was down to having the support of friends and family outside and, partly as a consequence of this, a determination to get better.

In late October my appointment with Dr Scholl came through and I made my way to a little NHS enclave on the outskirts of Harrogate, of whose existence I had previously been unaware.

Dr Scholl was a pleasant enough man, of about 50. Curiously, he reminded me of Dr Merrydew, except that he was much more smartly dressed and was also able to look you in the eye. In fact, it was something that he was able to do with a degree of prowess, and indeed he did it with a studied application all through our brief conversation, as though looking for the slightest sign that I might have been prone to relapse. He specifically asked if I had been to see my GP since coming home and I told him that, yes, I had gone to see Dr Gordon because I had only a limited supply of olanzapine. I told him how Dr Gordon and I had agreed that I might begin to wind down on my dosage of olanzapine and, indeed, take it only when I felt a particular need.

Now, you know how they talk about people expressing surprise by raising their eyebrows. Well, to suggest that Dr Scholl raised his eyebrows when I imparted this news to him would be to fall so far short of describing what he actually did with his eyebrows as to be meaningless. In fact, I swear I saw his eyebrows accelerate up his forehead at such speed that they carried on right down the back of his head and disappeared beneath his white shirt collar.

'I'm not at all sure that that was a wise step and I'm going to prescribe you more olanzapine. You can carry on taking them only when you feel you need to but I really don't want you to feel inhibited because you only have a limited number of these left. GPs are very good at what they do, but ours is a specialist branch of medicine and our decisions are founded on good evidence based on past experience. Do you understand?' I felt this was about as close to a rebuke as you would ever hear one physician deliver to another in front of a patient.

Michaela treated me to an I-told-you-so look when she came home that evening and I told her about Dr Scholl's reaction to my consultation with Dr Gordon. Then, about three weeks later, around the same time as I got the all-clear on my bran scan, I received a patient's copy of a letter sent by Dr Scholl to Dr Gordon. After going through the formalities of my condition, it changed tone and spared few niceties:

I understand from Mr Turnbull that you advised him that he could unilaterally reduce his dosage of olanzapine. It appears that he indeed followed your advice.

That he did so and then suffered no ill effects is down more to good fortune than to good medical judgement. The incidence of relapse in patients presenting with Mr Turnbull's symptoms is extremely high and psychosis is a frequent consequence of unplanned withdrawal from medication.

Clearly this did not occur in Mr Turnbull's case, but I state again that this is largely thanks to luck and not to judgement.

I remain yours with a sense of deep relief.
Dr Anthony Scholl FRCPsych

The other big bit of news in the last few months has been Ayanna's decision to leave Ripon and return with Erasto to Leeds. This had quite a big impact on my state of mind. While I had been in hospital, so much of the focus had been on finding quick and easy solutions to complex problems. But finding a home for my brother's belle and her son had been an act of finding a quick and logical solution to a problem that Michaela and I had found quite some time before I had gone mad. The idea that such an apparent win-win solution should have now unravelled depressed me. Michaela tried to persuade me that we had done the right thing in offering Ayanna some stability while she came to terms with what had happened, and that it was always inevitable that she would at some point 'move on'. For whatever reason, it didn't feel like that to me.

I think it was this event that prompted me to review so much of what I thought had gone on while I was in hospital: I created a spreadsheet with, down the left, a list of things that I thought had happened, with a timeline and comments in the cells to the right. This in turn prompted my first attempt at turning my experiences into some kind of narrative.

It began like this:

It's hard to pin down when I started to create the more extreme fantasy world... At its more benign, it was simply built on relaunching the Persona business off the back of legal suits and thereby doing right by the team: not just Stella, Rog and everyone in the office, but also Charley and the other 'remote' workers. There was the elaborate hosting of Smart staff and taking them on familiarisation trips across the North of England, but then there was something of a leap to the extravagant wedding celebration that Michaela and I enjoyed in the company of Newcastle United stars and to the accompaniment of some of Northumbria's best musicians.

Sometime during my first week in hospital I felt relieved that I never had to worry again about whether I would ever appear on Desert Island Discs: it was a now a given. But so too was the notion that Michaela and I would be perpetually on the run from the forces of evil, with our informal HQ starting at Wasdale Head, then moving to the Scillies and going on to include La Digue and, finally Jacqhou, in the Channel Islands. I need to know what Michaela's reaction was to this news, though I think I can now guess...

I'm unsure to what extent Dave tempered or fed my delusions: I taught him herbs and he told me the wasps were stealing the bees' nectar and bore the tormented souls of those in purgatory. My business would be able to fund research into this, I decided.

Then there was The Man Who Stalked His Cats and the film that would be made by Gerry and Tom. Of course we'd fly First Class to Oz to make it, as part of a travel policy that would be run by an old friend of mine from the airline industry.

My 'religious moment' in the hospital chapel echoed the previous one in Ripon Cathedral – I was unaware of the wider extent of the hospital and its other wards and thought people had come from all over Ripon in the wake of Malcolm's miracle. I wanted to lead the service and broke down on the floor. I need to talk to Nat about this (missing people) and to Dave.

I recall telling my sister Charlotte that Newcastle would be the UK's second city within ten years – something to do with all the pilgrimages and the Persona business's world HQ, next to Sage. Charlotte's eyes did pop out of her head the first time she saw me in hospital and I need to check with her what I said to her and when.

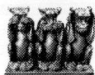

I think writing this down probably created the germ of the idea that I am now, in January 2011, thinking about nurturing further as part of my quite far-reaching list of New Year's resolutions.

Actually, the single biggest item on my resolutions list is not my idea at all: Michaela recognises that my spirit is tarnished and needs polishing, with something that we don't between us possess, if it is to regain its lustre. A colleague of hers at work has talked enthusiastically about how her daughter has been visiting a talk therapist, called Anton, up in the Eden Valley, in Cumbria. She's been having what's called Cognitive Behavioural Therapy, or CBT.

Unlike 'traditional' psychiatric treatments, which may look for sub-conscious causes of mental illness, CBT is focused on solving problems – helping people to change patterns of behaviour that are behind their difficulties and, consequently, changing the way that they feel.

I'm happy to give anything a go, now that I am coming to recognise that I am depressed, not just by the reality that my business is not in the greatest shape, but by the simple fact that I recently thought I had superpowers and now I know that I do not. It's possible to get a referral for CBT through the NHS, but this takes time and, anyway, Michaela really wants me to see Anton. She says she'll pay for me, which is very touching, especially after all I must have subjected her to these past months. I hope to see Anton quite soon.

In the meantime, I have been going through lots of things that I created on both my phone and my laptop while in hospital. There are things that I was sure that I had done, but now it seems I hadn't, and things that I thought I might not have done that, in reality, I did more than once. For example, I have found three separate entries in my phone's address book for Clare in the Community, that is Marius. I must have thought I was being so funny that I couldn't help but keep putting the joke in my phone.

On the other hand, as I was getting saner before leaving hospital, I had looked at what I thought was a long reading list for everyone who was going to be joining the Aurora Foundation team. It is no more extensive now than it was then, with its three incongruous book titles and an odd collection of films. Another list that I thought I had drawn up in hospital concerned grammatical errors committed by people who really should know better. I had thought this was going to comprise myriad instances of such misuse by radio announcers and so on. In reality I now find that it lists only the 'sins', of which I have collected no examples at all. These sins include the use of a plural verb when the subject is singular, simply because a plural crops up somewhere else in the sentence, and the increasingly widespread failure to understand sequence of tense or the use of the subjunctive in English, which too many people now seem to think does not even exist. It does and it enriches the language! I think about collating examples of these bad usages and making up for my failure while in Priestley House. I reflect that this is perhaps not the most urgent priority right now.

Meanwhile, having resolved that I need to make a full record of my illness, I set about organising all the different bits of material I have been assembling, lest my memory of it all – which remains currently quite vivid – should start to fade. I have an idea as to how I might present all this in the form of a novel: this might be a novel of two narrative strands, of which one is a more or less chronological record of how I got ill and then got better (already I am thinking in terms of becoming completely 'cured', you see, so perhaps writing this book will be useful therapy in itself). The other strand will be set in the future – in the fantasy world that I built while I was at Priestley House. I'm thinking I can use this as a vehicle for telling parts of the first story strand from different perspectives, and maybe also to provide some relief from what might otherwise be a rather dull story.

And so I set myself these preliminary tasks:

1) To send copies of all my emails during my episode to a new folder in one of my email accounts.

2) To make sure that all the pictures I took on that defining night in the Cathedral are also saved to a new folder.

3) To back up all this material to a dedicated hard disc.

4) To work up the idea of the Persona-in-the-future story line and the associated foundation.

5) To do some work on how I might present my meeting with Malcolm in fictionalised form.

From now on, I shall start to make notes of aspects of my illness as they come into my mind and try to order these.

It is Sunday January 16, 2011, and this is a significant day, because today I have downloaded a novel-writing programme and begun to load into it all the raw materials I have been gathering together. I have also started to write an occasional diary to help me to collect and present my thoughts. Here is today's entry.

Sunday January 16

My illness was wonderful for finding neat solutions and synergies: the amazing garden plan, with its garden of rest for Malcolm and nice peaceful sitting area for Michaela and me and the Hermit, if he didn't take up our generous offer of relocation and maybe wants to come out of his shell!

Then there was the idea of setting up surveillance on the garden shed… and using the cameras to record the movements of Bafta and Nada as part of the documentary, The Man Who Stalked his Cat.

Monday January 17

I must remember my theory about how the prostate is a two-way switch, more complex than biologists give credit for. My maxim during the build-up to my episode: Look into a person's eyes and you can gaze right into their soul.

Thursday January 20

Here are some quick fixes and action points that I came up with in hospital…
• Charley and me to help Gloria Turnbull — this will give me a route to a peerage. Five-year plan for Gloria!
• Me to be secret backer of plan to instal a supporters' chairman at Newcastle United, as I shared with the guy in the gym.
• Me to acquire St Kilda and save it for the National Trust for Scotland – with the sole condition than I can hold an annual party there for all my friends, with transport by my helicopter.
• Puns and the evolution of language
• Jung and coincidence – must read up on Jung's theory of synchronicity and see how this dovetails with my own Iceberg Theory (that for every coincidence of which you are aware, there are nine others that you've missed, meaning that, overall, there's an improbable number of coincidences).

Friday January 21

I've rounded up a selection of text messages from my mobile before and during my hospitalisation. I have not attempted to correct the English as the mistakes are symptomatic of my state of mind at the time. Looking at these now, it's clear friends, family and colleagues must have concluded that I had really lost the plot long before the medical people confirmed that I had. However did Michaela put up with this for so long?

Just take a look at this lot!

Aug 29 0709am: Sent to my nephew, Rory.

Hi R;ory, I am disappointed. U are not listening to me: u are treating me as part of the probelm rather than the solution. I am your godfather, please pause and reflect on that and on the bond I have always had with your brother.

There's a follow-up text from me and a reply from Rory, but I think I may have mentioned these at the time I sent them, when I was in hospital.

On **September 3** I appear to have sent a text to all the Persona staff at quarter to three in the morning, telling them it's time to go home now. I go on to say that I am very happy but that Michaela misplaced my meds last night, but please not to tell her I said so...

At 8.20 pm on September 14 I text Phil and Jean:

Hi both, gr8 to hear you're coming down to c the poor sick man on Sat! I shd be able to get day leave or a passy-out as we used to call it! U can admire the grapes on my vines & help strip the brambles & alder! Plus quince etc! Truly amazing fruit year! Beware! Great North Run on Sun so trains cd be unusually busy! Anyways, look forward to seeing & talkng Welsh with J! Yours in anticipation! The Vic of many tongues! X

At 10.26 on September 17, to my friend Danny Mason, in London: *How art thou? The fun is fainlly turning to bordom here... Suppose I shd be creative but Dave out today adn I'm unsure if it'll be*

Mon for me or, slim chance, today… Anyways, hd gr8 afternoon with sis Leanne then T at home with Michaela. Gr8 to c u: look forwArd to Simeon waaks… Mebbes IoM?? Much love to a gr8 m8! Vic

Not much later that day I sent a crazy text to everyone in Iceland, which I think I did mention at the time. The team at Persona have told me since that relations with some contacts there have been unexpectedly cool.

Finally, there's a text to Charley that I don't seem to be able to date:

My dear Charley
This is the story of my 'illnes'
It has, for reasons that will become a apparent a very joyous ending.
I will tell this story in one page instalments. It is a a story that may challenge the very basis of the beliefs up[on which you base you base your whole life and belif structe.
I am atheist and have been for some time.
Thfiis was because I couldn't see ratonal scientific explanto for it.
However I have always been intrgued to say the least what makes people believed they god's a authority.
I have also beeen very interested in things like quantum physics and chaose theory.
Ity is now time to tell the next instalment. However I have learned that this story is capable of making people ill with worry and so it's important that it be digested in very small bit-sized chunks, so please ow pause, sit down with Tim [her partner] and when you are ready, come back and read the next gpage. This very prosaic and practical and contains absolutely no shocks, sdo don't feel afraid to open it ….. Becase of this I hope it wont' take too long to get over the intial shock, but maybe take the dogs for a walk (I think it's going tobe another scrocher like yesterday)!

And now, from my spreadsheet, here are a few things that I am pretty sure did happen.

I did mislay things at a stone circle on Orkney.

I did get close to getting Michael Holbeck to invest in the company.

I did have some sort of 'religious moment' in Ripon Cathedral; and another in the hospital chapel.

I stalked the cats.

I got into trouble at the Co-op because my behaviour made me look like I was shoplifting.

Newcastle United did beat Aston Villa 6-0.

I still believe that I could look into people's eyes and gain some insight and this could encourage people to behave in a more open way.

My company, Persona Communications, did receive unwanted attention from a company called Smart Ideas, in Slough.

Comment: Smart felt we were treading on their toes and didn't like the fact that we had support from UK Trade & Investment to launch our Knowledge America portal.

I did conduct a survey of our garden with my friend Alice, with a view to creating a remembrance area for Malcolm and everyone else.

Comment: The ideas were fanciful and predicated on getting the Hermit on board. Oh, and on spending non-existent money.

I did have some ideas of at least some merit while I was mad: the elasticity of time; the idea that it was high time that Michaela and I got married. I'm really struggling to add to these, though…

I found a good friend in Dave.

I do believe my reflexes were sharper and that I could play better snooker, table tennis and football.

Comment: I know that Michaela and other members of the family doubt this and would insist that I simply THOUGHT I was better.

I do believe my ear was better attuned to language, as evidenced by my ability to understand old Jimmy when the nurses couldn't. And to converse in Franco-Italian with Valentina.

Comment: I'm not sure if the family would buy this one either.

My illness was caused by a physical accident that altered the chemistry of my brain and this makes my own illness distinct from that of other people who have suffered manic episodes.

Comment: I am resolute in my belief that I am 'safe' from a recurrence of my mania.

And here's a list of things that I now recognise may have not happened.

There was no industrial espionage or sabotage on the part of Smart Ideas.

There was no legal action by Immerhutts or anyone else against Smart Ideas or any individuals who may or may not have crossed my business path in recent years.

There was no big campaign to find all the missing people and I could have had no idea as to the whereabouts of Stella's sister.

I did not organise a campaign for Gloria Turnbull's leadership bid. Consequently, I do not expect to receive a peerage or appear on Desert Island Discs.

There was no crazy trip to find an island for the Hermit.

I did not become Chairman of Newcastle United. In fact, the popular revolt among fans that I thought had propelled me to that position never actually existed, if we are honest.

I did not buy St Kilda.

I was not suddenly able to play the Northumbrian pipes with no further tuition.

There has been no big wedding on Holy Island or anywhere else; no worldwide list of guests.

There has been no communications strategy meeting in the Lake District regarding the management of the release of information about my meeting with my dead brother, Malcolm.

There is not and never shall be an Aurora Group or an Aurora Foundation.

Michaela and I will not be pursued by vengeful Masons, or anyone else for that matter. Ergo, there will be no island refuges.

Nobody has made the documentary, The Man Who Stalked His Cats, and Two Flew Over the Cuckoo's Nest: The Unsequel will only ever exist as a couple of pages forged in the midst of madness.

I begin to find this list a bit depressing, as my current reality is so mundane in comparison with the parallel 'reality' that I have to now accept was no more than a figment of my imagination.

I think the jury is still out on these ones.

That I genuinely did meet the soul of my dead brother and that he asked me to seek his beatification.

That there are areas of natural selection that may just merit further study.

That we might, just might, retain a sixth sense about people being in our vicinity but out of our line of sight; and that those lumps some of us have on the back of our heads just might have something to do with this.

That maybe, just maybe, time could indeed be elastic and that this might emerge as we begin to understand the rules that govern our world at a sub-atomic level.

That maybe even Jung was wrong and perhaps there are just too many coincidences.

That I might just be able to tell this story in a way that engages people and might help in their understanding of psychosis, and thereby ensure that the treatment of mental illness is not deprioritised.

Putting all these things into words helped me to decide that, for the sake of my recovery, I must concentrate on those areas in which I think the jury might be out. At the same time, I recognised that I had indeed been more depressed than I had allowed myself credit for. Michaela was as good as her word and I have already had a couple of consultations with Anton.

Something else has come up: there is something quite strange about these stone circles and I'd like to understand more. I am not really sure I buy the received 'wisdom' in this field as so much of it feels like self-serving conjecture on the part of 'experts' on that period of unwritten history. The 'received wisdom' to which I refer is the idea that these circles are all about sacrifices to 'gods' to give thanks for the sun and the seasons. To me this feels like putting two and two together and getting five or six – where's the real evidence? Quite what I should do next on this one, I am unsure of.

CHAPTER 26

The banks of the Sabarmati

Saturday, October 16, 2021

Felix reflected with amusement on the contrast between his arrival at lonely Wasdale Head just one short week previously and his chaotic entry to Ahmedabad and subsequent check-in at a modest hotel in a new development on the other side of the city from the airport. It was his first visit to India and, while everything he had read about the country had referenced the chaotic mix of both order and disorder in its fast-growing cities, he had still been unprepared. Cautioned by the TravelKnowledge portal as to the wisdom or otherwise of hiring a car, he had – once he had emerged from a security check on exiting the airport that appeared every bit as demanding as any corresponding check upon entry – found a 'proper' taxi and foregone the alternative of a motorised rickshaw tuk-tuk.

He was glad of his choice upon reaching the city itself: at each major intersection the tuk-tuks would approach in droves from four directions simultaneously at full tilt and yet, somehow, would contrive all to miss each other, their paths criss-crossing like the warp and weft of a giant loom. Appropriate, reflected Felix, given the city's claim to be the cottonopolis of India. He chose to sit and watch the crazy city go by from the comfort of the back seat of his Hindustan and began to feel reasonably good about the world, despite the fatigue of getting down to London and fighting the scrum at the Air India ticket desk at Heathrow. He was especially pleased that, in all the days he and Michelle had been stuck at Wasdale Head, Jameela's brother or brothers had failed to appear. It didn't occur to him that, just as they had been unable to get out of the dale, so others might have found it equally difficult to get in.

At Heysham, he had dropped Michelle in good time for the afternoon ferry to Douglas.

'Good luck!' she said in his ear as they kissed each other's cheeks. 'I don't think we make such a bad team, do you?'

They'd agreed to communicate only by encrypted messages on Blather, with a view to reuniting in ten days or a couple of weeks, most likely in the Seychelles. Felix had then headed across the country by Clitheroe, Skipton and Harrogate and back home to York. He'd kept the radio on for company and the airwaves were full of the 'sensational' news about the leak of the Blair-Bush telephone conversations, with countless commentators adding their two-pennerth. Felix's main surprise was that it had all taken so long to come out, given all the other material that had been hacked and released by the likes of Edward Snowden and the Russians.

He'd had only enough time in his flat to feel a little saddened at the absence of Mr Merryweather, but had thought better of contacting Wendy as he could easily guess what she would have to say to him. And so he had repacked with such clean and reasonably suitable clothes as he could find for an extended journey, thankfully drawing on the summer wardrobe hanging in the cupboard and adding to it underwear that he'd run through the fastest programme on the machine. He wondered how well equipped Michelle's wardrobe was, given that she must have left with little idea either of where she would be going or, indeed, when she would be back – although she had taken a chance on leaving her heaviest wet weather gear with Felix when they parted company at Heysham.

On the train to London, Felix again reflected on the romantic pursuit that had become his mission: did he really know enough about Jameela to justify the time, the expense and the risk. He also thought very hard about Michelle: he had enjoyed his few days in her company and recognised there were depths to her character that he found very appealing. There was their shared sense of humour on the one hand and her admirable ability to remain unruffled in the face of provocation or uncertainty on the other. And he really liked her smile.

On the flight he had awoken from a fitful sleep, alarmed to realise he had enjoyed a quite explicit dream about Michelle in which she had emerged from behind a palm tree on the very beach he had shared with Jameela, clad only in the loosest cotton wrap, beneath which, to appreciate every detail of her body required but the scantest imagination. She had smiled at Felix, turned, and beckoned him to follow her, but Felix had encountered all manner of obstacles until the pursuit became impossible, so tied up was he, first in tangled mangroves and then in red tape and missed buses, trains and planes. On being roused by the arrival of a tray of food (more curry, but he wasn't complaining) he wished with all his heart that he hadn't had the dream. He wasn't Jesus and he didn't need to prove himself by being impervious to temptation. But Michelle's words – which he had taken purely at face value at the time – were now ringing in his ears: 'I don't think we make such a bad team.' He reflected that, even if both Jameela and Kenny were located, he and Michelle now had such an important a shared experience that it would be hard simply to abandon it. It was an opportune moment to remind himself just exactly why he had decided to spend his savings on chasing after Jameela: in just their briefest time together far from home (in the most beautiful surroundings, yes) she had kindled in him a spark that had lain dormant for as long as he cared to remember. It was a spark that had ignited the conviction that Jameela was, indeed, 'the one'.

~ 483 ~

At his hotel, Felix gained a distinct impression that his arrival had been expected in more ways than simply because he had booked his stay through TravelKnowledge. He felt a distinct over-attention on the part of the concierge and his team. 'Oh Yes, Mr Merry… weather (?), that is correct? Yes? We are so very pleased indeed to be seeing you here at last at our Hotel Hydrangea. I am at your beck and call and you must call me simply Concierge. Be pleased to be making yourself very much at home with us and then we shall be offering you all assistance in locating those addresses that I am sure that you will require to visit during your stay in our handsome city of Ahmedabad.'

As he sat in his room and watched the back of a macaque that had taken up residence on his window sill, he thought carefully about how he had made his booking. He had logged on to TravelKnowledge and entered Ahmedabad and – although various hotel options had come up – he had been seduced by a 'Travelknowledge offer exclusive to you, Felix!' and booked the Hydrangea. He was reluctant to feel paranoid but all of a sudden the idea that someone within the Aurora Group, which after all owned TravelKnowledge, was at the very least guiding his choices, was beginning to gain traction in his mind.

The afternoon and evening were still his own and he thought he might seek Concierge's advice on some sight-seeing. The Ahmedabad address that Vic had left with Greta had been in an office block and, on checking, Felix recognised that it was somewhere close to Gandhi's Ashram, on the banks of the Sabarmati. He wondered just how surprised Concierge might be if he were to ask for this address specifically…

'Yes, yes, of course, Mr Weather, this is an address that we know well but it is not somewhere that you should be visiting unaccompanied. If you will only wait two hours then I will be only too happy to accompany you and to ensure that you are able to arrive at the correct location.'

Felix did not feel in any position to decline an invitation that was verging on an instruction and so decided to find a quiet corner in the (alcohol-free) bar where he might communicate with Michelle. He called her on an encrypted Blather video link and attracted a rapid response. It was, he reflected, good to see her face, which prompted stills from his previous night's reverie to come flooding back.

'Not like you to be lost for words, my dear!' she said, cheerily.

'No, no, it's not is it? I guess I just hadn't expected to get hold of you so quickly... Any exciting news?'

'Well, that probably depends how you define "exciting", but, anyway, I went straight to the accountant's office in Douglas and, given all the secrecy around offshore banking, he was remarkably forthcoming. He told me exactly what Michaela had requested of him and the services they had provided...'

'And they were?'

'I'm sorry, Felix, but if I tell you that I shall have to kill you.'

'Ha ha! I've got men on the way to the Isle of Man already, just to take you out!'

'Ooh, I hope it's somewhere nice! But seriously, what I learned is that the Aurora Foundation runs a portfolio of investments not just from the Isle of Man but from a variety of other offshore places that might be thought of as, to a greater or lesser extent, "dodgy" or, at best, not consistent with the ethics of a charitable foundation committed to good works.'

'Well, I guess it's useful to have any suspicions confirmed in that regard, but are we any further down the road towards finding Jameela and Kenny's trail?'

'Well Felix, I did manage to work out where Michaela stayed when she was here, but that didn't really add much to our sum total of knowledge, so I left the Isle of Man and travelled to the Scilly Isles and, boy, was that a challenge... I had to fly to Manchester, then on down to Newquay and then I got on this tiny plane to St Mary's, which is where I stayed last night. I know it's not Ahmedabad, but it still feels like a long journey.'

'So what's your plan now?' asked Felix.

'Well, weather permitting, I get a boat to Bryher and check in at a guest house called Hydrangea Gardens.'

Michelle saw the surprise on Felix's face and looked at him quizzically.

'I'm at the Hydrangea Hotel here in Ahmedabad,' he said.

'No way! It's like déjà vu all over again, as they say!'

'I know: these things are really starting to freak me out. How did you book it?'

'On TravelKnowledge…'

'Hmm, why does that not surprise me?' said Felix.

'Anyway, to get back to the price of fish,' continued Michelle. 'Victor and Michaela stayed at the Hell Bay, which sounds a lot less romantic than Hydrangea Gardens. But romantic it certainly is and I wasn't sure even our generous budget would stretch to £300-odd a night, even if they'd had a room. And, besides, what's the point of staying at one of the most romantic hotels in the UK with no-one to share it with?'

'What indeed?' said Felix, wondering for half a moment if he would ever spend a romantic weekend there with Jameela. Or anywhere else for that matter. And, indeed, whether Michelle might perhaps spend a romantic weekend there with Kenny. He deliberately suppressed any thoughts of himself sharing romance with her, Michelle, at Hell Bay.

'Felix, do you think any of this is getting us anywhere?'

'I really don't know, 'chelle,' replied Felix, shaken from his musings. 'I still wonder if we're being taken for a ride. A long and devious ride. I get the strangest feeling at this hotel that they were expecting my arrival. But how could that possibly be so unless someone a) knew I was coming and b) had tipped off the hotel to that effect… and told them what to do with me when I got here.'

'Why do you say that?'

'Well, apart from greeting me like some long lost friend when I got here, Concierge knows all about the address I was given by Greta. And, he intends to go there with me when he comes off duty a little later.'

Felix watched Michelle frown as she then added, 'Well, it all seemed a bit too easy on the Isle of Man, too, if I'm honest. I mean why would an accountant betray client confidentiality? So do we play along and act like we suspect nothing, or do we try and do something they won't expect?'

'You mean we pull some kind of rabbit out of the hat and refuse to be nudged towards wherever they might hint?

'Exactly! They suggest Barbados, we go to, I don't know, Canvey Island!' ventured Michelle.

'Ugh! Must we?!

'No, not really, but, you know, a metaphorical Canvey island, maybe.'

Felix ventured: 'OK, so how about I go with Concierge and you find out what you can on Bryher, and then let's see if we can come up with something a bit more left-field?'

'OK, I guess…'

And so, as the sun began its tropical kamikaze plummet towards the horizon, Felix was joined by Concierge, who ushered him towards a Hindustan, the back of which was elaborately equipped with brightly coloured woven cotton seat covers and pictures of the Hydrangea Hotel on the backs of the front seats. The flowers in the pictures looked altogether more resplendent than the slightly tired ones Felix had seen in the hotel garden, and he wondered whether the normally luxuriant plants were happy as the dusty city edged towards the dry season. Concierge shuffled onto the bench seat alongside him and, as the driver pointed the car's big nose into the river of taxis and tuk-tuks, he said, 'So first we visit Gandhi's Ashram by the Sabarmati river, Mr Felix.'

Again, Felix recognised that Concierge was not seeking his opinion, merely advising him what he would be doing. After half an hour of what felt to Felix like a fairground dodgem ride, the Hindustan pulled off the road near the river, where Felix observed that, notwithstanding the twilight, women still stood knee-deep in the water with their laundry. Concierge marched him quickly along a walkway by the river until the hot, dry hubbub of the city was suddenly punctuated by a green and quite pleasant public park, where citizens wandered relaxedly, some arm-in-arm, as though the crazy city were a million miles away.

'We must be arriving before six thirty, Mr Felix,' said Concierge, urging him to quicken his pace, and it was just a few minutes before that time that they entered the simple building, just as the greater numbers were going in the opposite direction.

'You see, we have an "arrangement",' said Concierge. 'The Ashram is ours after all these people have gone home.' Concierge took Felix round the building's simple rooms and showed him where Gandhi would sit cross-legged at his spinning wheel. He then ushered Felix to sit opposite him at a simple wooden table.

'You see, Mr Felix, Gandhi is the most treasured person to have come from our state of Gujarat. You may think of Gandhi as the person who freed my country from the harsh yolk of imperialism. Perhaps you may know of how he instigated the Salt March from this very place in protest at the iniquitous British monopoly on salt, which was most profitable and most unfair. But also most very important in the life and teachings of Gandhi are his views on religion. The Mahātmā believed most firmly that all religions were different paths to the same truth and conflict between faiths grieved him deeply.

'You see, Mr Felix, I – like your friend Miss Durrani – am a Muslim by birth and by education. But if you peel away my skin then my soul that is being beneath my skin is no different from that of my neighbour, who is a Hindu.

'Gandhi had much time for Islam, Mr Felix, because of my faith's contribution to our motherland, and also because of its adherence to the idea of the Oneness of our God and of the notion of the Brotherhood of mankind.

'And of Christianity, Gandhi is much praising of Jesus because he was one of the greatest teachers the world has ever known.

'Hinduism tells every man and woman to worship God according to his or her own faith. So Hinduism is a religion that is, or at least should be, at peace with all the religions of our world. And that is why I am finding that this idea of "Hindu nationalism" is not a thing of logic, for it must tend to make people of different faiths to practise discrimination.

'And now, Mr Felix, are you aware of the events here in Gujarat that occurred in February 2002?'

Felix – who had somehow managed to betray no emotion at Concierge's unexpected reference to Jameela – confessed to being ignorant of the incidents to which Concierge referred.

'These events, Mr Felix, have cast a terrible stain over modern India. Today people argue much about the cause and they argue also about the events that followed, but the truth is that in 2002 my fair state of Gujarat saw Hindu and Muslim pitched into battle against one another in a most terrible way. A way the likes of which had not been seen since the darkest days of the Partition.'

Concierge sighed and continued: 'On that terrible day there was a fire aboard a train that was carrying Hindu pilgrims from the sacred site of Ayodhya. This site is long disputed between Hindus and Muslims and the days when both faiths could be found to be worshipping there together are long past. Indeed it is nearly 30 years now since Hindu nationalists destroyed the mosque on the site, and the burning of the train ten years later may have started as an act of revenge, or then it may have been orchestrated as an excuse for the many days of rioting that followed. Or it may even have been an accident: all we know for sure is that at least 1,000 people died in those riots and perhaps more than 2,000, and the majority of these were Muslims.'

All of this was new to Felix but he wondered increasingly why the concierge at a hotel at which he happened to be staying should wish to tell him it. He wondered about this every bit as much as he wondered how it might be that Concierge seemed very possibly to know more than a little about Jameela, and so he decided to ask.

'So are you part of the organisation for which Jameela works?' he ventured.

'And what organisation, pray, might that be, Mr Merry?'

'I think you know the organisation to which I refer,' continued Felix.

'Ah Mr Weather, you speak of organisations while I speak of morals, of truth, of ethics and of faith. Trouble yourself not further with these things and remember again the teachings of the Mahātmā, when he said that religion should pervade every one of our actions.

'Gandhi was very careful to make most forcefully the point that religion must never mean sectarianism – it must never mean the desire to promote one faith, one route to God, before another. It should mean rather a belief in ordered moral government of the universe. It is not less real because it is unseen and it harmonises the worldly expressions of religion that are symbolised by the "faiths" and gives them reality.

'And so now I must quote to you in the precise words of the great but most humble man when he stressed that humanity should be at the heart of religion: "Religion is to morality what water is to the seed that is sown in the soil. Just as the seed is choked under the earth when it is not duly watered, so too the morality which is devoid of the fertilising influence of religion gets thin and dry and is ultimately destroyed. In other words, morality divorced from religion would be an empty thing."

'And so now, Mr Felixweather, let us pause to reflect briefly on the humanity of Gandhi and on the true meaning of his teachings and how they remain important today. Indeed, Mr Merry, how very relevant they are to your own quest.'

'My own quest? What do you mean when you say "your own quest"?'

'Why, my dear Mr Merryweather...' Concierge said his name deliberately in a way that clearly suggested that all his previous 'mistakes' had been quite calculated. '...it is the quest for the truth and, more importantly I believe, for the true meaning of love. Now come with me!'

Confused and undermined, Felix followed Concierge from the Ashram, through the little park and out onto the busy street. He wondered why he and Michelle had even attempted to maintain a veneer of secrecy. It was all feeling like a complete waste of effort and, whatever Concierge might say, he was quite sure that he must be an integral member of the Aurora Foundation.

The pair arrived at a concrete block, probably built 20 years previously. Its ground floor was replete with open-fronted shops, mostly selling colourful cloths from which one might, given the skills and the inclination, produce a sari. People were, it seemed, everywhere and buzzed back and forth in a frenzy of activity that might or might not have been productive. Felix couldn't easily tell.

'And now Felix, if I may be permitted so to address you, we shall enter the more modern centre of teaching that is working on these notions of each faith being but one route to an eventual truth.'

Concierge took him to a thoroughly unprepossessing dingy door, which opened onto a small, yet luxuriantly planted, courtyard, whose existence behind the door would have been hard to predict. He then led him to another, tidier and more modern, door at one corner of the little precinct.

'And so you are placing your hand here on this pad while looking into the camera.'

Felix did as he was bidden and was astonished when a green light shone and invited him to push the door open, Concierge following closely behind him after, in turn, registering his identity.

'So how did someone get hold of my hand print and a picture of my irises?' demanded Felix, feeling, well, violated.

'Oh dear Felix, do not be fretting so. The organisation has its ways and it is, as you must know, only a force for the good.'

He ushered Felix into a lift and took it up to, Felix noted, the fifth of six floors, where they exited to a modern open-plan office. Or at least that was the only way Felix could find to describe it as he thought already of how he would tell Michelle of his unexpected adventure. The space was air-conditioned and seemed to exist quite apart from the city outside. It had windows but these were covered with white blinds and indeed the whole space had a rather white, almost clinical, air to it. Perhaps 30 or more people were mostly clustered in groups, all seemingly engaged in different degrees of animated discussion. At the far end of the room, Felix perceived a kind of presentation area, featuring a small cinema screen with a wide semi-circle of chairs arrayed before it. The whole space had the air of an ante room at the United Nations, such was the diversity of the people occupying it.

On seeing Concierge and his guest, a Chinese-looking woman broke away from one of the groups and approached them.

'Concierge, how are you?' asked the woman who, Felix noted, appeared to be maybe in her late 30s and was unusually tall for being Oriental. He did not hear Concierge's reply as the woman put an arm round his shoulder and led him away to begin what was clearly a very private conversation. Felix, who was amused to find that the whole world seemed to know his new companion simply as 'Concierge', was left alone to shuffle from foot to foot while everyone else in the room continued about their business.

Concierge turned back. 'Please be accepting my wholesome apologies, Felix,' he said. 'Mia had some information that she needed to impart to me. Now, let me explain the work that goes on here.'

Concierge took Felix to a computer screen and explained to him how everyone in the room could access a huge data bank containing, he said, a majority of the world's great scriptures.

'Look here, for example, here we find some of the Gathas, which are verses said to have been composed by the prophet Zoroaster,' said Concierge, after landing, seemingly at random on a particular page. 'These form part of the Avesta, which is the holy book of the Zoroastrian faith. Did you know, Mr Felix, that Zoroastrianism is among the oldest, possibly the oldest, of the monotheistic faiths? It is more than 3,500 years old and was once – indeed almost up to the birth of Mohammed himself – the great religion of what was known in those days as Persia?' It was merely a rhetorical question and Concierge quickly continued: 'The Zoroastrian faith has been finding itself obliged to evolve as indeed society has evolved and in response to, for example, the influence of Christianity. And yet it remains fundamentally a good and peaceful doctrine. It is only perhaps unfortunate that it is also a dying religion...'

Felix wanted to ask why this was the case, but Concierge had already put the screen to sleep and turned to look Felix in the eyes before embarking on another monologue.

'The organisation has an important centre, the location of which is secret, where linguists work on these volumes and seek to identify, as Gandhi himself might, the essence of their original meaning. That is to say their meaning as we might imagine it to have been handed down by God and not after it has been over-interpreted and reinterpreted by so-called religious people who may be having their own agendas.

'Your friend Miss Jameela would have spent some time here learning about all these different faiths and then about the non-violent, non-sectarian, non-confrontational kernel that is at the heart of almost all the faiths. It is the job of the people here to take that kernel and then to cultivate it in a beneficial way, if you follow my metaphor. Now, because you are a serious man with a serious and important mission, Felix, I will share with you that Jameela was working on the dissemination of a version of the muslim faith that is closer to the original teachings of the Prophet Mohammed than those that people I shall call amateur theologians choose to propagate.

'You see Mohammed too was a very wise man and a fine teacher but he did not ask that people should elevate him to the status of a god in his own right; nor that they should practise all manner of discrimination and bigotry in applying the lessons that he taught...'

Concierge was in full flow again now, but a single word had caught Felix's attention and so he interrupted: 'Concierge, you said Jameela WAS working on this; why did you say was, rather than is?'

'Oh Felix, that is because Mia is just telling me that, before she left here yesterday, Jameela requested that all work be stopped on the Islamic programme...'

~ 493 ~

Felix had to interrupt again: 'Wait a minute: you said Jameela was here, in Ahmedabad, YESTERDAY...'

'Oh yes, Mr Merry Weather, she was here for some time perhaps one month ago and then she returned here on business five days ago. But now she is left. She is gone.'

'Gone?! Gone where for God's sake?'

'Ah, now that I can not tell you and indeed I do not know the answer but I am thinking perhaps she is gone to Marie Galante. Yes, that will be where she is gone.'

'And just where is that?' demanded Felix, now raising his voice so that the hitherto quiet little groups gathered in the room were now all turned towards him.

'Oh Mr Merry Weather, you know neither your geography nor your history. You need to research where Christopher Columbus made landfall in what they used to call the New World.'

'Concierge, thank you, but I think I have had enough of your riddles now and I'd like you to take me back to my hotel.'

On getting back to the hotel – a journey that he completed with Concierge in sullen silence – Felix wondered what best to do next. Of one thing he was now reasonably sure: he would not be travelling to Marie Galante, wherever that might be. At the same time, he was disinclined to discuss his or her next moves with Michelle, even if the link were encrypted. He was reasonably sure that Michelle would head for Jacqhou when she had found out what she could on Bryher. So he was minded to travel to Vulcano, which would leave only the Seychelles and the Faroe Islands on the list of bad anagrams they had solved at Wasdale Head.

Wary enough to use a different search engine to the Eureka vehicle of choice, he identified a café on the edge of Victoria, in the Seychelles and – equally mistrustful of Smartmail and Blather – he sent a simple text message to Michelle with the suggested rendezvous and advising her neither to reply nor to contact him by other means. He hoped such precautions would be sufficient.

He didn't see Concierge again that night and set about booking his passage to Vulcano on Expedia, rather than TravelKnowledge.

Early the following morning there was a confident knock at his door, where he found Concierge standing with a cup of tea, nicely presented on a tray, alongside an envelope, which Felix took to be his bill. On opening the envelope, however, it turned out to be travel documents to take him to Guadeloupe and to a location on the island of Marie Galante.

'I have taken the liberty of booking the next leg of your journey,' said Concierge, to which Felix replied: 'That's very thoughtful, Concierge, but I've already booked my travel.'

'But I have seen no booking to Marie Galante!' exclaimed Concierge.

'Oh really, I didn't think you would have expected to have any involvement in my travel booking, Concierge. It was getting a bit late so I booked on lastminute.com,' he lied.

Felix collected his belongings together and, rather than risk any further inquisition from Concierge, he left enough money to cover his bar bill in an envelope and slipped down the fire escape at the rear of the hotel, then out of a side gate onto a back street. He hailed a tuk-tuk and asked for the Gandhi Ashram.

It wasn't easy retracing the previous evening's steps to the Aurora offices but eventually he saw a stall selling a familiar and slightly unusual pattern of sari material. The entry to the office courtyard was close by. He held his breath as he presented his eyes and hand, but the security system was happy still to accept him.

On arriving at the fifth floor he returned to the big white room and was surprised to see that Mia was still there: she seemed equally surprised to see him.

'I thought you were travelling to Marie Galante today, Mr Merryweather,' she said.

'Change of plan – I decided to do a bit more sight-seeing in Ahmedabad and I'm not travelling till tomorrow now, so I thought I would just call by as I was revisiting the Ashram. You see, I'm just a little curious why Jameela Durrani was here so recently…'

'I can't tell you about that as that is Foundation business, Mr Merryweather.'

'Is there anything that you CAN tell me that might be helpful to me if I want to see her?'

Mia paused for a moment and frowned, but then she looked very deliberately directly into Felix's eyes and said, 'Here we learn who to trust and how much to trust them and I can see that you have a genuine reason to ask me the questions that you do. I will permit you one hour to look at some of the less sensitive areas of our work here and after that all I can say to you is that, whatever anyone tries to tell your head to do, you must ultimately follow your heart.'

She installed him at a computer and enabled his access using an identity that would not permit him to enter more sensitive areas.

In reality, the access granted to Felix did not afford him any huge insight. Each of the world's major religions could be located via a drop-down menu and, once in such a religious section, the viewer could then access all the major and not-so-major theologies and sects within that religion.

A separate menu was entitled simply Divergence: it summarised the core tenets of the faith on the left-hand side of the screen, while, on the right, could be found a summary of the evolution of the faith and, specifically, the imposition of strictures that could not be found in that faith's original definition or blueprint.

There was, for example, under the Muslim faith, a great deal of analysis about the meaning of the word jihad, so generally taken to mean 'holy war' and a supposed obligation upon Muslims to force non-Muslims to convert to Islam under threat of violence. The narrative asserted that such a meaning was never contained within the original holy text believed to be the very word of God, as recorded by the hand of the Prophet Mohammed himself. Indeed, many Muslims interpreted jihad as the internal struggle of the individual in seeking to lead a more righteous life while ignoring the temptations all around.

There followed an extensive debate about strands of Islam that did not advocate violent jihad and which of these might be the best belief system to encourage.

Christianity received a similar treatment, with much debate about that faith's own Holy War against Islam in the Middle Ages. What particularly struck Felix was the very obvious degree of dissent within each faith – dissent that appeared to be every bit as capable of fomenting conflict as the differences between each faith. Protestant and Catholic; Shi'a and Sunni to name but the two most obvious.

Felix summoned Mia and asked, 'Do you really believe it could be possible to persuade hardened advocates of, say, one branch of Islam to turn their backs on a lifetime of belief in favour of some new structure?'

Mia responded: 'You describe it too simply, Felix. The process by which this is done is far more subtle; subliminal even.'

'Explain it to me; show me!' said Felix.

'I'm sorry Felix: you are asking now about things that go to the very heart of what we do here and I can tell you nothing more.'

It hardly seemed that an hour had passed when Mia told Felix to begin wrapping up. He logged out and, if he was surprised then to see a home screen on which a number of other identities in the organisation were presented, his heart missed a beat upon realising that one of the individuals listed was one Jameela Durrani. He was even more surprised to then notice other names, including Kenny Marchant. Katie Brown, Monique de la Rochelle, and Nils Boateng were others that stood out on a list of about 50 names. Realising that time was of the essence, he clicked on Jameela's icon and was asked to provide a password. He took a punt and typed his own name, Felix, and was astonished when the profile opened to reveal an email account, diary and folders of files. He clicked on the diary and quickly saw that Jameela was, apparently, scheduled to visit Vulcano and La Digue, in the Seychelles, in the coming days. More, she was due to visit the Lindisfarne retreat on Jacqhou the very next day – the very day indeed that Michelle would be there, but too soon for Felix to be able to make it there too.

He was poised to read Jameela's recent emails when two things happened: first, a rare commotion began to bubble up in the office – it was as near to panic as could easily be imagined. And then his VSP rang – surprising in itself, given that the office was intended to be sealed from external communications.

He quickly recognised that it was Greta, calling him from Wasdale Head.

There was no disguising the dismay in her voice as she said, 'Felix, it's Ned: he's disappeared. I think he may have been kidnapped!'

CHAPTER 27

The mind is a mysterious universe

Monday, January 24, 2011

Well, I have to say I was apprehensive about how the weekend would go, but in the event it all turned out OK – or more or less. In principle I am now recovered, but I think people recognise that I remain fragile, so it was quite brave of Michaela to get everyone together for my birthday. We were quite a gathering: Larry, Lisa; and Nat even managed to drag herself away from Amsterdam. Both my sisters came too, Charlotte and Leanne. And, on Saturday evening, we were joined by some of my friends and colleagues, including Stella, back from Australia for a brief post-New Year visit, and Charley and Danny, both up from London.

I still get quite nervous when too much drink is taken, although I can now just about manage a glass or two myself, to be sociable. As a consequence, when everyone started to shout over each other, I retreated to the living room for a few moments' quiet contemplation. I was consequently chastised by Michaela for being antisocial and it does seem a paradox that she's often the one to urge me to take things easy and avoid stress, but can sometimes seem blind to the things that actually cause me stress.

It is the contemplation of the lack of self-control associated with taking too much drink that makes me feel so... so *allergic*, yes, I think allergic is the word. I'm trying hard to deal with the allergy by introducing just small amounts of alcohol. Anton, who is teetotal, understands and has spoken with Michaela on my behalf, but I guess it's to be expected that my allergy will be overlooked or forgotten at times. I really don't know how recovering or former alcoholics manage, I really don't.

Before I retreated to the living room, I had been the butt of jokes about my episode. I guess it's a positive thing that we can all laugh about aspects of it now, as this must signify that people no longer really expect me to relapse.

For example, Larry told everyone about the day he had to rescue me from the store detective and the grumpy old dear in the Co-op.

'You poor thing,' said Leanne. 'How on earth did you get him home?'

'I told him to walk home; to walk straight home, and not to stop anywhere on the way,' said Larry. 'But he did get an awful lot worse before we finally called for the men in white coats. One morning he was sitting in his shorts and T-shirt on the grass in the garden, with his mirror propped up against a tree, when the postman arrived – he must have thought he'd come to a madhouse owned by a narcissist!'

'You must have been really worried,' said Charlotte. 'How did you manage to stay sane yourself?'

'Well, you know me, Auntie Charlotte, I'm not the world's greatest reader, but I read the entire Harry Potter series non-stop. It seemed a saner kind of fantasy world and it helped me escape at night.'

Then Nat chipped in: 'How bad did it all get?'

This time Michaela responded: 'Well, on the day he got taken in, the Friday, he called me at work and said he felt terrible and couldn't think straight, and would I PLEASE come home. So I got home as quickly as I could and I found him sitting on a rug on the lawn. He said "thanks for coming home" but he said he was hungry, so Larry took him some cheese and biscuits...'

'Yes, big mistake,' said Larry. 'He took one look at it and said "what do you call this: I need carbs on a proper size plate, not blinis on a saucer".'

Larry and Michaela then relived their little private joke, roaring 'BRING ME CARBS!' in unison.

'Yes, Dad decided he was a lion,' continued Larry. He said he was weak with hunger and didn't feel well, so Michaela and I persuaded him to let us take him up to bed. But he kind of flopped on the stairs and it was like all the strength went out of his legs and ended up in his voice, 'cos he'd started to roar like a lion. We were really relieved when we'd finally got him into bed...'

'Except that it turned out to be only the beginning,' resumed Michaela. 'After about ten minutes the phone rang. Vic had called the house phone on his mobile and was demanding food again, so, having learned our lesson, Larry took him a bowl of pasta...'

'How did that go down?' asked Lisa.

'Well, not very well, sis,' said Larry. 'He turned his nose up and said it was no meal for a hungry lion – I was so stressed!'

Michaela took over: 'Larry took charge and found the biggest pan he could, and the biggest bowl and he filled the pan with all the different kinds of pasta we had in the house.'

'Yeah, that shut him up,' said Larry. 'And that gave the two of us time to talk about what we should do next.'

'In the end,' said Michaela, 'I called the Crisis Team and told them we thought Vic needed to be admitted to hospital.'

'Did you tell Dad what you were doing?' asked Lisa.

'Yes, I explained to him that the doctors were going to come, but I didn't explicitly talk about admission to a psychiatric unit...' said Michaela. 'Your dad decided he'd get himself a bit spruced up ready for his visitors and he ran himself a bath. Only, when he'd had his bath, he then decided he'd like a shower too and he disappeared into the shower for what seemed like an eternity. Of course, in the meantime the crisis team turned up, with Dr Gordon, the GP. That was OK at first because your dad was nicely out of the way while I talked with them about his symptoms. And then the phone rang...'

'So who was it?' enquired Lisa.

'It was your dad, calling on his mobile again... Dr Gordon asked "Does he normally do that?". He thought it was a sign of complete madness that your dad would telephone me from upstairs, and when I said "Oh yes, that's perfectly normal in this house" they all just looked at each other like maybe I needed to be taken away as well!

'Anyway, your dad had been ringing to say he was on his way down and he did, eventually, find his way downstairs and sat, in his dressing gown, in front of that enormous mirror of his, cross-legged on the living room floor...

'I went in to speak to him but then he started ranting and saying he wouldn't speak to me because I was conspiring with the doctors to get him taken into psychiatric hospital...'

'And I persuaded you to go peacefully, didn't I, Dad?' interjected Larry.

'You did, son – you were good,' I said. 'You explained calmly how they would section me if I didn't go to hospital of my own free will and even in the state I was in then I knew that being sectioned was a very bad idea...'

Then Michaela got to talking about how she'd been warned that, in my deluded state, I might spend loads of money that I didn't have and how she'd carefully hidden all my credit cards and cheque books in different parts of the house. Even now I haven't managed to find them all.

And then she got onto what I'll call 'the Bagpipes Episode' – the day I went out with Charlotte and I then borrowed some money from her for a Northumbrian pipes loan, and then we planned a new bookshop with the girl at Waterstones, in Harrogate.

'Michaela gave me hell for doing that,' said Charlotte, with a slightly hurt expression.

'Well, I was convinced he'd committed to buying a brand new set of pipes for at least a couple of grand,' Michaela sought to justify herself. 'I was terrified of what he might do. It's like when he went out to HG1 with you, Danny. I was horrified that you could have let yourself be so easily manipulated,' she said, turning to face the sheepish Danny. 'You knew EVERYONE goes to HG1 and it could have been a disaster...'

'Yes, yes, the loony on the loose!' I chip in. 'Don't you think it might be time you all found someone else to laugh at?' I added. 'I think it's the moment I should take refuge in my own company.' And I left them all to get slowly more tipsy while I closed the living room door behind me and watched a programme about big game safaris on National Geographic. I did not feel there was any danger I would morph into a lion again. Not today. Not ever.

It is now Friday January 28. I won't need to tell you what a relief it feels that February is just around the corner and that the days will at last start to draw out. I won't need to remind you that the Indian summer of my days at Priestley House gave way first to autumn and then to the bitter freeze of late November and December – the second big freeze of the year, following the Siberian curtain-raiser that had been the previous January.

I reflect that the weather has, to a degree (now would that be Celsius or Fahrenheit?) mirrored my state of mind. The balmy days of my loony September, followed by a disappointingly uneventful autumn and then the depressive gloom of December and the challenge of somehow getting through Christmas.

The thing is, it has actually taken me a while to confirm my progressive recognition that, yes, I am depressed. Not depressed as in suicidal, but depressed like having to look at the brightest star in the sky through dark glasses. I have lost my lustre. I have also lost the last of the props provided to me by the NHS since my discharge from Priestley House, after Jenny and I agreed before Christmas that I was doing OK and there were probably others in the community more deserving of her time. I miss her weekly visits.

My sessions with Anton reflect, in part, a recognition by me that I am depressed and that I need help to put myself properly back together again. And already Anton has helped me to recognise that, just because I must accept that, sadly, I do not have superhuman powers, that doesn't have to mean, ergo, that I am not a special person.

It was down to Anton, for example, that – as I mentioned earlier – I took my first practical steps towards recording in my own way the story of my manic episode. Specifically I bought novel-writing software and began the task of importing into it all the material I could find, so as to build up the most complete evidence-based picture of my mind spinning out of control.

Yesterday, for example, I returned to all the emails and text messages I had sent in between my accident with the five-bar gate and my eventual admission to Priestley House.

Another thing I set about doing yesterday was to return to the lists I had drawn up while in hospital – lists of essential reading and viewing for my followers, my 'disciples'. It is still a shock to me that these lists appear not really to exist, amounting to no more than the odd book title and a couple of films. Because I'm sure I did create much longer lists in my head, I have added new titles that I think help to reflect my world view in the context of my illness. To Auto da Fé and its chilling depiction of how it feels to go mad, I have added Gabriel García Márquez's One Hundred Years of Solitude, on the basis that its magical realism reminds us that reality is, if you like, in the eye of the beholder. And Ursula K Le Guin's The Dispossessed, because – on one level at least – it is a very hopeful book, suggesting as it does that society does not have to be based on competitive destructionism. As a nod to the importance of our emotional selves, I've added J P Donleavy's The Beastly Beatitudes of Balthazar B as a reminder that – just as I was convinced when in hospital that there was some kind of positive conspiracy of good fortune designed to place me with Dave and use the skills of my team for the greater good – so, equally, fate can sometimes deliver a real bad hand, and destine the likes of our Balthazar to a life in which happiness is repeatedly snatched from his grasp. Then there's John Fowles's The Magus, in its original version, as a reminder that the freedom of the individual to act independently is fundamental to the human condition. I also have a 'long list' of lots of other books I've enjoyed over the years, but I have elected to pause for the time being as I don't think I had ever intended these lists just to reflect my likes and dislikes. They were supposed to be about inspiring understanding of the world and encouraging ambition.

Similarly, after thinking about poems, films and music, I have decided to 'park' these lists as well, for now at least.

It is the criteria for moving from the long to the short lists that are occupying my mind as I set off for Anton's. I have returned to work four days a week since the start of the year, but Friday is my Anton Day and – by the time I have driven up there and back and attended my consultation and then rested on my return home – it does take pretty much the whole day. I have taken the A61 out of town, joining the perpetual building site that is the A1 to the A66, at Scotch Corner.

Thankfully, the deep Arctic blast that blanketed the country in snow before Christmas is behind us now. Otherwise, the idea of visiting a CB therapist in the Eden Valley in winter would lie somewhere between impractical and potentially dangerous. Indeed, as I begin the steady climb towards Bowes Moor and the Stainmore Gap, the air is crisp, the sky blue, and the moors and hills resplendent beneath a veneer of frozen snow that shimmers in the low light of a winter sun.

As I cross the watershed at Stainmore, a strange thing happens: I accidentally flip the radio button on the steering wheel and it goes from Radio 4 to Radio 2; and what should be playing but the Rolling Stones' remake of the Chuck Berry classic, Route 66. You might chuckle at the coincidence and so, in normal circumstances, might I, but today it feels really quite spooky and I get the strangest momentary feeling, as though I am suffering from one of those petit mal episodes. It's as if I am suddenly here, in this place, but at some quite different time. And then, as quickly as the sensation came, it fades, just as the thumping rhythm of Get Your Kicks on Route 66 also fades away to some American guy waxing lyrical about the musical and literary significance of 'the Mother Route'.

I am just getting into the narrative when, bizarrely, the station flips back to Radio 4. I tune back to Radio 2 and it's Ken Bruce chatting. No Stones, no Chuck Berry, no American commentator. I wonder if I am going mad, but then reflect that I've been there, done that, got the T-shirt. And it didn't feel like this.

As I descend into the Eden Valley, the snow covering gives way to a coating of frost in the shadow of the Pennines. The sun is not yet high enough to turn the fields from white to green and the car's external thermometer suggests it's actually hovering around freezing. For want of any better strategy, I push the Route 66 episode to the back of my mind and concentrate on the road conditions. Anton lives in the red sandstone village of Dufton, whose position on the Pennine Way delivers a steady if modest flow of long-distance walkers to boost the numbers enjoying the traditional hospitality at the Stag Inn. The most direct route to Dufton is to drive along the road that crosses the army practice ranges at Warcop, and I decide to take a chance that the army may have gritted it. They haven't and I find myself obliged to drive gingerly across polished sheets of ice through a landscape that alternately reflects an urban scene from Northern Ireland during the Troubles, and then an Iraqi desert. Except for the small detail of the weather, of course.

My cautious progress means I arrive at Anton's house, on the green just a couple of doors from the Stag, a few minutes late.

'Come in, come in,' he urges. 'How have you been? I've just been playing Fat Controller,' he smiles, indicating the detailed model of the Isle of Man railway system that occupies what, in a more normal household, might have been called the living room. 'Just come on through... Coffee? Tea?'

Anton's coffee is instant and terrible, so I choose tea as I make myself comfortable in his little consultation room, heated by a generous open log fire. I wonder whether I should tell him about my Route 66 petit mal but decide this might distract us from addressing the bigger picture of the legacy of my illness. At times it doesn't seem very scientific: I sit and talk to Anton; he prompts me occasionally; and then I write him a cheque.

'So, Vic,' he begins, having presented me with a mug of quite passable tea and a fig roll. 'Last time we talked about how it makes you feel when you reflect on your time in hospital and compare that with the way that you feel now…'

'Well, it all seems very surreal now,' I begin. 'They were good times. I was happy. I was full of energy. I could change the world and I had certainty that I would change the world, I really did. It's been hard to come to terms not just with recognising that this was a completely false reality, but also with taking on board the simple fact that, actually, I have no superpowers at all. I'm not Clark Kent and I don't wear my underpants on the outside.'

'So how does that make you feel now?' says Anton, his bright blue eyes engaging me from above a sympathetic smile. He looks reassuring in the flickering light of the fire and his salt and pepper hair suggests a comforting maturity, notwithstanding the hobby that some might dismiss as juvenile.

I pause and reflect before replying: 'Sad; nostalgic; depressed; a bit worthless…'

'Now let's get things in perspective, Vic. You're a man who can be justifiably be proud of his achievements – you've kept a small business afloat on the global oceans of uncertainty through some of the most difficult economic times of our lives and now – through your account of your illness – you will bring new understanding to the world of these questions of mental health that blight so many lives.'

'So you think there really is value in me telling my story?'

'I do, yes, absolutely. And I believe the way you described to me last week your idea of weaving together a factual and a fictitious thread could prove inspirational. All that is needed is for you to truly believe in your exceptional abilities and this will surely happen…'

'You know, Anton, that I believe my illness was caused by a farm gate collapsing under me when I vaulted over it. But Michaela thinks that, even if this hadn't happened, then something else would have. She thinks my mind and body had together hatched some sort of a plan to make me step back from the stresses of life. She felt I was burning the candle at both ends and that it couldn't go on…'

Anton rubs the not-so-designer stubble on his chin and frowns before delivering his carefully measured response: 'We are hard-wired to survive, Victor. Some people will survive by the brain shutting down – fainting, or a panic attack…

'Other people may go into a bipolar state – post-traumatic stress disorder is a classic case, where the brain's wiring goes into overload but until you sort out the causal factors you can't cure it. It's like trying to keep the electricity on in your house when you know there's a short-circuit somewhere and it will keeping tripping out. Whether it's your home electrics or the human brain, you must come back to the absolute root cause and once you start working on that and resolve the remaining issues, then the brain will have the chance of the trip-switch, if you like, staying reset.

'That's what we are doing with talk therapy: giving people understanding of how they came to be where they are now – it gives them a very powerful tool for self-management.

'Sometimes something more than talk therapy needs to be undertaken to give reasoning and understanding and a greater chance to be embedded in the individual's day-to-day thinking. A combination may be called for for an individual patient… talk therapy, drugs, ECT, exercise, diet…'

'ECT!' I exclaim. 'I sincerely hope not. And anyway, I'm so much better. I'm just a little bit sad sometimes…'

'Indeed, Victor, but statistically speaking you are now susceptible…'

'Yes, that's what Dr Scholl told me back in November,' I interrupt.

Anton picks up almost without pausing for breath, in a way that suggests he is well rehearsed in this narrative. 'If such a breakdown were to recur there is no guarantee that it would be so enjoyable. It might become depressive rather than manic. In cases of bipolar disorder both states are terribly frightening – especially to others. But of the two, when such a person is on the road to recovery, what they miss is the manic up-side. One has such freedom to be, to do and to act with no fears because one has such a great sense of one's omnipotence. Some people lose their inhibitions and they think they can fly so they try to fly.'

I immediately think of young Tony at the hospital, trying to fly from a height of all of two feet.

'Your manic state was your brain's way of helping you survive that crescendo of stress,' continues Anton. 'It was waiting to happen. You were under great psychological assault at that time – and there may be lasting effects, like greater forgetfulness.'

'Oh no!' I say, reflecting that – while I can recall in some detail everything that happened to me during my episode – much of what has passed in the weeks since is a bit of a blur.

Anton continues: 'The brain is highly plastic, but once you punch something that's plastic it can take quite some time to recover its proper shape. But the brain's plasticity is fantastic...'

'Do you think that American politician who was shot in the head will get better?' I interject.

'Gabrielle Giffords?' says Anton, referring to the near fatal assassination attempt in which six others died outside a supermarket in Arizona. 'It's far too early to say, but the brain does have a capacity to recover that at times seems beyond our understanding.'

Anton starts to get quite technical now, explaining the role of neurotransmitters – dopamine, serotonin, adrenaline, noradrenaline – in delivering the brain's functionality. Alongside all this scientific stuff, I am struggling to understand how our little chats about life, the universe and everything might possibly be of any help. But, as if reading my mind, Anton continues: 'With talk therapy we are making new neural connections to give that sense of rationale and understanding... to look upon the episode dispassionately without the fear of going back there.'

I am reminded in this notion of being on the outside looking back, of the very real sense in which I felt I was looking down at myself when I first began to feel really, really ill prior to my episode. I describe to Anton how it felt as though my skull was just an empty shell and its contents were looking down on my body from somewhere up near the ceiling.

'Well, there are, of course, many documented instances of these out-of-body experiences in which people describe looking down on themselves. The rational explanation is that this occurs when there is an excess of carbon dioxide in the bloodstream; when people are genuinely experiencing closeness to death...'

'So you think I was close to death?'

'That's a big leap, Victor and it's not 100 per cent my field, but it may be indicative of just how unwell you had become at that point.'

'I'd like to understand more,' I venture, and Anton rises from his chair and heads for one of the many shelves of books that line the walls of the study-cum-consultation room.

'You could start with António Damásio,' he suggests. 'He's arguably the world's leading expert on affective disorders.' He pulls from the shelf a couple of titles: Descartes' Error, and Looking for Spinoza. The former is subtitled Emotion, Reason and the Human Brain. 'Or try Lewis Walport's Malignant Sadness. Or this one's very good – An Unquiet Mind, by Kay Redfield Jamison.'

The sub-title on this one is A Memoir of Moods and Madness and I'm unsure whether dipping into these – or indeed putting on my metaphorical swimming trunks and fully immersing myself in them – will increase my understanding of what happened to me and, therefore, be a positive thing or if, alternatively, they might just make me rather depressed.

'Borrow them, Victor,' urges Anton. 'In my experience there is no downside to having a better understanding of how the mind works and then applying the lessons to your own experience.'

'Have you ever suffered from depression?' I venture.

'Oh yes, Vic. That's why I do what I do now. I want to share with people like you the positives I have been able to draw from my own experience. Like recognising the triggers, and being able to take steps to halt negative trends before they become all-consuming...'

'Does playing the Fat Controller help?' I ask.

'Well, I know you probably think it's silly and maybe a bit

childish, but, you know, there's something deeply satisfying about railways. A train goes where the points and signals determine that it shall. It's not like an aeroplane or a car, which can deviate from the prescribed path at the whim of the pilot or the driver. So I find my little excursions to the Isle of Man can be extremely therapeutic.'

'What does your wife think?'

'She knows that it contributes positively to my mental health, just like a good stride up to High Cup Nick on a summer's eve can stimulate the production of positive chemicals in the brain in a quite different way. And, in any case, she attends her knitting circle…'

Driving home again I realise that I forgot to raise the subject of my Route 66 episode with Anton, even later in our consultation. I'm pleased, however, that I now have a truly relevant reading list and real books to back it up. The sessions are quite hard work but with the sun having peeled back the frost to reveal tired pastures yearning for the arrival of Spring, I feel a creeping flicker of optimism.

I'm home comfortably in daylight and decide to stimulate the production of some good brain chemicals by cooking a curry with plenty of turmeric (active ingredient curcumin, impedes the onset of dementia).

'That was great,' says Michaela. 'I thought you'd lost interest in cooking…'

'I had, but Anton made me think today about a few things. And he's given me a great pile of books to read!'

'That's great! You know I really have seen a difference since you started going to see him. I see the old you coming back, my love.'

'Yes, I think you're right, though I wouldn't have admitted it before today, I don't think… And you know, he's crazy too. He stays sane by playing with a train set. He's got the entire Isle of Man railway system in his sitting room!'

'His poor wife!'

'Oh, she just goes out knitting!' I tease…

'Michaela,' I add tentatively. 'Something a bit weird happened to me today…' I describe to her exactly how the radio switched channels this morning. Michaela looks somewhere between nonplussed and rather worried.

'Victor, my sweet. I think maybe you'd better just keep taking the tablets!'

CHAPTER 28

Kidnapped

Tuesday, October 19, 2021

After ten minutes, Felix eventually dared to remove the dark silk cloth he had wrapped round his face to resemble a hijab. The tuk-tuk was weaving swiftly through the slower traffic and he was increasingly confident his departure had as yet passed unnoticed. He had weighed up various alternative strategies, including feigning departure on the itinerary planned for him, to the island of Marie Galante; but he was unsure how comfortably that would sit alongside what he had told Mia at the Aurora building. He had been obliged to spend quite some time with her, following the panic that had erupted there and his own phone communication from Wasdale Head.

Rightly or wrongly he had decided to declare his intention to return to the UK on the grounds that he was no longer convinced of the wisdom of his globetrotting quest to find Jameela. He had not been convinced that he was being believed at the time and hence he was now worried that this disbelief on Mia's part might have been shared with others in the Aurora network.

He had no longer needed to return to the hotel as he had left with his bags, but he would have loved just a few minutes' access to the Internet to communicate with Michelle to bring her up to speed with his discovery of Jameela's appointment schedule. As it was, he had every hope that his partner in endeavour would, right now, be heading for Jacqhou. But he could not know this for sure. And he wanted very much to share with Michelle the bizarre news about Ned. He resolved to head straight for the airport and jump on the earliest possible flight that would take him, one way or another, to Europe, where he would head in the most direct route possible for the island of Vulcano.

BEEP, PEEP, BIP, BEEEP!!! The defiant horn of his tuk-tuk woke him from his reverie as his driver won a battle of nerves with another tuk-tukkist approaching at right angles. The sudden shock cast Felix rather arbitrarily into a contemplation of his current dilemma: was he enjoying this extraordinary and unpredictable international adventure, or would he rather be sitting at home with Mr Merryweather? Was the elusive prize of domestic bliss, or perhaps some other form of relationship with Jameela, worth all the stress, heartache and (let's be frank) money? At this moment, he felt he was unsure of the answer to the fundamental question of his present life. And so he closed his eyes and cast his mind back to those all too brief moments on the beach in Australia. The practical Felix was once again wanting to know if that fleeting encounter could really form a sound practical foundation for his subsequent decisions. And yet Felix the romantic continued to present strong evidence that indeed it could do just that; and that, far from being an alternative to Jameela, his whimsical wonderings about Michelle were no more than Satan's efforts to lure him into hedonism and away from his true path.

It was after midnight when the tuk-tuk finally arrived at the airport and Felix hastily entered the terminal and placed his luggage on the X-ray machine. It occurred to him that the Foundation could easily have spies in place – and so he dodged into the loos, where he once again put on his 'hijab', while being very much aware of its incongruity alongside his other, decidedly male, clothing.

Had he not chosen that precise moment to perform his

identity change, he might just possibly have noticed a familiar figure exiting the airport…

And, then again, but for that short delay, he might already have boarded his flight and switched off his phone before the moment at which Michelle chose to Bleat to him the following message: 'My dear Felix, take a look at your Nimbus page. Especially your Lifeline.'

Felix had had time to do little more than glance at his Lifeline and curse that he had wearied some time previously of living his life in the very public forum of modern social media. Had this not been the case, he might have seen the mysterious new entries there from as long ago as October 9 – fully nine days ago. In fact, the time that had subsequently elapsed felt like far longer, such had been the circuitous geography of the emotional and physical paths he had followed since then. Sitting in the cosy little room at the Wasdale Head Inn with Michelle he could not have imagined then what the coming days would bring. Now that evening had a decidedly distant feel to it and seemed like a simpler, more gentle place – one that Felix might indeed be tempted to yearn for.

He would consider what was on the page more thoroughly during the nine-hour stop that awaited him in Abu Dhabi. He wanted also, very much, to return Greta's call during the layover but felt, increasingly, that his communication channels were simply too compromised to contemplate making any kind of direct contact – especially given the manner in which he had made his exit from the Aurora offices in Ahmedabad.

It had turned out that Greta's call and the simultaneous commotion he had detected in the office were, in fact, connected. As too was the fact that the call from Greta had found its way past the offices' protective telecoms shell.

'Give me your phone!' Mia had demanded, after almost running from the other end of the office. Such was the force of her command that Felix meekly handed her the VSP. Her face was a picture of fury as she fiddled with the device to try to discover who had been on the line to Felix.

'Why is Ned Tackler calling you?' she machine-gunned at him after no more than a few seconds of fiddling with the VSP. 'This building permits calls only from Aurora insiders. Why are you receiving a call from Ned Tackler?'

'Ned Tackler!' exclaimed Felix, with genuine surprise. 'I received a call from a woman called Greta; she's a friend of mine back in the UK…'

'And this Greta woman must know where Ned Tackler is, because she used his phone to call you, Felix Mister Happy-Wotsit, whatever your name is!'

And it was this undeniable fact that had signalled the start of an uncomfortable hour, during which he had found himself subjected to what amounted to an interrogation by Mia and two of her colleagues.

How had he come to know Ned Tackler? When had they first met? What was the relationship between this Greta woman and Ned Tackler? When had he last seen Ned Tackler? What had Ned Tackler said to him? Where had they gone together?

Mia had visibly winced when Felix told her of his trip on the mini-submarine and he immediately regretted having shared this with her, but he had figured that the reality must be that there was very little that she did not already know about his movements. And he surmised that the wince might, in fact, have been no more than an act, designed to disguise from him the true extent of her knowledge.

Eventually, Felix had suggested that the best course of action for Mia if she wanted to find out what had happened to Ned would be to call his number and speak to Greta or, failing that, to call Greta at the Wasdale Head Inn. Felix would have liked to have been party to that conversation but had had to be content with piecing together its substance as best he could. From what he heard, it appeared that the Inn had been visited by two men dressed in dark suits, who had at some point got into conversation with Ned. The next time Greta had noticed Ned – or rather not noticed him – both he and the dark-suited strangers had gone, leaving behind only an unfinished pint and his VSP still tucked into the pocket of his familiar waxed jacket, which remained on the back of the chair he'd recently occupied. His tweed cap lay on the table as though waiting for a new head to adorn, so emphatic and abrupt had been Ned's departure.

Felix had been able to paint such a detailed picture mostly because Mia had insisted on repeating back to Greta everything she had been told and so this picture was the product of the former's interpretation of what she had been told by the latter.

Mia may have had no more than the haziest notion of what the English Lake District might be like, but she had rightly concluded that two men in dark suits would have looked very out of place there. 'Did you ever see anybody unusual?' she had quizzed Felix. 'Or perhaps somebody who may have spoken American?'

'No, I didn't,' responded Felix truthfully, unaware of those he and Michelle had passed on the road out of Wasdale days previously. In an effort to appear cooperative he had added that he had, in more than one location not including Wasdale, caught sight of a young man of Asian features and had been slightly surprised at Mia's dismissive response: 'That is not important!'

He had then been taken to a room on his own, where Mia had locked the door behind her, leaving Felix to presume he was now a prisoner of Aurora. However, after just a few minutes one of her colleagues had opened the door, handed back his VSP, and said: 'You're free to go now, Mr Messyheather.'

First, you should follow your heart
Each day on the road that you travel
Let no other keep you apart
If your fate you so wish to enravel
With moonbeams shot thro' by ol' cupid's dart.

Felix sat on the plane staring at the verse that had mysteriously appeared on his Lifeline. Mysteriously, because it was untagged, save for the date of posting and, when he had tried to reply to it, the usual Nimbus protocols had been missing. So he'd pasted the entire verse into Google and discovered the following entry in Cyclopedia: 'Short verse by the 19th century English poet and lyricist, Saville Walton.' The strange thing was that, when he subsequently put Saville Walton into Google, he could find no reference to any such poet…

'Could you switch that off now, Sir, we're about to take off,' said the cabin attendant, leaving Felix without further enlightenment. And so it was that Felix arrived in Abu Dhabi none the wiser as to how or why the entry had appeared on his Lifeline. By the time, another flight later, he had found his way through border control and security at Fiumicino and boarded a domestic flight from Rome to Catania, Felix was seriously starting to wonder if people he passed on the travelator might actually be him on his way back again.

It was dark, but nevertheless still reasonably warm, when he finally arrived in Sicily and discovered it was a two-hour drive to Melizza, the ferry port for Vulcano and the other Aeolian Islands. Flinching at the likely cost of a taxi, he rented a car, booked a hotel room at the port and set off on the drive north. He quickly reflected that he might, perhaps, have been wiser to look for a room in Catania: he was finding the monotonous drone of the route finder on his VSP soporific and, more than once, was alerted to his lack of attention and drowsiness by the kerklunk-kerklunk of the wheels of the little Topolina as he drove over the studs at the edge of the autostrada. It was after nine o'clock when he finally pulled up outside the Hotel Ortensia, an unpretentious little guest house on the edge of the port.

'I thought you were well travelled and worked in countries all over Europe,' said Michelle, slightly accusingly. She and Felix were risking an encrypted video call from computer terminals in their respective hotels, Michelle at a rather attractive establishment on the edge of the Jersey capital, St Helier, called Au Jardin des Hortensias; Felix in the somewhat less salubrious Hotel Ortensia, 1,500 miles to the south-east. 'It's the same in Italian and French, you dope! Just the French has a silent H at the beginning. But they both mean Hydrangea and that, to me, seems more than a little bit odd!'

Felix was nonplussed: he couldn't begin to imagine the scale of a coincidence that had seen two people staying at four hotels called Hydrangea within the space of a few days. And yet he had carefully avoided using TravelKnowledge to book his hotel.

'What booking engine did you use?' he asked Michelle.

'TravelKnowledge,' she replied.

'Well at least that halves the odds,' mused Felix. 'I've been avoiding TravelKnowledge and anything else that's even vaguely connected with Aurora…'

'So, I take it you didn't Eureka that funny poem on your Lifeline?'

'No, I used Google. Why?'

'Because I think Eureka, as the name suggests, might help you to find out more…'

'Tell me!' said Felix. 'I'm not going to go on Eureka.'

'Well Felix, if you used Google, you might have drawn a bit of a blank on Saville Walton, the elusive 19th century lyrical poet,' began Michelle. 'But, if you put it into Eureka, you not only get a reference to the letters from Robert Walton to his sister, Margaret Saville, which are the basis of Mary Shelley's original Frankenstein, but you will also find a complete biography of Saville Walton, albeit a completely fictitious one…'

'Fictitious?'

'Yes, because Saville Walton never existed: I'll text you what it says, if you like.'

'I think you'd better not do that,' said Felix, still pensive and bemused. 'Show me when we meet.'

'Anyway,' resumed Michelle, 'I'm off to Jacqhou in the morning.'

'And I'm off to Vulcano!'

At Felix's insistence they agreed to maintain 'radio silence' until they met in the Seychelles in four days' time. Felix quickly looked for accommodation in La Digue, in the Seychelles and was, by now, unsurprised to find that the most popular small hotel on La Digue was Villa Hortensia, risen Phoenix-like since a catastrophic fire in 2015.

He booked two rooms and texted to Michelle: 'Friday night is cocktail night: Villa Hortensia, La Digue!'

Felix checked out early from the Ortensia to a bright, clear autumn morning and, leaving his car at the hotel, walked through the little port to the dock. If he didn't have a mission to accomplish, he thought, it would be hard to imagine a more idyllic existence than globetrotting like this. But, for all the exotic beauty of the Great Barrier Reef, or the drama of Wasdale, it would be hard to imagine being anywhere better than on a boat sailing to a tiny Mediterranean island. Felix drank in the fresh sea air and, for the first time in several chaotic days, he reflected how good it was simply to be alive.

It wasn't too long before the ferry turned towards the port, situated at the point at which the barren volcanic landscape tapered to a narrow isthmus that joined it to the sister islet of Vulcanello. The little port was a hotchpotch of mismatched buildings and Felix reflected that, for whatever reason the archipelago had been named a World Heritage Site, by Unesco, it could not have been on account of its architecture. Nor could it have been because of the clarity of its sea air: the fresh ozone Felix had so much been enjoying had by now been replaced by a seemingly all pervading whiff of rotten eggs. As Felix trained his eyes more closely upon the island's rocky flanks, he could see small clouds of vapour venting here and there before dissipating into the clear blue sky. He hoped that he would, as the Internet guides suggested, quickly become used to the smell.

The onslaught upon his olfactory senses might have sharpened Felix's overall perceptions, or it might on the other hand have encouraged him to see things that were not actually there. In either event, a deep chill passed down his spine at what he believed he saw as the foot passengers queued to disembark and drivers returned to their vehicles: it was the young man slipping into the passenger seat of a white van… there was something just too familiar about the way he comported himself for it to be mere coincidence.

'How could I have been so naïve as to think I had shaken him off?' Felix reprimanded himself as he tried to come up with a strategy for giving the young Asian the slip. The best, indeed only, idea he could come up with was to rummage in his little rucksack for his hijab, which he then hastily wrapped around his head. Initially this seemed to achieve nothing more than to draw attention to himself, but then people clearly began to think him odd and started to leave a space around him. Neither result was what he had wished for, but to remove the headwear now would only attract further attention.

His salvation came with the melée that greeted him on the quayside: it was easy to lose himself in the centre of the scrum as it shuffled forward and he was able to remain there as the vehicles drove off the boat. Having evaded his tail, for the time being at least, Felix then wondered how best to address the awkward fact that, having arrived in Vulcano, he had absolutely no idea where on the island he should go. Perhaps he should Eureka 'Hydrangea Vulcano' and see what came up…

As things turned out, Felix had no need to use his VSP: a woman of perhaps 45 or a little older was standing on the quayside holding a placard marked Ned Tackler. Not for the first time did he feel he was little more than a minor character in some remake of the Truman Show.

'So, you're expecting Ned Tackler, are you?' Felix found himself saying to the woman, who, he noticed, was wearing a lot of black: skirt, a loose headscarf, shoes.

'Yes,' said the woman. 'But I do not think you are Ned Tackler.'

'No, I'm just a friend.'

'A friend? For how long have you known him?'

'Oh, quite a while,' lied Felix. 'We have connections in the Lake District, in England.'

'Wait here with me: perhaps he comes soon.'

Felix had not seen Ned on the ferry and doubted that he could have been on board, unless he'd been keeping deliberately out of sight.

'He's not coming,' he said to the woman, as the last pedestrians made their way ashore.

'No, I think not: I must come back for the next ferry. Perhaps you want to wait with me?'

The woman led Felix a hundred metres or so from the port, before inviting him to sit on the patio beneath the gently warming rays of the late October sun. She ordered him a cappuccino and a double espresso for herself.

'So, you are not Ned Tackler. So, who are you and what do you do in Vulcano?'

'I was hoping to find Victor Turnbull here,' ventured Felix.

The woman's eyebrows rose visibly. 'Victor? He has been here only once and that was quite some time ago.'

'What about Jameela Durrani?' risked Felix.

'You ask too many questions, Mister... What is your business here?'

'Mr Merryweather. Felix Merryweather. My colleague and I are looking for Jameela and other people who seem to have joined the Aurora Foundation and then disappeared.'

'Not disappeared, Felix. Merely disappeared from, shall we say, public view. But, please, be discreet. Walls have, how do you English say? ears?'

'There are no walls,' harrumphed Felix, gesturing towards the thin cord that defined the edge of the patio. 'And, anyway, it's your turn now. How do you know Victor Turnbull and why are waiting for Ned Tackler who, I happen to know, was kidnapped no more than three days ago.'

Taking note of Felix's inside knowledge, the woman began:

'You will know of Victor's personal story and how he came to establish Aurora and the Aurora Foundation?'

'Yes, he had a manic episode, which gave him the inspiration to turn a failing business into a world leader.'

The woman continued: 'Well, when he was in hospital he became friendly with a woman who worked some days on the reception desk. Victor believed his ear and his mind had become more finely tuned and that he could quickly learn new languages. He would talk with this woman in French and she would reply in Italian. He was a kind, gentle and funny man and I was that woman. I was living in Yorkshire with my daughter who was 16 at the time, but then my mother fell ill and I had to return to Sicily.'

The woman sighed. 'Family duties, you know. I did not want to come. I lost touch with Victor: he was discharged from hospital and, by the time he came back to visit, I had left. I was employed by an agency and so it would have been difficult for him to find me. But he did find me. He came all the way to Sicily to see me...'

'How romantic,' interjected Felix.

'No, it was not romance. He was, by this time, as you know, married. But he had said nice things to me and after he went to so much trouble to track me down, he said he had done so because I was one of the people who had really helped him with his recovery from illness. And he wanted to repay what he saw as a debt to me. This was at the time he was setting up the Aurora Foundation and he was creating what you might call "safe houses". He asked me to create a safe house in Italy for him and for his wife, Michaela, and he gave me a generous allowance and a salary for doing this. I was living in Messina, so Vulcano seemed like a natural choice, and I was able to find a suitable place here and still spend time at my mother's, and I had the money to pay for the additional care that she needed when I could not be with her. He changed my life.'

'I see,' said Felix. 'But you haven't told me your name, nor why you are expecting Ned Tackler.'

'I am Valentina, Felix. And the Foundation negotiated Ned's release from his captors. He will arrive today at some time...'

'And Jameela? What can you tell me about her?' asked Felix, dipping his biscotto in his coffee.

'She was here recently: I think Victor wanted to remind me that I am still part of the organisation. She is a nice woman. We talked.'

Felix's ears pricked up. 'About?'

'About life; about love; about the universe. She is a woman who needs some certainty in love and so that is why I believe she chose career before love.'

'I'm trying very hard to change that, Valentina.'

'Hah! Then I must wish you luck, Felix. Does your name mean "happy", in English? If so, I must wish you also happiness.'

'And Valentina, if your name means love, then I must wish you love!'

Valentina laughed. 'I am afraid it means healthy and strong, but I am happy to be healthy and strong, even if I have been unlucky in love!'

'Why do you wear black?' continued Felix.

'Because my dear mother died not so long ago and I wear some black out of respect for her memory. But now, Felix, we must return to the dock.'

'Nay lad, it weren't t'foundation 'at bargained me release!' pronounced Ned as the three of them walked towards the Aurora safe house. 'Aa did that missen!'

'What do you mean, Ned?' asked Valentina.

'He means he secured his own release,' clarified Felix. 'He can be a little difficult to understand at times.'

'Ah well, t'outcome were t'same whate'er language tha' puts it in!'

'Explain to me, Ned!' said Valentina.

'Well after they'd tekken me to somewhere in Italy, they said I 'ad ter tell 'em where t'Foundation's servers were, so I telt 'em. I telt 'em exactly where t'Foundation's servers WERE...'

'You did WHAT!?' demanded an incredulous Valentina.

'I telt 'em aboot t'owld servers as've bin shut doon...'

'He says he told them about the old servers that have been shut down,' helped Felix.

'Aye, t'ones in Svalbard,' said Ned.

'Does Victor know this?' asked Valentina.

'He shall do, just as soon as tha' tells him, lass!'

The safe house boasted, or rather acknowledged possession of, an unprepossessing frontage, on the edge of the northern side of town. It stood at the base of an upstanding knoll of volcanic rock, its rear wall being actually formed by the cliff of lava. What could not be guessed by looking at the little house – which Felix was unsurprised to note was called La Casa delle Ortensie, despite there being no garden – was that, since acquiring the property, the Foundation had tunnelled into the rock to create a suite of well appointed secure rooms, equipped with a full communications facility.

'We had to remove all the rock by darkness,' explained Valentina. 'It was a big job, but we managed somehow to keep it secret.'

She escorted Felix and Ned back to the front of the house, where she suggested they enjoy the fresh (or not so very fresh) air while she spoke with someone at Aurora. In the meantime they were each given a glass of wine from the neighbouring island of Lipari. It was a syrupy dessert wine, but that didn't seem to put off Ned, who was soon helping himself to a second glass.

'I don't think Victor thinks it was a great idea when you did tell these men about our old servers,' said Valentina. 'He wishes for you to stay here until he is able to come to, how do we say, "debrief" you.'

'That'll not cause me ower much 'ardship, lass,' smiled Ned. 'Just so long as aa can hiv plenty o' this poison!' he added, brandishing what was left of the bottle of wine. 'But tha' knaas, they'd o' had me finger nails oot, them fowks, so I figure I did t'best thing int'circumstances…'

It wasn't long before Ned was dozing off in the sunshine, and his cheap Italian cigarette smouldering in the ashtray, and so Felix took the opportunity to quiz Valentina further so as to glean even the smallest tidbit of knowledge about Jameela. Valentina told him very little of importance, preferring to share more generalities about life and love in general. He gained the impression, however, that Valentina, for all her lack of recent face-to-face contact with anyone at Aurora, knew more about Jameela's movements than she was prepared to let on. He wondered aloud whether she might perhaps accompany Victor to Vulcano for Ned's debriefing, but that enquiry was met with a categoric No.

'I know that Jameela is working closely with Victor but there are simple issues around security protocol that would prevent both of them being here, or indeed anywhere outside the UK and the Channel Islands at the same time.'

Felix indulged himself by taking a dip in the mud-bath near La Casa delle Ortensie, followed by a swim in the sea. The sun was still ascending high enough to warm the black volcanic sand, and the water in the bay was heated at intervals by sulphurous fumeroles on the seabed, one of which scalded his foot as he swam past. As the warmth went out of the day, he climbed the flanks of the volcano, passing countless yellow molehills, each angrily spouting boiling sulphurous fumes. He was unsure if he could learn to ignore the smell and wondered how people learned to live with it. He had seen nothing more of Jameela's brother and he began to wonder if he might, in fact, have been mistaken.

He would have liked to have stayed on the island and perhaps confronted Victor himself on his arrival, but – as Felix sat sharing a last meal with Ned and Valentina – there was something that the latter said that made him decide against this and catch the last ferry back to Sicily instead.

Her VSP bipped and as she looked at it, she turned to Felix and said, 'That is Victor – he is on his way here now and Jameela is travelling to the Seychelles, also right now.'

The journey to the Seychelles saw Felix retrace his vapour trails back to the Middle East, where he boarded an Air Seychelles flight from Dubai to Mahé. From there he caught a local flight to the island of Praslin, where he spent a surprisingly inexpensive night at the Berjaya Beach Hotel.

It was in the Vallée de Mai coco de mer forest the following morning that Felix saw him: this time he was quite sure who he had seen slipping behind one of the giant trees with the enormous buttock-shaped nuts and grotesquely long, dangling catkins.

The forest was dense and dark, and so it wasn't too difficult for Felix to weave an erratic path before, he hoped, throwing off his pursuer by doubling back the way he had come. The only trouble was that, in the process, Felix too lost his bearings, and when he eventually emerged from the forest, he was on the opposite side to his hotel. By the time he finally found his way back, he had little time to spare to catch the ferry for the short crossing to La Digue. He prepaid a second night at the hotel and instructed the receptionist that he was going to rest in his room and on no account was he to be disturbed. He then gathered his belongings, exited via the back door and made for the neighbouring hotel, from where he summoned a jeep to take him to the south of the island.

'Felix, has it not occurred to you that if Jameela's brother, or indeed brothers, intended to do you harm, he or they wouldn't hide every time you catch sight of them?'

It was a simple question and yet not one that had hitherto occurred to him.

'Supposing you're right, what other reason could there be for following me?'

'How about, Rahman would like to see Jameela just as much as you do?'

'Well, I guess it's possible…'

'My suggestion, Felix, is that, the next time you see him, you stand your ground and call his name. Perhaps we could even pool our resources!'

Felix decided to mull the idea over and ordered another piña colada. Villa Hortensia was on a west-facing hillside above the nearest thing to a town on the tiny island. A little further down the coast was the private estate, on which the Aurora Foundation premises were situated. A little further still, the equatorial sun was well into its descent to the western horizon. As a place for a mutual debrief, it would be hard to better.

Felix and the newly arrived Michelle had begun by bringing each other up to speed on their respective itineraries.

'So your trip to Jacqhou didn't take us much further forward,' suggested Felix.

'No, not really,' agreed Michelle, who had described how she had chartered a boat from St Helier to sail to the private island; how the boat had landed at the private Turnbull jetty; and how it had then been obliged to depart again. Her captain had then successfully attempted a landing in a sheltered cove on the other side of the island. Michelle had waded ashore as the boat returned to sea, and climbed the steep path up the cliffs at the back of the bay. Confronted by a high wall, she walked in one direction, only to find the wall intercepted a sheer drop to the sea. She retraced her steps and set off in the other direction, only to be apprehended by two guards, who then escorted her back to the main harbour.

'They weren't rough; they weren't unpleasant, but they were, shall we say, firm and resolute. There was no way I was going to get to see Victor Turnbull or anyone else.'

The guards radioed her boat, which came to collect her. Soon after setting sail, Michelle and the captain saw a helicopter arrive.

The captain trained his binoculars on the aircraft and said, with some confidence, that he had seen Victor Turnbull get on board before it took off and turned towards Jersey.

'And your Vulcano trip was a bit of a damp squib too, was it?'

'Well, I guess I gained a few new insights, and at least I do now know that Jameela is safe and, I presume well, even if it may be true that she's thought better of getting together with me.'

'And you think you were right to leave? What if this Valentina was lying to you? What if Jameela was due to arrive there with Victor.'

'Well Michelle, in that case I would feel a bit of a fool, that's for sure.'

Then Michelle showed Felix the information she had found about the mysterious poet, Saville Walton.

Saville Walton (1793-1872) was an English romantic lyricist and poet. He is chiefly known for his short verses on the subject of love unrequited.

Less well known is his interest in the emerging genre of Gothic horror and, in particular, his acquaintance with the author Mary Shelley, who wrote Frankenstein.

Walton saw in this no contradiction. Indeed he even penned a few verses on the more macabre subjects. Typically these comprised four lines of verse made up of two simple rhyming couplets, such as in the following verse, entitled Life After Dark.

In yonder churchyard after dark;
But in the gloom before the lark;
The spirits oft will dance and sway;
Returning to their graves by day.

The entry concluded with a bibliography listing various poems, conveniently divided into Romantic and Lyrical Verses, Gothic Rhymes, and Other Works.

'Does that poem ring any bells with you, Felix?'

'No, I don't think so…'

'Do you remember when Greta gave us the four addresses she had been given by Victor and Michaela? Did you ever see the other side of the paper?'

'No, I don't think I did. It was just scribbles, wasn't it?'

'It's what was under the scribbles that's interesting,' said Michaela, as she opened her purse and took from it the original piece of paper. 'Look, you can just make out the words, see...'

'They're the same, or pretty much, aren't they?!'

'Exactly. And I'll tell you something else. You didn't read everything that came up when you searched for Saville Walton, did you?'

'What do you mean?'

'Well, when I Eureka-ed him, I found a little lower down the entries, several that mentioned two people: Margaret Saville and Robert Walton. And do you know who they were?'

'I've no idea, but I'd be very surprised if you didn't tell me with that smarter-than-thou look on your pretty face...'

'Well, as you must know by now, Felix, I am indeed far more than a pretty face, which is why I can tell you that Robert Walton's letters to his sister, Margaret Saville, are the basis of the original version of Frankenstein, written by Mary Shelley.

'And...?'

'Well, that's where I thought you might be able to contribute your bit. Can you think of anyone with an interest in either lyrical poetry or Gothic horror?'

Felix scratched his chin, before replying: 'I think that's Jameela...'

'You THINK it might be Jameela? My God, let's hope you two never appear on Mr and Mrs, then!'

'We are but pawns on the chessboard of life,' mused Felix over breakfast the next morning.

'That's not another one by our friend Saville, is it?'

'Very likely,' replied Felix. 'We've been played for a pair of fools, haven't we? I no longer think I know whether the Aurora Foundation really is a quasi-secret organisation dedicated to the triumph of good over evil or if it is just the concoction of an over-fertile imagination dedicated to having a laugh at our expense.'

'Felix: I think it would be a very expensive joke if that was all that this was about, don't you?'

'It's certainly been expensive for us!'

'And fun at times, too,' suggested Michelle. 'Listen, we're going to continue what we're doing and that means, first of all, visiting the Aurora facility over there and then, I think, going to Svalbard to follow the lead that Ned Tackler seems to have let slip when you were on Vulcano. Where is that, by the way?'

'It's in the High Arctic, on the way to the North Pole. It'll be very cold and probably completely dark too at this time of year. I'm shivering even just thinking about it.'

'Well, let's see what happens in the next half a day: you never know, perhaps we might be able to stay here in paradise and wait for Jameela and Kenny to come to us.'

While the Aurora facility stood within a secure compound also housing a ministerial residence for visiting heads of state, the building itself was in the traditional Seychellois style of, essentially, no walls or doors.

Michelle and Felix had not so much penetrated the outer security ring as simply walked through it.

'We're here for Victor to debrief the staff on the Tackler incident,' pronounced Michelle boldly.

'Go to the Aurora building and ask for Nils,' suggested the guard.

'That could be Nils Boateng,' suggested Felix.

'Perhaps Kenny's here!' rejoined Michelle excitedly.

The pair wandered through the open peripheral rooms of the Aurora building to where they found a man mixing himself chilled cordial. A woman's voice called out from another room:

'Nils, c'est Jameela à l'appareil. Elle est avec Victor, à notre maison sécurisée, en Italie.'

'Merci, Monique. J'arrive!'

CHAPTER 29

When small is too big to grasp

Monday, February 7, 2011

So, it's ten days and one consultation since Anton gave me his collection of books about depression and manic behaviour. Despite my initial apprehension, I have delved into each one, with the aim of at least getting a flavour.

'I did find all of them quite useful in varying degrees,' I told him at our session on Friday. A session during which I felt Anton had really picked up on the modest steps forward I had made a week previously, and was working hard on making me feel better about my abilities. In fact, I have made some progress, albeit modest, in recording the 'adventure' that was my episode. I've decided that's what I'll call the 'contemporaneous' strand of my narrative, which will stick just as close as possible to my recollection of what actually happened to me, backed up by the evidence of diary notes, emails and so on. I'll change a few names and locations, of course, but that's all. I've decided to start the story not from the beginning, but from the moment when my mind actually started to fall apart, when I was up in Scotland. I have read and re-read it a few times and like what I've written. I've also created the bones of what I'll call my 'future extrapolation' and placed the opening scenes in a fictitious paradise off Australia's Gold Coast. I quite like this too.

I shared all this with Anton and even showed him what I'd written.

'This is fantastic, Vic, you really are so well placed – with your background, your abilities, your training, your contacts – to significantly extend the frontiers of people's understanding of mental illness, or affective disorders.'

The books that Anton loaned me are informative to the process of my understanding of the range of afflictions that fall beneath the broad umbrella of affective disorders or – in 'old money' – mental illness.

Let's begin with António Damásio and his Descartes' Error. The 'error' that Descartes – the 17th century French philosopher and scientist – committed, according to Damásio, was to assert that the mind and the brain were, in essence, separate and capable of independent operation. Drawing upon lots of examples of people who, for example, suffered brain injuries in accidents or through illness, Damásio seeks to prove that the two are in fact inseparable. Or that, to put it simply, the concept of a 'mind' independent of the brain is a nonsense.

Looking for Spinoza, whose worthy subtitle is Joy, Sorrow and the Feeling Brain, I found a little more challenging: breaking down the twin concepts of 'emotions', on the one hand, and 'feelings' on the other and then translating the former into neural pathways. All worthy stuff, but not 'stuff' that I felt was really leading me to a greater understanding of my 'condition'. Just for the record, emotions, says Damásio, are instinctive reactions shared by humans and other species, whereas feelings are what we as sentient creatures think about our emotions – or indeed the bodily states that we observe in ourselves while we feel these emotions. Damásio seems driven by the notion of bridging the scientific and the philosophical, hence the Spinoza of the book's title. He was a Portuguese Jew, who fled his homeland for the Netherlands to escape the Spanish Inquisition, and Damásio uses his fascination with Spinoza as a vehicle to further explore his theories about emotions and feelings.

'I thought the Walport book was kind of "everything you ever wanted to know about depression but were afraid to ask",' I ventured to Anton on Friday. Malignant Sadness describes how Walport, a successful scientist who had flirted with 'the blues' but never known serious depression, found himself suddenly completely debilitated by extreme depression – to the point at which he became unable to carry on with his work and family life and even contemplated suicide.

'I thought it was quite positive, in that he recovers, thanks to psychotherapy and drug treatment,' I said to Anton. 'And positive for me in that my own condition is no more than a superficial scratch to his gaping wound. But his description of the shame and stigma he suffered are quite depressing.'

'And that's why,' said Anton, 'the people at your hospital will have spent a lot of time doing their best to minimise your contact with the "outside world". They would have been protecting you from yourself in your most extreme moments. How did you find the phone and Internet connections at the hospital?'

'Terrible,' I said. 'They weren't too bad at the Reception desk and the far end of the garden, but otherwise, it was a case of sticking the phone out of the window…'

'And you think that was an accident of the telephone system? I've heard Priestley House is on top of a hill,' continued Anton with a wry smile.

It is the Friday after the Monday on which I wrote the above and, once again, I am making the long drive over the Pennines on a balmy February day.

My consultations with Anton have, I realise, evolved considerably since my first visit. Back then it was all about Anton lighting a touch paper and blowing it gently so that my brain would spark into life and I would begin to talk about the complexities of my episode.

Now, I recognise, our conversations are, indeed, conversations.

We have a dialogue, rather than a Victor monologue. In fact, I reflect, it is today Anton who is doing the bulk of the talking. And it is a wide-ranging monologue on his part. If I am to dissect its purpose, then I guess it's about further encouraging me to think dispassionately about that rather complex thing that is my brain.

Today we begin with a man whose musings on the more trivial aspects of daily life are often seen as spawning the entire 'philosophy industry'. When Michel de Montaigne took 'early retirement' at the tender of age of 38, back in the late 16th century, he began writing for his own amusement and that of his friends and family. These days we'd call it 'stream of consciousness' writing, or recording your thoughts as they come into your head.

Instinctively, this feels to me like a post-Medieval version of Tweeting while on the toilet. But Anton asserts that it was a watershed and quite revolutionary, in that it not only changed the place and direction of philosophy in thinking society, but also kick-started the Modernist era in art, by freeing artists from the constraints of being obliged to reflect history, and enabling them instead to reflect life.

'Montaigne wrote reams on just about every trivial aspect of life, from the things we do to the parts of our bodies,' says Anton. 'Smells; why we wear clothes; our thumbs; why and how we post letters; even penises…'

'Penises? Did they have them in 16th century French philosophy?' I ask.

'Oh yes, take a look at this,' says Anton, pulling from his extensive bookshelf a volume replete with protruding yellow Post-its.

The book falls open easily at a page on which the following is marked with an orange highlighter:

Till possession be taken, a man that knows himself subject to this infirmity, should leisurely and by degrees make several little trials and light offers, without obstinately attempting at once, to Force an absolute conquest over his own mutinous and indisposed faculties. Such as know their members to be naturally obedient, need take no other care but only to counterplot their fantasies.

'So he's having a debate with his own willy? I can understand how that might have been seen as ground-breaking back then but, these days, what's it all got to do with the price of philosophical fish?' I wonder.

'Well, Victor, perhaps a little more than you might think, especially in the light of what we have discussed about the various scriptures, their rigid interpretation and the appalling problems such fundamentalist views cause us all,' Anton replies. 'I see Montaigne as having been very much ahead of his time in this regard. He lived in turbulent times – his mother was Jewish but had been forced to convert to Catholicism, and two of his siblings became Protestants. Montaigne himself remained a Catholic but his private musings led him to question the very meaning of truth.'

'You mean he became sceptical?'

'Yes, Victor, he recognised that truth was not an absolute but actually something that was a bit squishy and intangible; something that might vary depending upon the perspective from which you viewed it. Of course, this view was not one that would necessarily sit all that comfortably with the great thinkers who followed him,' continued Anton. 'Take our friend Descartes again, for example. He comes along and says Truth is absolute. The Word of God, if you like. And once we have actually discovered the Truth, then that is that. No turning back. Pascal is little better and sets about dissing Montaigne as a bit of a lightweight who flits from subject to subject.'

I interject: 'So did anything Montaigne did actually change things in the real world, as opposed to in his head?'

'Well, that's the remarkable and modern thing about him,' replies Anton. 'As I said, these were very turbulent times. Montaigne himself came from a family of Jews who had been forced to convert and he insisted that the so-called "wars of religion" weren't religious at all, but political disputes dressed up in religious clothing. He acquired a reputation as something of a moderator, even between "religious" factions at opposite ends of the spectrum.

'And his modus operandi was to begin by asking the question "How do we know what we know?". So he would look at contentious elements in disputed religious tracts and seek areas of potential accommodation between factions. He was driven in this by a compassion and humanity, the likes of which feel very much at odds with his time.'

Now it is my turn to rub my chin and reflect. 'I think I might have rather liked him. All this is so very much like the fantasy world I created when I was ill: teams of people all dedicated to teasing out the humane elements of the scriptures and getting rid of the provocative and incendiary bits so often added by later "interpretations" and never intended by the original prophets...'

'Indeed, Victor, indeed...'

'Look, I had always thought of philosophy as a bit of a luxury: you know, thought for thought's sake... Now I'm wondering if pure science, with its absolutes, might not exist in something of a more dynamic relationship with philosophical reflection. I mean, I hear what you say about Pascal, and yet he was a nailed-on empiricist as well as a religious thinker, surely? I mean, he invented his Triangle, for God's sake!'

'Well, to be fair, Vic, Pascal rejected both empiricism and rationalism, but he did set out to demonstrate that Christian faith was indeed a rational thing. And even today we can see religious faith and atheism co-existing among our greatest thinkers.'

I suggest: 'Like, say, Dawkins and Hawking, on the one hand and, I don't know, didn't the Higgs boson guy specifically say that science and religion were compatible? In fact, when I was in the nuthouse, that was the central pillar of my new belief system: that faith could be either scientifically or religiously based. Dave's Rosary or my Three Monkeys.'

'Not nuthouse, Victor, please. You were in a heightened state of consciousness but words like "mad" or "nutty" should be applied with extreme caution,' Anton chides me. 'But yes, Peter Higgs has had a go at Dawkins for his absolutism and both he and Brian Cox suggest that science and religion are indeed compatible.'

'Well, I have my own issues with scientific absolutism,' I say. 'I think we should maintain an open mind on many things. For instance I think it's only right that the NHS should fund some alternative therapies when there's good evidence they make people feel better, even if we don't yet understand why this should be so.'

'Hmmm,' says Anton, leaving me to wonder if we are on the same page here. But he moves swiftly on: 'If you take a step back you can see that some of the greatest scientific discoveries begin with abstract thought and so we have the long search for the Higgs boson, expressed in shorthand as looking for the God Particle. Because in this, as in all scientific quest, until we have proof we can have only ideas and theories…'

'Which brings us back to Montaigne…'

'Indeed, the Holy Grail of theoretical science is the quest for a Grand Unified Theory, or Theory of Everything. The Theory of Everything will combine in a single equation the physics of the big with the physics of the small – the physics of cosmology with the physics of quantum dynamics.'

'Like a modern equivalent of $E=mc^2$?'

'Indeed, yes, but it's gravity that's the fly in the ointment, so to speak. In the Theory of General Relativity, gravity behaves itself and follows the rules, but in Quantum Field Theory, gravity is not compatible with the behaviour of the other three forces – strong and weak nuclear forces and electromagnetism. It's about finding something that will bring together the science of the big with the science of the very small, or the sub-atomic.'

'So, if they can prove the existence of the Higgs boson at CERN, will that do it?'

Anton laughed. 'No it's just one more piece in a big jigsaw, but it will prove that Higgs's abstract thinking – the way he came up with a theory – could advance our understanding of the universe, both the big and the small.

'But, even if the existence of the Higgs boson is proven, you still can't find a mathematical way of linking gravity – which falls into the physics of the big – with the physics of the small. You keep ending up with these infinities. And physicists don't like infinity because it's a cop-out.'

'So I guess they wouldn't like my great theory of the elasticity of time, then. The one I came up with in "the hospital"… Two to the power of infinity equals infinity to the power of two [$2^{\infty} = \infty^2$].'

'No, it's all about things like "fantastical" and "embroidered" mathematical formulae; String Theory; M theory; Membranes; P-branes; multiverses; and Bob's your uncle.'

'Or maybe Albert's your uncle,' I say.

'Poor old Albert. But he's your great great granddad's uncle now. All these new theories postulate many more dimensions than the original five or so. Now quantum scientists are talking about nine, ten or even 13 dimensions.'

'I can't persuade my brain to go beyond space and time,' I say. 'What on Earth are they all?'

'Well, Victor, just to be pedantic, the fifth dimension isn't Space. It's the dimension of Possible Worlds: a dimension in which we might find a parallel Planet Earth – the same as our own, but maybe slightly different…'

'You mean a dimension in which the fantasy world that I extrapolate from my manic episode really does exist, for example.'

'Yes, I think that's exactly the kind of thing they have in mind; or a world of Sliding Doors, where just a slight shift in time could precipitate a quite different outcome.'

'That sounds like my Iceberg Theory of Coincidence: things that so very nearly happen but about which we know nothing…'

'Indeed!'

'So what about all the others?'

'Well, they're all, in one way or another, about different but parallel possible worlds, until you get into the really high numbers, and then it all gets a little difficult for ordinary mortals like you and me to grasp. For example, the Tenth Dimension comprises infinite possibilities…'

'I thought you said physicists didn't like infinity.'

'Ah, touché!'

As I drive home, this conversation continues to revolve in my brain, most particularly the moment at which we later got onto talking about the late Douglas Adams, author of the Hitchhiker's Guide to the Galaxy series of books and, crucially, the ill-fated quest to answer the Ultimate Question. 'You know! Life, the Universe and Everything.' The answer, of course, was 42, which, I observed at the time, looked rather like $2^\infty = \infty^2$. So I am intrigued by Anton's suggestion that Professor Brian Cox may actually have taken Douglas Adams to view the Large Hadron Collider, at CERN.

My head is still full of it all when I arrive back home in Ripon.

'How was it today, Hun?' asks Michaela, who is home early from work.

'It was pretty amazing, actually,' I say. 'Did you know that there are up to 13 dimensions, not just the four or five we always thought there were?'

'Really? And how does that make you feel?'

'Pretty small, my darling; pretty small!'

It is February 14, Valentine's Day. More importantly to me, it is the anniversary of the death of my brother Malcolm and thus cause for sad reflection. In particular it is cause for me to reflect on how I came to meet with Malcolm around the onset of my episode. My meeting with Anton a week ago was very much about the quantum dimension to what was going on in my mind, and it was a source of comfort to me that the constructions of my mind might even somehow be realised in some parallel universe. But if anything shines out of the darker side of my experience, it is the recurrent wondrously plaited thread of the religious and spiritual, on the one hand, and the scientific and rational on the other.

That is why, tomorrow, I am meeting with a business colleague with influential connections in the Church. I am after a clear perspective on what the Church might make of my claim to have met with my dead brother, and to understand better why the letter that I wrote and left in Ripon Cathedral that night went unanswered.

It is March 1 and I have just got off the train at Durham, where I plan to kill two birds with one stone. I shall begin by visiting a senior cleric at Durham Cathedral. It is a meeting that has evolved out of the one I had a couple of weeks ago with a colleague well connected in Church circles. I am deeply appreciative, both of the intervention by my colleague, who – it turns out – has on occasions felt the presence of his late father, and to the senior figure who has made time to meet with me and help me better to come to terms with the experiences I had at the onset of my manic episode.

The more water that has flowed beneath the bridge since my emotional evening at Ripon Cathedral, the more extravagant my account of my meeting with Malcolm has seemed to me each time I reflect on what I told people about it, or each time I look at my subsequent notes or at the scribblings I photographed nearly six months ago now. With every passing day on which I have edged closer back to normality, so these scribblings progressively have acquired the status of the rantings of a fool.

As I walk up Durham's historic Bailey towards the magnificent Romanesque Cathedral, I feel I might be near to closing another open loop in my life since my manic episode. But closing this particular loop feels like a much bigger challenge than the very much more mundane issues I've already got to grips with, like completing my business accounts, and home finances, and hacking away at my overheads. Today, for the first time, I am about to expose my soul and I fear I might appear ridiculous…

I mentioned to Anton, when I saw him last week, my plan to meet this important Churchman as part of my quest to find answers to the beyond-the-grave encounters I had with Malcolm. Anton rightly pointed out that I was now seeing my behaviour in the days leading up to and during my hospitalisation in sharp relief; I could now take a more dispassionate view of things I did, said or wrote amid the frenetic urgency of mania.

But just because I am now able to question my sanity, does not necessarily mean I am feeling robust enough to sit down with a stranger and permit them to pass similar judgement.

Durham Cathedral sits atop a peninsula formed by a loop in the gorge of the River Wear. It's surrounded by some of the older departments and colleges of the university and road traffic on the narrow Bailey, which climbs up from the market place, is limited by a system of tolls. So there's a feeling of isolation from the pressures of work and commerce, which becomes the more acute on reaching the south side of the Cathedral. Here, an imposing stone archway gives access to solid-looking buildings and gardens around a 'village green'. To the left is the Chorister School, where a young Tony Blair received his education. To the right, a narrow lane leads to the Cathedral cloisters; and part way down this lane, a wooden gate in a tall wall carries a tiny sign that bears the title of the man with whom I have my appointment.

I find myself in a well tended garden: a tranquil enclosure within a tranquil enclosure in an area already cut off from the city hubbub. I climb a short spiral of stone steps and ring the bell at the imposing door. What if there's no-one there? The cleric's PA comes to the door and smiles. 'Mr Turnbull?' She takes me through to the most wonderfully peaceful sitting room, whose walls are festooned with hundreds of books. There are so many that all sound in the room is muffled. Books defineth the man and this collection tells me that here is a sympathetic and intelligent man with many interests outside his ministry.

I await his arrival, sitting on an unpretentious sofa that may have seen better days. He enters and sits on a straight-backed chair a couple of metres from me, placing his tall frame casually behind a small round mahogany table. His secretary brings tea and, but for my enduring nervousness and reticence, I would probably be chuckling at finding myself part of an archetypal scene from countless ecclesiastical sitcoms. My insanity would chime nicely with any of them: Derek Nimmo tries to hide my presence from the ferocious dean in the 70s classic, All Gas and Gaiters; Dawn French indulges my madness in the Vicar of Dibley; only Father Ted is dafter than I am.

The important man I am meeting, however, is well briefed as to the reason for my attendance and is a good listener as I tentatively embark on the story of those crazy few days that led to my breaking down in Ripon Cathedral that August Bank Holiday evening. I ask myself what I am looking for from this meeting: I want to know that my cry for help, if that's what it was, in the scribbled letter I wrote to the Canon at Ripon did not simply fall on deaf ears, or blind eyes. I want to know what the Church's view might be on meetings with loved ones beyond the grave; what its perspective might be on the good works my brother Malcolm carried out in his lifetime. And, I decide, what might be a believer's view of the notion that my brother might somehow have anticipated the approach of his death, prompting my mother, in turn, to talk about some kind of premonition of her own.

At no time as I hesitatingly embark on the story am I made to feel stupid or that I might in any way be wasting the time of a senior cleric with what, at the end of the day, might be dismissed as the fevered product of a troubled mind. He nudges me gently towards more rational explanations for my experiences, but they are explanations that nonetheless permit the excitement, mystery and mystique around the notion of some form of 'contact' with a lost loved one. I tell him of having found myself in a swirling vortex, in which channels of communication had been opened up, providing direct links not just with the matter from which my brother and indeed my most distant ancestors were hewn, but also with the very instructions that informed the behaviour of that matter, in a way beyond the current ability of science to understand. He listens attentively, but then he offers more prosaic, terrestrial interpretations.

'The channels opened up might be channels into your own subconscious,' he ventures. In my 'heightened spiritual state' I might have been more open to engaging in a dialogue with a subconscious, in which my brother's legacy resided: less a guardian angel and more a reminder of my better instincts; of my defining moral DNA.

'I am clear that events and dialogues happen within ourselves,' he says. 'We need to notice that we are in a heightened state: we can be quite dysfunctional in some ways; be deeply distraught, but we can be quite open to hearing things that we might not otherwise hear. So it does not mean that what you heard should be discounted; you may have had a manic episode, but it does not discount what happened. God is able to speak to us through our dysfunction, mental trauma or bereavement. Probably you do need to do something about this.'

I tentatively venture to raise the subject of my mother's premonition. Had Malcolm himself perhaps forseen his own demise?

'There is good evidence of people sensing they may die.' He tells me a story of a woman he had met once, only to hear that she had died of a massive heart attack two days later, despite having no previous symptoms. The following day he received a letter 'as if from beyond the grave' in which the woman spoke of her conviction that she was going to die. 'The body has a sense,' says the cleric. But, I wonder, can the body really sense that it is going to be killed in a road accident in a few weeks' time?

I find it helpful to listen to a man of faith gently coaxing me to look, seemingly paradoxically, for more rational explanations both for my brother's death and for my 'meeting' with him.

We move on to my conviction that my brother asked of me that I visit Archbishop Desmond Tutu and seek Malcolm's beatification. The cleric corrects me on my misapprehension that beatification means much the same as canonisation. I guess I'm relieved to learn that I perhaps do not need to travel to South Africa, as beatification may comprise more a simple blessing, albeit one that, in Roman Catholic terms at least, may be a first step on the road to canonisation.

But perhaps the best thing about our chat is one of those coincidences of which I have become increasingly and so deeply aware… This emerges as I tell the cleric about childhood visits to the town of Alnwick, in Northumberland, and how Michaela and I discovered a beautiful little church at Old Bewick, out on the moors, when we were trying to make sense to ourselves of Malcolm's death.

'I know it well,' he says, recalling an earlier time in his own ecclesiastical career. He begins to speak of his own interest in the Scottish saint, Margaret.

'My mother's name,' I interject. The cleric continues, explaining that St Margaret was wife of King Malcolm III of Scotland, and mother of David. Margaret, whose Malcolm was present at the laying of the foundation stone at Durham Cathedral in 1093. Malcolm, who, with another son, died in battle with the English at Alnwick, where a cross commemorates the event, this being followed soon afterwards by Margaret's death, perhaps from a broken heart.

Margaret; Malcolm. It is all starting to feel a little uncanny.

The Dean urges me to visit St Margaret's Altar while there is still natural light in the Cathedral, and to view the painting commissioned by the Cathedral of Margaret and David, as part of its ninth centenary in 1993. It is by the British-based Portuguese artist, Paula Rego, and, I am warned, I may find it sinister or disturbing. But the senior Churchman sees the painting rather as inspirational, and testimony to the hardship of its time, and indeed the lot of women in those days.

Eager to see the work, I bid my farewells. 'I'm sorry if your initial cry for help didn't induce the response you needed at that time,' says the Churchman. 'Come and see me again,' he adds, shaking my hand warmly.

Rego's Margaret, painted in oils, on aluminium, shows a gaunt, hollow-eyed Margaret not long before her death in November 1093, aged just 48. She looks 90, if she's a day. As my new acquaintance himself put it in a sermon in 2005: 'She is gazing into the far distance, as if her sights are already set on the next world.'

Margaret and Malcolm are, of course, not the only important figures in the history of Northumbria with strong connections to Durham Cathedral. This is where the followers of St Cuthbert eventually arrived with his remains, after their long, long meanderings throughout what we now call northern England and southern Scotland.

And so I kneel at the shrine of St Cuthbert and reflect on my own small place in this very large, perhaps infinite, cosmos. It is some time since I last visited the Cathedral and so I venture also to the Lady Chapel at the opposite, western, end of the building. There I find a Muslim family, paying homage to Mary, and I am reminded very clearly of the common heritage of the so-called Abrahamic faiths. Mary was, of course, the divine mother of the post-Abraham Muslim prophet, Jesus.

I take the main door out of the Cathedral, cross College Green, where students are now returning from lectures to the more traditional Halls of Residence in the old city. My own lecture is yet to begin, however. For I am on my way to hear a talk by the world-renowned cosmologist, Carlos Frenk, who is Director of the Institute of Computational Cosmology, here at Durham University.

That I am able to combine these two disparate missions here today in Durham is the product either of good fortune, coincidence or divine intervention. I make no judgment one way or the other.

I take my seat towards the front of the lecture theatre and am thankful that I have been able to arrive in good time. Professor Frenk is clearly a big ticket!

I am here because, as ever, I am fascinated by the confluence of the rivers of faith and science, and what better bit of science to look at than the very huge bit that is the Cosmos itself. And

Frenk is huge within the field of cosmology: he and three colleagues are credited with proving the existence of cold dark matter, thereby offering an explanation of the distribution of the tens of thousands of galaxies within the known universe.

Frenk is going to talk this evening not just about cosmology, but also about his work in the context of the great seat of learning in which we find ourselves, and in the context of the universal quest for knowledge that has driven religious and non-religious thought across millennia.

Professor Frenk arrives at the podium and begins to talk without notes: he speaks English like I presume he must speak Spanish, which is his first language, having been brought up in Mexico. That is to say he talks quickly, eliding his words, but exuding immense enthusiasm for his topic.

He begins with the very unrevolutionary observation that, yes, the universe is very big. Very, VERY big, in fact. 'But it is actually essentially a simple entity. Size and complexity are very different things, and one of the great mysteries is that the laws of nature, the laws of physics that we have discovered here on Earth, for some very profound reason, seem to apply everywhere in the universe.'

Frenk and his colleagues did their work on proving the existence of cold dark matter back in the 70s and 80s at a time, he reminds his audience, when cosmology barely existed – at least as a serious and respected branch of science. 'We knew about the Big Bang, but that was all we had. We didn't know what the universe was made of and we had no idea whatsoever of how galaxies had come about. That was a big mystery.'

He tells how his team explained that mystery; the discovery that dark matter was responsible for the cosmic web – the intricate pattern of filaments holding galaxies together in 'clusters'.

He recalls the challenge his team faced in achieving recognition for their almost heretical theories, but, he says, 'We progress in science by eliminating possibilities until, if you are lucky, you are left with the correct one.'

I think of Holmes instructing Watson: 'When you've eliminated the impossible, whatever remains, however improbable, is the truth.'

'We were heretics,' he continues. 'Scientists are about the intellectually nastiest people around, and that's the way it has to be. Science is organised scepticism and that's the power of science. If an idea gets through this filter then there must be something to it.'

I sense in this echoes of my discussion with Anton about Montaigne. Scepticism is as essential a component of what I might venture to call 'good religion' as it is of science, surely? And, as if on cue, Professor Frenk moves on to the question of 'why in Durham?'.

'Durham,' he says, 'is a very unusual place: a place with immense history and architectural heritage second to none – and an incredible Cathedral that dominates the city. And the kind of work that we do at the Institute for Computational Cosmology resonates with the work that they do at the Cathedral. We think about the universe; we think about the beginning of everything. Well, that's what people in the Cathedral also worry about.'

I walk back up the hill to the station feeling uplifted. When I arrived at Priestley House I was obsessed with this idea of twin paths to Faith – a rational, scientific path and a spiritual, religious one. Now here was one of the greatest scientists in the world saying the same thing. And this on a day in which a great religious man felt bold enough to suggest to me that there might actually be a scientific explanation to my meetings with Malcolm.

CHAPTER 30

To the hall of the mountain king

Friday, October 22, 2021

'So, once again, we arrive at the dock after the boat has sailed,' said Felix, as he and Michelle took on board the apparent news that Jameela was now in Vulcano, with none other than Lord Lindisfarne himself.

'No, Felix, this time YOU left the dock only for the boat to arrive the next day…'

'But Valentina was so emphatic about Victor and Jameela never travelling together…'

Michelle held up her mint julep in front of Felix's eyes: 'And what colour is this, my dear Felix?'

'Green…'

'And green means?'

'OK! Enough, enough, don't you think I feel bad enough already? And anyway, Little Ms Perfect, it's not like you've never been tricked on this journey of ours?'

'Really, and when was that?'

'Michelle, that's enough – it's getting us nowhere. Let's look at this new stuff on my Lifeline.'

Felix and Jameela were no nearer solving the mystery as to who might have created the fictitious poet, Saville Walton, but the bard had posted again on Felix's page.

'Twas in the land of midday dark;
Intrepid voyagers did anchor drop;
And there, where civilised life doth stop;
On adventure true did they embark!
SW 1852

'To me, Felix, that feels like one very good reason why we should NOT go to this Svalbard place, wherever it is. We know this Saville Walton guy is just a scam, but we don't know whose scam or why.'

'But on the other hand, there's what we overhead from Monique and Nils, which seems to suggest maybe we should go there…'

In truth, what they had overheard was snatches of a conversation, including such phrases as 'drone attack'; 'Svalbard servers'; 'Ned Tackler'; 'they mustn't be allowed to go there'; 'we can cut them off!'; 'they'll struggle to get there at this time of year'; 'what they're doing is a clear threat to the programme'; 'Jameela is going to go there herself'.

Of course, half a conversation could lead to a half correct conclusion and Felix, however green, was prepared to accept that the case for heading the High Arctic was at best circumstantial.

'How about we split up? I can stay here on the beach while you put your thermals on and go to Svalbard.'

Felix gave her a withering look.

'More seriously, Felix, I could go to Vulcano…'

'Curiously, both of these would appear to be somewhat hotter than Svalbard. Should I view that as coincidence?'

'OK! While, seriously, I think that Svalbard is the worst of all the bad ideas you have had so far, I actually think it may just be the right thing to do. And, for the sake of solidarity and mutual support; and because I have never been to the Arctic, let alone in darkness, I think I should go with you.'

She continued: 'I think we're getting towards the end-game and I'd be worried if you went alone – seriously! I don't want something awful to happen to you and I don't like this talk of drone attacks.'

With this much agreed, they reflected on what Nils and Monique had told them after their presence in the Aurora building had been recognised. About their reasons for going beneath the radar, both were candid: an Aurora-stimulated disappearance suited their personal lives for different reasons – Monique to escape overbearing parents; Nils, because his father's activities in apartheid South Africa had been exposed and he felt extremely uncomfortable about them.

Further confirmation that Kenny was alive and well was also a welcome boost. But on the subject of Jameela they had been utterly unforthcoming and were certainly not ready to share further information as to the nature of the telephone conversation that had been overheard.

The journey to Svalbard was going to be a bit of a budget-buster, but at least they wouldn't need to hurry too much to catch the evening flight the following day, from Mahé to Doha. Rightly or wrongly, even the suspicion of the end-game approaching seemed to give Felix and Michelle licence to push the boat out a little and, well, get drunk...

Having accomplished this, Michelle had one of those rare moments of lucidity that can occur in the midst of inebriation and, rummaging among the contents of her day bag, produced once more the piece of paper that Greta had given to them at Wasdale Head.

'Look at this,' she said with a note of triumph, turning the paper over to reveal the four-line verse that had been scribbled on the back.

Ye may travel all ower t'world
In a quest for both knowledge and love
But your guidance shall come from above
Born upon the wings o' a dove.

'My god, Michelle, it's our friend Saville Walton!' said Felix.

'Or our friend, Ned Tackler, perhaps,' suggested Michelle. 'Maybe an early prototype penned in the walkers' bar at Wasdale Head.'

'In which case we really are being led by the nose,' said Felix.

It was with heavy heads that they signed in for breakfast the following morning. Felix kept it simple, with fruit, a small bun and toast from the communal kitchen; Michelle kept it simpler still, with fruit juice and a dry cracker.

'We are idiots on 7,000 different counts, Felix, my dear! We should let our loves be; let these putative relationships remain unrequited forever. Or fly off to the Moon together; whatever. I feel really rough and we've more than a day of travelling ahead of us!'

But Felix was barely listening. 'What was it you said about not running away the next time something happened, Michelle? Look over there! Oy, Rahman! Come here! NOW!!'

This time the young man did not run away, but slowly raised his head from below the railings around the verandah, where Felix and Michelle were taking their morning-after snack.

'Come here, please Rahman,' repeated Felix. Rahman slowly climbed over the railing and walked towards Felix, who gestured to him to sit on an empty wicker chair.

'Why have you been following me?'

'Because I am hoping that you will take me to my sister.'

'Are you alone?'

'Yes. I have left home.'

'You've travelled half way round the world on your own? You can't be more than about 16 or 17…'

'I am 18. I am much younger than my brothers and than Jameela or my other sister.'

'Where did you get the money from?'

'I drew from my savings on my 18th birthday. Before that I was with my cousin, but he tired of all this…' Rahman made a sweeping gesture, as though to sum up the entire thus far fruitless pursuit of Jameela across continents and oceans.

'You must love your sister very much.'

'Mr Felix. My brothers and my mother believe my sister is being punished for betraying her faith and marrying an Englishman. I am young but I believe I can make my own choices. Suppose my sister did do something wrong. Is it right that I too should be punished for that? That my whole family should be punished? She has been most unfortunate and perhaps she made bad choices, but I believe our Lord is a forgiving God and he would not wish her to suffer further. I do not believe he would wish our family to suffer further for no good reason.'

'Why did you keep running away from me'?

'I thought you would send me home...' Rahman bowed his head, as though ashamed.

'I probably would have,' said Felix. 'But now I wouldn't have the heart to do that. However, the place we are going to next is not for a young man like you. And if anything were to happen to you I could not live with the guilt or with the accusations of your family.'

He turned to Michelle. 'What to you think?'

'I think Rahman should stay here until we tell him where to go to meet Jameela.'

Rahman did not protest, but merely shrugged.

'We will communicate with you by an encrypted thread on Blather and we'll update you each day until we know where she is,' said Michelle. 'Do you have enough money left?'

'I still have £1,000.'

Felix sighed, knowing that, with the flights north, their own funds were now running low. 'I will leave my credit card details with the owners here but, please, do not abuse it.'

'I will respect you,' said Rahman, who then looked Felix in the eyes and asked, 'Why are you travelling with a beautiful woman if you are in love with my sister?'

Felix laughed: 'Michelle is my sister in unrequited love, Rahman. She is looking for a man called Kenny who may be with your sister. There is no sin in a man and woman travelling together…'

Rahman merely shrugged. 'You have shared a room together,' he said accusingly.

'My god, you have been watching us closely! Yes, we did share a room. In fact, we had to share a bed together but nothing more: she was on her side of the bed and I was on mine…'

'I wouldn't do it again, Rahman,' said Michelle. 'He snores!'

It was at the absolute insistence of the hotel owner that Felix, Michelle and their new companion found themselves aboard an ancient Mini Moke, heading out of the village and over the hill towards Anse Source d'Argent.

'You can NOT leave La Digue without seeing it,' she had insisted. 'It was where they filmed that famous Bacardi commercial. Go there now before the crowds arrive.'

They reached the beach by descending a long but surprisingly straight track, arriving at the little bay of white sand, punctuated by sculpted red and grey granite blocks. It was, as promised, quite stunningly beautiful.

'Do people still drink Bacardi?' queried Michelle.

'I think we've moved on to designer drinks produced by small companies that could never afford to bring a film crew out here,' Felix replied.

Had he not been told about the ad by the hotel owner, Felix was sure that some subliminal memory of the location and its distinctive crossed palm trees would have been stirred.

The beach was already busy with bathers taking selfies and Felix wondered what it would be like if it got really busy. He and Michelle disappeared behind separate palm trees to change into their swimming costumes and wash the remaining cobwebs away. The idea of staying here rather than heading for the Arctic was acquiring growing appeal, and it was perhaps fortunate that the tickets had already been paid for. Indeed, even Michelle's suggested trip to the Moon would probably be more pleasant than Svalbard in late October.

Rahman was sticking closer to Felix than to Michelle, and Felix couldn't help thinking that he was being very closely observed, lest he demonstrate anything more than 'professional' interest in Michelle, who – Felix had to concede – did look pretty good in her bikini.

He doesn't look bad in trunks, really, thought Michelle, as she emerged from behind her tree. Maybe we should have just stayed here. Even that trip to the Moon feels more appealing than Svalbard...

The shallow waters were very warm, and alive with brightly coloured fish of many shapes and sizes. Felix wished he had a mask and snorkel; and more time. But even this quick dip in paradise was enough to remind him that it was good to be alive.

'I found a message in a bottle,' said Rahman, casually, when Felix walked back up the beach. He was holding up what Felix recognised as a vintage Bacardi bottle, with its telltale bat logo and wispy italic type.

'Where did you find it?' he asked.

'It was under the roots of this tree,' replied Rahman, pointing to where the sea had undermined the palm.

'Do you think it was washed there, or did someone deliberately put it there?' asked Felix, just as Michelle joined them.

Rahman shrugged and passed the bottle to Felix, who removed the cap easily. The bottle may have been old, but it had not spent 30 years in the ocean, of that much he was sure.

'You can buy vintage Bacardi bottles online for a couple of hundred quid, tops,' said Michelle.

'How on Earth do you know that?'

'I'm a barmaid, remember!'

Felix pulled a twig from the scrub at the back of the beach and poked inside the bottle until he was able to edge the note inside towards the neck. He inserted his finger and hooked it out. It was written on paper that had the look of having been deliberately aged.

Felix unrolled it, revealing a faded picture of what looked like a Soviet housing complex, somewhere in Siberia. Behind it rose a triangular mountain, while – in the foreground – there was a broken down bus, its tyres flat and windows cracked. It had that round shape and sloping back, reminding Felix of illustrations in those post-War Soviet feel-good picture books.

Beneath the picture was a single word in capitals, in Greek or, more likely, Russian: ПИРАМИДА.

Beneath that, Felix read the words: Bon voyage, mes amis!

And below that it said: N'importe quand; à n'importe quel endroit; n'importe où.

'No matter when; no matter which place; no matter where... What's that supposed to mean?' said Felix.

'Any time, any place, anywhere!' said Michelle. 'Don't you know your classic drinks ads. 'It's the right one, it's the bright one, it's... MARTINI?? It's the wrong bloody drink!'

'Someone is going to an awful lot of trouble, don't you think?'

'Someone who must be on this island, surely.'

'Someone in Aurora, methinks.'

This time, they had been unable to get beyond the outer security at the Aurora base and so the question as to who there might have planted the message in the bottle remained unanswered. With the clock ticking and their important questions still unanswered, Felix and Michelle headed back to the jetty, leaving Rahman to walk back up to the little hotel.

Before long they were back on Mahé, from where the onward journey proved a little less onerous than they might have anticipated, thanks to their remaining in similar time zones and travelling through the night.

From a rain-washed gloomy Oslo, it was less than two hours to Tromsø, where they made a short ground stop, before heading out over the Barents Sea.

Even in the orange early afternoon twilight before the onset of Polar Night, the view on the approach to Longyearbyen was mind-blowing, with endless ranges of snowcapped mountains filling the windows.

The Captain came over the Tannoy to warn passengers that the landing might be a little bumpy, owing to frost damage to the runway. But – in the event – Felix felt it had hardly merited the mention and suspected the announcement was just a way of telling those on board they were arriving at the edge of the civilised world.

The taxi was smart and black: the driver, rather less so. He sported a huge white beard, from which protruded an unlit pipe.

'Have you booked a room,' he asked, in perfect English. He let out a long sigh when Felix replied that they had not.

'I will take you to the Radisson Blu and there you may take pot luck, my friends. It is busy in Svalbard, even in October, these days.'

The hotel had once served as athletes' quarters at the Winter Olympics, in Lillehammer, before being dismantled and transported north. It nonetheless had more the feel of a trendy downtown city boutique than of a frontier post just a few hundred miles from the North Pole.

'You are most fortunate,' said the smartly dressed receptionist. 'We have a cancellation, so you may have our last double room.'

'We're not a couple,' said Michelle.

The receptionist shrugged.

'It's a good job Rahman didn't come,' said Felix.

'You'd better not snore,' replied Michelle.

Showered, changed and refreshed, Felix and Michelle returned to the reception desk with the photograph from La Digue.

'That is Pyramiden,' said the receptionist. 'It is an abandoned Russian or Ukrainian mining town. Do you wish to visit? It is not so easy to get there at this time of year.'

'How difficult is not easy?' asked Michelle.

'Well, there's even a hotel close by now, but it is closed for winter. But you could go to the offices of Spitsbergen Travel, on the main square, and see if you can charter a helicopter or a fishing boat, but both of these will be expensive.'

'Or?'

'Well, perhaps you could go over to the Karlsberger bar and ask around and see if someone could take you more cheaply. Sometimes there are Russians coming by boat from Barentsburg and they might take you for a price… And you will need to advise the Sysselman and take a gun.'

'Soosselman? Gun? What's all that about?'

'I've no idea 'chelle. Really, I haven't. Let's go and speak to Spitsbergen Travel.'

'People go to Pyramiden in the Summer, or they go in the Spring by skidoo, when the fjord is frozen,' said the travel agent. ' You would need to hire a helicopter and travel at mid-day.'

'How much would that cost us?'

The woman sucked her lip and made a clucking noise before replying. 'You will need to speak to the company at the airport, or I can do that for you, but I would say about 10,000 an hour.'

'Ten thousand!' exclaimed Felix. 'Pounds or dollars?'

'No, Sir, kroner. About $1,500 dollars for each hour.'

'We were told we might find somebody who could take us on a boat if go to a bar.'

'Karlsberger? Yes, or in Svalbar. You may find Russian fishermen there, but it is not something I can recommend. Or perhaps you may find someone who will hire you a RIB, but I can not recommend that either. Not in October. It is not safe.'

'And if we go, we have to tell someone called Soosselman?'

'The Sysselman. Yes, the Governor. If you go outside the city limits at Longyearbyen, the Sysselman must know. And you must take a gun… for the polar bears,' she added in response to Felix's quizzical expression.

'I see…'

As Felix and Michelle left the agent's office, they were greeted by a sight that had crept up in the short time they had been inside: the dark sky above them was filled with great shimmering curtains of dancing green light.

'Wow Felix, the Northern Lights – amazing!'

They watched spellbound as the lights came and went and rods of other colours briefly appeared. All around them people came and went, casting their eyes skyward only for a short time. For the 'natives', it seemed, the Northern Lights had lost their novelty.

It was just a short walk to the pub and a blast of chatter hit them as they edged open the door.

The clientèle comprised an odd mix of young people in trendy expedition clothes and older men, possibly miners. A third group comprised men, of varying ages and talking Russian.

Buying beer at the bar, Felix and Michelle then took the bull by the horns, moving between the Russians in turn until they found one who could speak English.

'Pyramiden?' frowned the fisherman through a thousand weatherbeaten wrinkles. 'They no longer wish us to sail to Pyramiden.'

'Who doesn't?'

'The people at Barentsburg. The mining company no longer holds the lease there, so they do not wish Russian citizens to travel. I could take you, but there is a risk, so it would be expensive.'

'How much?' asked Michelle.

The man scratched his chin. 'Fifteen thousand.'

'Kroner?'

'No. Dollars, my friend.'

The milky rays of the sun illuminated the southeastern sky as Felix and Michelle surveyed their surroundings the following morning. If you could ignore the patches of slush and snow, the overhead mining relics and water pipes conveyed on stilts above the permafrost, Longyearbyen – Longyear's Town – might have been a Wild West frontier post. But this was the Nasty North, at once untamed and yet, in places, deceptively serene.

They had risen early, to snow flurries, and visited the travel agent, where they had booked a helicopter for two hours, starting at midday. Then they had visited the Sysselman's office and discovered that 'he' was not a man, at all, but a woman of perhaps 60.

'We do not advise travel to Pyramiden any more,' she told them. 'The Russian mining company was looking after the site but they have put this in the hands of a third party and they are not receptive to visitors.'

'Can you stop us going there?'

'No, I can only advise. And my advice is that you do not go. If you insist on going, your pilot should await you with the rotor turning. And your pilot will take guns for all of you.'

It took no more than 20 minutes to fly across the fjord to Pyramiden, where the snow-covered flanks of the conical mountain (the pyramid) glowed orange in the faint sunlight, refracted from beneath the horizon and seeping over the mountains to the south.

The town itself was deserving of its 'ghost town' tag. The helicopter landed close to the chunky Soviet housing blocks. Between blocks, a bust of Lenin faced down another monument depicting a polar bear. Towards the east stood the skeleton of wooden staiths that must have served to load vessels with coal until the mine closed after the collapse of the Soviet Union. Beyond the dock you could see a glacier. Dirty debris suggested it had retreated some distance in recent years.

There appeared to be no sign of human habitation as Felix and Michelle walked from building to building, Felix carrying a loaded rifle on his shoulder. Most of the doors were unlocked: one revealed an abandoned sports hall, a vaulting horse still standing amid its rubbish-strewn floor. An empty swimming pool, its tiles cracked and falling, occupied another building; a surprisingly well maintained cinema, a third.

The residential blocks too had the air of eerily awaiting new occupants.

It was a story that repeated itself until Felix and Michelle arrived at a long, quite low, white building, towards the foot of the mountain. This time, the door did not give. It had a small box fitted just to one side of the door, however, which opened easily to reveal a shiny metal pad.

'I just wonder,' said Felix, placing his hand on the pad and looking into a camera above the door, similarly shielded from the weather. To his surprise, the door gave a click and a buzz and swung open.

'How on Earth did you do that?' exclaimed Michelle, astonished.

'My Midas touch! It's a trick I learned in Ahmedabad.'

Felix and Michelle entered the building and then went through a second door to a large room replete with banks of computers. The room was filled with light but was eerily soundless.

'The lights are on but nobody's home,' said Michelle.

'We know from Ned that these are Aurora's "old servers", but the place is clearly maintained, so where is everyone?' said Felix.

'Do you think Ned would have told his captors about this place if he had known there were Aurora staff on site?' wondered Michelle.

'That's a good point. But let's take a look at that last block.'

Felix was referring to a smaller building not far away. Once again the door responded to his magic touch. On a further door inside, a sign hung from the handle. It read: 'Back in five minutes!'

Inside they found a neatly arranged sitting room and then a series of bedrooms. All were recently tidied, as though the owners had gone on holiday and didn't expect to be back any time soon.

They went outside again and crossed to an ugly, square building, which thrummed to the sound of a generator. A huge oil tank stood beside it, and heavily insulated pipes carried the fuel to the generator building. A gauge on the side of the building suggested enough fuel to last for quite some time.

Felix and Michelle returned to the helicopter and asked the pilot if he could fly the short distance to the dockside. There they found a RIB moored beneath the tall structure. It could not have been there long, as waterproof thermal suits lay haphazardly across its seats.

They returned to the dock side and looked over towards the glacier, the view partially obscured by an old bus, like the one in the picture. They walked over to it and then round to the other side.

'Don't look!' shouted Felix. But Michelle had already seen what he had seen: a huge red stain spread across the thin snow that covered the ground.

'Oh my God, Felix, I think I'm going to throw up!'

The source of the colour was clear: Felix guessed he was looking at the remains of two people, but there was not a great deal left, save two skulls with pieces of flesh hanging off and vacant, staring eye sockets. There were pieces of torn clothing, the odd bone and three boots.

'I think they must have forgotten their guns,' said Felix.

At the pilot's instruction, they had taken pictures of the bodies and the pilot had radio-ed ahead to the Sysselman's office.

'You must report there as soon as we return to Longyearbyen. They are on their way to investigate the crime scene and pick up the bodies now.'

'Crime scene?' said Felix. 'Will they charge a polar bear?'

'We don't know if these people were already dead when the bear found them,' said the pilot.

Not for the first time, Felix began to wonder what they had actually got themselves into – their experiences had ranged from the mundane to the bizarre, from the quietly safe, to the decidedly edgy.

'This is a very serious matter, Mr Werrybether,' said the Sysselman, stern-faced. 'People have been found dead on Norwegian soil and we do not know who they are. And it appears that the guardians of Pyramiden have disappeared without trace.

'You see, when a settlement is abandoned here, the rules require that it be demolished and the site be returned to nature after ten years. So ten years after mining stopped and the people had all returned to the Ukraine and Russia, the mining company, Arktikugol, took a look and decided it would be cheaper if a small number of people returned here so that they could say that the site was still in use. That was the way it was for nearly another decade until Arktikugol passed responsibility for managing the site to another party. We do not know who this other party is,' she concluded, with a resigned shrug.

I do, thought Felix and Michelle together.

'So,' continued the Sysselman, 'if there is anything at all that you can tell us, then it is essential that you do so. And I would ask that you do not leave the island until we have concluded our initial investigations.'

'I think I would have preferred to be held against my will in the Seychelles,' said Felix, sipping from a glass of Spanish Bodegas, which, he had noted, came in at a cool 1,400 kroner. That said, there were many more expensive wines on the extensive list at Huset, which claimed to have "one of northern Europe's largest wine cellars".' He took another sip and oozed in his poshest voice.

'But I have to say this one goes quite exceptionally well with the Svalbard reindeer, darling!'

'Yeuch, you beast!' said Michelle, who had opted instead for the local Isfjord cod.

'I could have chosen the Svalbard bearded seal,' retorted Felix, to a withering look from his companion.

Michelle had played hardball with the Sysselman on learning of what she called their 'house arrest' and insisted that they be given a 'subsistence allowance' for as long as they were held without charge.

Huset, which had once been the town's only pub, and a pretty down-to-earth one at that, was now, without the slightest shadow of doubt, the finest restaurant within 600 miles of the North Pole.

'Before we both get utterly drunk on ridiculously expensive wine, we need to work out what we're going to do,' said Michelle.

'I think we need to tell someone, anyone, at Aurora what's happened. I can't really believe that the Norwegians don't know who's running the show at Pyramiden. How long do you think it will be before they know if those guys were shot by a bear or by a human?'

'Dunno,' said Michelle. 'I guess that may depend on whether they have to bring in forensic guys from the mainland.'

'Could be days, then…'

'My suggestion is that we call Ned, because we can…'

'I'm not sure that we can do that. Greta had his VSP. And anyway, do you think we can we trust him?'

'No, we can't, but I don't see that we really have any alternative.'

And so it was that Felix called Ned's VSP number, which was still on his own VSP.

'Hello, this is Ned Tackler's VSP…'

'Greta, do you have any way of getting hold of Ned? It is very important.'

'Why, hello Felix. It is nice to hear your voice. What is your trouble?'

'My trouble, Greta, is that Michelle and I are being detained in Norway in relation to a potentially suspicious death at a location associated with the Aurora…'

'Oh my goodness, Felix. That does not sound so good.'

'That is an understatement, Greta. Listen, you have Ned's VSP and on it there must be big names at Aurora. You must tell them that we think that the men who kidnapped Ned have been killed, possibly murdered, but possibly by polar bears. You must ask somebody to contact us urgently.'

'Yes, yes, that is understood, Felix. I am on the case, as you say, right now!'

'Mr Meredith, we have a second room available now, if you require.'

'What do you think, big boy? said Michelle.

'Behave yourself! Look, we're starting to run out of funds, Michelle,' said Felix. 'There's a limit to how many helicopters we can hire. I think we should stay in one room.'

'He's the last of the great romantics, my boyfriend,' said Michelle with a knowing wink to the receptionist.

They were now on Day Three of their enforced captivity on Svalbard.

'Why don't we go and have a look at the world seed bank?' suggested Michelle.

'Because you can't actually go inside it,' replied Felix.

'Even so, we may never come here again in our lives!'

'Even that would be too soon for me!'

'Oh Felix, how could you? It's beautiful and extraordinary. Don't tell me it doesn't excite you!'

'OK, OK, I know. I'm grumpy because I would have preferred to stay here of my own free will...'

'Mr Meredith! There is a call for you!' interrupted the receptionist.

It was the Sysselman. 'Mr Werrymether, the forensic examination of the bodies has proved inconclusive and we are going to have to send the remains to Oslo to get more answers. I thank you for the information that you gave to me in your statements, but I am wondering if there might be any more that you can tell us to help in our processes of identification. Perhaps you could come once more for a chat…'

Felix was unsure what more they could tell the Sysselman without disclosing to her a secret that they both suspected she already shared. It was a game of double-bluff.

'We are both looking for our lovers, who appear to have run off together,' began Felix. 'We believe her father is after them because he disapproves and he has been following us to try to reach them.'

'No, Felix,' said Michelle. 'You can't say that. It would be a disaster. It would be better for us to just deny that we have any knowledge at all…'

She was interrupted by a call on Felix's VSP.

'Felix Merryweather?'

'Yes.'

'This is Victor Turnbull.'

Later that same day, Michelle and Felix were on their way again, bound for Oslo, then on to the Faroe Islands, via Copenhagen. Things had moved quickly after the unexpected call from Vic Turnbull – a call that had culminated in an invitation, or perhaps an instruction, to meet with him in the Faroe Islands, and had quickly been followed by a call from the Sysselman saying they were now free to leave Svalbard.

'I think it's important that we meet, Mr Merrydew,' Victor had said. 'I've been impressed by the tenacity of the pair of you, but there are important things that you need to know. And, equally, there are important things that I need to learn from you.'

Perhaps the best thing, in Felix's eyes at least, was that Victor had paid for their Business Class flight to the Faroe Islands.

'I'd been starting to really worry about our kitty, 'chelle, I don't mind saying.'

The trip from Svalbard also included two, yes two, rooms at the Radisson Blu, at Gardemoen Airport, and when Felix and Michelle went to eat, they were pleasantly surprised to learn that dinner was on Vic too.

'So, all of a sudden, we are not secret squirrels in pursuit of some mysterious transnational fugitive – we're VIPs. What's going on Felix?'

'I no longer know, Michelle and nor do I think I really care. I think we at last have our goal in sight!'

The Airbus swung into the tight fjord to the north-west of the airport on the island of Vágar, on the western edge of the Faroe Islands, marooned in the North Atlantic between Scotland and Iceland.

'That was some approach,' said Felix, as they held onto their coats and battled through the wind towards the elegant little terminal building.

'If you say so,' Michelle replied. 'I had my eyes shut!' The Faroese passengers descended in a big scrum upon the duty free shop, leaving Felix and Michelle to reclaim their bags and make their way through Customs.

As promised, a young man was waiting for them, with a sign that said Merrydew and Merrydew – Victor's idea of a joke, since it was only hours since Felix had corrected him about his name.

'Rog Reid,' said the young man. 'I look after things here for the organisation.'

He appeared to carefully avoid mentioning Aurora by name, as he left them under the canopy outside the terminal, while he went to fetch his car. Powerful gusts of wind buffeted the car as they drove through a couple of villages and over a hill, before descending into a deep tunnel.

'We're now on the island of Eisturoy,' said Rog, when they emerged after a few subsea kilometres. More, shorter tunnels followed, before Rog took a right turn onto a road that climbed steeply up the mountainside. There was so little flat land to be seen that Felix and Michelle wondered how space had ever been found to construct an airport.

'This is where it might get a bit hairy,' said Rog. 'It's very windy, as you'll have noticed, and the road is high up and can get a bit icy. The main road to Tórshavn goes straight through the mountain now, but we are on the old road…'

Another ten minutes or so and they had arrived in one piece at a single-storey turf-roofed building. Even in the fading twilight, they could see that it commanded an exceptional view down a long fjord. The enigmatic Victor Turnbull was waiting for them at the door.

'Come in, come in! Welcome to my humble abode – or one of them!' he ushered them inside and asked Rog to take their luggage to their rooms. 'We don't stand on ceremony here,' said Victor. 'Go freshen yourselves up and I'll see you in, say 20 minutes, in the dining room.'

The dining room had been decorated in what they took to be a traditional local style – a long wooden table dominated the room, while the walls and floor were of white-stained wooden boards. Knitted pieces of artwork interrupted the white, alongside dramatic sea and landscapes, which Felix was admiring when Victor came into the room.

'William Heinesen,' said Victor. My favourite Faroese artist: I have several of his works. He was a man of very many talents: landscape painter, cartoonist, novelist, poet, playwright. But, you know, this is one of those places where necessity often commands that people have more than one job! I myself lead a global philanthropic organisation but I am also a regular nice guy… Ho, ho! Now, let's begin with a rhubarb beer, then we've a few Faroese nibbles for you. There's some fermented lamb, which you may find a bit of an acquired taste. My wife can't abide it, but she's in Australia at present, so we needn't worry about her. Rog and I have become quite partial to it! Then there's nibbles of bacalao and local crayfish and horse mussels, so enjoy! Rog will join us in a moment.'

As the meal progressed – with slow-cooked Faroese lamb and then a crumble of local rhubarb – the whole thing appeared to Felix to be more and more surreal. It seemed like they had just happened to call in on an old friend, while they just happened to be passing through a remote archipelago in the middle of the Atlantic. He tried to catch Michelle's eye, but she had by this time enjoyed her Faroese aquavit chaser and was already oblivious to the niceties of formal conversation. He watched Victor and Rog for a few moments, and it appeared that neither of them was exercising much restraint either.

Oh, what the hell!? he thought and tipped back his aquavit.

'So, Felix, my friend; Michelle – here's to all of us, eh?!' Victor raised his glass and chinked each of theirs in turn. 'I believe some of my people have not been making your lives too easy of late…' He left his observation hanging in the air, so Michelle thought that perhaps she should try and fill the vacuum.

'Exactly which of your pipple, I mean peeeple, are you referring to?' asked Michelle, her cognac glass swishing in her hand.

'Well, Michelle, I'm not sure I wish to name names, but you maybe have an idea. One or two of them have taken the idea of protecting colleagues from the cut and thrust of the outside world rather to extremes. But I've been impressed by the determined way in which you've responded and there might well be positions for both of you in the organisation should you choose…'

Felix couldn't believe what he was hearing.

'Now, hang on, are you telling me this crazy expedition we've been involved in hasn't come from the top of your organisation?'

'That is precisely what I'm telling you, but we must, for the moment, put that to one side as matters of far greater import have arisen. Let's begin with the unfortunate incident with our friends from the American mafia and their little adventure up in the Arctic. One of our operatives sent them up there on a bit of a wild goose chase, but he was wrong to do that... he thought it was a non-operational base, but it was, and still is, operational. We have obligations to the Russians, who own the mine, and ultimately the Norwegians, who are the sovereign power. So we had to get our people out and then arrange for a bit of an unfortunate accident to happen. It's just lucky there are a lot of hungry bears around until the sea freezes over for winter. The Sysselman has been very understanding, I must say! Lovely woman, lovely woman! But having to put all the servers up there on standby wasn't a great thing and the timing really couldn't have been worse. You see, we find ourselves privy to a lot of, shall we say "conversations" around the world that we get to "overhear" thanks to our equipment. It's all purely a by-product of the work we do on taking the sting out of some of the more, shall we say, "fanatical" religious orthodoxies. But enough of that for now! You must both be very tired – we'll start at eight and Rog will take you up the mountain and bring you up to speed.'

For once, Felix regretted having his own room: how he would have loved to pool his thoughts with those of Michelle and come up with a shared interpretation of a bizarre evening.

In the absence of such shared reflection, he might have hoped that they could at least compare notes the following morning. But it was only at 7.45 that Michelle eventually appeared, somewhat the worse for wear and, by this time, Felix was already finishing breakfast at the table with Victor and Rog.

At eight on the nail, Rog took Felix and the fragile Michelle and ushered them into a Land Rover. They retraced their route from the previous afternoon, before turning onto a narrow twisting, and, at times, vertiginous road. Striped poles on either side of the road suggested it would at some point be under snow, but today it was just wet, though not so windy as it had been on their arrival at Vágar.

After a few kilometres, the narrow road became more determined in its ascent, passing first through an electronically operated gate and then angling up the steep, rocky flanks of the mountain until, finally, they entered into a large cave that had been hewn out of a near vertical cliff face.

'Welcome to Sornfelli!' said Rog. This used to be known as ISCOMFAROES, back in the days when it was part of Nato's forward radar defence system.' He pronounced the acronym 'I-com Faroes' and explained that it meant Island Communications Faroes.

'Nato moved out with the end of the Cold War, but the civilian Faroese authorities still manage the radar in the white dome, which you will have seen as we drove up. You can reach the dome, up this ladder, or by the little "railway".'

The 'railway' to which he referred looked like a railway, but actually rose vertically up the cliff face and, today, disappeared into cloud.

'Let's go in,' said Rog. 'Apparently there were a lot of myths back in the Nato days about just what existed inside the mountain and new myths sprang up when Nato left. One of these was that Nato filled the whole labyrinth up with concrete before leaving.'

'And did they?'

'Well, yes and no,' said Rog. 'They didn't fill it up with concrete, but they did seal off some tunnels that may have contained equipment that was sensitive at the time and might have proved too difficult to dismantle and remove. But, at the end of the day, concrete is less hard than granite, if you get my meaning...' he added enigmatically, as he escorted them into an anteroom.

'OK, Rog,' said Felix, 'let's cut to the chase... What actually goes on here and what are we doing here today? Why does a secret organisation suddenly admit two people to its darkest secrets?'

'Darkest secrets? Yes, I suppose you might say that,' said Rog. 'But first, a little bit of history. So far as the Faroese people are concerned, we conduct research here into the whale species – and, specifically into the sustainability of pilot whale populations and whether or not heavy metal pollution impacts on the local population are recent or endemic, and what the effects might be of the consumption of such pollutants by humans.'

Felix thought he had caught all of that. Michelle, handicapped by an acute, if temporary, brain impairment, did not.

'But what are you actually doing?' asked Felix.

'We are Aurora's Anti-Fundamentalism Unit,' said Rog. 'And the unit does pretty much what it says on the tin. We seek to propagate, via social media and other channels, the most benign versions possible of all the world's great faiths for the express purpose of rooting out, or maybe shouting down, extremism.'

'You are kidding me!' said Felix. 'I thought Aurora was all about practical aid in the Third World, saving the rain forests and promoting good science and stuff…'

'That's exactly what you are supposed to think! Our cover's actually pretty good!'

'But does it work?'

And here, Rog chose to pause and reflect.

'One of the reasons why Victor is here now is because I requested a meeting with him. And his presence here is also indirectly related to your friend, Jameela.'

Felix's ears pricked up and even Michelle focused on listening a little better.

'Vic wanted Jameela on the team because of concerns that I had raised that, if you'll pardon the expression, some of the very "fundamentals" of the anti-fundamentalist initiative were actually flawed.'

'For instance?'

'Well, to be blunt, it seemed we were actually making things worse, rather than better. For example, we did a lot of messaging that was designed to promote the practice of Sufism in Islam, which reflects, if you like, a desire to return to the primary tenets of the faith through devotion to Allah. Now, before you tell me that that sounds like fundamentalism by any other name, the really crucial thing is that Sufism transcends both the Sunni and Shia branches of Islam, and that, as you can imagine, was critical.'

'So what went wrong?' asked Felix.

'Well, it was never our intention to create a "new prophet", but by channelling a lot of messaging through a supposed learned teacher that we had created, it did open the door to the interpretation that there was indeed a new prophet and that in turn stimulated a movement that set out to find this new prophet, whose whereabouts were, unsurprisingly, unknown. You will not be astonished to learn that some of those with vested interests in the status quo chose to see this evolution as a threat and branded it heretical. That is why you may have heard about the persecution of the Hakimists.'

'No, I hadn't.'

'Well, the "prophet" we had inadvertently created came to be known as Abd Al Hakim, or servant of the wise.'

'Where has this persecution been? I've heard nothing at all about it.'

'Well, I think that with all the other big stuff that's been going on across the Muslim world it probably got rather lost, but there have been killings – I hesitate to say massacres – in both Sunni and Shia countries and, most recently, a minibus full of Hakimists was forced off the road in Gujarat.'

'In Gujarat? That's a bit close to home!' said Felix.

'Yes, it was. This happened only just after you left Ahmedabad, Felix. A day or so later and you would undoubtedly have heard about it.'

'So you mentioned Jameela's involvement…'

'Yes, her view is that the entire notion of influencing people's thought and trying to nudge religions back towards a "truer path" is flawed and always doomed to failure.'

'I suspect she's right there.'

'Well, we have had some successes – in Pakistan for example. But on the whole I'm beginning to think she is, as you say, right. And certainly that is now Vic's view, which is why all work on the programme is currently on hold. The only problem with that is that it rather leaves me without a job!'

'Perhaps you should get back to the whales.'

'Well, actually, there is something else that we are doing here, which you may have heard about, and which I can show you. Follow me!'

They left the anteroom and returned to the entrance chamber, where Rog ushered them into a lift. Felix noted that there appeared to be a number of floors, both above and below the one on which they were now. Rog selected one of the higher floors and the lift shot up, leaving their stomachs behind. It was an ambiguous feeling for Michelle, given that she and her stomach were not on the best of terms.

'So, here we are, not far below the radomes on the mountain summit, and this is where we do our monitoring work.'

'Why do you do that? Isn't that what governments spend all their time doing.'

'It is, indeed, but what they don't do is then share the findings of this monitoring with their citizens.'

'And you think they should? That we should all know the minutiae of, say, what GCHQ finds out?'

'Well, yes and no. I can't support the wholesale release of information as happened in the Edward Snowden case, and Assange, of course, turned out to be just a crazy libertarian in the pockets of the Russians. But I am going to show you something...'

They entered a small room filled with computer screens, at which half a dozen men and women were working.

'Bella, can you show these guys the Waddington material?'

The woman called Bella made room for Felix and Michelle to share her view of her screen.

'OK, this is a drone pilot's view from the drone control room at RAF Waddington, in Lincolnshire.'

'You are kidding me?' exclaimed Felix. 'But if you can get in there, then so can others, surely?'

'Yes, of course,' said Bella. 'And they have: let me replay to you what happened two days ago in Kalamistan. As you know, the

Americans practise a "neither confirm nor deny" policy regarding what they are up to there, which means that a lot of what goes on there, if it ever reaches the mainstream media, is often routinely dismissed as "fake news". But what you are about to watch is not fake.'

Felix and Jameela observed as though from the 'cockpit' of the drone.

'This is the controller's eye view in Lincolnshire as the Reaper aircraft takes off thousands of miles away,' explained Bella. 'So far, so good: the drone is heading for a Taliban stronghold in Afghanistan; but now watch!'

Suddenly the aircraft appeared to bank steeply and head away in a quite different direction. 'This is the point at which the drone is taken over by the hackers. The RAF controller is doing everything he can to regain control, but without success.'

Bella fast-forwarded the footage. 'The drone is now flying south into Baluchistan, in southern Pakistan and on to Kalamistan, and what you can see coming into view is one of those American bases that don't officially exist. By this time the British have told their American colleagues that there's a rogue drone potentially flying towards the base, so watch what happens next…'

They watched as the drone sped on towards what was now clearly its target. They saw a helicopter take off from the base and turn languidly towards the drone, at which point the drone released first one, and then a second missile.

'These are Hellfire missiles and they're normally used to accurately target specific individual people on the ground, who are known to pose a threat. Remote summary execution if you like. But, as you can see, it seems to do a decent job as an air-to-air missile, too.'

Indeed, even as they watched, the helicopter exploded in a ball of flames. The drone swerved around the resultant fire cloud and dived towards the American base. After overflying the base the drone turned, as though to survey the damage it had caused.

'It's dropped two laser guided bombs,' interjected Rog. 'And, as you can see, it's not a pretty sight. Many casualties and, surprise, surprise, you have yet to hear a whisper about this!'

'But that's dynamite!' said Felix. 'The notion that foreign forces could hack into drones…'

'And that,' said Rog, 'is why you haven't heard about it. The trouble is that the south coast of England is just about within range of a drone based in Afghanistan. Of course, it could be shot down en route, but that would be very embarrassing, especially if the debris landed somewhere awkward on someone else's territory. So, the drone fleet is currently grounded until further notice and you're not allowed to know that. And nor do we know if "further notice" might actually mean forever. But now, let's take a break for lunch.'

They descended a short distance in the lift and exited into a corridor that led only in one direction. Felix judged this, wrongly, to be further into the mountain. However, after just a short distance, the corridor opened into a much larger room, whose far wall was built entirely of glass.

'This is our little window on the world,' said Rog. 'It's especially nice at sunset!'

Rog led them further towards the window, to a point at which the solid floor suddenly became a glass one, revealing a sheer drop to the foot of the cliffs far below.

Felix's head spun, but he gathered his rational self and walked carefully across the void to take his place at a table against the external glass wall.

'Close your eyes!' Rog instructed Michelle, as he led her shakily to the table.

'Felix, I feel sick,' she said. 'My head's spinning with all this information and with all this HEIGHT and all the drink and, oooh. I don't think I like it…'

'Eat something disgustingly unhealthy, that'll sort you out,' was Felix's not especially helpful advice.

Michelle opted instead for a comforting bowl of soup, while the men indulged in more unusual Faroese fare.

Miraculously, the clouds had now given way to bright, clear blue skies.

'That's the Trøllkonufingur, the troll's finger,' said Rog, indicating a rocky pillar on the island of Vágar, across the strait. 'And, over to the left, that's Koltur, the colt, with Hestur, the horse, beyond it.'

'Do people live on all these islands?' asked Felix, with a degree of incredulity: they appeared to rise without pause, as though straight from the depths of the ocean. 'There seems to be no flat land anywhere.'

'There are people living on 17 of the 18 islands,' said Rog, 'although some winter populations are very small. On Koltur they are talking about creating a nature park without sheep. The soil here is very thin, so no-one is sure what may grow without grazing. Perhaps there will be woodland. We don't know.'

'Do you like living here?'

'Yes, I do. The life is good here and people are happy. And I was never a big one for the sun or the beach. So I am happy with the amount of sun that we get here and even with the fact that temperatures rarely reach the high teens. And it doesn't even snow all that much, as it is mild here in winter.'

'I didn't think it was mild when we arrived yesterday.'

'Hah, that was nothing! But we're getting sidetracked into small-talk and there is something I must share with you in private.'

Back in the anteroom, in which they had first sat down, Michelle confessed to having begun to recover from her excesses and as Rog urged them to listen carefully and not be shocked, she said, 'I'm all ears now.'

'What if I told you that the footage we showed you earlier was only the beginning?'

'That would be very disturbing,' said Michelle.

'Well, you will remember 9-11,' continued Rog. To nods and frowns he continued. 'Well imagine something much worse: not just the hijacking of four airliners but an entire airline fleet that has been allowed to grow beneath the radar, so to speak, without anyone for one moment suspecting it was anything other than a legitimate airline.'

'And that's actually going on?' exclaimed Felix.

'Yes, we've picked up the Sigint. Have you heard of WCA? Worldwide Cargo Airlines?'

Felix and Michelle shook their heads.

'It's a transatlantic cargo airline with a hub in Riyadh and, over the years, it's picked up a whole range of US government contracts, so it's seen as pretty much part of the establishment.'

'And it's not?'

'No. The groups that evolved out of Al Qaeda have been playing a very long game, but now they are positioning themselves for a grisly conclusion.'

'Do you mean what I think you mean?' asked Felix.

'If you mean multiple attacks on the US mainland, then yes, that's exactly what I do mean.'

'So why hasn't US intelligence picked this up if you have been able to?'

'We think they may have, but we don't know for sure, as the communications have been very carefully encrypted.'

'Well they have to be stopped; the Americans must be told, surely?'

'Yes, Michelle. That's the conclusion that we've reached. It's just how do we tell them without putting our own operations at risk?'

CHAPTER 31

Full circle

Tuesday, May 10, 2011

My visits to Anton have become a little less frequent as I begin to feel that I have a full recovery in my sights. I recognise that the purpose of my consultations has been to provide me with an emotional parachute so as to help lower me gently back to earth. Without this parachute I might have fallen more precipitously and suffered injury in the form of more acute depression, or even another manic episode.

As it is, I do now recognise more clearly that I have been depressed, to the extent that all experience appears to have a dullness to it, as though I were looking at the world through dirty spectacles, or listening to birdsong with a swimming cap on my head.

I guess Anton has rescued me from this state of mind by encouraging me to think more positively about myself and by stimulating my interest in new subjects, including – I guess – the evolution of philosophy, which is, of course, one of Anton's own pet loves.

I now have the confidence to branch out a little myself: Michaela and I have begun to travel again. We have revisited together places of fond childhood memory, in an effort to help me to reconnect with my younger self; we have taken gentle recupcrative weekends at nice hotels across England and Scotland; and we have stepped further afield, to Amsterdam and Paris.

On my own initiative, I have explored new paths to self-discovery and have visited an alternative therapist who combines homeopathy with Eastern mysticism.

Indeed it was indirectly as a consequence of this last course of action on my part that I first began to feel that I had perhaps got close to the end of the road with Anton. It was back in March and I was eager to tell him about my new therapeutic adventure.

'What the hell are you doing that for, Vic? It's hocus pocus. Complete hocus pocus!'

I tried to explain to him that I found it helpful and uplifting, but he would have none of it, and started going on about evidence bases and such like. Now, I know that talk therapies are proven to work, but isn't that really just because someone has taken the trouble to measure and compare outcomes in a quantitative way? I would suggest that some so-called alternative therapies have not been thus compared for the simple reason that 'treatment' is very closely tailored to the needs of each individual 'patient'. So, it's not really possible to set up a control group and measure efficacy.

It wasn't so much what Anton said to me as the forcefulness with which he said it that began to persuade me that I could begin to do without his interventions and, so, I resolved to cut our weekly consultations to monthly. Since then I have visited him for my April consultation, at which we discussed time in some detail. Specifically I am, as you know, curious about the way in which time appears to pass at different speeds in different circumstances.

But this is about far more than simply the perception of time moving quicker when our minds are fully occupied; and indeed the converse inference that if we are bored, or perhaps depressed, time may appear to move more slowly.

Notions around the nature of time are of great interest to people in Anton's field, he reminds me. Specifically, it is about the relationship between the individual 'patient' and time that is key.

Talk therapy can seek to release patients from a form of captivity in which time has 'stuck', leaving them trapped and unable to embrace a more promising future.

I rather enjoyed the example that Anton gave me, quoting a therapist who had written on the subject of how, as a small child, he had dismantled the only clock in his parents' home to see how it worked. The therapist in question, Marek Gitlin, had been amazed to discover that Time 'still happened' even though its physical manifestation – the clock – no longer worked. It reminded me of the broken clock in my room at Priestley House.

This conversation steered us gently towards the concept of the passage of time in literature and now encourages me to consider our conventional parameters of time as something of a constraint upon our thinking. I think of the town of Macondo in Gabriel García Márquez's One Hundred Years of Solitude, where time seems to exist not like a river moving forward, but rather as simultaneous and recurrent waves; some characters seem over-endowed with memories, while others seem devoid of recollections that might provide them with context.

We slip to Proust and I ask Anton if he feels that it would be right for us to say that an event in the past never took place until such time as we chance to remember it and thus duly record it. Is this kind of way of looking at time just an extension of the paradox of Schrödinger's Cat? I wonder.

Similarly, is Karl Ove Knausgård's extraordinary biographical novel, Min Kamp (my struggle), a 21st century version of À La Recherche Du Temps Perdu? And, then again, is this collective navel-gazing just covering the kind of ground that Montaigne first trod?

'Of course,' Anton reminds me, 'all writers enjoy the luxury of playing with time. Take Ulysses. There is probably a degree course there, not on the study of Ulysses per se, but on how to read Ulysses. I've heard it makes more sense if you start in the middle.'

With such burning questions in mind, I have, since that session, looked at all these works and recognise that I am not yet sufficiently at peace with my own being as to lose myself in this kind of self-indulgent reflection. I retain as a legacy of my illness the idea of time not so much running out as running away from me – and leaving me saddened by my inability adequately to conquer it by achieving what I wish to achieve in the time sensibly allocated to doing it.

That is why today I shall conclude my relationship with Anton by taking some time to myself to explore themes that I have come to associate with the days and weeks leading up to my illness.

In particular, I am keen to satisfy my urge to understand more about what lies behind Neolithic stone circles.

In parallel, though quite separately, I am interested in the journey undertaken by the disciples of St Cuthbert: I have noticed that there are many churches dedicated to the Northumbrian saint in the Eden Valley, and some of these are close to Anton's home in Dufton. So, before I set out, I do a little research and discover that there are indeed at least 17 churches dedicated to St Cuthbert scattered across Cumbria, and a third of these are in the Eden Valley.

I decide that, after our session today, I shall visit just two of them – Dufton and Milburn – because they share in common their isolation from the communities they purport to serve and hence the probability that they were first built on much older sites of worship.

It has been a warm spring and – on our side of the Pennines at least – a dry one. Things west of the great divide have been a little less certain, but today is one of those magical ones upon which to crest the ridge at Stainmore is to see unfold before you surely the most remarkable vista in England.

Bizarrely, as I descend into the Eden Valley, there's a play on the radio that uses short snatches of Nat King Cole's Route 66 as scene-changers. I find myself reflecting on the extraordinary moment on a previous trip when my radio appeared inexplicably to change channels for the sole purpose of catching the Stones' version of that same classic. It is, perhaps, a measure of just how far I have come in the last few weeks that I am prepared to concede that I might just possibly have imagined the whole episode.

I have resolved that I shall take no crap from Anton today: I will stand my ground on subjects on which we may diverge. That's code for my saying that if I want to go and seek solace in the company of a Vietnamese snake charmer or a Cherokee porcupine breeder, then that's my decision and it's no-one else's place to criticise me for it.

In the event, my consultation turns out to be something of a damp squib: we spend more time talking about Anton's impending move to the other end of the country, precipitated by his partner's change in employment.

'So, if I need you, can I find you?'

'Of course, Victor, of course: I expect I will still come north from time to time to fulfil the needs of existing clients, but it's an exciting time for me – a new location, new patients, new challenges.'

I recognise this as a signal: the time has indeed come for me to slip my painter off and sail away.

In these days of declining church attendances you have to admire the tenacity of the parishioners in places like Dufton and Milburn, just a tad to the north.

Neither church obeys the loose rule that it should be at the heart of the community and Dufton's is probably a mile outside the village. While precise stories of the origins of both churches and the reasons for their location appear lost in the mists of time, what seems consistent is that both are supposed to have been built on the site of former sites of religious importance. Both can trace their origins to Norman times, but it's all a little hazy before that. But then we need to remember that the Normans did a good job of rewriting history.

Dufton apparently exhibits strong evidence of Celtic origins, while a small figure in the wall at Milburn is thought to be from Roman times. Only the latter claims specifically that St Cuthbert's followers paused on the site with his coffin.

I find both of them – St Cuthbert's, Milburn, at the very edge of the village, and St Cuthbert's, Dufton, in the middle of nowhere – extraordinarily spiritual and in each I sit a while and do something I haven't done for some time: I talk to Malcolm and light a candle in his memory. Some of you might call it prayer.

At Milburn, there's a small collection box, made of thick Perspex. My attention is drawn to a bank note inside it. It's not that long since I was in America and so I'm familiar with what a $10 note looks like. This one, however, does not look quite the same. I put my glasses on and get as close to the Perspex as I can and notice that it bears the tiny inscription 'Series of 1934 A'.

'How very strange,' I think. I look in the church's little visitors' book and am even more bemused to find that the latest entry is written by some visitors from America. From Amarillo, Texas, to be precise. Nothing too remarkable in that. Except that the date in the right hand margin is 1952.

'Must be someone having a joke,' I muse, leaving the church, singing to myself the words from the 70s Neil Sedaka song. Or was it Tony Christie. I forget. 'Is this the way to Amarillo?' I sing, but struggle to recall the next line. Something about a pillow. Or was it an armadillo? And then there's 'Marie, who waits for me…'

My reflective behaviour at the churches is indicative of a more general sentiment about this part of the world. I feel today that not without good reason is it called the EDEN Valley, such is its tranquility and feeling of connection with a world of mysticism.

And so it seems to me entirely fitting that my next stop this late morning will be at the stone circle known as Long Meg and her Daughters. The interesting thing about this particular circle is not just that it is the largest in Cumbria, but also that Long Meg – a monolith of local red sandstone, set apart from the circle itself – is of different stone to her granitic daughters, who are arranged in an ellipse to the north-east of her.

Arriving in the village of Little Salkeld, I stop at the old water mill, where they still grind flour the traditional way, and treat myself to a nice early lunch, with good coffee.

Long Meg is at the edge of the village, just a short walk from the mill, and I arrive to find just a couple of Druids, sitting in quiet contemplation at different parts of the monument.

It is a beautiful afternoon and I walk to the centre of the circle and sit facing the Pennines, to the east, with the sun on my right. The stones are casting only quite short shadows, reminding me that we are approaching midsummer. What a long way I have come in the nine months since my saga began.

I amuse myself by singing a little song to the tune of Lloyd George New My Father, or Onward Christian Soldiers, if you prefer.

Long Meg and her Daughters
Standing in a field
Hit them with a chisel;
They will never yield!

'Love the lyrics,' says a voice behind me. I turn, but I'm struggling to distinguish him too well, with sun shining so brightly from over his right shoulder. So I climb to my feet.

'Sorry mate,' I say, 'I hope you're not a Druid – you might find my little ditty sacrilegious!'

'No,' laughs the man, whom I put in maybe his late 30s. 'I'm just a curious visitor.'

'Where have you come from?'

'Just over the top, from York. I felt I needed a few days off and a bit of head-space to sort out some issues in my life…'

'It's a good place to come and sort out issues,' I say. 'I've had some quite big issues that I've had to deal with, but I'm on the winning lap now. I think this is a wonderful place to come and just reflect on life, don't you?'

'I really do, yes. It's the first time I've ever come here. Of course, I know about Stonehenge and all that, but this place is really a bit special, and so much more peaceful than the Big Daddy.'

'So tell me, I'm sorry, I don't know your name, why are you looking for head-space, as you put it?'

'OK, well it's kind o' personal, but I've been seeing this woman on and off for a long time. We used to be quite serious but then we finished it and now we're really just kind of friends. But since I moved up north, closer to where she now lives, I have a feeling that what suits me may not be enough for her.'

'And don't tell me: you don't love her and, worse, you don't think you ever will. Am I right … ?' I leave the blank space deliberately so that the man can fill it with his name.

The man misses my cue and instead goes straight on to answer my question. 'God, yes. I only wish I had been able to be as perceptive as you are. That way I might not have got myself into this stew.'

'Well, take it from me, if you have given enough time for love to blossom and it hasn't, then it never will. But you must stop giving her hope, because, for as long as you do that, she will for ever pin her hopes on you and that just would not be fair. My name's Victor, by the way.'

The young man looks at me in a slightly strange way. 'And mine is Felix. Felix Merryweather.'

I have the strangest feeling imaginable: it is like the strange moment on the A66 the other week only multiplied by ten. I feel a shiver as though someone was walking over my grave.

'Are you OK, Victor?' he asks. 'You look as white as a sheet…'

'Yes, yes, I'm fine. But I just had the most extraordinary case of déjà vu when you told me your name, as though I had met you before in some other life.'

'That's a bit weird,' says Felix. 'I've got to say I felt a bit the same myself, though not enough to turn me white… Do you think maybe it's something to do with this place.'

I think, maybe he's got something there. 'You could be right. You know local legend has it that Long Meg and Her Daughters were turned to stone for profaning the Sabbath, although in reality they arrived here long before anyone had even invented the Sabbath.'

'I think she must have profaned a lot more than the Sabbath to have had all these daughters. How many are there?'

'I don't know, Felix,' I say. 'My guess is about 60. What do you think?'

'I'm going to say 58, but let's count and, I tell you what, the one who's closest gets a pint.'

'OK,' I say, 'let's start at Long Meg and count round the circle in opposite directions.'

A few minutes later and we find ourselves facing each other back at Long Meg.

'I counted 59,' says Felix.

'I make it 61,' I say. 'I guess that means we'll have to have a recount.'

This time we set off in the opposite direction to our previous counts, once again returning to Long Meg.

'That's weird,' says Felix, 'I make it only 58 this time.'

'And I make it 62!' I tell him.

We count for a third time and this time I get to only 57 while Felix clocks 63, our highest tally yet.

'Let's ask a Druid,' I suggest, and we walk over to a strangely familiar woman who appears to have been mildly amused to watch our antics.

'So you don't know the full story of Long Meg? That if you ever count the same number of stones twice, the spell will be broken and the stones will come back to life?'

'That's extraordinary,' I say. 'I would have said "ridiculous" but seeing has to be believing!'

'Well, we'll just have to buy each other a pint, I guess,' says Felix. 'Where shall we go?'

'I dare say that will depend on what your plans are from here,' I say. 'I'm heading for Keswick to visit the stone circle at Castlerigg and maybe I'll stop at Mayburgh Henge on the way.'

'And I'm staying in Keswick too. There's a talk in the town tonight about stone circles and I fancied giving it a go, although I'm meeting friends later this afternoon for a coffee. They're on their way back down south from Scotland and I thought it would be good to catch up, so we're meeting in Penrith.'

'That sounds perfect,' I say. 'Let's go to Mayburgh together, then you meet your friends and I'll head for Castlerigg, and then we'll do the beer thing this evening, OK!'

'Perfect,' says Felix, and high fives me.

Felix is parked quite near the circle, so I show him Mayburgh on the map and say I'll see him there in 20 minutes or so. From Mayburgh, it's no more than five minutes into Penrith and maybe 25 for me to get over to Castlerigg.

So it's not so long before I find myself strolling with Felix the last hundred metres or so to the henge.

'So what's sparked your interest in stone circles, Felix?'

'I'm not sure, really, Victor. Look, I quite recently started work for a company with business interests all over Europe, so I travel a lot. Before I got this job in York, I worked for myself in London, in consultancy, and I didn't get much time just for me. So, between London and York, my personal life has tended to take a bit of a back seat. In fact...'

Felix pauses and so I help him out. 'Look, you don't need to feel that you're under any obligation to tell me anything but, for some reason, I did feel that we had some kind of a connection when you first told me your name. And, for what it's worth, I have got a little bit of life experience under my belt.'

Felix takes a deep breath. 'OK. You were right on the money earlier with what you said about how I might feel towards my sometime girlfriend. My "friend with benefits", I guess you might call her. I am extremely fond of Wendy but I've had more than long enough to fall in love with her and if it hasn't happened yet, then I can't really expect that it will happen... ever.'

'OK, and...?'

'How did you know there was an "and"?'

'The connection, maybe...'

'OK, there is an "and". It's "and" all the other women in all the other cities I've been meeting since I started this new job.'

'That sounds intriguing…'

'Well, there's a woman in Copenhagen, Katrina, who I met quite recently and we quite like each other. In fact, if it wasn't for the distance I'd be willing to give things a bit more of a go…'

'But you're frightened to do that in case she abandons her work, friends and family and comes to England and then things don't work out.'

'Yes, well read, Victor. And, if I moved to Copenhagen, I wouldn't want her to feel responsibility for me.'

'Ah Felix, have you never heard the expression: "Fortune favours the brave"?'

Felix laughs. 'Of course I have, but clearly I'm a commitment-phobe. It's just that what I want to find out is whether that's deep within my psyche, or if it's more just that my lifestyle isn't compatible with a serious relationship. And, anyway, there's more… There's Ute, in Berlin, and Genziana, in Florence.'

'My goodness, Felix, you are a busy boy! How do you feel about these two?'

'Well Ute's very pragmatic and, to be honest, I'm not sure she would really care either way. Now, Genziana… I can't really say. When I see her she's always very keen for us to go out together in Florence and really makes a point of us being seen in public, and she holds tightly on to my arm and kisses me a lot in public.'

'Ah, Felix. It can be so comforting when people's national stereotypes come to the fore… She's Italian, that's how she would behave. And I suspect the other two are probably behaving to type too! But has it never crossed your mind that you might be being just a little bit…' He pauses for effect. 'Greedy?'

'Yes, Victor, it crosses my mind like a busy shuttle in a loom. That's why I'm here – I'm trying to take a step back and reflect about where my life is heading on a personal level, and whether I might just place a heavier hand on its tiller.'

'You're a great one for the metaphors, Felix. I'm starting to wonder what's coming next.'

'Wow, Victor, it looks like a UFO must have landed here!' says Felix as the great henge at Mayburgh comes into view.

'I think that may be a simile, rather than a metaphor,' I tell him, provoking a chuckle.

We make our grand entrance to the vast banked circle. It's about the same diameter, I would guess, as Long Meg, but, rather than comprising a circle of monoliths, its perimeter is defined by a high rampart, which, I believe, was most likely built a few hundred years before Long Meg, from stones taken from the bed of the River Eamont.

Once inside the circle, it goes strangely quiet and we can no longer make out the noise of the traffic on the nearby M6, which some bunch of insane philistines and vandals permitted to be built almost right next to the monument itself. Within the circle stands a single monolith at the centre of the giant UFO landing pad, while trees have sprouted and grown tall in many places, their young leaves now gently rustling in the warm south-west breeze.

'It's quite something, isn't it?' I say. 'Just being here makes you thirsty to know more. You know, I think I might join you at that talk tonight, after our little pint!'

'I think you should, Victor. And when we take that pint, it'll be your turn to tell all!'

'Ha, we'll see...' I say.

We take a few more minutes to visit King Arthur's Round Table, which good old 'legend' suggests was once believed to have been the hero king's jousting arena. I know this part of the world has strong claims in the Arthurian legend industry, and maybe it really was his arena, but if that is so, then it was an opportunist Arthur taking advantage of a structure that had already been there for many centuries.

'I think perhaps we should have looked at this one first,' says Felix. 'It's amazing, but it's a bit of a disappointment after the sheer scale of Mayburgh Henge.'

'I know what you mean,' I say. 'That's why I didn't suggest we go to Little Meg…'

'There's a Little Meg?!'

'There is indeed,' I reply. 'Do you think they built small ones and then got more ambitious, maybe as their technology improved?'

'You know, Victor, we really know so very little about the world. And you know so much about me and I know so little about you!'

'Dog and Gun at 5.30, OK!?' I say. And we go our separate ways.

It's about 3.30 when I park at Castlerigg, next to the ice cream van. If Long Meg is the Alston market place of stone circles, this is their Piccadilly Circus. Or perhaps I exaggerate rather. That latter descriptor should apply to Stonehenge, for sure, so maybe this is just, I don't know, Whitby on a Bank Holiday. Anyway, if you haven't yet got the message, there are quite a lot of people around for a week day afternoon in May and they are huddled around the interpretation boards, climbing on the stones, climbing on the stile for a better vantage, standing in groups pointing out the fells to each other.

Now, if the siting of Long Meg seems pretty random, in landscape terms, the same could certainly not be said for Castlerigg, whose situation must have been determined to the last centimetre by those Neolithic town planners 5,000 years ago. This is one of the daddies of Neolithic monuments and those who built it seem to have chosen very carefully where to put it. We are on a small plateau above Keswick and some of the Lake District's most elegant fells frame the view on all sides: Skiddaw and Blencathra behind me to the north, Helvellyn to my left and High Stile in the distance to my half right.

I read the plaques that explain how the stones became a popular destination for parties of visitors in Victorian times and how, earlier, Wordsworth felt inspired by their location. I too feel inspired today. I shall say that again, because inspiration is a sentiment that I have found in short supply these past months. But now I feel I may just about have shaken off my depression. I breathe in deeply in the way I would urge my fellow guests at Priestley House, and am soon giddy with the freshness of the clean Lakeland oxygen.

'It truly is magnificent, isn't it?' says a voice at my shoulder. I turn to find myself looking at a middle-aged woman with quite short blonde curly hair and piercing turquoise blue eyes, set behind royal blue spectacle frames. I realise she's the 'druid' we met earlier at Long Meg.

'It is; truly magnificent,' I respond, turning back again to the view. 'Almost as magnificent as the enthusiasm that you appear to be radiating,' I find myself saying before I have time to question my impertinence.

However, she merely laughs and says, 'I shall never cease to be fascinated by stone circles, especially these early ones across Cumbria. It's not just that we know so little about their raison d'être, or our admiration for the efforts that must have been required to build them, or even just their general enigma. It's that extraordinary combination of energy on the one hand and total tranquillity on the other that they can impart to us simultaneously.'

'You know,' I say. 'That just sums it up for me as well. That's exactly how I felt at Long Meg and then Mayburgh Henge earlier today.'

'Ah, yes, I thought it was you. So you're a circle-bagger, then?'

'A circle-bagger? No, not at all: I just came here out of curiosity and for the peace.'

'I'm not strictly a circle-bagger either,' says the woman. 'But I have visited the majority of stone circles in the UK and France and I think I have probably read just about every word that there is to read on the subject. But I still don't feel I have all the answers.'

The woman sighs and becomes a little reflective. 'I've been here all afternoon, taking photographs and also watching people closely to see how each of them responds. And sometimes, like just now, I feel an urge to speak to one of them in particular.'

'Why is that?' I ask. I am very curious.

'Well, sometimes I just get a feeling. And I may see an aura. I'm one of those "lucky" people who can see others' auras, you know, their energy fields, though I don't know if it is lucky or not. I don't always see what I think the owners of the auras would like me to see.'

I am obliged to ask whether she saw my own aura.

'I did and I still do, and I can see that you have suffered recent difficulties, but now I can tell these are increasingly behind you and your aura is being successfully repaired.'

'You're actually quite correct: I'm impressed. Who else's aura have you seen today?'

'Well, that's an interesting question and I wouldn't normally single anyone out, but there was a young woman here earlier. The reason why I remember her so well was because she wore her aura like a broken heart. She was one of the loneliest people I have seen, although she was working hard to hide the fact.'

'Why had she come here?'

'Well, she told me that she felt she was obliged to pay the price for major errors of judgement in her life. She was an Asian lady who told me she had married an Englishman who had then betrayed her trust. But, of course, she had brought shame upon her family and now she finds herself in limbo, rejected by both her new and her old worlds. Like so many, she was looking for peace and space in which to reflect and perhaps to take a new turn at a crossroads.'

'Could you do anything to help her?'

The woman laughs. 'I'm not a therapist, Mr...'

'Turnbull, but call me Victor.'

The woman does not complete the sentence, merely saying instead, 'How very extraordinary; how very very extraordinary.'

'What's wrong,' I ask.

'I have just had the most extraordinary feeling of déjà vu,' she replies. 'It quite sent a shiver down my spine.'

I reply: 'I had that earlier when I met this guy at Long Meg. He's called Felix something...'

Now the woman's jaw drops. 'This really is very strange: I have a recurrent dream in which I meet a man called Felix Merry-something or other.'

'Merryweather, that's his name! I can assure you he really does exist! Now, you were telling me about the Asian lady.'

'Yes, I was telling you about Jameela Durrani.'

Now it is my turn once again to feel a shiver.

'You too?' asks my new companion. 'I'll tell you a little bit more about this Jameela woman: she got talking with someone else whose aura I could see – a woman called Anne Buchanan. They left together. Listen, I'm Flora Mackenzie and I'm giving a talk in Keswick at seven thirty this evening at the high school. It's a special late season addition to the Keswick Lecture Society's winter programme. I think Jameela and Anne will both be there.'

'And so will Felix and I. And, just by the way, I know Anne Buchanan.'

I meet with Felix as agreed at the Dog and Gun and can't wait to tell him about the extraordinary events at Castlerigg. The bar is busy with a mixture of walkers rounding off a pleasant day in the hills, and others who have changed out of their designer outdoor gear ready for a night of more applied drinking. Dogs on leads seem to be taking up an awful lot of the scarce floor space.

Felix listens patiently to everything I have to tell him and then says, 'I think you might find this a bit hard to believe.'

'I sense a "but" coming,' I say.

'But I have to tell you that I know Jameela Durrani and I think I know, I mean I do know, Anne Buchanan. I used to work with Jameela. She's a very nice woman, but she had some very difficult things in her personal life and I felt extremely sorry for her the last time we met.'

'Flora Mackenzie, the woman at the stone circle, gave me a bit of insight into that,' I say. 'But my impression was that this

Jameela woman had not met Anne Buchanan, the one it now appears that both of us know, before today.'

'That could well be the case – I wasn't suggesting that they had met. The reason why I know Anne is because she is the older sister of Wendy Buchanan: the Wendy you advised me to abandon.'

'Hey, now steady on,' I say. 'What I actually advised you to do was to be honest with Wendy and stop stringing her along because it's useful for her to be around for a bit of sex when you aren't in Copenhagen, Berlin or Florence, if I remember the list correctly. But look, if I'm honest I'm not looking forward to seeing Anne myself, either. Our last exchange was decidedly frosty.'

And so it is that I find myself explaining to Felix the ins and outs of the difficult subject that we didn't quite get onto earlier today, beginning with that dreadful day at the stone circle on Orkney when I called Anne in her office in Aberdeen. I then find myself wondering how on earth I am going to tell the story of today to Michaela without her thinking that I have, once again, completely lost the plot.

There is a very good turnout for Flora's talk a little later. She quickly demonstrates her encyclopaedic knowledge of her subject and, as I watch her there, a penny finally drops: she too has something in common with Anne Buchanan. The only reason why I have failed thus far to recall what it is they have in common is because I was so ill and unable to focus my attention when she had been the woman who returned my misplaced camera to me at Skara Brae, on Orkney.

This realisation causes me to try to piece together the bones of the telephone conversation I then had with Anne Buchanan that same day. My apprehension about meeting her face-to-face later this evening distracts me from what Flora is saying.

However, I am aware that she is, in effect, conducting her audience on a guided tour of Neolithic and Iron Age circles throughout the British Isles, with her sharpest focus reserved for the many Cumbrian monuments.

She catches my fuller attention when she recounts her experiences at Castlerigg, touching again on the circle's sense of great energy, combined with absolute tranquillity and serenity. And then she says, 'I know this may sound like a heresy when we are so very close to Castlerigg, but I have to tell you that there is another such circle in Cumbria that may just be Castlerigg's equal and perhaps even its superior. It is called Sunkenkirk, or Swinside – and that is not to confuse it with the settlement called Swinside, in Newlands Valley, so close to here. This Swinside is close to Broughton-in-Furness and its situation is almost as near to perfection as that of Castlerigg. But it has more stones than Castlerigg – and a sea view. It is no Mecca for visitors, as it is a little hard to get to, although that may change when new access arrangements are completed.'

Felix leans towards me and whispers, 'Why do you think it is that I feel I know all this already? This Swinside circle: I feel like I know it.'

'Shhh!' says an angry face turning from the row in front and causing far more disruption than Felix's whispered question to me.

I reflect on what Felix has just asked me and realise that it is just another symptom of the truism that there will always be more questions than answers.

I linger nervously after the talk concludes and suggest to Felix that perhaps we might cut and run and go and grab a bite to eat. But Felix is keen to stay, he says, and catch up with Jameela, even if he must also run the gauntlet of Wendy's sister.

Before long Flora joins us. 'I have remembered, Flora, that we too have met before: on Orkney, when you were good enough to return my camera to me.'

'I know that, Victor, but I didn't wish to remind you of that today: you were so very, very ill that day. I could see it in your aura, and that is why I was so very pleased to see you and your aura so much better today.'

Soon I can see Anne Buchanan and the woman I presume to be Jameela approaching us. Given all that I have heard today I am surprised to see that Jameela's face looks happy and relaxed: and then I realise that there is a reason.

'Felix! What on earth are you doing here? How wonderful to see you! What a truly amazing surprise!'

Felix's face is a picture: he is wearing the kind of contented smile more usually associated with cats and cream.

Anne's words for me are rather less effusive but equally not nearly so bad as I might have feared. In the first instance, she is clearly more preoccupied with the curious coincidence of her sister's sometime boyfriend appearing to be a long lost best friend of a woman she has only met for the first time a few short hours ago.

She begins: 'I reflected a lot after that telephone conversation of ours because I realised that you must have been in a pretty bad place before you would have even considered calling me.'

'I was, Anne. I was working up to a manic episode that saw me spending three weeks in hospital and quite a long time recovering afterwards. However, for a variety of reasons, I think that today I may just be better again!'

'I'm very pleased to hear that, Victor: life is too short for us to bear grievances or have hard feelings and I am sorry that I couldn't help you more that day. But, you know, my own life had gone a bit awry. I think you know I made surprising discoveries about my sexuality and, well, I'm still on a bit of a journey in that regard. To be honest, I think I rather like both men and women. Do you think that's greedy?'

I laughed. And smiled, partly with relief that there was no sense of conflict in the air. 'I really don't think greed comes into it!' I say.

'Now,' Anne continues. 'I'm not sure I can be quite so generous in what I say to this man,' she says, poking a sharp finger in Felix's ribs. 'When are you going to stop buggering about with my poor little sister?'

Felix turns a very serious face towards his interrogator and says, 'Anne, I understand your concerns and I have given a lot of thought to the way that I behave and the responsibilities I have to others, and the respect in which I should hold their feelings. All I can say is that I can do better and I will do better, but the most important thing is that from this moment forward, I shall act with fairness to myself and with honesty towards others.'

I see a collective dropping of jaws, Jameela's among them, but Felix isn't going to wait for others to seize his moment.

'Jameela,' he says. 'I think it would be nice if we went somewhere quieter together.' And with scarcely a nanosecond's reflection, they are gone.

'That's not supposed to happen,' says Flora. 'At least not yet!'

'What on earth do you mean by that?' I ask as Anne and I share baffled expressions.

'That's not for me to say, Victor, if you don't already know.'

Flora's enigmatic words still ring in my ears as I set off back to Yorkshire the following morning. After Felix and Jameela left us last night, Flora too went on her way, leaving me to share the remainder of the evening with Anne.

'What are you doing in the Lake District anyway?' I asked her.

'I needed to get out of the Aberdeen village for a bit and get some fresh air while I think about life, the universe and everything.'

I sighed deeply before telling her straight, 'You really, really shouldn't talk so lightly about life, the universe and everything. It's all far more complex than you ever thought!'

We didn't see Felix and Jameela again, so I can only speculate what they might have got up to. I think I have faith in Felix's new-found integrity, though. I only hope it is justified. I'd like to think I might see them both again and I guess it shouldn't be all that hard to track them down on the Internet. Then again, given what I now know about life, the universe and everything, a reunion may just chance to happen anyway, whether I organise it or not.

I have resolved to tell Michaela in very measured terms about the extraordinary events in Cumbria and, above all, not get too excited when I am telling her. I think that will be the best plan. After all, what has happened, has happened and surely I can't be turned in to the nutty police merely for telling the truth?

I feel good for having made this decision as the A66 takes me close to the places I visited yesterday. I decide to stop for coffee at the little Café 66, just beyond Appleby.

When I pull in to its tidy little car park, I am surprised to see it has been rebranded, and rather brashly at that. A flashing neon sign above the door says Mr Happy's Route 66 Diner. The car park is full of 1950s American cars: Cadillacs, Chevies, Buicks and strange retro pickups.

But this is only the beginning, as I discover when I push open the ranch-style half doors and see the sign asking me to please leave my gun at the door. The clientèle, mostly male, all seem to be wearing cowboy hats and there's not an English voice to be heard.

'Two fries, hash-brown, grits and eggs, sunny-side-up, with shakes – Coming up!' A young woman with blonde pigtails and a blue and white gingham apron collects the order and heads for a Formica table by the window. An ugly man with a huge moustache slaps her backside and makes an obscene gesture as she passes beneath the sign that says God Bless America. The jukebox is playing Elvis's Love Me Tender and a picture of the King is on the wall – next to a photograph of President Eisenhower.

A young woman heads for the door, followed a few paces behind by a man, who shouts, 'Marie, wait for me!'

I blink, then blink again but nobody appears to have noticed my presence.

As Nat King Cole's 1946 version of Route 66 succeeds Elvis on the jukebox, it slowly dawns on me that this is all too real to be any kind of practical joke. It is not an experience that I have any intention of sharing with Michaela.

CHAPTER 32

The beach

Jameela was beginning to find Ned's demeanour of injured innocence not just tiresome, but more than a little annoying.

'Ned, what you seem to have been forgetting in all this is that I am – look at me – a grown woman. I am, actually, as it happens, quite capable of looking out for myself. So your collusion with all these other people in this transglobal game of cat and mouse you've been playing with Felix is not in any way to be laid at my door.'

'Aye lass, but t'Foundation 'as allus bin careful to cover t' tracks o' its operatives an' mek shure t'owtside world disna' ken whet's gennin on.'

Jameela – who was also angry that Ned seemed deliberately to lay his accent on as thick as possible with non-Cumbrians – looked him between the eyes – insofar as she could do that on a Flexiscreen in a hotel room in Sydney. She continued: 'As you well know, that is what happens when the operatives in question request it for whatever reason. So you've got Nils Boateng and his embarrassing father, Monique de la Rochelle and her disapproving parents, Kenny Marchant and his complete inability to decide between two women…'

'Aye lass, 'n' tha' needs to remember that all we were doin' was ter protect ye from another disappointment after ye'd already chosen Aurora ahead o' that Felix fella.'

'And what if I might decide that I can have both? It's not like everybody in the Foundation is single or celibate, is it?'

'But,' began Ned.

'Oh look, just leave it for now, Vic's on his way to Eastertide with Rog and there are bigger issues to consider than my personal life…'

She walked to the window, leaving Ned's babble to ooze from the screen she'd hung on the wall behind her, and gazed out across the Harbour. She shut Ned's ramblings out of her mind and recalled with a certain nostalgia the way she had felt when she had met up with Felix after all those years – in another hotel not far from her next destination. She was still uncertain about whether she wanted things to go any further than they had, but, more importantly, she was determined that it was she who should be in control of events, and not Ned Tackler and his chums.

And then she found herself getting angry that she was permitting herself to be sidetracked by such personal trivia, when matters of life and death were at stake. Ned had travelled to Eastertide just as soon as Victor had completed his debrief on the kidnap episode. She was aware that Victor, for his part, had left for the Faroe Islands to meet up with Rog and, like her, was now on his way to Eastertide. Indeed he might well have already arrived. Now, however, Jameela was increasingly unsure what value there was in having flown Ned half way round the world – he'd been a hugely important element in the establishment of the Aurora Foundation, for sure, but things had now moved on, hadn't they?

'Ned,' she said firmly, returning to the screen. 'That's enough for now, I'm going to work through the WCA files and then I've got a plane to catch.'

Felix and Michelle had never known anything quite like it – the world of business jets was way outside their previous experience.

'I wouldn't normally take the Legacy on a long trip like this,' said Victor as they reached cruising altitude. 'But there are four of us, plus the relief pilot, and we can, just, make it in three legs, so it stacks up quite well in terms of both time and cost, against first class fares.'

'I still don't really understand why you want us with you,' said Felix. 'Why the big change?'

'Well, Felix, since Jameela joined my top team it's been a bit of a reality check for me… You see, I have to accept that, under my guidance, the Aurora Foundation has slightly lost its way and we have been operating inside a bit of a bubble. Perhaps it's time for us to burst that bubble.'

The Legacy made an almost imperceptible turn. 'We're just avoiding UK airspace – keep the air traffic control fees down!' said Victor, changing the subject.

Felix adjusted himself in the luxurious seat. He suspected Victor would have rather more to say on this subject. It was going to be a long conversation, he guessed, on a long, long journey: Dubai, Singapore, Eastertide Island. Michelle returned to her seat with a cup of coffee and she too settled herself, opposite Rog. As Victor noted her return, there was a sense that something of a 'big reveal' was about to follow.

'You will have read,' began Victor, 'about what I'll refer to as my "little episode" a decade or so ago. You'll know that this episode, if you like, stimulated my brain in such a way that I became a little bit "super clever" for a time. And that it was during this time that I was able to transform a fairly ordinary, under-performing technology and travel business into a global leader.

'You will also know, because I am on record many times for having said as much, that it is my view that great entrepreneurs need a lot more than just a good idea: they need the single-mindedness to pursue that idea and, perhaps above all, they need luck. In spades.

'What my episode gave me was the confidence to embrace a

very wide vision and the belief that I was absolutely right about everything, and therefore correct to pursue that vision.

'My luck was in having the right people around me, like young Rog here, for example. And in being able to acquire another business that gave us a huge leg-up just when we needed it.'

Victor paused, shifted in his seat a little and took a sip of water.

'Now, let us consider for a moment, what happens when entrepreneurs have become very successful and thus convinced that, because they have always succeeded, ergo they must always be right. Think of Sir Clive Sinclair and the death-trap called the Sinclair C5; think of James Dyson and his attempts to do an electric car better than electric car manufacturers and his obsession with the Brexit fiasco and moving UK jobs offshore; think of the disaster that was Donald Trump.

'What Jameela has helped me to realise has been the extent to which I have been becoming prone to falling into the same trap: I have tried to remain humble, but in reality I haven't been. And that is especially so with regard to the work that we do at the Aurora Foundation.'

Michelle now sensed the opportunity to tease out of Lord Lindisfarne information that might NOT have been in the public domain.

'Victor, I've read a certain amount about affective disorders and I know that you have always differentiated what happened to you from other people's experiences on the basis that your manic episode was caused by a physical injury. I'm just wondering how you found your mental health in the period immediately after your discharge from hospital. I mean, growing your business so rapidly must have been very stressful at the very time at which you were surely liable to regress into depression or even another episode…'

Victor did not respond immediately and, when he eventually did so, it was slowly and with careful consideration. 'I was very fortunate to have my deputy, Stella de Weld, doing most of the donkey work while I recuperated. But, yes, if I am really, really honest with myself and with you, what I really needed at that time was complete rest and a gradual reintroduction to the challenges of life. The way Aurora happened was the very opposite, as I think you have recognised. It did cause me stress; and sometimes that stress was simply about adjusting to my exceptional new life circumstances.

'The way that stress manifested itself was in, I now recognise, a degree of paranoia, and my defence was to protect myself and my family by building tall and thick walls of secrecy around our lives. Now, that's not actually all that unusual – Mark Zuckerberg, who created Facebook, for example, is deeply reclusive. And pretty nerdy. If you take us all, as a group, then I guess we exhibit all the personality aberrations of the population at large, but for some reason – perhaps the result of external factors, as in my own case – these "defects" become exaggerated.

'That exaggeration can be good or it can be bad: I'd like to think that, as far I'm concerned, it has, on balance, been good.'

'Do you think your personality is on the autistic spectrum somewhere?' asked Michelle bluntly, causing Felix to squirm a little uneasily, making the leather of his seat squeak.

Victor responded with a slight start. 'No, absolutely not. No, I really don't, although I do know where you're coming from. At the height of my episode I did engage in a single-minded pursuit of the goals that I created while I was in hospital: saving the world in seven days; defeating the incipient spread of the cancer to a fair society that is Freemasonry; even saving the bumble bee. But that does not make me autistic or Aspergic: these behaviours were no more than symptomatic of my mental condition at a particular point in time.'

Michelle was not to be sidetracked from her blunt line of questioning. 'Do you regret the anxiety that this must have caused at the time to those close to you,' she continued. 'Your wife, Lady Lindisfarne, and so on?'

'Of course I regret it, but that's a bit like asking me if I regret that my hair is a bit of a mousy colour rather than dashing blond or jet black. I was ill and, as in all illnesses, those close to me suffered some collateral damage for a time. But the other side of the coin is that Michaela, Lady Lindisfarne, shares in the rich new life that Aurora has brought to us, consequent in part upon my manic episode, and my sister Charlotte is part of the organisation and is doing work that she loves in a place that she loves…'

'Of course,' said Michelle. 'But isn't that a bit nepotistic?'

'Hah, you really are determined to have a go, aren't you? Michaela is a shareholder in Aurora and a Trustee of the Foundation, and my sister Charlotte was the best person for the difficult job that she does and – and this is key – I was able to trust her absolutely in a way that would have been difficult had she been recruited on the "open market".'

'If it all happened again, would you do things differently?'

'Of course I would, Michelle. Because now I have the benefit of seeing how my decisions work out in practice. There are a great many things I would do differently but I have very few real regrets: I have tried to do good – for people, for my region, for the planet. Had I not tried… had I, say, stashed all my millions in offshore accounts for my own personal use, then I would find it very difficult to sit here and defend myself.'

'And the offshore accounts?'

'OK… I don't disapprove of taxation, but I am very queasy about some of the things the UK Government does with our money. What I can absolutely guarantee to you is that not one penny of what the Foundation has ever invested offshore has ever been used for anything other than good, charitable purposes.'

'Like eavesdropping?'

Victor paused again. 'Well, that's the billion pound question, isn't it? That's what we are all going to sit down and discuss when we get to Eastertide. What are the rights and wrongs of our activities that have made us privy to huge secrets, and what would be the implications of sharing what we know or, indeed, not sharing what we know?'

'Or, in the words of Montaigne,' said Felix. 'How do we know what we know?'

'Indeed!' said Victor, impressed to find someone else who seemingly shared his own knowledge of the French philosopher.

'And the business jets?'

'Just one business jet, used when needs must. And would you rather walk?'

Bizarrely, it was only then, when the name Eastertide was specifically mentioned, that it occurred to Felix that Jameela would surely be at the meeting that Lindisfarne had called. However, he did not dare ask the specific question for fear that he might not get the answer for which he so yearned. He wondered if it would be too much to ask that maybe, just maybe, Kenny Marchant might be there too.

These and other questions – not least the one about who precisely had led him on a wild goose chase with Michelle, and the associated one about the extent to which Jameela was or wasn't aware of what was going on – he would be able to continue turning over in his mind for another 18 or 20 hours at least.

The business jet terminals at Dubai and Singapore had come and gone and the crew had rotated at each one, while the small band of passengers stretched their legs a little. Now, at last, Felix was finally able to look out of the window and see familiar Eastertide Island landmarks. As the Legacy made a sweeping turn onto the approach, he prodded Michelle awake and pointed out to her the Euphoria Hotel and the beach at Beverage Bay, where he had first worked out the identity of the familiar woman he'd seen at the hotel. The woman who, soon afterwards, had joshed him about his unusual name.

It was hard to believe that only about six weeks had passed since that day: it seemed more like an entire lifetime and he felt years older – and possibly just a little bit wiser.

'You'll be staying with us, in the Tower,' said Lord Lindisfarne, as they waited for their baggage. 'I want you both to observe our meeting, which I've convened for 2.30.' It was already about half past eleven. You can grab a couple of hours first if you want.'

Felix was too excited at the possibility of seeing Jameela again to relish a two-hour rest; he still did not dare to ask if she was already here on Eastertide.

Before too long, the four of them and the crew had cleared immigration and all were heading for the golf buggy 'taxi station'. The crew disappeared on a buggy in the direction of the Hotel Euphoria, while the drivers of a small convoy of buggies began to organise bags and people for the short ride to the Eastertide Tower.

It was just as Felix was about to board one of the buggies with Michelle that the arriving passengers on the commercial flight from Sydney exited the terminal building and began to look for their own buggy hotel transfers. Among them a youngish woman with a dark complexion and sensational long, sweeping black hair was striding purposefully towards their group.

'It couldn't possibly be THAT Felix Merryweather,' said the woman as the man she was addressing found himself quite lost for words. 'And who's this? Your girlfriend?' she added, with a nod towards Michelle.

The boardroom at the Tower was on the floor above the one on which Jameela had found herself staring out of the huge picture window just a few weeks previously. Like Felix, she suddenly felt the weight of the passage of a great deal of time – a huge, great lump of time that had somehow been crammed into a month and a half. Now, somehow, the clock had been curiously wound back to a moment before her momentous decision to throw her lot in with the Aurora Foundation's top team. She had not known then that the news of her decision would not be properly conveyed to Felix; poor Felix, who had for some reason seen something in her after a gap of so many years; something of which she herself had been unaware. Poor Felix, who was back here on Eastertide Island, for reasons of which she was only partially aware.

She had exchanged only a few words with him at the airport and then on arrival here at the Tower, where he had spoken of some kind of wild goose chase from one Aurora location to the next in the hope of tracking her down.

'Did you really care that much?' she found herself asking him.

'And did you not care at all?' he'd responded accusingly.

His words had been left hanging in the air as Jameela had said, truthfully, 'I'm sorry, but I have to prepare for an important meeting now.'

'We haven't told Rahman!' said Michelle, as they waited for the others to arrive in the conference room.

'Oh shit!' said Felix, reflecting that they had failed miserably to maintain daily contact with the young man as promised. In fact, amid everything that had happened, they had remembered only once to get in touch: from Oslo, while en route to the Faroe Islands. Now, Felix sent the encrypted Blather message he had said he would upon locating Jameela, referring disingenuously to a 'communications blackout'. He urged Rahman to travel as quickly as possible to Eastertide Island and make contact upon arrival.

One by one the senior members of the Aurora team arrived: Rog; then Stella de Weld, from the Aurora Group and about whom Felix felt he already knew so much; Michaela, Lady Lindisfarne; a woman of perhaps 50, called Charley; Jameela, of course; and finally Victor, Lord Lindisfarne himself; and a slightly older woman who looked rather like him, and was called Charlotte.

Victor called everyone round the large board table, conveyed apologies from a guy called Dave who was not well enough to travel, and explained to those assembled that Felix and Michelle were there as dispassionate observers. He thanked everyone for having travelled long distances at short notice and added that other, more junior, members of the Aurora team would arrive on Eastertide over the coming days for a personal briefing on the outcome of today's discussions. There could be room neither for ambiguity in the message nor any possibility that any detail of today's discussion might leak out. In such cases, said Lindisfarne, face-to-face discussion was the safest means of conveying decisions and plans.

His flow was interrupted only by the sudden arrival of Ned Tackler, who burst through the door behind where Felix and Michelle were seated, and looked in turn at the faces around the table.

'Good of you to turn up, Ned,' said Lindisfarne. 'Why don't you join us?' Ned pulled out the only empty chair, next to Felix. It was only once he had sat down that he gave a start, having noticed who was on his right.

'Eh lad, fancy seein' thee here!'

'Yeh, just fancy that,' replied Felix.

'OK, OK, let's get started, shall we?' continued Lindisfarne, who – for the benefit of anyone as yet unaware as to the reason for the 'summit' – then invited Rog to brief the room about the intelligence discoveries made at Aurora's various listening posts.

'So, let's get this straight,' said Stella de Weld, after Rog had presented to the table the same information that he had shared a few days previously with Felix and Michelle in the heart of a Faroese mountain.

'We believe,' continued Stella. 'No, we KNOW that there is an imminent attack planned against the USA and we know that it will be devastating, not just in terms of loss of life, but in a geopolitical sense and, knowing the unpredictability of America in these times, we are looking at something potentially far, far worse than their response to 9-11. But if we share our intelligence with America, we show our hand and disclose that we know more than we should and that in turn will unleash an unpredictable response against Aurora…'

'That about sums it up,' said Lindisfarne and Jameela in unison. 'Except,' continued Jameela, 'there's an added dimension that it is just possible that the Americans already know about this but are prepared to take the hit so as to justify a response that's already planned...'

'You mean like all those 9-11 conspiracy theories that George Bush knew beforehand?' interrupted Charley.

'Yeah, pretty much,' Lindisfarne replied.

'How about we tell the media and let them break the story?' suggested Charlotte.

'The downside to that is that the UK Government will move heaven and earth to locate the source and that could make life very difficult for the media,' said Lindisfarne.

'Well, surely that's their concern and, anyway, imagine the public backlash if the Brits ended up doing America's dirty work for it,' countered Charley.

And so the discussion continued until, after some time, Lindisfarne, in an effort to break the deadlock, suggested Felix and Michelle be invited to venture their opinions.

'I think you have an absolute duty to disclose what you know, and I believe the media is the best channel by which to do this,' said Michelle. 'But don't just use your own, that is Aurora's, media channels: take the story to somewhere unconnected that clearly has no axe to grind; the Phoenix, say.'

'And Lord Lindisfarne should himself ask for a meeting with the Editor and maybe they could talk about "sources close to the Government" or something like that,' suggested Felix. Then, pausing a moment for effect, he added, 'And maybe you need to think about whether it might be time for Aurora to return closer to its roots; stop playing God?'

Michaela was quick to counter. 'I'm not sure that we should stop, if this is an example of the kind of thing we can put a stop to!'

'And what if it's a trap designed to flush us out? An elaborate hoax?' asked Jameela.

'My team have checked out that possibility every which way we can and we don't think that's at all likely,' said Rog. 'But here's another option. I think we can create an alias for ourselves that looks like MI5 and alert the Americans that way and then we can monitor their response. And, in the meantime, Victor can be ready to deliver a secret brief to the Phoenix.'

'Are you as uneasy about all this as I am?' Felix asked Michelle in a quiet corner during a comfort and coffee break.

'You mean, do I find it all a bit hard to take at face value?'

'Yes, that's exactly what I mean. We only have one person's word for it that that drone strike we watched was genuine. If it did happen, it could have been something that wasn't exactly what we thought we saw; or equally, it might have just been an elaborate piece of CGI. And if that's not real then how do we know this other threatened attack is real?'

'The trouble is, Felix, we both know that deception, the manipulation of information and dirty tricks, are the new frontier in the battle between the various world orders...'

'So, Michelle, what are we supposed to do?'

'We just have to tell them what we think,' Michelle replied.

'How do you feel after that lot?' Felix asked Michelle after they eventually left the reconvened meeting an hour and a half later.

'A bit bruised,' Michelle replied.

'You did well, though... And it had to be said.'

Neither Felix nor Michelle could yet know the extent to which they had contributed to a pivotal moment in the history of the Aurora Foundation.

What had been clear to both of them was that – if it was indeed true that either the UK or US government, or both, had laid some kind of an information trap for the Foundation – there was actually very little that could be done about it. If the Foundation chose to say nothing, then – whether the supposed attack on the USA happened or not – it could be accused of not sharing information that might have prevented just such an attack. If, on the other hand, the Foundation revealed what it believed it knew and was actually responding to a false trail laid by agents of one or other of the two governments, then its own 'cover' would have been permanently compromised and action to shut down its operations would be likely.

Felix and Michelle had both found Rog's analysis highly plausible but could not judge whether or not it might be possible for it to be based upon a very elaborate subterfuge. The essence of the plot that had been identified was the establishment over a number of years of an air cargo operation within the USA. The conspirators had been playing a very long game: the cargo airline had operated legitimately within the USA for more than a decade and was above suspicion, thus concealing the identity of those Middle Eastern interests whose backing had supplied its initial finance.

The essence of the plan was now to execute a kind of 9-11 Mark 2 strike against military targets across the country, using aircraft charged with a lethal cargo of explosives.

Michelle had argued forcefully that the Foundation's only viable course of action would be to disclose what it knew, irrespective of whether it believed the plot existed. The best way to do this would be in the manner discussed – via an unattributable briefing to a news outlet – while hoping that no information trail had been laid that might lead back to the Foundation's door.

But this course of action also involved the implication that the Foundation might well be forced to retreat from some of its activities. This would, suggested Michelle and Felix, be no bad thing.

They had both been more than a little surprised that so little thought had been given to the question as to whether it was appropriate for a private organisation to become so deeply involved in the murkier areas of international affairs, not least because of the potential dangers implicit in such activity.

It seemed to Michelle and Felix that this was a very long way from what even the dodgier social media organisations – hopefully not including Blather – got up to, and far beyond the original desire to make life more difficult for non-governmental quasi-political organisations, like the Freemasons or the mafia.

Rog remained steadfast in his assertions that the Aurora intelligence was genuine. Lindisfarne maintained the air of someone who perhaps recognised that an era was drawing to a close, but appeared reluctant to take the actions necessary to accommodate change that was inevitable. One by one, other members of the group seemed to be coming round to the view, with greater or lesser degrees of apprehension, that there was no alternative for Aurora but to bring what it knew into the public domain.

Eventually, Lindisfarne called the meeting to a close and rose from his seat. 'I recognise the consensus that has emerged,' he said. 'And, while it is in some respects with a heavy heart, I know what must be done. I shall travel to London with Michaela on a scheduled flight just as soon as we can get a meeting set up. I'll be less likely to draw attention to myself that way than if I were to take the Legacy on my own.'

Then Felix's heart fell as he added, 'Jameela, Stella and Rog will come with us on the Legacy as far as Brisbane so as to ensure that we are all as fully briefed as possible on every aspect of this.'

Lindisfarne maintained a communications silence once the party had left Eastertide: not even encrypted Bleats were to be risked. So Michelle and Felix found themselves the beneficiaries of an unanticipated beach holiday while they awaited the return of Jameela and her colleagues from Brisbane. It was marred only by the all-too-frequent interruptions of Ned Tackler, who was exhibiting absolutely no desire to return to his little submarine in Wasdale.

However, at lunchtime on their second day spent mostly on the beach, they were greeted by a highly excitable Ned on their return to the Eastertide Tower.

"Ere – feast yer eyes on this!' he exclaimed, ushering them into the common area. The flat-screen TV was paused on an image of Lord Lindisfarne, while the running headline at the foot of the screen read: 'Aurora shares dive with competition scare.'

Ned hit playback and the BBC newsreader read: 'Shares in the British-based tech giant, Aurora, plunged today amid fears that the latest version of its Framboise VSP could lose market share in the USA ahead of a series of surprise Federal lawsuits, alleging anti-competitive practice.

'Although only about 25 per cent of Aurora shares are traded on the Stock Market, today's losses have already wiped £1 billion off the personal wealth of its founder, Lord Lindisfarne.

'Lord Lindisfarne today accused American regulators of bringing spurious charges for the sole purpose of benefitting Aurora's US tech rivals.'

The three looked at each other. 'That must have been yesterday in the UK,' said Felix finally. 'How come nobody from Aurora let us know?'

His question hung in the air as the announcer moved on. 'In other news, American security services have disclosed that a major terror attack on US soil has been thwarted after key intelligence was intercepted. No details as to the nature of the threat have as yet been revealed but sources say that had the attack gone ahead, there would have been major loss of life.

'And in a separate security issue, the Royal Air Force has confirmed that all of its drone fleet has been grounded following an IT glitch at a control room in the UK.'

'So there you have it,' said Michelle. 'Two apocalyptic events condensed into a few lines and reproduced uncritically and with no thought for the context…'

'Do you think the share price is linked to this?' asked Felix.

'You mean, do I think that the Americans have conjured up some legal charges to put Aurora in its place? Or to send a signal that they know exactly where the intelligence came from? Anything is possible.'

'Aye, owt can 'appen,' parroted Ned.

There was still no news either from Lindisfarne or from the team in Brisbane when Michelle, Felix, Ned and the remaining members of the Aurora team turned in for the night a few hours later. However, as they took a later breakfast the following morning, they were interrupted by the arrival of Jameela, Stella and Rog, who had returned on the morning flight.

'We don't yet know if the share price will bounce back,' said Jameela. 'It recovered a little with the threat of retaliatory action by Europe, but then fell back with talk of it all escalating into a tit-for-tat trade war. I haven't heard from Victor, but I think he must be quite despondent.'

'Aye, 'appen,' said Ned. 'Losin' a billion quid can 'ave that effect...'

Jameela ignored him and continued: 'So far as we can tell, the briefing went as planned: the story initially appeared at some length in the Phoenix online, but you won't find it there any more. The Government issued a DSMA Notice requiring its removal.'

'DSMA? What's that?' asked Felix.

'Defence and Security Media Advisory Committee,' replied Jameela. 'Since then, as you'll know, there have been stories on the BBC and elsewhere. These effectively acknowledge that there was a plot against the USA and that the drone incident in Afghanistan did occur, but their significance has been downplayed. And, of course, the conspiracy theorists have been out in force – although, for once, what they are saying is actually the truth, or very close to it.'

'And are we going to see action against the Aurora Foundation?' asked Michelle.

'I think you already have,' replied Jameela. 'Neither the UK nor the US likes private organisations playing at nation states. The factors that have led to Aurora's share collapse have been engineered, and very quickly. I think that if the Foundation is seen to stop monitoring high-level communications and acting like a world policeman, then the legal sanctions will evaporate. Until that time, if Aurora Group revenues are effectively strangled, then the Foundation loses its funding too.'

'And?' said Felix.

'And… I think we can most likely expect an announcement from Lord Lindisfarne before too long to the effect that, in the light of unforeseen revenue constraints, the Foundation will refocus its work on its core objectives of mitigating climate change, fighting corruption, promoting academic research, and nurturing the influence of the culture of the ancient Kingdom of Northumbria…'

A distinct cloud hung over the Eastertide Tower the following morning. It was a fug comprising apprehension about the future of the organisation and the world at large, uncertainty about people's individual wellbeing, and – in the case of Felix and Michelle – a sense of anticlimax. They had tracked down Jameela and, since the previous evening, were in possession of a confession from Ned that they had indeed been led on a wild goose chase. And a further confession from Ned that the whereabouts of Kenny Marchant were known.

But Felix's reunion with the object of his desire had been at best prosaic: there had been no opportunity to talk about what he at least had felt was the unfinished business of a potential love affair or, more to the point, a lasting relationship. He had begun to contemplate the possibility that he had blown everything out of proportion – imagining an outcome that had never actually been on the cards.

For Michelle, there was the sobering reality that, with the freedom to choose to be with her, Kenny had elected instead to conspire in his own apparent disappearance.

As Felix and Michelle had lain in their own separate beds, each had – unbeknown to the other – carefully weighed up the opportunity to wander a few paces along a corridor and seek comfort in the other's company. So close had they grown in adversity, the idea that they might take their relationship on to another level was not out of the question. If either had known how near the other was to acting that night upon latent desire, they might well have taken that short walk.

Jameela, for her part, was every bit as restless. She saw, on the one hand, her new life as a globetrotting ambassador for the Aurora Foundation very much in the balance. Then there was the terrible trouble to which she had unwittingly put Felix, bless him. She was unsure whether she could easily shoulder responsibility for that – she did not want to be wanted so badly by anyone that they would go to such lengths.

Ned Tackler too longed for simpler times: times before miniature submarines, video links, or kidnappings. Times when excitement was defined by crossing the finishing line in a fell race, getting a prize for lying, or supping an experimental ale in good company.

Stella de Weld felt she was in the wrong place: she was surely needed at the helm of the Aurora Group, managing the crisis that had blown up so suddenly.

Charley wondered if the bite on her leg might lead to Lyme Disease.

Charlotte asked herself if it had really been necessary for her brother to drag her half way round the world for a meeting to which she had scarcely contributed, but nonetheless was happy to pass some time sharing her experiences in Transylvania with Jameela.

As no-one knew the whereabouts of Lord and Lady Lindisfarne, or what might happen next to determine the fate of the Aurora Group and the Foundation, everyone was reluctant to do anything proactive.

What caused a decisive move from such lassitude to some sort of activity was a reminder circulated by one of the on-site Aussie staff that it was by now Saturday and, here on Eastertide, Saturday meant Barbie Day.

'Well, they certainly know how to throw a barbie!' said Felix to Michelle, who had linked arms with her companion to breathe the unmistakable aroma of singed meat and sizzling corn cobs.

'Yes. But I didn't come all this way with you to learn what I already know. I want to know what happens to us now?'

'You mean what happens to us, as individuals? Or US, the two of us?'

'Both, I guess…'

Felix realised that he was being asked to give serious consideration to the idle thoughts that had invaded his mind during the night. He wondered if Michelle somehow knew what he had been thinking. But the arrival of someone else interrupted this potentially perplexing line of thought.

'Am I interrupting something?' asked Jameela.

Felix started slightly and Michelle saved him the trouble of answering by saying, 'I think it's time you two talked.'

'Why did you go to such lengths to follow me?' demanded Jameela as they wandered away from the group by the barbecue.

'Because I felt I had just found something very special only for it to be cruelly snatched away. And I was genuinely concerned for your safety.'

He summoned up his courage, drew in a deep breath and, looking straight into Jameela's eyes, told her, 'Remember that night all those years ago, when we spoke and you told me about your failed marriage? Well, I came to realise after we met again so near to here that my heart missed a beat that night… But I didn't recognise what I felt at the time. I thought I was feeling grief for you; but in fact I was feeling love and didn't realise that until I saw you again and my heart missed the same beat and I realised that all other relationships, present or past, were as nothing to the light that shone from you.'

Jameela reddened, and said, 'I don't think anyone has ever said anything quite so touching to me. And now you must be so angry with me!'

'Angry? No, I'm more angry with myself that I may have presumed too much.'

Jameela resumed: 'And if I said that you had done nothing wrong, but that I had perhaps just taken what seemed like the easy way out? You know, Victor gave me the perfect opportunity to duck out of making a decision that I was pretty happy to run away from. When we left each other I had every intention that we should get together and at least explore whether there might be something for us. But then Victor made me an offer that would make it very easy for me to just slip from view. In fact, that's what the Foundation aims to do with its top people, as you know, though it is not intended to be an irreversible process. All of a sudden I felt all the pain of my first marriage flooding back and I thought "I can choose to be with Felix and risk being hurt again" or I can choose the Foundation and Victor.'

'So you chose the Foundation,' sighed Felix. 'Do you have any regrets?'

'I hugely regret that I hurt you and caused you to spend so much time and money chasing after me – even if Ned did make a difficult situation so much worse. And, yes, I regret that when I had the opportunity to be brave I chose instead to be a coward… I didn't set out deliberately to forget you,' she added. 'I even made you my new password.'

'Does that mean that you might possibly do things differently now?' asked Felix, choosing to ignore the password reference. There are some things it's best not to reveal that you know.

'Well, perhaps things happen for a reason and maybe the problems at Aurora are designed to offer me a second chance…'

Felix found himself replying in an unexpectedly robust manner. 'I really don't want you going all fatalistic and "Insha'Allah" on me, Jameela. You either want to spend time with me or you don't.'

'I know, I know,' she sighed. 'But I need to know that you won't let me down. And I know that you slept with Michelle, by the way, and I look at the two of you together, and you need to know that I can't live with you being unsure and maybe wondering if you would have had an easier time with her than you would with me.'

Felix gasped. How could she possibly have heard about that one night in Broughton-in-Furness?

'Ned had some woman friend of his watching you, before you ask…'

Felix sighed. 'We had to share a bed, but I didn't touch her and she didn't touch me. I was being faithful to you and I guess she was being faithful to Kenny. You can take that as a compliment if you want, but I'm certainly not going to have you or anyone else trying to hold me to ransom by misinterpreting information gained by spying on me. Maybe we should just forget all about the whole idea: I'll swallow my pride, cry about my lost savings and get on with my life…'

He turned as if to walk back to the Tower but had gone no more than two paces before Jameela instructed: 'Felix! Wait, please!'

And, as he paused, she walked towards him, put her arms around him and kissed him gently on the lips.

Felix and Jameela sat alone together on the beach. Felix's legs still felt like jelly and, rather than spoil the moment by engaging in deep and meaningful conversation, he preferred to relax and say little, content that perhaps, after all, the journey had indeed been worth it.

So absorbed were they in each others' company that they failed to notice who was approaching them.

'Look who I's foond!' Ned was not alone: a young Asian guy was approaching, half a pace behind him.

'Rahman?' said Jameela. 'Can it really be you?'

To say that the reunion had been emotionally charged, would be to understate the obvious. There had been tears; many tears; some of joy; some of anger; anger at the time lost; mutual anger at their mother and unwritten rules that had to be obeyed; anger at their father for not standing up for what his heart, if not his head, believed in.

And then their years apart were pushed a little to one side, as Jameela's curiosity got the better of her and she said to Felix, 'So, you went to my father's restaurant in Luton? Are you crazy? Did you think about what you were doing?

'Yes, yes and… no, not really,' blushed Felix. 'I really regretted what I'd done when I was worried that Rahman here wasn't just after me, but probably after you too. I was worried as to his intentions.'

'Well, you were right to regret,' said Jameela. 'If it had been one of my other brothers, things could have been different.'

'So do you think there could be a reconciliation with them, and with the rest of the family?'

'Huh. Maybe you should ask Rahman that…'

'Insha'Allah…' shrugged Rahman.

'But God and my brothers and mother won't be willing, will they?' said Jameela.

'No, probably not, but I shall come and live with you, because my love for you is greater than for them or for any sense of family "honour".' Rahman almost spat the word out.

'And then the family shall be even more divided,' sighed Jameela, without extending the conversation. 'Let's go back to the others. We can talk more later.'

Felix let Jameela get a little ahead of him before digging into his wallet and finding the business card that Jameela's father had given him. He drew a deep breath, then texted: *'I am with your niece, Jameela, and nephew Rahman. Just to reassure your brother that everyone is safe and well.'*

He felt it was the least he could do and hang the consequences, whatever they might ultimately turn out to be.

As they approached where the group was enjoying its barbecue, Felix could see that there had been other new arrivals. Indeed, Michelle could be seen smiling, arm-in-arm with a youngish man who bore more than a passing similarity to the exasperated chap Michelle had introduced Felix to in a Kentish village what seemed like an eternity ago.

Michelle high fived him. 'I think you might call that mission accomplished, Felix, don't you?'

Felix beamed, but could see, out of the corner of his eye, that Jameela was less certain. And the reason why soon became apparent: Somewhat bizarrely, Emily Black was among the other new arrivals.

'There's someone I really need to talk to, 'chelle,' said Kenny, rushing hurriedly to the edge of the group.

'Are you seriously telling me that the reason Kenny disappeared was actually because he couldn't decide whether he loved me or Emily Black?'

'Aye, that's aboot 't size o' it,' said Ned.

'And I've travelled all this way just to hear that?'

'Yes, but we did have fun…' ventured Felix.

Michelle gave him a withering look, just as Emily made her return.

'I came here because I decided my real family was actually the Foundation and because, more specifically, I wanted to put Kenny on the spot, yeah,' she said. 'And now, after all that, he says that, actually, you're the one for him…'

'I'm not sure I really care,' replied Michelle.

Later, as darkness began to fall, the group split, with some heading for their rooms in the Eastertide Tower and others for the Euphoria Hotel. Felix and Jameela were surprised to see that Rog was among those walking in the direction of the hotel.

'Is that Emily Black he's with?' asked Felix.

'You know, I think it might just be,' replied Jameela. Then, as they neared the Tower, someone else familiar came into view, walking in the direction of the Euphoria.

'Isn't that Clive, the Australian guy who was in my session at the Shared Ambition workshop?' suggested Jameela. 'What on earth do you think he's doing here?'

'More to the point, Jameela, what is SHE doing here? The woman who's with him?'

'Clive!' called Jameela. 'Good to see you! Whatever brings you back to Eastertide?'

'The sea, the sunshine. And this lovely lady, here, who's come all the way from the North of England to share it with me!'

'Well hello Felix!' said Wendy. 'When you left your cat with me to go off searching the globe for the love of your life, I really didn't imagine that you'd just be spending your time sunning yourself on the beach... And just before you ask, Mr Merryweather is staying with my sister.'

'Your sister!' gasped Felix. 'But she lives in Aberdeen, doesn't she?'

'Yes. And?'

'And I don't think she's too fond of me.'

'Er. No.'

'I hope she doesn't stick pins in him!'

'I think she quite likes cats, Felix. But she's not so fond of pigs.'

Felix chose to ignore the dig as, however fond he might be of Mr Merryweather, he was far more curious as to how Wendy came to be here on Eastertide Island. And with Clive, of all people!

'We met through a forum for jilted lovers, actually,' said Wendy. 'And I guess we just hit it off.'

'Yeah, Felix old man, she's real sweet!'

'Yes Clive, she is. She's a lovely woman. And just you be sure to be good to her.'

'Just like you were, eh Felix?' said Wendy.

Felix was not in the best humour when he and Jameela got back to the Tower. And his mood did not improve when he realised that there had been another improbable arrival on the island earlier in the day.

He'd recognised the shrill and by now irritatingly earnest tones of Flora Mackenzie long before he saw her, but was glad when none other than Ned Tackler saved him the trouble of asking what the hell she was doing here, by piping up: 'Aye, lad, mebbes aa forgot ter tell yer, but me n' Flora 'ave had a bit of a thing goin' on, so I thought "If I can just spin out my stay at Eastertide Island, 'appen my Flora'll be able to come an' join me".'

His smug grin etched annoying lines in the leather of his weather-beaten visage in a way that reminded Felix of just how much responsibility Ned bore for his long wild goose chase – even if the eventual outcome had been successful. Nonetheless he resisted the temptation to punch him and instead delivered nothing more hurtful than a withering look.

'Don't be too harsh on him, Felix,' said Jameela. 'After all, he did create the opportunity for you to make a pretty big gesture. And it is one that I appreciate; I really do. But, just for now, I'd like some time to wind down and reflect a little.'

'So where's the love of your life, dearest,' demanded Michelle, as Felix moved on to his next designer gin from the collection in the lounge.

'In her room reflecting on life, the universe and everything… I could ask you the same question.'

'You could indeed, and the answer you would get would be that I don't know and I'm not sure I care…'

'If it's any consolation, I thought you looked good together. Maybe you should give him the benefit of the doubt. Or maybe you should share him with Emily…'

Michelle cut him off. 'I really don't think so, Felix. I think maybe I'll just play hard to get and see what happens. After I've told his loving parents where I've found their toad of a son!'

On returning to his room, Felix was surprised to find on his VSP an email from Roger Smart, which read:

I thought I'd let you know that Luke has developed the encryption system you were after. And he's also located a hidden folder inside the Aurora system, called Les Disparus, whatever that means. Your friend Jameela and that Katie Brown are both in it. And there's a load of weird messaging between someone called Shell2021 and TopCat2021, all about jellied eels and rabbits, or something, if that means anything to you. I'll get Luke to draw up a bill.

Somewhat after the horse has bolted, reflected Felix, resolving that perhaps this was one bill he could afford not to pay.

'The thing is, Felix,' said Jameela, as she looked as though through his eyes and into his very soul. 'The thing is that this story about you chasing round the world after me hardly squares with your ex-girlfriend turning up here and what I've heard about you sleeping with your travelling companion...'

Felix realised that it must have been Flora Mackenzie who had relayed information about what had gone on in Broughton-in-Furness. 'Jameela, you have to believe me when I say I didn't know about Wendy and, once again, nothing happened between me and Michelle. We had to share a hotel room and that meant sharing a bed. That's all!'

Jameela's serious face unfroze a little as she responded: 'Actually Felix, I do believe you; I really do. But I just need you to know that if you ever do lie to me, I will see right through you, so be warned now!'

'What will it even matter?'

'It'll matter a lot if we're going to make a go of this…'

'A go of me and you?'

'Yes, Felix, me and you.'

Letter from Stella de Weld, Group Chief Executive, Aurora to Victor, Lord Lindisfarne, Monday, November 1, 2021

My dearest Vic

It is with the heaviest of hearts that I find myself writing this letter to you. A whole decade has passed since we began the adventure that has been the Aurora Group - longer if you also take into account my time at Persona Communications before you and then the whole world went just a little crazy.

It has all been a most incredible experience for me and I can never, ever thank you enough for trusting in me to act as your First Lieutenant and be there with you as we grew the businesses so rapidly.

However, I think perhaps you can feel a 'but' coming and there is indeed a but…

I think you'll agree that the events of the past few days leave both the Aurora Group and the Aurora Foundation at something of a crossroads and I can choose either to remain with you and help you rebuild, or I can choose to do something more for myself.

These days here on Eastertide have reminded me that there is another side to life, and while indulging more in that 'other side' will in no way fill the hole that will be left by my leaving Aurora, it is, I feel, a step that I must take for myself.

Rebuilding Aurora will present many challenges and I can not put my hand on my heart and say to you that I am the best person to guide the Group under these circumstances.

My preference is to leave with immediate effect by taking gardening leave. I know you've said before that it is important that we nurture our garden and whether that was intended literally or just as another of your metaphors, for me it now has a literal meaning as I have been offered the job of head gardener at the Euphoria Eastertide. I would really like to take up the offer!

With kindest regards and thanks for all the memories
Stella

Letter from Lord Lindisfarne to Stella de Weld, November 2, 2021

My Dear Stella

I was saddened to receive your letter though, I have to admit, not wholly surprised. These last days have indeed been seismic and they have caused Michaela and I to reflect on what we really want to do with the rest of our lives.

Although the fall in Aurora's share price means this is not the ideal moment for an exit, they have rallied somewhat with the partial lifting of the American legal threat, and so we have decided to effect a gradual sale of our shares until such time as we no longer hold a majority interest.

Please handle this information with the utmost discretion as we are doing this through third parties so as not to further impact on the Group's value. That's why we're in London, as I have been taking time with the brokers.

Even with the fall in value we shall, of course, be more than comfortable: the plan is to make a significant bequest to the Foundation and then to step away and leave it to concentrate on the less controversial aspects of its work. I also plan to reward Felix and Michelle for their dogged determination in pursuit of their dreams.

Then we shall think about where we might spend our retirement: after all, I am getting on towards 70 and Michaela is 60, so I think we deserve a quieter life.

I wondered about Vulcano but I'm not so sure about the smell. Or there's Jacqhou, though I'm uncertain I would relish the confinement and, after all, it was somewhere that came to us through someone else's misfortune so it was never really our own dream.

No, I think we might just find a nice place on the quieter side of the Lake District, with a lake view and a Lakeland garden, with hydrangeas. There would seem to be a certain symmetry in that – and it is a noble thing to cultivate one's garden as you yourself observe!

And, perhaps we might fast-forward a couple of centuries from Voltaire and Candide, to the immortal words of the late John Lennon, singing about God. 'The dream is over,' he says. And perhaps so is my own. Like John, I was a dream weaver but now the dream really is over… and, we just have to carry on, don't we?!

With fondest wishes and thanks (for all the fish, perhaps?).
Victor

The End

EPILOGUE

Monday January 9, 2017

I can scarcely believe it, but it is now more than six years since my episode, as I've come to refer to it. When I'm not referring, that is, to 'the time I went bonkers' or 'when I was in the loony bin' or, indeed, 'when I was in Butlin's for three weeks'.

Frustratingly, life and all its attendant difficulties and demands has reasserted its right to sit at the top table. From here it presumes to insist upon awkward necessities like earning a living, or managing the consequences of more complex ailments (of a physical nature) than those ever presented by my episode, for all its scariness.

Persona Communications did not become Aurora and, in reality, I found myself having to gradually wind the business down and let people go, to the point at which it is now, just me, Vic Turnbull, sole trader.

On a happier note, while Michaela and I did not marry as urgently as my imagined meetings with my dead brother might have beseeched, we did, finally, tie the knot in 2013 in a civil ceremony, followed by a blessing the following day by the senior Durham cleric who did so much to help me come to terms with lack of my superpowers. Fittingly, that took place at the Altar of St Margaret, in Durham Cathedral.

My desire to record my manic experience remains steadfast and what began life as Two Flew Over The Cuckoo's Nest: The Unsequel is now the somewhat less ungainly, The Episode. But it remains but two thirds complete and already threatens to be as long in the gestation as the Mousetrap was, or indeed is, in the performance.

For all that, I have a pretty keen sense of where The Episode is taking me, but still have a few loose research ends to tie. So today, I am to meet up with Clare in the Community, or Marius, to employ his more widely recognised moniker.

We're meeting in Skipton, at a pub called The Castle – Marius lives on a canal boat moored on the edge of town.

'I'd have to say Vic, that when I look back even over these last few years, you were probably very fortunate to be mentally ill at the time you were... That was 2010, yeah? Probably the very zenith of mental health within the NHS.

'We were reasonably well funded, people recognised the importance of our services, and with a lot of famous people "coming out" about their own mental frailties, we were very much front of the public mind.

'Things probably started to go downhill, however, pretty much on the day you went home. The trouble was, and still is, that politicians love to talk a good talk about mental health, but really it's no more than a smokescreen for the fact that they are actually doing nothing. Worse, they are sitting back and watching while the Byzantine machinations of the NHS systematically move resources away from unsexy mental health to higher profile things, like casualty and cancer care.

'Take my own case: I used be retained as fairly senior adviser by the Vale and Dales NHS Trust until they let me go in favour of cheaper options, preferably wholly outside the NHS, under the local authority umbrella.

'I couldn't find work in Yorkshire so I tried the North East and when things dried up there too, I went to West Cumbria. Health Services there are trapped in a seemingly terminal vortex of decline: it may be right next to the Lake District and yet no-one seems to want to work there, so the services decline and then they end up having to fill vacancies with expensive agency staff. Like me.

'I did a bit of work on the front line, in Workington: lots of drugs issues, lots of violence. To be honest, there were times I felt really quite unsafe…'

'You'd think people would jump at the chance of being so close to the Lakes, or living by the coast,' I venture.

'Well, Vic, I guess it's because changing perceptions is like trying to alter the course of a supertanker. And this particular supertanker is fuelled by the negative reputation of West Cumbria and headed for the great naval scrapyard in the sky, to extend the metaphor. And besides, there's no real understanding that the Lake District is actually next door to West Cumbria. The perception is rather of nuclear power, poverty and social decline.

'Anyway, I managed to get myself a more managerial gig, off the front line and I've been doing it for the past four or five years. I'm in charge of night-time emergencies: four nights on, three off. I've got myself a little chalet by the coast and a motor scooter, so I trundle up on the train all the way to Barrow and then up the coast, and commute from my chalet, near Drigg.'

'Do you think the whole funding issue is down to the signs of mental illness being often a bit hidden?' I ask.

'Well, absolutely. Cases in which mentally ill people cause harm in the community are actually very rare, even though they can obviously attract huge publicity if things do go badly wrong. Say, if a severely bipolar patient with occasionally violent schizophrenic tendencies is discharged but doesn't take his medication and stabs someone in the street…

'More normally, the work that we do is far more about protecting patients and their family and friends, from themselves: preventing them from doing permanent damage to their reputations through inappropriate behaviour in public.

'Often this can be about money: a patient believes she, or more usually he, has become very rich, so goes out and buys an expensive motor. Then he forgets he's just done that, so he goes and buys another one. And another. And another.

'I've spent a lot of my time persuading unscrupulous car

salesmen to cancel deals. Some of them will, but others will say, "No, sorry guv, he signed a contract". So then I have to get legal and talk about cooling-off periods and about people not being responsible for their actions and "See you in court!".'

Once again I raise with Marius a topic casually mentioned to me by John, the nurse at Priestley House. This is the observation that I was just one of quite a few seemingly 'middle-class' inmates at the time of my hospitalisation. Normally it's people with addiction or other problems, wrapped up with poverty, who go in and out of Priestley House in a perpetually revolving door.

'Yes, that was true,' says Marius. 'It was for a period after the financial crash and there was yourself and quite a few others who didn't fit the traditional profile. I remember there was one guy in particular: a very prominent local businessman who I can't, obviously, name. He was absolutely determined he was going on home leave to give his daughter away at her wedding. And he was resolute that he was going to make a speech. We had a small team secreted at the wedding venue ready to grab him and take him back to Priestley if he started talking nonsense.'

'And did he?'

'In the event, no, he was quite well behaved!'

'You see,' I rejoin, 'as I've said before, even in your darkest moments during an episode it's still possible to take a step back and look at yourself...'

'That's as may be, Vic, but this guy would have been finished if he'd said the wrong thing and his whole business could have gone down the pan and taken all his workforce with it!' Marius pauses, shakes his head gently, and adds, 'And the sad thing is, Victor, that in all likelihood, if you were have an episode now, there wouldn't be a bed for either of you locally.'

With that sobering thought, eventually our conversation peters out and I walk back through the town with Marius to see his boat, which is an attractively painted narrowboat on the broad Leeds and Liverpool waterway.

'You seem to lead quite a nice life,' I say. 'No women?'

'No, not really. A relationship would be a bad fit with the life I lead. Working away from home. At night. And when I've built up enough funds I usually head for Tarifa for the kite-surfing. And any free time I have back here, well, I've taken up Thai boxing, which is great for working out tension and stress. And I read a bit.'

'You can read The Episode when it's nearly finished,' I venture.

'I'd like to do that!' says Marius, as he stands on deck to wave me goodbye.

Monday January 9, 2017

By coincidence, Prime Minister Theresa May chooses today of all days to illustrate Marius's point for him, when she delivers a speech on mental health issues to the Charity Commission. Her words seem jarringly at odds with the real world, in which there are lots of promises about making more resources for mental health care available, but these promises can not be delivered upon because the NHS is actually a collection of underfunded independent fiefdoms all fighting for a share of dwindling resources.

May proclaims that her mental health reforms will 'focus on young people' and promises additional training for teachers, an extra £15m for community care, and improved support in the workplace.

The Government says one in four people has a mental disorder at some point in their life, at an annual cost to society of £105bn.

Figures show young people are affected disproportionately, with more than half of mental health problems starting by the age of 14 and three quarters by 18.

Mrs May says mental health has been 'dangerously disregarded' as secondary to physical health and changing that would go 'right to the heart of our humanity'.

She highlights the fact that young women are at the highest risk of mental ill health and says that one in four adults suffers from mental illness.

She goes on to promise a number of actions, each targeted at addressing some of the most acute policy and resource failings affecting both younger and older victims of mental health disorders.

The mental health charity, Sane, says the plans need to 'be matched by substantially increased funds to mental health trusts', while Mind says it is 'important to see the prime minister talking about mental health', but the proof will be in the difference it makes to patients' day-to-day experiences.

So, if you think scepticism is ill-placed and that the Government should at least be given a chance, ask yourself now what has actually happened since January 9, 2017. As Hugh Pym, the BBC's Health Editor, said at the time:

'There is no new Treasury money for the plans. Funding for care is still challenging.

'NHS Providers, representing mental health and other trusts, predicts the share of local NHS budgets devoted to mental health will fall next year.'

And Professor Sir Simon Wessely, President of the Royal College of Psychiatrists, added: 'We have a long way to go before mental health services are on an equal footing with those for physical disorders.'

Liberal Democrat Norman Lamb, a former health minister, said Mrs May was announcing policies already agreed under the Coalition Government and called it 'a puny response' to 'cover up for this Government's failure' of delivery, while Barbara Keeley, Labour's Shadow Minister for Mental Health, questioned why funding was not being ring-fenced.

Wednesday July 4, 2018

The Episode was a project that I initially thought I could comfortably wrap up in a few months. In reality it has been a creature prone to retreating into hibernation, then springing to life for brief periods of frantic activity. A consequence of this evolution is that events have in some cases overtaken the 'future' strand of the narrative, the Felix strand, if you like.

Who could have predicted the rise of ISIS, Brexit or the election of Trump? When I first drafted the future strand, I could not have dreamt that events in real life might ever have overtaken the fictions that I had sketched out, and which I intended to feature in my story. As a result, because I want to minimise the risk of The Episode becoming a hostage to a particular moment in time, some of the original 'future events' that I had planned have been downplayed or removed altogether. My story has been impacted upon by events on both the local and the global scale, including everything from archaeological discoveries on Orkney to major conflicts on the world stage.

Indeed the whole dynamic of the relationship between the three Abrahamic faiths, and between the various sub-divisions of each, has become – thanks to Trump, Netanyahu, Putin et al – far more fraught and unpredictable. In that context, the relationship between Felix and Jameela might be seen as metaphor for better co-existence and so I commend the writings of Saif Gjobash, former UAE Ambassador to Moscow, in his Letters to a Young Muslim, which deals with the challenges of being a Muslim in the 21st century. Or take a look at Ziauddin Sardar's quarterly magazine, Critical Muslim.

As for me, well, notwithstanding the warnings of Doctors Merrydew and Scholl, I have shown no signs of relapse, confirming – to my mind – my own diagnosis that The Episode was caused primarily by damage to my urethra. My most lasting health legacy is a near constant but very mild tinnitus, about which I can seemingly do nothing.

Something that I hoped I might be able to do something about, on the other hand, was the habit I seemed to have acquired of letting my bottom lip protrude below my top one – a kind of pet lip expression. However, even as I write now, I'm aware that the lip still keeps popping out.

June 2025

Extract from an article in this month's issue of Fortean Times, the British magazine that reports on 'The World of Strange Phenomena'...

<<Felix Merryweather recounts a curious tale of Neolithic stone circles, auras... and mobile phones!

The date of April 1, 2025 will be forever etched on my consciousness as the day on which the laws of probability, or even possibility, made a fool of me.

Nearly 14 years after a quite bizarre chain of events at stone circles in Cumbria had brought me together with my wife and soulmate, Jameela, perhaps I should have anticipated that any return visit to the area's rich Neolithic heritage might be marked by encounters with the unexpected.

That curious day in May 2011 began strangely enough but got only stranger as it wore on. To start with, I had gone to Long Meg and her Daughters, a fine stone circle in the Eden Valley. I'd gone there because I had a notion that to do so might just possibly help me to clear my head and acquire a clearer sense of what I should do with my life. Or, more specifically, my love life.

I had been juggling four relationships of convenience with different women – three overseas and one here in England. Some guys might have been jealous, but it was not a situation that caused me any satisfaction and I knew I had to haul myself out of the rut that I had fallen into.

As I contemplated the grandeur and serenity of Long Meg and her Daughters, a man of fifty-something struck up a conversation with me and very quickly persuaded me to open up to him about my 'predicament'. I had a very powerful but inexplicable sense of not merely knowing him but of his somehow having a window that opened onto my soul. He hardly had to ask me any questions before he had a clear grasp, not just of my situation, but also of my mental state as I wrestled with the conflicts I faced.

In short, I felt very much as if this man, Victor Turnbull, and I somehow knew each other quite intimately, as though in different lives in some kind of parallel universe.

Thus far, you may think, nothing too remarkable. But there is a legend associated with Long Meg to the effect that you can count her daughters but you'll never arrive at the same number twice.

We each counted the stones three times that day and, sure enough, we could never make our tallies match.

But it was when we met up later that day, having first visited Mayburgh Henge, near Penrith, that things became really strange.

Somehow, in the few short intervening hours, Victor Turnbull's path had crossed those of two women in my life – two women who, it seemed, had become best of friends as a consequence. One was the sister of a then girlfriend, with the former of whom Victor had once had a relationship – the other was Jameela, who would become my wife.

He had also met up with an expert on stone circles, called Flora Mackenzie, and it transpired that they had first met near the Ring of Brodgar stone circle, on Orkney, years previously. Flora Mackenzie claimed to be able to see people's auras and, on meeting Jameela at Castlerigg stone circle, near Keswick, she had recognised a quite damaged and unhappy person.

However, when she met me – at the end of a talk on stone circles that she was presenting in Keswick that evening – it was as though she had actually seen a ghost. She had already told Victor that she had been having a recurrent dream in which she met a man of my name. But when she saw me, she said, it was as though she knew everything about me. My face, she said, was exactly the way she had seen it in her dreams. The only explanation she could find was that our paths had somehow crossed in some other life in some parallel plane.

Extraordinarily, these curious events somehow injected me not with greater confusion, but with a remarkable clarity of vision, and I recognised that I must henceforward be fair and open with others in my life, while being true to myself. At the same time, while I had been wholly unaware that I carried any kind of a flame of Jameela, meeting her that day opened the door on a whole new chapter of my life. It was, if you like, love at first sight – even though we had met previously, albeit some years before.

So confusing were the events of that day that I chose not to dwell on them. Given that there could be no rational explanation for these bizarre coincidences or for the inability of Victor Turnbull and I to correctly count a circle of stones, expending further mental energy on the pursuit of an explanation seemed a waste of time.

Fast forward to early spring of this year. Both Jameela's and my own interest in stone circles had waned, but we'd rented a cottage for a few days in the South Lakes and now we both recalled Flora Mackenzie's reference in her talk to a stone circle, near Broughton-in-Furness, called Swinside, or Sunkenkirk. She had said that its situation was on par with that of Castlerigg, and so Jameela and I took a picnic there.

It was a beautiful spot, cradled in the hills and overlooking Morecambe Bay, in the mid-distance. The weather was pleasant and we lay with our backs against one of the standing stones. I noticed that a rabbit had been scrabbling at the base of the stone and I could see the edge of a metal box, lodged some way underground.

I pulled it out. Although rusted in places, I could still read on it the words 'Farrah's Original Harrogate Toffee'. I opened it and found inside a scribbled note that read: 'This box contained a time capsule left by Victor Turnbull, latterly Lord Lindisfarne, and his wife Michaela. It was found on Saturday October 9, 2021 by Felix Merryweather and Michelle Bell and contained an old-fashioned mobile telephone, which turned out to be just one of many clues that led the pair of us on an extraordinary journey to many parts of the world. We return here January 1, 2022 to mark the successful conclusion of that journey and to leave, for the sake of posterity, the sim card from that phone.'

My blood ran cold – surely there could not be two people with the unusual name of Victor Turnbull, any more than there could be more than one Felix Merryweather?

Getting information off that outmoded data card proved an immense challenge but eventually we were able to find someone with the necessary equipment. It contained records of many calls and many of these related to a period during which this particular Victor Turnbull had been hospitalised, thanks to a manic episode of some kind.

Victor Turnbull was by now in his 70s but was happy to renew his acquaintance with Jameela and me. We later visited him at the home he shared with his wife, Michaela, on the edge of Ripon, where I showed him what we had found on the data card.

He looked puzzled and yet, in a strange way, not so puzzled…

'Yes, I did endure a manic episode in 2010, from which I made a full recovery. And yes, during that episode I did acquire what felt at the time like superhuman powers. I did genuinely believe that my business had become a world-leader and that it was my job to use the profits from its supremacy to do "good works".

'After you have been through a manic episode you have to come to terms with the reality that you do not have superpowers and that can be quite difficult. Lord Lindisfarne? I did fantasise about being made a Lord by the Labour Party.

'But I'm not sure how I feel about being confronted with any kind of "evidence" that my "brave new world" was anything more than a figment of my overstimulated imagination.'

'Can you explain it?' I asked.

'No. And I think it's best if I don't try.'

And then he asked me if I was familiar with Voltaire's philosophical novel, Candide, in which the naïve young hero of that name undertakes a long and incident-packed journey in which he is constantly reminded not just that the world and humanity are full of unpleasant surprises, but that – at the end of the day – there is little that we as individuals can do to influence events.

'That's why,' he said, with a sweeping gesture of his arms that took in the attractively planted, if slightly wild suburban garden behind him. 'I genuinely feel that I'm better off just looking after my garden, as Candide also concluded.'

As we turned to leave, I noticed that banks of hydrangea were just coming into bloom and I saw what I thought were three rather incongruous and garish garden gnomes. On closer inspection I realised they were the three wise monkeys – Mizaru, Kikarazu, Iwazaru – who see, hear and speak no evil.

Jameela and I shared our puzzlement and cast a quizzical glance towards the owner of the garden. Only the faintest enigmatic smile crossed his lips. There was another story, I'm sure, but he'd be damned if he would be telling it.

• *Felix Merryweather works in international marketing and lives in North Yorkshire with his wife Jameela and two children.*>>

Thursday, July 5, 2040

Northern Echo online. It is with great sadness that the death is reported of Victor Turnbull, of Ripon, aged 88. Victor was well known in business circles, having run a travel marketing business, Persona Communications, from offices in Ripon for some years. He later attracted a small but loyal following as a writer of fiction, the first of his works, The Episode, being based on a mental breakdown he suffered in 2010. He leaves a widow, Michaela, and three grown-up children.

Monday September 29, 2053

Times multiverse edition – deaths. The former industrialist and Labour peer, Lord Lindisfarne, has died peacefully at home in Cumbria after a short illness, aged 103. Born Victor Pierre Turnbull, Lord Lindisfarne is best known for building the world-leading tech giant, Aurora, into a force that challenged American dominance in the field of personal communications. His Aurora Foundation has been admired and loathed in equal measure for charity works that have ranged from intervention to save the environment to, more controversially, dismantling the power of vested interests and secret organisations, such as the Freemasons.

The more controversial work of the foundation ceased in 2022 as a consequence of the spectacular decline of the Aurora business for reasons that have never been satisfactorily explained.

Luck and Judgement – the rise and fall of the UK's Internet giant. *Click link to obituary.*